THE WIZ BIZ II

CURSED & CONSULTED

RICK COOK

Wiz Biz II

This is a work of fiction. All the characters and events portrayed in this book are fictional, and any resemblance to real people or incidents is purely coincidental.

A Baen Books Original

Baen Publishing Enterprises
P.O. Box 1403
Riverdale, NY 10471
www.baen.com

ISBN: 0-7434-3617-2

Cover art by Clyde Caldwell

First paperback printing, July 2003

Library of Congress Catalog Number 2001043165

Distributed by Simon & Schuster
1230 Avenue of the Americas
New York, NY 10020

Production by Windhaven Press, Auburn, NH
Printed in the United States of America

Wiz looked at the setup and nodded. Ranked in front of him were twenty-one Emacs, all sitting cross-legged on the floor of the Bull Pen. All of them had their quill pens out and poised expectantly.

"**backslash**" he proclaimed.

"**?**" responded the first Emac.

"**fractalfind exe,**" Wiz said. The Emac on the far left turned to the others and began to gabble at them. The other twenty Emacs bent to their tasks immediately.

The air above the Emacs began to thicken and take on a bluish tinge. It grew denser and bluer until a neon blue cloud hung over their heads.

"It's working!" Danny said.

The form began to pulse and Wiz realized he was getting a headache. "Do you guys feel all right?" Wiz asked.

"I feel fine," said a large Saint Bernard with Jerry's voice. To his left a six-foot-tall cockroach waved its feelers in agreement.

"Well, I don't," Wiz sang with two of his mouths, creating a bell-like harmony. Vaguely he realized they were standing not in the Bull Pen but under an enormous crystal canopy that shimmered with pastel highlights. And wasn't he supposed to have only two arms and one body segment?

As he watched, dog, cockroach and canopy all began to melt and run together. He felt his own body grow indistinct at the edges and begin to flow.

"**SIGTERM!!**" Wiz screamed.

The universe, canopy, cockroach and dog all froze in a half-melted state.

"**UNDO!**" he commanded. Instantly Wiz, Jerry and Danny were standing in the Bull Pen again.

"I think we have a problem here," Jerry said.

BAEN BOOKS by RICK COOK

CONTENTS

THE WIZARDRY CURSED

ONE

CONTRACT

Beware of open-ended contracts. They are
hell to support.

—Programmers' saying

Torches flickered and smoked, casting fitful light
through the cavern. Tosig Longbeard, King of the
Dwarves—or at least the Mid-Northeastern Dwarves of the
Southern Forest Range—shifted on his carved alabaster
throne and eyed his visitors with distaste.

It was, he had to admit, a most unusual sight. Three
Troll Kings in the same room and not fighting. The sight
and stench would have been enough to gag a human; but
dwarves have a somewhat different aesthetic and King
Tosig's attitude owed more to the delegation's demands
than their looks or smell. He drummed his fingers on the
throne arm as he tried to figure a diplomatic way out of
this mess.

The smaller troll in the center did the talking. He was
unusually intelligent for a troll and their host had no doubt
he was the one who had organized this meeting. *Pox rot
him!* Tosig thought as he waited for him to run down.

"This is not a matter for me or my people," Tosig broke

3

in at last. "If this new human wizard bothers you, then destroy him."

"We cannot," the troll king replied. "This magic is too strong." His face split into a snaggle-toothed grin. "But dwarves have powerful magic. Dwarves can kill this new wizard."

His two companions nodded and growled assent. King Tosig glowered back and felt a tiny burning sensation kindle somewhere up under his breastbone. At that moment he truly wanted to kill the new wizard who had brought him all this trouble.

At that moment the new wizard wouldn't have been at all averse to being killed.

Like King Tosig's hall, the chamber was underground and dimly lit. But instead of rough stone, the walls were fine mosaics in subdued and tasteful patterns. There were no smoky torches here, only a diffuse radiance that seemed to emanate from everywhere in the room. And while the creature that faced the two humans across the table might be decidedly odd, by no stretch of the imagination could it be called either ugly or stinking.

But that did not mean the wizard was enjoying himself.

"Okay, look," William Irving Zumwalt said. "If the dryads mark their trees our woodcutters will leave them alone. But in return our people can cut other trees and use the forest without being harassed."

The being across the nacreous table cocked its head, as if listening to far-away voices. It was manlike, but then so is a gorilla if you stretch the term far enough. Parchment skin stretched over delicate bones. Fingers so long they were almost tentacles. Enormous dark eyes that slanted at the corners. Ears blood-pink and pointed. The thing was at once inhumanly beautiful and deeply disturbing.

The silence dragged on. Wiz shifted and fidgeted while the creature sat with its head to one side and its eyes focused on things far beyond its visitor. Elven magic could warp time to make centuries pass in a single night. But

Wiz was finding that non-mortals didn't need magic to make a night drag on for centuries.

"It will be done," the creature said finally. "The trees will be marked."

"But when?"

The other lifted a delicate hand and waved it airily. "Soon," it fluted.

Wiz took a tighter rein on his temper. "Soon" to a non-mortal meant any time in the next geologic eon—if then.

"But precisely when? I can't go back to my people and tell them just 'soon.' We've got to be able to go into the forests to cut wood and gather food."

"You wish it done soon. I say it will be soon. That is enough."

"Fine, but we need . . ." Wiz was talking to empty air. The being had vanished, leaving Wiz and his companion alone in the gently glowing chamber. Slowly and inexorably the light was dying, a none-too-subtle hint that the meeting was over.

"Well, then . . ." Jerry Andrews put his palms on the opalescent table and heaved himself up from the low chair. He had lost weight in the year or so he had been in this world, but he still outweighed Wiz by nearly 100 pounds just as he overtopped him by a head.

"Next full moon," Wiz agreed and got up as well.

I hope they will be here then, he thought as he followed Jerry through the fading light of the corridor and out into the clear frosty air outside the hill. There was no door or other obvious exit. One step they were within the enchanted hill and the next step they were outside, with the forest looming up behind them and the gently glowing magic barrier that cordoned off this place in front of them.

Reflexively they both inhaled deeply. There was nothing wrong with the air inside, but the air outside seemed sweeter. *The smell of freedom,* Wiz decided. It was just a few more steps along the moonlit path and they were past the barrier and back in the forest that belonged to men.

❖   ❖   ❖

"Mortals drive us from the forest," the troll king's voice echoed off the walls of the cavern. "We cannot hunt where we did."

Meaning you can't hunt mortals, King Tosig thought sourly. *Well, what did you expect, you silly nit? You go around eating people, even mortals, and naturally they'll object.* The burning in his stomach was stronger and he knew he would be up all night, walking the floor and drinking ground chalk.

He understood the trolls' problem in a general way. For time out of mind trolls had roamed the marches of the human realms, devouring human travelers and occasionally daring to attack mortal farms and villages. Then three or four seasons ago a new magician had arisen among the humans. Brought from outside the World, or so the story went.

At first this alien wizard had only used his power in human quarrels. But before long his vastly more powerful magic had begun to spread among mortals. Suddenly the humans had respectable magical powers and the trolls, who had almost none, had lost a major item in their diet.

Tosig tugged his beard. This was a pretty problem indeed. So far there had been little contact between humans and dwarves and he would just as soon keep it that way. His realms were far from the lands of mortals and his people had not suffered from the humans' new magic. However he had heard stories and they were not the sort to encourage him to stir up trouble in that direction.

Well, maybe he wouldn't have to. The king had been talking for nearly a day-tenth and hadn't yet . . .

"I call debt-right!" the troll king thundered. "Blood for my people."

A stillness settled over the hall. All the dwarves present knew that the troll kings' claim was legitimate. Tosig sighed and inwardly cursed the day he had contracted a debt to a gang of trolls. But contract it he had, and now the troll had made a formal demand. Debts must be paid.

There were practical considerations as well. The dwarves traded salt and iron to the trolls for hides, some forest products and the odd bit of booty. It was not a terribly profitable trade, but if the truth be known the Mid-Northeastern Dwarves of the Southern Forest Range were not a terribly wealthy tribe. They didn't need complications with the trolls now.

As if I didn't have enough problems! Tosig thought as the pain in his stomach gnawed and the silence stretched on. *As if . . .* Suddenly he stopped short and thought furiously.

Ignoring the burning inside he nodded to his visitors. "It pleases me to grant your request. The thing shall be done." He waved dismissal. "Now go."

"When?" the small troll demanded eagerly.

"Soon," Tosig said loftily. "Return to your forests." He repeated the dismissing gesture. The guards around the perimeter of the hall shifted and the trolls took the hint. Jostling and squabbling, they made their way out of the hall.

As soon as his unwelcome guests were gone, he motioned to his seneschal.

"Make sure they leave immediately," he said, rising from his throne. "And see that their rooms are fumigated. The last batch had lice."

The seneschal nodded and began to back away, but the dwarf king caught his sleeve and pulled him close.

"Send Glandurg to me in my chamber," he commanded in a low voice.

There was a flash of bewilderment on the seneschal's leathery face. Normally it was part of his job to keep Glandurg as far away from his royal relative as he could. But he nodded, sketched another bow and hurried to do his master's bidding.

Beyond the barrier, Bal-Simba was waiting. The enormous black wizard sat patiently on a rock, wrapped in a cloak against the evening chill. Beside him was Danny, the other member of the programming team. Huddled next to Danny was his wife June. Fortunately it was a large rock.

Bal-Simba was there because it was as close as he could get to the negotiations. Despite being the head of the Council of the North and as such the leader of nearly all the mortals in the World, the non-mortals would not treat with him. Wiz Zumwalt's new magic was stronger and to the non-mortals that made him the only mortal who mattered. They would tolerate Jerry, Wiz's cubicle mate from his days as a programmer in Cupertino, because Jerry was Wiz's right-hand man and also an expert with the new magic.

Danny was there because Wiz and Jerry were. Like Jerry, he had been magically brought to this world to help Wiz complete his magic compiler and like Jerry he had chosen to stay behind when most of the programmers went back. He had matured considerably in the year or so since he had come to the World, but there was still a lot of punk kid and hacker in Danny.

June was there because Danny was. If being a father and husband had matured Danny, being mother and wife apparently affected June not at all. She was still an almost feral presence; shy, silent and remote from everyone except Danny and their infant son. Even pregnancy and motherhood had not added a single pound to her painfully thin frame.

Sitting pressed up against Danny she reminded Wiz of a wild animal, unsure of her surroundings and ready to lash out at anyone who came too close. As she moved, Wiz saw that she had Ian with her, nursing under the cloak.

"Well, Sparrow?" Bal-Simba asked as they approached.

"They said they'd do it, but they won't say when. I think we're supposed to meet again at the next full moon."

Bal-Simba nodded. He had hoped for something definite to tell the farmers, but he had not really expected much more.

Wiz sighed. "Lord, do you think we're making any progress at all?"

Bal-Simba sighed in return. "How am I to judge, Sparrow? I know as little of dealing with these creatures as you do. Less perhaps." He rubbed his massive forehead with a meaty hand. "Still, they continue to treat with us and that is no small thing. Nor is there any sign of war by non-mortals against mortals and that is a large thing indeed."

Wiz nodded. His new magic had upset the balance of this World and sent humans thrusting out past their ancient boundaries in a wave of settlement, destroying magical creatures as they went. The non-mortals had reacted and the World had teetered on the brink of a war of extermination against humans. With the aid of a team of shanghaied computer programmers, Wiz had been able to stem the tide and temporarily confine the humans within somewhat larger boundaries, blunting the threat and removing the danger of war.

But to keep the peace the humans needed some kind of treaty with the World's non-mortals, something that would set out rules for both groups. The negotiations had dragged on for months with many different beings. Apparently most of the non-mortals either couldn't conceive of the idea of a general policy or weren't interested in negotiating one with the humans. So arrangements had to be made a bit at a time with one group of non-mortals after another.

It would have tried the patience of a seasoned diplomat and Wiz was a long way from being any sort of diplomat. Worse, he was the only mortal the elves and others wanted to deal with and to him the meetings were a form of exquisite torture.

"Well, now what?"

Bal-Simba heaved his bulk up off the rock and picked up his wizard's staff. "That we shall know at the next full moon, Sparrow."

❖ ❖ ❖

"You sent for me, Uncle?"

King Tosig looked up sourly at the young dwarf standing in the door of his study. His sister's niece's son was well-enough formed, with broad shoulders and powerful limbs. His beard was long and thick, as a dwarf's beard should be, and his craggy features bore a hint of the dwarf king's own.

The face was fine. It was what was behind it that was the problem.

Instead of digging, making, hoarding and other normal dwarfish pursuits, Glandurg's mind was forever on other things. Where the average dwarf is an intensely practical, rather unimaginative sort, Glandurg was a dreamer and a romantic.

The young dwarf knew that there was more to life than the tunnels and forges of his subterranean home. He just wasn't sure what. Being young, inexperienced and a romantic, he was convinced it was better than what was here.

Worse, he had gathered a group of young dwarves about him and converted them with his cockamamie chatter. They careened about the tunnels, refusing to listen to their elders and engaging in all sorts of undwarvish nonsense.

To Tosig, who was practical and unimaginative even for a dwarf, Glandurg and his friends were a constant source of trouble. If such a thing were possible Tosig would have suspected a taint of mortal blood in his ancestry.

The dwarf king forced his face into an unaccustomed smile and gestured at his visitor. "Come in, boy. And close the door behind you."

"Uncle, I really am sorry about the sewage tunnel," Glandurg began breathlessly. "But the survey showed . . ."

The dwarf king reddened at the thought of the stope flooded when that tunnel broke through, and his already perilous hold on his temper weakened. As if a dwarf had to rely on a survey to know where he was underground!

"Never mind that," he cut his near-nephew off. "I have another job for you and your friends."

"It's not another sewage tunnel, is it?" Glandurg began apprehensively. "Because if it is . . ."

"No, this is something else. Something more suited to your talents. Oh sit down, boy! Sit!" He shooed the young dwarf into a three-legged chair in front of his desk.

Apprehensive at this unprecedented honor, Glandurg sank into the chair, his eyes riveted on Tosig's face.

"Now then," said Tosig, composing his thoughts. "You know I had an embassy from the trolls this evening?"

Glandurg nodded eagerly. "Three mighty kings of the trolls—or so it is said." His face fell. "I was on guard duty on the peaks."

Tosig nodded. He did not mention he had given standing orders to keep Glandurg out of the throne room during audiences.

"The trolls came asking a great favor and for reasons of state I have decided to grant their request."

Glandurg leaned forward expectantly.

"The trolls are threatened by a new wizard who has arisen among the mortals. A wizard from beyond the World, bringing with him strange and powerful magic. Our allies the trolls suffer cruelly under his influence and they beg succor."

He fixed his young relative with an eagle stare. "You are to be their succor. I want you to gather a troop of hardy adventurers and kill the human wizard with the new magic."

Glandurg gulped. "You mean go Outside? Out into the World?"

"Well, you're not going to find him in our tunnels are you?" Tosig snapped.

"No, I mean, of course not, but . . ."

The dwarf king glared and the young dwarf trailed off. Glandurg was all for adventure and travel, in the abstract. But now that he was facing the possibility of leaving the tunnels where he had lived all his 184 years, he discovered he wasn't so sure he wanted to go.

"We'll need supplies," he said at last. "And gold."

Tosig's stomach flared again, but he nodded. "Anything you need. Within reason, boy! Within reason. Now, how soon can you leave?"

"I don't know. A week perhaps."

Tosig nodded. "A week if you must, then. Sooner if you can. Our allies depend on us in this and I am depending on you."

Glandurg's face glowed.

"Thank you, Uncle. I will strive to prove myself worthy." He bowed deeply and then whirled and raced out the door, slamming it behind him.

As the door reverberated behind his young relative, King Tosig allowed himself a tight little smile.

A debt was a debt and debts must be paid, even to trolls. *On the other hand,* he thought, *nowhere it is written what coin they must be paid in.* Clearly there must be an effort to crush this Sparrow, but if the effort failed and one of his blood relatives perished in the attempt, why, who could blame the king or his people? Even mortal magicians were not without defenses after all.

He shifted and the pain in his stomach came back, but not so bad this time. Maybe he wouldn't need the ground chalk after all.

"Dammit, they're stalling!" Danny said as the group picked its way along the trail in the moonlight. "They're just keeping us hanging."

"Why?" asked Jerry. "It doesn't get them anything."

"I dunno why," Danny said stubbornly, "but we're being stalled."

Wiz walked beside his fellows, too tired to join the argument. *Pointless anyway,* he thought. *No matter what their motives are we've got to keep negotiating with them. It's the best we've got.*

Behind them Ian made a tentative whimper. June quickly hushed him.

"I thought you were going to leave her home," Wiz said in an undervoice as he jerked his head back at June.

"Well, I tried," Danny said defensively. "But she came anyway. You can't argue with her. It's like she doesn't hear."

"If you can't keep her at home maybe it would be better if you didn't come to these things."

"No way, man. This is where stuff is happening. Besides, she's not a problem. She just sits with me." Wiz saw the angry jut of his jaw and decided to try a different approach.

"Okay, but it can't be good for the baby to be out in this weather. And it will be even colder next full moon."

Danny's expression cleared as he thought about it. "Yeah. You're right. Maybe I should stay home."

Wiz nodded. The new Danny could be just as obnoxious as the know-it-all kid who had come to this world a little over a year ago, but at least you could reason with him.

More or less, Wiz reminded himself.

At the base of the enchanted hill Bal-Simba motioned the party to halt in a clearing. They clustered together while he began the chant to transport them back to the Capital on the Wizard's Way.

A quickly spoken spell, a flash of familiar darkness and they were standing on the flagstones of the Outer Court of the Wizard's Keep, just inside the main gates of the castle.

Wiz blinked at the brightness of the lantern-lit courtyard after the moonlit forest clearing.

"You know, this is still wrong," Jerry said as the guardsmen hurried to open the inner gate that separated the Outer Court from the Keep proper.

"Looks fine to me," Wiz said as his wife Moira came through the gate to meet him. The mellow glow of the lanterns caught the coppery highlights in her red hair and warmed the creamy tones of her freckled skin. She was easily the best thing Wiz had seen all day and he hugged her tight and kissed her soundly.

"No, think about it," Jerry persisted as Wiz and Moira broke the clinch. "We just teleported in here. But what about the velocity differences caused by the rotation of the planet? There should be a speed difference. And there's the energy gradient, and . . ."

Moira's green eyes gleamed with amusement. "Has he been like this all evening, love?"

"Just since we got back," Wiz told her.

"But . . ." Jerry interjected.

Wiz was in no mood for one of Jerry's attempts to apply the finer points of physics to this world. "It's magic, okay?"

"Yeah," Jerry persisted as they went through the inner gate, "but magic has rules."

"But that doesn't mean we understand them."

"Still . . ."

"Look, there are a lot weirder things about this place than some missing energy when we teleport. Let's leave it, all right?"

Jerry looked at him sympathetically.

"You're really beat, aren't you?"

Wiz sighed and put his arm around Moira's waist. "Yeah, but at least that's over for another month. Maybe we can concentrate on writing software for a while."

"Oh, a week at least," Jerry said. "Then we've got a couple of other loose ends to deal with."

Wiz thought about those "loose ends" and glared at his friend. "You had to remind me, didn't you?"

TWO

DRAGON TROUBLE

The day was bright, the air was crisp and Judith Conally was off in a world full of dragons, elves and heroes.

So Prince Leopold slays the dragon Ferocious before he meets the wood elves, she thought as the trolley car jolted to a stop in front of the San Jose Public Library. *But then where does he meet Bronwyn Halfelven? It can't be in the troll's cave. That's too trite. And if he kills the dragon before he confronts Gorbash Fleshripper, why does Bronwyn agree to accompany him on the quest?*

She sighed and shifted on the hard fiberglass seat. Her fellow passengers ignored her. Their thoughts might not be as colorful as Judith's, but they were just as lost in them.

Externally, Judith was no different from the other passengers. Her clothing was more comfortable than stylish and while no one would have called her ugly, they wouldn't have called her beautiful either. Her long dark hair was lustrous, but it was caught back in a severe bun. Her figure was substantial rather than eye-catching, her jaw was square and her nose on the large side. She looked, well, ordinary.

Judith sighed again and rose with the rest of the passengers. Working out the details of a novel wasn't nearly as easy as she had thought. Maybe she could find a solution in the book on Celtic magic the library had gotten her through interlibrary loan. If not she would have to invent something that would be magically consistent with the universe she had created.

Problems, problems. She never knew being a successful fantasy author could be this difficult.

Well, almost a successful fantasy author, she admitted as she stepped down onto the trolley platform. The outline of her trilogy had caught the eye of an editor at Nemesis Books. The sample chapters had passed muster and now the editor wanted to see the completed manuscript of the first novel.

The other passengers had stepped off the platform to cross the street in either direction, but Judith still stood there, trying to decide.

For a moment she concentrated on dragons. Not dragons as they were—quarrelsome, nasty-tempered beasts that stank of sulfur and snake—but dragons as she had first seen them. Mighty, ethereal creatures printed against the pale pink glow of clouds at earliest morning as they swooped around the tower of the Wizard's Keep.

She was bound by oath not to reveal what she had seen in that other world. As part of the small team of programmers who had taken Wiz Zumwalt's crude magic compiler and turned it into a piece of production software, she had really experienced magic and dragons and the rest of it. She couldn't *directly* refer to her time in a world where magic worked and dragon riders were as common as 747s are here. But she could draw on what she had seen and done to make her novel come alive. And most of all she had the memories to sustain her as she struggled to write.

As always thinking about her time in another world refreshed her. Judith started to cross to the library, head high and still lost in thought.

Can I do it in two trilogies? she wondered as she stepped off the curb. *Or will I need to stretch it to three?*

❖   ❖   ❖

If Judith was lost in thought, the truck driver was just plain lost. He had driven the semi all the way from Minneapolis to deliver a load of exhibits to the San Jose convention center next to the library. But he had gotten his directions mixed up and instead of arriving at the back of the center and the loading docks, he ended up in front of the building, on a street that wasn't supposed to have truck traffic. He certainly didn't know the neighborhood well enough to realize that people on the trolley platform in the center of the street were given to crossing no matter what the traffic light said.

The blare of the horn and the screech of air brakes brought Judith half out of her reverie. Instinctively she jumped back as the driver yanked the wheel desperately in an effort to avoid her.

Together it was almost enough. Instead of receiving an obliterating blow from the truck's front bumper, Judith Conally was only kissed by the left fender. But the kiss was near as deadly as a blow. Her purse flew out of her hands in a high arc, opening in mid-air and spilling wallet, tissues, keys and coins along the curbside. Limbs flailing, Judith spun away and slammed headfirst into the curb.

She did not move again.

A woman and a dragon waited for them when they entered the programmers' quarters in the Wizard's Keep.

Of the two the woman was slightly the larger and by far the more formidable. Shauna was broadbeamed with brown hair and an easy gap-toothed smile. She had an infant daughter of her own and she was more than happy to nurse Ian—and mother June and Danny as well.

"My Lords, Lady," she curtsied. "I have a cold supper waiting."

"Thanks," Wiz said, "but I'll just have something to drink." He drew a mug of ale from the small cask at the end of the table and plopped down on a bench along the wall. It was something past midnight, but all of them were too keyed up to sleep. A light meal and light conversation had become a ritual after meeting with the nonhumans by the light of the full moon.

Shauna surveyed Wiz's thin frame disapprovingly. "You'll never put on any meat that way." Then she turned to June. "Here child, let me hold the baby and you get yourself something to eat."

Shauna, Moira and Danny were the only three people June would allow to hold Ian. Without protest June handed the baby to Shauna and went to heap her plate. Jerry, Danny and Bal-Simba joined her while Moira stayed with Shauna and Ian.

"It's a wonder you don't catch the ague, all of you. Out all night in the cold and damp consorting with uncanny beings. And taking the child to such doings, well . . ." Shauna peered under the blanket at the sleeping infant.

Ian awoke briefly, saw he was being made much of, accepted it as his due and drifted back to sleep.

Wiz took a pull on his mug and nearly lost it when the dragon rammed his head into his ribs.

"Well, what's your problem, Scales-For-Brains?" he said, reaching out to scratch the dragon behind its ears.

Shauna looked up from Ian. "Naming such a beast 'Lord,'" she said with a shake of her head.

"Not Lord," Wiz corrected as he dug his fingers into the scaly hide. "LRD." The dragon stretched his neck out luxuriously to expose a spot behind his right ear.

"LRD?"

"It's a TLA for Little Red Dragon," Jerry put in from where he was building a triple-decker sandwich.

"What is a TLA?"

"Three-letter acronym."

Shauna looked puzzled and Moira chuckled. "Never ask them for an explanation. You will only end up worse confused."

Shauna sniffed and turned her attention back to June and Ian. LRD reminded Wiz to keep scratching with a butt to the side that nearly knocked him off the bench.

As a two-foot hatchling, LRD had been as cute as a kitten when he wandered into the programmers' makeshift workshop and decided he liked the company. Now, a little over a year later, LRD was something more than six feet from snout to tail-tip and massive in proportion. Compared to the 80- to 100-foot cavalry mounts in the aeries below the castle, LRD was still tiny. Compared to the scale of the rooms and passages in the castle, LRD was definitely on the large side and getting bigger every day.

He had given up trying to sleep on tables after a couple of them collapsed under his weight, but he still liked to nudge people to have his head scratched. Of course what had once been just a firm, insistent push was now enough to knock a grown man off his feet. He was also beginning to show flashes of typically dragon-ish temper—which is to say he could turn nasty in an instant—and occasionally he would burp a little tongue of flame. Almost everyone steered clear of him and the only place he was really welcome was the programmers' workrooms and their living quarters.

The dragon decided he had had enough head scratching and ambled over to see how Ian was doing. Shauna eyed him disapprovingly but he extended his neck and sniffed the sleeping infant, giving nurse and baby a good snort of dragon breath in the process. Ian opened his eyes and cooed at the scaly monster looking down at him.

For some inexplicable reason LRD had decided he liked Ian. He would curl up next to the baby's crib for hours, dozing or watching the infant with an unwinking golden stare. If Ian was distressed or uncomfortable, LRD became frantic. When he wasn't with Ian, the dragon divided his time between chasing the castle's cats and sunning himself on any convenient surface.

He seemed mildly approving of June, and he and Shauna had arrived at an armed truce. Everyone else he ignored—unless he wanted his head scratched.

Wiz finished his ale and debated making himself a sandwich. He decided he wasn't hungry and putting food in his stomach would only dilute the soporific effect of the ale. He needed something to help him sleep after the hours spent under the magic hill.

Moira left June and Shauna and came over to sit by him. "You're not eating?"

Wiz took a moment just to admire her. Moira was broad-hipped, deep-bosomed and had a pair of wonderful green eyes set in a wide freckled face under a mane of red hair. The hedge witch was the first person he had seen when he had been kidnapped into this world and he had thought she was breathtakingly beautiful then. They had been married nearly two years and she still took his breath away.

"I want to make sure I can sleep tonight," he said, slipping his arm around her waist. Then he leaned close and nuzzled her hair. "What's the matter, do you want your ears scratched too?"

Moira turned and gave him one of her patented 10,000-volt looks. "Perhaps we should discuss that back in our chambers, my Lord."

Wiz rose and pulled her up with him. "Maybe we should at that."

Looks like the ale was wasted, he thought as they made their goodbyes to the others and headed off to bed.

Once again torches lit a meeting of dwarves in an underground chamber. But this was a much smaller gathering in much less impressive surroundings than King Tosig's audience hall.

It was, in fact, a storeroom for hides. The torches were leftovers plundered from wall sconces elsewhere in the hold and the twelve dwarves sitting on the smelly bales or lounging against the rough-hewn walls had no more right to be there than the torches did.

A minor detail, Glandurg thought as the last of his followers slipped into the room and closed the storeroom door. Anyway, now that he was acting under his uncle's orders, not even old Samlig, the keeper of the storehouses, would dare to question them.

Still Glandurg couldn't help looking over his shoulder. Samlig was a crusty one and he'd just as soon not put his new legitimacy to the test.

Taking a deep breath, he drew himself up to his full three-foot-eight and faced his men.

"Comrades," he proclaimed, but softly. "At last we have a mission worthy of us."

"Not another sewage tunnel, is it?" asked a dwarf named Ragnar.

Glandurg dismissed the question with a lofty gesture. "This is a mission to the Outside World. Beyond the tunnels of the Hold."

A couple of the dwarves exchanged suspicious glances, wondering what kind of unpleasant and menial chore had been arranged for them now.

"I have just come from a secret audience with my uncle, the King," Glandurg told them. "He has entrusted us with an important mission."

"I thought the King said he'd cut your ears off if you came next nor nigh him," put in a dwarf named Gimli who was so young his beard barely touched his chest.

Glandurg glared at him and planted his hands on his hips. "Do you want to hear this or don't you?"

Gimli wilted under his leader's stare and Glandurg adopted his heroic pose again.

"As I was saying, a secret audience with the King. He has commanded us upon a vital mission for all of dwarfdom."

He paused for effect and the other dwarves leaned forward expectantly.

"We are to penetrate the world of mortals to its very heart and there find and slay a wizard from beyond our World! It is a dangerous, desperate quest and in his hour of need my uncle the King has turned to us as the staunchest, bravest among all his subjects." He surveyed his wide-eyed followers and saw they were satisfactorily impressed.

"This isn't another one of your stories?" one of the dwarves asked at last.

"Why don't you go to my uncle the King and put that question to him?"

That settled it. None of them would go anywhere near King Tosig, but the assurance with which Glandurg issued the challenge told them that for once their leader was not exaggerating. At least not much.

"How are we supposed to get there?" asked Thorfin, always the practical one. "That's two hundred leagues at least."

"We will ride," Glandurg said loftily. "It has been arranged."

"I don't know about horses," a dwarf named Snorri said dubiously. "I'm not much for them."

"We will not ride horses. We will fly."

"I thought you said we'd ride," said Ragnar. "Which will it be then?"

"You'll see soon enough," Glandurg told him with a superior smile. He was pleased that he had thought of the transportation problem and he was even more pleased with the solution he had worked out in the few hours since meeting with the king. But he didn't want to tip his hand. His companions might not be as happy with his cleverness as Glandurg was.

"What about supplies?" Ragnar asked.

"Our every need will be supplied from the hold's storehouses," Glandurg said. He smiled at the thought of old Samlig's face when he issued out the carefully hoarded goods. "We shall have the weapons, the armor and the gold we need from my uncle the King's personal treasury."

He looked them over again. "This will not be easy. The alien wizard has mighty magic and his legions of mortal warriors are numberless and not to be despised. It will be a long, difficult adventure and danger awaits us at every turn."

The dwarves all nodded. Danger and adventure were fine with them.

"This will be to the death," he proclaimed. "Some of us—nay, all of us!—may not return."

He swept his gaze over his followers impressively.

"Now swear with me in blood!" Glandurg drew his knife and nicked himself on the wrist. He cut deeper than he meant to and winced slightly at the sudden pain. There was a lot more blood than he intended, but his sleeve reddened satisfactorily and the blood dripping off his wrist made a most impressive touch.

One by one the other dwarves cut themselves and mingled their blood with their leader's for the oath.

"To the wizard's death—or our own."

THREE

OPERATION 500-POUND PARAKEET

The problem with a kludge is eventually
you're going to have to go back and do it
right.
                            —*Programmers' saying*

"You're sure this will work?" Wiz asked for the fourth
time that morning amid the bustle of final preparations.
He was wearing a warm wool tunic and pants, a heavy
travelling cloak and a very apprehensive look.

"If you can remember to do your part of it," Moira
said a little sharply. Then she caught his expression and
placed her hand on his arm.

"Do not worry, love," she said softly. "The spells are
as simple and foolproof as we can make them. What was
your phrase?—'Idiots-and-English-majors' simple."

Wiz didn't object to the characterization. In spite of
the power his spell compiler gave him, he had absolutely
no talent for this world's magic. It had taken Moira and
Bal-Simba weeks to teach him what he would have to do
today.

Wiz was much more warmly dressed than necessary
for the Council chantry where he stood. But the clothing

24

didn't entirely explain the sweat beading on his forehead.

He was standing in the middle of a circle traced in
white powder on the flagged stone floor. Around him
stood eight of the blue-robed wizards of the Mighty, each
of them at one of the points of the compass. Late morning
sunlight pouring in through the stained glass windows cast
gaily colored patterns on the floor and the wizards, but
beside each of them burned a pair of tall wax candles.
Apprentices bustled around the edges of the room putting the finishing touches on preparations and sometimes
conferring in hushed low tones. On the dais at one end
of the room, Arianne, Bal-Simba's second in command,
was overseeing three Watchers hunched over their communications crystals. Next to the tall blonde woman stood
a pudgy little man in the blue robe of the Mighty, his
lips moving silently and his eyes focused far away as he
maintained contact with others of his fellows at their
assigned tasks.

"Are we prepared then?" asked Bal-Simba from his spot
on the circle.

"Lord, the patrols are off the beach," Arianne told him,
pushing back a stray lock of blonde hair.

"The other wizards are standing by," reported Malus,
the wizard next to her.

"Operation 500-Pound Parakeet is ready to go," Jerry
called from his place at the side of the room. Everyone
looked to the sun stick which cast a shortening shadow
on the marks on the opposite wall. The tip of the shadow
was inexorably approaching one of the marks.

Danny and Jerry stepped into the circle to clap Wiz
on the back and wish him well.

"I never did understand why you call this after a giant
parrot," Moira said as they waited for the last minutes
to pass.

"Parakeet," Danny corrected. "It's how you get rid of
cats. You get a 500-pound parakeet and teach it to say
'here, kitty kitty kitty.' "

Moira started to frown and then laughed as she caught the joke.

"So you call this Operation 500-Pound Parakeet."

"They call it Operation 500-Pound Parakeet," Wiz said sourly. "I had nothing to do with the name."

"Hey man, it's gonna be easy," Danny told him lightly. "All you gotta do is zip back to the City of Night, off a demon who's waiting to toast you, and then call for the cavalry—us. We handle the rest." He made a palm-down gesture as if sweeping aside minor details. "Nooo problemo."

"It is indeed simple if you remember your spells and execute them correctly," Moira agreed.

"I rest my case," Wiz said sourly.

"Crave pardon?"

"Almost time," Bal-Simba called from his place at the head of the circle. "Make ready."

"I mean you just proved my point. Oh well, if we're going to do this thing, let's get on with it."

He kissed Moira long and hard.

"Okay," he said. "Places everyone."

Moira, Jerry and Danny stepped back and out of the circle, being careful not to scuff the chalked lines. The seven other wizards looked at Bal-Simba and he watched the sun stick as the shadow crept the last fraction of an inch along its track.

Then all the wizards raised their hands and began chanting. Wiz gripped his staff and tried to breathe slowly and evenly as the chant rose around him and the air seemed to fill with smoke. The sound became louder and louder, then began to fade as the air around him became thick and opaque.

There was a flash of darkness and suddenly the air was so cold it burned his lungs.

Wiz Zumwalt clung to his staff and pressed his eyes tightly shut as waves of dizziness washed over him. When he opened his eyes he found he was nose to nose with a wall of crudely dressed black basalt. He turned and nearly fell when he stepped on a patch of ice in the wall's shadow. He scraped his palm as he caught himself against the rough wall. Then his vision cleared and the dizziness receded as he looked out over desolation.

Even at its height the City of Night had not been attractive. Its builders, the wizards of the Dark League, had cared much more for power than for beauty. Most of the city had been crudely built out of the volcanic stone of the Southern continent with no regard to appearance or city planning.

But when the Dark League had ruled here at least there had been a kind of sinister vitality to the place. In its ruin and abandonment the city was simply ugly. The cobbled street fell away steeply and over the roofs of the close-huddled buildings Wiz could see the steel-gray harbor merging at the horizon into steel-gray sky. Behind him the volcano on whose flank the city stood curled a thin plume of smoke to the leaden sky. Even the snow that capped the mountain was dirty gray.

Studded here and there around the city were gaunt black towers, several of them with their tops blown off. A few yards ahead of Wiz the street was blocked by rubble where one of the buildings had collapsed. Many of the buildings between him and the harbor were ruined, roofless or in a couple of cases simply melted.

He reached inside his shirt and pulled out a tiny bit of blue crystal he wore on a thong around his neck. "I'm here," he said into the communications crystal. "Start Operation 500-Pound Parakeet."

Then he looked out over his handiwork again and shivered, not entirely from the cold.

Directly or indirectly, Wiz was responsible for most of the destruction. In his first great battle with the Dark League he had used his mixture of computer programming and magic to rout the League and destroyed a good part of the city in the process. In the second confrontation, he had been kidnapped to this place by the remnants of the League. For weeks the enemy wizards had hunted him through the freezing ruins of the City of Night while a tracking demon waited to destroy him if he used the least of his new magic.

He had been rescued after he had incited a magical battle between the wizards and Bale-Zur, the invincible slaying demon who had once served them. The effect of so much magic unleashed had attracted the attention of the Council's Watchers and brought a patrol of dragons south over the City to his rescue.

However the battle had stirred up the slaying demon. Instead of staying in one place and killing whatever came to him, the Watchers reported Bale-Zur now roamed the City of Night ceaselessly looking for victims. Worse, it had begun to range beyond the City itself. If this kept up it was sure to use its powers to travel across the Freshened Sea to the lands of men.

Wiz knew he was safe enough, but he kept his back to the freezing wall anyway. The communications crystal used the old magic of the Mighty, not his new spell compiler that would activate the tracking demon. Even though it needed eight powerful wizards and a complicated ceremony, Bal-Simba had sent him along the Wizard's Way by conventional magic so he did not have to use his own spells.

Of all the mortals in the World only three were safe from Bale-Zur. The demon would not touch Wiz, Jerry and Danny because their full names—their true names—had never been spoken anywhere in the World. To Bale-Zur they were no more prey than a rock.

However Bale-Zur was only half the problem. The other half was the hunting demon the Dark League had created in their attempt to destroy Wiz. Unlike Bale-Zur it could not range much beyond the Southern Continent. However it was keyed to Wiz's special brand of magic and would attack and destroy anything that used it.

But spells built with the magic compiler were the only

kind Wiz, Jerry and Danny knew. If they tried to make magic the demon would be on them instantly.

It presented a pretty problem. Wiz, Jerry and Danny were immune to Bale-Zur, but if they used their magic they would be immediately attacked by the hunting demon. The hunting demon would not respond to conventional magic, but not even all of the Mighty together could hope to stand against Bale-Zur.

Until Bale-Zur was contained it was horribly risky for any mortal but Wiz or his friends to enter the City of Night and until the hunting demon was contained, they could not be safe here.

The demons weren't the only dangers in the City of Night. Remnants of the League's old magic remained and there were other monsters here as well. However none of those were the equal of a well-prepared magician— *well, probably not,* Wiz told himself—and most of them were not active by daylight in the open. *We don't think!*

Naturally they had backup. He was being closely watched by magical means, and several of the Mighty were poised to jump to his aid if he appeared to be in danger. There were two squadrons of dragon riders circling just off the beach. But he was still here alone and if anything went wrong he would be the first to know it.

Well, now I know how a worm on a hook feels, Wiz thought. He pulled his cloak tighter and set to work.

After hashing it over repeatedly, they had worked out a plan. It seemed like a good idea back at the Capital, but standing in the shattered city, Wiz was growing less fond of it by the minute.

He shifted his grip on his staff. The sooner they got this part of the operation over with the sooner he would be able to protect himself. *And the sooner I can use a spell to stay warm.*

He reached into his pouch, drew out four pieces of blue stone and set one at each point of the compass. Then he stood between them and began to scratch in the frozen dust with his staff.

Carefully he traced the figure in the dust as he had been taught. The old magic of this world depended for its success on precise execution. Everything had to be done just right and even the tiniest deviation from the rituals could mean disastrous changes in the outcome. The secret of the success of his magic compiler lay in the fact that it used extremely simple, reliable little spells that could be built up to produce complex, powerful effects with little or no talent on the part of the user.

With his new magic Wiz was easily the most powerful mortal magician in this world. But he was as natural a klutz as he was a computer programmer. Even this simple spell would tax him to the limit.

He finished the tracing and made especially sure the lines crossed to close the figure around him. The freezing wind whipped up little eddies of dust, but it did not erase the pentagram.

Finally he surveyed his handiwork one more time and reached back into his pouch. This time he pulled out a bit of forked, twisted root. Stepping to the edge of the circle, he lifted the root to his mouth and whispered to it the words Moira and Bal-Simba had spent so long pounding into his head. He leaned over and placed it outside the circle. Then he stepped back and waited.

He had barely reached the center when the root stirred in the dust. As he watched it seemed to untwist and swell until it became a tiny brown man shape, no longer than Wiz's thumb. It got to its knees and then to its feet and then shook itself once, as if to clear its head. It strode forward, placed its hands on its hips, threw back its head and began to shout.

Inside the circle Wiz heard nothing but the wind. He knew that the manikin was reciting a simple spell in the new magic. The spell didn't do much, but it should be enough to attract the demon. Wiz gripped his staff harder and forced himself not to hold his breath as he watched.

Suddenly, with an earsplitting roar, the demon arrived. A clawed foot crushed the mandrake manikin to the dust. The burning red eyes searched right and left and the horned, scaled, fanged head swiveled on the snake-like neck as it scanned for more prey. It stopped when it saw Wiz standing perhaps twenty feet away, seemingly unprotected and reeking of traces of the new magic. Without warning and without seeming to gather itself it leapt at Wiz, jaws gaping and talons spread. Its bellows rang off the surrounding stone walls.

Perhaps five feet from the human, the demon bounced. It stopped dead in mid-air and with talons scrabbling for purchase it slid slowly down the invisible barrier that lay between it and its would-be prey.

Again and again, the thing hurled itself against the invisible barrier that separated it from its prey. In spite of himself Wiz flinched and shrank back from its fury.

It was wasted effort. The demon clawed impotently at the barrier and scrabbled frantically against it, but it could not come close to penetrating it.

Wiz raised his staff and spoke. **"demon debug begone exe!"** he proclaimed.

The demon renewed its desperate attack on the magical barrier and its screams rose to a crescendo. Then the spell took hold. The demon became translucent. Its roars faded to the merely deafening, down through the loud and then trailed away like a locomotive whistle disappearing in the distance. It became transparent, faded to a mere outline and then it was gone.

Wiz let out his breath in a great gasping sigh and sagged against his staff.

"Okay," he said into the communications crystal. "Phase one is accomplished. Come on through and let's get the rest of this thing over with."

There were two soft pops behind him and there were Jerry and Danny, looking disoriented and a little sick, but clutching their staffs gamely. They were burdened with packs and hung about with an assortment of pouches, crystals, strangely shaped bits of metal and other less identifiable things. In addition Danny carried a large leather sack that pulsated and moved as if the contents were alive.

The contents of the sack were to help them in their search. Everything else Danny and Jerry carried was for protection or defense. Looking them over, Wiz reflected there was probably enough magical firepower between the pair of them to defeat the Dark League ten times over. Far more than they would need for anything they were likely to meet here.

Which was fine with Wiz. He had not the slightest intention of giving anything in the City of Night an even break.

"You okay?" Wiz asked as his friends seemed to become aware of their surroundings.

"Yeah," Danny mumbled. Then he shook his head to clear it. "Boy that's a weird feeling."

"It'll be a good feeling when we get out of here. And the sooner we start the search the sooner that will be."

Danny nodded and bent to open the leather bag.

Hundreds of things like dirty gossamer handkerchiefs half-flapped, half-floated out of the sack and wafted off in all directions. Behind them came a half-dozen things of the same stuff about the size of a bath towel. Finally Danny reached in and pulled out a crystalline object about a foot high. The facets flashed in the pale light and the thing began buzzing weakly as it started receiving data from the searching units.

"It will take them a few minutes to get some kind of search pattern set up," Wiz said into the comm crystal. "There's not a lot we can do until then."

"Just be careful doing nothing," Moira's voice admonished them. "That place is not safe."

"No kidding," Wiz said, thinking of the close calls he had when he was a fugitive in the city.

"They're spreading out fast," Jerry said, craning his neck and shielding his eyes with his hands to try to follow the searchers' progress.

All the things in the sack were variants of the system of searching demons which had been one of Wiz's first projects with his new magic. The smaller searchers had almost no intelligence or volition. They were passive receptors which passed information back to the bath towel things for concentration and interpretation. They in turn passed the information back to the crystal object which did the final evaluation.

Unlike Wiz's original system, this one was tuned to look for only one object, the heart of Bale-Zur. The demons had been trained on similar demon hearts held in the vaults beneath the Capital. When they found a demon heart they would report back to the humans.

Danny poked at the rubble with his staff. "What does the heart of a demon look like anyway?"

"It's a cloudy sphere about as big as your head," Wiz told him. "Anyway, that's how it was described to me."

"Do not worry about identifying it," Moira's voice came inside their heads. "Your searching demons will know it when they see it."

"If it still exists, it should be somewhere in Toth-Set-Ra's old palace," Moira's voice told them. "That is," she paused for a second while she translated what the Watcher's crystal was showing her into their coordinate system, "almost straight behind you."

"I hope it is there," Wiz said. "It will make our job a lot easier."

He motioned toward the palace and all three of them gathered up their magical paraphernalia and set off.

FOUR

COMA

"Hi. Uh, I'd like to see Judith Conally."

The nurse looked up from her paperwork and flashed a professional smile. "Are you a relative?"

"No, I'm a friend."

"I'm sorry, but only relatives are allowed to visit patients in the neurological unit."

"She doesn't have any relatives out here. I'm her best friend. Can't I please see her?"

The nurse looked him over. He wasn't much more than twenty. A pale and soft youth with brown hair and a complexion that bore a trace of adolescent acne. He was wearing an old flight jacket with several felt-tip pens in the left sleeve pocket and a T-shirt with a picture of a warrior in a horned helmet air-brushed on it.

He had laid a three-ring notebook on the counter with a couple of library books on top.

A student, she decided. Harmless and very earnest.

The nurse glanced at the chart. The visiting rule wasn't rigidly enforced in the neurological unit unless the doctor requested it and there was nothing on the chart about that. The patient hadn't had a visitor in a while.

She smiled again, a little less professionally. "I suppose it would be all right, but you'll have to be very quiet."

The searchers found the heart of the demon before Wiz and his friends reached the palace.

As they got close to the former seat of the Dark League's power the destruction got worse and the going got harder. In some places it was hard to tell the streets from the flattened houses and in a couple of instances it was easier to avoid the street and go over the remains of the buildings. Once they came to a place where the stone had melted into glassy slag with razor-sharp edges everywhere. Another time seeping water in deep shadows had formed a waterfall of ice nearly ten feet tall.

They saw no signs of life, but once they heard something scrabbling over the rubble as if fleeing their approach.

"Boy, what a mess," Jerry panted as they pulled themselves to the top of the latest obstacle.

Wiz shaded his eyes and looked ahead, trying to find the easiest route. "I don't remember it being this bad. On the other hand, I stayed away from this part of town as much as I could."

Danny consulted the crystal device. "It's over that way, in that big black pile of rubble."

Jerry scanned the horizon. "*Which* big black pile of rubble?"

"That one," Wiz pointed. "Let's go."

Another fifteen minutes of hard travel brought them through the shattered black gates of the palace. The going was easier here because there had been just one building set in an extensive courtyard. None of the roof remained and everything had collapsed in on itself, but enough of the walls still stood that you could pick out the general outlines of the floor plan.

"This guy sure had lousy taste," Jerry said, eyeing the remains of a strangely twisted mosaic on a partly standing wall.

"I think some of it's kind of neat," Danny said as he looked over a doorway shaped like the gaping mouth of a monster. He reached out and stroked the door jamb admiringly.

The door growled and Danny jumped back, landing sprawled on the rubble.

"I told you not to touch stuff," Wiz said.

"Yeah." He consulted the locator to hide his embarrassment. "Uh, what we want is down this way."

Another couple of hundred yards and the trio came to an archway that was still mostly standing. Through it they saw five or six searchers hovering around like a patch of smog, pulsing weakly as they sensed their quarry.

"I guess it's down there," Danny said.

"Great," Wiz said, eyeing the remains of the room. "The debris is only about ten feet deep in there. I don't suppose you guys brought shovels?"

Jerry looked down at the equipment festooned about him. "No. We've got enough stuff here to flatten this place in an eyeblink, but we don't have anything that will let us move the rubble."

"I could send shovels to you," Moira's voice said in Wiz's ear.

Wiz considered. "Let's try it bare-handed first. Where's Bale-Zur?"

"The Watchers say it is down by the harbor."

"Moving this way?"

"Not yet. We will let you know."

"Well, come on," Wiz said to his companions. "Maybe the heart is close to the top."

"Maybe pigs will grow wings," Danny said, eyeing the rubble.

"Around this place you never know," Wiz said as he cast the first stone.

As he followed the nurse down the hall, Craig felt like the place was closing in on him. Everything was hushed, like sound didn't carry here. The lighting was all indirect and the colors were all neutral browns or dark greens. It was like your senses didn't work right.

He didn't like hospitals anyway. They reminded him of the time he had spent in corridors, rooms and visitors' lounges waiting for his mother to die. But even for a hospital this place was spooky. It was visiting hours, but most of the room doors were closed. Only once did he catch a glimpse of someone sitting at a bedside, a dark form outlined in the flickering glow of a TV screen.

The nurse stopped before one of the too-wide doors, gently pushed it open and then motioned him to follow her in.

At first he thought Judith was someone else. She was wizened and shrunken down into the immaculate white sheets of the hospital bed. They had cut her hair short and shaved part of one side of her head. There was a tube in her nose and another one running from her arm to a bottle of clear liquid hanging by the bed.

Craig looked dubiously at the nurse.

"Can she hear me?" he whispered.

"Perhaps," the nurse said gently. "Try talking to her. You don't have to whisper."

"Thank . . ." Craig started to whisper and caught himself. "Thank you."

"I'll be at the nurse's station."

As she went out the door the nurse felt a flash of pity. The young accident victims were about the worst, second only to the little kids who had nearly drowned. Maybe the visitor would do the patient good, but she doubted it. After six years on Neuro she had a feel for the patients and this one probably wasn't ever going to come out of it.

At first the programmers didn't have too much trouble digging through the rubble. The pieces were about the size of Wiz's head; small enough to handle easily and big enough to make obvious progress. The stone was freezing cold, but their sturdy gloves protected their hands and kept their fingers warm.

The heart wasn't under the first layer of rubble, or the next. By now the job was getting harder. They started to run into pieces that took two or all three of them to shift. More and more of the pieces were locked together like jackstraws and could only be moved in order. Soon all three of them were sweating in spite of the cold and panting from the effort.

"You know," Jerry said as they took a breather, "logically the heart should be all the way at the bottom of this pile."

Danny picked up a pebble and chucked it against the wall. It bounced off with a metallic clang. "It'll take us days to dig down that far, even with picks and shovels."

"Well, we can't bring anyone through to do our digging for us," Wiz said. "We're the only ones the demon won't harm."

Jerry rubbed his thumb where he had mashed it between two stones. "This seems to be an ideal job for magic. We could use a summoning spell and just call the heart to the surface."

"We could also summon Bale-Zur right on top of us. No thanks."

"So?" Danny interjected. "He won't hurt us."

Wiz thought of the huge black demon with the yard-wide mouth and glowing red eyes. "You *seriously* do not want to meet this guy. I still have nightmares about what he did to those Dark League wizards. Anyway, we can't conduct the next phase of the operation with him right on top of us."

"May I make a suggestion?" Moira's voice spoke in his ear.

"Sure darling, go ahead."

Danny started and then realized Wiz wasn't talking to him.

"Jerry is right. Could you use magic to do your digging?"

"Won't that attract Bale-Zur?"

There was muffled noise over the crystal as Moira conferred with other wizards.

"Perhaps, but it is imperative we complete this before nightfall. Unless you want to spend the night there."

Wiz remembered some of the things that inhabited the City of Night after dark and he shuddered again. "No thanks."

"Besides, should worse come to worst we can lay the demon elsewhere."

Wiz weighed that. "Okay. We'll give it a try." He turned to his companions. "Now does anyone have any good ideas for a digging spell?"

As the nurse left, Craig pulled a chair close to the bed, wincing at the slight scraping sound.

"Hi, Judith. Can you hear me?" Always Judith. She hated to be called Judy and she had pinned his ears back when he slipped the first time they met.

The figure in the bed did not respond. There was not a flicker from the eyelids and the rhythm of breathing continued uninterrupted.

Craig wanted to bolt. This was too much like his mother had been, before she'd wake up and start screaming for her shot. The only thing that kept him in the chair was knowing he'd have to pass the nurse and she'd know he couldn't take it. He had to stay for a few minutes anyway.

He felt like an idiot for coming. None of the others had, not since Judith was transferred out of ICU. So he'd said he would at the last gaming session and then he was committed.

"Everybody misses you on Friday nights," he said brightly.

"Bill and Sheri are taking your place in the campaign, but they're really not very good."

Still no response from the bed.

"We had a really good game last Friday. Joe was

dungeon master and he set up a really nasty scenario. You
had all these flocks of dragonlets in a crystal cave and
they'd just swarm the party from all directions. But you
had to be careful what spells you used because a lot of
the crystals were Reflect Magic and you could get the
spell thrown right back in your face." His grin made him
look even younger. "Boy, you should have seen it! Dragons
diving on us everywhere. They'd make flame attacks and
then swoop down with claws and tail, ssshhhewww." He
imitated the motion with his hands.

Judith tossed restlessly and mumbled.

"Anyway we were up to our asses in dragons. Then
Howard's mage figured out you could use the Reflect
Magic crystals for bank shots and he started bouncing stuff
off the walls and hitting the dragons from behind! Hey,
did you say something?"

" . . . real dragons ugly," Judith mumbled. "Smell like
snakes . . . ride over the castle."

She was talking! For an instant Craig thought about
ringing for the nurse, but then he realized she probably
wouldn't give a shit.

" . . . tie into the saddle . . ." Judith went on. " . . . takes
years to learn to ride. No fun, anyway . . . better dragons
imagine . . ."

"Yeah, dragons are neat all right."

"Real," Judith said very distinctly.

"Huh?"

"Real dragons. Saw them myself come over the Wizard's
Keep first morning we were there. Real dragons . . ." She
settled back and trailed off into incomprehensibility.

Craig hunched closer to the bed.

"Tell me more, Judith. What about the dragons?"

FIVE

UNSOUGHT PROPHECY

It was late in the afternoon when they got the digging spell working. The wan sun was sinking toward the horizon, throwing highlights off the sullen gray surface of the Freshened Sea and sending dark shadows creeping out across the ruins. The cold deepened with the growing twilight and all three programmer/magicians had wrapped their cloaks tightly around themselves to try to stay warm.

"I'm not sure I like this," Jerry said as they huddled together for a final review of their handiwork. "We really should run a couple more tests."

"We don't have time. Unless you want to stay here all night?"

Jerry looked around at the menacing ruins and pulled his cloak tighter. "No thanks. I just wish . . ."

"Oh come on, we've tested the thing to death," Danny said. "Let's get this over with. I'm freezing."

Mentally Wiz reviewed the spell one more time. It simply checked each loose piece within its radius of operation to see if it was the heart of the demon and if it wasn't, tossed it aside. When it reached the demon's heart, it would stop. It was straightforward enough and Wiz couldn't find any flaws. Besides he was as cold as Danny was.

41

"Okay," he said. "Let's do it."

All three of them stepped back from the pile of rubble and out the collapsed archway. When they were in position, Wiz called:

"emac"

A three-foot-high demon with enormous ears popped up before him. **"?"** it said.

Wiz pointed his staff at the rubble choking the room. **"kill exe!"** he commanded.

The Emac turned toward the spot and gabbled soundlessly. Then it bowed and popped out of existence.

For a moment nothing happened.

"It takes a while for the effect to build up," Wiz explained unnecessarily.

"I just wish . . ." Jerry began. "I have this awful feeling we forgot something."

"It's working!" Danny shouted, pointing at the rubble. A single pebble detached itself from the pile and flew off in a flat arc. Then another pebble whipped off in another direction, and another and another.

As the three watched a head-sized chunk of material shook itself loose and lobbed away from the rubble. Then several more pebbles.

One of the pebbles flew over Wiz's head with an ugly singing whirr.

"Direction," Jerry said abstractedly. "Did we put anything in the spell to control which way the rubble would go when it left the pile?"

"No," Wiz said apprehensively, as another volley of material broke loose from the mound.

"Then hit the dirt!" Jerry shouted as a dozen big chunks of rubble came flying straight at them.

All three of them dropped and rolled behind the remains of the wall just as a half-dozen pieces of stone went through the spot where they had been standing, humming like angry bees. Then a torso-sized slab of black marble lofted over the wall and crashed into the frozen dust behind them.

Then all Hell broke loose.

The pile of rubble exploded outwards in all directions. The small stuff came off with the velocity of rifle bullets. The bigger pieces arced away like mortar shells. The three wizards pressed themselves against the base of the wall and tried to burrow into the dirt as debris landed all around them.

I am not a target, Wiz told himself as he tried to become one with the base of the wall. *This is not aimed at me.* He shifted slightly just as the remains of a large piece of furniture sailed over the ruined wall and crashed to earth a few feet from him. Abstractedly he realized there should be a simple command to shut the spell down, but it's hard to think when you're in the middle of an artillery barrage and impossible to talk when your mouth is full of dirt.

There were crashes and thuds and whizzes and occasionally a nasty *spang* as something hit the wall and ricocheted away. Once a big piece hit the top of the wall, knocking off chips and showering them down on the cowering trio. The dust grew so thick that Wiz couldn't see two feet in front of him—not that he was looking.

Then suddenly it was quiet.

No more crashes. No more earth-shaking thuds. Just a couple of zips from small stuff and then silence. Even the dust started to settle.

Wiz raised his head and looked around wonderingly. Then he realized Moira was screaming at him through the communications crystal.

"We're fine," he told her, looking at his companions. "The spell was just a little more effective than we thought."

"Oh man," Danny muttered. "Anyone got anything for shell shock?"

"It's the details," Jerry said to no one in particular. "It's always the details that get you in trouble."

Wiz made a feeble attempt to brush himself off and peered around the archway.

The remains of the arch were pocked and scarred with fresh blemishes, white against the polished black granite. But the room itself was as clean as if it had been excavated by a team of expert archaeologists and then scrubbed and vacuumed by a village of Japanese housewives. There, almost exactly in the center of the room, sitting on the newly exposed mosaics of the floor, was a cloudy gray sphere.

Wiz stepped through the archway and realized he was tracking dirt back onto the clean floor.

"Okay," he said into the communications crystal. "We have the thing located. If it's safe come on through."

Then he looked around and bit his lip.

Wiz didn't like *any* part of the operation, but this next step was his least favorite, even counting facing the golden demon. Moira was not immune to Bale-Zur, but she knew more about controlling a demon than any of the programmers. In addition to having more skill at natural magic, she had spent long sessions at Heart's Ease with Shiara the Silver learning all the former wizardess could tell her about such things. If their plan failed, Moira was their last line of defense.

"Sharp lookout everyone," he called over his shoulder. Danny and Jerry spread out, staffs ready, peering into the building gloom for any sign of trouble.

Two figures popped into existence on the polished floor, not just one.

"What the hell is she doing here?" Wiz demanded.

Moira frowned at the greeting and then she whirled. Standing behind her, not two paces away, was June.

"How did you get here?" Moira asked sharply. But June just smiled triumphantly and made a beeline for Danny.

"I thought you said she didn't have any magical ability," Wiz whispered to Moira as the couple hugged and June clung to Danny's arm.

"She does not—I think," Moira whispered back.

"Well then?"

Moira only shrugged.

"Let us get it over with," Moira said. With Danny, Wiz and Jerry forming a perimeter guard, she knelt by the heart of Bale-Zur and reached slowly out to it.

For a long time she stayed motionless, her hand hovering over the cloudy crystal sphere. At last she began to move her fingers slowly over the surface, caressing it without quite touching it. Her lips began to move as she started the chant she had been taught to bring the demon back under control.

With the point of her staff she marked a pentagram around the demon's heart. Then she stood up, backed off a step and raised her staff. Her voice rose to a wild cry as she gestured into the air. In spite of himself Wiz found his attention was drawn to his wife and her work.

The sphere pulsed and glowed with an inner light, casting a greenish-gray luminance around itself and Moira. It rocked back and forth as if seeking to break free of the imprisoning figure. Still Moira continued the eerie chant, bouncing the words off the ruined walls like bullets.

And then Bale-Zur was there.

Half-hopping, half-shambling, the huge demon moved into the circle of weird radiance. Its great horned head turned neither right nor left and its glowing eyes, red as the fires of Hell, stayed fixed on the hedge witch and the heart. For an awful moment Wiz thought the monster would reach out and grind Moira into a red smear, as he had done with a legion of wizards from the Dark League. Instead the demon approached her across its heart and sank down on its haunches to stare motionless at the woman and the sphere.

Moira continued her chant as if nothing had changed. She lowered her staff and pointed at the heart. Bale-Zur stayed motionless, great taloned hands resting on his misshapen horned knees. The hedge witch extended her staff and tapped the crystal sphere once, twice, three times. The demon leaned forward as if in special interest. Moira repeated the three taps and Bale-Zur cocked its head. Again the three taps and this time the demon seemed to shrink in on itself like a deflating balloon. Suddenly, noiselessly, it shrank and vanished without a trace. The glow faded and all that was left was a woman and a head-sized ball of some shiny black material.

Moira grounded her staff and sighed deeply. Then she sagged against it.

That broke the spell. Wiz rushed to her and put his arms about her shoulders. She leaned against him and he could feel her heart pounding even through the thick cloak she wore.

"Fine," she muttered. "M'fine. Just hold me, will you?"

Danny, Jerry and June all gathered around them in the deepening gloom of evening. Moira took a deep breath and straightened in Wiz's arms.

"It is done," she said in a surprisingly strong voice.

Wiz looked at the globe, now cold and dark. "That's it then," he said. "Bale-Zur is gone."

"May we never see its like again," Moira said fervently.

"Oh, you will not, mortals," said a sweetly mocking voice behind them. "I see that in your future."

All four of them whirled. There, standing poised on the ruined wall, was an elf.

Like all her kind, she was tall and slender. The delicate points of her ears peeked through the long dark hair that curved around her face and fell loose down her back. Her oddly slanted eyes were as blue as Moira's were green. In spite of the cold she wore a shoulderless gown of fine pale pink stuff that rippled in the chill wind and set off her pale skin and dark hair. She was as alien as she was beautiful, utterly relaxed and as menacing as a tiger poised to spring.

June screamed and sank back against Danny. Moira stepped to the side and held her staff aloft as if to strike. Danny clutched June to him and Wiz and Jerry simply goggled.

"Uh, hi," Wiz said, completely nonplussed. "Lisella, isn't it?"

The elf maiden arched her beautifully formed brows and pursed her red lips in a mock pout.

"You have forgotten me already. I am disappointed, Sparrow."

"Ah, not exactly." *I never forget someone who's tried to kill me.* The elf looked amused at his discomfort.

"So," he said at last, "what brings you here?"

Lisella smiled, bright and cold as the moon at midwinter. "Why, I came to renew our acquaintance, Sparrow, and to offer you a gift of prophecy. Shall I tell you your future?"

"Uh, no thanks."

"Ruin and loss," Lisella went on as if he had not spoken. "Your company shall meet your greatest enemy, one like you with powers as great as yours and allies greater than you can imagine." Her voice rang off the stones and the wind pulled at her skirt and hair. "At the crossroads of the worlds you and your companions shall meet him in a great battle. The mightiest among you shall die, each of your number shall suffer great loss and your enemy shall achieve his heart's desire."

She raised her arm and made a sweeping gesture that encompassed all of them. "That is your future, mortals. That is what lies ahead."

And then she was gone. The only sound was June's harsh sobbing echoing off the cold stone.

They looked at each other.

"Bitch!" Danny said fiercely as he clung to his wife. "Goddamn bitch."

"That's the one who was trying to kill you?" Jerry asked Wiz.

"Yeah. She kept trying to set up magical accidents."

"Why?"

"Who knows? I met her once at Duke Aelric's but by that time she'd been after me for months. I think it was some sort of cat-and-mouse game between her and

Aelric—with them as cats and me as the mouse. She'd try to kill me by accident and Aelric would help me escape by the skin of my teeth."

"Do you think she's after you again?"

Wiz looked apprehensively at the place on the wall where Lisella had stood. Then he shrugged. "Maybe."

Jerry followed his gaze. "It sounds like we're in for some real trouble."

"If she's right, maybe."

"Well, elves can foretell the future, can't they?"

"Foretelling and true speaking are two different things," Moira said firmly. "Elves can see truly but they are as false and tricksome as a piskhie maze. Clearly she means us no good and we had best ignore what she has said."

It would have been more convincing, Wiz thought, if her knuckles hadn't been white on her staff.

"Well anyway, I think we'd better wind up here and get back to the Capital," Jerry said. "Bal-Simba needs to know about this."

"I don't think he's going to like it much," Wiz predicted.

Wiz's prophecy, at least, was correct. The enormous black wizard heard them out and then led them back through their story time and again with sharp questions. At last he had no more questions and simply sat with his head sunk into his hamlike hands. The group of programmers sat clustered around the table, unsure what to do next but unwilling to depart without his leave.

"What do you think it means, Lord?" Wiz ventured at last.

"I wish I knew, Sparrow." He lapsed into silence again.

"There have been other elven prophecies to mortals," Moira said. "Or so the stories say."

"Not like this," Arianne said from her place behind Bal-Simba's chair. "Those stories speak of chance meetings and a prophecy given either as a reward or punishment."

"This was neither," Bal-Simba said. "She asked for nothing. More, she obviously sought you out at a time when you would all be together and away from the Capital and its protections."

"What should we do?"

"There is nothing we can do. The future may be open to elves, but to us it is closed and hidden. We can only live our lives as best we can and see what comes of all this."

"I wish I knew what her game was," Wiz said.

"I wish I knew why she wanted you dead," Moira replied.

"She hasn't tried to kill me since I was kidnapped to the City of Night. That's something anyway."

"True," Bal-Simba said. "It is something. I only wish I knew what."

SIX

QUEST COMPANION

Good help is so hard to find
nowadays.

—Personnel manager's lament

Craig paused at the foot of the stairs and went over his spiel again. He wanted to get this just right, otherwise Panda would think he was crazy.

For two weeks he had visited Judith every night, even missing two Friday gaming sessions in a row. Slowly and patiently he had worked the story out of her; where she had gone and what she had seen and done.

It was unbelievable. It was fantastic. Except that it made sense. When you put it together with other little things over the last year, it *had* to be true!

The exultation grew until a lump rose in his throat from sheer joy. *There were other worlds where magic worked!* It wasn't all just game scenarios and science fiction. Those places really did exist and you could get there from here! He shivered again at the wonder of it all.

Only—now he needed help.

Out on the street the traffic rushed by unheeded. Craig stared unseeing, while he went over his dilemma one more time.

Somehow he had to find a way to open that door into the other world. He wanted that more desperately than he had ever wanted anything in his life, even, he realized with a guilty start, more than he had wanted his mother to live. But he had to have a Quest Companion, someone to help him push that door open.

Who? He had spent most of the last three days going over possibilities and the list was disappointingly small. When you got right down to it, Craig realized, he didn't have any close friends except maybe Judith.

The gamers were the only people he actually knew. But he really didn't like them much and most of them thought he was kind of strange. Besides, they couldn't help him. The thought of Joe or Howard as Quest Companions on a real quest was silly and the rest didn't know enough about computers.

There were the others, the ones he met in the shadowy neverland of bulletin boards in his secret identity as Skullslayer, the master hacker. But he knew as little about them as they did about him. It would be embarrassing to confide in someone and then have it turn out to be a pimply faced thirteen-year-old.

There was one whose real identity he did know. A year and a half ago Panda had taken the unusual and dangerous step of contacting him in person. He was such an outtasight hacker that he'd discovered Skullslayer's identity and found that he used to work as a part-time operator in the University computer center. Not only that, he knew that Craig's password and login were still active!

The stuff about the virus, that had been an accident. Mikey had explained it all to him the night he showed up at his apartment and wanted help to cover it up. At first he'd been scared that Mikey was going to turn him over to the FBI, but Mikey just sort of mentioned in passing that he knew a lot about Skullslayer and of course if he was picked up he'd have to make a deal to save his own skin. Just this one favor, Mikey had promised, and we'll be square.

Actually it was a thrill and kind of an honor to be involved in something as big as the Jesse James Virus. So in a matter of ten minutes, from his living room, he had hopelessly muddled the trail that led from the out-of-control computer virus back to Panda.

They'd never met in person again, but they had become good friends over the BBSs. Craig followed Panda's exploits with admiration and more than a little awe. The guy was not only good, he was, well, *daring*. A dozen times or more Panda had boldly gone where no hacker had gone before, coming up with phone numbers and access codes to some of the most outrageous systems.

A woman with a bag of groceries in either arm came up the walk from the parking lot. She stepped off the sidewalk to pass well around Craig, eyeing him suspiciously as she did so.

She's gonna call the cops on me. Well, he couldn't delay any longer.

The name on the door was "Michael E. Baker," but Craig knew everyone called him Mikey—like in the cereal commercial.

"Panda? It's me. Skullslayer."

There was a muffled "just a minute" and the sound of a lock turning.

The door opened a crack and a blue eye peered out. "You alone?"

"Yeah. Just me."

The door closed and then opened wide.

Mikey was shirtless and barefoot. He was several years older than Craig, but Craig was already beginning to bulge and Mikey was lean without being skinny. His blonde hair was cut surfer style and wire-rimmed glasses hid mild blue eyes. While Craig looked like a computer nerd, nothing suggested Mikey Baker was one of the most accomplished hackers in Silicon Valley.

"Come on in." He turned his back on his guest and strode back into the apartment.

"Nice place," Craig said as he closed the door behind him. The living room was furnished in modern chrome-and-leather furniture. Brown leather that complemented the beige carpet and the darker brown drapes. One entire wall was taken up with an elaborate entertainment center, including a big-screen television that was playing soundlessly. It was fairly neat for a hacker pad. No printouts, no posters, no stacks of books and magazines, just the day's newspaper on the floor by the recliner and a couple of empty beer cans.

Mikey went back into the kitchenette and opened the refrigerator. "Want a beer?"

Craig plopped himself down on the leather-and-chrome sofa. "No thanks." Then he saw what was on television and his jaw dropped.

A luscious brunette was squatting before a man who was hung like a horse. The man's pants were down around his ankles and the woman was completely naked. The camera closed in tight on the man's crotch and the woman's mouth.

"X channel," Mikey said as he came back into the living room with a beer in his hand. "Satellite feed."

"Wow. I thought you couldn't get those here."

Mike smiled. "They're up on the satellites if you know where to look."

Craig watched the action on the screen some more. "Wow."

"How'd you find me?"

Craig tore his eyes away from the television.

"The day you—uh—came over to my place. I got your license number." He shrugged. To any true system breaker the rest was obvious.

Mikey grunted. "Pretty cute. So what brings you here?"

Craig tore his eyes away again.

"You know Judith Conally?"

"No."

"Well, I game with her and . . ."

Mikey grinned. "Is she a good fuck?"

Craig colored. "I never . . . I mean, I don't know her that well."

Mikey's grin got even wider. "So if she's not a good fuck why play games with her?"

Craig stopped dead. That was the thing about Panda. He had a way of derailing your train of thought. And you could never be *quite* sure when he was kidding.

"Well, she's in the hospital, see? She had a real bad accident. I've been going to see her and sometimes she, like, talks, you know? Like she doesn't know what she's saying.

"Anyway," he hurried on, "she's been talking about this world where magic works and there are dragons and wizards and all that kind of shit."

Mikey popped the top of the beer. "So?"

"So I don't think it's just a story."

"Get real!" Mike took a hefty swig from the can and turned back toward the TV. A skinny blonde with a haystack hairdo and basketball breasts was being caressed from behind by a black man.

"No, listen man. She went someplace last year, her and a bunch of other people. They were recruited at an SCA war and they were gone for maybe six months. Everyone who went has been real secretive. It was right after Judith came back that she started trying to write fantasy.

"And," he concluded triumphantly, "they got paid in gold! I remember Judith bitching about how hard it was to get it changed into money."

Mike turned back to his visitor. "And you think they went to Middle Earth or something?" he said contemptuously.

"They sure as hell didn't go to Redmond, Washington. Microsoft doesn't pay its people in gold."

Mikey turned back to the television. "Bullshit."

"Wait, there's more. They were recruited to, like, program magic. Over there you can hack magic the way you can computers. Programmers are super-wizards in that world."

"And you believe her. This cunt's wacked out of her mind in the hospital and you still believe her."

"I'm telling you it all fits!" Craig said desperately. "It's *gotta* be true."

"It's still bullshit. And even if it's true, so what? What's that got to do with us?"

"Don't you see, we can go there too!"

Mikey set the beer down. "Why the fuck would we want to do that?"

Craig stopped with his mouth open. In all his planning, in all his imagining this meeting, that question never occurred to him. "Well," he said lamely, "it would be an adventure."

Mikey snorted.

"There's gotta be all kinds of treasure and stuff laying around. They paid all those people in *gold*, man! And we'd be wizards. Super-powerful wizards over there."

Mikey stared at the television and said nothing. On the screen the blonde was pistoning up and down on the black man. Her breasts were flapping like tethered balloons, but not a strand of her haystack hair was out of place.

"So what do you want me to do?"

"I, uh, need help figuring out how to make the stuff work. I need someone who's even better than I am and Panda's the *best*!"

Mikey accepted the compliment without comment. For a long time he sat and drank his beer, watching the screen and saying nothing while Craig fidgeted in silence.

Finally he tilted the bottle and drained the last drops. "I want to talk to your friend."

Craig hesitated. "She's kind of hard to talk to."

Mikey smiled a 1,000-watt smile. All of a sudden he looked about fifteen and utterly charming. "I think I can get through to her."

"Hi, Sheila, we're here to see Judith."

The young black nurse stood up from the filing

cabinet and turned around. "Hi, Craig. One of you will have to stay here. Rules say only one visitor at a time."

"Oh, come on Sheila, it would only be for a couple of minutes."

"Please," Mikey said, flashing one of his winning smiles. "We'll only be a few minutes and I really think it would do her good to see us both."

He looked so sincere, so innocent and so vulnerable that Sheila hesitated and then nodded. "Well, all right. But don't tire her out. And if the supervisor comes around, you snuck by me. Okay?"

"Did you catch the ass on that nurse?" Mikey asked in an undervoice as they headed for Judith's room.

Judith had a roommate now, an elderly Italian woman who lay spread-eagled beneath the sheets and breathed in great, wracking gasps. Otherwise everything was exactly as it had been on Craig's first visit.

"Hi, Judith," Craig said brightly. "This is Mikey. He's a friend."

There was no response from the bed. Mikey glared at Craig.

"It takes a little bit to get her talking," he whispered. Then he turned back to Judith.

"Mikey's interested in dragons, Judith. Dragons and wizards and magic. You know, the stuff you saw in the other place."

The woman's eyelids fluttered.

"You remember the dragons you saw. The ones you could ride on."

Judith's lips moved. Out of the corner of his eye Craig could see Mikey sitting impassively.

"You remember the flying dragons, don't you, Judith?" Craig went on with a tinge of desperation. "The ones you rode?"

" . . . not ride," Judith mumbled. "Mad at me . . ."

Craig threw a triumphant look at Mikey, but Mikey's expression didn't change.

"Magic, Judith. You did magic there."

" . . . spell compiler . . . full of spaghetti code. Worked asses off to fix it." Her arms twitched restlessly against the soft restraints that tied them to the bed.

"The magic compiler, how did it work?"

"Weird language . . . hacked together." She drifted off into incomprehensibility.

"Have you got a copy of the code?" Mikey put in sharply.

Judith tossed and mumbled. " . . . secret. All secret . . ."

Mikey leaned closer to the bed.

"Have you got notes?" he demanded. "Where are your notes?"

" . . . notebook . . . projects."

"Where's the notebook, Judith?" Mikey persisted. "Where did you put it?"

Judith began to move her whole body against the bed.

"Hey, she's getting upset. I think we'd better leave her alone."

Mikey ignored him. "Tell me!" he hissed, grabbing Judith's hand and squeezing hard. Judith moaned and tried to pull away from his grip.

"Hey! You're hurting her."

Mikey squeezed harder, bearing down on each word. "Where. Are. Your. Notes?"

"Home," Judith gasped. "Desk." She was thrashing from side to side and breathing hard now.

Mikey released her hand. "That's fine, Judith," he said gently. "You did real good."

He turned to Craig. "You heard her. She's got stuff back at her apartment. Can you get in?"

"Well, yeah but . . ."

"Then come on." He stood up and headed for the door without another look at Judith. Craig followed more slowly. At the doorway he looked back. Judith was still moving restlessly, panting with hard, regular gasps.

It was almost like she was sobbing.

❖   ❖   ❖

Judith's apartment was on the ground floor of a two-story complex in a quiet residential neighborhood. There were maybe fifty apartments grouped around a big central terrace and pool. They had obviously been built in the '60s, before San Jose land values went crazy, but they were well-maintained. *Probably not a bargain,* Craig thought as he led Mikey through the wrought iron gate into the court, but still the sort of place that was passed down from friend to friend.

The apartment was dark and the drapes were drawn. One of the nearby apartments had a television game show on, but no one was in the courtyard.

"There's a key in the planter by the door, under one of those phony rocks," Craig said. "She showed it to me when I stayed here."

Mikey gave him a knowing smile.

"Not like that! I just crashed on her couch a couple of nights." He didn't add that it had been while his mother had been in the hospital and he couldn't face going back to the house alone. Somehow that wasn't the sort of thing you told Mikey.

He groped around, picking up rocks from the planter. "Shit. It's not here."

"May I help you?" a voice demanded sharply.

Craig jerked erect and whirled. A middle-aged woman was glaring at them from perhaps twenty feet away. She had a sweater thrown over her shoulders and a cordless telephone in one hand. Her thumb was ostentatiously posed over one of the phone's quick-dial buttons.

Before Craig could do more than flush, Mikey stepped forward smiling—far enough to establish contact but not close enough to be threatening. "Yes ma'am," he said as if he was genuinely glad to see her. "My name is Ralph Simmons. I'm Judith Conally's supervisor. This is Craig Scott, a friend of Judith's. We've just come from the hospital and Judith asked us to bring her a few things."

Some of the venom left the woman's stare. "I thought she was in a coma."

Mikey positively beamed. "Oh, she's come out of it. She'll be in the hospital a while, but she's already talking about going back to work. I don't mind telling you that's a relief to me—I mean aside from being happy she's going to be all right. Judith is the only one who really understands that code. Just between you and me, we've been hurting without her."

The woman shifted her stance and her finger moved away from the call button. "Hadn't she quit to write or something?"

"We'd brought her back on a consulting contract. You know, just for a few hours a week. You don't just let someone like Judith walk out the door."

The woman nodded reluctantly. "She always seemed like a real dedicated person."

"Very dedicated," Mikey agreed. "And a very good worker." Then he frowned ever so slightly. "But we seem to have a little trouble here. Judith told us she left a spare key under a rock in the planter, but we can't seem to find it."

"Oh, I took that in after the accident. Didn't seem safe."

"That was very thoughtful of you, ma'am. I wonder if you could see your way clear to let us use it for a few minutes. You see, Judith wanted to look over some of the listings and the doctor thought it would be good for her. Kind of therapy, you know."

"Well . . ."

Mikey turned up the wattage on the smile. "Oh, I know it's a lot to ask, but they never did find Judith's keys after the accident. Naturally if you'd like to call the hospital . . ." again the trace of a frown, "only Judith's not supposed to have phone calls and they'd probably have to track the doctor down."

"Just some papers, you say?"

"Yes, ma'am. She won't be needing clothes or anything for a while."

"I don't suppose it would hurt. I'm Mrs. Mapelthorpe, the manager. I can let you in on my pass key."

"Yes, ma'am. If you'd like to come in with us, just to make sure . . ."

Mrs. Mapelthorpe smiled. "Oh, I'm sure that won't be necessary." She fished in the pocket of her sweater and brought out a key ring. "Just stop by 102 and check with me before you leave. Oh, and if you could, remind her that her lease is up next month. She needs to decide what she's going to do about the apartment then."

Mike flashed that winning smile, again. "We will. Thank you."

The place smelled of dust and cool, stale air. Someone had obviously tidied up after the accident, but apparently no one had been here since. The place had the feel of being not quite lived in.

"This is weird," Craig said, looking around the apartment. Mikey made a beeline for the desk.

"If we're going to see the old bitch on the way out I don't guess we'd better take anything except the papers—unless she kept that gold here?"

"No, that's in a safety deposit box."

"Bingo!" Mike said, holding up a thick notebook triumphantly. "Right on top of the pile." He looked at the papers stacked beneath it. "And here's some more." He started scooping up the papers and stacking them on top of the notebook. "And some disks too. Find me a box to carry this shit, will you?"

They couldn't wait to get back to Mikey's apartment, so they took a corner booth in a coffee shop and set their box of plunder on the seat while they spread the papers out to study them.

"Boy, I didn't think that would work," Craig said. "When the old lady showed up I was sure we were dead."

Mike looked at him contemptuously. "All you have to do is act sincere and be polite. Then people will believe any bullshit you feed them. Especially the old farts."

Neither of them said anything as they studied the

papers and notebook. Their coffee arrived and Craig hardly looked up to add extra sugar and nearly a whole pitcher of creamer. Mikey sipped his black, apparently oblivious to the heat.

"It looks like the whole damn language is here," Craig said finally. "Weird-looking stuff, though."

"You expected maybe ANSI C? Of course this shit's weird. Look at what it does."

Craig put his hand down on the stack of papers and leaned across the table to Mikey, eyes glowing. "You know what this is? I mean really? It's the road to your heart's desire. Anything you want."

"So, what do you want?"

Craig hesitated. "I guess a better world. Where people really care about people, you know?"

Mikey looked amused. "No, I don't know. Tell me."

Craig fidgeted. "I dunno. But we went wrong here. I mean with all the pollution and shit. We've just squeezed the beauty out of the way we live. There's no magic in the world."

He toyed with the spoon in his coffee. "Maybe with magic we can build something better. Something that uses magic and technology both in the way they were supposed to be used."

Outside the traffic rushed by.

"What about you? What's your heart's desire?"

Mike grinned lopsidedly. "That's easy. I want to be master of all I survey."

SEVEN

JOURNEY

"Getting there is half the fun."
—*Wrong-way Corrigan*

"I thought we were going outside," Ragnar the dwarf complained as he puffed along under a pack nearly as large as he was.

"We are," Glandurg told him as he led his band up the sloping passageway. Each of the dwarves was nearly buried in weapons, food and other necessities for the journey.

"This doesn't lead to the gate. The only things up here are the watch posts."

"You will see," Glandurg assured his men. "Step lively now."

The corridor grew steeper until finally it challenged even the surefootedness of the dwarves, burdened as they were. The way was narrower here above the highest of the workshops and habitations and the walls and floor rougher. The tunnel began to turn more frequently as the very mountain narrowed toward its peak. Several times they passed doors leading to lookout posts on the mountain itself. The dwarves guarding the doors did not salute them as they passed, but they didn't try to stop them either. That was reassuring to Glandurg's followers, who still had trouble believing that King Tosig had trusted his ne'er-do-well relative with an important mission.

Finally, just when it seemed the trail couldn't get any steeper or the mountain any narrower, Glandurg stopped in front of an iron door set in the rock. Fumbling in his pouch he produced a large key and turned it in the lock. Soundlessly the door swung open and blinding daylight flooded into the tunnel.

Hard on each others heels the dwarves tumbled out onto the mountain top. They were standing on a broad, flat expanse of dark gray stone. Squinting off in the distance they could see the other peaks of the Southern Forest Range, most of them lower than they were now. Beyond the mountains in every direction stretched the dark green of the Wild Wood, cut here and there with the meandering silver thread of a river.

None of them had ever been this high on the mountain and most of them had been outside their home tunnels perhaps a half-dozen times in their lives. It was an intoxicating sight and they peered in every direction, jabbering excitedly as they pointed out features to one another.

Glandurg ignored his unsophisticated comrades and strode toward the edge of the open space. He reached into his pouch and produced a polished bone whistle, elaborately carved in dwarvish fashion. Placing it to his lips he blew loud and hard, but no sound came from it. He scanned the skies and then blew again.

The response came not from the air as he expected, but from behind him. There was a scrabbling sound and a griffin leapt lightly down into the center of the ledge.

There was a gasp from Glandurg's followers and they shrank away from the apparition which had appeared in front of them. Glandurg gulped, terribly aware that the griffin was between him and the door to safety. But he put on his best leader's manner and strode toward the beast in what he hoped was a good imitation of fearlessness.

The other dwarves were under no such burden. They moved back against the doorway, ready to vanish down their tunnel to safety at the first sign of a hostile move.

The griffin managed to look smug, amused and dangerous all at the same time. The dwarves were on her turf and they all knew it.

Dwarves and griffins shared the mountains in an uneasy truce. The griffins nested on the uppermost crags and the dwarves tunneled through the rock. Dwarf mothers frightened their children into obedience with tales of dwarf children who had wandered away and been seized and eaten by griffins. By the same token dwarves were known to enjoy the occasional griffin egg surreptitiously taken from the nest.

"I told you we would ride," Glandurg said as he strode to the griffin.

The griffin hissed loudly and backed away.

"But you agreed to take us to the human wizard," Glandurg protested.

The griffin nodded.

"Well," said an exasperated Glandurg, "if we don't ride how will you get us there?"

The griffin smiled—as much as a creature with the beak of an eagle can smile—and flexed its claws.

Craig scowled as he riffled through the papers spread out on Mikey's coffee table. The clock display in the upper-right corner of the television set showed it was after midnight, but he paid no more attention to that than he did to the old movie on the screen. He took another pull on the can of grape soda and slammed it down, slopping sticky purple fluid on Judith's notes.

"We got a problem."

Mikey looked up from the recliner where he was curled up with Judith's notebook. "Like what?"

"How are we going to get to this other world?"

"Judith got over there, didn't she?"

"Yeah, but someone took her."

Mikey considered for a moment. "What about that first guy, the one she called Wiz? He got there on his own, didn't he?"

"No, he was taken over too. By one of their wizards." Craig drained the last of the soda and threw the empty can in the general direction of the wastebasket. "Great! So we've got all this magic and stuff and we can't do anything with it."

Mikey laughed and shook his head.

"What's so goddamn funny?"

"You. You're talking like a system administrator. If it's not obvious or it's not in the manual, it can't be done. What you need to do is chill out and keep working on this stuff."

"What good does that do?" Craig asked, half-sullen.

"The more you learn, the easier it is to make things happen. That's the secret of hacking. You don't worry if something seems impossible. You just keep watching and learning and pretty soon it's not impossible."

He stood up and stretched on tiptoes, leaning far back to work the kinks out of his spine. "Now here, we can't get over ourselves, but maybe we can get someone to bring us over."

"How?"

"We make something like a beacon. Something that says 'here we are, come get us.'"

"Can we do that?"

"Your friend thought so. She worked out a way to do it."

He flipped open the notebook and put it on the coffee table. "See?"

Craig studied the block diagram scribbled on the page. "I don't think that's gonna be easy."

Mikey grinned lopsidedly. "So? Nothing that's worth having is."

Craig was right. It wasn't easy. Judith's notes had no more than outlined the beacon spell. It was broken down into modules, but half the modules hadn't been written and several of the ones that had been needed modification.

Worse, they were flying blind. They had no way of testing anything because the magic compiler didn't work in their world. All they could do was check and re-check their work manually and hope they had everything correct.

They didn't have much in the way of tools. Judith had started work on a cross-compiler for the magic language that would run on an MS-DOS computer, but it was only a skeleton. She had written sort of a syntax checker for the magic language that worked something like *lint* for C. But like *lint* it flagged all possible errors. Since there was no way of running a test compile, they had to be "more Catholic than the fucking Pope," as Mikey put it, and correct everything that the checker flagged.

Mikey ended up picking the basic approaches and doing the broad outlines while Craig did the detail work and coding. Partially this was because Craig wasn't very good at the big-picture stuff and partially because that was just the way it worked out, somehow. That meant that while Craig spent hours sweating over the grunt work, Mikey lounged around the apartment drinking beer and playing computer games.

Since both of them were system breakers they worked essentially around the clock, catching naps when they felt like it and ordering in from fast-food joints when they got hungry. Thus it was nearly three o'clock in the morning when Craig came in to tell Mikey they were finished.

"I'll get some sleep and then we can go over the whole thing one more time," he said to Mikey's back. "What are you playing anyway?"

"Empire."

Craig nodded. He was familiar with the game. You explored an unmapped world, captured cities and built armies and fleets while the computer did the same thing. Eventually you met the computer's forces in a climactic battle for control of the planet.

"Looks like you've got him on the run," Craig said, surveying the map on the screen. "One or two more turns and he'll surrender."

"He surrendered a while ago," Mikey said, maneuvering about thirty aircraft to attack the sprinkling of enemy armies in the upper left corner of the screen.

"So why are you still playing?"

"Because I want to crush the motherfucker," Mikey said as his legions of aircraft tore into the opposing forces. Most of the armies went down under the onslaught, but one beat off five separate attacks.

"Die, you cocksucker!" Mikey snarled as he used the mouse to mass even more air forces against the remaining red marker on the screen.

"I always quit when the computer surrenders," Craig told him as he watched over his friend's shoulder.

"I don't want surrender. I want him wiped out," Mikey said without taking his eyes off the confrontation.

Craig took a swig of soda. "Takes too long that way."

"Yeah, but when it's over I'm the only one left standing."

The computer beeped as its final army vanished under the combined attack of nearly twenty aircraft.

This is extremely undignified, Glandurg thought as he watched the green forest sail by beneath him. *Warriors should ride into battle, not be carried along like a sack of meal.*

Behind him came eleven more griffins, each carrying a dwarf dangling from its talons.

Still, there are advantages, he admitted. *It would be hard to hold on riding griffin-back.*

❖   ❖   ❖

Craig looked at the stuff laid out on the coffee table dubiously. Some of it, like the sheets of typing paper with the spell written on them, was perfectly ordinary. Others, like the hibachi full of glowing coals, were ordinary but out of place. Still others, like the roots and powders he and Mikey had scoured Chinatown to find, were just plain odd. The table had been shoved to the center of the room and a circle drawn around it in blue marking chalk.

Mikey had just finished placing the black, white and red candles at the points of an invisible star outside the circle. He used the tape measure to check the distances between them and then did a quick calculation on his HP calculator.

"That should do it," he said, carefully stepping over the chalk mark to join Craig at the coffee table.

"Give me your hand."

"What do you want that for?"

Mikey picked up the Exacto knife lying next to the hibachi. "I don't, I want some of your blood."

Craig winced as Mikey drove the point into his fingertip. "Hey! Not so rough, okay?"

But the blood flowed freely and Mikey held Craig's hand over the hibachi, letting the dark red drops drip onto the glowing coals.

Craig wrinkled his nose at the odor, but Mike didn't seem to notice. He reached into the coffee cup, picked up a four-finger pinch of the powder there and cast it onto the coals where Craig's blood still sizzled. The powder sparkled as it hit the charcoal and heavy sweet-smelling smoke boiled up out of the hibachi.

Craig coughed and his eyes watered, but he grabbed Mike's outstretched hands in his across the glowing coals. Then he looked down at the notes to the side of the hibachi and both of them began to chant, reading the words in unison.

The smoke got thicker and thicker until Craig could hardly see the paper and the sweetish, pungent odor made his head swim. He shut out the discomfort and chanted for all he was worth as the room began to shimmer and dissolve around him.

EIGHT

THE OLD ONES

The enemy of my enemy is my friend.
                        —*Old Arab proverb*

So with friends like these, who needs
enemies?

                        —*Old Jewish proverb*

Smoke and fire and candlelight . . .

At first Craig thought the place was on fire. There was
smoke or fog everywhere and a dim red light coming from
the wrong angle. Between the smoke and the dim red
light, Craig couldn't see very well and somehow he was
very glad for that. What he could see was *wrong*, like an
optical illusion.

They were in a cave, or maybe on a mountain crag.
The ground under them was rough rock, kind of, and it
sloped away so steeply that Craig was afraid to take a step.
The air was thin and hard to breathe, or maybe just so
full of smoke there wasn't much oxygen in it. His chest
heaved as he sucked great, unsatisfying lungs full. He
clutched Mikey's hands tight in his own. Mikey squeezed
back so hard Craig's hands hurt.

70

Craig was scared. For the first time in his life he was so afraid the very marrow of his bones chilled. He didn't care about treasure, or adventuring, or magic. This place played on dark half-realized places in his psyche in ways that were horrible. He just wanted *out*.

Then he realized they were being watched.

It loomed above them in the fog, tall and manlike. There was a hint of distance about it as if it was enormous, but there was no way to tell. In the smoky red haze Craig could make out the outline, including the pointed ears. There was a suggestion of body hair, or maybe fur. Worst of all, it seemed to twist and flicker like an image in a mirage. Looking at the thing made Craig's eyes hurt, but he couldn't make himself look away.

Craig wanted to moan in terror, to yell a warning, to scream, but he couldn't get his breath to do any of it. All he could do was stare at the half-seen creature and cling to Mikey's hands for dear life.

"Who are you?" Mikey finally got out.

We are what was and what might be. The voice filled Craig's head like ringing thunder until he wanted to clap his hands to his ears to shut it out. *We are what will be again.* The voice pressed on. *We are the dawn and nightfall and deepest night. We are . . . Ur-elves.*

"We, ah, we weren't expecting this."

We know, the voice came again and there was amusement in the rolling words. *But you called and we answered.*

"Why did you bring us here?"

To serve.

"Then you want to make a deal, right?" Mikey said, the words low and fast, as if he was desperate.

We have a bargain, the voice thundered inexorably. *Sealed in blood.* Craig thought of his finger, still throbbing where Mikey had pricked it, and moaned aloud.

Your talents will serve us. Your magic will be the spearhead of our power. You will bring down those who stand between us and our fulfillment and lay waste to their world.

Craig closed his eyes tightly and moaned again. The thing and its words were awful and terrifying and . . . Attractive.

NINE

WORLDS' MEETING

Come closer, the thing said. *Come closer and watch.*

As if moving through a zoom lens Craig and Mikey were sped to the side of the Ur-elf. Craig still couldn't form a clear impression of what it looked like and for that he was just as glad.

Craig had the impression of two huge, shaggy hands cupped before him, hands with claws for nails. There was something glowing in the hollow, like a living coal. The radiance expanded and grew brighter until his face was bathed with yellow light. The light turned cloudy. Then it cleared and they were looking down on a world held in the Ur-elf's palms.

There was deep blue ocean and spotted through it were islands. As Craig watched the islands formed as faceted images, then smoothed and took on color and texture. Vaguely he sensed that one end of this place connected to his own world and the other end to the world of magic.

Again the zooming effect and they were falling toward a large island in the center of the ocean. The place was long and narrow, with reddish brown desert shading from mountains at one end down through brown-yellow plains in the center to lush gray-green at the other end.

Faster and faster they fell, closer and closer to the

mountains at the desert end. Craig sucked in his breath
as the mountain peaks rushed up toward them.

Then suddenly they were standing on the tallest peak
of all, looking out over the mountains and desert.

In this place the magic of both worlds works, the voice
inside their heads told them. *It is yours for now. Make
good use of it.*

And then they were alone on the crag.

Craig tasted bile on his tongue. His head hurt with a
roaring, throbbing ache that threatened to take the top
of his skull off with every beat of his hammering heart.
Mikey didn't look too much better.

The two looked at each other for a long moment while
the chill mountain wind whipped around them and tugged
at their clothing.

"Come on," Mikey said at last. "Let's get to work."

The amazing thing was, Craig realized, he already *knew*
this stuff. He didn't have to think about how to do it,
he could already make magic.

Working alongside Mikey, he sketched out the form
of their new home, the citadel and fortress which would
be their base for the attack into the new world.

Shadowy cloud forms hovered around the peak as the
pair pushed and shaped the outlines of their castle. It
would be small at first, covering no more than the top
of the peak. But already Craig could visualize its spread
as a great stronghold and arsenal to pour forth the sin-
ews of conquest.

It was somehow *right* that they should conquer this
world of magic. It was the natural order of things, meant
to be. As he shaped and formed, Craig realized in the
back of his mind he hadn't always felt that way. But that
was immaterial, like a long-ago dream. This was fated and
he would bend all his talents to seizing this other world.

Something told him that those talents were now
considerable.

A push, a twist, a sudden shimmering coalescence and

their magic castle was *done*! Craig breathed a sigh and admired their creation.

The walls soared straight up out of the sides of the peak. Towers and turrets sprouted everywhere, flags flew from the staffs and whipped in the incessant wind. It was magnificent!

At least it was magnificent for a first effort. He had to admit that the walls leaned askew in a couple of places and that some of the towers slumped as if half-melted. Some of the windows were funny shapes too. And somehow it wasn't as *big* as he had imagined it would be.

"Needs a lot of work," Mikey said.

"It's pretty good for a first effort."

Mikey shrugged. "Come on. Let's get the hell out of this wind."

Together they strode over the canting drawbridge and through the lopsided gate of their redoubt.

Craig looked at his handiwork sitting in the flagged stone courtyard and suppressed a pang of disappointment. It was smaller than he had thought it would be, maybe ten feet from wingtip to wingtip. The color was a nice battleship gray, just like a real F-15, and the twin tails stood proudly above the jet exhausts, but somehow it didn't look just right. It looked kind of like an F-15 Eagle, or maybe a Russian Foxhound or Flanker interceptor, or maybe even a Navy Tomcat. He tried to remember just exactly what an F-15 looked like and found he couldn't separate the images of twin-engine, twin-tail interceptors in his mind.

Well, all right, it would have to do. They needed air defense, didn't they? This might not be exactly right, but it could fly and it could fight. That was good enough.

Anyway, there was some good stuff. The conformal fuel tanks along the sides of the fuselage under the wings were right. And the missiles and drop tanks hanging from the pylons beneath the wings and body looked right. Who cared if it wasn't perfect? It was wicked and it was all his.

"Hey Mikey," he yelled, "look what I've got."

"Yeah?" Mikey came out of the main keep, wiping his hands on a rag.

"There," Craig gestured proudly. "It's a robot F-15."

Mikey walked over to the plane. "Bullshit."

"Huh?"

"Bullshit. Look, you've got a missile under the left wing and a drop tank under the right."

"So?"

"So what happens if you drop the tank or fire the missile? You've got an unbalanced load on the plane. And anyway, that missile isn't off an F-15. It looks Russian or something. And you've got the center drop tank painted with a red nose, like a bomb."

"So who the hell cares? It will fly and it can fight. All right? That's what's important, isn't it?"

"Who's it going to fight?" Mikey demanded. "We're the only people in this world. You think the Russians are going to come swarming in here or something?"

"We're here to fight someone," Craig said stubbornly. "*They* told us so."

"Oh yeah," Mikey agreed. "We're gonna have to fight all right. But shit like this," he gestured at the plane, "isn't going to be what decides that battle."

"Oh yeah? Well, what will decide that fucking battle, hotshot?"

Mikey got that sneering smile Craig had come to hate. "Something a lot more powerful than any robot airplane. You'll see when the time comes."

Well, fuck you very much! Craig thought as Mikey disappeared back into their lumpy castle. He picked up a loose stone and threw it against the castle wall with all his strength.

He needed a better way to do this. He'd created the F-15 just by imagining it, but the problem with that was that you had to imagine all the details at once. That was too hard.

Okay, so what about breaking it down? Suppose you could imagine something one part at a time, like drawing it out on paper? Or on a computer screen! Yeah. Like a workstation!

What he needed was a magical workstation. Already the image was forming in his mind. He'd never seen a jet fighter up close, but he knew exactly what a workstation was like. Of course, he'd want to make a few improvements.

Craig left the misshapen fighter sitting in the courtyard. He'd do a hell of a lot better the next time, but he was going to build that fighter anyway. Squadrons and squadrons of them, just on principle.

It took him nearly three days, but at last Craig had his workstation. The "screen" was a gently glowing rectangle nearly a yard across. There was a keyboard and a mouse, of course, but the system also had voice input. If he really wanted he could just think hard at the screen and make things happen.

The display was an engineer's dream. Infinite resolution, at least sixteen million colors, three-dimensional, fully shaded modeling and redraws at better than sixty frames a second. He could design anything on this baby!

Craig stared at the glowing surface and tried to think of his first project. Maybe jet fighters were a little old fashioned for what they needed to do. They needed weapons that were more far-out, more science-fictional.

Like giant robots! Yeah, now there was something he could really get into. He'd always liked Robobattle, where the gamers slugged it out in twenty-fifth-century robot war machines. Now he could actually build something like that.

Instinctively he reached for the mouse and began to sketch designs on his super-workstation. More accurately, he tried to remember what the warbots in Robobattle were like. They were nice and impressive and in the game they had a lot of firepower. Then there were the giant intelligent tanks from Orc. And magic! Yeah, what would it be like to have a couple of hundred megaton/seconds of firepower and the destruction spells of a Seventh-Level Mage? That would be really something.

Working with bits and pieces from computer games, role-playing games and old television shows, Craig began to fashion his engines of destruction. It never occurred to him that he had the power to do something original.

"See?" Craig said eagerly. "I can design stuff here on the screen and then build it magically."

Mikey looked over Craig's workstation and didn't say anything.

"I don't have to imagine it all in one piece. I can work on it a piece at a time, and . . ."

"So build me a planet buster."

"Huh?"

"Come on. Whip me up something that can blow up a whole planet." He smacked his fist into his palm. "Pow! Just like that."

"It doesn't work that way," Craig said uncomfortably.

"Why not?"

"You've got to have at least a general idea of how something's supposed to work before you can build it."

"You mean we've got to sit down and fucking design all this shit?"

"No, not that bad. But we've got to know how the stuff functions or it won't work."

"Jesus fuckin' Christ," Mikey muttered. "What a pile of shit."

"You wanna go back and tell them that?" Craig snapped. "I sure as hell ain't gonna."

Mikey grinned in that nasty, superior way of his. "Maybe I will do that the next time I talk to them."

Craig's jaw dropped. "You've been *talking* to them?"

"They're around, if you want to make contact."

"But Jesus, I mean . . ."

"They're real interesting too. I'm learning a lot from them."

The way he said it made Craig uncomfortable. "You mean magic and stuff?"

Mikey grinned again. "Oh, I'm learning lots of things."

Craig knew he needed to learn more about how magic operated, but the thought of even seeing an Ur-elf again made him weak in the knees.

"Look, suppose you concentrate on the theoretical stuff and I'll keep working on the robots and shit."

"Okay," Mikey said with a little smile. Craig had the uneasy feeling he'd been outmaneuvered again.

Mikey stopped at the doorway and turned back to Craig. "Oh, if you want to do something useful, redesign this fucking castle and make it more livable."

Okay, Craig thought, turning back to his workstation and away from thoughts of Ur-elves and magical theory. *Let's really turn this sucker into something!*

Craig stood at the topmost point of the highest tower, surveyed his work and found it good.

The skimpy, saggy little castle they had formed out of pure magic was long gone. Now the entire top of the mountain had been terraced and leveled. What had been the original castle was now just the central piece of an elaborate structure. Even it was much changed.

Caermort—the Castle of Death, he thought. *That's what we'll call it.*

It certainly looked deadly enough. Energy cannons poked their ugly snouts out of domed turrets on the stone ramparts. The central tower of gleaming steel soared to neck-craning height, glittering like a mirror in the afternoon sun. Several of the courtyards had been roofed over with domes of crystal. Random bolts of lightning flew between towers and played over the domes. Further up the air sparkled and flickered as the protective magical shell around the castle interacted with random dust motes which were wafted into it.

Within the castle itself hordes of servants, robots and living creatures hurried to do his bidding. In the caves dug into the mountain giant robots worked with monster tools to assemble more of their kind and other engines of destruction to boot.

It still wasn't absolutely perfect, he admitted modestly. If he did not work a thing up in complete detail on his screen the details were likely to be filled in haphazardly.

But all in all it was a marvelous engine of destruction. All this power aimed at a single goal. Conquest. Already his drones scouted the limits of this world and his robot legions formed in the huge caverns beneath the mountain or exercised on the desert plains. Mikey might sneer, but he'd stop when Craig's mechanical armies marched across the border between the worlds.

The border between *both* worlds, he amended silently. Why limit himself to the one where magic worked? There was no army on Earth that could stand against his creations.

Better to be Lord of Three Worlds, than Lord of Two, he decided.

TEN

WRECK'S WARNING

The programming team was up to its elbows in source code when Arianne came into their workroom.

"Forgive me, my Lords, my Lady," the tall blonde lady said as she entered the room. "Are you occupied?"

Wiz turned toward the door. "Occupied, but not super busy. What's up?"

"Bal-Simba sent me to request your presence."

"Sure. In his office?"

"At Oak Island off the south coast. A strange thing has washed ashore at the village. Bal-Simba asks that you examine it."

Wiz looked over at the pile of scrolls and the shimmering letters hanging above his desk and paused. A summons to meet Bal-Simba here was one thing. A jaunt to a distant village to look at something was another matter. Even walking the Wizard's Way, such a trip would probably eat the rest of the day.

"Can't we just send one of our searching units?" he asked. "We do have to get this stuff done before—"

Arianne hesitated. "Lord, I think you had better see this personally."

"What is it?"

"We do not know. But from the description I think it owes more to your world than ours."

❖   ❖   ❖

Wiz smelled salt and mud. They were in a hollow between two sand dunes. Gray-green sand grasses and little twisted shrubs grew here and there around them and even in this sheltered spot a breeze ruffled the vegetation and their clothing.

There was a man waiting for them, a rough, grizzled fellow dressed in the bulky knit sweater and canvas trousers favored by the folk who made their living upon the Freshened Sea.

"My Lords, welcome," he said, bowing perfunctorily, as if unused to the exercise. "I am Weinrich, the mayor of Oak Island."

Moira curtsied and the rest bowed. "Well met, Lord. I am Moira and these are the wizards Sparrow, Jerry and Danny."

Weinrich's face cleared, as if a burden had been lifted from him.

"Ah, well met indeed. They said you might come."

"Well, we're here," Wiz said a trace sharply. "Let's see the thing that's causing all the fuss."

With the growing importance of Wiz's new magic, and the spreading word that he was from beyond the World, there was a growing tendency to ascribe anything out of the ordinary to the new magic. Normally Arianne and Bal-Simba did not take the villagers' reports this seriously, still . . .

As they climbed the dune Wiz saw four dragons flying complex figure eight patterns off the beach, obviously on guard.

"If this is another piece of driftwood," he muttered to Jerry as they toiled up the sand dune, "I'll . . ."

Then he came over the rise and saw what was down on the beach.

The villagers had dragged it further up the beach, above the tide line. Now they clustered in knots at a respectful distance.

Off to one side the village hedge witch conferred

nervously with a blue-robed wizard of the Mighty. Occasionally he would look over at the thing as if to make certain it had not moved under its own power.

It was worth looking at, Wiz had to admit. To the fisherfolk of this isolated island it must have seemed strange beyond all imagining.

One wing was crumpled under it and the other canted into the air. The front of the body was stove in, apparently from hitting the water. As they got closer Wiz could smell the sharp chemical reek of gasoline.

"An airplane," Danny said.

"Perhaps, but there is magic here as well," Moira said.

Wiz didn't have his wife's nose for magic, so he fished out the magic detector he carried in his pouch. The crystal glowed a strong green as he pointed it at the craft.

Magic all right. But gasoline as well. He felt the hair begin to rise on his neck. Whatever this thing was, it was very, very wrong.

"Moira, you and the others stay back. Jerry and I will go in for a closer look."

Moira nodded. "Be careful, love."

"Very careful."

Wiz and Jerry half-stumbled, half-slid down the seaward face of the dune, oblivious to the sand that was trickling into their shoes. As they got onto the beach, they split up. Wiz approached from the tail and Jerry eased toward the crushed nose. There was no sign of movement.

The sea breeze swished through the grasses at the edge of the beach, drowning out the villagers' whispers and dulling the wizards' conversation to an unintelligible murmur.

"Look at this!" Jerry called. "It's got a gasoline engine."

As Wiz ducked under the wing of the plane to join him, Jerry reached out and gave the cowling fasteners an expert twist. Then he flipped the cowling back to expose the power plant.

"High output two-stroke," he said looking it over. "That thing probably puts out ninety horses in spite of its size."

He looked further. "No muffler. If that thing was a two-stroke the villagers should have heard it coming for miles."

"It had to be running," Wiz said. "But that's impossible."

"Maybe not," Jerry pointed to the front of the plane. "Look at the prop. Only one blade bent. That means it wasn't turning when it went in."

Wiz knelt down beside the propeller. "If it crashed here it's not surprising. That engine couldn't possibly run in this World."

"Do you think it was sucked through from our world?"

Wiz shrugged. "Maybe, but how? And why? Anyway, the thing's obviously not dangerous now. Let's get the others down here."

Moira and Danny quickly joined them at the wreck. The other wizards kept their distance.

"It's our technology, all right," Wiz said as the others came up. "No cockpit, so it was a drone of some kind."

"What about the magic?" Moira asked.

Wiz looked at his magic detector. "That seems to be concentrated in the boxes in the mid-section."

"If I didn't know better I'd say that was an instrument bay," Jerry said, ducking under the up-tilted wing and squatting down beside it.

"Don't be too sure you know better."

Jerry popped the fasteners and lifted the covering. Inside was a wild tangle of wires and printed circuit boards leading back to several oddly carved lumps of pearl-gray material.

"Cute," Jerry said at last. "Some of this stuff is obviously electronic, but the guts of it," he pointed to the pearl-gray lumps, "are obviously magical."

"We can probably untangle the electronics, but the magic?" He looked over at Moira.

"That is likely to be difficult, my Lord. We do not know who made those things or what they are supposed to do." She frowned and concentrated. "I can tell you that the spells are most powerful, however."

"So the magic's fine," Jerry summed up. "It's the engine that doesn't work."

"Of course the engine doesn't work," Wiz said irritably. "It couldn't work here. The whole thing's impossible."

"Oh yeah?" Danny retorted. "Take a look at those exhaust pipes."

Wiz followed Danny's pointing finger and saw that the pipes were discolored where they came out of the cylinders.

"Heat did that. That sucker ran and it ran for a while."

"But if the engine worked, then the guidance system and the imaging stuff wouldn't. They're based on magic."

"Wait a minute," Wiz said. "Let me try something. **emac!**" he commanded.

"?"

"list"

The Emac took the quill from behind his ear and scribbled furiously in the air. Lines of fiery symbols appeared and scrolled upward from the Emac.

"carat S" Wiz pronounced and the Emac froze in mid-line.

"Hey, I recognize that!" Wiz peered closely at the glowing letters of fire. "Not only are they magic, they're *our* magic. These spells were written with our magic compiler or something damn like it."

Four pairs of eyes met over the wreckage and no one said anything.

"This will do," Glandurg puffed, looking around the grove.

"High time too," Thorfin wheezed, coming up behind him nearly bent double by the climb and the weight of the enormous pack he carried.

One by one the other dwarves filed into the clearing and dumped their packs. The griffins had left them off at dawn on the other side of the forest and they had been walking ever since. The wooded land was a collection of craggy hills cut by little valleys and laced with brooks and streams. Generations of firewood gathering by mortals had left the woods open and parklike under the spreading trees, but it was still hard going, even for dwarves.

Glandurg had led his band almost entirely through the forest to a wooded bluff overlooking the river that ran by the base of the Capital mount. Just a few hundred yards and a stretch of placid water now separated the dwarves from the enormous bluff that bore the capital city of the North on its back and the Wizard's Keep at its very tip.

As his followers rested behind him, Glandurg surveyed the scene. From here they could watch the Wizard's Keep and the comings and goings of their quarry and stay concealed in the forest. A perfect spot to plan an ambush.

"How are we supposed to know this wizard when we find him?" Gimli asked from where he lay against his pack under a spreading tree. "Mortals all look alike."

"No they don't," Snorri said with a superior air. "There's men mortals and there's women mortals. You can tell them apart easy."

"That only cuts it down by half," Gimli said. "We can't go around killing all the male mortals we meet, can we?"

Glandurg turned back to his band. "That will not be necessary," he said loftily. "I thought of this before we left and I obtained from my uncle the King a means to infallibly identify this mortal."

He drew from his pouch a handful of hazelnut-sized lumps. "Each of you will have one of these. They will always point the way to this foreign sorcerer, be he a hundred leagues away."

Each of the dwarves came forward and took one of the seekers from his hand.

"It's dark," said Thorfin, staring into his palm.

"Mine's not pointing any way at all," Snorri chimed in.

Glandurg scowled and grabbed for the more powerful version of the device that hung around his own neck. Cupping his hands to shield it from the light he saw that it glowed only very dimly. The arrow within pointed waveringly south.

"He must be more than a hundred leagues from here," Glandurg said weakly.

"We aren't going to fly after him, are we?" Thorfin asked with a dangerous edge to his voice. The other dwarves muttered in agreement.

"No. There is no need for that. He will return soon enough. Meanwhile we will scout around us and wait."

Bal-Simba was waiting for them at the crest of the dune. Outlined against the sky with sea breezes whipping the edges of his leopard-skin loincloth the big wizard was a most impressive sight. Wiz, who was a little chilly in spite of his traveling cloak, wondered how he managed to keep warm.

He heard their breathless report gravely and without comment. "We will have the thing taken back to the Capital for study," he told them. "Unless you think it is unsafe?"

"No reason to think that, Lord," Wiz said. "Although since we don't even know where it came from I can't guarantee anything."

Bal-Simba pursed his lips. "I think we may have a clue as to that. I have been talking to Weinrich and the other villagers. They say there has been a change in the weather recently."

"The weather?" Wiz said blankly.

"Folk who live by the sea are always sensitive to the weather. This far south on the Freshened Sea the pattern of wind and weather is constant, year to year."

"Village folk are usually wise in the ways of the immediate surroundings," Moira agreed. "But you say a change?"

"A fog bank about a day's sail to the east. A fog that does not lift and does not move. A place where a sailor can get lost because neither compass nor magic works properly."

"And they think this thing came out of the fog?" Wiz asked.

"It seems to have come from that direction."

"Lord, if I were you I'd search the hell out of that fog bank."

"That is already in train, Sparrow," Bal-Simba said.

Dragon Leader looked over his formation again and then turned his eyes back to the sea below. Two days ago his entire wing of almost fifty dragons had been brought together from their scattered patrol bases and sent hurrying south to Oak Island. Yesterday had been spent frantically setting up a makeshift base among the fisherfolk and putting out the first hasty patrols to try to define the edges of this strangeness.

Now Dragon Leader was taking his flight into the heart of this new thing. Every rider and dragon was at the peak of alertness. He could tell from the way they were flying that none of them liked it at all.

Even the formation reflected that. Instead of putting his dragons in line abreast or an echelon to cover the maximum territory, he had his first element above and behind his main formation for top cover. The rest of the patrol was pretty much line abreast, but they were closer together than normal so they could support each other quickly in case of trouble.

Every man and woman in the patrol understood the significance of that. This was a fighting formation, not a scouting one. Dragon Leader was going into this strange place loaded for bear.

Dragon Leader and his troopers were used to flying into the unknown. In a world where maps were components of spells rather than guides to terrain, he had often struck out over uncharted territory. He was used to magic as well. Save for the death spells on their iron arrows and a few odds and ends, dragon cavalry did not use magic. But they dealt with it constantly and most of them had faced it on more than one occasion.

Not that they had seen any magic here. So far he had seen nothing but sun-dappled sea and the occasional wheeling sea bird. Just what they should have seen, in other words.

But it wasn't right. There was something odd about this stretch of ocean, something that made his eyes hurt to look at it and made him queasy the deeper the patrol penetrated. It was like trying to look at two things at once, he decided. Two pictures that were almost but not exactly alike.

His dragon sensed it too. Whatever there was about this place, his mount didn't want anything to do with it. He signaled his patrol to extra alertness and pushed on. Then he reached for his communications crystal to report.

There—again there was strangeness. He managed to reach the Watcher on Oak Island, but the voice was weak and there were gaps, requiring several repeats to get the message through.

Interference? he thought as he replaced the crystal. But that didn't seem right either. He knew the effects of jamming spells on communications crystals. He had felt them often enough during the years of war against the Dark League. But this was more as if someone had sub- stituted a poorly ensorceled crystal for his own. It was as if the spell on the crystal had suddenly become much weaker, less competent.

He noticed that the rhythm of his mount had changed as well. The dragon's wingbeats had increased, as if they were climbing instead of flying level. The beast wasn't exactly laboring, but he was definitely working harder. He did a quick calculation and decided that if this contin- ued, the extra effort would reduce his patrol's flying time by one-third.

Down below the sea seemed the same, but this place was definitely different.

Off to his right one of the dragons flying top cover waggled its wings to attract attention. The riders on the right wing caught it as soon as Dragon Leader did and used hand signals to pass the information on to their commander.

Dragon Leader kneed his mount gently and his dragon banked gently left and right to acknowledge. Craning his neck he saw the rider rise in her saddle and raise both her arms above her head in the signal for land.

Dragon Leader hesitated for an instant and then signaled the entire patrol to turn toward the land.

The patrol was barely halfway into their turn when three gray shapes hurtled down on them out of the clouds.

"Break! Break!" Dragon Leader screamed into his communications crystal. The warning was unnecessary, already the squadron was scattering like a flock of frightened chickens as the screaming intruders dived on them. Riders fumbled for their war bows as they twisted and dove in every direction, trying desperately to get away from their attackers.

In the end it was biology rather than maneuvering that saved them. Dragons have poor radar returns and the targeting radars on the robot fighters were unable to get a lock. Craig hadn't thought to equip his creations with cannon, so the planes were impotent against the dragons.

Of course the dragons were equally impotent against the planes. The aircraft were too fast and too unexpected. They swooped through the formation before a single rider could draw a bow or a single dragon could breathe fire. The planes made a tight curving climb back into the clouds and then they were gone.

The dragons didn't hang around either. The entire squadron dove for the wavetops and ran for home as fast as their wings could carry them.

"That," said Wiz grimly, "is definitely a jet fighter."

The recording had been frozen at the moment that the plane was climbing away from the dragon squadron. The view was almost from directly above and the outline and details were unmistakable.

"Looks like it was drawn by a fourteen-year-old," Danny said contemptuously. "It's a combination of a bunch of different planes."

"Notice that it's unmanned," Jerry said, sticking his finger into the image to point at the place where the cockpit should be. "Either these guys are real cautious about risking their necks or there aren't very many of them. Maybe only one or two."

"The main thing," Wiz said, getting up from the table, "is that we've got both dragons and jet fighters in the same air at the same time." He turned to Arianne, who had brought them the recording.

"You say the dragon riders were having trouble communicating?"

"Their voices were weak. And they said their dragons tired easily."

Jerry gestured and the image started moving again.

"Those planes don't look like they're doing any too well, either."

"Basically then," Wiz said, "both magic and technology work in that place, they just don't work very well."

"Sounds like an IBM shop," Jerry said.

"Whatever. Anyway that explains the drone. It was only designed to work in that world and it got in here by accident."

"But it does not tell us who sent it," Moira said. "Or why. Those are the things we most need to know."

"It seems to me," Bal-Simba rumbled, "that we have two ways to find out. We can sit here and wait for whomever or whatever is sending these things to come to us or we can send our own scouts through to spy out this new world."

"Lord, that's not much of a choice," Wiz said. "So far these things aren't hostile, but they're sure not friendly. If we wait we may not like what we get."

"My thinking precisely, Sparrow. So we must go and see."

"Forgive me, Lord," Moira said, "but might that not

be taken as an unfriendly act? True, they have not sent us embassies, but they have done us no harm either."

"Unfriendly, perhaps. But no more so than what they have done already. If you have a better suggestion, Lady, I am anxious to hear it."

"No, none, Lord. But I would not have us blunder into war unnecessarily."

"Fear not, Lady. We shall be very circumspect."

ELEVEN

A WALK IN THE WOODS

Across the river from the castle mount a line of hills ran down to the water's edge. Because the land was so rugged it had never been farmed. Instead it was left as a source of firewood, mushrooms and herbs for the denizens of the Capital.

It also made a pleasant place to walk on an Indian summer afternoon. Which is why Wiz, Danny and Jerry were picking their way through the woods as the sky started to darken from twilight to evening.

"I still think we ought to try to catch one of those drones," Danny said as the trio made their way down a trail that skirted the edge of the bluff.

"For the tenth time, no," Wiz told him. "And watch your step here, it's steep."

"We already have one drone," Jerry said, stepping to the side of the trail away from the cliff. "What do we need another one for?"

"Yeah but . . ."

A small black-clad shape hurtled out of the trees above them, screaming and waving a samurai sword as he came. The trio watched open-mouthed as he passed a good four feet to their left, missed the path completely and went over the edge of the cliff.

There were a couple of bounces, a thud and then something that sounded like a particularly inventive brand of profanity.

"What was that?" Jerry asked, peering over the edge.

"I think it was a ninja dwarf," Wiz said wonderingly.

Danny frowned. "That sounds like a character out of a D&D game." He thought for a second. "A *bad* D&D game."

Bal-Simba looked up from the scrying stone and blinked as if to clear his vision.

Wiz leaned across the table eagerly. "Well?"

"I sense malign influences aimed at you and a definite violent intent." The big black wizard rubbed his temples. "It appears, Sparrow, that someone is trying to kill you—again."

"Who?" Wiz asked. "And why? And why a dwarf, for Pete's sake?"

"That I could not discover," Bal-Simba said. "There is deadly intent and fixity of purpose. There are indications that non-mortals are involved, but that is all I know."

"Lisella?" Jerry suggested.

"Perhaps," Bal-Simba said slowly.

Wiz shook his head. "I don't think so. Lisella is subtle. There's nothing subtle about a dwarf jumping out of a tree waving a sword."

"Nothing very effective either," Danny said. "He missed us by a mile. Well," he amended under Wiz's glare, "a good six feet."

"Maybe that was Duke Aelric protecting you."

Wiz snorted. "More likely it was incompetence."

Bal-Simba stood up. "Whatever it was, I think it would be best if you stayed within the Wizard's Keep for a space."

"Fine by me. I've got more than enough to keep me busy for a couple of weeks."

"It may be longer than that," Bal-Simba told him. "Until we know who or what is behind this attack, you should stay where we can protect you."

"How long then?"

"I do not know. But my magic tells me whoever is after you is not easily discouraged. Until we have found the guiding hand you are in danger."

"You had to go after him yourself," Glandurg said disgustedly. "You couldn't wait for the rest of us."

"Well, you said he had to be slain quickly," Gimli said defensively. "There he was coming along the trail and there I was, so . . ." He shrugged.

"You're lucky he didn't turn you into a rabbit," his leader told him, "instead of just throwing you over the cliff."

"Didn't throw me," Gimli said sullenly.

"You jumped, I suppose?"

"Well . . ."

Glandurg looked around at the other dwarves. "Listen to me. No more striking half-hearted, do you understand?"

"Not much chance of that," Snorri said. "The wizard hasn't stirred from his castle for days."

"Then we have run him to earth and trapped him like a rat!" Glandurg gloated.

"Begging my Lord's pardon, but how do we get him out of the trap now that we've got him in it?"

The dwarf leader frowned. There was more to this business than he had imagined and some of the details were proving quite annoying.

"We could tunnel in," one of the other dwarves suggested. "That whole bluff's nothing but limestone."

The others shifted and murmured approval. Tunneling was something dwarves were comfortable with.

"How long would that take?" Glandurg demanded.

The dwarf who had made the suggestion eyed the distant cliff and castle.

"If we can sneak in close and drive the shaft steep up from the river level—oh—not more than two, three years, I should think," he finished brightly.

The leader shook his head. "That will not do, then. Our king promised the trolls speedy action." Besides he knew in a general way that two or three years was a long time for a human to stay in one place.

"You got a better idea then?" the other challenged.

"Of course I have."

"What then?" the other persisted.

The leader reddened. "Don't be impertinent!"

"I'm not being impertinent, I just want to know what your idea is."

"I . . ." Over the shoulder of his questioner, the leader saw a flight of river swans glide down to the smooth river surface, their wings extended and motionless. As the swans touched down he had an inspiration.

"Backwards!" he proclaimed. "We will come at this alien wizard backwards!"

TWELVE

PICNIC

Wiz paced to the window, looked down into the court-yard, paced back to his chair, sat down, picked up the scroll, got up and strode to the window again.

"I've got to get out of here," he said turning to face his wife.

Moira kept her eyes on the blouse she was embroidering with a pattern of moss rose and holly leaves. "So go."

"No, I mean I've got to get away from the Wizard's Keep."

Moira looked up from her work. "You never wanted to go outside the castle before."

"Yeah, but I knew I could do it any time then. Now I'm cooped up here and its getting to me. I'm going stir crazy."

Moira put down her needlework and frowned. "With assassins about that is not safe, but if you feel you must, I can summon a troop of guardsmen . . ."

"No. That would be worse than not going out at all."

"Then you must stay in, I am afraid."

"Look, I could rig a spell that would protect me."

"Against what? Dwarves are clever and we do not know when or how they will strike again."

"We don't even know if they'll strike at all," Wiz said. "That may have been a fluke."

97

"Bal-Simba does not think so."

Wiz growled.

Moira took his hands in hers. "I am sorry, my love. I do not mean to sound unsympathetic. It is just that here you are safe. Outside the castle you cannot be protected."

"I feel like I'm wrapped in cotton wool and it's suffocating me," Wiz protested. "It's affecting my work. I just want to get away from everyone for a while."

Moira twisted her mouth sideways as she thought.

"I will speak to Bal-Simba," she said finally, "and see if he thinks it is safe."

"Where are we going anyway?" Wiz asked for the fifth time as Moira threw a light cloak over her new dress.

She smiled at him in the mirror as she adjusted the cloak on her otherwise bare shoulders. "To a special place. You will see."

Wiz stepped up behind her and put his hands around her waist. "Darling, any place is special with you. Especially in that dress."

"I am glad you like it, my Lord. I had it made specially for today." Then she turned practical in a flash. "But come, we do not want to be late for our own picnic. And bring the basket."

Moira didn't tell Wiz where they were going even when she took them on the Wizard's Way, so Wiz was completely unprepared for the place where they popped up.

A familiar flash of darkness and they were in a sunlit dell. Clear water leapt off the rocks above and splashed musically into the pool beside them. Sunlight poured into the open space about the pool and dappled through the trees and bushes around it. The grass was bright green and tiny orange and red flowers spangled the meadow. In a quiet side of the pool, sweet blue irises reared above swordlike stands of green leaves. The bushes were blooming in clusters of pink and white and sometimes blood red. Where it was not stirred by the fall, the water was so clear Wiz could see minnows darting among the pebbles on the bottom.

"This is beautiful," Wiz said looking around him.

"Thank you, my Lord. Bal-Simba suggested it as a favorite picnic spot for those in the castle."

She forbore to mention Bal-Simba had also suggested it because it was easy to defend. Nor did she tell him the area had been swept by a troop of guardsmen and wizards only moments before their arrival. Nor did she mention the other precautions which had been taken.

Watching from the hilltop, Snorri the dwarf could not believe his luck. When they weren't working on Glandurg's contraptions, the dwarves had been scouting through the forest and surrounding countryside, hoping for something that would give them any entry into the castle. He had suspected something when he saw the guardsmen searching the dell. He had hidden himself among the bushes and now his patience had been rewarded.

Their quarry himself! Without guards and completely at his ease. The dwarf's hand crept to the sword strapped across his back. A quick charge and . . .

Then Snorri paused and frowned. There was magic about this strange wizard, and powerful magic at that. He did not recognize the spell, but its import was clear enough. Not only was the wizard shielded from violence, but any attempt at it would bring swift and deadly retribution. Protected as he was he could not be shot, cleaved, hacked, bashed or in any other wise attacked.

The dwarf bit his lip in frustration. He was closer to his prey than any of the party had been since the first day when that idiot Gimli tried. Yet he was as blocked from overt violence as if the wizard was still within the castle.

But that was only *overt* violence! Slowly, very slowly, Snorri put his hand into his belt pouch and felt the small tightly wrapped packet at the bottom. Then he turned his attention back to the protection spell. Finally he smiled. If his face had not been hidden by his hood it would have been a most unpleasant smile.

A fraction of an inch at a time, Snorri began to crawl forward toward the pair on the blanket.

Even if Wiz had been looking for the dwarf he couldn't have seen him and Wiz's mind—and eyes—were on other things.

Moira had laid aside her cloak and was bustling about spreading the blanket and laying out things from the hamper. As she came past, he reached out and pulled her to him for a long kiss.

"I thought you said you were hungry," Moira said, slipping from his grasp.

Wiz looked deep into his wife's green eyes. "There are all kinds of hunger."

"Food first," the hedge witch said firmly. "Then we shall see what else this blanket is good for."

She settled herself on the blanket with Wiz beside her and took out a green bottle.

"Currant wine for me," she said as she set the bottle to one side, "and for you, blackmoss tea." She wrinkled her nose as she pulled the earthen jug from the hamper.

"How you can stand to drink that stuff is beyond me," she told her husband, as Wiz poured the dark brew into a mug. "Especially when it is cold."

"Iced tea is a tradition where I come from. And it really isn't that bad once you get used to it."

"Ugh!" said Moira.

Wiz raised his mug. "To us."

Moira raised her goblet in response. Both drank and their eyes locked. Wiz eased closer, gazing deeply into his wife's wonderful green eyes.

"Pig's feet!" she said suddenly.

"Huh?"

"Pickled pig's feet." Moira turned and reached into the basket. "Shauna sent some along."

"And you don't like blackmoss tea," he said, setting his mug down.

Moira unwrapped Shauna's contribution. "But black-moss tea is disgusting," she said seriously. "Shauna's pig's feet are delicious."

"Ugh," said Wiz firmly.

Neither of them noticed the black-gloved hand that snaked out of the bushes behind them and passed over Wiz's mug. Nor did they see the surface of the tea roil briefly and then settle back into oily stillness.

Worming his way backwards Snorri kept his eyes on the couple. Wizard the Sparrow might be, and lucky he certainly was, but neither wizardry nor luck would save any mortal who consumed the powerful corrosive in that cup. Even gold itself would dissolve under the puissant acid formed when the magic powder met water.

Snorri was clever, but common sense wasn't his strong point.

"Well," said Moira, "I also brought along some of those meat pies you are so fond of."

"Now that's more like it. Darling, I don't know how to thank you for setting this all up. It's wonderful."

Moira picked up her goblet and took a sip. "I am glad you are enjoying yourself. And as for thanking me, perhaps we can think of something."

Without taking his eyes off Moira, Wiz picked up his mug and raised it toward his lips.

At which point the bottom fell out of the mug and the tea splashed all over the blanket.

"I think I made it too strong," Wiz said dumbly.

"Wiz, look!" Moira pointed at the blanket where the tea had splashed. The fabric was dissolving in smoking ruin and bare black earth was showing through beneath.

"Definitely too strong."

"You ninny, it's been poisoned!" Moira raised both her arms and gestured. Instantly five guardsmen and a blue-robed wizard popped through about them. The guardsmen surrounded Wiz and Moira and the wizard swung his staff over his head, throwing a glittering circle of protection around the group. Already Moira had started the spell to take them back to the castle along the Wizard's Way.

Back in their quarters Wiz and Moira surveyed the ruins of their picnic. The guardsmen had brought the basket and utensils back, but the food and drink had been disposed of as possibly poisoned. The remaining contents of the basket had tested safe, Arianne assured them. But somehow it didn't make up for the rest.

Moira looked sadly at the still-smoldering remains of the blanket. For a moment Wiz thought she would cry.

"I'm sorry about the blanket, darling."

Moira looked up at him, smiled and clutched his arm. "I'm glad it was only the blanket."

THIRTEEN

AIR ATTACK

Glandurg put his hands on his hips and surveyed the results of his men's labors. The forest clearing had been converted into an impromptu woodworking shop as dwarves dragged felled trees into position, rived them into billets and shaped the billets according to his direction.

His original idea had been to have the griffins fly them into the castle, but the griffins had flatly refused. Well, so be it. This would work just as well and in truth he had more confidence in dwarvish craftsmanship than he did in griffins.

Already four frames lay scattered about under the cover of the trees, complete except for their covering. The covering had arrived this morning, borne by griffins from the hold of the Mid-Northeastern Dwarves of the Southern Forest Range. The bolts of spider silk had been accompanied by a letter from King Tosig complaining about the expense, but Glandurg had barely glanced at that. It was just like his quasi-uncle to be preoccupied with such trifling details.

Glandurg moved among his companions, instructing them, pointing out defects and in general making a nuisance of himself as the other dwarves fitted and tied the pieces together. He paused to inspect the hide glue soaking in a cooking pot off to one side of the clearing and for the twentieth time that morning congratulated himself on his plan.

"Brilliant," he said to no one in particular. "They will never expect us to attack from the air!"

"Bloody good reason for that," muttered one of the dwarves as he bound a rib to a wing spar. The leader glared at him but he did not raise his head to meet Glandurg's eyes.

For several hours after their return, Wiz and Moira moped about their apartment. It was like going on a picnic and being rained out, Wiz thought glumly.

"Look at this," Moira said ruefully, "I have stains on my gown."

She held the garment up for Wiz to see. Sure enough, the back and one of the sleeves were stained with the red wine that had slopped out of her goblet.

"Looks like a job for a cleaning spell," Wiz said.

"Alas, the gown itself is magical."

"I wondered how that thing stayed up."

She smiled roguishly. "Men are supposed to wonder, my Lord." Then she looked down and sighed. "But the magic of this gown interferes with the spells we use to clean clothes. My Lord, do you know any cleaning spells?"

Wiz considered. For the mightiest wizard in all the world his repertoire of magic was rather limited. He could think of a dozen ways to incinerate the gown, but offhand he didn't know a single one to clean it.

"Well, I haven't been looking for one." He stopped and snapped his fingers. "Wait a minute, I know what you need. A detergent!"

"What does it deter?" Moira asked blankly.

"Not a deterrent, a detergent. Something that will lock onto the particles of stain and bind them to water so they will rinse away. I'll need to talk to Danny and Jerry. But we should be able to whip something up."

❖   ❖   ❖

In a few minutes of quick conversation and some scribbles on the ever-present slates the three programmers had worked out a spell to make a detergent.

"We need something to mix it in." Wiz started toward the kitchen.

"You are not experimenting in one of my pots," Moira said, stepping in front of him.

"How about a bucket?" Danny suggested. "There's one out in the hall."

"One of the maids must have left it there," Moira said. "Honestly, I think they become more slovenly every day."

"In this case it's a good thing," Wiz said as he made for the door.

The bucket was half-full of dirty water, but that didn't bother Wiz. "After all, when we get done with the spell it won't be water," he explained to the others.

A few quickly done spells, a quick call for an Emac and the spell was under way.

"You know, this gets easier all the time," Jerry said. "I don't ever remember being able to whip up programs this fast back in California."

Wiz shrugged. "Superior tools."

Jerry looked unconvinced.

"I think the system is actually helping us," Danny said. "Sometimes when I'm putting a spell together it's like the magic is reading my mind."

"In your case that's scary," Wiz said. "Whoops. Here's the operating demon."

The demon was small but muscular. It was clad in a white T-shirt and tight-fitting pants. Its eyebrows were white, its head was shaved and a gold earring dangled from one pointed ear.

"This is like watching old television commercials," Jerry said.

"Just be glad it wasn't a big arm punching out of the bucket," Wiz said.

The demon nodded at them and dived into the bucket. There was a trace of a splash and suddenly the dirty water had turned to something clear and viscous. There was no sign of the demon and the stuff looked like machine oil and smelled like nothing in particular.

"That's it?" Moira asked.

"I guess so."

Danny dipped his forefinger into the liquid. He tried to force his thumb and forefinger together and they slid over each other quickly and silently.

"Boy," Danny said admiringly, "that stuff's slicker than greased owl shit."

"Detergents generally are," Jerry said.

"So we use this in place of water?" Moira asked.

"Good grief no! You'll only need a dear little bit of it, maybe a few drops, in a whole bucket of water."

Moira frowned. "At that rate, I think we have enough to clean the entire castle for the next year."

"Oh," Wiz looked abashed. "That's not a problem, is it?"

"Not really. I will get a bottle from the stillroom tomorrow and for now we will leave the bucket in the alcove with the mops and brooms." She nodded to a tapestry hanging in the corridor near their apartment door. Such hangings were used to conceal this World's equivalent of broom closets. "It will be safe there on the shelf."

"It's simple, you see," Glandurg said, gesturing to the newly completed wing. "We'll just fly over the walls of the castle, as easy as birds."

"We're not birds," said Thorfin.

"Anyway we don't know how to fly them," Snorri added.

"You built them, didn't you? You can fly them."

"I built a cradle once," another dwarf said. "That doesn't mean I know how to have a baby."

"All right then," said Glandurg in disgust. "We'll practice until you do know how to fly them."

All the dwarves looked expectantly at their leader and Glandurg realized he had just backed himself into a corner.

"Here we are," he said with more confidence than he

felt. "You pick it up like this, grab the holding bar like this and you maneuver by shifting your weight or twisting the bar. Now what could be simpler?"

"Telling isn't showing," Thorfin said dubiously.

"Well, keep watching," Glandurg snapped. He hoisted the wing, ran forward and leapt into the air.

The result was a sort of grotesque hop that carried him perhaps two feet up and six feet forward. He barely got his feet down in time and half-stumbled on landing.

"Not much flying there," said Snorri.

"Well, I didn't get going fast enough. Here, let me show you again."

This time Glandurg went to the far end of the clearing and came pounding across the open space at a dead run. He reached the top of a small hillock and again jumped into the air. The result was a flight of perhaps a dozen feet.

"There, you see," he puffed triumphantly as he came back to join his followers.

"Not very well," Snorri said. "Can you do it again?"

Glandurg glared at him. "I will not. You do it."

"Don't know how," Snorri replied.

Glandurg glared at him. "Not enough, is it? Very well. I'll show you some flying." He turned and made for the largest tree at the edge of the clearing. "Come along," he flung over his shoulder. "You'll see right enough."

When he reached the base of the tree he started to climb. With a lot of grunting and heaving he managed to reach the branches about thirty feet up. From there he swarmed upward until he was nearly a hundred feet above his fellows.

"Pass the wing up," he shouted down.

"How?" Thorfin shouted back.

Glandurg bridled. "Don't be insubordinate."

Finally, with the aid of a line thrown to Glandurg, they were able to get the wing up to him. The others watched as Glandurg wormed his way into the contraption while balancing precariously on a branch.

"Watch," he commanded, and launched himself out into empty air.

Considering he had never flown in his life, it wasn't too bad. He dived too steeply and had to pull back sharply to keep from ploughing into the ground. He overcorrected and soared up again, slipping off to the right as he lost longitudinal control. He managed to bank sharply left, thereby avoiding the trees at the edge of the clearing and he was still turning when the ground came up to meet him. He moved further back to bleed off more airspeed, brought the nose up too far and came down in something that was more a poorly controlled stall than a landing.

The shock rattled Glandurg's teeth and drove him to his knees. It also snapped the left wing spar just outboard of his left shoulder.

"You see?" Glandurg said as he staggered to meet the pack of dwarves running toward him. "You see how easy it is.

"Here now," he said to Thorfin. "You try it."

"Will not."

"What?"

"I ain't going," Thorfin said stubbornly.

Glandurg marched over and stuck his face in Thorfin's. "I'm the leader here and I say you bloody are going!" he roared.

"You can be the leader all you want and I'm bloody not going," Thorfin said in the same unyielding tone. "No way I could handle one of them things. I'm scared of heights."

"'S truth," Gimli said. "I watched him on the flight here. Fair like to mess his pants, he was."

Thorfin glared at the purveyor of this unsought bit of support, but he stood firm. "I ain't going up in one of them things. Not even for practice."

"You would betray your oath?" Glandurg heaped scorn into his words.

"I ain't going back on my oath, but the oath didn't say anything about playing at being a bird."

Glandurg sensed that he was facing his first command crisis. He decided to resort to his ultimate threat.

"You will or you'll be sorry."

"You can't make me sorrier than I would be if I took one of those things. What could you do to me that's worse?" The other dwarves shifted uneasily and one or two murmured support for Thorfin.

Glandurg considered the question. It dawned on him there really wasn't anything he could do. The members of his band were sworn to kill the wizard, but Glandurg had not sworn them to obey him—in part because he doubted they would take such an oath.

However a successful commander remains flexible in the face of unexpected opposition.

"All right then, you won't have to fly. You and anyone else who feels the way you do can create a diversion by attacking the castle from below. There won't be as much glory in it, of course." He let the scorn drip from his voice. "But when the attack starts you can swim the river and climb the castle walls."

Thorfin nodded. "That suits," he said stolidly.

In the event two other dwarves decided they'd rather swim and climb than fly. That left Glandurg and eight others to practice gliding out of trees.

By the end of the day each dwarf had made five flights. It was a most successful training session, Glandurg decided. They were all alive and they still had half the wings undamaged. They could even land in the general direction of their target most of the time.

They needed more training. But meanwhile they could continue to practice with the remaining gliders and work on repairing the damaged wings.

It wasn't the woods, or even the streets of the Capital outside the castle, but there was solitude in this place, and a lovely view.

Well, Wiz thought to himself, *at least I'm safe up here.*

❖   ❖   ❖

Glandurg shifted uneasily and grasped his holding bar even tighter. This had seemed like a brilliant inspiration when he had both feet on the ground. Now, dangling hundreds of feet above the river he was less certain.

The wind whipped loose a strand of hair from under his hood and slapped it across his eyes. Instinctively he reached to push it away and for a heart-stopping instant he nearly lost his grip. He clutched the holding bar and squeezed his eyes tightly shut to blot out the scenery passing below him. Above him the griffin flew on, oblivious to his cargo's antics.

I am the leader, Glandurg reminded himself. *I must see where I am going.* He forced his eyes open. The castle was coming up fast. Carefully he reached into his shirt and removed the indicator. The glowing arrow inside the crystal sphere pointed straight at the battlements. Glandurg squinted through the wind. Yes, there was a lone figure high on the castle walls.

For an instant the dwarf was so exhilarated he forgot to be afraid. The Sparrow himself and out in the open! Truly this was his lucky day.

"Release the wings," the dwarf commanded.

Off to the west Wiz saw a flock of pigeons or turkeys or some other kind of heavy-bodied birds. As they came closer to the castle he could see they were too large to be pigeons. Turkeys then.

Hey, wait a minute! There aren't any turkeys in this World! Not only that, but each one seemed to have two sets of wings. *Biplane birds?*

Then each of the birds seemed to split in two and half of each bird dove toward Wiz.

The dwarves had taken good care to build their wings strong and light. They had taken less care to learn how they reacted in flight and no care at all to understand the mass of thermals, updrafts and cross currents that swirled around the castle on a warm autumn afternoon.

Nine dwarves aimed themselves straight at the lone

figure on the parapet without hesitation or thought for consequences. So naturally the nine dwarves went everywhere *but* to their target.

In his eagerness to reach his prey Glandurg had dived too steeply. He came in fast and low, headed straight for the castle wall. Frantically he pulled back on his control bar in an effort to avoid smashing into the stone. His wing swooped up, lost airspeed and teetered on the verge of a stall as it approached Wiz. Then Glandurg hit the updraft along the face of the wall, rose like an elevator and sailed majestically over the wall a good twenty feet above his gaping prey to drop into the courtyard behind.

Ragnar took a lesson from his leader's approach and set his height correctly. But his griffin had been well behind Glandurg's and he had to turn to the right in order to come in on Wiz. The turn brought him into the turbulence in the lee of one of the wall towers and he was tossed like a leaf to land nearly a hundred yards further down the wall, almost at the feet of an astonished guardsman.

By the time Ragnar had untangled himself from the wreckage of his wing the guardsman had drawn his sword. The dwarf scampered off with the guard in hot pursuit.

Meanwhile the other flying dwarves had arrived. Some went left, some right and some high. One or two threatened to smash into the wall and had to abort, hauling their wings around in tight turns and then dropping away into the valley.

The Wizard's Keep was boiling like an overturned anthill. Alarm horns rang out from the towers along the walls, guardsmen raced frantically to their stations, dragon cavalry poured out of their cave aeries and Wiz was surrounded by guards and wizards and hustled away to safety.

Off in the distance the griffins circled in a tight knot, watching intently and making noises that sounded suspiciously like laughter.

❖   ❖   ❖

Thorfin wrinkled his nose in disgust. The wind must have shifted and now he would have to breathe dragon stink all the rest of the way up the cliff.

Nasty beasts! No one but a mortal would think of keeping them. And as for riding them . . . He shivered involuntarily. Still, the dragons were all in their caves and his target was above him.

He levered himself up onto the outcrop and found himself nose to nose with a dragon.

It was not a very large dragon, but then Thorfin was not a very large dwarf. More to the point, the dragon was safely resting on a ledge and Thorfin was clinging to the cliff face by his toes and fingers. His sword was strapped across his back in a position more picturesque than practical and the blade wasn't designed for dragon slaying anyway. All things considered, the dwarf was at a serious disadvantage.

Thorfin did the best thing he could think of. He squinched his eyes tightly shut, turned his head away and pressed himself as tight against the cliff as he could manage.

Because they are both greedy for treasure, dwarves and dragons are natural enemies. However like cats and dogs, this is learned behavior. Thorfin had enough experience to know about dwarves and dragons. The Little Red Dragon had never even seen a dwarf before. It divided its time between roaming the programmers' quarters of the castle and sunning itself on the ledges on the cliff beneath the castle walls.

The dragon nudged the black-clad figure experimentally. It went "whoof" in a satisfying fashion.

Little Red Dragon nudged harder. This time he was met by a louder "whoof" and a string of interesting words.

This was more fun than annoying the castle cats! The dragon braced all four feet against the rock and pushed with all his strength.

Under the impact of the head butt Thorfin lost his grip

on the rock and went hurtling down toward the river, screaming curses as he fell.

"We chased six of the little buggers out of the castle, Lord," the guard captain told Wiz as they made their way back to his quarters that evening. "Plus a couple more that never made it over the walls. That was all of them, we think."

"You think?"

"That's why we are here, Lord."

"This is weird," Wiz said. "I've never even *met* a dwarf, I mean socially, and now there are a bunch of them trying to kill me. Why?"

"Ask us after we capture one. But by tomorrow this castle will be dwarf proof."

Wiz knew that Jerry, Danny and several of the Mighty were already erecting a dwarf-repellent spell around the Wizard's Keep. "I just hope it works," he said as they came up the back stairs and into the hall that led to his apartment. "I've been jumped, poisoned and attacked from the air—or they've tried to do all that anyway. I'm getting tired of it."

Fear not, mortal, thought Ragnar as he watched the party approach from the curtained alcove where he lay hidden. *You will not be tired of anything much longer.*

With so many mortal soldiers about there was no hope of fighting his way clear. So be it. He would fulfill his band's vow at the cost of his own heart's blood. They could kill him but not even twice that number of mortal warriors could protect the strange wizard from a pantherlike spring from his hiding place.

Ragnar crouched and drew his sword with a flourish that knocked a bucket off the shelf above him. The humans started at the noise, but Ragnar, oblivious to the liquid that drenched him, leapt forward with his sword brandished above his head. The guardsmen went for their weapons, but the dwarf was already in their midst and his blade was flashing toward his sworn foe.

His blade was still flashing when his feet shot out from under him and he went scooting between the startled guardsmen flat on his back with his arms and legs waving in all directions. His sword made glancing contact with one guardsman's mailed thigh and then he was through them and sliding down the corridor, his passage lubricated by the super-detergent that had soaked him and his clothes.

Wiz watched stunned as the dwarf whisked down the corridor, trailing curses, until he reached the stairs, where his cries ended in a *bump bump bump*.

One of the guardsmen moved to follow and immediately went to his knees in the trail of detergent Ragnar had left behind. Two others went more cautiously, hugging the walls of the corridor. Four others pushed Wiz back against the wall and stood shoulder to shoulder around him, protecting him with a wall of living flesh.

"It seems there were seven dwarves, my Lord," the guard captain said sheepishly. "Perhaps we had better stay with you until the wizards finish their spell."

"Yeah," Wiz said shakily. "Perhaps you had better."

It was a battered, dispirited group of dwarves that met in the clearing that night. Ragnar was the last to return, stripped to his loincloth to rid himself of the effects of the super-detergent and undwarvishly clean from swimming the river with traces of it on his body. While he dried himself by the fire and swilled down a mug of steaming soup, his companions considered what their next move should be.

"We learned much today," Glandurg said as he paced up and down before the fire.

"We learned dwarves are not meant to fly," came a voice from the edge of the circle.

"We learned the plan of the castle and of our enemy's defenses," Glandurg shot back, determined to put the best possible face on the day's events. "If we did not accomplish our objective, at least we gathered valuable knowledge."

"And how do we use that knowledge?" asked one of the other dwarves.

"We will find a way, but first we need a new strategy."

"We need a new leader," Snorri muttered.

Glandurg reddened. "Someone who attacks with poison and kills the cup no doubt."

It was Snorri's turn to redden.

"Can't we just say we tried and go home?" asked Gimli, the youngest of the dwarves.

"No!" Glandurg roared. "We are sworn to this quest. Our honor and the honor of all dwarfdom rests with us. Others may turn and run, but I will pursue our pledge to the bitter end."

"Bitter it is likely to be," said Thorfin sourly, nursing an arm in a sling.

"That is as it is," Glandurg said loftily. "The important thing is how we may fulfill our vow."

"Well, we're not going to fly in," Ragnar said from the fire.

"The human wizards have been busy," Thorfin said. "Now the whole castle is closed to us."

"Unlikely it is that this Sparrow will venture beyond the walls," Snorri added.

"We must think," Glandurg said. "We must await our opportunity and think in the meanwhile." He dropped down on a stump and ostentatiously rested his chin on his fist in a pose meant to suggest to all deep thought. In their own ways all of his followers imitated him.

It was a very imposing sight, but none of them had the faintest idea what to do next.

FOURTEEN

VIRTUAL UN-REALITY

"This is hopeless," Wiz said finally. "We've just got to have more information."

The dusty smell of hay and cattle still clung to the programmers' workroom, legacy of its days as a cow barn. Most of the stalls along the walls were no longer used as programmers' cubicles and the people who were left could have fitted into a room inside the keep proper, but the programming team kept the Bull Pen, partly because it was easier than moving and partly because of the aptness of the name. In a little while they were settled around the long plank table down the center. "We can't very well go knocking on the gate," Wiz said.

"Perhaps we can do exactly that," Moira said slowly. She turned down the table to Arianne. "Lady, does magic work within that castle?"

Arianne's brow furrowed as she considered. "As best we can tell. We cannot see through their barriers, but they seem to use magic within it."

"Then perhaps someone can go knocking at the gate of the castle. Or at least the semblance of someone."

Arianne's jaw dropped. Then she beamed and nodded. "Of course! Yes, Lady, I think that would work very nicely."

❖   ❖   ❖

"When I proposed this, I did not have you in mind," Moira grumbled as she watched the preparations. She, Wiz and Arianne were jammed into Arianne's workroom off the main courtyard of the keep.

As one of the Mighty, Arianne rated a tower to herself, but as Bal-Simba's assistant she spent most of her time doing administrative work and she preferred a place closer to the meeting halls of the main keep.

"Come on, darling, you said yourself this isn't dangerous," Wiz said from the stool in the middle of the room.

"She said no such thing," Arianne said sharply, looking up from her work table. "She said you cannot be harmed physically. But there will be a psychic link between you and the simulacrum."

"Not like a video game, huh?"

"Not a game of any sort," Arianne repeated firmly. "So be very careful and pull out at the first sign of trouble."

"That's right about now."

"There are many others who could go."

Wiz shook his head. "Nope. We need someone who knows enough programming to understand what he sees. That's me or Jerry. I'm higher ranking so they're more likely to talk to me."

Arianne nodded. She reached under the workbench and produced a bag of black velvet.

"Put this over your head."

Wiz looked at the hood dubiously.

"Is this necessary?"

"Not absolutely. But it will help you concentrate."

"Let's do without it then. That looks too much like what they put on someone before they hang him."

Arianne shrugged. "Your choice, Lord. But I will leave it around your shoulders should you want it."

She stretched to reach a shelf above her workbench and took down a carved wooden box about the size of a cigar box. Opening it, she hesitated over the contents before reaching in and removing a gnarled, forked root about the size of her hand.

"I have never seen one so large," Moira said as she came from her place by the door to get a closer look.

"Plucked from the earth by the full moon of mid-Winter," Arianne told her proudly. "It is the best I have."

"The bigger the root, the better, eh?" Wiz said from his stool.

"There are other factors, but basically yes. Now, if everyone is ready?"

Wiz nodded, Moira stepped back to the door and Arianne laid the root on the stone floor. Then she produced an ebony wand decorated with silver leaves and jeweled flowers.

Suddenly she spun and jabbed the wand at Wiz. He started and flinched at the unexpected move. Slowly and carefully she brought the wand away from Wiz and pointed it at the mandrake root, all the while keeping it perfectly level as if balancing an egg on the end.

Wiz looked down at the root. It seemed the same, but he felt dizzy and lightheaded, as if he hadn't eaten all day. He thought about trying to clear his head and decided against it.

Again Arianne turned and jabbed the wand at Wiz. Again a wave of lightheadedness rose up in him. As she turned back toward the root he could hear the spell she was muttering more clearly, although she had not raised her voice.

A third time she jabbed and pointed at the root. Wiz felt as if he was dividing like an amoeba. He saw the workroom from two perspectives at once, as if his vision had doubled. He closed his eyes, but both sets of eyes closed and he was completely in the dark. For a moment he felt nauseated and he took two deep breaths at once to try to settle his stomach.

With his eyes kept tightly shut, he reached up with all four of his hands and groped for the hood. He pulled it over his head and opened his eyes to darkness and to light.

He turned and faced himself and the two women.

"This is sooo weird," he said wonderingly in reverb duet.

"You will get used to it," Arianne said. "Concentrate on the simulacrum and try to ignore your body."

Wiz tried to move around the workroom to get the feel of his new body. At first both his standing body and his body on the stool tried to move together. He concentrated fiercely on the standing body and bit by bit his other body relaxed. Finally his "vision" fused completely into his new body. Distantly and dimly he could feel himself sitting on the stool and his breath sucking through the black velvet hood but he had to concentrate to feel it.

It wasn't a perfect illusion. His sense of touch worked very poorly and his sense of smell seemed to work not at all. But he could see and hear perfectly and his balance was good enough.

He faced his audience and spread his arms.

"Ta-DAH," Wiz said. He made a low bow and instantly regretted it as a wave of dizziness washed over him. He barely managed to avoid falling on his face.

"Can you move all right?" Arianne asked.

"I'm still kind of clumsy." He took another turn around the room, more confidently this time. "Okay, let's do it."

With Arianne and Moira trailing, he stepped out into the bright sunshine of the courtyard. He was particularly proud that he didn't trip over the raised sill of the workroom.

Jerry was waiting in the chantry with Bal-Simba and a couple of other blue-robed wizards. They had decided to have someone else send the simulacrum to the castle because Wiz was afraid he might transport himself instead of his image if he tried to walk the Wizard's Way unaided.

As "Wiz" and the others came into the room Jerry squinted at him.

"Gee, it really isn't you, is it? I can't tell even this close."

"Let us hope no one else can either."

Bal-Simba reached out and clapped the image on the shoulder. Then he grinned broadly at Arianne, showing all his pointed teeth.

"It even feels right! A work of art, Lady."

The usually unemotional wizardess dimpled and dropped a curtsey in return.

One of the other blue robes, a lean man with thinning dark hair named Juvian, bustled forward. "Everything you see and hear will be recorded." He tapped the glowing blue sphere he held in his palm. "It will not be necessary to stare or to overtly memorize anything. Keep your eyes moving and try to see as much as you possibly can."

Arianne stepped up beside him. "You know the recall signal. Use it at any sign of danger. We will be watching and if we see anything we will pull you back." She laid a hand on his shoulder and her brown eyes bored into his.

"Remember Sparrow, even though your body remains here you can be hurt. Do not become careless."

Wiz gulped and nodded.

A flash of darkness and Wiz found "himself" standing in front of the huge gate of the castle.

The doors were gigantic. Throwing his head back and squinting up, Wiz estimated they were at least a hundred feet high. They were made of some greenish metal with a zig-zag crack down the center where they met. The portal they were set in was made of some smooth pale blue substance with softly rounded forms and no joints anywhere, as if it and the walls of the castle had been cast in a single piece. The whole thing reminded Wiz of something out of a 1930s' comic strip.

There was no sign of a knocker or a doorbell. He thought about knocking, but if the thing was as thick as it looked he doubted he would be heard inside.

Well, nothing ventured . . .

He stepped up to the door and pounded three times

with his fist. The door boomed and rang from the blows in a way that made Wiz's whole body shiver.

For a minute nothing happened. Then he stepped back from the door and a motion on the portal caught his attention.

What he had taken as parts of the rounded decoration were futuristic gun turrets. The barrels poking out of the turrets were equally futuristic, with cooling fins and streamlined muzzle brakes. There were at least six of them and all of them were pointing directly at him.

Okay, so now they know I'm here. He decided the best thing to do was to act nonchalant, as if he went calling on strange castles every day. He thought about trying to whistle, but he wasn't sure he could. So he settled for folding his arms and looking around.

Around him the red sand desert stretched away in gentle folds. The landscape was dotted here and there with dark green spindly bushes and an occasional clump of something that looked like it might have been cactus if it had known what a cactus was supposed to be. The sun was high in the sky and the reflection off the greenish metal of the gates was enough to make him squint.

Oddly, when you got this close to it the castle wasn't very impressive. Standing next to it was like standing next to a mountain instead of something manmade. Even the gate was huge and impersonal. Somehow that made it less imposing, not more.

Well, it's not their taste in architecture I'm concerned about.

Wiz couldn't sense temperature very well through the simulacrum, but the glare of the sun and the bright reflection off the gate told him it had to be hot out here. He wondered if he was sweating.

Then the door started to move. Wiz opened his mouth and nearly choked on his carefully prepared greeting when he saw what was behind it.

The robot was eight feet tall with glowing red eyes and

a glossy black skin. It was human-shaped, but it wasn't what Wiz would call reassuring.

"You rannggg?" it asked in a voice like the bell of doom. It would have been even more impressive if the robot had been talking to the visitor instead of the gatepost.

Wiz dredged up the last of his nonchalance. "Yeah. I'm Wiz Zumwalt and I'm here to see the boss."

The robot paused as if considering the information. A crackling blue nimbus played over its head and down its right shoulder.

"Commeee," it commanded.

The head cocked to one side and jerked upright. The arms jerked up, elbows bent, bringing the hands to shoulder level. The robot spun on its heel, nearly lunged into the gate, recovered and strode off, weaving from side to side like a drunken sailor.

"Lead on, Lurch," Wiz said to the robot's departing back, then hurried after him. The guns tried to track him even inside the portal.

The hall beyond the gate was so gargantuan that Wiz couldn't make out the other end. High above shafts of sunlight washed down through the haze that hid the ceiling.

A rather thick haze, Wiz noticed as he strode along after his jerking, zig-zagging guide. It wasn't just that the place was big, it needed a good vacuuming. He noticed that both he and the robot were leaving footprints in the film of reddish dust on the marble tiled floor.

After a few hundred yards they turned off into a side corridor. Its proportions were more to human scale, but it was round and a trickle of water down the center made the going harder. The robot splashed along unconcerned, but Wiz tried to keep his feet dry by staying to the side. He had to hurry even more to keep up with the robot.

Even though Wiz's temperature sense didn't work very well, it was so cold he shivered a bit. The metal walls of the tunnel were filmed with condensation which trickled down and accumulated at the bottom of the corridor.

That's where the water comes from, he thought. *They need a little work on their climate control system.* He looked down at the water in the center of the tunnel and saw it was slimed with green algae.

Not to mention their housekeeping.

A short way down the corridor was a door, round and massive like a bank vault's. The robot stopped short and waited as Wiz came up beside him.

Just as Wiz reached the robot the door popped open and clanged against the corridor wall. Wiz jumped back to keep from being crushed. His guide remained impassive even though the door missed him by a fraction of an inch.

A few other little things they need work on, too. As he set off in pursuit of the robot he wondered if that was supposed to have been an automated door opener or a man trap.

Another few hundred feet brought them to a bank of elevators that looked like something out of a New York office building—if you ignored the remote-controlled machine guns covering the lobby and the gargoyles perched over the elevator doors.

After a brief wait one set of doors banged open and Wiz and the robot stepped into an elevator—more accurately, they stepped *down* into an elevator, since the car had stopped about a foot below the floor.

It took a long, long time to reach the top. Wiz wasn't sure whether that was because they were going so high or because the elevator worked about as well as the robot guide. They jerked, lurched, sputtered, speeded up and slowed down until Wiz lost all sense of how far they had come. He wasn't even too sure they had gone straight up.

At last the doors flew open and they stepped out into another corridor. This one was broad and clean, at least. The floor was tiled in jade-green material, the walls were malachite and the ceilings and wall decorations were in polished gold. It was like being inside a Faberge Easter egg and it removed any last lingering doubts Wiz might have had about his hosts' taste.

The robot lurched drunkenly down the corridor and caromed off the wall, knocking off chips of malachite and bending a golden wall sconce.

At the end of the hall was a bronze portal. The robot stopped before it and made a motioning gesture with its arm that nearly took Wiz's head off. Then it froze.

Wiz recovered from the accidental assault, realized his guide had signaled him through the door, saw that the robot wasn't likely to make any other dangerous moves, and stepped past.

The room was as out-of-scale as everything else in the castle. One whole side and half the ceiling was picture-window-size panes of glass giving a panoramic eagle's-eye view of red desert and sere mountains. The place was fitted out like a laboratory, or perhaps a control room, with panels of dials and switches everywhere, the odd arc of electricity here and there and huge pieces of unidentifiable apparatus scattered about. The whole room reeked of electricity and danger.

There were two humans waiting for him there.

The younger one reminded Wiz a little of the way Danny had looked when they first met, kind of soft and unformed. The other one was a few years older, harder and leaner. He was sitting on one of the control consoles with his legs dangling. Even though he was relaxed, there was something predatory in the way he looked at Wiz.

For a minute no one said anything.

"Uh, hi. I'm Wiz Zumwalt. From Cupertino." His voice was almost lost in the huge room.

"We know who you are," the older one said. He reached behind him, picked up a beer bottle and took a swig. No one made a move to offer Wiz a drink.

"Lurch there is really something," Wiz said brightly.

"He's an early model," the younger one said. "The ones we build now are a lot better."

His companion grinned nastily. "*Much* better."

"Very impressive."

The silence stretched on.

"I'm Craig Scott," the young one said at last. "This is Mikey Baker."

"Craig talks too much," Mikey said conversationally. "Don't you, Craig?"

Craig wilted.

"Pleased to meet you," Wiz said.

"Yeah?"

Again the silence stretched out.

"Anyway, I thought we should meet, you know, talk."

"So talk."

"You know you upset a lot of people when you showed up."

Mikey smiled. A not at all pleasant smile. "No shit? Well, we're going to upset a lot more people, aren't we Craig?"

"We sure are."

"What are you going to do? What do you want?"

"We're going to build a whole new order," Craig said. "We're going to combine magic and technology into a system that really works for mankind. When we get done things will be better than they have ever been."

"Only you won't be around to see it, man," Mikey said.

"We're going to . . ."

"You talk too much, Craig," Mikey repeated without heat. "Now shut up and let the grownups talk, will you?"

He took another pull on his beer.

"You see, you're squatting on a prime piece of real estate, you and your friends. Now it so happens we need that place. So in just a little while we're going to come over and take it."

Wiz went cold. "Hey look, we can negotiate . . ." But Mikey cut him off with a sharp bark of laughter.

"What's to negotiate?" he said, sliding off the table and stalking over to Wiz. "We're here and you're history." He jammed his face into Wiz's, so close Wiz could see the pores on his skin. "We're gonna get your whole flicking *world* before we're through, baby, and there's not a damn thing you can do about it."

"The hell there isn't," Wiz flared back. "Technology doesn't work over there, remember? And we've got magic the likes of which you've never seen."

Mikey smiled. "Wanna bet?"

Then his expression softened. "But maybe you're right. Maybe we should negotiate this thing like adults." He smiled again, a more relaxed, gentle smile. "After all, there's plenty for both of us. Two whole worlds, right?"

"Well . . ." Wiz didn't want to break the moment, but he didn't like the idea of giving away half the World. "I'm not empowered to negotiate directly, but I can take an offer back to the Council of the North."

Mike nodded and his smile grew wider, almost radiant. "Of course. So here's the offer I want you to take back to your Council."

He flicked his hand up and a wave of fire washed over Wiz.

Wiz screamed as the flames hit him. He dropped to his knees and then fell to the floor, the center of a white-hot ball haloed in orange. Thick black smoke roiled off the body and disappeared.

Then the inferno vanished and nothing remained but a tiny blackened thing lying on the laboratory floor.

Craig was white with shock at what his friend had done. "It wasn't him," he said dully. "He wasn't really here after all."

"Shit!" Mikey picked up the charred bit of root and threw it against the wall. "Shit, shit, *shit!*"

FIFTEEN

FIRE WITH FIRE

Reverse engineering is the sincerest form
of flattery.
—*Engineers' saying in Silicon Valley*

Wiz screamed.

His very eyes were on fire. Heat singed his hair and beat on his brain through his skull. The flesh melted and ran off his face. The palms of his hands and the soles of his feet throbbed with pain as the awful, searing heat destroyed the nerve endings.

Somewhere far beyond the wall of terrible pain he was aware of Arianne gesturing wildly. Then waves of coolness washed over his body.

"Oh my God," Wiz moaned. "Oh my God."

Arianne held him in a way that combined professionalism and compassion. "You will be all right, my Lord," she said soothingly. "Try to relax."

Wiz relaxed one tiny, knotted muscle. The expected flare of pain did not come. He relaxed a few more muscles and still no pain.

"Jesus," he breathed out raggedly. Arianne released him to another's arms. Moira. Instinctively he reached out to touch her hair.

"I warned you that the psychic effects could be painful," Arianne said.

"Yeah, but . . ." He gasped for breath again. " . . . my God." Moira hugged him to her and he felt her tears on his cheek.

"I'm all right now, darling," he said with a smile he did not feel.

"*They* will not be if ever we meet," his wife said fiercely.

"I am sorry we did not get you out sooner, my Lord," Arianne told him, "but we did not realize what was happening."

Wiz sucked another racking breath. "Sucker punched. That son-of-a-bitch sucker punched me."

The tall blonde sorceress shrugged. "Name it as you like. They have no honor."

Wiz was still shaking a few minutes later when the programmers and such of the Mighty as were in the castle assembled hastily in the chambers of the Council of the North. They took their places haphazardly around the long oak table without regard for the carefully established rules of place and precedence. That alone told Wiz how seriously the wizards took this.

"They're programmers, all right," he told the group. "From our world or one very much like it."

"Do your people make war against us?" demanded Juvian.

"Definitely not. I could tell that much just by looking. But they're trained in the same discipline we are."

"That's bad," Jerry said.

"Worse than you know, perhaps," Bal-Simba rumbled. "They have some powerful magical force behind them."

"The Dark League again?"

Bal-Simba snorted. "Much more powerful than that. Non-human I think, and mighty even for non-humans."

"Elves?"

"Perhaps."

"That must be what they've been up to," Danny said. "They've been stalling the negotiations while they got this thing set up."

Wiz frowned. "I don't know. There was magic all over the place, but it didn't feel like elf magic."

"May I remind you, Sparrow," Bal-Simba said, "that you have not met many elves?" Then he shook his head. "But you are correct. Elves can make time and space run strangely, but I have never heard of them creating a whole new World."

"Well, whoever it is has found themselves a couple of people who understand programming. They seem to be pretty good at it."

"They are," Danny said.

"You know them?" Wiz demanded.

"One of them. Mikey Baker. Well, I didn't really know him but I used to see him around on the nets. His handle was 'Panda,' you know?"

"No, we don't know. Tell us."

"Well, he was into hacking and phreaking—system breaking and shit like that."

"Don't call it hacking," Wiz said sharply. "People like that aren't 'hackers,' they're worms."

Danny shrugged. Unlike Wiz and Jerry he didn't have the true hackers' deep contempt for computer vandals who used their skills to break into computer systems. Nor was he offended that the media insisted on calling those criminals "hackers."

"Whatever. Anyway, no one liked him much."

"I can see why. But was he any good?"

"Oh, I guess so. But he was like nasty-nice, you know? Real sweet and easy-going on the surface and just rotten underneath."

"He sure as hell wasn't sweet to me!"

"He wasn't like that before. It seems like he's changed a lot."

"Well, what else do you know about him?"

"Not a lot. The people I knew didn't like him so I

steered clear of him. There's a rumor he had something to do with the Jesse James Virus."

Wiz looked puzzled. "The Jesse James Virus?"

"That was after you left." Jerry shook his head. "A variation on the Panama Virus. Very sophisticated and real nasty. If this guy was behind it, he's got talent."

"I'd say there's a lot of talent behind that place," Wiz said. "Face it. We're not unique. There are a lot of competent programmers who could do pretty much what we've done if they knew about this place and how to get here."

"Yeah," Danny said, "but *how* did they find out about this world?"

"Perhaps they did not," Moira said. "Perhaps they were brought here as the wizard Patrius brought you here."

"Mikey told me they came here voluntarily."

"I wouldn't trust anything that guy said," Danny put in.

"Maybe, but someone turned them on to magic programming and our magic compiler. They didn't pick that up on their own."

No one said anything for a minute.

"There's only one place they could have gotten the compiler," Wiz said at last. "It had to come from here."

Bal-Simba frowned like a thundercloud. "A traitor?"

"Not exactly," Jerry said. "I've been studying the code from that recon drone we found. The compiler they're using isn't exactly our compiler. It doesn't have the extensions we've added in the last year and it's got a couple of features we don't."

"So they got an earlier version of the code and they've been working on it independently," Wiz said. "Can you tell roughly when they got their version?"

"No 'roughly' about it. I know exactly when. They're working with the last version the full programming team worked on."

"One of the programmers after all," Wiz said. "But we'd ruled that out."

"I fail to see how," Bal-Simba said. "That—ah—

'nondisclosure agreement' you had them sign is not enforceable in your world."

"Meaning we can't sic that demon named Guido on them," Wiz agreed. "But we thought of this before and we checked."

"Between Worlds?" Bal-Simba looked skeptical.

"Even in our world there are ways of checking, although they aren't absolutely accurate."

"We had to make a couple of phone calls," Danny said.

Arianne looked at him strangely but said nothing.

"And you checked everyone?"

"Not everyone. One person, Judith Conally, is very ill. She was hurt in an accident a few months back and she's still in a coma."

"She's out then," Wiz said. "People in comas don't talk."

"That's not true, you know," Bronwyn said from where she sat at the end of the table.

"Huh?"

"People in comas can sometimes talk. It is not common, but . . ." She shrugged.

"If she talked," Moira said slowly, "there might have been ears to hear."

"Well, we pretty well know that no one else did," Jerry said.

"I think," Bal-Simba said, "it is time for another Great Summoning from your world."

SIXTEEN

RESCUE

Three A.M. is a bad time in hospitals. Normal life processes are at their lowest ebb. If it is busy it is because things have gone to hell and if it's quiet it's hard to stay alert. Fortunately things were quiet on Neuro, so the nursing supervisor was having trouble staying awake when Sheila came up to the station.

"We've lost Conally." Sheila's voice was so low and tight the supervisor had trouble understanding her.

The super looked up from her charts. "What?"

"Conally, the patient in 314. We've lost her."

The supervisor looked sharply at the young nurse. She seemed to be taking this one very hard.

"Too bad," the supervisor said sympathetically, reaching for the phone. "I'll get a resident up here to pronounce and then we'll . . ."

Sheila shook her head. "You don't understand. She's not dead, she's gone! Not in her room."

It was the supervisor's turn to go white.

The bed was in place, the bedclothes rumpled but not thrown back and the bed was empty.

"Did you check the other rooms?"

"I've looked everywhere in the ward. I can't find her."

It wasn't unknown for Neuro patients to get out of bed and wander around. That was why the unit was built secure. Except for emergency exits with alarms, the only way in or out was past the nurse's station and the door could not be opened from the inside unless someone at the nurse's station buzzed you out.

"Well, search again."

"I've already got Doreen and Lupe doing that."

"We'd better alert security to search the rest of the hospital," the supervisor said at last.

As she turned away from the empty bed she thought regretfully of the cigarettes she had left in her locker. This was going to be a bitch of a night.

Bronwyn looked up from the still form, her lips pressed into a tight bloodless line. "What have those damned barbarians done to her?" she demanded.

"How should I know?" Wiz said. "I'm not a doctor."

"Neither are any of them by the look of it. They kept her clean and fed, but they did nothing to heal the damage to her brain."

"I don't think we can," Wiz said. "Head injuries are hard for us to handle."

"Barbarians," Bronwyn repeated and motioned her assistant to her. "Now leave us. And don't expect to talk to this one for a couple of days at least."

In the event, it was three days before Bronwyn would let Wiz and Moira in to see her patient.

Judith was lying in bed propped up with pillows. She still looked terrible, but she was conscious.

"Hi, Judith. How are you feeling?"

"Wiz, Moira," she said weakly. "I dreamed about you." Then she frowned. "I feel funny. Arms and legs don't move right and my eyes don't wanna focus."

"That is normal," Bronwyn said. "Magic can only do so much safely. You must heal the rest of the way naturally. That will take time and work on your part."

"Not complaining," Judith said muzzily.

"You said you dreamed about us," Moira said gently.

"Dreamed about this place a lot. I think."

"Do you remember answering questions about this World?"

Judith's eyes flicked from side to side, as if searching. "I, I might have. It seems like I went over and over things about this place."

"She will never have complete memory of that time," Bronwyn whispered in Wiz's ear. "There was too much damage."

"Did you have any notes about our system of magic?" Wiz asked.

"Notes?" Judith seemed confused. Then she pressed her fingers to her forehead in an effort to think. "Yes, I did make some notes after I got back, but I didn't show them to anybody. They're in my apartment."

"We'll check on that," Wiz said.

"What's wrong?" Judith asked.

"We think you talked while you were in the hospital," Wiz told her. "We think someone got most of the system of magic out of you. I'll bet we won't find those notes in your apartment either. Do you know a guy named Mikey Baker?"

"No."

"What about Craig Scott?"

"Yes," Judith said hoarsely. "He's a friend of mine. We furp together all the time."

"Furp?" Moira asked.

"FRP—fantasy role playing games," Wiz explained absently.

"What's happened? What's wrong?"

"Craig and this Mikey character are here. They're raising all kinds of hell."

Judith went even whiter. "No! I couldn't have!"

"That is enough," Bronwyn said firmly. "She needs to rest."

"Right," Wiz said. "Listen, you just concentrate on

getting well and don't worry, okay." He patted her hand and left.

"Moira?" Judith said weakly as the hedge witch turned to go.

"Yes, my Lady?"

"I screwed up, didn't I? I really screwed up."

Moira smiled and patted her shoulder. "It is all right," she told her. "It doesn't really matter."

Then she turned away so Judith would not see how much that statement cost her.

SEVENTEEN

A NEW ALLY

Wiz was in the middle of analyzing a module from the crashed recon drone when Bal-Simba found him in the Bull Pen.

"My Lord, you have a visitor."

There was something in the way he said it that made Wiz snap around, the intricacies of the code forgotten.

"Who?"

"Duke Aelric."

Wiz's jaw dropped. Only once before had the elf duke sent his image into the Wizard's Keep. The times Wiz had met him it had been in his own elf hill. No mortal understood how the elf hierarchy worked, but Aelric was called "duke" and stood high among the elves. Whatever this was, it had to be important.

Without another word Wiz left his code and hurried out the door of the Bull Pen, but when he turned toward the main keep and the Watcher's Hall, Bal-Simba placed a hand on his shoulder.

"Not there. The main gate."

"Why did he send his image there?"

Bal-Simba looked at him strangely.

"He did not send his image, my Lord. He is here in person."

❖   ❖   ❖

There was no room in the Wizard's Keep deemed grand enough for receiving an elf, but the Wizard's Day Room was quickly put right, Malus was awakened from his afternoon nap and shooed out, and Wiz and Duke Aelric retired there.

Even in leather breeches, boots and a simple tunic of dark blue velvet brocaded in silver, Duke Aelric was as out of place as a president in a pig sty. But he contrived to put Wiz so much at his ease in the short walk from the main gate that Wiz didn't notice—almost.

"What can we do for you, my Lord?" Wiz asked after his guest had been seated and refused refreshment.

"It is more a question of what I can do for you, Sparrow," Duke Aelric said. "Or perhaps what we can do for each other."

"Oh?" was all Wiz could think of to say.

"You have already met the new arrivals from your world?"

"Mikey and Craig?" Wiz said grimly. "Yeah, I've met them."

"Then you agree they must be dealt with?"

"Yeah. That's what you might call at the top of my to-do list."

"I also want to see them dealt with. And what is behind them. Better to work together on this, do you not agree?"

"I'd be honored, Lord. But why . . . ?"

Aelric cocked a silvery eyebrow. "Why am I interested? Because what you are doing is important. And because I think you will need my help. In fact, you will need all the help you can get."

The way he said it made Wiz's blood run cold. He knew the business with Craig and Mikey was serious, but if Duke Aelric was interested it had to be even more serious than he imagined.

You will meet your greatest challenge, Lisella had said. He forced the rest of the prophecy out of his mind.

"Okay, what do you suggest?"

"First, I think, we must pool our knowledge. There are things I can tell you which will help and other things I wish to learn from you."

"Sure." Wiz reached for the silver bell to summon a servant. "Let me get the rest of the team in here."

Duke Aelric made small talk while they waited. Wiz was too astonished by the whole situation to do more than respond half-heartedly. He was very glad when Jerry burst into the room.

"They said you wanted to . . ." He stopped short and goggled at the guest. Duke Aelric rose and bowed exquisitely, obviously amused by Jerry's reaction.

"This is, uh, Duke Aelric," Wiz said lamely. "I've told you about him."

"Honored."

"Ye . . . yeah," Jerry replied weakly. "Uh, forgive me. They didn't tell me . . . I mean, they just said Wiz wanted to see me."

The door opened behind him and Danny came in with June beside him.

"And this is Danny . . ." Wiz began, but he was cut short by June's shriek. She shrank back against Danny, white and open-mouthed.

Aelric bowed again. "My Lord, my Lady."

June turned away and buried her face in Danny's shoulder.

"Uh, Danny, why don't you take June back to your room?" Wiz said desperately. "I'll talk to you later, okay?" Danny threw Aelric a venomous glance and led his shaking wife out.

"Now then," Wiz said, turning back to Duke Aelric, "here's what we know so far."

It was several hours later when Wiz hunted up Moira.

"How is our guest?" she asked as soon as he came into their apartment.

Wiz kissed her perfunctorily. "You heard, huh?"

Moira looked at him. "Not much of a greeting, my Lord."

"I've got a problem. You know June saw Aelric and nearly went into hysterics?"

Moira nodded. "So I had heard."

"It's the same thing that happened the last time she met an elf," Wiz went on. "At the time I thought it was just Lisella. The way she popped up was enough to scare anyone and June's easy to frighten. But Aelric was just sitting there and she's more afraid of him than she was of Lisella."

Moira nodded. "Certainly she is terrified of elves. But you are concerned about more than June's feelings, I think."

"I'm concerned about making this thing work. Right now Danny wants to tear Aelric's heart out because of the effect he has on June. We can't build a team with something like that going on."

"What can I do to help you, love?"

"You're closer to June than anyone. Do you have any idea why she's so afraid of Aelric?"

"Nothing specific," the hedge witch said slowly. "June is afraid of many things." She smiled ruefully. She is hardly what you would call normal in the best of circumstances."

"Amen to that!"

"But still . . ." Moira trailed off and stared away. Then she looked up at her husband. "You know her history. She was found wandering on the Fringe of the Wild Wood a few years ago, much as she is now. No one knew her or whence she came and she cannot, or will not, tell us."

"So?"

"She is terribly afraid of elves. Perhaps she has had dealings with them before."

"That doesn't make sense. Elves don't deal with humans."

"They deal with you."

"So I've got an elf magnet in my pocket. June sure doesn't."

"There is one case where elves do deal with humans regularly. They take human children to act as bond servants within elf hills."

"And you think June . . ."

"Time passes strangely under an elf hill. It seems like a season or two but when the servants have fulfilled their bond and are released centuries have passed. Their family, their friends, even their village are dust and gone."

"It makes sense," Wiz said at last. "It would explain where she comes from and a lot about why she is so strange."

Moira said nothing.

"What else? There's something you aren't telling me, isn't there?"

"My Lord, I do not know any of this. It is all surmise."

"But you suspect something. Out with it."

Moira stared into her lap. Wiz waited. "Do you know why June needs Shauna to help nurse Ian?" she asked at last.

"I never really thought about it."

"Because she does not produce enough milk."

"As flat-chested as she is, I can believe it, but so what?"

Moira snorted. "My Lord, contrary to what lechers like you believe, the size of a woman's breasts has little to do with her ability to feed an infant. No, June does not produce enough milk because her breasts are damaged. There are scars around both her nipples. Many little scars, as if she had been bitten repeatedly."

Wiz went cold. "Meaning what?"

"You recall I once told you elves prefer human nurse-maids for their infants? It is said that elf babies are born with all their teeth."

Moira looked at him levelly, green eyes intent and serious. "It is also said those teeth are sharp enough to draw blood."

Duke Aelric was on the castle wall, watching the setting sun turn the clouds orange and the hills purple.

In his own unearthly way he was as magnificent as the sunset and Wiz watched both for several minutes before he got up the courage to approach him.

"My Lord, I need to talk to you."

Aelric turned from the sunset and inclined his head. "Of course, Sparrow."

"It's about June, Danny's wife."

A graceful frown knitted the elf duke's brow. "Ah, the one who was so upset? Forgive me, I thought she was a servant."

"Was she?" Wiz asked harshly.

"I beg your pardon?"

"Was she one of your servants?"

Duke Aelric made a throw-away gesture. "I really do not know, Sparrow. There have been so many."

"She was some elf's servant. Now she's terrified of elves because of something that happened to her."

Duke Aelric said nothing.

"Doesn't that bother you at all?" Wiz demanded.

The elf duke raised a silvery eyebrow. "Why should it? If she did serve the ever-living I can assure you she was not deliberately mistreated. If she was a servant it was because she was offered a bargain and she accepted. I assure you the bargain was kept." He cocked his head. "Forgive me, but I do not see the relevance of an old bargain with one mortal—if bargain there was. Nor do I understand why you are so concerned about it."

"Some bargain," Wiz said bitterly. "Parents would 'foster' their children into elf hills in return for the protection they needed to survive."

"Nonetheless, she would have entered our domains as all mortals enter them. Of her own will."

"And came out to find that centuries had passed."

Aelric cocked his head and said nothing.

Wiz could only stare. When they had met before Duke Aelric had been gracious, even charming, if somewhat frightening. Wiz knew that elves could be cold and cruel, but this was the first time he had ever seen it in Aelric.

And the worst of it was, Wiz realized, he wasn't being cruel at all. He honestly did not understand why what had happened to June should be any of his concern. He began to appreciate, vaguely, just how un-human elves really were.

"Now she's terrified of you and her husband would just as soon murder you as look at you and I've got to work with both of you."

The elf turned to Wiz and gave him a look that rooted him where he stood. "Her husband cannot find the necessity one-tenth as distasteful as I do." Aelric's fine features drew up in a sneer. "Sparrow, do you think I *like* coming here; associating with mortals?"

"Then why did you come?"

"Sparrow, listen to me. There are *things* in this World that are not of it. Ancient things whose very nature you cannot comprehend." His eyes bored into Wiz. "I told you once that you had upset a very delicate balance. Even after all that has happened I still do not think you understand what you have done.

"Magic in the hands of mortals is dangerous, Sparrow. Unlike the ever-living, you are not inherently magical. You do not really understand magic.

"But your new magic is very powerful. That arouses certain—things—" He trailed off, as if thinking. Then he resumed briskly. "Now those things must be dealt with. For this we will both need to bend all the powers we possess to the task."

He was afraid, Wiz realized. Duke Aelric was actually afraid of whatever it was they were facing! Something cold and hard grew in Wiz's stomach.

It was fully dark by the time Wiz went to visit Danny. He was alone in his room, Shauna having taken June and Ian off someplace to try to calm her down.

"Has he gone yet?" Danny demanded sullenly.

"No, and he's not going."

Danny bounced up off the bed. "Fuck that shit! He's

going if I have to throw him out of here on his goddamn ass!"

Wiz moved in front of the door. "You're not going anywhere. You're going to sit down and we're going to talk."

"Fuck that." Danny tried to force his way past Wiz, but Wiz grabbed him and pushed him back into the room. "Listen to me. This is a war, not a popularity contest. Right now we need all the help we can get and he's about the most potent help we're likely to find.

"Maybe something happened between June and Aelric once. But that's over. Now we need each other. That means if you're going to be part of the team you're going to have to work with him." He looked hard at Danny. "Right now Aelric is a lot more valuable to this project than you are. If you can't handle it, I'll have to replace you."

"With who?" Danny sneered.

"With one of the wizards we've been training. Malus, maybe. He may not be as talented as you are, but he can get along with Aelric."

Danny didn't say anything.

"Well?"

"I still don't like him," Danny said sullenly.

"You don't have to like him. You have to work with him. Now, can you do that?"

"Yeah, I guess so. Just keep him the hell away from June."

Wiz released Danny's shoulders. "He doesn't have to come anywhere near June."

"Okay then," Danny said. "Anything else?"

"Not now. We'll have a staff meeting at noon tomorrow to figure out approaches."

Duke Aelric did not stay the night in the Wizard's Keep but he returned early the next morning. Again they met in the Wizard's Day Room: Wiz, Jerry, a sullen but cooperative Danny, and Bal-Simba as the head of the

Council of the North. The huge wizard said little and
Aelric generally ignored him.

Yesterday Wiz and Jerry had done most of the talking as they filled Duke Aelric in. Today it was the elf duke
who dominated.

"Lord, it sounds as if the simplest approach would be
to close off the gate into our World somehow," Jerry said
when Aelric had finished.

"Simple indeed," Aelric said with a trace of amusement,
"if we but had the key."

"Is there a key?"

In response Aelric lifted a finger and an elaborate,
convoluted shape blossomed in the center of the table.

"That is a simple representation," he told them. "There
are actually eleven directions, not just three. The narrow
part at the top represents the situation when the gate was
first opened. Here at the bottom," he gestured at the
wildly intertwined strands that seemed to grow out of the
table top, "is the situation as it is now. If I knew the total
shape, it would be possible to construct the key and so
close the door beyond opening again. But . . ." He smiled
slightly and shrugged.

"Wait a minute!" Jerry said thinking hard. He scribbled
frantically on a slate while the others watched in silence.
"That's a fractal!"

"I do not know that word," Aelric said.

"It's a self-similar figure with fractional dimensions."

Aelric arched an eyebrow.

"Just a minute," Wiz put in. "Are you sure that's a
fractal?"

"Pretty sure. Look." He passed the tablet over to Wiz.

"Yeah," Wiz said slowly. Then he looked back at the
elf. "Look, when you say 'know the shape,' do you mean
'describe mathematically'?"

Aelric frowned. "I do not understand you, Sparrow.
When I say 'know the shape,' I use the words as mortal
magicians do, I think."

Wiz turned to Bal-Simba. "Lord . . ."

"If the Sparrow means what I believe he means, then yes. A mathematical description is sufficiently precise."

Aelric turned back to Wiz. "Can you do this?"

Wiz nodded. "Fractals have another characteristic. They are generated by iteratively applying a function—that means applying the function over and over—and a lot of those functions are pretty simple."

"There are image compression systems that use fractals," Jerry said. "Rather than store the actual image they store functions that generate fractals to mimic each part of the picture and then combine them. You can compress an image ten thousand to one or more that way."

"Show me," Aelric commanded.

The elf was leaning forward looking at them so intently Wiz almost thought he was going to spring at them like a lion at an antelope.

Slowly and carefully Jerry and Wiz led Aelric through the process that would yield the solution. Although mathematics was an alien language to the elf, parts of it he grasped intuitively. Other parts had to be broken into tiny pieces and gone over and over.

At last his face split into a broad smile. "Brilliant. A whole new way of looking at such things. Thank you both." Then he sobered. "Yes, I think this," he tapped the slate, "is a fair representation of the problem of closing that door. But if I understand you, it is a problem almost beyond solution."

"Almost isn't the same as impossible," Jerry said. "There are ways you can simplify something like that. In principle it is solvable. It is just a matter of putting enough computer power to work on it."

"Now that's something we can do," Wiz said. "Our spell compiler isn't adapted to solving mathematical problems but demons can be made to calculate as well as work magic."

Danny shook his head. "I dunno. This isn't going to

be easy." It was the first thing he had said all morning
and he looked at the glowing model rather than Aelric
when he said it.

"So it's not easy," Wiz told him. "We can do it anyway."

"Okay," Wiz said three days later, "I was wrong."

The same group, less Aelric and with the addition of
Moira and Arianne, was assembled in the Bull Pen to
review the project. After the initial flurry of writing code,
things had settled down to running the program. It had
been running day and night for the last two days and as
they met the Emac controlling it sat on Wiz's desk in a
stall behind them, scribbling away furiously at line after
line of glowing "printout."

"This isn't going to work," Wiz said tiredly. "We can't
do the calculations fast enough. The problem with the
magical compiler is it's slow. We're getting maybe 200
MOPS, absolute tops."

"MOPS?" Moira asked.

"Magical Operations Per Second."

"Two hundred spells a second does not sound slow to
me," Bal-Simba said.

"It is for this kind of work. What we're doing here isn't
so much spell casting as it is mathematical analysis and
that takes a lot of computing power, magic or no."

He sighed. "Back home I used to work on machines
that could do five or six million instructions per second
and we had access to some that could do two hundred
million."

"That is a great deal of calculation," Bal-Simba said.

"The fractal resembles a Mandelbrot set in some
respects, although it's defined by a completely different
function," Wiz told him. "What that means is there is not
an analytic equation which will give us the boundary—
which is what I was hoping for. What we do have is a
procedure for calculating whether a given point is inside
or outside the set."

"I will take your word for it," Bal-Simba said.

Wiz sighed. "What it comes down to is that we can find the shape of the key to any desired degree of precision, but we have to do it by calculating one point at a time. That takes computing power."

"Wait a minute!" Jerry said. "What about parallelism? Each of those points is calculated independently of the others, right? So why don't we get a bunch of copies of the program working on the problem simultaneously and feeding results to each other?"

"Well, machine resources are essentially free," Wiz said. "But it would mean rewriting part of the compiler to handle the parallelism."

Jerry nodded. "That's doable. But before we do that we can test it with just a few copies active and one copy acting as supervisor. Kind of like running multiple virtual machines."

"Virtual machines?" asked Moira, catching a phrase in the mass of technobabble that almost sounded familiar.

"That's like a computer that isn't there," Jerry said helpfully.

"It's something that acts like a computer only it isn't," Wiz added.

Moira regarded both of them coldly. "I see. Like your explanations."

Wiz shook his head. "No, our explanations are real. A virtual explanation would be something that acted like an explanation, but wasn't."

Moira nodded. "I rest my case. Well, never mind. Just tell me what you will need to make this machine that is not a machine and I will see about getting it for you."

Wiz looked at the setup and nodded. This wasn't going to be pretty, but it was strictly a proof-of-principal device.

Ranked in front of him were twenty-one Emacs, all sitting cross-legged on the floor of the Bull Pen. All of them had their quill pens out and poised expectantly.

"This will take a while," he told Jerry and Danny quite unnecessarily. "We've only got twenty processors here and that key is a twelfth-order function. On the other hand, our algorithm will converge on that function. We'll start seeing a representation almost immediately, but it will be real fuzzy."

"And the more processing time we put on the sharper the image will get," Danny interjected. "We helped you write the damn thing, remember?"

Wiz blushed, nodded, and raised his staff.

"You know . . ." Jerry said slowly.

"What?"

"I don't know. I have a feeling about this. Like the one I got in the City of Night just before we used the digging spell."

Wiz lowered his arms. "What is it that bothers you?"

"I can't put my finger on it. But there is something about this whole business." He thought hard and then shook his head. "No, I guess not. Go on with the spell."

Wiz looked around for a convenient cover in case he needed it. Then he raised his staff again.

"backslash," he proclaimed.

"?" responded the first Emac.

"fractal_find exe," Wiz said. The Emac on the far left turned to the others and began to gabble at them. The other twenty Emacs bent to their tasks immediately.

The air above the Emacs began to thicken and take on a bluish tinge. It grew denser and bluer until a neon blue cloud hung over their heads.

"It's working!" Danny said.

Wiz just stared at the slowly coalescing shape and wondered why everything the Emacs turned out was in such violent colors.

As the cloud solidified it began to show hazy lumps and hollows. It wasn't even solid enough to be called a shape yet, but already Wiz could see similarities between it and the thing Duke Aelric had called up on the conference table. The process was slowing as the algorithm had to work harder and harder to discover which points were part of the shape and which were not.

The form began to pulse and Wiz realized he was getting a headache. He looked away, but the afterimage remained burned in his retinas. His vision grew dark around the periphery and everything seemed fuzzy. He shook his head to try to clear it but that only made things worse.

"Do you guys feel all right?" Wiz asked.

"I feel fine," said a large Saint Bernard dog with Jerry's voice. To his left a six-foot-tall cockroach waved its feelers in agreement.

"Well, I don't," Wiz sang with two of his mouths, creating a bell-like harmony. Vaguely he realized they were standing not in the Bull Pen but under an enormous crystal canopy that shimmered with pastel highlights. And wasn't he supposed to have only two arms and one body segment?

As he watched, dog, cockroach and canopy all began to melt and run together. He felt his own body grow indistinct at the edges and begin to flow.

"SIGTERM!!" Wiz screamed.

The universe, canopy, cockroach and dog all froze in a half-melted state.

"UNDO!" he commanded. Instantly Wiz, Jerry and Danny were standing in the Bull Pen again.

"My God," Danny said shakily. "I mean, well, my God!"

"I think we have a problem here," Jerry said. His voice was calm but he was white and breathing in long, deep gulps.

"I think we just got closer to being inside a system crash than I ever wanted to be," Wiz replied, collapsing onto a bench before his legs gave out.

"You know," Jerry said, "this may not work after all."

Danny collapsed on the bench next to Wiz. "Right now, I'm just glad everything's back to normal."

"Oh yeah?" Jerry said, "look."

Wiz followed his pointing finger. Where the Emacs had

been stood twenty mice, all dressed in blue-and-red band uniforms, complete with frogged jackets and plumed shakos, and carrying musical instruments. The twenty-first mouse, wearing a tall bearskin hat, raised his baton. The mouse bass drummer struck three quick, sharp beats and the entire mouse marching band charged into song.

Who's the leader of the club . . .

"**UNDO!**" Wiz, Jerry and Danny yelled simultaneously.

It was afternoon the next day when a tired, dispirited team of programmers met with Moira, Bal-Simba and Duke Aelric.

" . . . and we still don't know what happened," Wiz concluded. "One minute everything is fine and the next minute the world goes crazy."

Aelric looked at him strangely. "You honestly do not know?"

Suddenly Wiz had the feeling they had missed something very obvious.

The elf duke sighed. "Forgive me, Sparrow. I had forgotten I was dealing with mortals and I simply assumed . . ."

"What did happen?" Jerry asked.

Aelric paused, weighing his words. "The object we call the key is in some sense a representation not only of the gate, but of this World as well. As your spell moved closer and closer to producing the shape of the key it began to have an ever-stronger effect because it became an ever-more exact replica of the World."

"And by the Law of Similarity, like things affect each other," Wiz said. "So it began to affect the universe."

"That is—ah—a not incorrect way of putting it. Quite frankly I wondered how you would deal with the problem. It never occurred to me you had not realized what would happen."

"Why didn't the shape have any effect when you showed it to us?"

"What I showed you is powerful enough, believe me,

Sparrow. But it was incomplete; only the part between the Bubble World's creation and that moment. I did not attempt to reproduce the entire shape of the key."

"I told you guys it was a hardware bug," Danny said, running his hand through his disheveled hair.

"The question is, how do we fix it?" Jerry said.

"I know of no way to fix it," Aelric said. "Any spell which can produce that shape must inevitably affect the World in a chaotic fashion."

For a minute no one said anything.

"You know," Jerry said finally. "This thing acts like some kind of quantum effect at a macro level."

"So maybe we need a quantum mechanic," Wiz said. Jerry groaned, Danny scowled and Moira and Bal-Simba looked blank.

"Just trying to lighten the mood a little. Sorry."

"You should be," Jerry told him.

"Sparrow, there are times I think it is a blessing I do not always understand you," Bal-Simba rumbled. "But I take it that this approach is not practical?"

"I guess not," Wiz said. "Damn! And it looked so perfect."

"Just a minute," Jerry said. "You say that it is the *spell* which affects the World?"

Aelric inclined his head. "Just so."

"Well, suppose we did it without using a spell?"

Aelric thought hard. "You mean using no magic at all? Yes, I suppose that would be possible."

"The calculations could be done by hand," Jerry said.

Danny snorted. "Man, there isn't that much time in the universe. What we need is a Cray or something."

"Computers won't work here," Wiz protested. "Nothing high-tech works in this world."

"Craig and Mikey seem to be doing all right."

"Yeah, but they're not in *this* world, they're in that bubble universe."

Danny shrugged. "So we get ourselves a supercomputer and we set it up in our own bubble universe."

"Do you know how to create such a thing?" Bal-Simba asked.

"No," admitted Danny.

"Nor do I," said Bal-Simba.

Everyone turned to look at Aelric.

"It, ah, would not be practical for us to do it either."

"Whoever is helping those two is powerful indeed," Bal-Simba said.

"Well, there's gotta be a way," Danny said a bit sullenly.

"Maybe there is," Jerry said. "Suppose we help ourselves to a corner of their universe?"

Wiz, Moira and Bal-Simba stared hard at Jerry.

"My Lord, how long has it been since you slept?" Moira asked.

"Twenty-eight hours or so, but what's that got to do with it?"

"If you get a good night's sleep, I suspect the connection will occur to you," the hedge witch said tartly.

There was a lull in the conversation while everyone considered.

"Well, it does seem to be a pretty big place," Wiz said at last. "Lots of islands and no one in most of it."

"We've been able to set up scout bases for our dragon patrols," Danny pointed out. "Why can't we just take over one of the deserted islands?"

"You can't be serious!" Moira snapped. "You mean hide like a mouse in the corner while you do your work?"

"Hey, it's there and they're not using all of it," Danny said. "Why not?"

"For a beginning you could all get killed. None of you know what lurks in that place nor how it is guarded."

"I do not believe it is guarded at all," Bal-Simba said. "Our scouts have found no sign of watchers or guardian spells. Indeed, their biggest problem seems to be to keep from straying into that universe unintentionally."

The hedge witch's mouth dropped open. "You are actually serious! My Lord, I cannot believe that you are actually considering this."

"My Lady," Bal-Simba said gravely. "In times like these we must consider many things we would rather not."

She turned to Aelric in mute appeal, but the elf only shrugged. "It does seem to present a solution, Lady."

"There's another little problem," Wiz said. "Where are we going to get a supercomputer?"

"We can't just issue a purchase order, can we?" Jerry said finally.

"I don't think Dun and Bradstreet has a current report on us."

"I take it," Bal-Simba said, "we cannot simply pay for this in gold, as we paid the programmers?"

"Not that simple," Wiz told him. "First, I don't think they'd take gold. Second, these things are built to order and most manufacturers have backlogs. Third, they're still under export controls and there is a lot of paperwork you have to fill out before you can buy one."

"Well," Jerry said slowly, "the regulations have gotten a lot looser since you left. Anyway, legally we *are* entitled to an export license. We're not on the list of proscribed countries, after all."

Wiz looked at him. "You want to fill out the application? And then explain it to the State Department?"

"Just a thought."

Danny shrugged. "So we swipe one."

"I don't think so. At five million a copy, people would talk."

"So what? The Russians do it all the time."

"We're not . . ." Wiz started and then stopped. "You know, you may have something there, in a backhanded sort of way." He stared off into space for a minute and chewed on his lower lip.

"Assuming we can make our searching demons operate . . . yeah."

"We're gonna swipe one?" Danny asked eagerly.

"If we can find the right one," Wiz told him. "After all, a fair robbery is no exchange—or something like that."

"And then you are just going to walk into this bubble universe and set it up," Moira said disgustedly. She picked up the jug of fruit juice and sniffed it. "Are you sure you did not turn this into something stronger when I was not looking?"

EIGHTEEN

INTERNATIONAL COMPLICATIONS

Generals are not known for their sunny dispositions. Just now this general's disposition was as frigid as the Alaskan snowbanks lining the runways outside. His staff didn't look like they were having much fun either.

"Okay, so whatever these things are, we haven't been able to get good radar signatures on them. Are we even sure they are real?"

The other officers in the room shifted uncomfortably. At last the intelligence officer spoke up.

"Sir, we're not sure. But they act like they are."

"Analysis shows there's about an eighty-five percent chance they are real," said the officer responsible for the base's powerful radar chain.

The general glared as if he wanted to kill someone. Now.

"Well, if they're real why the hell can't our pilots find them?"

"By the time we can get there they are always gone," the intelligence officer said. "Besides, that whole area is a fog bank."

"That's unusual in itself, isn't it?"

"No, sir, not exactly," the base weather officer put in. "As you know fog's not unusual in that part of the Bering Sea. More like the normal thing."

155

"Is it normal for the same patch of ocean to stay fogged in for weeks?"

The weather officer shrugged. "Not quite so far north, no. But it's not unheard of either."

"What's causing that?"

"Cold air moving over warm water. Telemetry shows the water's somewhat warmer there than in the surrounding parts of the ocean."

"Why?"

Again the shrug. "We don't understand the weather patterns in this part of the world that well. An upwelling current, a vortex breaking off one of the regular warm currents, we just don't know."

"And you don't know what's playing hide-and-seek with our radar?"

"Whatever it is, it's not meteorological."

The general turned to his radar officer.

"And you don't know either?"

"No, sir. I can tell you something is showing up intermittently and whatever it is is probably not an artifact of the equipment, but that's all I can say."

"And patrols through that show nothing?"

"Nothing but fog. Sometimes our equipment works perfectly. Sometimes everything goes to hell. Radar, radios. I even had one case where the inertial navigation systems started acting up."

He scowled at the thought. This far north compasses were unreliable. If the INS failed, the pilot was reduced to dead reckoning and quite possibly a very chilly bath.

The general nodded again. In peacetime the base only kept one pair of F-15s sitting as CAP—combat air patrol— and they were not launched except at definite targets. They were well positioned to intercept something coming in to the Alaskan mainland, but not to go chasing things out over the Bering Sea.

He looked over at his intelligence officer, who merely shook his head. "It doesn't match anything we know of."

The general thought hard. "Thank you, gentlemen."

The officers rose to go, but the general motioned his intelligence officer back into his chair. "Matt, stay behind for a minute, will you?"

"Now," the general said when the others had filed out and closed the door behind them. "What do you think this thing is?"

The intelligence officer frowned and shook his head.

"I don't have the faintest idea. If it is Soviet, it's stealthed well beyond what we thought they could do and it's carrying one holy hell of an electronic counter-measures suite. I don't know anything that could produce returns like that, or the kind of interference that's coming out of that area." He paused significantly. The northern border was so sensitive that if the intelligence officer at this base didn't know, no one in the Air Force knew.

"I'll tell you something else," he went on at last. "From what I'm hearing, I don't think the spooks know what those things are either. CIA and NSA don't tell us everything, but the reactions I'm getting tell me they're in the dark and they're plenty worried."

It was the general's turn to frown. "Why so?"

"The arms control talks. If the Soviets can produce something that good without our having an inkling of it, then our 'national technical means of verification' aren't worth a damn. If we can't catch them with our satellites and spy planes then we can't make sure they aren't cheating." He made a throw-away gesture. "Poof, no treaty."

The general didn't say anything for a long, long time. "Would they really blow a treaty over some anomalous returns?"

"It sure as hell wouldn't help."

"But why the hell would the Soviets take something like that out over the ocean? Haven't they got enough places to test it where it would be secure?"

The intelligence officer shrugged. "Ask me another one. But don't be surprised if we get some company before long. Important company."

The general cracked the knuckles in one fist and then

the other, like a man preparing for a fight. Then he smacked his right fist into his left palm and stared out into space.

"All right," he said finally, "what you're telling me is that it's vital to the security of the United States that we find out what the hell these things are?"

The IO chewed that over for a minute and then nodded. "Not 'vital' maybe, but damned important. Yessir, that's my assessment."

The general slammed his palm down on the desk. "Then we're by damn going to find out, and soon! I want some F-15s prepared with long-range ferry tanks and recon gear up the wazoo. Damn, I wish I had some EF-111s!" He looked over at his intelligence officer.

"The next time that thing shows its nose we're going to be ready. We're going to find out what this sucker is and we're going to nail him!"

NINETEEN

MOUSEHOLE

"Behold, the Mousehole!" Wiz Zumwalt said, standing in the lobby of his new secret headquarters and gesturing grandly. Moira, who was standing beside him, only sniffed.

The Mousehole—no one could remember who came up with the name—was a one-story complex of glass and stone raised overnight by magic. It meandered beneath the trees in a small valley like a giant's game of dominoes. In addition to the labs and workshops, the complex included wings of private quarters for the programmers, wizards and their servants and helpers, storerooms and, most importantly of all, a room for their soon-to-be-acquired computer.

Wiz put his hands on his hips and surveyed the scene. With its airy spaces, hidden fluorescent lighting and non-static carpeting, the complex would not have looked out of place in a Silicon Valley industrial park. Of course, it did have a few features most Silicon Valley complexes lacked—such as windows that opened and the smokeless torches in brackets along the walls because the electricity wasn't hooked up yet.

"You know," Wiz said, "the Wizard's Keep has a lot of atmosphere, but this is still pretty neat."

"This is still madness," Moira responded grimly. "I just hope we do not all live to regret this."

"You mean you hope we *do* live to regret it."

"You know perfectly well what I mean!" the hedge witch snapped. "And *here* on this island, of all places!" She growled in frustration, crossed her arms and turned away.

Wiz came up behind her and put his arms around her. "I don't like it either, darling. But we've got to be able to use a computer and that means taking risks."

He felt her stance begin to soften. "And they don't patrol this island regularly. So we're safer here than anywhere else. Besides, we've taken precautions."

In fact the precautions had taken more time than the buildings. Not only was the glass carefully dulled to avoid any hint of reflection and the stone colored to match the surrounding rock, but powerful blocking spells had been erected over the place. From the air the valley appeared as simply another hill. Magical emanations were blocked. Even infrared, UV and radar signatures were tightly controlled.

Moira sighed. "Oh, I know, love. But on the same island as our enemies!"

"It's a big island. We're nearly a hundred miles away from them. As long as we don't have dragons flying in and out of here or something we'll be safe enough."

"I suppose," Moira said in a tone that suggested she supposed nothing of the sort. But she relaxed and turned back toward Wiz.

He smiled down at her. "Besides, look at the bright side. In this world there are no dwarves trying to kill me."

Glandurg was bent over his locating talisman. For two days there had been no sign of the Sparrow even on his searching device. Now he was attempting a difficult spell to increase its power temporarily.

His followers were crowded around the stump where he sat, watching as he poured all the magical energy he could muster into the device. The sweat was running down Glandurg's brow and even Gimli was uncharacteristically quiet.

The device pulsed, flickered and then lit with a faint blue glow. Within it a shadowy arrow pointed south.

Glandurg jumped up off the stump so quickly he almost knocked Ragnar over. "South! The alien wizard has gone south." His face split in a wide smile. "Excellent. We have driven him from his hole and now we can follow him. He will not be so well protected in his new lair." He jumped up on the stump and struck a heroic pose.

"This time we shall not fail!" he proclaimed in ringing tones.

The other dwarves listened politely, but with a notable lack of enthusiasm.

"This means the griffins again, doesn't it?" Thorfin asked glumly.

"I don't see why we don't just grab the thing now," Danny complained as he and Wiz made their way back to their quarters. "It's been nearly a week since we got here and we can't do anything until we get that computer."

It was well past midnight and the halls were deserted. The support staff was small and was not on duty around the clock. Even Jerry had turned in an hour ago, leaving Wiz and Danny to finish reviewing the results of their search for a "candidate" computer system.

"Because it's still legal," Wiz told him. "They haven't done anything they aren't supposed to yet."

"But we know they're going to."

"But they haven't. So we don't touch it."

"Like, the KGB is really going to use a supercomputer in the United States."

"It's the GRU—military intelligence—and they're still legal."

"Bullshit!"

"Maybe," Wiz said firmly. "But that's the way we're going to play it."

They walked on in silence. Their feet made no noise on the carpeted floor and the dim light from the ceiling panels had a bluish cast that made it seem even dimmer.

As they came around a corner, they saw movement ahead. Instinctively they both froze. Then Wiz realized it was June.

June was always cat-quiet when she moved, edging along the walls of a room as if she was afraid something would grab her. Now she was moving even more stealthily. She kept her back to the wall and stepped sideways with large cross-body steps that carried her along utterly without sound.

Danny moved to say something, but Wiz put a cautionary hand on his arm. As silently as she had come, June disappeared down the cross-corridor.

"What's June doing sneaking around like that?"

"She's not sneaking!" Danny fired back.

"All right, she's not sneaking. What's she doing?"

Danny dropped his eyes and didn't say anything.

"Danny . . ." Wiz began dangerously.

"She's . . ." He took a deep breath. "Well, she's watching."

"Watching who?"

"That elf dude. She doesn't trust him."

"That's obvious. Any special reason?"

"Because he's dangerous. Because he doesn't belong here."

"He's our ally."

"How do we know that? Because he says so?"

"Because he is," Wiz told him with a lot more firmness than he felt.

"Look man, June knows elves. She lived with them for hundreds of years, right? She doesn't trust him and that's good enough for me."

"He's saved my life a couple of times and that's good enough for me," Wiz retorted. "Look, I told you once before you don't have to like him, but you're going to have to work with him. If you or June can't handle that, I'll have to send you back to the Capital."

Danny just snorted and turned away.

❖   ❖   ❖

The only thing worse than flying over the ocean, Glandurg decided, was flying over the ocean at night. It was bad enough to look down and see nothing but water beneath you, but it was worse to look down and not see the water you knew was there.

This whole trip was worse than anything he had imagined. He was cramped and sore after hours of hanging from a griffin's talons. He was mortally tired, but he could not get any sleep. He was chilled nearly to the marrow from the night cold and wind. He was still half-airsick from the terrible fog bank they had gone through a while ago where everything was suddenly *wrong*. Now the griffin that bore him was laboring and wheezing as if from exhaustion.

Well, at least Thorfin had stopped moaning and Gimli wasn't retching any more. *The next time I make a journey like this I will insist on a flying carpet*, he declared to himself. *It costs more, but the extra comfort is worth it*.

The truth of the matter, he admitted to himself, was that he didn't want to make a journey like this. Not ever again. Not even the quest was worth this misery. He would have gladly ordered the griffins to turn around and take them home if it didn't mean flying for hours and hours more.

A sudden move by the griffin jerked him out of his misery and sent a new thrill of terror through him. The griffin had banked and seemed to be losing altitude. Glandurg's heart jumped into his throat at the thought of going down in the ocean.

Then his dwarvishly keen nose caught a new smell mingled with the iodine-and-salt odor of the ocean. A smell of mud and decay that was like perfume to him. Land! There was land ahead.

Glandurg fumbled with half-numb fingers for the thong around his throat. The talisman was glowing brightly and the arrow pointed sharp and clear straight ahead of them.

❖   ❖   ❖

"We have got to do something about June," Wiz told his wife the next morning over breakfast. "Now she's taken to sneaking around after Duke Aelric."

"I know," Moira said calmly.

"Huh?"

Moira laid down her slice of bread. "Love, not everyone is as oblivious to what goes on around them as you are. And more importantly, Duke Aelric knows as well."

"He said something?"

"He is an elf. He knows."

"Great!" Wiz sighed. "All we need to do is insult Aelric."

"Has he told you he is insulted?"

"No, but you know how touchy he is."

Moira reached for the jam. "Just so. If he were insulted, you would know it. I take it he has said nothing?" She cocked her head. "No? Then it does not concern him and should not concern you."

Wiz grunted. "Anyway I'm going to send June back to the Capital."

"Danny will not like that."

"Then Danny can go back too. Dammit, she's not supposed to be here in the first place!"

Moira looked amused. "Perhaps not. But do you seriously think you can keep her and Danny apart?"

Wiz considered that. "With a moat full of crocodiles, maybe."

"I would bet on June over the crocodiles. No, love, I am not sure even death could separate those two."

"So I send them both back."

"Wiz, I do not mean to tell you how to mind your business," his wife said in a tone indicating she was about to do exactly that, "but I think that would be unwise for two reasons."

Wiz started to say something, but Moira held up her hand to stop him.

"First, what can Danny accomplish back at the

Capital? He needs to be with you and Jerry to be effective, does he not?"

"Yeah, but . . ."

"And second, do you think anyone at the Capital can control him?"

Wiz thought about that. "Right. He doesn't listen to anyone except Jerry and me and half the time he doesn't listen to us." He sighed. "Okay, he stays and that means June stays. But for Pete's sake will you use whatever influence you have with her to get her to lay off Aelric?"

"I have already spoken to her and I will do so again. But I fear she is even more resistant to direction than Danny. Besides, in this case she has a very strong motive for following Aelric."

"Danny says it's because she doesn't trust him."

"I am sure that is true. But I think there is more to it. She spies on him because she fears him."

"And that's why she doesn't trust him."

Moira shook her head. "Again, I think that is true in part. But mostly I think she follows him because it is a way to rise above her fear. She somewhat controls the thing she fears, you see."

"Not exactly, no."

"Nevertheless it is so."

"Sheesh! I dunno. This whole thing used to be so simple. There were good guys and bad guys and it was easy to tell the difference. Now . . ." He shrugged.

Moira reached out and took his hand. "You have managed well enough so far."

"Yeah, but you'd think this saving the world business would get easier with practice. It just seems to get harder and more complicated every time."

"Let us hope this is the final time, love."

"Yeah," Wiz said fervently and squeezed her hand.

"Besides," Moira went on brightly. "There is a positive side to this, you know. You said we needed to do something about June. June is doing something about herself. It is helping to heal her."

"That's something, I guess."

They ate in silence for a while.

"Moira?" Wiz said at last.

"Yes, love?"

"Do you trust Duke Aelric?"

The redheaded witch considered. "Not trust, exactly. I think that as he says, his goals and ours run together on this thing. Besides, Bal-Simba says he is worthy in this and I trust Bal-Simba."

Wiz hesitated. "You really don't like him, do you? Aelric, I mean."

Moira paused. "Nooo," she said at last. "I do not like him."

"You seemed to like him well enough when we met him in the Wild Wood."

"He saved our lives in the Wild Wood."

"But you never said anything that indicated you don't like him."

Moira sighed and bit into her bread and jam. "Liking or not liking an elf is like liking or not-liking a mountain," she said around the mouthful of food. "An elf or a mountain simply *is* and you must accept that."

"Well, *I* like him," Wiz said firmly. "And I trust him too."

He turned back to his own breakfast. *Just maybe not as much as I used to,* he thought as he reached for the butter.

Even for humans, the place was strange looking, Glandurg thought as he crouched on the hill looking down on his enemy's new lair. It was only one story, even if it did run out in all directions. The stone of the walls looked solid enough, but the place had windows as big as doors! Not a moat or a crenelation to be seen.

Not even a log palisade. He snorted silently. The place was defenseless.

There was a tiny noise in the bushes and Ragnar

slithered back into view. Glandurg and the others crowded around him.

"Dwarf-proof!" he said disgustedly. "Whole bloody place is spelled against us."

Glandurg wanted to beat his fist in the dirt in frustration. But it would not do to lose control in front of his followers. "Then we will wait and watch," he said between gritted teeth. "The wizard cannot stay within forever."

TWENTY

MEETING BY MOONLIGHT

Unlike the Wizard's Keep, the small staff at the Mousehole did not work around the clock. By nine P.M. the hallways were deserted and by midnight the place was as silent as a tomb.

It was well past midnight when a shadow slipped into the lobby and paused at the main door. A remarkably well-dressed shadow.

Aelric's cloak was blue at the shoulders fading to purple and finally to black at the hem. Here and there upon it gems sparkled like stars in fading twilight. As he turned June saw his tunic was dove gray and his hose pure white. He turned fully and she caught her breath and shrank back into the shadow. But his face remained as serene as always and he gave no hint that he knew she was there.

Then liquidly, noiselessly, he opened the door and slipped out into the night. June waited for a moment and then followed, not nearly so graceful but just as soundlessly.

Aelric did not sneak, but nonetheless he moved quickly and gracefully in an odd twisting fashion that was hard for a human eye to follow.

About a half mile from headquarters the path wound through a thick patch of ferns and then dropped into an open glade. June hesitated for a moment and when Aelric did not emerge on the path that came out of the depression, she dropped to her hands and knees and crept forward.

She knew the glade well enough. By day it was a pleasant spot and once or twice she and Danny had come this way to picnic and make love. Under the full moon their pleasant little picnic spot was transformed into something completely different.

Through a break in the lacy foliage June caught a glimpse of movement in the glade. Oblivious to the damage to her dress, she pressed herself flat to the earth and slowly wormed her way forward through the over-hanging ferns.

The moon was high and its silvery light poured into the clearing. Duke Aelric stood in the middle of the open space and he was not alone. There was another cloaked figure beside him, nearly as tall as he was. Then Aelric moved and June saw it was Lisella.

She was near as pale as the moonlight itself and her hair cascaded down her back dark as the forest shadows. Like Aelric she was wearing a cloak with the hood thrown back. To a normal mortal she would have been heartbreakingly beautiful, but June dug her fingers into the soil and pressed herself flatter at the sight.

Neither of the elves spared a glance for their surroundings. They were deep in conversation. The liquid tones of elf speech did not carry well, but June could see clearly enough.

Lisella was speaking quickly, her eyes focused on Duke Aelric's face. Aelric heard her out without changing expression and then said something with a half-smile that made her draw back and bite out a retort.

From her hiding place June watched intently. Normally elves were impassive or half-mocking when they spoke to each other. She had never seen them talk together like this.

Lisella faced Aelric square on and said something.

Aelric half-nodded, as if agreeing with her, and then responded calmly. Lisella seemed to have trouble controlling her temper. She said something short and sharp.

Aelric made a chopping motion with his hand and turned away, as if to leave. Lisella's voice caught and held him. He turned back to her. Without moving closer he spoke firmly to her. She looked at him closely and then shrugged.

Lisella cocked her head and said something with a mocking little smile. Aelric nodded.

She arched an eyebrow slightly but he said nothing and stood firm. At last she nodded and spoke. He bowed formally and she responded with a half-curtsey. Then she turned and swept out of the clearing. Aelric stood watching her for a moment and then took the moonlit path back toward headquarters.

June remained flat on her belly under the ferns for a long time before she rose cautiously and slipped back to the fortress.

Wiz got an early start the next morning and by the time Danny arrived in the lab he was deep in his latest project.

"You know your buddy, the elf dude?" the young programmer said as soon as he stepped into the room.

"It's elf *duke*," Wiz said without looking up from the code he was debugging.

"Whatever. Anyway you know Lisella, the one you said was trying to kill you?"

Wiz looked up cautiously. "Yeah?"

"Did you know Aelric's meeting her here?"

"What? How do you know that?"

"June saw them out in the forest last night. She says it looked like they were arguing about something."

"So June's still following Aelric."

"You ought to be glad *someone* is," Danny snapped. "Didn't you hear what I said? He's meeting with the one who's trying to kill you!"

"She's not trying to kill me anymore."

"She sure wasn't trying to do you any good when she showed up at the City of Night."

Wiz laid down the scroll he was holding. "Look, I don't know why Aelric's meeting Lisella. But right now we can't afford to alienate him. So tell June to lay off, will you?"

Danny stared at him, hard. "Man, you're goddamn blind! You just don't want to see, do you?" With that he turned on his heel and stomped out of the lab.

In the next hour Wiz got maybe two lines of code written. Finally he gave it up and went to find Moira.

Moira was in the storeroom, overseeing the stocking of a load of supplies which had been brought over the Wizard's Way that morning. While the servants bustled about, Wiz took her off in a corner and told her June's tale.

"A human spying on elves?" she said when Wiz had finished. "It seems unlikely. They can pass unseen by mortals as easily as they breathe."

"Yeah, but if anyone could do it, it would be June. Besides, magic doesn't work as well here, remember?"

The hedge witch wrinkled her brow. "To be sure it is an unlikely tale for her to concoct. Well, if it is true, then we must be even more careful with our elf duke."

"I thought you trusted him, more or less."

"Less now than before."

"I don't know, though. If he wanted to harm us there are a lot easier ways to do it. Why go through all this rigamarole of pretending to ally with us?"

"Well," Moira said, "it is said that elves are tricksome and strange."

TWENTY-ONE

THE GREAT PLANE ROBBERY

Ivan Semonovich Kuznetsov, major in the GRU, snapped awake and sought groggily for the thing that had awakened him.

The four big Ivchenko turboprop engines on the wings of the AN 12 transport beat steadily as the plane bore east and a little north toward Leningrad. His cheek was slightly numb from the cold and vibration where it had rested against the metal side of the cabin.

But there had been something . . .

He shook it off. Too much vodka last night, that was all. Truly it was a terrible thing to grow old. Not that thirty-three was old, but he could no longer drink the night away and rise fresh with the dawn.

But this dawn there was cause enough for celebration. Snug in the belly of the aircraft was the newest, fastest graphics supercomputer the Americans made. In a few hours it would be in Leningrad and Major Ivan Kuznetsov could expect to share in the rewards of a job well done.

The computer had traveled a long and shifty path from the factory in Texas. It had originally been ordered for a research institute in England, but by a carefully staged "coincidence" it had been diverted to Austria and from there on to what had been East Germany where the

Soviet intelligence service still had friends. Kuznetsov had some small part in all of that. Now he was accompanying it on the last leg of its trip to the Soviet Union.

Where it would go once it reached Soviet soil he did not know and would never have dreamed to ask. There were many important projects in the motherland that required computers which were beyond the current abilities of the socialist nations to build. Since the Americans still would not sell such computers openly, the nation relied on the GRU, the intelligence arm of the Red Army, to acquire them in other ways.

"Comrade Major . . ." Kuznetsov jerked fully awake. Whenever one of his subordinates addressed him as "comrade" he knew something had gone wrong.

"Yes, Sergeant?"

"The computer . . ." Vasily began. In a flash the GRU major was out of his seat, thrusting the man out of the way and diving headlong through the door into the cargo compartment.

"It's gone," the sergeant's voice echoed after him.

Kuznetsov didn't need Vasily to tell him that. The webbing that had bound the computer tightly in place was a tangled limp mass on the floor. The wooden pallets were exactly as they had been, but the crates were gone.

"Yo momma!"

Like a wild beast Kuznetsov spun and sprang for the cockpit door. His sergeant pressed against the bulkhead to let him pass as he squeezed into the cockpit. Before the pilot could turn to him he grabbed the man's shoulder and tried to twist him around in his seat.

"The cargo door," he demanded. "When did it open?"

"It didn't open," the pilot, Volkov, protested. "There's an indicator . . ."

"The devil take your fucking indicator," the GRU man roared. *"When did that door open?"*

"It didn't! We would have felt it in the controls. Comrade Major, I swear to you on my mother's grave that door did not open."

"*Don't lie to me!* That door opened. *Now when?*" He took a deep breath, pulled his pistol from its holster and pressed it against Volkov's head, just in front of his earphones. "If you do not tell me the truth immediately I will blow your brains all over this cabin."

The co-pilot and flight engineer had their eyes studiously glued to their instrument panels. The pilot looked at the pistol out of the corner of his eye and Kuznetsov jammed the gun against his head even harder.

"Major," Captain Volkov said with quiet dignity, "you may arrest me. You may shoot me here and now. But that door did not open. It could not have."

"Very well," Kuznetsov said softly, so softly he was almost inaudible over the roar of the engines. "Very well, the door did not open." He took the gun from the pilot's head. "Then would you please tell me *where is the fucking cargo?*" His voice dropped again to a near whisper. "That is all I want to know."

Volkov blanched and started out of the pilot's seat. Kuznetsov moved to block him and then thought better of it. He nodded curtly. "Sergeant, accompany him."

As the two scrambled aft Kuznetsov stared moodily at the cloudscape below him. They were somewhere over Estonia, he knew, and the Estonians were notorious through the USSR as the biggest thieves of state property in all the republics. The Georgians were bigger black marketers and the Azerbijaniis were more violent, but over the years the Estonians had stolen everything from a freight train to an entire fleet of fishing trawlers. "Well, this time those damned Estonians have gone too far," he muttered to himself.

"Sir?" asked the co-pilot. Then he withered under the GRU man's glare.

"Sir, should I radio Leningrad and declare an emergency?"

"No, you idiot! The last thing we need is to have Leningrad Center shouting questions at us."

Although the questions would come soon enough, he

realized. Chill fear clutched at his stomach as he thought what those questions would be like.

Just then the intercom squawked. "Major," Vasily's voice came over the loudspeaker. "Major, I think you'd better come down here and take a look at this."

Kuznetsov looked down at the co-pilot and flight engineer and decided he was not going to leave them alone in the cockpit to do God-knows-what.

"Come with me," he commanded. The co-pilot opened his mouth to protest and Kuznetsov touched his holster. "Now," he ordered, "immediately." Wordlessly the men slid out of their seats and preceded the major down to the cargo deck.

Volkov and Vasily were squatting over the heap of webbing where the computer had been, staring intently at one of the pallets. As Kuznetsov made his way back to them, bracing with one hand against the side of the plane, he saw there was a small pile of something shiny and metallic in among the straps and buckles.

"When we looked closely we found this," Vasily shouted to make himself heard over the din of the engines. He handed Kuznetsov an object off the stack, an object that glinted like summer sunlight even in the gloom of the aircraft deck.

Kuznetsov had never seen gold before, but no one had to tell him this was gold.

"But where did it come from?" Volkov asked, bewildered.

"That is a very good question," Kuznetsov said, kneeling down to study the pile of gold bars. They were surprisingly tiny, each one fitting neatly in the palm of his hand and weighing about two kilograms. There were no identifying marks of the kind usually found on bar gold, not even assayer's marks.

"How much do you suppose it is worth?" asked the co-pilot.

"If I had to guess, I would say perhaps ten million American dollars. That was the value of our cargo."

"What was our cargo, anyway?" the pilot asked.

The GRU man glared at him. "That is none of your concern."

Volkov did not flinch. "If my career is to be ruined I would at least like to know what over."

Kuznetsov considered and then nodded. "Very well. It was an American supercomputer. The latest model of supercomputer and one that took us nearly two years to acquire."

The pilot's mouth dropped as he realized the enormity of the loss. "Boishemoi!" he breathed.

The GRU man nodded curtly. "Just so."

"What I don't understand," the co-pilot said, "is why go to the trouble of leaving the gold after stealing the computer?"

"That too is a very good question," Kuznetsov said sourly as he braced himself against the plane's gentle bank to the right. "Does anyone have any more good questions?"

"Just one," Vasily said hesitantly as the craft began to bank more steeply. "Who is flying the plane?"

Volkov and Semelov gaped at each other and both dashed for the cockpit.

"Well," Wiz said at last for want of anything better to say, "there it is."

Sitting under the lights on the concrete floor were two dozen boxes full of computer and supporting equipment, all cocooned in foam and cardboard, wrapped around with clear plastic and bound with metal straps.

Moira followed the programmers' admiring looks and tried to be enthusiastic, but it all looked so *ordinary.* The way Wiz and the others had been talking she expected a nimbus of power around the boxes, or lightning bolts or something.

None of the programmers noticed her disappointment. They were too busy swarming over the pile, touching cabinets and opening boxes.

"I hope the installation instructions are complete," Danny said dubiously. "I've never installed anything bigger than a 386 PC."

"Voila!" Wiz stood up from a newly opened box waving a black oblong. "A complete installation course on video tape. Just sit ourselves down with some popcorn and get educated."

"Wiz."

"Yeah, Jerry?"

"Where are we going to get a VCR?"

"Lift one out of a store the same way we lifted the computer," Danny said.

Wiz frowned. "I dunno. That would be stealing."

"Wiz."

"Yeah, Jerry?"

Jerry gestured at the $10 million pile of crates. "What do you call this?"

"Well," Major Ivan Kuznetsov said, hefting the bar of gold absently, "what do we do now?"

The occupants of the cockpit looked at one another and no one said anything. By now it was painfully obvious they would all share the same fate.

"Think, comrades," Kuznetsov urged. "Think as if your lives depended on it." *As they well may*, he didn't have to add. "What could have possibly happened to that computer?"

"It was fine when we loaded it aboard," Vasily said. "I checked and rechecked it myself."

"And I also," Semelov put in. "The webbing was secure and there was nothing unusual about it."

The pilot and the major nodded. They had also checked the cargo and the mountings before takeoff and Kuznetsov and Vasily had been on the cargo deck for takeoff.

"And there was nothing out of the ordinary when you left to go to the latrine?" Kuznetsov asked Vasily.

"Not the least little thing."

Kuznetsov said nothing. Technically both he and the

sergeant were supposed to have been on the cargo deck
at all times. But rank has privileges and he had chosen
to ride up front where it was warmer and quieter.
Abstractedly he realized that would be seen as derelic-
tion of duty by his interrogators, but he did not think it
would matter much. He turned to the pilot.

"And you are sure the cargo doors did not open in
flight?"

"Major, I swear to you on my mother's grave that
none of the aircraft doors opened after we left the
ground," Volkov said. "For that matter the load did not
even shift. We would have felt the alteration in the
center of gravity."

Kuznetsov looked at him with contempt. "So one
moment it was there and the next it vanished like winter
fog?"

Volkov shrugged and spread his hands helplessly.

"It was there when I left and gone when I returned,
not two minutes later," Vasily said.

"Where does that leave us?" asked the co-pilot.

"As traitors to the Motherland," Kuznetsov snapped.
He furrowed his brow and grimly, desperately, tried to
think.

"What are our options?" Volkov asked.

"We should call Leningrad Center and report this
immediately," Vasily said when no one else spoke up. "It
will go harder on us the longer we delay."

Kuznetsov shook his head. "Report what, Sergeant?
That our cargo seems to be missing and we have acquired
a pile of gold instead? Perhaps we had better consider
the situation first."

Besides, Kuznetsov thought, *it can't go any harder on
us than it will already.*

"At least we have the gold," Semelov pointed out.

Kuznetsov snorted. "Leningrad Center isn't expecting
gold. It is expecting a computer. May I remind you,
comrades, computers such as this you cannot buy at a hard
currency store?"

"I don't suppose there is any chance they will believe us?" Volkov asked tentatively.

Kuznetsov snorted again. "Would you? Besides, it makes no difference. The computer was in our care. We lost it. We are responsible."

Volkov licked his lips. "What do you think they will do to us?"

For a moment there was only the roar and vibration of the engines. "I doubt they will shoot us," he said at last. "Not when we give them the gold. But we will undoubtedly be interrogated—rigorously." He paused, remembering the courses he had had on interrogation techniques. Then he tried to shove those images out of his mind.

"They will doubtless conclude we sold the computer for gold. Nothing we could say or do will convince them otherwise. Then they will want to know who we sold it to. Eventually we will tell them."

"But we haven't sold the computer!" Volkov protested.

Kuznetsov grinned mirthlessly. "My friend, you do not appreciate scientific socialist interrogation. By the time they get done with us we will have confessed anyway— over and over again. Eventually we will come up with a confession they will choose to believe."

"And then?"

"Then we will spend the rest of our lives at hard labor in a prison camp. I understand that under Perestroika conditions in even the severe regimen camps have improved greatly. Now the average prisoner lives as long as seven years."

No one said anything.

"I have a wife . . ." the co-pilot began.

"She is disgraced," Kuznetsov cut him off. "She will doubtless be arrested and interrogated as well, probably sentenced to prison." He thought of his own Yelena and tried not to.

"Comrade Major . . ." Vasily began.

"Yes?"

"Sir, I . . ." He stopped, licked his lips and took a deep breath. Then the words came with a rush. "Sir, they do not imprison the families of defectors do they?"

All five men froze, not even breathing. Then their eyes darted around to the faces of the others, seeking some sign of their thoughts. Finally the other four looked straight at Kuznetsov.

"No," the GRU man said slowly. "They are disgraced and interrogated, but not rigorously. They are not imprisoned."

"And," Volkov added eagerly, "if we landed some-place in the West, they would assume the Americans had reclaimed their computer and were lying about it not being aboard."

Kuznetsov said nothing at all.

"There are even," Volkov went on carefully, "places in, say, Sweden, where you can land an aircraft like this and not be discovered for, oh, long enough to hide something in the woods before anyone arrived."

Kuznetsov hefted the gold bar thoughtfully.

"Comrades," he said finally, "I understand Sweden is lovely at this time of the year."

Volkov looked at Kuznetsov, Vasily looked at Semelov and the co-pilot looked at his charts. Then they all looked at the bar of gold in Kuznetsov's hand.

Without another word, Volkov reached up and flipped off the radar transponder. Then he pushed the wheel hard forward and shoved on the rudder pedal, sending the plane diving for the deck and, as soon as they were below radar, turning north toward Sweden.

TWENTY-TWO

INSTALLATION

"Hey Moira," Jerry called. "Can you come in here and help me for a minute?"

"Of course," Moira said. "But what are you doing?"

Because the room had no windows the only light came from a torch on the wall. Jerry was on his hands and knees with a string and a piece of chalk. With exaggerated care he marked a tiny dot on the concrete.

"Did Wiz ever explain to you about 220-volt single-phase 60-cycle AC?"

"No."

"Then I'm drawing on the floor. Anyway, I need to mark out a pentagram. Can you stand in the center and hold the line exactly on this dot while I swing a circle?"

"Of course," Moira said as she took the string and stooped to hold it on the point Jerry had marked, "but why do you need to be so precise?"

"This spell multiplies a mass times a length and divides it by time. I've got to get the units exactly right or we won't get the output we need. So the pentagram has to be just the right diameter."

"Forgive me, my Lord, but that is a circle, not a pentagram."

"Special kind of pentagram," Jerry grunted.

"It is *not* a pentagram. It is a circle."

"A pentagram approaches a circle for sufficiently large values of five. Now, step out of the way, will you? And don't muss the lines."

As Moira moved out of the way, he deftly sketched a shape in the center of his creation.

"That is not any kind of pentagram," Moira insisted. "That is a circle with a sideways S in it."

"It does the job of a pentagram," Jerry said. "Stand back." He turned to the Emac which was standing nearby. **"backslash,"** he commanded. **"power_up exe."**

A puff of bright blue smoke billowed into the diagram on the floor, coalesced, condensed and solidified. The demon was about two feet tall and looked like a stick figure. Except instead of straight lines, its arms, legs and body were composed of neon blue lightning bolts. Its nose was a 150-watt light bulb.

"bzzzzp bzzzzp ready," it said in a buzzing voice.

Jerry nodded and flipped the switch on the wall. The fluorescents in the ceiling flickered and caught, bathing the room in a cold bluish glow.

"Okay. Douse the torch, will you? We've got power."

"Of that I make no doubt," Moira said, eyeing Jerry's creation dubiously.

TWENTY-THREE

GREMLINS

"Where does this go, Lord?" asked one particularly lanky guardsman as he and his fellows rolled a tan metal object through the opened double doors.

Wiz looked up from the sea of packing material, pallets and computer parts scattered across the floor of the computer room.

"Oh, that's part of the air conditioning. It goes in that room over there. And be careful of the stuff on the floor. There's metal strapping all over the place."

Moira looked over the slowly growing computer in the middle of all the litter. It still wasn't very impressive. There were four tan metal cubes, each about waist high, that stood all in a row. Next to them were a couple of taller cabinets. At the other end was a large desk with a workstation sitting on it—the "console" the programmers called it, although what consolation it might be Moira couldn't imagine. There were a half-dozen other workstations, a thing Wiz told her was a printer and some other equipment scattered around the room.

"Forgive me darling, but the problem with your world's magic is that it just doesn't look impressive."

"It's not supposed to," Wiz told her. "If it looks impressive it scares the suits."

Moira thought about that and then did what she usually did when the conversation lapsed into incomprehensibility. She changed the subject.

"What does that part do?" She nodded toward the box being maneuvered through the just-big-enough doorway.

"That's the climate control system. It's not really part of the computer at all. It just keeps the room at constant temperature and humidity. These things are picky that way."

"This could be done by magic, you know."

"I know, but the computer is designed to work with this system and as long as we have electric power, why not use it?"

"Magic would be more reliable," Moira said dubiously.

"Magic doesn't work as well here as it does at home. Besides, machinery can be just as reliable as magic."

Moira arched an eyebrow skeptically, but she said nothing.

"Hey Wiz," Danny called out. "I think I've got the cabling problem whipped. Come look at this."

Danny had several sections of the raised floor up to expose one of the cable runs. "You know you said it would take us a couple of days to get all the cabling spliced right? Well, I found a way around it."

"emac" he said, and one of the yard-tall editor demons appeared beside him.

"**?**" said the Emac.

He reached behind him on the floor and handed the demon the wiring manual and printout of the installation chart. The little demon staggered under the pile of paper nearly as tall as he was. Then Danny gestured down into the hole and commanded **"backslash untangle exe."** A foot-tall demon wearing work clothes and a tool belt popped up in the cable run. The Emac flipped open the wiring chart and started to gabble furiously. The demon in the cable run whipped out his tools and began splicing wires so fast its hands were a blur.

Wiz shook his head in admiration. "Danny, that is a truly tasty bit of work."

The younger programmer shrugged, but his face lit up at the compliment. "I figure it will take maybe a couple of hours to get the cabling done."

"What does that do to the rest of the schedule?" Moira asked.

Wiz thought for a minute. "We should be able to hook up the climate control this evening. Once we turn it on that's about all we can do tonight. We need to let the temperature and humidity stabilize before we try to bring the system up. That'll take six or eight hours."

The programmers were in fine fettle the next morning. They were days ahead of schedule and best of all, the hardware installation was almost done. All of them were much more at home with software and they were looking forward to the next phase.

"Well," Wiz was saying as they came down the hall, "if everything passes the hardware checks we should be able to start loading system software by this evening."

"That'll be a relief," Danny said. "I'm getting sick of messing with hardware. What's the matter?"

Wiz had stopped dead and was frowning off into space. "Is it my imagination or is it humid in here?"

"Humid," Moira said.

"Definitely," Jerry said.

Wiz looked at the others. "Come on." He wasn't quite running as he headed toward the computer room, but he wasn't far from it. The others were right behind him.

Smoke was pouring out of the computer room.

"What the hell?"

"The place is on fire!" Wiz shouted.

Danny ran forward as if to dash into the room. "That's not smoke," he exclaimed. "It's cool and wet."

"Fog," Jerry said wonderingly. "The room's full of fog."

Wiz took a deep breath and charged into the computer room. The air was so clammy he could hardly breathe and the fog swirled around him like the special effects in a bad monster movie. Batting at the swirling mist he fought his way to the back of the room. Thick white clouds of vapor were pouring out of the air conditioning duct at the rear of the room.

"Shut off the climate control," he yelled over his shoulder. "And get a fan in here to clear this stuff out."

Almost instantly a wind rushed through the room, sucking the fog out faster than it could pour in through the vents. By the time Wiz reached the door again, the air in the room was clear. The relays clicked over and the air conditioning died.

Moira was standing in the doorway with her staff in her hand and the wind she had raised tugging at her skirt and tousling her coppery hair. As Wiz emerged she gestured and the winds died away instantly.

"My Lord," the hedge witch said with a smug little smile and arched eyebrow, "explain to me again how reliable mechanical contrivances are."

She looked so lovely with her hair in disarray Wiz forgave her.

It took the programmers and their helpers nearly two hours to get things under control. Water had to be vacuumed out of the soaked carpet, books and papers had to be spread out to dry and a dehumidifying spell was used to help dry out the equipment. Fortunately there wasn't much damage, but there was a lot of work to be done.

"Okay, " Wiz said grimly. "Somehow the air conditioner and the humidifier both got stuck on. The low temperature turned the high humidity to fog."

"We're lucky we didn't take two days off," Jerry said. "We probably would have had ice all over the equipment."

"I'm damn glad we hadn't powered up the computer," Wiz replied. "That would have been a real mess."

"Hey guys," Danny called from the back of the room. "These things didn't get stuck on. Someone reset the thermostat and the humidity thingie."

Wiz and Jerry crowded around him quickly. Sure enough inside the clear plastic box covering the controls both dials were at their maximum positions.

"I could have sworn I set those properly," Jerry said.

"You did," Wiz told him. "I double-checked before I left the computer room last night."

"Someone must have messed with them," Danny said.

"Inside the locked cover? I don't see how."

"Magic," the young programmer retorted.

"From where?" Wiz asked. "Moira, did you . . ."

"Certainly not!" the hedge witch said indignantly. "Nor did any of the other wizards here. Believe me, my Lord, if there is one thing any apprentice learns early it is not to tamper with another's magic. Those who do not learn it do not live long enough to become magicians."

Wiz put his hand on her arm. "Of course you didn't darling, it's just that . . ." Then he stopped as he caught sight of something over Moira's shoulder.

A line of seven little figures marched across the top of the computer console, their arms swinging and their bodies swaying in time to the song they were bawling out at the top of their tiny lungs. Their voices were so shrill that the words were lost, but the tune came through clearly, as if hummed by a chorus of mosquitoes.

eee-eh, eee-eh
eee-eh heh heh heh heh
eee-eh heh heh, eee-eh heh heh
eee-eh—heh heh heh heh

As Wiz watched, the creatures disappeared through an open inspection panel into the guts of the computer. The last one, evidently realizing it was being watched, waved gaily to Wiz before it dived after its fellows.

"Uh, folks," Wiz said just a shade too calmly. "I think we've found our problem."

For a moment no one said anything. For a long moment.

"What in the World was that?" Jerry demanded finally.

"I have seen their like before," Moira said. "The mill

in my village had one. How the miller would curse when the thing played tricks on him! He had me down there nearly every new moon to try to rid the mill of it."

"I take it you didn't have much luck?"

"No. Sometimes it would quiet down after I came. Sometimes not. Once it dumped near a barrel of flour on the miller and me as we left the mill after the exorcism."

She paused and shrugged. "I do not know what to call them. They are so rare they do not have a name."

"Gremlins," Wiz supplied. "We have gremlins in our computer. Wonderful."

"Gremlins?" Moira asked.

"Little magical creatures that live in machinery and cause trouble." He jerked a thumb at the infested computer. "You know, gremlins."

Moira frowned in the especially pretty manner she had when she was confused. "Love, how is it you have names for these things if they do not exist in your world?"

"They didn't exist so we had to make them up."

Moira raised an eyebrow. "That makes less sense than most of what you say."

"That's because you've never worked around complicated equipment. Believe me, it's enough to make you believe in gremlins even when you know they don't exist."

The hedge witch sighed. "I will take your word for it."

"The real question is, how do we get rid of them?" Jerry asked.

"I do not know. I was not very successful with the one in the mill. Perhaps one of the Mighty will know more."

"What can you tell us about them?"

Moira pursed her lips and tried to think. "Not a great deal, I fear. They are very uncommon."

"You said there was just one in the mill," Wiz said, "I just saw seven of them go into the computer."

"That is very unusual. I have never heard of more than one at any place."

"I'm surprised you don't have them around the Capital with all the magical apparatus there."

"Only mechanical things attract them. Aside from that," she shrugged, "I know only that they are somewhat like the other Little Folk, the ones you call Brownies."

"Wait a minute," Wiz said. "Do you think Brownies could give us some pointers on handling these pests?"

Moira considered. "I do not know. We have no Brownies here to ask."

"No, but there are Brownies at Heart's Ease. Lannach and his people, the ones I rescued in the Wild Wood."

The hedge witch nodded. "They are in your debt then. It is worth a try, yes."

The brownies arrived the next day, brought along the Wizard's Way by Malus.

"We are here, Lord," Lannach said, hopping down from Malus's pack onto the table and bowing deeply.

Wiz bowed back to the little manlike creature. "Thanks, Lannach. If you can help us we'd really appreciate it."

Behind Lannach, Breachean, Loaghaire and Fleagh jumped down to the table. Then Meoan climbed out of the pack and Brechean and Fleagh helped her down.

Wiz's eyebrows went up. "Meoan too?"

The little woman looked up. "Am I unwelcome then, Lord?"

"No, not at all. I just thought you'd stay at Heart's Ease with your baby."

"Lord," Meoan said gravely, "we owe you our lives. Small we may be, and with scant powers. But we do not forget our debts."

"Well, if you can keep these little bleeders under control you can consider the debt paid in full."

" 'Twere best we were about it then," Lannach said.

While Wiz and the others watched from across the computer room, Lannach knelt by a ventilation grill in the base of the console. He called out in a language that sounded like an excited mouse. Then he cocked his head and listened intently.

Although Wiz heard nothing, Lannach apparently got

a reply. While Wiz and the other humans fidgeted Lannach conducted a long and seemingly involved conversation in mouse-squeak. Finally he stood up and dusted his hands on his moleskin breeches.

"Your device is inhabited, Lord," he reported, hopping up on the table next to Wiz.

"We know that."

"They thank you most gratefully. They say they have never seen a more fitting home for their kind."

"So we've got seven of them living in there?"

The brownie's tiny face creased in a frown. "Seven? Oh no, many more than that, I think."

"We only saw seven."

"Ah, well they are shy creatures so doubtless you did not see them all. Besides, they multiply quickly when they are in a place to their liking."

"Look, we don't mind them living here, but we can't have them interfering with our work. Is there any way to keep them in line?"

The little creature shook his head. "We can try, Lord. But they are flighty and chancy beings. They will not keep their word even if they can remember from one minute to the next what they have sworn to."

"I don't suppose a repulsion spell like **ddt** would do any good?" Wiz asked hopefully.

"Little, I fear," Lannach said. "As you may know, Lord, non-mortals differ in their susceptibility to such things. These are especially resistant. They are hard to dissuade and they would even be hard to kill by magic."

"Great," Wiz muttered.

"We can do this, Lord. If my kin and I work together we can probably dissuade them from their worst mischief."

"That would be something anyway," Wiz sighed. "Okay, Lannach. Do your best. Meanwhile Moira will show you your quarters and fix you up with something to eat."

"We have a place for you in the kitchen," Moira said as she led the gaggle of brownies out the door, "and bowls of milk for you all."

"Wonderful," Wiz said as the brownies left. "We got cockroaches. Insecticide-resistant cockroaches."

"Just think of it as working with beta version hardware," Jerry said helpfully.

Wiz glared at him. "Is that supposed to make me feel better?"

"No, it just puts the problem in perspective."

Wiz groaned.

TWENTY-FOUR

AIR INTERCEPT

Ozzie Sharp drained the last of his cold coffee and paced down the line of radar and communications operators. He briefly considered going forward and getting another cup, but his tongue felt like it had grown fur, his stomach was starting to go sour and the combination of the coffee and the cabin noise of the aircraft was making his bladder twinge already. Better save it until he needed the caffeine.

He looked for a place to set down the cup, but most of the flat, stable surfaces in an AWACS aircraft are for work. He kept the cup clenched in his brown fingers and turned his attention back to the radar displays.

Ozzie wasn't a big man, but he was built like a fire-plug. There were traces of gray in his curly black hair, but he still moved in a way that suggested that if there was a brick wall between him and where he wanted to be it was too damn bad for the wall. Like the crew, he wore a dark blue Air Force flight suit. But there was no insignia of rank on Ozzie Sharp's flight suit because he had no rank.

"Anything?" he asked the operator at the end of the line.

"Not a thing," the operator said, never taking his eyes

off the screen. The operator didn't add "sir" and Sharp understood the significance of that perfectly.

Well, fuck 'em. Ozzie Sharp had been sent here from Washington because he was one of the best trouble shooters in the agency. This was trouble and he meant to get to the bottom of it.

So far he was just a passenger. The general had set this operation up before he arrived and all Ozzie had to do was ride along. The general might be content to command from the ground, but Ozzie Sharp wanted to be where the action was.

The AWACS was further west than usual. Whatever was out there was tricky. Moving the plane out over the Bering Sea made it easier to burn through the jamming and pick up the weak radar returns.

Orbiting nearby were two F-15 Eagles with conformal fuel tanks for extra range and Sparrow and Sidewinder missiles to deal with whatever they encountered. Perhaps more importantly, the fighters also carried a variety of sensors including special video cameras to record what they found.

Back at the base were more Eagles, two KC-10 tankers on alert, and another AWACS, ready to take up station when this group reached the end of their endurance. They had been doing this for four days now, but no one was getting bored.

The operator, a skinny kid with a shock of dark hair, turned to his passenger and tapped his screen. "Ivan's out in force today."

"What's that?"

The radar operator grinned. "Our opposite number. An Illuyshin 76 AWACS."

"Observing a test?"

The operator shrugged. "Maybe. But if I had to guess I'd say they're looking for something in that fog bank— just like us."

"With just the AWACS?"

"Nossir, that's not their style. But they like to hold their interceptors on the ground until they've got a target and then come in like gangbusters. Their birds are probably faster than ours but they don't have the range."

Sharp nodded. It was a well-known fact that the Soviets were years behind the West in jet engine technology. What the Americans achieved by sophisticated engineering and advanced materials, the Russians got by brute force at the cost of higher fuel consumption.

But high-tech or low-tech, the effect was the same, Sharp reminded himself. When those interceptors came they could be damn dangerous.

"Make sure our people know about this," he told the operator.

"Already done," the operator replied, pleased he had anticipated the civilian.

The operator turned back to his screen, scowled at it, then reached over and fiddled with the controls.

"Hello, hello," the operator said to himself. "Looky here." Then he thumbed his mike.

"Okay, we've got contact. Bearing 231 and range approximately 220 nautical miles. Height 500."

The pilot's voice squawked in his earphones. "Five thousand?"

"Negative. Five hundred."

"Understood," the pilot came back. "Five hundred feet."

"Eagle Flight," the flight controller's voice came on the circuit, "you are cleared. Now go!"

"Eedyoteh!" Go!

Senior Lieutenant Sergei Sergovitch Abrin of the PVO—the Soviet air defense forces—eased the throttle on the Mig 29 Flanker forward. The plane rolled down the rain-slick runway gathering speed as it came. In his rear view mirror he could see his wingman behind and to his right. He was vaguely conscious that the second pair of his flight was taking off on the parallel runway several hundred meters to his left.

The weather was abominable, fog and occasional flurries of snow and rain. But that was nothing out of the ordinary and Senior Lieutenant Abrin had nearly a thousand hours flying out of this base.

As they passed the critical point, he eased back on the stick and the powerful interceptor lunged into the air. Even as he climbed into the overcast, Sergei Abrin ran another quick check of his systems.

A Mig 29 had the range for this mission and no Soviet interceptor carried a more powerful or sophisticated radar than the one in the nose of his Flanker. Whatever those things were they were damn hard to pick up on radar and he would need all the power he had.

Satisfied, he watched the altimeter wind up and considered what he and his men were heading into.

For weeks now the powerful warning radars along the coast of Siberia had been getting anomalous and faint returns from out over the narrow sea that separated Russia and Alaska. Recon flights had shown nothing and previous attempts to intercept these things had failed. After the usual dithering and indecision, Moscow had decided to make a serious effort to discover what was happening on this most sensitive of borders.

An early warning aircraft had been assigned and interceptor squadrons were given permission to depart from their regular training plans to investigate in force the next time something was sighted. They were also fitted with long-range fuel tanks and given full loads of fuel— a departure in the defection-conscious Soviet air force. If that wasn't enough to convince the pilots how serious this was, the KGB showed up and installed a number of very black boxes in each aircraft.

Senior Lieutenant Abrin thought of himself as a man of the world, as befitted the son of a medium-high party official. He had his own theory about this thing.

It was no accident that nearly invisible aircraft were flying along the US-USSR border. Obviously the United States intended this series of provocations as a tactic to wring further arms concessions from the Soviet negotiators in Vienna.

Well, they would learn the folly of their ways. For longer than Sergei Abrin had been alive, the men and machines of the PVO had stood between the Motherland and the Capitalist aggressors. If they wanted to play games over this narrow sea they would find that the Red Air Force could play also—and far better.

Still, he thought as his interceptor raced out over the ocean. This was a bitch of a day to be flying.

"Go!"

Patrol Two kneed the dragon and pulled on the reins. In response the beast swept into a wide, gentle turn. He was obviously happy to be going home and so was Patrol Two.

The squadron leader's instructions had been explicit. Head out on this track for four day-tenths, then reverse course and return to the temporary base the dragon riders had established on one of the small islands. Each rider had set out alone on a slightly different course to cover as much of this strange new world as they possibly could in the least amount of time. The squadron leader didn't want to stay on the island too long for fear of discovery and for once Patrol Two fully agreed with him. They would pause another day to rest their dragons and then they would leave this ill-begotten place.

This particular corner was worse than most, Patrol Two admitted as the dragon's strong wingbeats bore them along. Not only was there the strangeness here that made dragons uncomfortable and dampened the effect of magic. Here there was also constant fog mixed with freezing rain and snow from thick, low-hanging clouds that forever darkened the sky. Were it not for the dragon's homing instinct and the fact they had flown a straight course out, Patrol Two wasn't at all sure they could find their way back to their fellows.

A weak sun broke through a ragged hole in the clouds,

turning the sea the color of fresh-beaten lead. Patrol Two frowned. The sun seemed to be in the wrong place. Then a shake of the head. Well, it wasn't the only thing that was wrong here.

A window popped up on Craig's screen. In it, in full color and three dimensions, was a robot.

"Ready, master," the robot intoned.

"Ready for what?" he snapped. All his worker robots looked alike. Then he saw the designation in the status line under the window. "Oh, the jammer! Then turn it on!"

The robot nodded and winked out while Craig turned his attention back to the warbot he was designing. But now he was smiling.

He had suspected all along that the dragon riders who flitted around the edges of his realm had some kind of communications system. It was magic rather than radio and it had taken a lot of work to discover just how it worked. Once he knew, he had set his robots to work building jammers. Now he had just cut his enemies' communications link.

Maybe that will clear those damn dragons out of my airspace, he thought as he went back to work on the warbot.

"Now go!"

Major Michael Francis Xavier Gilligan grunted and broke out of the holding pattern. A quick check of the cockpit panels, a fast glance to the right to make sure Smitty, his wingman, was still in position and he concentrated on his descent. Five hundred feet wasn't a lot of altitude for a high-performance fighter in this kind of weather. A few seconds inattention and you'd fly right into the water.

Bitch of a day to go flying, Gilligan thought to himself. Then he turned his full attention to the job at hand.

❖   ❖   ❖

Patrol Two looked down at the now-useless communications crystal and swore luridly. Between the winds and the fog, the rider and dragon were perilously close to being lost. And now this!

This, thought Patrol Two, *is turning into one bitch of a day.*

Sharp hunched over the operator's shoulder, staring at the big screen as if he was about to dive into it.

"Incoming aircraft!" one of the other operators sang out. Sharp jerked erect and hurried to the man's console.

"We got four, heading our way from the East." The operator looked at the screen again. "Probably those tricked-up Flankers." He studied the radar signature analysis. "Yeah, four Flankers incoming."

"Are they after us or Eagle Flight?" Sharp demanded.

"They're heading into the area Eagle Flight is going for. Uh oh!" The operator spoke quickly into his mike. "The Soviets just lit up their air intercept radars."

"Are they after our guys?"

The operator studied the screen intently. "They're headed in that direction. No, wait a minute. I don't think so. They seem to be after the same targets we are. The IL-76 must have picked them up just after we did."

Ozzie Sharp scowled mightily at the screen. All of a sudden the air over that God-forsaken patch of ocean was getting awfully crowded.

"Smitty, check your ten," Gilligan called to his wingman. "Do you see that?"

Off to their left and slightly below them, something dark was threading its way through a canyon between two banks of clouds.

"What the hell is it?" Smitty demanded a few seconds later.

"I don't know. I don't think it's doing a hundred knots and it keeps ducking in and out of those clouds."

Gilligan touch-keyed his mike to transmit the report, but there was silence in the earphones.

He tried again. Still nothing. He switched radios. Nothing. He tried different frequencies, he checked the circuit breakers, he ran the radio checklist. Still nothing. He could get Smitty but that was all. Meanwhile the thing appeared out of another cloud.

"Smitty, can you raise anyone?"

"Negative, sir."

Gilligan considered for a minute. Whatever this jamming was it apparently wasn't strong enough to block him from talking to his wingman, but there was no way to reach anyone else. It had been made crystal clear to him that one way or another the information he collected *had* to get back.

"Smitty, have you been getting this on tape?"

"Yessir."

"Then make sure you've got a good image and then split off. I'm going in for a closer look."

"The hell you say!"

"As soon as you're sure you've got a good image, split off and get the hell out of here. That information has got to get back."

There was a long crackling silence on the radio.

"Am I supposed to say 'yes sir'?" Smitty said finally.

"You're supposed to get that damn information back. Anything else is up to you. Now, have you got it?"

"On the tape."

"Then go. Remember. No matter what happens to me, you've got to get that data home."

Gilligan watched as his wingman broke off. Since his first day in flight school he had been drilled that a fighter never, ever, flies alone. Suddenly it was awfully lonely.

Well, the sooner I do this, the sooner it will be over. Reaching down, he activated his camera. Then just to be on the safe side he armed the two Sidewinders hanging under the fuselage. He left the Sparrows unarmed. That thing might have a fuzzbuster tuned to the targeting radar's frequencies and he didn't want to fight unless he absolutely had to. Finally he checked the status of his 20mm cannon.

One good pass, Gilligan told himself. *One pass so close I can see the color of their eyes.*

It was the sound that first alerted Patrol Two. The hissing roar that sliced through the eerie silence of the fog banks. The dragon rider had only a brief glimpse of something moving up behind and to the left. Something very, very fast and headed straight at them.

To a dragon rider that meant only one thing: Dragon attack! No time to turn into it and fight fire with fire. Patrol Two grabbed an iron seeker arrow out of the quiver and brought the bow up with the other hand. Twisting around in the saddle even as the arrow fitted into the bow and not waiting for the seeker to get a lock, Patrol Two got off one shot. Then the rider pressed flat against the beast's back and yanked the reins to throw the dragon into violent evasive maneuvers. The dragon, unsettled by the roaring monster, responded enthusiastically and dropped into a writhing, spiraling dive into the fog.

The arrow's spell wasn't capable of making fine distinctions. It had been launched at a moving target and that was sufficient. The arrow flew straight to its mark and hit the plane's right wing about halfway out toward the tip.

As soon as the point penetrated the thin aluminum skin the arrow's death spell activated. It didn't know it was trying to kill an inanimate object and it was as incapable of caring as it was of knowing.

Like most things magic, the spell didn't work perfectly in this strange halfway world, but it worked well enough.

"What the fuck?" Mick Gilligan yelled, but there was no one to hear. His radios, like every other piece of electronic equipment in his Eagle had gone stone dead. Unlike the F-16, an F-15 does not have to be flown

by computers every second it is in the air. But everything from the fuel flow to the trim tabs is normally controlled by electronic devices.

As a result Major Mick Gilligan didn't fall out of the sky instantly. But everything on the plane started going slowly and inexorably to hell.

One of the things that went was the automatic fuel control system. Normally the F-15 draws a few gallons at a time from each tank in the plane to keep everything in trim. When the electronics died, Major Gilligan's plane was drawing from the outboard left wing tank. Rather than switching, it kept draining that tank, lightening the wing and putting the plane progressively more out of trim.

Gilligan didn't notice. He was too busy dealing with the engines. Losing the electronics meant they were no longer automatically synchronized. Almost immediately the right engine was putting out more power than the left. By the time Gilligan had taken stock of the situation, the exhaust gas temperature on the right engine was climbing dangerously and the left engine was going into compressor stall.

He didn't waste time cursing. He put both hands on the throttles and started jockeying the levers individually, trying to get more power out of his left engine and cut back the right before the temperature became critical.

It wasn't easy. Without the electronic controls the throttles were sluggish and the engines unresponsive. Gilligan was like a man trying to take a shower when the hot water is boiling and the cold water is freezing. It's painful and it takes a lot of fiddling to get things right. Gilligan was fiddling furiously.

Gilligan looked up and saw the windshield was opaque with dew. The windshield wipers had quit working along with everything else. He also saw by the ball indicator that the plane was banking right and descending. Instinctively he corrected and put the throttles forward to add power and get away from the water. The engines seemed

to hesitate and then they caught with a burst of acceleration that pressed Gilligan back into his seat.

It almost worked. In fact it would have worked if
Gilligan hadn't forgotten one other automatic system.
When the power came on, the Eagle's nose came up. Too
far up. The Boundary Layer Control System that is supposed to keep the F-15 from stalling at high angles of
attack was also dead. The nose went up and then back
down as the Eagle stalled and plummeted toward the
ocean.

Senior Lieutenant Abrin had lost contact with his base
and the rest of his flight, but his radar seemed to be
working perfectly. He watched on the screen as the
Americans performed the highly unusual maneuver of
splitting up and one of them turned back. Then he saw
the other plane make a pass at something and then disappear from the screen.

That was enough. He quickly turned his plane in that
direction to see what had happened.

Patrol Two broke out of the clouds almost in the
water. Frantically the rider signaled the beast to climb
for everything he was worth. The dragon extended its
huge wings fully and beat the air desperately to keep from
smashing into the sea. Spray drenched dragon and rider
alike, but somehow they avoided the ocean.

The dragon beat its wings strongly to climb away from
the water and suddenly roared in pain.

Fortuna! Patrol Two thought. Somewhere in the last
minute's violent maneuvering the dragon had injured
himself. The rider touched the communications crystal
worn on a neck thong, but the bit of stone remained cold
and dead.

Gilligan reached for the yellow-and-black handle next
to his right leg. *I hope to Christ this still works,* he
thought as he pulled the ejection lever.

The ejection seat was designed as a fail safe, electronics or no. The canopy blew off and Gilligan was blasted into the air scant feet above the water.

There was a whirling rush and then Gilligan was kicked free of the ejection seat. Suddenly he was dangling under his parachute, floating down in a clammy fog to the water he knew had to be below him.

Below and off to one side he saw a tiny splash as his ejection seat hurtled into the Bering Sea. Then the fog closed in around him and all he could see was cottony grayness.

Gilligan cursed luridly. In the personal effects compartment of his ejection seat was his map case and in that map case were several letters he had intended to mail—including the alimony check to his ex-wife which was already a week overdue.

Sandi's lawyer is going to kill me! he thought as he floated soundlessly through the fog for an unknown destination.

Patrol Two was in no better shape. The dragon was favoring its right wing in a way the rider knew meant the beast would not be able to bear them up much longer.

Pox rot this place! Patrol Two swore silently and then concentrated on trying to remember the way to the nearest land. It was a terrible place to set down, but from the way the dragon's chest muscles tightened with each wing beat Patrol Two realized they would be doing well to make it at all.

Lieutenant Smith hadn't seen Major Gilligan go in, nor had he heard the distress cry from the F-15s transponder. But the major was supposed to make a quick pass and come back to join him. As the minutes ticked by, the lieutenant became increasingly worried. Something had to have happened to his commander.

Smith hadn't gotten a good look at whatever it was, but he knew his video camera had it all down. That part of the mission was over. Now all they had to do was get back safely. He concentrated on guiding his plane back on what he was pretty sure was a reciprocal heading while he kept running through the channels on his radios. Mick would be along, he was sure. And if he wasn't then that video tape was doubly important.

Suddenly Smith's radar and radios were working again. Quickly he shifted to his assigned frequency, keyed his mike and began reporting what had happened.

Lieutenant Smith wasn't at all sure what he had seen down there, but he was reasonably sure the Soviets didn't have anything to do with it.

Patrol Two stayed in the open to make searching for land easier, but the rider also kept close to the clouds to hide quickly if need be. Off on the far horizon, the rider saw a thin line that seemed to be land. The dragon saw it too and surged forward, its wing beats picking up strength as it flew.

Patrol Two was just starting to relax when another of the roaring gray monsters burst out of the clouds above and in front of them less than half a bowshot off.

Instantly, the rider rolled the dragon right and ducked into the clouds. As the misty gray swallowed them up, Patrol Two had a quick glimpse of the thing rolling into a turn to follow them.

So stiff, Patrol Two thought. *Its wings don't move even in a turn and the rest of the body stays rigid as well.* Whatever the things were, they weren't dragons.

Senior Lieutenant Abrin spent the next ten minutes dodging in and out of the clouds looking for the thing again. Although his plane did not have a video imaging system like the F-15s and it had all happened so quickly he hadn't had time to turn on his gun cameras, he had gotten a good look at the object before it disappeared.

Lieutenant Abrin had no doubts about what he had just seen. His most prized possessions were a Japanese

VCR and a bunch of bootlegged American movies. The more he thought about it the more obvious it was to him what was going on.

"Comrades. Do we have any information on Spielberg making a movie in this area?"

TWENTY-FIVE

MAROONED

Warm! Mick Gilligan thought as he spluttered his way to the surface. *The water's warm.*

By rights it ought to be nearly freezing. But it was nearly as tepid as the Caribbean.

Nothing but surprises, he thought as he pulled his seat pack to the surface with the cord attached to his leg. *At least this one is pleasant.* He unsnapped the cover on the top half and inflated his raft.

Wait a minute! There are sharks in the Caribbean. He redoubled his struggles to get into the raft.

It wasn't easy. An Air Force survival raft is about the size of a child's wading pool and it is designed to be stable once the pilot is in it, not to be easy to get into. Gilligan was encumbered by his arctic survival suit, his G-suit and his flight suit. He wanted to hurry for fear of sharks, but he didn't want to splash too much for fear of attracting them. If there had been anyone to watch, it might have been fairly amusing. But there wasn't and Gilligan himself wasn't at all amused.

Once he had flopped into the raft he tried to orient himself. The one thing that hadn't changed was the fog. It was dense and thick everywhere. The air was a good deal colder than the water, so that wasn't astonishing, but it didn't explain *why* the water was so warm.

He pulled the seat pack into the raft and set it on his lap while he undid the catches on the bottom. Inside was a standard Air Force survival kit, including food, medical supplies and a lot of other necessities. Right now he was most interested in the radio and the emergency transponder.

The radio was about the size of a pack of cigarettes. Eagerly Gilligan extended the antenna and trailed the ground wire over the side into the water. Then he tried the radio. Only a hiss and crackle of static came out of the speaker.

Grimacing, Gilligan carefully clipped the radio to the breast pocket of his flight suit. Next he pulled out the transponder and examined it.

The transponder was bigger than the survival radio, but it did more. When it received a signal indicating an aircraft was in the area it transmitted a powerful homing signal. Just now it was silent as the grave.

Gilligan punched the self-test button on the receiver and watched the LED indicator light up. Then he studied the other indicator for a few minutes and his expression got grimmer and grimmer.

Every military aircraft and almost all airliners and business aircraft carry beacons which would trigger his transponder. Gilligan knew for a fact that an AWACS and several other aircraft should have been within range. If even one plane was above the horizon, the device should have been screaming its little electronic heart out. Yet the self-test said it was working.

Either the self-test was lying or there were no planes above the horizon. Considering what the rest of this business had been like, Gilligan didn't think the transponder was broken.

He pulled out his compass. He didn't expect it to work this far north and he wasn't disappointed.

There was one very non-standard item in Major

Michael Francis Xavier Gilligan's survival kit. A 9mm Beretta automatic with three fourteen-round magazines and a black nylon Bianchi shoulder holster to match. He inspected the pistol, slammed one of the magazines home and jacked back the slide. Then he struggled into the shoulder holster's harness.

Then he felt a lot better.

Back at the base the people were feeling worse as the minutes ticked by.

The general wasn't happy, Ozzie Sharp wasn't happy, the squadron commander wasn't happy and unhappiest of all was the young captain who ran the base's rescue operation.

"We got on his last known position quickly and flew an expanding spiral search," the captain explained. "Then we did it again with a different aircraft and crew. We have had aircraft on top almost constantly. There is no voice communication and no transponder signal."

"What about the Russians?"

"They say they haven't seen any sign of him."

"And you believe them?"

"It's credible," Ozzie Sharp said. "The Russians returned to their base with all their missiles still on their wings." No one bothered to ask how he knew.

The general grunted. Then his head snapped up and he transfixed the young captain with a steely-eyed stare.

"Why the bloody hell can't you even find the area where he went down?"

"Sir, this is a very unusual situation. He had sent his wingman back, so we don't have as much information as we normally do." The captain thought about explaining how well they were doing to have gotten this far in the few hours since the missing pilot's wingman had broken out of the dead zone. Then he caught the general's eye again and decided not to.

"Have your crews found anything unusual?" Sharp asked. "Any unusual readings or problems with your instruments?"

"None, sir. As far as we can tell, there's nothing in that fog but more fog."

The expression on Sharp's face made the general seem mild by comparison.

"We're going over the area again," the captain offered quickly. "But so far there's no sign of Major Gilligan or his plane."

"Nothing on the transponder?" the general asked.

"Nossir," the officer said.

"Captain, I thought this sort of thing wasn't supposed to happen."

"It isn't, sir."

It's as if he dropped off the face of the earth, the captain thought. But it was bad form to say something like that.

Major Gilligan drifted through the fog and tried to figure out what the hell had happened to him. He didn't have the faintest idea where he was, but increasingly he doubted it was anywhere near Alaska. There was still fog all around him, but when the sun broke through it was bright, warm and too high in the sky, totally unlike anything he had experienced in Alaska.

He could hear the sound of surf off to his left. Surf usually meant land of some kind, so that was as good a direction as any. Besides, the fog seemed to be marginally thinner that way.

Major Michael Francis Xavier Gilligan began paddling grimly toward the sound of the waves.

TWENTY-SIX

GILLIGAN'S ISLAND

Gilligan saw the land almost as soon as he broke out of the fog bank. One minute he was paddling along surrounded by whiteness and the next he was out under sunny skies with only an occasional puff of fleecy white clouds. Behind him the fog looked like a wall.

Ahead of him he could see a shore fringed with trees, and hills behind. Between him and that shore waves beat on a reef, making the noise that had drawn him here.

Gilligan studied the situation as best he could sitting in his raft. Fortunately the current wasn't strong here and the tide was high. He thought about trying to find a channel, but he decided that would cost him more energy than he could afford. So he picked the best-looking spot and paddled toward it.

It took perhaps an hour for Gilligan to negotiate the reef and another forty-five minutes or so to cross the lagoon behind it. As he crossed the lagoon, Gilligan had a chance to admire "his" island. It was worth admiring, he had to admit. The black sand beach was smooth and unmarred. The trees behind it were tall and tropic green. The place looked like a travel poster.

A travel poster for a deserted island, he thought. There was no sign of footprints, tire tracks, roads or trails. The detritus along the tide line included not one beer can, plastic jug or bottle.

Reflexively he scanned the sky for contrails. There were very few places in the world where you could not see jet tracks in the sky, but apparently this was one of them. Except for the clouds and the fog on the water behind him there was nothing in the sky but the bright tropical sun.

Wherever I am, with scenery like this there's sure to be a Club Med or something close by.

After pulling his raft up on the beach above the tide line, Gilligan stripped off his life vest, arctic survival suit and G-suit, stowed his gear, checked his radios again and started off down the beach. Either this place was as deserted as it looked or it wasn't and he stood a better chance of finding either people or food if he stayed on the beach.

After almost an hour of walking he found nothing to show that the place was or ever had been inhabited. He had stopped twice to empty the sand out of his boots. Finally he tied the laces together and slung them around his neck so he could walk barefoot through the fine black sand.

Crabs skittered across the beach, gulls wheeled over the water and an occasional brightly colored bird flashed through the trees. But there was not a single sign of human life.

Damn it, he thought, scanning the sky again. *Places like this just don't exist anymore.* He looked down the long, pristine stretch of beach. *And if they do, I want to retire here!*

He had been walking perhaps half a mile barefoot when he found a place where a boat had pulled up. *Not a boat,* he corrected, *an amphibious tractor.* The signs were clear enough. The place where it had come out of the water had been washed away by the tide, but he could clearly see where it had pulled up above the tide line, and then the tread marks where it had churned over the soft sand and in among the trees. Between the tread marks was a furrow as if the vehicle had not retracted its rudder. Following the line he could even see where several branches had been broken off in its passage.

Gilligan paused and considered. An amphtrack implied military. Even in backwaters like this civilians didn't own them. That meant there was an element of risk in meeting the tractor and its crew. On the other hand, there was also the possibility of rescue.

He studied the marks carefully. Although he was no expert, he knew that the amphibious tractors of the U.S. Marines drove through the water on special treads with extra-deep cleats. Soviet equipment used regular treads and either propellers or water jets. But the sand was much too fine and soft to give him any clue. He could only see that something big and not wheeled had come this way.

What the hell, this is the era of glasnost. We're all supposed to be friends these days. He sat down on a tree root and put his boots on. Then he checked his pistol. *Still, it never hurts to be careful.*

Cautiously, Major Mick Gilligan set off into the forest in pursuit of the vehicle.

The trail was surprisingly difficult to follow. The amphtrack had not torn up the forest floor as much as he expected. There were no clear tread marks and in many places broken branches offered clearer indications than the tracks. Still, you can't move something that big through a wooded area without leaving a plain trail.

Except for the breeze in the trees and an occasional bird or animal call, the woods were silent. There was no sound of an engine, which made Gilligan even more cautious. But there were no voices, either. Perhaps they were too far ahead for him to hear.

Gilligan was a pilot, not a woodsman. He had to divide his attention between trying to follow the trail, trying not to walk into a tree and trying to scout ahead. So it wasn't surprising he stepped into the clearing without seeing Patrol Two standing in the trees on the other side.

Then the dragon rider shifted. Gilligan caught the motion and looked up. Then he stared—first at the weapon and then at the wielder.

The bow was nearly as tall as she was and the limbs were of unequal length. Gilligan remembered seeing something like that when he had been stationed in Japan and he had gone to a demonstration of traditional Japanese archery. But the person carrying it was anything but Japanese.

To Gilligan she looked like something out of a Robin Hood movie. She wore thigh-high boots of soft brown leather, tight breeches that bloused out at the thigh and a fleece-lined vest over a close-fitting tunic. She was tall, nearly as tall as he was, and slender. Her hair was cornsilk blonde and freckles dusted her nose. The eyes were pure, pale blue and very, very serious. The arrow in her bow was aimed straight at his midriff.

"Uh, hi," Gilligan said.

TWENTY-SEVEN

ENCOUNTER

Karin studied the stranger carefully without shifting the aim of the arrow. He was a big man, broad shouldered and apparently well muscled, although it was hard to tell through his clothing. He wore a drab green coverall with straps, pockets and strange black runes scattered over it. The thing in his hand was black and shiny and he handled it like a weapon, although Karin had never seen its like.

In all their patrolling, the dragon riders had never seen a human in this place. Indeed, they had been told there were only two humans among the enemy and they never left their castle. Where did this one come from?

He didn't act like one of the enemy, she thought. In fact he seemed more confused than hostile. Still better to be safe, so she simply nodded to him without moving the bow.

"I'm Major Michael Gilligan, United States Air Force. I, ah, had a little trouble back there and I need to contact my unit." He stopped, as if expecting a response. "Um, I don't suppose there's a phone around here anywhere?"

"Air Force? You are a flier then?"

"Yes, ma'am. Only, as I say, I had a little trouble and came down in the water."

"And your mount?"

"Down at sea."

The poor man's dragon had drowned! To Karin, who had only narrowly avoided the same fate, the tragedy was doubly poignant.

"I'm very sorry," she said, lowering her bow. "I am called Karin and I too am a flier."

Slowly and with exaggerated care, the man put the black metal thing in a pouch under his armpit. "Pleased to meet you, ma'am. Ah, about that phone . . . ?"

"I do not think you will find one here," Karin told him, not quite comprehending what a "phone" was.

"I kind of figured that," he said. "Where are we, anyway?"

"I am not quite sure," she admitted. "I think it is the western shore of the main island in the Bubble World."

"Bubble World?" he asked blankly.

"The World between the Worlds. I do not pretend to understand it, but our wizards say that it is connected at one end to our World and at the other end to the World from whence came the Sparrow."

"Sparrow? Excuse me, ma'am, but I'm just plain confused."

"Of course! You must be from the other World, the Sparrow's World." She smiled. "This must all be very strange to you, I know."

"Yes, ma'am!" he said fervently. "It certainly is that."

"Well, come back to my camp then and we can talk. Oh, and stop calling me ma'am. I am neither a witch, a wizard nor an elder and I am called Karin."

He looked at her in a way Karin found rather pleasant. "No ma'am—I mean, Karin—you are definitely not an *old* witch!"

This, Major Mick Gilligan told himself firmly, *has gotta be a hallucination*. He was probably lying in a hospital bed somewhere drugged out of his skull after being fished out of the Bering Sea. He wondered if his nurse looked anything like Karin.

Still, he thought, *hallucination or not, I've gotta play it like it's real.* So far it hadn't been too bad. Stuck on a deserted island with a beautiful girl, even a beautiful girl who thought she was William Tell. No, that wasn't half bad for a hallucination.

"My camp is just over there," Karin said, pointing toward an especially thick clump of trees.

"Where's your vehicle?" Gilligan asked.

"No vehicle, only Stigi and myself," Karin told him as they stepped into the camp.

"But we've been following . . ." Gilligan began.

Then he saw the dragon.

Stigi was only average size for a cavalry mount—which is to say he was eighty feet long and his wings would probably span as much when fully extended.

An eighty-foot wingspan on an airplane wouldn't have impressed Gilligan particularly. Eighty feet of bat wings on a scaled, fanged monster who looked ready to breathe fire at any second was *very* impressive.

Gilligan's jaw dropped and he licked his lips. "That's, that's a . . ."

"That is Stigi," Karin supplied, strolling over to the monster and patting its scaly shoulder just in front of its left wing.

The dragon raised its head about ten feet off the ground and regarded Gilligan with a football-sized golden eye.

"Does it fly?"

"Of course he flies," Karin said. "How else would we get here?"

"Hoo boy," said Major Mick Gilligan. "Oh boy."

Karin's camp was well off the beach, in a fold in the ground well-shaded by trees. The dragon took up a good half the space, but there was still room for a small fire and a simple canopy made with something like a shelter half.

"This is pretty cozy," Gilligan said as he looked around.

"I am a scout," Karin explained. "There is always the

possibility of being caught away from my base and having to forage. So," she shrugged, "we are prepared."

"There aren't many places we can land away from our bases," Mick told her. "If something goes wrong we have to bail out."

"Bail out?"

"Use our ejection seats."

"Ejection seats?"

He looked over at the dragon. "Yeah, I guess you don't have much call for those."

"Now," Karin said, settling herself on a log by the fire, "what happened to you, Major?"

"It's Mick, as long as we're on a first-name basis."

Karin frowned prettily. "I thought you said your name was Major."

"No, that's my rank. My first name's Michael, but everyone calls me Mick."

"Ah," Karin said. "When Stigi and I are in the air we are called Patrol Two."

"That's like a call sign. I was Eagle One on my last mission."

"What happened to you?"

Gilligan sighed. "Kind of a long story. Basically we were getting some peculiar—ah, indications—from an area out over the ocean and they sent us out to look. My wingman and I found something, but we couldn't communicate with our base. I sent him back and went on in for a closer look. There was a little tussle and I came out on the short end."

It was Karin's turn to sigh. "That is more or less what happened to me. I was out on single patrol, near the great fog bank where this World connects to yours, when I was attacked from behind. I managed to avoid the attacker and I even got a shot off at it, but in the maneuvering Stigi sprained his wing."

"Sprained it?"

"Our dragons seldom hurt themselves so, but this is a strange place and things are not exactly as they are in our world."

"They're not as they are in our world, either," Gilligan said, looking over at Stigi. The dragon's head was resting on the ground but one unwinking yellow eye was fixed on Gilligan.

"What jumped you, another dragon?" he asked as he turned so he didn't have to look at the dragon looking at him.

Karin frowned. "Something strange. It was all gray and roared as it came. I did not get a good look at it."

Uh-oh, Gilligan thought. *Gray and roaring and came at her from behind. Hoo boy.*

To cover himself he asked the first non-personal question that came to mind. "You keep talking about different worlds. What do you mean?"

"There is our World, where magic holds sway. There is your World, where I gather magic works poorly or not at all?" He nodded and she went on. "And there is this World, where both the things of our world and the things of your world work after a fashion. But this World is new. Some say it was created by our enemies."

"Your enemies?"

"Powerful wizards who command legions of non-living beings," Karin explained. "It is said they prepare war against both your world and ours. But surely you know this?"

"All we know is that there's something funny going on out over the ocean. We thought maybe it was someone from our world. That's why I was sent to investigate."

The dragon rider frowned. "If that is all your people know then surely you must return to bear word to them."

"That's my plan."

Karin sighed. "I wish I could contact my base, but my communications crystal stopped working just before I was attacked. I am sure my squadron commander would know what to do."

"You seem to be doing all right," Gilligan said, looking around the camp site.

Karin smiled. She had a wonderful smile, Gilligan

noticed. Then she sobered. "Thank you, but I feel so inadequate. I have been a rider for just two seasons. I have never been in combat before. In that time there has been no one to fight."

"I know the feeling," Gilligan told her. "I've been in for ten years, I've got about 1800 hours in F-15s and I've never been in combat either." He had missed Iraq because he'd been in the hospital with hepatitis, but he didn't tell her that.

Karin looked astonished. "Ten years and never a battle?"

"We've been at peace all that time," Gilligan said. *Well, more or less.* "Actually we've been at peace for almost twenty-five years and we haven't had a major war in nearly fifty."

"Forgive me, but if that is so then why do you maintain fighting fliers?"

"Because for most of that time we've been close to war. My nation and another great nation were ready to go to war at a moment's notice."

"Yet you did not? You must be remarkably peace-loving in spite of it."

Gilligan grinned mirthlessly. "Not peace-loving. Scared. We got too good at it. We developed weapons that would let us destroy cities in an eyeblink. Weapons we had no defenses against. All of a sudden a major war didn't look real cost effective."

Karin shivered. "I do not think I would like to see war in your world."

"Neither would we," Gilligan told her.

"But," Karin said thoughtfully, "with such weapons you would be powerful allies against our enemies."

"Maybe. I don't make policy, but I'm sure willing to carry the word back to the people who do."

"We must get you back to your World, then."

"You mean you can get me home?"

"The Mighty at the Capital certainly can. The Sparrow knows how."

"But first we've got to get to your Capital. Are they going to come looking for you?"

Karin shrugged. "Probably. But they dare not search too long or too hard. Magical methods work poorly here and we are too close to our enemies' hold to risk many riders and dragons."

"So they aren't likely to find us."

"No, but I do not think that will matter. Once Stigi's wing is healed, he will be able to carry us back to my people."

Gilligan looked over at the snoring dragon. "You mean that thing can really get us out of here?"

"In easy stages, of course. Stigi can carry two for a ways and there are many reefs and islands where we can rest."

"That's something to look forward to, anyway."

"Meanwhile," Karin said, getting up. "It is late and morning comes early. Let us to bed."

Mick Gilligan fell asleep that night and dreamed about flying and girls with blonde hair and freckles.

TWENTY-EIGHT

IMAGE ENHANCEMENT

Quite a collection of brass, Willie Sherman thought to herself. It wasn't the biggest group she'd ever worked with and it wasn't the highest ranking, but it was still two generals, a gaggle of colonels of both types and a brother who was obviously some kind of high-up spook. Pretty impressive.

Not that Master Sergeant Wiletta Sherman was impressed. After being in for eighteen years there wasn't a lot left that could impress her.

Less than twenty-four hours ago she had been at Edwards AFB in the California desert helping to test a new filmless imaging system. She had been ordered to Alaska so quickly she'd just had time to throw a winter uniform into a suitcase and grab a few toiletries.

Unfortunately whoever was responsible for this building had never heard of the DOD energy conservation guidelines. It had to be eighty-five degrees and she was already sweating in her heavy blue wool uniform.

If it weren't for all the brass she would have taken her jacket off. But no one else had, so she just sweated.

"Everybody here?" asked the ranking two-star. "Okay, pull it up and let's see what we got."

Willie hit a couple of keys to call up the file on the

screen. Before she got here someone had already gone through the tape, picked out the best images and digitized them. So all she had to do was the processing.

The workstation she was using wasn't much bigger than a personal computer tied to a compact refrigerator, but it had cost the government nearly a million dollars. She didn't know how many millions had gone into the software, but it obviously hadn't been cheap. For Willie, who had started her career analyzing photographs of North Vietnam with a binocular microscope, it was a lot more impressive than her audience.

After a couple of seconds the image flashed on the screen. Willie looked at it and her eyes went wide. Some asshole was playing tricks, in front of the goddamn generals, no less!

The picture was obviously taken at long range but it was clear enough. Against a background of fleecy gray clouds a dragon sailed along with its wings extended. There was a rider on its back just forward of the wings.

Beautiful job, though. There was no sign of a matte line or the kinds of shadow inconsistencies that usually trip up faked photographs—not that that was going to save the poor bastard who was responsible.

Willie braced for the inevitable explosion. It didn't come. All the generals and colonels were staring at the picture as if it made sense. Some of them looked sideways at each other, as if they wanted to say something, but none of them opened their mouths.

"Hmm, ah yes," the major general said. "You're sure this is, ah, correct?"

"I unloaded the tape and digitized the image myself," said the colonel in charge of the base's imaging section.

"And this is the best image that was on the tape?"

"Ah, yes sir," said the colonel. "None of them are any better and they all, um, show the same thing."

The major general looked over at the black man in the flight suit with no insignia and the brother looked back at the general. Not a muscle in either man's face moved.

"Well then," the general said briskly. "We'll have to use this one." He peered at the screen again. "Although it is a little out of focus."

It's a dragon, you fucking moron! Willie Sherman thought. But in the Air Force there are times when you protest and there are times when you keep your mouth shut. In her climb to master sergeant she had learned which was which and this was definitely a time to shut up and soldier.

"Let's check it against known aircraft first," the head of the image processing section said.

Try checking it against Saturday morning cartoons, Willie thought. But she entered the command anyway.

Quickly the machine ran through the profiles of Soviet and NATO aircraft.

"No match, sir," Willie reported without taking her eyes off the screen. Even smiling would be bad form and she wasn't sure she could keep a straight face if she met someone's eyes.

The major general nodded. "A new type then."

"That's what we suspected all along," the man with no insignia said.

"Let's see if we can get some more detail," the imaging colonel said. "Try stretching the contrast."

Without comment Willie used the mouse to indicate the new contrast range. Instantly the dragon and rider seemed to fuzz and smooth out as every shade of color broke down into sixteen closely related shades.

"Look there along the trailing edge of the wing," said one of the other colonels. "That's obviously some different kind of material."

"Radar absorbing," said the spook. "If you look at the way the trailing edge is scalloped you'll see that it has some resemblance to the trailing edge of the B-2."

"Might also be radiators to dump infra red," one of the other colonels said.

The brigadier general rubbed his chin. "Plausible. Okay, assume they're radiators. They'd be flat black, wouldn't they?"

The imaging colonel nodded. "That gives us a color reference. Make them flat black."

I can't believe you people are taking this seriously! Willie thought. But what she said was, "Yes, sir."

Making the rear of the wings flat black changed the colors on the rest of the image, muting them and fuzzing the details even further.

"Okay," the two-star general said. "Now, where are the tail surfaces?"

"If you look closely at the tail boom you'll see it's somewhat flattened," the imaging colonel told him. "The entire thing is apparently an empennage."

"Enhance that, will you?" the brigadier asked. "Let's see if we can bring out the detail along the boom."

"Try compressing the tones there," suggested the imaging colonel.

Willie marked out the tail with her mouse and compressed the colors. Now four or five shades on the tail were rendered as one. The thing on the screen didn't look like a dragon anymore, but it didn't look like much of anything else either.

Slowly and gradually, one change at a time, the gaggle of officers used a million-dollar workstation to enhance a clear picture of a dragon into something they could accept.

By the time they broke for dinner they were arguing over the serial numbers on the tail.

TWENTY-NINE

HUNTING PARTY

It was still cool and gray when Mick awoke, but Karin was already stirring. She had taken the quiver from the pile of harness and slung it over her shoulder.

"What are you doing?" he asked, throwing back the blanket.

"I must hunt to feed my mount," the dragon rider said, holding her bow horizontally and sighting down the string.

Mick Gilligan compared the monster before him to his dog at home and then computed the amount of dog food it would take to make a meal for a fifty-foot-long golden retriever.

"An elephant a day?"

"Not so much," Karin shook her head and then brushed a wisp of golden hair off her forehead. "Dragons are related in part to lizards and magical besides. They do not eat as much as you would suppose."

"Still, its going to take a lot of meat."

"I know where to find that. There is open country not far from here and large game to be had. Will you hunt with me?"

At home Mick had gone deer hunting occasionally, without much luck. On the other hand the thought of being stuck in camp all day with an overgrown iguana with a sore wing didn't appeal to him either.

"Sure," he said. "Let me get boots on."

Karin led off at a brisk pace through the forest. Trailing behind her Gilligan found himself admiring the way she moved lithely through the undergrowth—and the swing of her hips in her tight riding breeches. He shook the thought off and tried to concentrate on business.

Gradually the trees thinned and the underbrush diminished until the forest became almost parklike. Once a herd of deer or something like them went bounding away at their passage. Karin ignored them, obviously intent on bigger game.

After perhaps three miles the forest petered out altogether and they moved out onto a broad plain. The trees were reduced to occasional clumps and the grass varied between knee and waist high.

Karin stopped and raised her head as if she was sniffing the air. Then she pointed off to their left and, motioning Gilligan to silence, she started off in that direction.

Gilligan heard their prey before he saw it. The wind brought crackling and crashing as if a number of large animals were moving about. As they got closer he could smell them as well, a faint odor that reminded him of nothing so much as the elephant house in the zoo.

The dragon rider moved through the grass silently with a grace that made it seem effortless. Gilligan, trying to move quietly, found it wasn't effortless at all. He had to keep his eyes on the ground in order to keep from stepping on dry leaves or twigs. He was so intent on trying to move quietly he almost ran into Karin when she stopped suddenly. Then he looked up and saw what they were hunting.

Dinosaurs! Gilligan thought. There were about a dozen of them in a clump of trees perhaps a hundred and fifty yards off. They were bipedal and balanced themselves with their long tails while they used their smaller forearms to pull branches down to the small heads on their snakelike necks and then nipped off the leaves and buds. They were striped dusty gray and green and they didn't look like any dinosaurs he had ever seen pictures of. But they were definitely large and reptilian.

While Gilligan had been staring at the animals, Karin had slipped to one side and dropped down on one knee. Slowly and carefully she drew the bow to full extension, string and arrow kissing her lip. Then she released.

Suddenly an arrow sprouted from the flank of one of the dinosaurs. The beast stopped feeding, looked down at its tormentor, honked once and then dropped like a sack of sand.

Instantly the other dinosaurs fled, honking and bellowing, knocking over a small tree in their flight.

As the noise of the herd faded into the distance Karin and Mick moved up to the carcass.

"They have no fear of humans," Karin said, surveying her kill. "If all the beasts on this island are like that I will have no trouble keeping Stigi fed."

"As long as they don't stampede toward you when you shoot one," Gilligan said.

"Such animals almost always run upwind when frightened," Karin told him. "That way they can smell what is ahead of them."

"Great," Mick said, looking at the kill. "Now, how do we get it back to camp?"

"That will not be necessary. Stigi can walk. I will go and get him. Can you stay here with the kill?"

"Sure."

"Oh, and do not let predators get at the carcass. Stigi expects to be first on a kill and it upsets him when he is not."

Mick thought of Stigi angry. "Right," he said.

Karin nodded and strode off the way they had come.

"Hey, wait a minute! How do I keep predators off this carcass?"

Karin turned back to him. "Use your weapon," she called and then disappeared in the brush.

Mick drew the 9mm automatic and looked at it sourly. Then he looked over at the elephant-sized monster he was supposed to be guarding. Then he thought about the kind of thing that was likely to prey on something the size of an elephant.

"Right," he said again.

The sun was close to the horizon when Stigi waddled out of the forest with Karin alongside. Mick moved to meet them, but Stigi drew back his head and hissed like a jet engine starting up. Mick took the hint and backed off.

"He does not like you," Karin said, quite unnecessarily. "Perhaps it would be better if you gathered wood for a fire. It looks as if we shall have to camp here tonight." Mick noticed that both his and Karin's packs were tied to the saddle.

Mick retrieved the hand axe and started gathering firewood. After he saw Stigi tear into the carcass he spent as much time as he could with his back to the dragon. Stigi's manners ran to the enthusiastic rather than the polite and Mick, who hated the chore of field dressing a rabbit, was a little put out by the sight.

By the time Mick had a double armload of firewood Stigi had finished his meal. The dragon followed docilely behind Karin and settled down near the fire with a belch that smelled like smog in a butcher shop.

Their own dinner was a thick stew of parched grain, dried fruit and jerky from Karin's pack. By mutual agreement they had decided to save Gilligan's rations against future need.

While they ate Stigi washed himself with his tongue like a giant cat and then curled up and went to sleep. With his belly full he snored astonishingly loudly.

Around them the plain was alive with the sounds of night birds and the roars of hunting predators. Gilligan took to running his thumb over the butt of his pistol and searching the darkness.

"Nothing will come close to us," Karin told him, catching his expression. "They are afraid of Stigi and the fire."

"What about scavengers after the carcass?"

Karin shook her head. "Especially not the scavengers. Besides, if something did approach Stigi would sense it instantly and waken."

"What's left of that carcass is going to get pretty ripe in a couple of days."

"We will not be here that long. Indeed, we would not have camped here tonight if darkness had not caught us. We need to be back among the trees for safety."

"Doesn't that just make it easier for things to sneak up on us?"

"Not the predators." Karin pointed outside the firelit circle. "That."

Mick followed her arm with his eyes. Off in the distance there was a greenish glow against the sky, as if there were a city lit entirely by mercury vapor lamps just over the horizon.

"What is that?"

"Our enemies' hold," Karin said grimly. "A great castle and fortress."

"So close? They must be on the next island over."

"No," Karin told him. "They are on this island."

Mick started. "Then what the hell are we doing sitting around a campfire?"

"Keeping off predators," Karin said sharply. "Without the fire they would be a danger, Stigi or no."

"Besides," she added, relaxing slightly, "those of the castle do not hunt by night."

"If you say so," Mick said neutrally.

"Such has been our experience."

Despite the roaring and the snoring, Mick finally got to sleep that night. But he didn't sleep easily or comfortably and his dreams weren't nearly as pleasant as they had been the night before.

THIRTY

GRAND REVIEW

Craig looked down from the balcony and out over the serried ranks of his handiwork.

The narrow valley was full of rank upon rank of war machines. There were warbots ranging from two-ton Fleas to 200-ton Deathbringers, there were tanks and armored cars and artillery and jeeps and scout cars and missile carriers and on and on. They were there by the companies and battalions and regiments, by the hundreds and the thousands. They packed the valley and spilled back through the enormous portal at the valley's head into the very bowels of the mountain. And over it all, perched on a reviewing stand carved out of living rock, was their creator.

Looking them over, Craig reflected he had come a long way since those first crude robots.

Now for the test. He had marked off hundreds of square miles of desert south of the castle for a proving ground. There he would pit his creations against each other to test his tactics and designs. When the battles for the control of the new world began he wanted his armies to be perfect.

Flanked by his robot servants, Craig shifted in his elaborately carved chair. The other chair on the platform was empty. Mikey had sent word at the last minute that he would be too busy to watch the show.

As if he's done anything since we got here, Craig thought. Aside from a few robots he had whipped up for his own use, Mikey had never touched his engineering workstation. Craig seldom saw him anymore and he palmed him off with vague explanations when he tried to ask about his work.

Even if he was busy, he could have taken a couple of hours to see at least part of the parade, Craig thought. He realized that part of it was disappointment. He was sure Mikey would be impressed when he saw the super-weapons he had whipped up. *But no, he's too busy even to come to the damn parade.*

Well, it didn't matter. He'd created all this and now he'd work out the winning tactics on the game board of the desert. When the time came Mikey would be plenty impressed with how his armies performed in battle. That was really all that mattered.

He turned to the robot to his right. "Move out," he commanded.

The valley filled with the ear-splitting noise of ten thousand engines starting up. Clouds of dust roiled over the scene as Craig's army began to move.

On wheels, on tracks, on legs and on cushions of air, the forces Craig had fashioned out of magic and engineering began to pass by their creator in review. In spite of the noise, the choking dust and the diesel and gasoline fumes, Craig hung over the balcony rail and watched entranced for hours.

THIRTY-ONE

PICNIC ON PARADISE

Karin was as good as her word. They were breaking camp at dawn and by the time the sun was full up they were back in the forest. By mid-day they had found another camp site. The hillside Karin chose was not far from the plain and its plentiful supply of dragon fodder, but the trees were tall and broad enough to provide cover even for a dragon. There was a rock outcropping with an overhang that would shield their fires from prying eyes and could serve as a lookout spot as well. At the foot of the hill a small stream wound through the forest.

By the time they had returned to their old camp site and brought their goods to the new spot, it was late in the afternoon. This time Karin insisted on gathering the firewood and she brought in several armloads of dead branches.

"The wood is neither green nor rotten," she explained as she threw down the third load. "It makes almost no smoke."

Dinner that night was a stew of dried meat, grain and dried fruit, all from Karin's rations. Tomorrow they could explore and see what kinds of food they could find in the forest. For tonight it was easier to eat what they had.

"So tell me about dragon riding," Gilligan said as they scraped the last of the stew out of their bowls.

"It is much the same everywhere, is it not?"

Gilligan shrugged. "I wouldn't know. We fly airplanes, not dragons."

Karin looked at him strangely.

"Machines," Gilligan explained. "Non-living flying things."

"I see," Karin said slowly and then seemed to gather herself. "Well, it takes several years to become a flier. You must bond with your dragon, of course. Then you must learn how to maneuver, how to fly in formation and combat tactics."

"You mean you actually fight air-to-air combat on those things?"

"Yes."

Gilligan whistled. "That must be something to see. I imagine your tactics aren't anything like ours."

"Well," Karin said slowly, "there are many things to consider. In general, the rider who starts with the best position will win. That usually means diving on your enemy from above with the sun at your back. But of course there are many other things you must consider. Relative strength, level of training."

"It's the same with us," Gilligan told her. "If we get in close we try to have the advantage in height and position. Diving out of the sun is a favorite tactic."

"We do that also," Karin said.

"Do you break off after one pass?"

"We might. It depends on numbers and your dragon's fighting potential. Some dragons, like Stigi, are very strong and fierce. In a melee I would have a considerable advantage." She paused and frowned. "Still, there are a great many things which can happen in such a situation. Diving on an enemy and past him is surer."

"Have you ever been in a dog fight?"

"Crave pardon?"

"That's what we call short-range air-to-air combat. Dog fights."

Karin considered. "I see. Yes, the expression is somewhat apt. But no, I have never been in battle of any sort."

She hesitated for a minute. "Mick, may I ask you something?"

"Sure."

"Are you bonded to another?"

Mick looked up from the fire. "I beg your pardon?"

"Bonded? I do not know your customs, but do you have a life companion, a mate?"

"We get married," Gilligan told her. "I was. Not any more."

"Your wife died? I am sorry."

"No, we're divorced—that means we ended the marriage."

Karin grew solemn. "Among us that is not a thing done easily."

"It isn't easy with us either," Gilligan said, thinking of the lawyers, the interminable conferences, the constant phone calls and the months of aching, gaping hurt.

"Forgive me for asking, but how did your wife displease you?"

Gilligan smiled mirthlessly into the campfire. "She didn't displease me. I displeased her. I think. Or maybe we just displeased each other. Anyway, she had her choice of rotating to Alaska with me or leaving me, so she left." He snapped the twig and threw it into the fire.

"Look, it was nobody's fault. Okay? It's just that I'm a pilot and an Air Force officer and she couldn't handle that."

For a while neither of them said anything. "I understand, somewhat," Karin said slowly. She sighed. "I was to be married once, while I was in training. But Johan wanted me to give up flying. I could not do that."

The fire turned the pale skin of her cheeks ruddy and painted reddish highlights into her blonde hair.

"I couldn't either. God knows I loved Sandi, but I just couldn't give it up."

Karin looked up at him and smiled slightly. "We are two of a kind then."

"Guess so," Gilligan agreed.

They sat by the fire for a while in companionable silence.

The next morning Karin took Stigi out into the open and carefully exercised him. She was frowning when she led him back into camp.

"How's the wing?" Mick asked, seeing her expression.

"Not good. It is healing, but only slowly. It may be another half-moon before Stigi is strong enough to bear us away."

"Is it infected or something?"

"Nothing like that. It is simply taking more time than it should to heal. If I did not know better I would think he was not properly fed." She sighed. "As it is, I suspect it is simply the nature of this place. It is harder for dragons to stay aloft here, you know."

"I hadn't noticed."

She led Stigi back to his resting place and spent the next hour or so grooming him and talking to him. To Mick, lounging under the overhang, the sight was remarkable. *Beauty and the Beast,* he thought.

Karin was still frowning when she left Stigi and came to sit beside him in the shade.

"Something else wrong with Stigi?"

"No. Nothing like that." She dropped down beside him.

"What then?"

Karin bit her lip. "Mick, there is something else you should know. After last night . . . The way you describe your mount . . . I think I am the one who brought you down."

"I know."

She turned to him wide-eyed. "You knew? And you did not tell me."

"I pretty much figured it out the first day. I got a better look at you than you did at me and unless there were other dragon riders in the area it pretty much had to be you."

"And you made me gather up my courage to tell you! Thank you very much, I am sure."

"Hey," he said, laying a comforting hand on her shoulder, "I was the one who hurt Stigi. I wasn't sure how you'd take that."

"Yes, but you did not mean to."

"And you didn't mean to shoot me down." He grinned. "We're even. By the way, how did you bring me down?"

"With this," Karin said, reaching behind her and drawing an arrow from the front part of the quiver.

"Do not touch it," she admonished as she held it up for his inspection. Gilligan saw the whole arrow, from head to fletching, was made of iron.

Karin pointed to two black dots, one on each side of the broad arrow head. "These crystals on either side of the head are eyes," she explained, pointing to the shiny black buttons. "When both can see their target the arrow's aim is true. There is a spell to keep the target centered in each crystal."

"Like a guidance head," Gilligan nodded. "But that still doesn't explain how an arrow brought down a twenty-eight-million-dollar aircraft with triply redundant everything."

"The death spell," Karin told him. "It paralyzes anything the arrow strikes."

"So that's why my electronics went to hell." He shook his head. "I'm damn glad Congress is never going to hear about this."

There was very little they could do. They did some exploring, hunted a bit and gathered berries and other wild foods from the forest. But that did not take much time. Karin spent an hour or two working with Stigi every day and another half hour or so grooming him. Mostly they lazed around camp and talked while they waited for Stigi's wing to heal.

There was one chore that needed to be done regularly.

Stigi was very efficient at converting dragon food into dragon droppings. Although he was partially housebroken and used a spot down hill from the camp, the spot had to be shoveled out and spread around, well mixed with earth. Otherwise the smell and insects would have made the camp uninhabitable.

Using her hand axe, Karin made them two wooden scoop shovels. They looked a little odd to Gilligan and the handles were too short for his taste, but they were much better than using hands.

Every two or three days Karin or Gilligan would "clean the catbox," as Gilligan insisted on calling it. It was hard, dirty work but it was at least something to do.

"Well, this part of the woods should be green next year," Gilligan said, stretching backwards to try to get the kinks out of his back. "You know this is one thing we never had to worry about with an F-15."

Karin tamped down a mound of mixed earth and dragon dung and looked up.

"Back at the Capital the grooms and stable hands would take care of such chores. But it is part of dragonriders' training to be able to care for our mounts in the field."

"Does that include making shovels out of expedient materials?"

"Expedient . . . ? Ah, I see." She smiled in a way Gilligan found utterly charming. "No, I learned that from my uncle when I was growing up on the farm. He would make such implements to take to the village and sell." She looked down at the scoop beside her. "I think he would find these a little crude, though."

"You grew up with your uncle?"

"My parents died when I was young," Karin said. "A hard winter, not much food and some malevolent magic." She shrugged. "Life was hard before the Sparrow brought us new magic."

"Who's this Sparrow?" Mick asked, as much to keep her sitting beside him as to keep from going back to shovelling.

She turned to him, her blue eyes wide. "You must know the Sparrow. He comes from your world."

"The only Sparrow I know is an air-to-air missile."

"This Sparrow is a mighty wizard. Near four years ago he broke the entire Dark League of the South in a great battle of magics. Since then his new magic has spread across the land, driving back the dark."

"From my world, you say? Do you know where?"

" 'Tis said from a place called the Valley of Quartz."

"Silicon Valley? Yeah, I suppose if we had wizards that's where they'd be. Have you ever met this guy?"

Karin shook her head. "I am not stationed at the Capital. I have seen him once, though. He and his fellow wizards, Jerry and Danny." She stopped. "Are those more of your air-to-air missiles?"

He smiled. "If they are I never heard of them."

"Well, no matter," the dragon rider said with a glance at the horizon. "It grows late. If we do not finish soon we will have to bathe in the dark."

Gilligan stood up. "I guess you're right." He reached down to help her up and when she stood up they were almost nose to nose. He held on and their eyes locked. Then Karin dropped her hands and broke away.

"Quickly," she said with a breathless little laugh. "We would not want to have to finish on the morrow."

Even working at their best pace, it was still nearly dark when they got back to their camp. Karin went to the stream to bathe first and Mick stayed behind to build the fire and start dinner. Once the fire was going and the stew was bubbling in its pot, he had nothing to do but stare into the flames and think.

Karin came back from the stream with her clothes over her arm and her blanket wrapped around her.

"I feel cleaner without them," she explained. "They need to be washed."

"I wish to God you'd put them on," Gilligan said tightly, keeping his attention riveted on the fire.

"Why?"

"It's easier to take." He looked up at her. "Dammit, lady! Do you have any idea how hard it is on me to keep my hands off you anyway?"

"Then why try?" Karin asked softly, letting the blanket drop.

The flames traced out the curve of her hip and the swell of her breast and the light put a ruddy glow in her cheek and highlighted the pale strands of her hair.

Mick sucked in his breath at the firelit vision before him. Then he stepped forward and clasped her to him.

"I never did get my bath, you know."

Karin giggled and nuzzled the pit of his shoulder. "You smell all right."

"And if you keep that up, I'm not going to get any sleep either."

"Are you complaining?"

Gilligan leaned over and kissed her. "Hell no. Just observing."

The fire had long since died and the only light came from the stars that powdered the sky. There was not enough light to see, but that didn't matter and hadn't mattered for hours. Being shot down, the dragon, none of it mattered. He hadn't felt this good since Sandi . . . well, not in a long time. And maybe not even then, come to think of it.

As he bent to her again he noticed that Stigi had very ostentatiously turned his back on them.

At last they both relaxed, soft and sleepy and warm in each other's arms.

"What is it?" Karin said, feeling Mick tense suddenly.

"I've got to go back, you know," Mick said softly. "If I can find a way out, I've got to go back."

Karin shifted and snuggled more closely to him. "I understand. I too have my duty."

"So where does that leave us?"

"It leaves us with meanwhile," Karin told him. "We have meanwhile."

"Yeah," Mick said, reaching out to caress her. "We have meanwhile."

Karin giggled. "Remember today is a hunting day. We will be walking and away from camp almost the whole day."

"So?"

"So you said you needed sleep."

"Right now," Gilligan said into her ear, "there are things I need more."

THIRTY-TWO

THE ULTIMATE WATER BALLOON

Craig was deep in the design of a new kind of battle armor when one of Mikey's robot servants came for him.

"The Master commands your presence," the robot said in a Darth Vader voice of doom.

"You mean Mikey?"

"The Master. Come." With that the robot pivoted on its heel and marched out the door with Craig hurrying along behind.

Mikey was up on the battlements, standing next to a troughlike contraption and looking out over the valley.

"What's shaking, dude?" Craig said as he puffed up with the robot guide.

"Shaking? A whole lot. I want you to see my latest invention."

Since Mikey had ignored everything he had done since he made the giant robot, Craig didn't think this was quite fair. But he didn't object. Instead he bent over and inspected the device.

"What is that thing?"

"It's a water balloon. The best goddamn water balloon you've ever seen."

It didn't look much like a balloon to Craig. Just a featureless silvery sphere, like those mirrored balls people used to put on pedestals in gardens. The sphere was resting in the trough and there were some springs and some other, less identifiable, bits of machinery underneath.

"What does it do?"

"Watch," Mikey told him. "But put these on first." He snapped his fingers and the robot stepped forward and proferred a couple of smashed ham sandwiches.

"Not those, you fucking moron!" Mikey said. "Give him the goddamn goggles!

"Jeez, Craig, you need to do something about these robots. They're so fucking stupid."

Craig started to tell him it wasn't one of his robots, but Mikey had already slipped on a pair of dark goggles and was looking back out over the valley. Craig took the pair of goggles the robot was holding out to him, wiped the mustard and mayonnaise off the lenses and slipped them on.

Mikey threw a lever on the side of his device and the silvery ball whisked down the trough and out over the valley in a high, lazy arc. Craig watched the ball shrink to a dot and then lost it in the sun.

Suddenly the world exploded.

Castle, valley and mountains all disappeared in a blaze of blinding radiance. Craig squinched his eyes shut but the sight was burned into his vision. He opened his mouth but he was bowled over backwards as if he had been slapped by a giant hand. Sand and bits of rock stung his skin and the wind whipped insanely about him. The parapet shook beneath him until he was sure the castle was coming down. The noise shook him like a terrier shakes a rat. All he could do was lie curled up in a ball and scream at the pain in his ears and the red after-images in his eyes.

Then it was over. As suddenly as it had come the noise and the shaking stopped. Cautiously, Craig opened his eyes and tried to climb to his feet.

Mikey was standing at the battlement braced like a sea captain facing into a storm. His hair was blown back and his clothes had been whipped about, but he stood firm and unrelenting, looking out over the valley. As he gazed on the roiling clouds of dust and debris below his smile reminded Craig of a picture he had seen once in Sunday school, of Moses looking out over the Promised Land.

Craig shook himself and looked around. The pennants on the castle towers had been torn to shreds by the blast. Half the roof tiles had been blown off the conical roof of the nearest tower and the chamber below gaped up. His robot guide lay in a twitching heap, unable to rise.

Mikey said something, but it didn't register on Craig's numbed and ringing ears.

"What?"

"I said, 'Neat huh?'" Mikey half-shouted.

"What in the hell was *that*?"

"Like I said, a water balloon."

"Like hell!"

Mikey's smile grew broader. "Nope. Take a sphere of water—just ordinary water—and squeeze it real hard. Pretty soon the atoms disassociate into hydrogen and oxygen. Then if you squeeze it hard enough those hydrogen atoms are forced close enough together that they fuse." He threw up his hands. "Poof! Instant H-bomb."

"Jesus Christ," Craig said. Then he looked out over the dust-filled valley. "Jesus H. Fucking Christ on a goddamn rubber crutch!"

"Hey, that was nothing. The castle's shields took most of the blast so we only got a little of it. And the best part is that the spell to compress that water is so simple I can make my H-bombs any size I want. A hundred megatons, two hundred, even a thousand megatons, no problem."

Craig leaned against the battlement to ease his shaky knees. "That's some water balloon. You ought to put one of those things in the nose of an ICBM."

"ICBMs? We don' need no steenkin' ICBMs. Combine that with the teleportation spell. What do you think would happen if you shoved a mother big bomb down into the planet's crust?"

"Jesus," Craig breathed. "You could sink half a continent!"

Mikey's smile grew wider. "If you do it right you should smash the world." He looked out past Craig, past the fortress and past the dissipating cloud.

"The whole fucking world," he repeated dreamily.

THIRTY-THREE

A FRIGHTENED DRAGON

In spite of the night's activities, Karin and Mick got an early start. Mick caught a quick bath in the freezing stream at first light while Karin spent time with Stigi. Then they set out on the hunt as dawn turned the sky red.

The pickings weren't as easy as they had been. The dinosaurs had learned to be wary of the humans and keeping Stigi fed now involved more stalking. Fortunately Karin was adept at hunting with a bow.

Still it was nearly noon before they found a likely looking herd and moved into position downwind for the stalk.

Karin was just sizing up the situation when a second sun blossomed in the northern sky. In an instant the world turned overexposed blue-white with stark black shadows, as if a gigantic flashbulb had gone off behind them.

"Get down!" Mick yelled and pulled Karin down beside him.

"What . . ." The dragonrider tried to look back toward the source of the flash, but Gilligan reached out and forced her head down.

"Don't look! Keep your head down and close your eyes."

"I . . ." Karin begin, but her voice was drowned out when the shock wave hit.

Gilligan pressed his face into the dirt and screamed at the top of his lungs as the wall of dust and flying debris passed over them. The wind yanked at his flight suit and the wind-driven sand stung his exposed skin. He kept his head down and his eyes screwed shut until the gale ceased.

When he opened his eyes Karin was staring at him in shock. She tried to get up but at that instant the ground shock wave hit them and she was knocked first to her knees and then flat as the earth trembled beneath her. She lay on her stomach and clutched at the ground with clawed fingers as if she was afraid the shaking would throw her off.

Gilligan waited until everything was still and probably quiet—his ears were ringing so he couldn't tell—before he climbed shakily to his knees and looked around.

Dust stained the sky an ugly mustard yellow and dimmed the sun to a reddish disk. One of the nearby trees had been blown down and limbs had broken off several others. In the distance a herd of reptiles stampeded blindly, bellowing their panic across the plain.

"Okay, you can get up now."

Karin's face was white where it was not smudged with dirt and her freckles stood out starkly.

"Mick, what was that?" She clung to his forearms to hold herself erect.

"Let's get out of here," Gilligan said grimly.

"But Stigi needs to eat."

"He'll have to hunt for himself if we both die of radiation poisoning. Now let's get the hell out of the open!"

She bent and retrieved her bow. "He will be frightened," she said by way of agreement.

He's not the only one, Gilligan thought.

❖   ❖   ❖

Karin was right. Stigi was blundering around roaring in fear and pain. The campsite was a wreck where the dragon had lumbered through it, flattening shelters and mashing things into the dirt.

The dragon rider set about the task of trying to calm her mount while Gilligan gathered everything of value and flung it under the overhanging rock for protection from fallout. He kept his eye on the skies, looking for rain clouds.

"Karin, get over here!"

"But Stigi needs me."

"Bring him here then. But get the hell under cover."

She led the dragon over to the rock shelter, still patting his great scaled neck and talking to him in soothing tones.

"Get in here with me and have him lay down next to the overhang so he blocks the entrance," Gilligan commanded.

For once Stigi did not object to Gilligan's proximity. It was hard to imagine an eighty-foot monster cowering, but this one was shivering from fang to tail tip. Karin kept patting his back and talking to the dragon even after it lay down.

Gilligan checked his shoulder holster and found that about a handful of sand had gotten into it when he hit the dirt. Rummaging through the haphazard pile of equipment he found his cleaning kit and proceeded to field strip and clean his Beretta.

Objectively it didn't help much, but it made him feel better.

"You said you would tell me what that was later," Karin said after a time. "Is now later enough?"

"It was an air burst," Gilligan said tightly. "I don't know how big because I don't know how far away."

He looked out around the quaking dragon at the sky. "Pretty far, I think. There's no sign of blast-induced rain."

"It wasn't natural, was it? I mean it isn't something that just happens here?"

"No, it's manmade. Or *something* made anyway."

Karin eyed him sideways. "And you have seen them before?"

"Never. I always hoped I never would." He slid the pistol back into its holster. "You remember I told you that we would fight an all-out war with weapons that could destroy a city in the blink of an eye? That was one of those weapons."

"Then your people . . . ?"

"*No!*" Karin jerked back as if she had been slapped at the violence of his reply. "I told you we'd never use them unless we were attacked. Nobody would. We're all too afraid of them."

"I can see why."

"Besides, if we did use them we wouldn't set one off over a deserted plain like that and we wouldn't use just one of them."

"But you are expecting more of them. You make us stay under the rocks."

"If there were going to be more we never would have gotten off the plain. We're here because of fallout."

"What is that?"

He turned to her. "Nuclear weapons don't just make a big explosion. They produce all kinds of poisonous byproducts. Even if the blast doesn't get you you can still sicken or die. That stuff will be coming out of the sky for the next few hours and it will be dangerous for the next few days. That blast was a pure air burst so there won't be as much fallout as there could have been. The wind is generally away from us so the plume may not reach us. We may be safe, but I don't want to take chances."

"What about Stigi?"

"You see any place around here that could shelter him?"

Karin shook her head reluctantly.

"Besides, he may not be as affected by this stuff as we are." *For all I know he's got a nuclear reactor in his gut,* Gilligan thought. He wondered if anyone had ever worked out the dose response tables for a firebreathing dragon.

There was no rain that night, and no more explosions. Sometime on toward dawn Gilligan finally drifted off into an uneasy sleep. He dreamed of ruined deserted cities and Karin with her hair falling out.

He awoke numb and muzzy headed. The sun was above the horizon, Karin was gone and so was Stigi.

He cast about frantically for a moment, but Karin's pack and Stigi's saddle were still where he had piled them. Obviously Karin expected to be back soon. Gilligan forced himself to sit down under the overhang and wait.

Perhaps an hour later Karin led Stigi back up the path and into the wrecked campsite.

Heedless of the possibility of fallout or Stigi's steam-whistle snort, he raced across the clearing to meet them. "Karin, I was worried about you," Gilligan said as he took her in his arms. They kissed deeply and then Karin broke away.

"Stigi was restless so I took him to the stream for a bath," she explained. "It always calms him."

"That wasn't safe. We don't know we're out of the fallout plume."

"Oh, but that thing did not leave poison here," Karin said almost gaily.

"What makes you so sure?"

"This," she said, digging into her pouch and producing a small object apparently carved out of jet. "Scouts carry these because sometimes we must forage abroad. It tells us if something is safe to eat or drink. I checked everything I could find and there was no sign of harm."

"I don't know how good it is at detecting fallout," Gilligan said dubiously.

Karin returned the amulet to her pouch. "It has never failed us."

Mick nodded. It was possible serious fallout hadn't

reached this far and they had nothing to worry about. If the fallout had reached them they were already facing a bout of radiation sickness. Logically there was no reason to believe Karin's magic rock was telling the truth, but it felt better that way.

He hugged her again "I was worried about you," he said with his nose and lips buried in the hair on her neck.

"I am sorry, love."

"That's the first time you called me that."

Karin pulled her head away and laid her fingertips on his cheek.

"Well?"

"Well, I like it." He kissed her again.

After a long moment Karin pulled away. "Mick, we have to talk."

"Okay, about what?"

"What happened yesterday. We cannot stay here now."

"You got that right. The best thing would be to move to the opposite end of the island, as far away from that castle . . ."

"No," Karin cut him off. "I need to go the other way. I need to get as close to that castle as I can to spy out its defenses."

Mick dropped his arms to his sides.

"One of those 'defenses' you're talking about is nuclear weapons. That's crazy!"

"Nevertheless," Karin said quietly, "I must."

"Look, at least wait until Stigi's wing is healed. That's, what, another week?"

"Longer than that, I fear. He apparently tried to fly yesterday in his panic and re-injured it."

"So you're going to walk?"

"I have no other choice."

"The hell you don't! You can stay here like a sensible person. Until help arrives or until that dragon can fly."

"And meanwhile the ones in that castle will be brewing up who knows what kind of horrors," Karin blazed back. "No. I have my duty as a scout and flier and I will not shirk it to lie around here while my very world is threatened."

"I don't know how it is in the dragon cavalry, but in the Air Force a recon pilot's first job is to get the information back to his base."

"A scout's first job is to gather information. Having no way of getting anything back, I can only gather more."

"I'll bet you've got some kind of regulation against this kind of behavior," Gilligan said with a shrewdness born of desperation.

"There is also a regulation saying regulations are guides and must be applied with wisdom. This is an unusual situation and I must take unusual action."

Like me sending Smitty back and pressing on alone, Gilligan thought. Somehow he felt that the universe was getting even with him for that.

"What about Stigi?"

Karin frowned. "That is the thing which made it so hard. I will take Stigi with me. He can walk and dragons can keep a fairly good pace."

"Okay, you feel you've got to scout ahead. You could do it faster once Stigi's wing heals."

"It will heal just as well on the march as here."

"And if you're caught in the open?"

"That is a chance I must take."

Gilligan opened his mouth and found he didn't have any more arguments. Karin obviously wasn't thinking straight, but that didn't matter. She was driven by an overpowering urge to do something, anything, except the intelligent thing, which was sit and wait.

Intellectually he could understand that. He felt the same way. But the kind of training it takes to fly a high-performance jet had drummed the value of patience into him. Dragon riding didn't demand the same qualities, or maybe Karin was still too inexperienced to have learned them.

Gilligan considered knocking her out and tying her up. But Karin was lithe and strong. Then he considered Stigi's likely reaction if he tried it and quickly discarded the notion.

The dragon rider set her jaw defiantly. "You have your own rations and equipment. I am sure that you will have no trouble reaching the far end of the island. I will give you a note so that your story will be believed should you meet one of our patrols. Then you can send help on to me."

"You're crazy, you know that?"

Karin shrugged. "I have my duty."

Mick stepped forward and grasped her hands in his. "I'm not going to let you do this. Not alone." Karin looked at him and then smiled.

Hell of an expeditionary force, he thought as he pulled her close and kissed her hard. *Two crazies and a gimpy dragon.* Then he opened his eyes and looked at the woman in his arms.

Still, he thought, *there are compensations in being crazy.*

They spent the rest of the day packing and headed out across the plain the next morning. Karin took the lead with Gilligan beside her. Stigi followed at her heels like an overgrown hound.

The morning was bright and the sky was painted pastel blues and pinks by the rising sun. Except for an occasional broken limb or an uprooted tree there was nothing to suggest what had happened here two days ago. The plains animals had returned to their normal habits and several times they passed herds of them grazing in the distance.

Once Stigi bridled and snorted as though an animal had come near, but he quickly relaxed and resumed walking. Either there had been nothing there, Gilligan decided, or whatever it was had gotten a look at Stigi and decided not to try anything.

THIRTY-FOUR

RECON BATTLE

For three days they trekked across the plain. The tree-studded veldt gave way to grassy savanna and the grass grew shorter and sparser. The soil was brick red now and vegetation grew poorly. Water was something you found in greenish sinks instead of rivers or streams and trees became a memory.

Several times they saw large columns of dust to the north, as if distant armies were on the march. They tried to go between them and saw nothing. The herds had been left behind them on the veldt and now even the antelopelike runners were scarce.

There were signs, however. Twice they crossed ground which had been torn up by treads. Once the tread marks were accompanied by what appeared to be enormous footprints, as if some unimaginable two-legged beast had been following the vehicles.

On mid-afternoon of the third day they were approaching a low ridge of reddish earth when Karin called a sudden halt.

"Wait." She held up her hand and dug something out of her pouch. "There is magic ahead of us."

Gilligan reached for his gun. "What kind?"

"It doesn't tell me that, only . . ."

With a thundering roar a tank burst over the hill. Beside it came three two-legged robots, springing forward on back-flexing limbs. While the tank nosed up and over the hill, the robots leaped over the ridge like giant grasshoppers.

Stigi reared back, wings spread and neck extended, and roared a challenge. Karin dropped to one knee and had the bow off her shoulder and an arrow nocked in one fluid motion. Without seeming to aim she fired at the tank.

The arrow hit the tank's armor without seeming effect. With a roar of its engine it continued down the hill straight at the party.

"Run for it!" Gilligan yelled and dashed to his left to try to circle the attackers. Seeing his action, Karin broke right.

Stigi had a different idea. The dragon inhaled and blasted a gout of flame straight ahead, bathing the tank in fire. The flame splashed off the tank, but here and there it caught. A tiny tongue of orange licked out of the deck behind the turret. It spouted thick black smoke and grew larger. The tank stopped and the tongue turned into a gout of orange and black as something in the machine's engine compartment caught.

Meanwhile Karin had dropped to her knee and fired another arrow at one of the robots. Again her aim was true and again the robot continued to advance apparently unheeding.

Karin tried to run again, but as she rose she got tangled in the lower limb of her bow and went sprawling into the sand. She rolled to the side and threw her arm up in a futile attempt to shield herself from the advancing robot.

The robot never noticed. It continued unerringly straight toward the place where she had been. Then it emitted a despairing whine and toppled into the sand beside her.

Karin looked up, shook sand from her eyes and tried to locate Mick and Stigi.

Mick's sudden dash had attracted the attention of two of the robots and now he was frantically dodging blasts of energy from their snout cannons. By a combination of broken-field running and dive-and-roll, he had managed to stay ahead of them so far, but the robots had split up and they were coming at him from different directions.

Karin grabbed another arrow, but Stigi reached Mick first. With a roar, the dragon charged full on into one of the robots, catching it at knee level in a way that would have earned him a clipping penalty if they had been playing football. The robot lurched forward onto its snout, then got its feet under it and tried to rise.

It got halfway up when a whipping blow from Stigi's tail hammered it to the ground again. This time the robot didn't try to rise. It swiveled its body around to face the on-rushing dragon and let loose with a bolt from its cannon.

Fortunately energy cannons don't work any better than regular ones when the barrel is full of sand. There was a muffled "whump" and the cannon barrel glowed cherry red and went limp. Stigi grabbed the fifteen-foot-tall robot in his powerful jaws and shook it the way a terrier shakes a rat, slamming it into the ground and tossing it into the air until pieces began to fly off.

Meanwhile, Karin's arrow had found the third robot. It took two more steps and collapsed with the iron arrow sticking straight out of its back.

Craig frowned at the glowing display. He had sent a light scout force scooting along the southern edge of the play area to try to get behind his opponent's main body. Now something had knocked them out.

Sending a stronger force south to engage whatever his scouts had hit was bad strategy. It would dilute his main strength. He decided to send a recon flier south to check it out. Then he turned his attention back to the battle that was shaping up between his warbot columns and his enemy's main force. If he worked quickly enough he might be able to catch them in a pincer.

❖   ❖   ❖

"Mick, are you all right?"

Gilligan put his hands on his knees and bent forward to take deep, heaving breaths. He was too winded to talk so he shook his head and made a waving off motion to Karin.

Mechanically, Karin walked over to the third robot and pulled her arrow out of its back.

"Stigi, release!" she commanded. With a clank and a clatter, the dragon reluctantly dropped its much-mangled new toy so Karin could retrieve her arrow.

By this time Mick had gotten enough breath back to stand up and look around. Off in the distance he could see plumes of dust rising into the burning sky. Karin was staring intently at the flaming mass that had been the tank.

"Come on!" Gilligan grabbed her arm.

"But my arrow!"

"We don't have time," he panted. "Let's get the hell out of here before reinforcements arrive."

She nodded and they set off, Karin at a fast walk, Gilligan at an exhausted shamble and Stigi, prancing from pride, bringing up the rear.

After about a half a mile, they stopped for a moment to get their bearings and let Mick catch his breath.

"Were those more of your people's creations?" Karin asked.

"The only place I've seen stuff like that is on Saturday morning cartoons." He caught her puzzled look. "No, we don't have anything like that."

"The enemy then."

"Whatever they were before it's a safe bet they are our enemies now." He looked out at the dust clouds in the distance.

"I'll bet they are not alone either."

"Probably not," Karin said in a small voice. Then she put her head up. "We must go more carefully and quietly," she added more firmly.

"What we must do," Mick told her, "is get the hell out of here while we still have the opportunity."

"You are free to go."

"Look, we dodged the bullet this time, but only barely. What do we do if we meet a bigger force? And another thing. That unit is going to be missed. This place has about as much cover as a billiard table and when they start looking we're going to stand out like bugs on a plate."

"We must find out more," Karin said stubbornly.

Mick threw up his hands.

"All right, but if we're going to commit suicide, let's at least do it intelligently. Let's find some cover and rest while we work out the best approach."

Finding cover turned out to be easier said than done. Finally they discovered a deep wash that offered some protection from ground level observation. Stigi hunkered down against the bank and made like a rock and Karin and Mick sat in the shade near his head.

"We had best move only at night from now on," Karin said as she dropped down next to Gilligan. "That way they cannot see us."

"Don't bet on it. There's a real good chance at least some of that equipment has infrared sensors. At night we will stand out even better."

"What do you suggest then? Aside from turning back?"

"I think we'd better look for cover. The land's been getting drier ever since we left our old campsite, so I don't think we're going to find any forests. But its also been rising. I'd be willing to bet that there are places not far from here that are cut up by arroyos and canyons. That's not as good as trees but it will give us some cover."

Karin nodded. "Since the land rises off to the east, that is the way we should go then."

She stopped and frowned. "What is that sound?"

Gilligan's hearing was damaged from years around jet engines, but he heard it too, a low, hissing whine. Unlike Karin he knew what it was.

"Get down!" he shouted.

The black bat shape glided over the gully without stopping or turning. There was no time to hide. Mick and

Karin froze where they were. Stigi opened an eye and for an awful moment Mick was afraid the dragon would stick his head up to see what was going on, but there were no interesting smells or sounds so the dragon decided it wasn't worth the effort.

Eventually the flier meandered off to the south and finally over the horizon. They stayed frozen a long minute more and then relaxed.

"A scout?" Karin said shakily.

"Probably. Trying to find those things we knocked out."

"Then we had best move quickly. Perhaps we can reach those hills you spoke of by nightfall."

She signalled Stigi to his feet and Gilligan shouldered his pack.

"What the hell is that?" Mikey demanded. He had taken his time coming in answer to Craig's urgent summons and he obviously wasn't happy about being called to give a second opinion on a piece of metal.

"I think it's an arrow. We found it sticking in the hull of a burned-out tank on the edge of the wargame area," Craig told him. "I don't know how it works yet, but it's magic somehow."

"And all metal, too. What have you got out there? Robot Indians?"

"Whatever it is did a number on one of my Troll class tanks and three Springer Warbots. One of them was all messed up, like it had been run over by a bulldozer."

"So what do you want me to do?"

"I just figured you should know about it."

"All right, I know. What are you going to do?"

"I'm going to send some more patrols down that way. And mount more sensors on the stuff I'm testing." He paused. "Oh yeah, I'm going to send drones out to map and scout this whole fucking island. Maybe there's something out there we ought to know about."

He looked at Mikey. "I thought maybe you had some

magic or technology or something that could help," he said hesitantly.

"Shit," Mikey said informatively.

"Huh."

"I said shit. S-h-i-t. Shit. That's what all this robot stuff is. It's shit."

"How are we going to fight without weapons?" Craig demanded.

"And you call those weapons?" Mikey sneered. "Things that can be wiped out by arrows."

He came around the table and moved close to Craig. "Listen to me, little man. The ones who brought us here have got power you can't imagine. They gave us the ability to create fucking anything and what do you do? You waste your time with comic book toys."

"They're not toys!" Craig yelled. "They're the most powerful weapons man has yet devised!"

"*Man* has yet devised," Mikey mimicked. "That's how limited your thinking is. This hasn't got anything to do with *man*. We're beyond *man*." He stepped back and grew calmer. "You were a mistake, do you know that? Instead of spending your time really learning about how to dominate worlds, you hide down here with your *toys*. Why don't you come up to the real world and let the Ur-elves show you what power is?"

"I don't like them," Craig mumbled. "They make me uncomfortable."

"And because you're uncomfortable you won't take advantage of what we're offered. Christ Jesus! Play with your toys. You're too fucking pathetic to do anything else!" With that he turned and stomped off.

He stopped at the door. "Oh yeah. From now on, if you've got anything to say to me, you come see me."

"Goddamn motherfucker sonofabitch!" Craig screamed at the door. That arrogant bag of shit! Just tossing it off like all the work he'd done was nothing. Just didn't count next to *his* high and mighty projects.

He grabbed the iron arrow off the table and threw it against the wall. It clanged off and the wastebasket scuttled under it to catch it as it fell.

Goddamn that sonofabitch! Why, he could take on NATO and the Warsaw Pact and stomp them both with what he had here. There wasn't an army on earth that could stand against what was here in the castle and out in the wargame area.

With an angry gesture he turned on the scanner. The central display showed the arrays of forces in neat green and gold symbols. Around the edges were six smaller screens, each showing a view of part of the battlefield in full color. The units were poised and ready. Except for scouts nothing had moved since he found the destroyed patrol.

Looking at the main map he saw that a platoon of green tanks was just over a small rise from a battalion of yellow armor. Perfect situation for the kind of fast-moving ambush he loved. With the mouse he turned both units on and took control of the green force. Quickly he moved them into position hull down behind the ridge and opened fire on the advancing battalion at barely 200 yards.

Six yellow tanks died in the first salvo and four more before the yellows could return fire. Their first shots were ineffective but they were maneuvering for cover and the next green shots only destroyed two more tanks.

Twelve to nothing. It was the time to scoot, but Craig held his ground, firing salvo after salvo into the deploying yellow forces.

Now it wasn't all one-sided. The yellow battalion had taken cover and was returning accurate fire. The battalion's SP battery opened up, walking volleys of tank-killing shells toward his platoon's position. First one and then another of his green tanks blew up and turned dark.

"God*damn you!*" Craig yelled and ordered his remaining tanks to charge directly into the lead elements of the battalion, all guns firing. He lost two more tanks in the wild charge and then he ran the survivors head-on into the remains of the battalion's transport section. Tanks ground over jeeps, butted trucks off the road and smashed scout cars. Then the battalion artillery began firing into its own supply train and in seconds it was all over.

Craig screamed in frustration and scanned the board. There was a section of warbots in the next hex over, 130-ton monsters with limited flight capability. They were also on the gold side, but that didn't matter. Taking direct command of the unit, Craig sent them hurtling toward the armored battalion even as it reorganized for the march.

The battalion was massacred before it could even deploy again. Salvo after salvo of missiles tore through the armored column. Multi-gigawatt battle lasers raked it from end to end, blowing up tanks and simply melting smaller vehicles. Finally the warbots themselves closed, smashing tanks beneath their enormous feet and picking up vehicles and flinging them for hundreds of yards.

"Yes!" Craig yelled and hunched over the screen. As fast as he could move the mouse he ordered a general engagement. Everything was to attack everything else.

What had been a relatively well-planned large-scale exercise turned into a mechanical armageddon. From one end to the other the central plain of the exercise area blazed with explosions, laser blasts and burning vehicles and robots. Artillery batteries fired on the units they were supposed to be supporting or turned their guns on each other. Recklessly tanks crashed together. Warbots tore other warbots limb from mechanical limb.

Where the battle wasn't fierce enough or the destruction great enough, Craig took direct command of his units, overriding their carefully programmed tactics in an urge to slaughter. Blind and unheeding, robots charged forward in obedience to their master's command. They didn't even break stride when they reached laser range. Instead they slammed into each other, flailing with their arms and butting their heads against each others' armored carapaces.

Finally it was over. On all the plain there were no more

units capable of movement. Every damaged unit had fired off every available round, even if it meant beating the bare earth senselessly with machine guns. The few units that had ammunition they could not fire set it off in the magazines in an orgy of self-destruction.

Looking down on the destruction he had caused, Craig felt more relaxed. His fury at Mikey had died to a dull resentment. The guy was an asshole, but hey, it didn't matter much. They'd go into battle soon enough and when they did, Craig would show him what this stuff was worth.

As he rose from his command chair Craig remembered about the scouts. He still needed to scout the rest of the island. Well, he'd start making more tomorrow.

THIRTY-FIVE

COSMIC SQUARE DANCE

The blue thing on the screen wove and interwove. It divided, branched and rejoined in a complex, twisting pattern that hinted at an order beyond human imagining.

"How goes the work, Sparrow?"

Wiz jerked his attention away from the screen and saw Duke Aelric standing behind him.

"About like you see. We're making progress, but it's slow going." He reached for the keyboard and called up a second program with a couple of quick commands. Now a yellow thing joined the blue one on the screen. It wove in a complex and elaborate pattern that almost matched the blue one. Wiz moved the mouse and the two shapes melded together into a single form that was mostly green. Here and there, however, patches of yellow and blue still stood out vividly.

"The blue is what we're producing. The yellow is the pattern you gave us," Wiz explained.

The elf duke nodded. "Very good, Sparrow. You make excellent progress."

They watched the shapes for a while without comment.

"Lord, you said there was something stronger behind Craig and Mikey," Wiz said. "What?"

Aelric took his eyes from the screen. "Does it matter,

Sparrow? More to the point, do you think you would understand the explanation?"

"Yes," Wiz said levelly. "I think it does matter. As for the explanation, try me."

"Very well." Duke Aelric stared into the screen and stroked the line of his jaw with a long pale forefinger.

"Perhaps it would be easiest to say that the World as it is today exists because of choices, a multitude of choices made since the first instant of primal chaos. But each of those choices meant that other things were not chosen. In that dance of choose and choose again, some became strong and flourishing while others were made weak or even nonexistent. The patterns of the dance are not to the liking of all and there are those who would alter them."

"So they've set themselves up against the caller in this cosmic square dance?"

"Cosmic . . . ? Ah, I see. No Sparrow, there is no caller to this dance. It is blind chance working itself out through the interaction of chaos and such forces as came out of chaos. But yes, there are—those—that would have things work another way and they seek to alter the pattern, given a lever to work through."

"And Mikey and Craig are the lever?"

"So it would seem."

"And we don't know what it is these others want?"

"I would not wager that they could be said to 'want' anything at all, any more than a river 'wants' to run downhill. However I doubt very much that the World could survive in a pattern that would be more to their liking."

They were both silent for a minute.

"Aelric," Wiz said at last. "My Lord?"

"Hmm?"

"If Jerry and Danny and I can match their programmers are you strong enough to fight the ones who are behind them?"

The elf duke looked down at him with eyes gray and

cold as a winter's sea. "No Sparrow, I am not. Not I and all my kind could stand unaided against them."

"Oh," said Wiz in a very small voice.

"Nor is it needful that we do so," Aelric continued. "The World as it is exists because it is stronger and more stable this way than in any other form it could easily reach. To say that a thing came about by chance is not to say that it can be altered effortlessly once it has happened."

"You can't unscramble an egg," Wiz agreed and then frowned. "Only here you *can* unscramble an egg."

"That does not mean it is equally easy."

"So there's something like an energy gradient these others will have to cross before they can settle the universe into another stable state."

The elf duke paused as if tasting Wiz's words. "That would not be an incorrect way to put it. Perhaps it would be more nearly right to say they seek to create the conditions necessary to tunnel through the gradient to another state."

"Where did you learn about solid-state physics?"

Duke Aelric smiled. "Where did you learn about magic, Sparrow? We teach each other, I think."

Wiz thought that Aelric knew a lot more about physics than he had ever taught Wiz about magic, but he didn't pursue the point.

"You know this sounds an awful lot like cosmology."

"What is cosmology?"

"One of our sciences. The branch of physics that deals with things like the beginning and end of the universe."

The elf duke smiled. "Then this is cosmology."

Wiz turned that over in his mind and then returned to the main point.

"What you're saying then is that we can take them."

"What I am saying, Sparrow, is that there is a chance that we can take them. But first and above all else, you must wrest this new lever from their hands."

"That doesn't sound very hopeful."

"It is not hopeless, Sparrow. Leave it at that."

He nodded with mock gravity. "Now, are there any other matters on which I may set your mind at rest?"

Wiz took a deep breath. "Yes. What does Lisella want?"

Again that marrow-freezing stare. "What the Demoselle Lisella wants is none of your concern, Sparrow. She has not bothered you again, has she? No? Then dismiss her from your mind."

"But you've met her here."

"How do you know?"

"Someone saw you."

"Sparrow, you would do well to concentrate on matters of import, not my intrigues by moonlight. What is between the Demoselle and myself is none of yours. Now, is there aught else?"

"Just one other thing. Are those dwarves who are trying to kill me part of the Others' plan?"

Aelric's laugh was like the peal of a silver bell. "Believe me, Sparrow, they are not." He sobered. "No, that is a matter between you and others of this world, mortal or non-mortal, I think. But be wary of them, Sparrow. They can be dangerous."

THIRTY-SIX

A VISIT WITH MIKEY

Craig couldn't really name the impulse that drove him
to visit Mikey. He hadn't seen him since Mikey had
called his weapons "toys." He didn't really have anything
he needed to talk to him about. But he still decided
to go. Maybe he could explain to Mikey about his new
robots. Maybe Mikey would apologize for the things he'd
said. Maybe whatever, he hadn't talked to anyone but
robots for weeks.

Craig hadn't been in Mikey's part of the castle for a
while and Mikey had made some changes since then.
Where Craig's work area was modelled on a laboratory,
airy and brightly lighted, Mikey's wing was gloomy as a
smoggy twilight. The further he penetrated the dimmer
and redder the light became until he felt he was pushing his way through blood-soaked gloom.

He turned the corner and started climbing stairs. The
walls fell away as he climbed until the staircase seemed
to stretch up into a bleak, blood-lit, starless sky. *Come
on*, he told himself, *this is just an illusion. You know
you're still inside the castle*. But somehow that only made
the illusion stronger. The wind whistled around him,
tugging at his jacket and whipping his jeans against his
legs. There were hints of shapes in the sky above him,

huge dark-on-dark things that shifted and twisted in ways his eye couldn't quite follow.

Craig shivered and stayed close to the center of the railless staircase. He thrust his hands deeper into the pockets of his windbreaker and kept his eyes on the stairs under his feet.

Suddenly he was there. There was no door, no anteroom. Just a pool of light at the top of the stairs and Mikey hunched over a desk in the middle of it.

As he reached the top Mikey regarded him in a not-quite-hostile manner.

"What brings you here?"

Craig shifted uncomfortably. "Well, I hadn't seen you in a while and I just felt like coming to see you, you know?"

Mikey grunted and turned back to his work. Craig stood uneasily as the silence stretched out and the wind whipped and whistled around them.

"This is kinda spooky," he said at last.

"I like it," Mikey said without looking up.

The silence dragged out as Craig stared at Mikey's back.

"You look like you've been learning a lot." Craig tried to flog his enthusiasm. "It must have taken some real magic to put this place together."

"Yeah," Mikey said. "I've been learning. That and a whole lot more."

"Oh?" Craig asked brightly. "Like what?"

"Like philosophy, man. I've really clarified my thinking." He smiled and for an instant the old, charming Mikey flashed through. "You know who really owns something? The person who can trash it. Just fucking ruin it completely. That's how you know the real owner."

"But what about the guy who can use it? You know, build something with it?"

"So what? If he can't protect it, he doesn't really own it. It's like a computer. The name on the paper may say it belongs to IBM or Pac Bell, but that doesn't mean shit.

The people who really owned those computers were people like me who could get at them any time we wanted to."

Craig laughed nervously. "Man, you're getting heavy."

Mikey smiled. "Heavy times. Our friends now, they understand that. You know what those guys are really? They're the greatest goddamn hackers of all!" The smile grew wider, dreamier. "Man, this is gonna be great."

"Yeah, but there are people out there, you know?"

"So? If they can't protect it, they don't own it. Simple as that."

"Yeah," said Craig desperately, "but you don't have to destroy something to prove you own it, right? I mean it's enough to know that you can do it, isn't it?"

"Yeah," Mikey said with the same dreamy smile. "Sometimes that's enough."

"So all this is really theoretical, isn't it?" Craig pressed. "I mean it's not like you're actually gonna destroy anything, are you?"

Mikey came out of his trance and regarded him closely. "Sure it's all theoretical." He turned away from Craig and back to the crystal thing on his desk. "Just theoretical."

Craig hesitated, torn between a desire to press his companion for more assurances and the fear he might not get them. Finally he turned away, mumbled something about needing to get back to work, and started down the dark and twisting stairs.

Mikey didn't even grunt goodbye.

THIRTY-SEVEN

CHUCK JONES'S CAT

"Not only is the universe stranger than you imagine, it is stranger than you can imagine."

— *J.B.S. Haldane*

"And so are all the other universes."

— *Wiz Zumwalt*

Jerry and Danny listened intently when Wiz related what Duke Aelric had told him.

"That's weird," Danny said when Wiz had finished. "I wonder how much of it is true."

Jerry leaned back in his chair and put his feet up on the console. "What I want to know is what stirred these things up. If they've been around forever why did they pick *now* to start causing trouble?"

"Duke Aelric talked about that some when he first joined us," Wiz said. "He thinks it's because of us. Our brand of magic apparently triggered something." He glanced past Jerry's feet to the console screen where the convoluted blue shape slowly rotated.

"I think the whole thing's crazy," Danny said. "Is he still around?"

"Aelric? I don't think so. I think he left again right after I talked to him."

"Pity," Jerry said. "I would have liked to ask him some questions about this."

"Bet you wouldn't get any straight answers."

Before Wiz could reply the door opened and Moira came into the computer room carrying a wicker basket with a cloth over it.

"Forgive me, my Lords, but I thought you might enjoy some refreshment," she said as she put the basket down on the console.

Wiz started to object to covering up the stacks of papers, but then Moira folded back the cloth and he goggled instead.

"Doughnuts! Where did you learn to make doughnuts?"

"Jerry took me to a doughnut shop while I was in your world. I liked them, but it took me some little time to master the recipe."

Wiz grabbed a chocolate-frosted chocolate a fraction ahead of Jerry's and Danny's reaching hands. He took half of it in one bite and closed his eyes in bliss.

"You sure got it right. This is wonderful."

"You said it," Danny enthused, spewing crumbs from his second choice over Moira's skirt.

The hedge witch dimpled and bobbed a curtsey. "Thank you, my Lords. Now, if you will excuse me, I must see to the unpacking of our latest load of supplies."

"Won't you have some with us?" Wiz asked his wife.

"Thank you, no. I, ah, sampled several while I was making them. I fear I am more than somewhat full." She turned toward the door. "Do not eat too many and ruin your appetites. June is preparing something special for dinner." Behind her Wiz nodded and reached for his third doughnut.

For several minutes the only sound in the computer room was working jaws. Eventually a combination of sated appetites and an increasingly limited selection made the three more talkative.

"If she can whip up doughnuts why can't she make coffee to go with them?" Danny asked.

"She didn't like coffee when she tried it," Jerry told him. "She liked doughnuts."

"Okay, but why so many maple ones? Everyone hates maple."

"I think they were her favorites."

"Anyway," Wiz put in, "isn't there something about looking gift horses in the mouth?"

"Yeah. Sorry," Danny said perfunctorily.

"You know," Jerry said after a moment, "what Aelric said almost makes sense in a quantum mechanical sort of way."

Wiz looked around. "I'm not sure *anything* makes sense here," he said.

"They've been saying that about quantum mechanics for years," Jerry said. "Anyway, this might, if you looked at it right."

Wiz picked through the basket and selected a jelly doughnut as the best of the remaining batch. Then he turned back to his friends. "I'll bite. What does quantum mechanics have to do with these bad guys?"

"Okay, you know that in quantum mechanics you deal with the position of a particle in terms of probabilities? There's a probability wave and the particle is most likely to be found at the wave's greatest magnitude and less likely to be found at lower magnitudes. But the point is, you don't know exactly where it is."

Danny rummaged through the basket. "So? Are there any more chocolate ones?"

"I think you ate them all, but as I was saying, we already know that something like quantum effects occur here on a macroscopic scale. Remember when we tried to play cards? The shuffled deck was in something like a quantum indeterminate state. We had to create a demon to collapse the state vector by looking at the cards before we could play. Otherwise the deck would respond to everyone's mental desires and you'd end up with everyone holding four aces or the like."

Jerry took another swig of tea from his mug. "It's as if the line between reality and unreality is drawn at a higher level here. Some things don't become real here until someone becomes aware of them."

Wiz took a bite of his doughnut and chewed thoughtfully, dribbling powdered sugar down his chin.

"How does that tie in with these—things—that want to destroy the World?"

"Well, there's an alternate interpretation of quantum mechanics from a guy named Everett which says that what we're really seeing is multiple worlds, all equally real. What collapsing the state vector really means is that we've chosen among them. One of them becomes 'real' because we've taken that branch of the skein of parallel universes and that makes the others unreal."

Wiz put his doughnut down on the console behind him and rubbed his chin thoughtfully, leaving white streaks on his cheek.

"That would explain a lot about this place. For instance, why there are some operations that seem to be basic that we can't use in our magic language because they're unstable."

"Yes," Jerry said slowly. "We've been beating our brains out because we thought they have to be composed of several simpler operations. Maybe there's some kind of uncertainty principle at work and those *are* primitives, they're just one thing one day and another thing the next."

"Well, the appearance of demons is sure influenced by the operator's mental state, unless you specify what they look like in the spell." Wiz wiped at the sugar on his cheek thoughtfully, smearing it out more evenly. "And so these things that Duke Aelric's worried about come from one of these parallel universes?"

"I suppose you could say that they represent a universe with a low-probability wave function that overlaps ours," Jerry said. Then he brightened. "Hey! If I work out the mathematics on this, will that make me the Niels Bohr of this universe?"

"You know . . ." Wiz began and reached behind him for the doughnut. When he couldn't find it he turned to look.

A mouse-sized gremlin was halfway down the desk with the doughnut clasped in front of him. The prize was nearly as big as it was and the gremlin was bent backwards under the load as it staggered away.

"Hey!" Wiz yelled.

The gremlin looked over its shoulder at Wiz, grinned, and broke into a wobbly run. Right to the edge of the desk and several steps beyond into empty air.

Suddenly the grin faded. The little creature looked down and saw it was standing on nothing. Its face fell and its bat ears drooped to its shoulders.

"Uh oh," it squeaked. Then gremlin and doughnut plummeted to the floor.

As the gremlin scuttled away, Wiz walked over, picked up the doughnut, brushed it off and took a second bite.

"I don't know if that makes you Niels Bohr," he began again, "but if you're right I think Chuck Jones is the Erwin Schrödinger of this universe."

"Who's Chuck Jones?" asked Jerry.

"Who's Erwin Schrödinger?" asked Danny.

Halfway to the hills Mick and Karin met a ruined army.

They smelled it before they saw it. The stink of burning rubber and insulation, of overheated metal and cordite. Of dust churned up in the heat of battle.

But there was no sound of combat. No artillery, no engines. Not even the shouts of men. Cautiously, Karin and Mick eased to the top of a rise and peered over it.

The panorama was so big and so torn up it was hard to tell what had happened here. Gilligan thought of the pictures he had seen of the destruction at Mitla Pass in the Sinai during the Six-Day War. But this was worse than any of those pictures. It seemed that the destroyed equipment spread over the plain for miles in front of them.

His first instinct was to go around, even if it meant walking for miles. But there was no hint of movement anywhere on that enormous battlefield, no contrails in the sky. Except for the occasional crackle of flame and the whistle of the wind there was nothing.

"Well?" Karin asked.

"I say go across. It's risky, but we're low on water. Besides, we'll be harder to spot out among all that junk than we would be out on the plain."

The dragon rider nodded and went back to get her mount.

It took hours to cross the battlefield.

They walked past a line of what looked like self-propelled guns—if self-propelled guns had barrels made of glass that would droop and melt under the effects of enemy weapons.

Here a half-dozen tanks in various stages of destruction confronted the remains of a fifty-foot-tall robot they had pulled down like wolves on an elk. Further on were the remains of a missile battery caught on the march and burned while trying to deploy.

But there were no bodies. The wind brought the smell of burnt vehicles but not a trace of the sweetish stink of burning flesh. Not even the carrion birds seemed interested in this plain of dead machines.

"Mick," Karin asked at last, "why do they do this? Do our enemies fight among themselves?"

"I think it's more likely they're just conducting live ammo practices."

"But they are killing their own creations!"

"These things weren't ever alive. They're machines, like my F-15, not living beings like Stigi. I doubt a single living creature lost its life here."

"Still, there is something . . . obscene about all this."

Gilligan shrugged. "For us, war is a material-intense business. You go through a lot of equipment."

But looking over the carnage, Mick tended to agree with her. Even if these things weren't alive, it had taken ingenuity to design them and time and resources to build them. He had been taught that in a war you expended your equipment wholesale in an effort to win. If you struck hard and fast with overwhelming strength you minimized casualties, or so the reasoning went.

Gilligan had always accepted it unthinkingly. Now, wandering among acres of scorched and twisted ruins, he began to appreciate what that meant.

Besides, he thought, *this wasn't a battle. This was an exercise, a test. You don't need to wreck all this just to test it.*

"Mick?" Karin said after they had trudged on in silence for several minutes more. "The people who do this, why do they do it? Why like this?"

"I don't know," Mick told her sadly. "I don't understand their thinking at all."

THIRTY-EIGHT

TRAP

Wiz Zumwalt sat on a rock under a spreading tree and savored the experience. It was cool and pleasant here. The late afternoon sun did not quite reach down through the leaves and the forest around him was alive with birdsong and the skitterings of squirrels and other little animals.

Wiz wondered what season it was. It looked like late summer, but the Bubble World didn't seem to have seasons. *How can a world shaped like a burrito have seasons?* he wondered.

For once the pressure was off. The visualization program was running well, Lannach was keeping the gremlins under control and everything else he could think of to do was done. So he had slipped out of the Mousehole for a couple of hours to do a little exploring.

It was the first time he had really been outside the Mousehole since he arrived and he was enjoying it. No gremlins, no brownies, no elves and no dwarves.

Glandurg could not believe his luck. After all the weeks of hunting and the long weary days of waiting, there was the Sparrow, not two hundred paces away, with his back turned!

And better yet, there was no sign of the protection spell

Snorri had reported. Nothing that would do violence to an attacker. There was magic about him, of course, but after all he was a wizard.

Glandurg nearly hugged himself with glee.

He dropped to his belly and wormed his way forward through the fallen leaves. He moved with exquisite care as he eased his silent way toward the sitting figure. Fifty paces and still no move from his quarry. Twenty. Ten.

Glandurg rose with a rush, took two steps and leaped toward the defenseless Sparrow.

He didn't exactly bounce, but he certainly vibrated. Glandurg had leaped directly into the center of an enormous spider web that sprang up in his path. His sword fell to the leaves, but he remained thoroughly stuck in the mass of sticky strands.

Wiz turned around at the noise and gaped. There was a dwarf hanging upside down in a giant spider's web. The dwarf was struggling frantically and cursing luridly. Wiz didn't speak dwarfish, but it sure sounded lurid.

Wiz waited until the dwarf ran down.

"Now," he said. "Just what is this all about?"

"A protection spell," Glandurg spat. "I might have known."

"You didn't think I'd come walking in the woods without one, did you? I hoped I'd seen the last of you back at the Capital, but I wasn't taking any chances."

Actually Wiz had devised the spell against any wild animals that might be lurking in the forest. He didn't want to kill them, so he had settled for something that would immobilize an attacker.

"You know, I'm sort of glad you did show up," Wiz said. "Now maybe you'll tell me what this is all about."

Glandurg nodded and the gesture made his beard fall in his face. He shook his head to clear his eyes.

"Meet it is that you should know the cause and agent of your doom," he said in his best skaldic voice. Or at least the best voice he could manage suspended upside down in midair.

"I hight Glandurg; son of Megli, praised above all smiths; son of Famlir, who fell in the battle of Breccan's Doom; son of . . ."

"Yes, I'm sure you're from a very distinguished line," Wiz cut him off, "but that doesn't explain why you're trying to kill me."

The dwarf glared. Mortals had no sense of family and no appreciation for skaldic recitation.

"My uncle is Tosig Longbeard, King of the Dwarves. To fulfill a debt he has commissioned me to seek your death. To this end I have sworn mighty oaths that my quest shall end in your death or my own."

"Uh, I don't suppose we can talk about this?"

The dwarf looked uncomfortable. "I am sorry, Wizard. You are brave and honorable and you are working for the good of all our World. But I have sworn a quest and you must die to satisfy it."

Wiz bent and picked up Glandurg's fallen sword.

"I can't very well let you go, you know. I can't be looking over my shoulder at every moment."

"Wait," Glandurg said quickly. "I cannot forgo my sacred mission but I can postpone it. If you release me, I swear to take no action against you," he made a motion as if to cross his heart, "until you have fulfilled your own work."

Wiz considered. He didn't have much stomach for killing anyway.

"All right," he said finally. "Swear to that and I'll let you go."

Glandurg moved his hands again. "I do swear that I shall not try to slay you until your battle with your enemies is over. I swear by the moon for as long as it is in the sky."

"Fine," Wiz said. He turned and started to walk away.

"Wizard," Glandurg called, "what about me?"

"Oh, the web will dissolve in six or eight hours," Wiz told him. "I'm sorry, but I can't get rid of it before that."

Besides, he thought as Glandurg's curses died behind him, *I'm not sure how far I trust you.*

❖   ❖   ❖

"Well, that's one less problem anyway," Wiz said as he walked into the Mousehole's lounge. Aelric and the other programmers were nowhere to be seen, but Bal-Simba and Moira were there.

Bal-Simba looked up at him quizzically.

"The dwarves," Wiz said, plopping down on a sofa. "I just got them off my back."

"They are here?" Moira demanded.

Wiz nodded. "Their leader just tried to jump me. He ran right into my protection spell and before I'd let him go I made him promise he wouldn't try to kill me any more. At least," he amended, "not until this business with Craig and Mikey is finished."

"You made a deal with a dwarf," Moira said slowly.

"Uh, yeah."

"Sparrow," Bal-Simba said slowly, "what *precisely* did the dwarf swear to?"

"He promised he wouldn't kill me until this business is over."

"Can you remember his exact words?"

"Yeah. He said, 'I will not slay you until your battle with your adversaries is over.' Well, that's pretty close anyway."

Moira moaned.

"Is something wrong?"

Bal-Simba put a huge hand on Wiz's shoulder. "Sparrow, there are scant dealings between mortals and dwarves, but this much we have learned. A dwarf keeps only his exact, literal word. They are slippery as river eels and will wiggle through any least little hole left in an agreement."

"There's a hole in this one?" Wiz asked in a sinking voice.

"Sparrow, how many dwarves are we dealing with?"

"About a doz . . . oh," Wiz said in a small voice. "And he promised only for himself."

The black wizard nodded. "He only swore that he

himself would not kill you. He did not even promise he would not help the others."

"Oh," Wiz said again.

It was almost nightfall by the time Glandurg's followers found him. The wait had done nothing to improve his temper.

"What happened to you?" Gimli asked in awe at the sight of his leader hanging enmeshed in sticky ropes.

"Never mind that, get me down!"

"He tried the Sparrow alone, he did," Ragnar told Gimli. "I recognize the signs."

"Now," the red-faced Glandurg ground out, "now I shall have him."

"Looks as if he had you," Ragnar observed. "Trussed you up like a spider to a fly."

"Just cut me down," Glandurg growled.

The dwarves set about it, but it was a sticky, tedious business. While they hacked and sawed Glandurg fumed and muttered.

"I will have his heart's blood."

"Can't very well do that," Thorfin said from the tree limb where he was cutting away at one of the last strands of the web. "You said you swore an oath you wouldn't harm him until after he's completed his own quest."

"I swore so long as the moon was in the sky," Glandurg amended.

Ragnar gaped. "He let you get away with that?"

"I am cleverer than any mortal wizard," Glandurg said smugly. "It was the first oath I offered and he took it."

Thorfin looked up at the darkening sky where a sliver of waning moon hung high. "And the moon has, what, eight, nine more days? Then it will be the dark of the moon and it will be gone completely." While he was looking up his knife severed the strand and Glandurg fell heavily to earth.

The dwarf rose and brushed off the last clinging bits of web. "Mark you, I shall use the time well. I have sent to my uncle the king for a thing which will finish this Sparrow once and for all."

And maybe this time he'll let me have it, Glandurg thought to himself.

Tosig Longbeard, king of the Mid-Northeastern Dwarves of the Southern Forest Range, fidgeted uneasily on his alabaster throne and waited for his visitor to get down to business. The smoky torches flared in their wall sockets, throwing distorted shadows dancing over the carved and inlaid walls of his audience chamber, but there were none but himself and his visitor to see. His court, his seneschal and even his guards had been withdrawn because Aelric, the most powerful elf west of the mountains, had "begged the favor" of a private audience.

Dwarves and elves have scant dealings and Tosig had absolutely no idea why one of the greatest elves should come to call. He noted his guest was carefully treating him to every shred of courtesy and respect to which he was entitled. Somehow that was not reassuring.

First there were the formalities to get through. Elves are notoriously punctilious and dwarves are sticklers for forms and honors, so that had taken time. Further, elves are as courteous and delicate as trolls are rude and direct. After half a morning's pleasantries, Tosig almost preferred the trolls.

At last, when Tosig was ready to scream, the elf turned to the subject at hand.

"I understand your nephew has undertaken a quest to fulfill a promise you made to the troll kings."

"He's not my nephew," Tosig snapped. Then he softened. "But, ah, yes, a minor kinsman of mine is off doing some small service for the trolls."

Aelric said nothing for a space. Tosig watched him warily. This elf was known to consort with mortals, including even this strange wizard the trolls wanted dead. Were he to take a hand in the business . . .

"The honor of dwarves in keeping their promises is

well-known," Aelric said. "It would be tragic if such an important promise were not kept because your relative was not given full support."

"I've supported that insufferable young pup to the limit of my purse and beyond!" Tosig burst out. "Oh, if you only know what this thing has cost me first and last. The supplies, the gold paid to griffins because he and his friends were too good to walk like ordinary dwarves. And always more demands. More supplies, more treasure. More gold to the griffins. More . . ." He stopped and beat his chest to relieve the burning pain. "I have supported him," he finished.

"But perhaps not with everything asked for?" Aelric murmured. "There was mention of a sword, I believe?"

"Blind Fury?" Tosig screamed. "Never! Never in a thousand lifetimes I tell you!" He dissolved into a choking fit.

"A great treasure to be sure," Aelric agreed. "And yet after all you have done it would be ironic if you were blamed for—lack of support."

"Greed," Tosig grated. "Say it outright! Dwarves are miserly and for my miserliness I would not risk giving Glandurg the sword Blind Fury."

"*I* would never say such a thing."

"But others would and you wouldn't correct them. Bah! Even for an elf you're mealy mouthed."

Aelric only nodded gracefully in a way that indicated he was much too well-bred to argue with his host.

Tosig drummed his fingers on the throne arm. He could afford to turn his back on his debt to the trolls if he had Glandurg for a sacrificial goat. But to have an elf telling such a tale . . . Well, it would ruin his tribe's trade for generations.

"The thing's cursed, you know," he said at last. "And the boy's incompetent. He's had a score of chances at this alien wizard and muffed them all. Sword won't do him a bit of good."

Aelric made a throw-away gesture with one elegant

hand. "As you say, I am sure. Yet the point is not whether your nephew . . ."

"Don't call him my nephew!" Tosig barked. "He isn't my nephew, rot him!"

"Your relative then. The point is not whether he accomplishes his mission, only that you cannot possibly be blamed for his failure." The elf arched a silvery eyebrow. "Besides, the wielder of Blind Fury is invincible in battle. Who knows what even your—relative—might accomplish with it?"

Tosig glared at the elf and continued to beat a tattoo on the throne arm. He was trapped and they both knew it.

"Why are you so interested in this anyway?" the dwarf king demanded. "I thought you had dealings with the wizard."

"Oh, I do," Aelric told him. "However there is the matter of a prophecy. It were best if it were fulfilled." A strange expression flashed across the elf's face. "Fulfilled in all its particulars."

"Behold the sword Blind Fury!"

Glandurg brandished the weapon aloft and the other dwarves crowded around. They had all heard stories of the great treasure of their tribe, but none of them had ever seen it before. Never in the memory of a living dwarf had the enchanted sword left the deepest, strongest treasury.

It was worth seeing. The golden hilt gleamed, throwing sparks and highlights where the sun's rays caught a bit of carving or granulation at just the right angle. The rubies and sapphires set in the hilt glowed with inner fires and the fist-size emerald in the pommel flashed and flamed.

In fact, it was downright gaudy.

That was fine with the dwarves, whose taste for gaudy is perhaps exceeded only by Las Vegas architects. But it was also deadly. The double-edged blade glittered in the

sunlight with a sinister brilliance that threatened to out-
shine the hilt. The blade was as wide as a man's palm
and nearly as long as a dwarf was tall and the magic of
it twisted the air around it like heat waves in a mirage.

Glandurg could not conceal his glee. "One stroke! One
stroke and the Sparrow is finished! Nothing can stop Blind
Fury and he who wields it cannot be harmed in battle."

"Can we see?" Gimli asked eagerly.

"Yes," Ragnar said. "Show us."

The others took up the chorus. "Yes. Yes. Show us."

Glandurg smiled and nodded. Obviously the sword had
gone a long way toward restoring his tattered prestige with
his followers. He didn't tell them he had asked King Tosig
for it before setting out and received a rebuff that singed
his beard.

He marched to the edge of the clearing where a log
nearly two feet thick lay against a head-high boulder.

"Observe the log," he said. He wound up and swung
at the log with all his strength.

Blind Fury whistled through the air and Thorfin
jumped back as the tip removed the bottom six inches
of his beard. With an evil hiss the weapon missed the log
completely and bit deeply into a boulder, cleaving the rock
to the ground.

The dwarf looked around. Thorfin was fingering the
end of his newly trimmed beard and several of the other
dwarves were looking at the newly split boulder with a
combination of wonder and skepticism.

"I meant to do that," Glandurg told the watching
dwarves. "Now stand back and give me room."

The others needed no urging. They backed off to give
him a good twenty feet of room in every direction.

Glandurg hefted the sword. In the back of his mind
it came to him that there were stories about how Blind
Fury got its name.

"Now watch," he said. This time he did not specify a
target.

Again he raised the sword over his head, braced his

feet apart and swung a mighty blow. He was aiming at
the boulder but the blade's arc flashed past the stone and
on around and into the oak tree beside him. Glandurg
was dragged along helplessly but Blind Fury sliced through
the three-foot trunk as if it wasn't there.

Slowly, majestically, the tree rocked, teetered and began
to fall—straight toward the watching dwarves. Dwarves
scattered in every direction as the oak crashed down on
them. The trunk itself missed Glandurg by scant inches
where he stood holding the enchanted sword.

Wiz looked up from where he was checking some
wiring in the computer room. "What was that crash?"

Jerry, who was closer to the window, looked out. "Just
a tree falling up on the hillside."

"Oh," Wiz said, turning back to the wiring. "Nothing
important then."

A curse! Yes, that was it, Glandurg remembered. There
was a curse on the sword. Dwarfish faces began poking
out among the still-shaking leaves of the fallen tree.
Somehow they didn't show the respect they had a few
minutes ago.

"Well, that's enough of that, isn't it?" Glandurg said.
"Hand me the scabbard, will you?"

THIRTY-NINE

PROTECTION

It was just after dawn and Wiz was finishing up an all-nighter on a workstation when a shadow swept over the window. He jerked his head up in time to see a dragon land almost at the front entrance of the Mousehole.

It looked like a league dragon, but Wiz grabbed his staff and headed for the main door anyway. The dragon scouts were under strict orders to stay away from the Mousehole lest the coming and going of the dragons should attract attention.

By the time he reached the entrance Moira was already there. Of the other programmers or wizards there was no sign, but one of the guardsmen was holding the door for their unexpected guest. As he strode in, Wiz recognized Dragon Leader, the commander of all the League's dragon cavalry.

Dragon Leader was a bowlegged, solid little man with pale blond hair and eyes like the fog off an arctic glacier. He was dusty and he and his flying leathers reeked of the snake-and-sulfur odor of dragon.

"My Lord, my Lady." His head bobbed in something more than a nod and less than a bow. "Forgive me for coming here, but we have a problem I thought you should hear of immediately."

"I understand," Wiz said. "We're still trying to find what's causing the trouble with the communications crystals."

"Thank you, my Lord. But now we have a new problem. In the past two days we have started to encounter enemy scouting demons over the island—well south of their usual routes."

Wiz gripped his staff tighter. "Do you think they know we're here?"

Dragon Leader considered. "So far as we know they have not tried to come this far south. But they are searching the island. That means you are in danger of discovery."

"Well, danger or not we can't leave."

Dragon Leader nodded. "Your decision, Lord. But understand we cannot protect you this close to our enemies' base."

"Understood."

"You should be safe for another ten-day or so. Their scouts are thorough but they do not move as quickly as dragons." He shrugged. "Perhaps they will not come this far south. Or if they do your disguise may fool them."

"But you wouldn't put money on it."

"As I say, Lord, their scouts are thorough."

"Anything else you can tell us?"

"Nothing not in our regular reports. There is constant activity around the castle, but no sign of any more great explosions."

"Okay," Wiz sighed. "Well, thanks for the warning. We'll do what we can."

"Will you stay for refreshment?" Moira asked. "Perhaps a bath?"

"Sorry, my Lady, but I have to rejoin my patrols." He sketched a bow, turned on his heel and strode from the room. A minute later they watched through the windows as man and dragon lifted off in a cloud of dust.

"What is that guy's name anyway?" Wiz asked as they watched their guest dwindle into a dot in the sky.
"Everyone just calls him Dragon Leader."

"Ardithjanelle, which means 'shy flower of the forest,'"

Moira said. "The story is that his parents were expecting a girl child."

Wiz watched the dot for a second. "I think I'll just call him Dragon Leader."

It was less than half an hour after Dragon Leader departed that the still-sleepy programmers, Moira and Duke Aelric met in the day room. Wiz outlined the situation to them and then posed the question on everyone's mind.

"Well, what do we do now?"

"How much longer do we need?" Moira asked.

"Maybe another two weeks, if Lannach can keep those damn gremlins at bay."

"There really isn't much we can do," Jerry said. "We have got to have this place to keep using the supercomputer."

"We could move to another island," Moira suggested, in a tone that indicated she didn't think much of the idea.

Wiz shook his head. "We'd have to stop work, get the system into a stable state, back up everything, move it all and then try to get up and running again. I know companies that have gone broke in the process and they could get spares from the manufacturer if they broke something. Besides, I think those patrols already cover the other islands." He grimaced. "Probably the best we can do is continue here for as long as we can and be ready to cut and run as soon as we're discovered."

"We may have more time than you think," Aelric put in from where he stood. "Our enemies seek something toward the middle of the island. I do not think they will come this far south."

"How do you know that?" Danny asked. Aelric shrugged elegantly.

"Anyway, we need to be ready to bug out if they do find us," Wiz said.

"We can put together some really righteous defenses," Danny said brightly. "I've been working on some ideas."

Moira shook her head. "Not as many as you might think. Defenses attract attention. Powerful ones are likely to shine like a beacon to anyone who can sense magic."

"We discussed this once before, Danny," Wiz said. "The logic still holds. Stealth is better than weapons."

"Shit," said Danny and scowled down at the table top.

"One thing we ought to do is to get as many people off the island as we can," Jerry said. "If we can't defend this place we don't need guardsmen and there is no reason to have as many support people as we have."

"We can all do our share of the cooking and laundry," Wiz agreed.

"Or do it by magic," Moira said to her husband. "Forgive me, Lord, but no one but a goat could stomach your cooking."

"Hey, I lived on it for years."

Moira leaned over and kissed him lightly. "I rest my case."

"In any event," Jerry said, "it's getting too dangerous to keep anyone here who isn't absolutely necessary."

He carefully avoided looking at Danny and so did everyone else in the room.

The brownies hadn't attended the council, so as soon as the meeting broke up, Wiz went to tell them. He found Lannach in the computer room, crouched on his haunches at the rear of the console and apparently talking to someone inside the computer.

"Lannach, we're going to have to pull your people out."

The little man stood up and dusted his knees. "Why, Lord? Are you dissatisfied with our work?"

"No, nothing like that. But Mikey and Craig are getting close to finding this place. We're sending everyone we can spare back."

Lannach frowned. "Forgive me, Lord, but you cannot spare us if you want your computer to work."

"We can't protect you if they find us and attack."

"Lord, we will not leave. Not just for our own safety."

"I don't want that on my conscience."

"It is not upon your head, Lord. It is our decision."

"Thanks, Lannach." Wiz held out his hand. Gravely Lannach took his first two fingers in both his tiny hands and pumped them up and down.

"Look, you've got to go."

It was late and the hall lights had long since dimmed, but Danny and June were still at it.

Again June shook her head so hard her mouse-colored curls beat against her forehead. "You come," she said with undiminished firmness.

"I told you, I can't. I've got to keep working."

June planted herself on the edge of the bed and crossed her arms. "You will not be rid of me," she said fiercely.

He pulled her up off the bed and held her in his arms. "Honey, I don't want to get rid of you, I want to save your life."

Ian stirred restlessly in his crib and started to whimper again. He wasn't used to hearing his parents argue and he had been crying off and on all evening.

June turned her back on her husband and scooped Ian out of the crib. For a moment all her attention was concentrated on soothing him while Danny tried to think of something more to say.

"Just this once," he promised. "Just this once you've got to leave me."

June shook her head wildly and clung to Ian.

"Dammit, you can't stay here," Danny said desperately. "If not for you think about Ian."

June looked down at the child and her eyes filled with tears but she shook her head again.

Wiz was trying to find a way to squeeze more speed out of the algorithm when Danny came into the lab the next morning. His eyes were red, his skin was pale and blotchy, as if he'd been crying. Even his hair was a worse mess than usual. He looked like he hadn't slept at all last night.

"I had it out with June," he said dully.

Wiz put down the sheaf of papers. "Is she going back?"

Danny snorted. "Fuck no. That silly little bitch is determined to stay here and get herself killed." He growled in frustration and slammed his fist down on the desk. "God*damn* her and her stubbornness."

"I'm really sorry, man. I could ask Moira to talk to her."

"What for? She won't listen. She just rocks back and forth and shuts out the world."

Wiz couldn't think of anything to say. When he had come to this World Danny had been a self-centered twerp who did what he wanted and didn't care about anyone. Now he had others to worry about and he was having to make hard choices. Wiz could sympathize. He'd had a fair measure of twerphood in his makeup when he first met Moira. But there wasn't anything he could do to make the choice easier.

"She's sending Ian back with Shauna," Danny said finally. "That's something anyway."

"But she won't go?"

Danny bit his lip. "It's real simple. Where I go she goes. And I've got to be here."

"Hey look, you could handle some of this stuff from the Capital."

"Bullshit," Danny said without heat. "The only place I can do any good is here."

"But the risk . . ."

"Moira's staying here, isn't she?" He looked up at Wiz with a ghost of a smile. "Besides, I want a World for my kid to grow up in." He looked down. "Shit. I left my notebook back in my room. I'll be back in a minute."

Danny brushed past Jerry as he went out.

"What was that all about?" Jerry asked after Danny disappeared down the hall.

"I think," Wiz said wonderingly, "that was Danny growing up."

❖   ❖   ❖

By the time Danny got back Wiz and Jerry were hip-deep in trying to find something to make the algorithm work faster. By noon they considered and rejected at least four approaches.

Outside the computer center the Mousehole was abuzz with activity as nearly everyone else got ready to leave. Guardsmen, servants and wizards went back and forth in the hall carrying boxes, bags and piles of clothing. They finally took a break when Moira came in to discuss details of the move.

"You know," Jerry said as he pushed back his chair, "I could think a lot better if I didn't feel like I had a target painted on my back."

"Well, we're stuck with it," Danny said angrily. "We gotta stay and if they find us we can't fight. All we can do is hope we can get outta here in time."

"Wait a minute," Wiz said slowly. "Maybe there is something we can do."

"Like what?"

"Protection spells. Really heavy-duty protection spells. You know, like force fields in the science fiction movies."

Danny's eyes lit up. "Hey, cool!"

"Do you think that would work?" Jerry asked.

"It might. At least it would be better than nothing."

"Such spells are powerful magic that stands out strongly," Moira said dubiously.

"They stand out strongly in your World," Wiz said. "But magical senses don't work as well here. Besides, Craig and Mikey don't use magical detectors the way your people do."

"We hope," Moira corrected. "And in any event, where do you propose to get the time to create such a spell?"

"Oh, I've got most of the groundwork done already," Wiz said. "I've been working on it off and on ever since I was rescued from the City of Night. Believe me, there is nothing like being nearly killed a dozen times over to make you think about ways to protect yourself."

✧   ✧   ✧

"Voila!" Wiz proclaimed and placed five rings on the table like a handful of jacks.

"They look like something out of a Crackerjack box," Danny said dubiously.

"Well, as a matter of fact . . ." Wiz began. "Never mind. It isn't what they look like, it is what they do."

"They are certainly charged with magic," Moira said, eyeing the pile of trinkets. "Even in this place they have powerful auras."

"They've got more than that," Wiz said smugly. "This is a truly tasty hack, if I do say so myself."

Danny reached out and poked one of the rings with his forefinger. "So what do they do, shoot lightning bolts?"

"Nope, they generate a stasis field. Basically the spell is an amplified variation of that spell we used to stretch out a night and get more programming time while we were working on the magic compiler. Except instead of stretching nights out two-to-one, this spell stretches time out sagans to one."

"Sagans?" asked Jerry.

"Yeah, you know. Like 'SAY-guns and SAY-guns of light years.'"

"Oh, right," Jerry said, catching the imitation of the famous astronomer.

Moira frowned. "One moment. You say this spell slows down time enormously?"

"Yep."

"Then how can you move when the spell is active?"

"You can't. It freezes you solid. But nothing can hurt you."

"Still, the spell can be broken, can it not?"

"It automatically shuts off when malevolent magic goes away. Kind of like the protective spell I used against those dwarves."

"So at the first sign of trouble you slip on the ring and turn into a statue?"

"Well, no. We wear the rings all the time. They activate

automatically when you're under direct attack and they stay active as long as you're in danger. The rest of the time they're inert."

"These things are like bullet-proof vests?" asked Jerry.

"More like an airbag in a car. Nothing happens until you need it."

Wiz passed the rings around and each of them slipped one on. Then Danny turned and held one out to June. But she hissed and shrank away as if Danny had offered her a scorpion.

"June, please." But June's face was white and she refused to touch the ring.

"It is not like the enchantment in the elf hill," Moira said, coming over to her and laying a hand on her arm. "It will serve only to protect you." Still June shook her head and turned away.

Danny held up his hand to display the ring he was wearing. "Look, if I wear this and you don't, we'll be separated if something happens. But if we both wear one we'll always be together. Please darling, wear it for me."

Hesitantly June reached out a shaking hand and clutched the ring Danny extended to her. With a sudden move she jammed the ring onto her finger and then jerked her hands back into the folds of her skirt. Danny grabbed her and hugged her to him.

"Oh yeah, I almost forgot," Wiz said a shade too brightly. "There's another way to turn the ring on and off."

He held up his hand and mimed twisting the stone. "If you want you can activate the spell by turning the stone in the ring a quarter turn to the right. You can deactivate the spell in the presence of danger by having someone turn the stone a quarter turn to the left."

"What kind of a moron would want to turn off the spell when he's in danger?" Danny asked.

Wiz stopped short. "You know, I never thought of that."

"Feeping creatureism," Jerry said.

"What kind of creature?" Moira asked.

"A feeping one," Danny explained. "That's one that has too feeping many . . ."

"What it means is that I've added features just to add features," Wiz interrupted. "It's a spoonerism on featurism."

"If you expect me to ask you about spoons, my Lord, you will be sorely disappointed. Nevertheless I understand the idea."

"Yeah," Wiz said sadly, "and that took more work than all the rest of the spell put together."

"So now we can continue to work even under the strongest magical attack?" Moira asked, eager to get the conversation back to something that halfway made sense.

"Not under actual attack, but right up to the minute it begins."

Moira looked down at the ring on her finger. "I hope it works."

"I hope we never find out," Jerry said fervently.

FORTY

RAID

The drone had come so far south only by accident, cut off from its base by a line of strong thunderstorms and blown well past the point where it should have turned for home. Nevertheless it kept recording what its sensors recorded and transmitting it back to the castle.

There wasn't much. This part of the island was mostly low hills covered with open forest. It had been hours since the drone had seen anything even as interesting as a herd of animals. Just the occasional bird, a motion in the branches that might be an animal and the mixture of trees and grassy clearings.

The sun was almost to the horizon and the shadows had lengthened and begun to blend together into the beginnings of dusk. The drone was a already headed north, back toward its home when its infrared sensor recorded a patch of anomalous heat off to the right. True to its programming, it turned away to investigate.

A quick scan found nothing in the visual band to account for the heat, no sign of sun-heated rocks or hot springs. The machine was too simple-minded to be puzzled, but it did have contingency programming for something like this. It shut down its engine, switched on its full sensor array and turned to glide over the hot spot.

Beneath the trees and magical camouflage a lone guardsman was shifting the last of his troop's equipment into a neat pile for transport back to the Capital. He looked up as the shadow swept over him, caught a glimpse of something like a large bird and then bent again to his task.

He didn't even consider the incident worth reporting.

It took time for the drone's report to filter up the chain of command at Caermort. Craig had just finished a dinner of magically produced tacos and Coke when the notification popped up in a box on his screen. He glanced at it, frowned, and wiped the grease from his mouth and hands before he hit the key to get more information.

A strong source of IR and magic emissions under what appeared to be a perfectly ordinary hill at the far south of the island. Craig chewed at his lip. That wasn't that uncommon. There were a lot of centers of magic in this world and some of them had funny effects on the non-magic sensors.

But this magic fell off fast. Right over the site it showed up strongly on the drone's sensors. As soon as the drone moved off the spot it faded fast. A few hundred yards from the hill the magic was too weak to pick up.

Without taking his eyes off the screen, Craig balled up the taco wrappers and threw them in the direction of the wastebasket. The basket sensed the incoming object, saw that it would miss, and scuffled over to catch it. Craig was too preoccupied to notice.

That kind of fall-off *was* unusual. Magic usually faded out evenly, following a kind of inverse square law. Still, it was more curious than anything else and a long way away besides.

"Ah, what the shit," Craig muttered at last. He had plenty of drones and besides, there were a couple of new types of recon robots he wanted to try out.

❖   ❖   ❖

"Well, that's the last of them," Wiz said, looking at the spot where the guardsmen had just winked out.

"Gonna be lonely around here," Danny said from where he was lounging against the wall. June, who was standing at his side, bit her lip and nodded. Shauna had taken Ian back four or five hours ago and it was the longest June had been separated from her son since he was born.

The storeroom, which had been packed with equipment and supplies, was mostly empty now. The departing guards and staff had taken much of the material back with them. Two of the three residential wings of the complex were completely shut down and only a few rooms in the other residential section were still being used.

"Yeah, at least until tomorrow night," Wiz agreed absently. Moira had gone back earlier to reorganize the supply effort to fit the new and much smaller operation. Only Wiz, Jerry, Danny, June and the brownies were left in the complex.

And who-knows-how-many gremlins, Wiz added to himself.

"Well," said Jerry, "now that we're alone what's for dinner?"

"Moira left us bread, cheese and cold roast beef in the kitchen," Wiz said. "I think we'd better enjoy it while we can."

He looked sourly at the stack of waxed cardboard cartons next to him. Each one was stenciled "Meals, Ready-To-Eat" and a lot of government-sounding gobbledygook. Wiz didn't know where Moira had gotten them, but he hoped she got back soon with some real food.

Noiselessly the metal spider crept toward the darkened buildings. At the edge of the tall grass it paused, bobbed slowly as if testing the air, and then skittered across the open space to the concealing shadows.

Carefully lifting only one leg at a time it eased its way

along the wall, every sense alert for any sign of danger
or alarm.

Danger there was none. The building's spells discouraged animals, kept away insects and were proof
against dwarves. But there was nothing to keep away or
warn of a robot.

There was a door halfway down the wall. Standing on
its hind pair of legs and balancing itself with its left and
right pairs, the robot stretched its front pair full out to
try the knob. When it found the door locked, the robot
retracted its legs and lowered its egg-shaped body to the
ground. There it sat, listening intently for several minutes. A sliver of moon appeared through the scudding
clouds, faintly illuminating the building. The robot stayed
pressed to the ground, looking like a rock and a couple
of sticks to the casual observer.

At last the moon disappeared into the clouds and the
robot stretched up to the doorknob again. It swiveled its
body and a beam of blinding red light lanced out of its
underside to trace around the knob and lock.

If there had been anyone in the wing the brilliant light
and the smell of burnt paint and scorched metal would
have alerted them. But there wasn't. No one heard when
the spider robot wrenched the lock free and no one saw
when the thing pulled open the door a crack and slipped
through.

It was pitch dark in the corridor, but that didn't matter
to something equipped with image intensifiers backed by
ultrasonics. Slowly, carefully the robot moved down the
deserted hallways, its front pair of legs extended before
it like antennae.

At the end of the third corridor, the spy droid detected
a light far off to the right. It eased down the corridor,
becoming more cautious as its sound sensors began to pick
up voices.

" . . . and he used Interrupt 21h for error handling!"

There was a burst of laughter and then a second voice
started to tell another joke.

Ahead was a doorway letting warm yellow light out into the hall. The robot pressed itself hard against the wall and crept ahead one tentative step at a time, moving sideways like a steel crab.

It paused again at the door and then with exquisite caution it eased a single leg around the corner so the video sensor in the "ankle" could scan the room.

Wiz was sitting in the console chair with his feet up on the console, tearing a bite out of an oversized sandwich. Danny was perched on the edge of the console drinking from a mug and Jerry was over at the table building himself another sandwich.

" . . . so, anyway," Wiz said around the half-chewed sandwich, "the physicist says, 'First assume a spherical chicken of uniform density.'"

Jerry roared and Danny broke up in a coughing fit when some of his drink went down wrong.

Very funny, Craig thought as he looked at the image his scout was sending back. *Laugh while you can.*

Come on, damn you! Wiz stared hard at the computer screen. *We're running out of time!* But the twisting, convoluted blue shape looked no different today than it had before.

"I *hate* asymptotically converging algorithms," he growled. "The closer you get to the solution the longer they take."

"If you've got a better algorithm it's not too late," Jerry said mildly.

Wiz just snorted. "I'm just on edge. It's a combination of being a little kid waiting for Christmas and the fact that the longer we're here the riskier it gets."

"Plus, Moira's not here," Danny said from the table where he and June were sitting. "When's she due back anyway?"

"She said probably late this afternoon." Wiz swiveled back to the monitor, but the shape still looked the same. Irritably he started flipping through the views, each of which showed three of the shape's dimensions at a time. But the effect started to give him a headache.

June stiffened and grabbed Danny's arm.

"Noise," she said.

"I don't hear anything," Jerry told her.

Danny was frowning and listening hard. "I do. Kind of a whine."

"Are we losing a bearing on the disk drive?" asked Wiz. He bent and pressed his ear to the case. "No, I don't think it's coming from there."

By now the whine was louder.

"I think it's coming from outside," Jerry said and all four of them moved to the window.

There was a flash and the window blew in with a roar. Pieces of glass the size and shape of knives scythed toward them in a glittering rain. But they shattered or bounced off when they struck the four immobile figures. Clouds of dust from the explosion roiled through the empty window frames. But not one of the four moved so much as a muscle.

They stood still and silent as the doors to the computer room flew open and three hulking robots marched in, tracking mud behind them.

Then came Craig in a suit of power armor and lastly Mikey wearing jeans and a T-shirt.

"What's wrong with them?" Craig's voice was tinny through the battle armor's speaker.

"They were like that when I came in." Mikey looked them up and down and smiled nastily. "It's a spell of some sort." He turned his back on the group and went to the computer console. The screen still showed the weaving blue form of the key.

"Son of a bitch," Mikey said, open-mouthed.

Craig stomped up to peer over Mikey's shoulder. "What is it?"

"Something that makes this whole business worthwhile. Something that gives us just what we need."

Mikey smiled. Not one of his half-sneers or tight little mouth quirks, but a big broad smile like a child on Christmas Day.

He left the console and went around in front of the impromptu sculpture garden where he could stare directly into Wiz's eyes.

"Thanks for the computer. It will save us a lot of trouble."

He turned to Craig. "Have the robots pack all this up and load it on the ship. Then search the place and grab anything else that looks useful."

"What about them?"

Mikey looked at the frozen group. "Finish them."

Craig raised his arm and pointed the laser in his suit's right forearm at the group. A brilliant beam of red light shot out and played across Wiz and his friends. The wall behind them smoked and scorched but the four statues were unaffected.

"What the hell?" Craig raised both arms and two laser beams converged in a spot of blinding incandescence that moved over the forms. The concrete wall behind them pocked and spalled and the aluminum window frame with its remaining shards of glass melted and ran. But still Wiz and his friends were unharmed.

"Oh shit, just leave them," Mikey said. "Later we'll see how well that spell stands up to a nuclear fireball. If that doesn't work we'll just drop them in the Sun. But get the computer on board first."

With one last look at the object on the screen, he left the computer room.

Quickly Craig brought the system down, cursing the clumsiness of his armor's steel fingers on the keyboard. For a space there was no sound save the clicking of the keyboard. Neither the programmers nor the robots stirred.

Gradually the room began to fill with dense black smoke from a fire elsewhere in the Mousehole. Craig, protected by his armor, barely noticed.

After several minutes the system blinked and died.

Craig ordered the robots to begin dismantling and removing the computer. Then he went over to stand in front of the four motionless figures.

"Greatest wizard in the world, huh?" he said to Wiz. "Man, you were easy." Wiz did not twitch. Not even the look in his eyes changed.

Craig turned from one to the other, savoring the moment. So this was what it felt like to be a winner, a real winner. He tried to burn the feeling into his memory so he could relive it over and over for the rest of his life.

But why have just a memory? Why not a souvenir to help keep the memory fresh. In fact, why not *four* souvenirs?

As the robots returned from moving the computer, Craig gave them new orders.

Outside the Mousehole was a ship, a golden cigar shape lying on its side and pressing into the earth. One by one the robots carried their burdens up the gangway and carefully stowed them in one of the holds.

"Okay," Mikey said as he came back into what had been the computer center. "Let's get going. Hey! Where's Zumwalt and the others?"

"On the ship. I'm gonna build a trophy room and they're going to be my first trophies."

Mikey snorted and shook his head.

"Have it your way. Just make damn sure they stay frozen. Now have you got everything? Then let's haul ass."

As soon as they were aboard the gangway withdrew into their ship and the airlock doors swung shut. With an ear-piercing whine the golden craft rocked slightly and then rose straight up.

In the cockpit, Craig and Mikey lounged back in their acceleration couches and watched the ground fall away. Once they were high above the valley, Mikey used the mouse to line the crosshairs up on the now-deserted Mousehole. Then he pressed the left button quickly three times.

"Bombs awaaaay," he called as three dots detached themselves from the ship and plummeted to Earth.

Three blinding, shattering explosions came as one, making the ship's screens darken for an instant and filling the world below them with boiling, churning dust. The ship rose and fell slightly in the blast wave and then sailed serenely out of the billowing mushroom cloud, made a right-angle turn and headed north.

The cloud of smoke rose high in the air behind them.

From the hillside where he lay, Glandurg cursed as the airship vanished in the distance. "Balked again!" Then he straightened. "Come. We must follow these strangers to their lair."

"Don't see why," Snorri grumbled. "Seems like this Sparrow is bloody well finished."

"He was alive when he was taken from his abode."

"Didn't look none too healthy," Thorfin said. "All stiff like that."

"But he was alive. To fulfill the quest we must kill him ourselves or make certain of his death."

"Lot of extra work, if you ask me," Snorri said.

Glandurg turned on him, red-faced. "Who's leading this quest, you or me?"

"Oh you are," Snorri said sullenly. The other dwarves stood in a silence Glandurg chose to interpret as assent.

"Too right I am! And I say we track the wizard down."

"How far do you reckon they'll take him?"

"That's immaterial. We will follow our prey to the ends of the World."

"We're a good bit beyond those already," Thorfin muttered.

Glandurg ignored the remark. "Besides, I doubt these newcomers will have their lair ensorcelled against us. We should be able to penetrate easily."

"Does this mean griffins again?" Gimli asked plaintively.

"We would be too easy to see. No, we shall follow on foot. Now quickly." He looked down at the cloud of smoke roiling out of the valley. "There is nothing left here for us."

Gathering their packs the dwarves set out toward the north, following Glandurg's magic indicator toward an unseen foe.

There was no sign of life in the room where Wiz had met Craig and Mikey. Now the glass wall showed the night sky clear but oddly devoid of stars. There were just a few sprinkled around, making it hard to tell where the sky left off and the shadow of the mountains began.

Aside from the weak starlight, the only illumination came from the console monitor which spilled a squarish puddle of pale light onto the tiled floor. The only motion was the slow ceaseless rotation of the strange shape on the computer screen as the system ground inexorably closer to the final solution.

The door opened and a robot guard clanked in, sensors swiveling left and right as it probed the darkness, the laser turrets on its shoulders tracking restlessly back and forth. It was the very picture of mechanized death, even if a thin stream of oil was leaking from a blown knee seal, leaving oily footprints in its wake. Every time the robot took a step the piston in the leaking hydraulic damper slammed against the stop, making a distinct "clank." But the noise only made the black metal thing more menacing.

Twice it circled the computer, alert for any sign of life or anything out of order. Finding nothing, it clanked around the room once more and left. The dim light glinted faintly off its shiny black carapace as it turned the corner and the sound of its passage faded into the silence and stillness of the night.

Long after the guard's last echo died something moved in the deepest dark at the base of the computer. Slowly and oh so cautiously a smaller patch of darkness separated itself from the computer's shadow. As it scuttled along the base of the wall a stray glimmer of light caught it and resolved the patch into a tiny man-like figure.

The gremlin squeaked inaudibly at the light and scurried back into the shadows. There it paused, casting this way and that, its leaflike ears flapping and its long pointed nose quivering.

Machines! It was in the middle of an enormous collection of machines with a variety and complexity it had never imagined. In every direction beyond these stone walls was a gremlin king's ransom of machines. The computer that had been such a regal home just a few days ago was shabby and threadbare by comparison.

A broad, snaggle-toothed and beatific smile spread over the little creature's face.

Suddenly it was a *very* happy gremlin.

FORTY-ONE

LOSS

"Nothing?" Bal-Simba demanded. "Nothing at all left?"

Dragon Leader shook his head. "A smoking crater, Lord. We landed and searched for survivors, but we found only one."

He gestured at the brownie standing on the council table.

"Breachean, my Lord." The little man hung his head. "It is my great shame that when the invaders came I ran away."

"It is our good fortune that you did," Bal-Simba said kindly. "Else there would be none to tell us what happened."

"I cannot tell you much, my Lord. I was outside when the metal creatures arrived and I ran. From the top of the hill I saw them carry out the thing the gremlins loved and put it in their ship. But then I ran over the hill and saw nothing more until the explosion."

"The computer?" Moira demanded from her place behind Bal-Simba's chair. "They took the computer?"

"Aye, my Lady. The metal things carried it out."

"But you saw no people?"

"No, Lady, either yours or my own."

The giant black wizard was silent for a moment, his

head sunk on his chest. Up and down the long table the wizards of the Council of the North simply stared. One seat at the table was conspicuously vacant.

"Very well," he said at last. "Thank you, Breachean. Dragon Leader, keep what watch you can on the area in case someone else did survive, but do not endanger your riders."

Dragon Leader saluted and left with the brownie at his heels.

Bal-Simba sighed and looked back at Moira. "Child, I am sorry," he said simply.

The hedge witch was white, her freckles standing out vividly. "They will pay for this," she said softly. "By the World, the sea and the sky above they will pay!"

"Indeed they shall," the wizard Juvian said from his place near the head of the table. "Lady, the Council extends its deepest sympathies to you in your bereavement."

"He is *not* dead," Moira said fiercely. "The others perhaps, but not Wiz. I would know if he was."

The wizards did not point out that psychic bonds worked poorly between the Worlds.

"Remember the elf Lisella's prophecy," another wizard said. "All would suffer great loss, the mightiest among them would perish and our enemy would gain his heart's desire."

"The first part is fulfilled," Bal-Simba said. "Let us see if we can prevent the rest from coming true."

"We still have the wizards and apprentices that Jerry was training," Arianne pointed out.

"Even the best of them is more promising than skillful," Bal-Simba told her. "They are but half trained and none of them is close to being a match for any of the off-worlders." He nodded to Malus and Juvian. "Meaning no offense, my Lords."

"None taken," Juvian replied. "You speak only the simple truth."

"What about the elf?" Honorious asked.

"Aelric? There is no sign. Perhaps he perished or perhaps he has returned to his own domains."

"Well then," Agricolus said. "We must still face these others. What chance have we?"

"If they have the computer they can take the Sparrow's work and turn it against us," Bal-Simba said grimly. "Now time is on their side. We must deny them as much of it as we can."

"You mean attack them now?" Arianne asked.

"As soon as we can. They will only grow stronger."

The wizards shifted in their chairs. Arianne opened her mouth as if to ask another question and then thought better of it.

"Well," said Juvian at last. "I see no way to better our position by waiting."

No one at the table was under any illusion about their chances. That was written in their faces. However cowards do not gain the magical power that lifts a man or woman into the ranks of the Mighty, still less are they chosen to sit on the Council of the North.

"Very true," said Malus with a completely uncharacteristic seriousness. "With the Sparrow and his friends gone there is no one left who is truly a master of the new magic."

"No, wait!" Moira shouted. "There is another!"

FORTY-TWO

A NEW PLAYER

Judith was awake and sitting up in bed when Bronwyn and Moira came in.

"Hey Bronwyn, look at this." She held up her right arm, clenched a shaky fist and beamed. "Not bad, eh?"

Then she caught her visitors' mood and sobered. "Is something wrong?"

"A great deal, I am afraid," Bronwyn told her.

Moira stepped up to the bed. "My Lady, you know that Wiz and the others were hiding in the halfway world to use a computer?"

Judith nodded, eyes wide.

"They were . . ." Moira stopped and took a deep, ragged breath. "They were discovered there and apparently overwhelmed."

"Oh shit!" Judith breathed. Her eyes began to fill with tears. "I'm really sorry, Moira."

Moira reached out and patted her hand. Then she gathered herself. "Our one chance now is to strike quickly against these other two wizards from your world, but we have no one who is expert with the new magic."

"You have me," Judith said quietly. "I may not be in Wiz's league, but I helped write the compiler and I'm a pretty damn good programmer."

Moira sighed. "Thank you, my Lady. I had hoped you would say that."

"There is more," Bronwyn put in sharply. "Lady, before you can do anything, you must be further healed. The spells to do so are dangerous and could harm you."

Judith didn't say anything.

"I know this is difficult," Moira said sympathetically. "Craig is your friend."

"Ex-friend," Judith said coldly. She looked up at Moira, her face white and her lips pressed into a bloodless line.

"Do you understand what he did to me?" she asked, her voice shaking. "He came to me when I was helpless and he *used* me! He pried things out of me I never intended to tell anyone. Then he took that information and he turned it against my friends." Her eyes glittered with a mixture of tears and rage.

"I feel like I've been raped. If there is anything I can do to get back at that son of a bitch, I'm for it."

"Even at the cost of your health?" Bronwyn asked sharply. "Understand Lady, this healing spell could leave you worse than you are now with no hope of recovery."

"I don't care if it leaves me confined to a goddamn iron lung! If I can take that slimy little bastard down with me it will be worth it."

Bronwyn nodded and motioned Moira to one side.

"Well?" Moira demanded. "She is willing."

"She is blinded by anger," Bronwyn said coldly. "She is not thinking rationally." She held up a hand to cut off the protest. "But nevertheless I will do it."

It was the work of a few moments to prepare for the spell. Bronwyn summoned her two most senior assistants and they prepared the brazier and candles while the chief healer traced the warding circle about the bed.

Judith sat in the center of things and watched. "This isn't the spell you used on Wiz, is it?" she asked.

Bronwyn finished the warding circle and looked up. "You are more seriously ill, Lady." She stepped back and regarded Judith carefully. "You may still withdraw."

"Not on your life."

Bronwyn nodded. One assistant reached into the sleeve of his robe and pulled out a packet of herbs which he threw on the brazier. As the fragrant smoke billowed up, Bronwyn and her other assistant raised their wands and began the chant. The first assistant joined in in a minor key. Judith's eyes widened and her mouth formed a little "O" of surprise as the spell took effect. She lay back on the pillows and jerked spasmodically, her breath coming in short gasps. Moira caught her breath, but Bronwyn and her assistants continued the chant uninterrupted.

The chant soared, dropped and finally died away like the after note of a great bell. Judith twitched once more and lay still. The smoke dissipated and Bronwyn ritually defaced the circle before stepping to the bedside.

"Is she all right?" Moira demanded.

"Only time will tell that," the healer said.

"But the convulsions . . ."

"Nerves knitting together and forming new pathways. I have seen worse."

Judith's eyes fluttered and she breathed in great wracking gasps. Moira reached to her, but Bronwyn placed a hand on her arm.

"Can you hear me, Lady?" the healer asked gently.

Judith opened her eyes and her mouth worked convulsively. "Wwww . . ." she gasped.

"Yes, Lady?"

"Wwwater," Judith forced out.

"Here, Lady," Bronwyn took a bowl from one of her assistants and held it to Judith's lips. "Sip, now. Just sip." Judith slurped the liquid in the bowl, choked and spluttered.

Bronwyn removed the bowl. "That is enough for now," she said. Judith sank back against the pillow and breathed strongly and regularly. In a moment she was asleep and snoring gently. The healer nodded and motioned for them to withdraw. Already her assistants were carrying out the brazier, candles and other paraphernalia.

"She will probably sleep for a few hours," Bronwyn told Moira as they left the room. "We will know more when she awakens."

"Do you have any idea?"

"Well," the chief healer said judiciously, "she is not dead. That is something."

Moira couldn't bear the thought of going back to the apartment she had shared with Wiz, so she went to her office off the programmers' quarters. She hoped that work would help, but after she went over the same list of supplies three times without being able to remember what was what from the top to the bottom of the tablet, she gave up the idea of doing anything useful. Instead she contented herself with trying to file some of the stacks of wooden tablets and sheets of parchment that had accumulated on her desk while she was in the Bubble World. Vaguely she realized she would probably never be able to find half the material again, but she didn't really care. At least it kept her from breaking down completely.

"Hi."

Moira looked up from her filing and saw Judith standing in the door of her office.

"Lady!" she whooped, knocking over a pile of files in her haste to get around the desk. "Are you all right?"

"Never better," Judith said as the hedge witch hugged her tight. "Hungry as hell, but I feel great and I don't think I've weighed this little since I was sixteen." She stood back and patted her now-concave stomach. "Hell of a way to lose weight, though."

"I'm so glad."

"Bronwyn says I'm fine, so I thought I'd come and surprise you. Now let's go get some dinner. I haven't eaten in—oh—fifteen minutes." Her voice hardened. "And then we need a council of war."

✧   ✧   ✧

In the event, the council was combined with dinner. For the first half-hour or so, Judith tore into a heaping selection of meats, fruits, bread and cheeses laid out on the table in Bal-Simba's study while Moira, Bal-Simba and Arianne filled her in. Then as she started to dawdle over her food instead of wolfing it, she began to ask questions and contribute information.

"You say you have pictures of some of these robots Craig and Mikey have been producing?" she asked, polishing off another hunk of bread. "Can I see them?"

In response Arianne gestured at the tabletop and a miniature tableau sprang into existence among the bread crusts and fruit rinds. On a barren landscape of red hills and sand perhaps a dozen metal creations were locked in mortal combat.

"Well, what do you know?" Judith said wonderingly. "Warbots."

"You recognize them?" Bal-Simba asked.

"I'll say. That's a Murderer. That one's a Red Terror. That thing over there is a Fer de Lance tank. And a couple of King Cobras. I don't know what that one is, but it looks like a Preying Mantis with a couple of laser pods added."

She looked up from the display. "They're game pieces. Imaginary fighting machines. Only it looks like the little shit's made them real here."

"They are real enough, Lady," Arianne said.

Judith examined the display again. "I wish I had my rule books; then I could tell you exactly what they're capable of. But I can remember enough to do pretty good without them."

"They look powerful," Juvian said dubiously.

Judith twisted her mouth to the side and rubbed her chin. "Well, yes and no. They're sure nothing to mess with, but they have a lot of weaknesses."

Absently, she picked up a pear and bit into it.

"Look, I don't know this Mikey, but I know Craig. I know how he thinks and I know how he fights." She wiped a dribble of juice off her chin and took another big bite.

"When you do a long campaign with someone you get to know them pretty well. Craig is not very original. That's why we didn't let him DM. He was too predictable."

"DM?" Juvian asked.

"Dungeon Master. The person who sets up the game. Anyway, Craig's strictly a by-the-book player and he expects everyone else to be the same way." She stopped talking, demolished the remaining pear in three bites and wiped her chin before she went on.

"So maybe we can surprise them." She grinned nastily. "In fact, I know we can surprise them. And I have a few ideas on how."

"How long will it take you to—ah—arrange your surprises?" Bal-Simba asked.

"The longer the better, but I can have some stuff ready in a few days."

The black giant turned his attention to Moira. "And you said that Wiz believed we had at least two weeks?"

"So he said, Lord."

"Then we had best postpone our plans for an immediate attack. A few days will make us much stronger without appreciably strengthening our opponents, I think." He turned to Judith. "When can you begin?"

Judith took an apple out of the fruit bowl. "How does right now sound?"

In the event, it took a few hours longer than that to clear off her old desk in the Bull Pen and get started. It was after midnight when Malus and Juvian reported to her there.

"Moira tells me you're pretty good with the spell compiler."

"We are hardly what you might call skilled, Lady," Juvian said. Malus stifled a yawn. He hadn't been up this late in years.

"Okay, I want you to pick out the best of the apprentices and journeyman wizards. No, let that wait until morning. There are a couple of things I want you two to start on right away."

"You mean tonight?" Malus asked.

Judith smiled. "Get used to it. The time-expansion spell only works from sundown to dawn and we're going to need all the time we can get."

The morning sun was streaming into the Bull Pen when Moira came calling. Juvian and Malus had dragged themselves off to bed some time before, but Judith was still hard at work.

"My Lady, Bal-Simba sent me to see if you are in need of anything."

"Just fine, thanks. But if you could have the kitchen send over some more food, I'd appreciate it."

"And a quantity of blackmoss tea. It is already being prepared."

Judith leaned back away from her desk and put her arms behind her head. "Bronwyn told me the healing spell would make me hungry, but I didn't have any idea it would be like this."

"The healing process takes energy, Lady. The body must replenish itself."

"Anyway, I'm not tired and that's useful. Look what we whipped up last night."

Over on the center table sat a vaguely familiar object. Except instead of being made of coiled straw basketwork it was made of shiny metal. The shape was different, too. As if two of them had been placed bottom to bottom. The result was something like a football, if a football had been two feet long and made of steel finished to look like coiled straw.

"Malus did the critical part of the spell," Judith explained as she reached down to the object and detached a tinier thing. This she held up for Moira's inspection.

It was a shiny piece of metal no bigger than the first joint of Moira's finger. She looked closely and realized it was a perfectly formed metal insect, a bee to be precise. She became aware of a muted buzzing coming from inside the larger thing, as if it was full of thousands of steel bees.

"They'll ignore you unless you're moving fast," Judith explained. "But they home in on anything going faster than about 800 feet per second and destroy it."

Moira handed the robot bee back to Judith. "That is clever, but I am not sure I see the purpose."

"That's because you don't know our weapons. The most common ones are guns that shoot pieces of metal at very high speeds."

"Wiz told me about those. He said they were very destructive."

"They are. And they're going to be one of Craig's prime weapons. But our little killer bees can destroy bullets and shells before they can hit anything. So when we attack, we saturate the area with a bunch of these beehive rounds."

"But that thing is not round," Moira said. Then she looked narrowly at Judith. "Or does it approach round-ness for sufficiently large values?"

Judith looked blank. "I don't understand."

"Neither do I," Moira sighed. "It was something Jerry said."

She stopped and for an instant Judith thought she was going to cry. But instead she said, "If there is nothing more you need I will leave you to your work."

Judith leaned forward to her desk again. "You know," she said absently, "I've worked on mission-critical soft-ware before. But this is the first time I've had the whole world on my shoulders."

"How does it feel?"

Judith gave her a tight little smile. "I don't like it." She sighed and turned back to Moira. "People are going to get killed in this, aren't they? Probably a lot of people."

Moira nodded gravely. "This troubles you?"

"Yeah. A lot. Before when I've fought a campaign it's been a game. At the end you picked your pieces up and put them back in the box until next time. Here there won't be any next time and I'm sending people to their deaths on the strength of my bright ideas."

"They will go with or without you, Lady," Moira told

her. "The best you can do for them is to give them the tools so they may win."

Judith grimaced as if she was tasting something sour. "Yeah, but that doesn't make it easier."

"I am told that it never is easy, Lady."

"Lady, this is fantastic," Bal-Simba said as he looked over the plans. "I am astonished that you have accomplished so much in so little time."

Judith shrugged. "Mostly it wasn't any harder than hacking out some simple BASIC subroutines. Besides, I had Malus, Juvian and some of the apprentices to help me."

"Still, I remember how long it took a dozen of you to produce what we needed the last time you were our guest."

"That's why it took so long. What we did then laid the groundwork for what I'm doing now." She smiled. "The secret of good programming is that you spend ninety percent of your time up front building tools and maybe ten percent on the actual job—plus the other ninety percent of the time it takes to debug everything, of course. Unlike most of the people I've worked for, you were smart enough to stand back and let us spend the time on the tools. So now . . ." again the shrug, "it's easy."

"You said you also wanted to discuss strategy. My guard commander tells me your suggestions are, um, somewhat unorthodox."

Judith smiled. "I'll bet he did."

"Well, he did put the matter—ah—somewhat more strongly."

"I can understand that. But I know Craig and Craig's a gamer."

Judith rested her elbows on the table and leaned forward. "Look, one of the problems most gamers have is they spend too much time worrying about hardware and not enough on C3—command, control and commu-nications. If I know Craig, he's got some horrendously effective hardware. But he's weak on the things that will let him use it effectively.

"Now," she went on judiciously, "we could try to match him on the hardware. But we really can't because he's had longer to play with this stuff and he has control of the Bubble World. So mostly we won't bother. Instead we'll use pretty much the weapons and tactics your people already know—plus the new magic—and we'll primarily use technology to enhance the C3. We may not be as powerful as he is, but we'll be better coordinated."

Bal-Simba grinned. "Excellent, Lady." Then the grin faded. "But you have laid your plans in terms of only one of our enemies, this Craig. What about the other one? The one called Mikey?"

Judith's frown matched the wizard's. "I don't know. So far we haven't seen anything that isn't in Craig's style. Either Mikey is just like Craig or he's up to something that hasn't shown up yet."

"Ah," said the wizard Malus, "you sent for me, my Lord."

Bal-Simba looked up from his desk and eyed his tubby little colleague.

"My Lord," he inquired pleasantly, "have you ever flown on a dragon?"

Malus blinked. "A dragon, my Lord?"

"Yes. Have you ever flown on one?"

"Why, ah, no. No I haven't. That is . . ."

"We need wizards with the dragon cavalry in the attack. You are among the best qualified of the Mighty for the job." Bal-Simba forbore to mention that Malus's main qualification was his weight. In spite of his girth, he was the lightest of all the Mighty—save for Juvian, who suffered from an airsickness no spell could cure.

Malus half-bowed, torn between honor and trepidation. "Well, thank you, my Lord, but I mean, after all, a wizard on *dragonback* . . ."

"It is voluntary, of course," Bal-Simba said blandly.

"Oh naturally I volunteer, but, ah, wouldn't a levitation spell work just as well?"

"Dragons do not like to have other flying things near them when they are on the wing. Especially not something so unnatural as a flying wizard."

Malus deflated like a cold souffle. "Oh."

Bal-Simba beamed and clapped the smaller man on the shoulder. "Excellent. Now, report to the Master of Dragons in the main aerie. He will see to your training as a dragon rider. Later the Lady Judith will brief you on tactics and teach you the new spells you will need."

As the pudgy wizard bowed and turned toward the door he remembered that he was deathly afraid of heights.

Judith pushed a strand of dark hair out of her face as she bent over the map again. Her lower back ached from the time she had spent standing like this and she was hoarse from talking all morning, but at last the plan seemed to be coming together.

"Okay, that leaves the communications relay *here*." She stabbed her finger down on the three-dimensional map that occupied the whole table top. "If we lose that we lose most of our ability to coordinate between the attacking force and the Capital."

Moira checked her stack of wooden tablets. "We have an entire squadron of dragons assigned to protect it. They carry your new weapons. The squadron leader is waiting outside should you wish to meet her."

Judith stood up from the map and stretched to try to get the kinks out of her back. "Yeah. There are a couple of things we need to go over." *And it'll give me an excuse to sit down.* She was still studying the map when she heard the door open.

"Reporting as ordered, my Ladies."

Judith looked up at the sound of the voice and gaped.

The squadron leader was a fresh-faced brunette with a fine dusting of freckles and one of those complexions that no one over the age of twenty can ever have.

"Have they explained your mission to you?" Moira asked, apparently oblivious of the effect the squadron leader was having on Judith.

"Yes, Lady. We have been running training exercises every day for as long as our dragons can fly."

"And the weapons?"

The dragon rider grinned. "Amazing, Lady. The dragons do not like them, but . . ." She shrugged.

"Okay," Judith put in. "Remember those things are most effective against metal—robots or flying machines. Don't use them against biologicals unless you have to. Also keep in mind there is a maximum and a minimum range. Also, the closer they get before you shoot the better your chances of hitting, but the fewer shots you can get off before they are too close."

"We have been practicing these things, Lady."

"Good. Now if we're lucky they won't detect the communications platform at all and you won't have to fight." The expression that flashed across the squadron leader's face showed she wouldn't consider that lucky at all. "If you do have to fight, you'll probably be in—ah—a target-rich environment. Keep in mind your job is to protect the relay, not shoot down attackers."

The girl nodded gravely. "I understand, Lady."

"Okay. Anything else? Then you're dismissed. I'll try to talk to you later about last minute details."

The squadron leader bowed and closed the door gently behind her as she left.

"Our apprentice squadron," Moira explained as Judith scowled at the closed door.

"Hell, she can't be more than fourteen!"

"Closer to sixteen summers."

"A goddamn kid!"

"What would you? The alternative is to send them into the thick of the battle. Besides, young riders and dragons are adaptable in ways that older ones are not. Believe me, my Lady, if they must use those weapons of yours, the dragons had better be the most adaptable ones we have."

FORTY-THREE

YOU BASH THE BALROG, I'LL CLIMB THE TREE

The four frozen statues stood in a neat row, like the pieces in some gigantic game.

In truth, Craig's trophy room was only a storeroom off in one wing of the castle. Wiz and his friends were dumped there and left to gather dust against the day when Craig would have a proper trophy room to display them.

Once or twice in the succeeding days Craig came down to look at them and gloat. But mostly they were left alone to stare sightlessly at the stone wall across the room.

"Hhsst," a tiny voice squeaked. "Hhsst! my Lord."

But Wiz flicked not so much as an eyelid.

Lannach tiptoed into the room, keeping his back to the wall. He reached out to touch the hem of June's dress, he tugged on Wiz's pant leg. There was no response.

The protection spell! Of course. They were still in danger in this place so the protection spell still held them fast.

The brownie danced up and down in frustration. He and his companions had spent days searching for their friends and now they could do nothing for them. The castle was constantly patrolled by warbots and other strange creatures and Lannach knew it would only be a matter of minutes before he was discovered. Danger of discovery aside, any one of the four was far too large for even all of the brownies together to move.

Then he remembered the rings and what Wiz had said when he gave them out. Lannach had been busy with the gremlins then and hadn't paid much attention, but he did remember that the spell could be turned off.

If he could get to the rings.

Lannach stepped back and considered. Both Danny and Jerry had their arms raised and away from their bodies. June had both her fists jammed in her mouth. Wiz's arms were out, slightly away from his body. Clearly it would be easier to reach his ring.

But even with his hands down, Wiz's ring was still easily at three times Lannach's height. The brownie looked around frantically, but there was nothing he could use as a ladder anywhere in the room.

Lannach reached above Wiz's boot and touched his leg. The fabric of his pants moved easily under his tiny hand. Not ideal, but it would have to do. Carefully he stretched up and grabbed Wiz's pant leg, pulling himself up to stand on the top of Wiz's boot.

He had just reached belt level when a shadow in the hall told him someone was coming. It was too far to jump to the floor and there was no obvious place to hide. But Wiz's jerkin was the kind that laced all the way down the front. Quickly he wiggled his way beneath the jerkin, clinging to the shirt for dear life.

The guard's little red eyes shifted back and forth as it scanned the room. Lannach pressed himself close and dared not to breathe. He knew he must make an unsightly bump on Wiz's stomach. He just hoped the guard didn't notice it.

Finally the creature gave a piglike grunt and shambled out the door, trailing his halberd behind him. Lannach closed his eyes and sighed in relief. He lost his grip and squeaked in terror as he almost slipped out of the jerkin. Then he resumed his ascent of Mt. Wiz.

A quick reach and grab gave Lannach a double handful of Wiz's shirt sleeve. Resolutely ignoring the drop below, the brownie swung his body out until he could wrap his legs around Wiz's forearm. Then he shinnied down the arm feet-first, locked his legs around Wiz's wrist and reached out with both hands for the ring.

It was an awkward position and the stone was stiff. It took all of Lannach's strength to turn it.

Suddenly Wiz relaxed and dropped his arms, nearly dashing Lannach to the floor.

Wiz shook his head, felt the weight on his right arm and looked down to see Lannach clinging to his shirt sleeve for dear life. He put his left hand out to support the brownie's feet.

"Thanks, Lannach," Wiz said.

"We pay our debts, Lord."

Quickly he set the brownie down on the floor and moved to free his companions.

"Where are we?" Wiz asked the brownie.

"In your enemies' castle, Lord. They attacked the Mousehole, stole the computer and then destroyed the place."

"Damn!" Wiz breathed. "What about the rest of your people?"

"All here, Lord. Save only Breachean. We think he got away."

"Thank God for that."

"There is more, Lord," Lannach squeaked. "The Council is preparing to attack this place with everything they have."

"They'll be slaughtered!"

"Perhaps, but with you and the others dead, they saw it as their only chance."

"Can you get word to them that we're still alive?"

"Alas, Lord, their magic blocks us here."

"Damn!"

"Doesn't make much difference," Jerry said grimly. "If we don't stop Mikey and Craig right now we're cooked anyway."

"Damn!" Wiz said for the third time. He thought hard. "Okay, I guess our best chance is to do all the damage we can in here. The first thing we've got to do is take out that computer."

"That will not be easy," Lannach said dubiously. "It is heavily guarded. Besides, your enemies get little enough use of their prize. When they brought the computer they brought the gremlins with it. Now the whole castle is infested."

"The gremlins are here?"

"In greater numbers than ever, I fear."

"Hey Lannach," Danny said. "Do you think you could, like, stir those gremlins up a little?"

The little man grinned. "You mean encourage them to cause trouble? Easily, my Lord."

"Then do it," Wiz commanded. "Let's turn this place into a gremlin jamboree."

"With pleasure. But what will you do?"

"We," said Wiz, "are going to stage our own jamboree."

With Wiz in the lead the group made its way down the hall. Lannach had told them the computer was in the central tower and that meant they had to go to the center of the castle to reach it. That wouldn't be easy, Wiz knew. Not only was the place enormous, Lannach said there were guards everywhere.

Don't think of it as a problem, Wiz told himself. *Consider it a challenge.*

Their first challenges were just around the corner. Three of them, all nearly seven feet tall. Their faces were piglike with tusked snouts and red eyes that looked mean even as they laughed uproariously at something one of them said. They were wearing armor of fantastic designs and carrying an assortment of wicked-looking polearms. Curved swords and daggers hung from their studded metal belts, and nickel-plated machine guns were slung over their backs.

Wiz peered around cautiously and then jerked his head

back before they could see him. Danny, Jerry and June also peeked around.

June laid a hand on Danny's arm and looked at him quizzically.

"We're going to sneak up on them and knife all three of them when they're not looking," Danny whispered sarcastically.

Wiz signaled his companions into a huddle twenty feet or so back from the corner.

"We've got to go this way," he whispered to them. "Lannach says this is a blind corridor and there's only this one way out."

"Can we distract them?" Jerry asked.

"Without them raising the alarm? How?"

When they looked back, June was halfway down the corridor. All three motioned frantically for her to come back but June ignored them. Then she whipped around the corner.

"Oh shit! Come on." Danny set off at a dead run with Wiz and Jerry pounding after him.

As they came around the corner June was walking back toward them, wiping her knife on her skirt. Behind her were three large steel-clad forms lying in a heap.

"Now what?" she whispered to Danny.

"Uh, now we keep going," Danny whispered hoarsely. Wiz and Jerry just goggled.

Just past the guards was an open door leading to a room with masses of wires running down the walls.

"What do you suppose all this is anyway?" Danny asked, looking around the room.

"Hard to say, but if I was to guess I'd say it was a wiring closet for their phone exchange."

Wiz looked over the mass of wiring speculatively.

"I'd say it was a good place to start sabotage then." He raised his hands. "Let's see how long it takes this stuff to melt."

"I got a better idea," Danny said. "We've got a couple of minutes, don't we?"

Wiz looked down at the bodies of the three guards. "Uh, yeah."

Danny grinned. "Good. Let's see what happens when they get their wires crossed."

Wiz looked at the wall of hair-fine wires dubiously. "I said a couple of minutes, not a few hours."

"Oh, I'm gonna have help. **Emac!**"

Instantly one of the little demons stood before him. **"backslash,"** Danny commanded.

"?" the Emac responded.

"list spaghetti exe"

As Wiz and Jerry watched the demon scribbled furiously, filling the air with glowing symbols. Danny knelt down and began giving the creature commands in a low voice.

"You know," Jerry observed, "it's kind of handy carrying your own software development environment with you wherever you go. Kind of like having the world's niftiest laptop—except you don't get tired lugging it through airports."

Wiz eyed his friend. "I think you've been here too long."

With a final whispered **exe!**, Danny stood up. There was a quick swirl of air and another little demon stood next to the Emac. This one wore a blue denim work shirt, jeans and construction boots—much like the one Danny had produced to connect up the computer. However this demon bore a striking resemblance to Alfred E. Neuman.

Danny pointed at the wiring panel. **"Kill!"** he commanded.

The demon grinned and swarmed up the panel, clinging with its feet while it swapped wires with both hands.

"That was fast work," Wiz said as the quartet left the wiring room. Behind them the demon was still furiously switching connections.

"It's something I've been kinda working on for a while," Danny admitted.

Wiz shook his head. "I don't think it's *ever* going to be safe to let you go back to California."

✧   ✧   ✧

A line of dwarves came out of the desert. They were footsore, dusty, travel-worn and thirsty. Glandurg was in the lead, limping slightly, and the rest were strung out behind him.

"Let us rest before the final assault," Glandurg commanded. His followers needed no second order. They threw themselves down in the shade of a red earth hillock.

While they rested, Glandurg and Thorfin crawled to the top and looked out at their target.

"Big enough," said Thorfin, craning his neck to try to see the top of the central tower.

"Our magic will let us locate our target no matter how big it is."

Thorfin looked ahead dubiously. The desert had been singularly unappealing and the castle before them looked less appealing than that.

"Not what I was thinking of," he muttered.

Glandurg started to say something but he was interrupted by one of the other dwarves.

"Hsst! Someone's coming."

Quickly the party concealed themselves as only dwarves can.

What this time? Glandurg thought. *More of those big metal walking things? Or the ones that roll over the ground?*

Then he heard the crunch of walking feet. The walkers again; two small ones from the sound of them.

But it wasn't the walkers. Instead it was two mortals and a dragon, looking as tired, dusty and footsore as the dwarves. While the dragon rested behind the hillock the humans climbed to the spot Glandurg and Thorfin had vacated just moments before to spy out the castle.

"Now," said Major Mick Gilligan, "we can see the whole place from here. Is this close enough for you?"

Karin frowned. The trickles of sweat down her face left clean tracks through the reddish dust. "But we cannot see clearly. We must move closer."

Gilligan licked his lips and tasted grit. "From here on

the land's flat as a pancake. We get any closer and we're going to stick out like three sore thumbs."

Karin smiled. "You only have two thumbs, silly."

Mick leaned over and kissed her on her dusty, sweaty cheek. "Two sore thumbs and a sore big toe, then. Anyway, we're not going to have any cover."

"I think we must risk it," Karin said seriously. "We won't learn much watching from here." She shaded her eyes and scanned the plain before them. "Besides, there is some cover out there. Enough to hide a person if you are careful."

Gilligan glanced back at Stigi and didn't say anything.

Karin scanned the plain. "At least there do not seem to be any robots out there."

Fine, Gilligan thought, *so it's a killing zone.*

"Okay, but remember what I told you. We keep spread out, drop at the least sign of trouble and be on the lookout for mines."

Karin nodded. They slithered down the hill, collected Stigi and started out onto the plain.

Now what was that all about? Glandurg thought as he watched the humans and the dragon go. He signaled his own group to assemble and they too started out on the plain.

The plain before them was not only flat, it was wired. There were pressure sensors in the soil, motion sensors concealed in rocks, capacitance sensors masquerading as bushes and an invisible network of radar, laser and ultrasonic beams lacing back and forth so tightly not even a field mouse could move without being detected.

Neither group was more than a hundred yards onto the flat ground before they were picked up, marked as hostile and targeted.

In pillboxes disguised as hillocks of red earth, shutters slid off firing ports and machine guns poked out their ugly black snouts. Artillery buried in the base of the castle swung around as automatic loaders delivered shells and

powder charges to their gaping breeches. Firing impulses
raced at the speed of light along buried wires to fields
of mines.

Suddenly the earth erupted in flame and smoke and
flying pieces of metal.

"What was that?" Karin asked.

"Barrage," Gilligan told her shortly. "About a mile to
our right. Come on. Let's move!"

"What was that?" Glandurg demanded as the explosions
and gunfire rang out over the plain.

"Dunno," Snorri said. "But it's about half a league over
yonder." He pointed to the column of smoke and dirt
boiling up well to the dwarves' left.

"Well, let's not wait around to find out, shall we?"

The wiring closet had been heavily guarded because
it was the concentration point for the sensors and fire control systems for the outer defenses of the entire southern quadrant of the castle.

The wiring was automatically monitored, but the computer doing the monitoring could only detect breaks and
bad connections. It wasn't bright enough to realize that
connections were being switched at the rate of hundreds
per minute. So it didn't go to the backup.

Not that it would have mattered. The gremlins had
been at the backup all morning.

"What the hell?" Craig muttered as the alert box
popped up on his screen. Quickly he called up the display for the outer sensor array. The map showed possibly hostile contacts at half a dozen shifting points in the
southern quadrant. They were being fired on but as fast
as one winked out another appeared somewhere else.

Not another herd of those damn grazing things, he
thought and called up the security camera displays. The
cameras in the area showed a wild jumble of confused

flickering images, but the ones mounted on the castle walls showed several tiny figures out on the plain. But they weren't any place close to the target zones.

"Shit!" The damn system was messed up again. He switched over to manual control and ordered a battery to fire on one of the groups of dots.

The guns fired, but the shells landed a couple of miles from where they were supposed to be. He tried to correct his aim and a different battery fired at a point well behind the targets. In rapid succession the same command fired other batteries.

Craig growled in frustration. He switched to his backup control system, only to get a message on the screen saying it was inoperative. He gritted his teeth and tried to sort out the mess by experimenting with the controls. But the demon in the wiring closet was changing connections at random much faster than Craig could fire ranging shots. At that point coincidence could be defined as the same command firing the same weapon twice in succession at the same target.

"*Shit!*" Craig yelled. Then he reached over and sounded the general alarm. The lights flickered and one wall of the room slid back to reveal a wall-sized map of the castle and its approaches. "Guards to the perimeter," he barked into a microphone. "We have intruders approaching from the south."

Then he threw himself back in his chair, crossed his arms and watched the screens. "All right, suckers. Let's see you evade that!"

Slowly and cautiously Wiz and his friends made their way toward the center of the castle. They saw no more of the live guards, but several times they had to hide from heavily armed robot sentries. Fortunately they were so noisy the quartet could hear them coming and June was particularly adept at finding hiding places.

Finally they **found** the elevator.

Wiz eyed **the number** painted on the wall across from

the elevator doors. "From the looks of this, we're pretty low in the castle. I'll bet what we want is further toward the top."

Off down the corridor there was a distinct *clank clank clank*.

"Robot coming. Everyone in quick." They piled in and Wiz pressed the button. "Okay, going up."

The elevator doors jerked towards each other, slammed back and then jerked together. The car twitched spasmodically, almost throwing its occupants into a heap.

"Maybe," Wiz amended. But the car began to rise, slowly and jerkily at first and then faster and jerkily. All four of them braced themselves against the sides of the car and tried their best to stay upright.

"Hey," Danny said after a few minutes, "isn't there something about being trapped in an elevator?"

"Huh?"

"In the spy movies. Aren't people always getting trapped in elevators?"

"Don't be morbid."

"I'm not being morbid, I'm being practical."

"If you're so damn practical why didn't you think of that before we got on the frigging elevator?"

Danny just shrugged.

"Wait a minute," Wiz said, looking up, "there is something we can do. Jerry, see if you can reach the ceiling of the car."

Jerry extended his hand experimentally. "Sure. Now what?"

"See if you can find the service hatch."

Jerry prodded at the ceiling as the car continued its jerky climb. Finally one of the ceiling sections flipped back to reveal an opening perhaps two feet square.

"Okay," Wiz said, "we climb up on top of the car."

"Is that safe?" Jerry asked dubiously.

"Safer than meeting a reception committee. Now hoist Danny up, will you?"

With Jerry's help Danny easily wriggled through the

hatch. June followed lithely with a slight assist from Danny. Wiz followed June with an easy leap and a quick chin up. That left Wiz, Danny and June on top of the elevator and Jerry in the car.

Since Jerry weighed nearly as much as Wiz and Danny put together this presented a problem. Since Jerry was not exactly light on his feet, it presented a serious problem. The first attempt to hoist Jerry through the opening nearly pulled Wiz and Danny back into the car. Finally, Wiz dropped back into the car to push from below while Danny heaved from above. With much tugging and shoving, they were able to get Jerry onto the roof of the car.

Then the elevator ground to a stop and the doors started to open.

Wiz leaped for the hatch and wriggled through just as the doors ground open. Before they could close the panel two goblin guards strode into the elevator with drawn laser pistols. As the four humans held their breath the guards looked around suspiciously, their weapons tracking their head movements.

One snorted like a bull and drew in a deep breath, as if testing the air. His companion grunted something to him and he exhaled with a grunt. They looked around again, but they did not look up.

Finally the pair backed out of the car and the doors closed. After a moment, the elevator creaked and jerked and started upward again.

Wiz let out a deep breath and nearly collapsed with relief.

"It's the helmets," Jerry said after a moment.

"What?"

"The helmets. They're so ornate the guards have trouble looking up." He shook his head. "Bad design. Like a lot of this place."

"Personally I think it's great design," Wiz said sharply. "It just saved our bacon."

"Aw, we could have taken them easy," Danny said. "A few lightning bolts and, hey—" He made a gun with his finger and mimed shooting at the door. There was a flash of blue spark from his fingertip and a large scorch mark appeared on the wall of the shaft.

Danny looked down at his finger in surprise. "I didn't know it was loaded."

"Well, holster it. And remember we're just a little bit outnumbered here. We don't start throwing fireballs until we absolutely have to."

"Get ready then," Jerry said, looking up at the indicator over the door. "We may have to. We're almost there."

Quickly the three magicians arranged themselves to have the best field of fire when the door opened. All three of them muttered preparation spells so they could come out shooting if they had to. Then they waited.

The elevator creaked and swayed, jerked twice more and then expired with a sigh. The doors started to open, slammed closed, and then slid all the way open with a despairing groan—leaving them looking at a blank stone wall.

Wiz looked down through the hatch and out the open door. At the bottom of the door there was a narrow slit of corridor visible, perhaps eighteen inches wide. The elevator had gone almost completely past their intended floor.

"Shit!" Wiz muttered and all of them quickly dropped through the hatch into the car.

Jerry reached out and punched the elevator button. The car lurched and groaned again, but did not move.

"Reminds me of the elevator at a Star Trek convention in Denver," he said.

"We'll have to squeeze out through that space then," Wiz said.

Jerry eyed the slit. "I don't know if I've got that much octopus blood in me," he said dubiously.

"Maybe there are working controls outside," Wiz said as he knelt to slip through the crack. He eased through the opening and felt for the floor with his feet. The elevator was just high enough that he couldn't keep his weight resting on his elbows in the car and touch the floor at the same time. He eased out further and for a terrible second kicked his legs over empty air in the elevator shaft. Then his left foot caught the floor and he eased himself down on solid footing. He sighed and turned around to face down the corridor.

And found himself face-to-face with a goblin guard.

The guard roared a challenge and swung his halberd two-handed. Wiz ducked and the halberd knocked chips of stone off the door jamb. Snarling, the guard swung the weapon back over his head and down toward the crouching programmer. Instinctively Wiz lunged forward as the blade descended. He hit the goblin in the knees just as the halberd came down with the full force of the monster's body behind it. The combination overbalanced him, and the guard went sprawling headfirst down the elevator shaft, screaming as he fell.

Wiz collapsed forward on his face, sucking great lungfuls of air. Somewhere in the distance a siren began to wail. Behind him he heard his three companions drop to the floor of the corridor. Then Jerry and Danny reached down and pulled him to his feet.

"How'd you do that?" Jerry panted, red-faced from the tight squeeze.

"I don't know," Wiz gasped. "Now run!"

The four of them pounded down the corridor, turned a corner and headed off in what Wiz hoped was the right direction. After several hundred yards they ducked into a side corridor to catch their breath.

All four of them leaned up against the wall gasping. Off in the distance, faintly, they could still hear the siren. Then another siren sounded and another and another until the castle reverberated to the sound.

"Guards to the perimeter," the speakers in the wall above them squawked. "We have intruders approaching from the south."

"What's that?" Danny panted.

"I think," Wiz said slowly between gulps of air, "that all hell just came unshirted."

FORTY-FOUR

FOR FAITH, FOR LOVE, FOR HONOR

The Wizard's Keep boiled with activity. From the tallest towers the trumpeters blew "Assembly" over and over. Down on the drill ground armored guardsmen fell in rank by rank while the drummers beat the Call To Arms on the great bass drums that hung by the reviewing stand. From the aeries below wing after wing of dragons rose and circled and grouped themselves into larger formations.

In the Watch Room every post was manned. The Watchers on the main floor murmured into communications crystals or peered into scrying glasses for some sign of the enemy. On the wall behind them glowed a huge map of the northern end of castle island, casting an eerie bluish glow over the proceedings.

On the dais at the opposite end of the room groups of wizards hovered over their own crystals and muttered spells and incantations. Bal-Simba was there, seated in his raised chair where he could watch and command everything. Judith was there, seated next to Moira at a small table to Bal-Simba's right. Arianne was at his left and next to her, the elf duke.

Aelric stood tall and terrible in shining silver mail of elven metal. His helm, intricately and carefully wrought, extended down over his cheeks and neck, unlike the conical helms of the Council's guardsmen. But save for the nose guard it left his face unprotected.

"Is there aught else?" Bal-Simba asked the people clustered around him. Arianne and Moira shook their heads and Aelric said nothing.

"My Lady Judith?"

"We're as ready as we'll ever be. The dragon riders have got the new spread-spectrum communications crystals so they can cut through the jamming, the guardsmen have the last of the special weapons and the scouting demons are deploying now." She took a deep breath. "It's going to be rough, but Craig's in a world of hurt unless he can make a saving roll."

"Saving roll?"

"Uh, unless he gets lucky."

Aelric smiled without warmth. "Fear not, Lady; luck they shall not have this day."

Bal-Simba looked around the group once more. "Aught else? Then we are ready."

Aelric bowed to the group. "If you will excuse me, I have my own part to play. This battle will not be fought entirely in the World you know and my own role comes—elsewhere." He started to go and then turned back. "One other thing. You may find you have acquired some unexpected allies. I would suggest that you simply accept such help as you are given." He picked his way off the crowded dais and strode toward the door.

Moira followed him and caught up with him in the corridor.

"You came back."

Aelric looked down at her. "Did you doubt that I would, Lady?"

She stopped. "Lord . . ." The elf duke turned back at the sound of her voice.

"Lord, I have not properly thanked you for your aid. I have been surly and ill-natured to you and," her eyes begin to fill with tears and the words came with a rush, "and I am sorry and thank you. That is all I wish to say."

"You are most welcome, Lady," Duke Aelric said, ignoring her tears. "Truly this has not been easy for any of us."

"I wish there was something I could do to make up for everything."

"Bend every power you possess to our victory," Duke Aelric said. "Then hope that it is enough."

The dwarves were panting and exhausted by the time they reached the base of the castle. The explosions and beams of burning light had never come close but they had taken them as a hint and crossed the plain at a dead run. Since dwarves are too short and stumpy for distance running they were pretty well worn out.

A dozen dwarves slumped down in a row beneath the towering walls of living rock and gulped great lungfuls of air. Out on the plain the explosions continued unabated.

"Now that we're here," Thorfin gasped after several minutes, "how do we get inside?"

"Place isn't spelled against us," said Snorri. "Don't see any gates, though."

"Gates would be guarded," Gimli pointed out.

"There are openings further up," Glandurg shaded his eyes and craned his neck. "Leave your packs here and bring only what we shall need for the final assault."

Thorfin and Snorri looked at each other and shifted uneasily. "You mean those openings that spout fire and explosions every so often?"

"You have a better idea? I thought not."

The wall was solid rock and so steep it was only a few degrees off vertical. But dwarves are creatures of the mountains and if they cannot run they can climb like flies.

Glandurg lifted Blind Fury high above his head with both hands.

"Forward!" he proclaimed. "For glory and honor!" Glandurg turned and began to climb the wall. Behind him his loyal followers hesitated and then started after him.

❖   ❖   ❖

It took Mick and Karin longer to cross the plain. Mick insisted on going flat every time the artillery came within a few hundred yards of them. Fortunately the fire never got really close and their only injury was to Stigi, who received a scratch from a shell fragment.

"Well, we're here," Mick said as they rested in the shade of the wall. "Now are you satisfied?"

"I wonder if we can get inside?" Karin said thoughtfully.

"Even for you that's a crazy notion. We've done too much already."

"Let us work our way along the wall and see if we can find a gate," she went on as if she had not heard him.

Mick looked at her, sighed and nodded.

The things men do for love!

"The scouts are in position," the Watcher reported.

Bal-Simba looked up at the display. Already it was beginning to show the information pouring in from tens of thousands of scouting demons like the ones Wiz and his company had used to locate the heart of Bale-Zur in the City of Night.

Unlike those demons, these absorbed everything that happened around them and transmitted the information back to dozens of concentrators floating well to the south out of the battle zone.

Circling off the southern end of the island was a thing like a gray tarp, a relay for communications and the concentrators. It absorbed the information, did some preliminary filtering and fed it back to the relay. The relay in turn passed the information back to the Watchers in the Capital.

As one, the controllers in the pit looked up at Bal-Simba. The giant wizard took a deep breath. Then he nodded.

The controllers turned back to their crystals and the attack was on.

FORTY-FIVE

BATTLE ROYAL

"Dragon Leader, you have an allied force approaching to your right. I say again, you have friendlies approaching from widdershins high."

What the . . . ? There were no more friendly forces. Save for a couple of squadrons on guard duty Dragon Leader had the entire cavalry of the North with him. Anything else in the air had to be hostile.

"Dragons at widdershins high," the scout on the right flank sang out.

"Can you identify?" Dragon Leader barked into his communications crystal. He hated surprises in the middle of a battle.

Silence.

"I say again, can you identify the dragons?"

"Uhhh . . ."

"Dammit, speak up!"

By now the formations were at almost the same level and closing fast as the newcomers pulled into a shallow dive.

Dragon Leader craned his neck to see the approaching force. Whoever they were, they had the most ragged-ass formation he had ever seen. They looked more like a flight of geese than a squadron of cavalry.

Dragon Leader's mount bridled and nearly bucked as the flight approached. It took a moment to bring the animal under control and when Dragon Leader looked up again the leader of the new force was flying next to him.

Dragon Leader glanced. Then he gaped. Then he nearly fell out of his saddle. Flying beside him was the biggest dragon he had ever seen in his life.

This was no adolescent cavalry mount. It was a full-grown, fully intelligent dragon and a monster of its kind at that. It was easily twice the length of his own mount and might have reached 200 feet. Behind and above came dozens more wild dragons.

A great golden eye regarded Dragon Leader and his dragon with amused contempt. Then with a flick of its tail, the giant reptile winged over and dived for the deck. The rest of the wild dragons followed their leader down.

Dragon Leader licked lips suddenly gone dry. "Uh, central," he croaked into his communications crystal. "The allied forces have taken the lead position and are going in low."

"Allies lead and low," the controller's voice came back. "Acknowledged."

Fortuna, Dragon Leader thought, *what have we gotten ourselves into?*

Out on the edge of the plain the warbots waited. There were 100-ton Murderers, 30-ton Hellfires, Skysweeper anti-aircraft units, a couple of 200-ton Gargantua fire support models and a dozen or so Springer scouts, all in a loose grouping just behind the military crest of the ridge. They were being held as a mobile reserve, ready to sweep down off the ridge and deal any attacker on the plain a crushing blow to the flank.

The Springer nearest the crest of the ridge turned its head. Its sensors had picked up something. . . .

With a rush the lead dragon swept over the hill scant feet off the ground. A blast of dragon fire destroyed the first robot before it could even face its foe.

The second warbot had time to half raise its laser before the hurtling mass slammed it to the ground. The warbot next to it had only half turned when the massive tail caught it in its midsection and sent it sprawling.

By now the engagement was general as a dozen more dragons topped the ridge and piled into their metal enemies. Laser blasts and gouts of dragon fire lanced through the air and parts of robots and pieces of dragon bodies flew in every direction.

Then there were no more robots. Seven of the dragons lay motionless amidst the carnage and one dragged a wing.

As one, the unharmed dragons galloped forward and took to the air again. The one with the broken wing followed on foot.

Without warning clumps of guardsmen and wizards popped up all over the plain. Immediately they spread out into long, loose lines and started moving toward the castle.

Kenneth, at the head of his group, squinted at what lay ahead. *Fortuna, what a mess!* he thought. The wizards had been able to bring them no closer than a league to the castle because of interfering magic. They would have to cross the distance on foot, possibly under fire and almost certainly against enemies.

Kenneth felt especially naked without comrades at either shoulder. But they had been warned that concentrations which gave defense against sword and spear would only serve as targets for the weapons of these foreign sorcerers.

Well in front of the attacking forces a half dozen football-shaped metal containers popped into existence and split open on the red sand. A dark cloud poured out of each of them and dissipated in the air.

That was the signal. Kenneth raised his arm and motioned his men to move forward.

I wish I had a drink, he thought.

❖   ❖   ❖

"Mikey! Mikey!" Craig beat on the door frantically. Finally it opened a crack.

"Yeah?"

"Why the hell didn't you answer the net? I've been calling you for fifteen minutes."

"I told you. If you have business with me, you come to me. I'm not answering your goddamn pager." The door started to swing shut.

"Goddamnit, we're being attacked!" Craig yelled. "We've got dragons and infantry and shit all over the place."

The door swung open and there was Mikey wearing only a pair of pants. In the back of his mind Craig realized he looked terrible, all thin and sort of stretched out. He moved like a speed freak, all jerky, uncontrolled energy. There was a predatory gleam in his eye that Craig didn't remember seeing before.

"Yeah?" Mikey said. Then he paused as if listening to something that only he could hear.

"Come on, man! I need all the help I can get."

"You keep them busy. I've got something to set up."

Craig nodded and raced for his command center.

"We have isolated their control links," one of the Watchers called out to the group on the dais.

"Transfer the characteristics to my station," Judith called back. Instantly the Emac sitting cross-legged in front of her began to write in the air.

Judith smiled tightly. "Time to jam." She turned to the Emac.

"backslash"

"?" the Emac responded.

"blackwatch exe"

The Emac gabbled and several dozen demons appeared on the table. They were fashioned like men but each wore a skirt and shawl of dark green patterned with black. Several had drums and the rest had odd contrivances with several shiny black tubes extending over their shoulders. The leader carried a silver-tipped staff near as tall as he was and wore an enormous hat made of some black fur.

"Give them 'The Black Bear,'" Judith commanded. "Then 'Scotland the Brave,' 'The Highland Brigade at Maggersfontein,' 'The Southdown Militia,' 'The Earl of Mansfield' and 'Lord Lovett Over The Rhine.' After that use your imagination."

The tiny drum major nodded, turned to the demons behind him and raised his staff. The pipers inhaled as one, the drummer struck the beat and the skirl of the pipes reverberated off the stone walls.

"Let's see them even *think* through that," she said viciously.

"I hope it is as effective on the enemy as it is on us," Bal-Simba boomed over the noise.

Judith looked up and realized everyone in the command center had stopped work and was staring at the table. Several of them had clapped their hands over their ears. Judith made a gesture and the sound died to a whisper.

"Sorry Lord, I keep forgetting it's an acquired taste."

By the time Malus's dragon approached the castle the fat little wizard was half-seasick and thoroughly miserable. Normally a dragon could not carry two people for very long. But the wizards had added their magic to the animal's natural flying ability so they were able to keep up with the other dragons.

Not that it was much comfort to Malus. He was strapped into a second saddle back on the dragon's shoulders. The beast was too wide to straddle comfortably at that point and the insides of his thighs ached terribly. Although the straps holding him to the saddle were secure, the saddle itself had a tendency to shift alarmingly whenever the dragon maneuvered suddenly. For Malus's taste there had been far too many sudden maneuvers. The blue robe of the Mighty, which was so impressive on the ground, was totally unsuited for dragon riding. The wind tugged at the hem and tended to flip it back above his knees. The cold air whipped up the robe and around his legs. Probably the only part of him that was still warm was his seat, which was protected by the saddle. But he couldn't tell for sure because it had gone to sleep long since.

He tried to shut out the discomfort by concentrating on the back of the rider and not looking down. Above all, he didn't want to look down.

The castle erupted in flame and smoke as every weapon fired on the attackers. Artillery and mortars of every description fired and fired again as fast as the automatic loaders could feed them. Streams of tracers fountained up into the sky as anti-aircraft batteries sought their targets. Lines of laser light swept back and forth over the plain and sky.

Between the killer bees and the messed-up control system in the southern quadrant it wasn't nearly as effective as it should have been. What ought to have been annihilating was merely deadly. Men went down like tenpins and dragons fell from the sky under the impact, but still the others pressed on.

From ground and air the attackers returned fire. Lightning bolts and fireballs flew from the wizards' fingers destroying emplacements and blinding sensors. Then two squadrons of dragons peeled off and let fly with heat-seeking missiles. The missiles went for the hottest things in the castle, which were the barrels of the artillery and the firing tubes of the lasers. A series of explosions blossomed on the castle walls and here and there the secondary explosion of a magazine made a section of castle wall bulge outward and slump.

Still the attackers came on.

Circling above the battle Malus groped in the sleeve of his robe and brought out a crystal sphere just large enough to fit comfortably in the palm of his hand. It was held in a net that was tied to his wrist so he would not lose it and the netting made it harder than normal to concentrate. Still the picture was clear enough.

Peering into the crystal he saw that there were a number of other things in the air, but little enough magic.

Fumbling in his other sleeve he produced a light hazel wand. It wasn't as powerful or as impressive as his normal staff, but it was much easier to handle on dragon back. He kept his eyes fixed on the crystal as he raised his arm above his head and began to chant.

Craig's screen started to fill with magically generated hash. He quickly applied a filter function to the image and some of the interference faded, but what was left pulsed rhythmically and seemed to beat against itself like a badly tuned instrument, creating irregular patches of dark and light on his screen.

The magical sensors were worse. The screen filled with glowing blobs of amorphous color that made it look like a neon lava light. Craig swore under his breath and started combining the output of various kinds of sensors and tinkering with filters until he got his best picture.

Vaguely Craig realized he hadn't been smart in setting this system up. Everything flowed back to his command center, but he could only concentrate on a few facets of the battle at one time. There was too much happening for him to coordinate the defense. He would have to rely on the sensors and programming built into his warbots and other weapons. Which was fine, only there was no way for those weapons to coordinate without direct orders from his command center.

Still, he had a lot of weapons.

"What's going on up there?" Gilligan demanded.

Karin shaded her eyes and squinted. "I cannot see. No, wait! Those are dragons. Ridden dragons and they are attacking." She looked at Gilligan. "Those are my people."

"Can we signal them?"

"They are too high and too fully engaged." She picked up her bow and started back toward the castle. "Come on. We must help them."

"How?"

She looked over her shoulder. "We will think of something, now come if you are coming." She trotted off with Stigi humping along beside her. Gilligan had to run to catch up.

Thorfin looked at his leader's boot soles and scowled. It seemed as if they had been climbing for hours. First up the steep outer wall, then in through a gun port and finally up through the castle's ventilation ducts. There was plenty of room, but the wind was almost strong enough to pluck a dwarf from the wall and every few hundred yards they had to unfasten a grating that blocked the duct. Twice they had narrowly avoided the whirling blades of huge ventilation fans that threatened to turn the whole expedition into dwarf tartare. And still they climbed onward. Glandurg stopped every few minutes to check his locating talisman, but it always told them the Sparrow was above them.

I never realized glory was such hard work, Thorfin thought as Glandurg missed a foothold and kicked him in the face.

"Look," said Jerry. "Do you have any idea where we are?"

The four of them were standing at the crossing of four identical corridors. There were no floor numbers, room numbers or anything else to give them a clue.

"One of the upper floors of the castle," Wiz told him.

"In other words we're lost, right?"

"No, I know where we are. I just don't know where the computer is."

Jerry growled. "Okay, let's do this systematically. Lannach says the computer is in the room where you met

Craig and Mikey, right?" Wiz nodded. "We know the room has an outside wall because it had a big window, right?" Again the nod.

"So let's go to the outside wall, put our left hands against it and follow it around, checking every door as we go. Eventually we've got to find the right room."

"There are hundreds of rooms on this floor," Danny protested.

"All the more reason we need a system."

"Okay," Wiz said. "There's the outside wall. Let's do it."

All four of them put their left hands on the wall and started walking single file. The first room they came to was empty. The second held a mass of machinery that was obviously not the computer.

"This looks more like it," said Wiz as they came to the third door. It was wider than the others and almost as high as the corridor.

Wiz opened the door and looked inside. Ranked along the walls in the dark were a dozen heavily armed robots, all motionless. Suddenly the lights came on, the robots jerked erect and a dozen metal heads swiveled toward the door.

The programmers didn't wait for the rest. Wiz threw fireballs, Danny threw lightning bolts and Jerry hit them with some kind of spell that made them crumble to powder. A couple of laser beams flashed over their heads and left burning furrows in the wall behind them. The heat activated the fire sprinklers, drenching all four of them with water.

June looked up at the rain magically coming from the ceiling and laughed at the wonder of it all. Wiz choked on the smell of fried, electrocuted, powdered robot and shook his head to get the water out of his eyes.

He glared up at Jerry. "You and your system."

"There's nothing wrong with the system. It's just that if you follow it you are certain to find everything on this floor."

"Most of which we don't want to find. Okay, we'll keep following the wall, but from now on we don't open any doors unless they look really promising."

Karin stopped so quickly Mick almost ran into her. She turned, put her finger to her lips and gestured around the corner. Cautiously Mick peeked around. There was a door there, set at the end of a narrow corridor back into the wall. There were also six things out of someone's nightmare guarding it. They were big, ugly, armored, and armed to the teeth.

He ducked back and looked at Karin. Go the other way? he pantomimed and Karin nodded.

Just then Stigi decided to see what was so interesting. He stuck out his neck, thrust his head fully around the corner and snorted in curiosity.

With a wild yell the guards charged forward.

"Shit," Gilligan said, fumbling for his shoulder holster. Before Karin could draw her bow, he stepped around the corner, dropped to a semi-crouch and fired two-handed.

Eight shots rang out in the confined space and all six of the guards were down.

Karin's eyes widened at the sight.

"Well done," she said. "Now, shall we use the door they were guarding?"

At that moment the door flew open and a solid mass of the manlike monsters charged out waving swords, spears and other less identifiable, more nasty, weapons.

Instinctively Gilligan dropped into his shooters' stance, but Karin grabbed his arm and pulled him down.

With a *whoosh* and a roar Stigi let go with a blast of flame.

The effect on the packed mass was instant and appalling. The things shriveled, screamed, burst into flame, and died in the ranks.

Again the *whoosh* and another lance of dragon fire struck the remaining attackers. Black smoke boiled off charred flesh and the stink was appalling. Here and there came a series of explosions as ammunition in guards' bandoleers ignited.

And then there were no more attackers. Gilligan looked at the blackened mass in front of him and was almost sick. He'd seen people burned to death in air crashes before, but not on this scale. Karin had gone deathly pale under the layer of reddish dust.

"Let's get inside," he said. Carefully they picked their way through the grisly remains, trying to touch as little as possible.

"My God," Gilligan breathed, "will you look at this place?"

The room was enormous. The ceiling was at least a hundred feet above them and it stretched out proportionally in all directions. In the center of the brightly lit area were half a dozen huge robots in various stages of construction with smaller robots swarming over them like worker ants. As they watched a traveling crane maneuvered a torso section over the legs and hips of one of the robots.

"It's a factory," he said, awed.

None of the robots paid the least heed to their unexpected visitors. They kept right on working.

Gilligan motioned and led Karin and Stigi along the wall and around the assembly area.

"There's got to be another way out of here. No way those robots could get through the door we just came through."

They were halfway around the room when another giant robot stepped out of the shadows behind them.

Karin screamed, Stigi whirled, inhaled and spouted a gout of flame. The robot stepped forward inexorably and raised its laser arm.

Craig had designed the robot with a magic power source, a magically reinforced body and magic sensors and control links. But the design was essentially technological.

He hadn't considered what might happen if his creation stepped in front of a giant flame thrower.

The robot's first bolt went wild into the ceiling, knocking hot rock down on the three and burning a red afterimage in Mick's vision. Then the chips in the control circuits overheated and failed. The robot pinwheeled its arms wildly and its glittering torso twisted from right to left and back again. Then the seals in the hydraulic cylinders in its legs and hips failed from the heat and contact with the boiling hydraulic fluid. The thing lost hydraulic power in a gush of robotic incontinence, tottered and fell face-first into a puddle of smoking hydraulic fluid. The floor shook, but the robot workers paid no attention.

Stigi stalked forward and sniffed disdainfully at his kill. Then he stepped daintily around the puddle—or as daintily as you can when you're eighty feet long and in a confined space—and continued on his way.

The main door out of the assembly area was on the same scale as the rest of the factory. Fortunately it was also open.

"Now, where do we go from here?"

"Up I would think," Karin said. "Their commanders would want to be as high as possible to see as much as they could."

Gilligan didn't bother to point out to her that it didn't work that way when you had radar and advanced sensors.

"Think we can get Stigi upstairs?" he asked.

"Oh yes, Stigi is not afraid of heights." She frowned. "Though this place is so tall it may take us hours to reach the top."

Remembering how high the fortress looked from the outside Gilligan thought that was a wild underestimate.

Then he caught sight of something. "Wait a minute, we may not have to walk. Look at this."

Set in the far wall was a freight elevator big enough to take a semi. "They must use this to move robots. If it will carry one of them it will sure hold Stigi."

It took a little doing to get the dragon into the elevator. If Stigi wasn't afraid of heights, he wasn't very fond of confined spaces and to him an elevator big enough to move the Space Shuttle was still a confined space. He started alarmingly when the elevator began to move and for a moment Gilligan was afraid he was going to crush them both. But Karin stood by his head, stroking him and telling him what a good dragon he was.

Stigi calmed down but every so often he would glare over at Gilligan in a way that said he understood perfectly well Mick was to blame for all this and some day he would get even.

The elevator lurched to a stop and the doors opened. "End of the line," Gilligan said.

He drew his pistol and peered out. They seemed to be in some sort of service area. The floors were bare concrete and the light fixtures were Spartan. Scattered about were a number of pieces of equipment Gilligan didn't recognize and a thing like a metal octopus that was obviously a cleaning robot of some kind. At least it had a floor buffer built into its base.

As Craig studied his screen, a new symbol sprang up at the very bottom. One of his scouts had located the attacker's main communications relay.

"Get that relay," Craig screamed into the screen. On the periphery of the battle a demi-wing of two squadrons wheeled and raced to do his bidding.

"Shield flight, you have sixteen enemy incoming. I say again, sixteen incoming."

"Understood. Sixteen incoming," Elke repeated into her communications crystal.

There were only five other dragons and riders at her back.

What was it the strange sorceress had called this? A "target-rich environment." To hell with that. She called it being plain old-fashioned outnumbered.

She signaled her command and the dragons wheeled and spread out into the attack formation they had practiced so many times at the Capital. Off in a far corner of her mind Elke realized she wasn't frightened, just terribly, terribly busy.

The fighters came in hugging the ground to escape radar detection, but that did nothing to shield them from magic. Elke and the Watcher both saw them coming.

Almost directly beneath their quarry the flight of metal shapes arrowed upward, jets thundering as they climbed toward their target.

Far above them Elke winged her dragon over into a steep dive. Out of the corners of her eyes she saw the dragons to her left and right fold their wings back and follow her down.

Her instructors might not have approved. The formation was loose and dragons were slowed by the objects they grasped in their talons. But it was closing with the enemy and that was all that mattered.

The targeting spell for the new weapons she carried began to sing. Before her eyes lines of glowing green merged into cross hairs and rectangle of her target sight. She kept staring intently at the specks below her, moving her head slightly to center them in the crosshairs, listening intently all the while. Then the squadron leader heard the bone-quivering hum in her ear that told her the weapon had locked on. She reached out and touched a stud on her saddle.

A trail of smoke sprang from the box in the dragon's claw as the air-to-air missile leaped free of its launcher. Beside and behind her other trails of dirty gray smoke streaked the sky as the rest of her flight fired.

The squadron leader eased back on the reins and hauled her dragon around into a tight spiraling turn. Below her fourteen missiles raced toward their targets. In spite of their magical components, the guidance systems were essentially technological. They looked for the brightest radar returns in the sky. Dragons and the relay they were guarding returned only small echoes but the climbing fighters stood out sharply.

The fighters were hardly sitting ducks. Their radar sensors picked up the missiles as soon as they launched and the attackers broke and jinked all over the sky in an effort to break the radar locks, scattering flares and packets of chaff behind them.

For half of the fighters it was enough. Eight of their companions exploded in balls of black and orange as the missiles found them but the others continued to climb toward the relay demon.

Elke counted the explosions and nodded to herself. Well, they'd been warned that some might get through. But the survivors had lost momentum. That gave her squadron opening enough.

Again she led her dragons into a screaming dive into the midst of the attackers.

The fighters filled the air with ECM, flares dropped free with magnesium radiance that briefly outshone the sun and chaff bloomed everywhere around them.

None of which mattered in the slightest. Dragons, even missile-armed dragons, don't carry radar and the forces were too close for missiles. Now the defenders relied on the traditional weapons of the dragon cavalry. Bursts of dragon fire ripped at the metal shapes. Then the great bows sang and iron arrows leaped toward their targets. Planes cartwheeled across the sky or dropped like stones as flames and death arrows found their marks.

One lone fighter pulled away from the melee, climbing toward the relay station. Elke lined her dragon up on the metal enemy and touched the second stud on her saddle. Again smoke streaked from the dragon's claws as a second missile sprang free. But there was no pulse of radar energy to warn the aircraft. Instead Elke held the missile on course by manipulating the stud with her thumb, always keeping it centered in the glowing orange rectangle. The missile traveled up the plane's tailpipe and blew it out of the sky before the aircraft or its controllers even knew it was there.

❖   ❖   ❖

In his castle, Craig cursed and pounded his fist on the table. But he had other things to command his attention.

Well, it wasn't the first time he had lost heavily in the early moves and gone on to win the campaign. The enemy couldn't do jack shit unless they could penetrate his fortress. They hadn't hit his outworks yet. When they did things would be different.

Vaguely he wondered where the hell Mikey was and what he was doing.

The wind whistled and whipped like knives of ice around the high, dark spire where Mikey stood. He could sense rather than see the formless shapes that pulsated and moved in the freezing distance beneath his feet.

A single wan pool of yellow light illuminated his workbench. For the last time he checked the spell before him.

It was a complex shape about the size of his head and so dark as to be beyond black.

Mikey caressed the thing, oblivious to its piercing chill. At last it was ready.

We are prepared. The voice pulsed in his ears like his own blood. *We wait.*

With a gesture Mikey killed the light on the workbench. Then he clasped the sphere to him and started down from his high place.

The guardsmen and wizards advanced in loose order over the barren ground.

Actually, Donal thought, "loose order" was a misnomer. A "swarm of gaggles" was more like it.

But this was the formation they had been advised to use. Having seen pictures of their likely opponents Donal was all for it. Absently he reached back and touched the tube slung across his back. He hoped it was as good as advertised.

So far they had met no real opposition on the ground. The shelling had died down to a background rumble.

Once a cluster of gray metal things swooped down on them with fire and explosions. But between their wizards' lightning bolts and the timely intervention of a wing of dragons there had been very little damage done.

Up ahead a door opened in the castle wall and several things shaped like men stepped out.

Either we're a hundred paces from the castle, Donal thought, *or those things are giants.* He signaled his squad to spread out and take cover. Seemingly oblivious to the oncoming metal giants, the guardsmen responded as they had been drilled.

A lance of fire slashed into the earth so close to him he could smell the ozone stink. Behind him bullets beat a tattoo into the dirt. Donal jammed the point of his sword into the ground and brought the dull green tube slung across his back around and over his shoulder. As methodically as he had been taught he flipped up the sights and lined them up on the giant robot.

The tube bobbed up and down as he followed his target and then he squeezed the trigger. The tube bucked slightly and Donal dropped and rolled just before another blast of laser energy rent the place where he had been standing.

When he looked up the robot was swaying uncertainly, its right knee a smoking ruin. Before he could get to his hands and knees two more explosions blossomed on the giant torso. It swayed forward once more and then toppled like a felled tree.

In his tower Craig swore viciously. His warbots were programmed to fight other warbots or dragons, not infantry with anti-tank missiles. He'd have to override and run this action himself. He slapped a button on his console, but nothing happened.

"Get me a control link!" he yelled into his microphone.

"We are trying, dread master," came a voice in his ear, "but there is something wrong in the transmitter."

"Then switch to the alternate," Craig yelled.

"That was the alternate," the voice said. "Maintenance estimates it will have the primary repaired in three point oh eight minutes."

"Shit!" Craig slumped back in his chair. This was like playing on a night when you couldn't make a saving roll for love or money. Well, three minutes wouldn't make that much difference in that part of the battle and there were plenty of other places he could put his time.

Meanwhile, was it his imagination or did he hear a high-pitched sound coming from his display console—a sound like a very small giggle?

"My palm's sore," Danny complained.

"Well, don't drag it along the wall," Jerry told him. "I didn't mean that literally anyway."

Even investigating only the likely looking doors it seemed that it was taking forever to check out the rooms. Even this high up the castle was much bigger than Wiz had imagined.

The next set of doors didn't look like anything Wiz remembered, but they were big and probably important. He was just about to punch the button when they slid open and he found himself face-to-face with a dirty, unshaven man in a tattered flight suit waving a pistol. Over the man's shoulder Wiz could see an equally dirty and disheveled woman and a large dragon.

"Who the hell are you?" he demanded.

"Major Michael Gilligan, United States Air Force. Who the hell are you?"

"This is the Sparrow," Karin put in, stepping forward. "He is the mighty wizard I told you of." She sketched a curtsey. "Well met, my Lord."

"What are you doing here?"

"Raising hell," Gilligan told him.

"My Lords, the League is attacking the castle," Karin said breathlessly.

"I know. Look, can you get a message back to the Capital? They need to know we're alive."

Karin's face fell. "Alas, my Lord, the enemy is jamming our communications."

"Damn," Wiz said, entirely without heat. "All right. We're searching this floor for a computer these guys are using to cook up something really nasty. Can you help us?"

"Of course, my Lord." Karin bobbed another curtsey.

"Okay by me," Gilligan said. "You really from the USA?"

"Cupertino," Wiz shrugged. "It's pretty much the same thing."

"Hot damn!" Danny said, looking up at Stigi. "Firepower!"

"You might say that," Gilligan said, thinking of the pile of charred bodies by the gate.

"Come on then, and keep your eyes peeled. We've run into all sorts of things."

A couple of hundred more yards and two more uninteresting rooms and they came to a broad cross corridor that was carpeted in a different color and more richly finished than any they had seen so far.

"I recognize this!" Wiz said. "This is the way to the computer room."

"Great!" said Danny as he stepped in front of Wiz and out into the center of the corridor. "Let's go . . ."

A bolt of green radiance lashed down the corridor and caught Danny square in the back. He pitched forward and dropped like a sack of sand. June screamed and rushed toward him, heedless of the bolts of energy crackling around her.

Down the corridor came a packed mass of goblin troops, the ones in front firing ray guns.

Gilligan stepped forward, dropped to one knee and braced the pistol in both hands, elbow resting on knee. Three well-placed shots dropped the leaders and the rest hesitated for a moment.

Then Wiz started throwing fireballs.

"Stigi," Karin's voice rose over the noise. "Forward."

Stepping past June kneeling over Danny, the dragon shouldered Gilligan and Wiz out of the way and advanced down the corridor. The guards reformed and came on, energy bolts scoring the walls ahead. If any of them hit Stigi he didn't show it. Instead he breathed deeply and sent a gout of flame washing down the corridor.

That was the final straw. The attacking guards broke and ran.

Wiz bent over Danny, but June bared her teeth and hissed at him. The young programmer's shirt was burned away and the flesh beneath was charred and smoking. Wiz could see the white of bone from his ribs and spine. He was still breathing, but his breath was coming in great harsh gasps.

"He's dying," Jerry said quietly. His eyes were big and his face pale.

"Lord, unless you have powerful healing spells I am afraid this one is done for," Karin said quietly to Wiz.

"No," Wiz said without taking his eyes off Danny. "Nothing like that."

"Then I am truly sorry, my Lord."

"Goddamn!" Wiz breathed. If skilled healers could reach him in the next few minutes he still had a chance. But there were no healers among them and no way to get Danny to a healer in time. They could not walk the Wizard's Way from inside the castle. The opposing magic was too strong. There just wasn't time.

Time!

Quickly Wiz knelt again and reached for his friend's arm. June bared her teeth again and fumbled in her skirt for her knife.

"I'm trying to save him, dammit!" June looked hard at him, but she relaxed slightly.

Wiz reached out and touched the ring of protection Danny still wore on his right hand. Before June could object he twisted the stone and Danny froze in stasis as the protection spell took hold.

"He's all right," Wiz said to June. "Don't you see? The

spell will keep him safe until we can get him back to a healer." June looked down at her husband and bit her lip, but she made no move to touch the ring.

"Help me carry him further down the corridor." He turned to Karin. "I don't think there are any more branches off this corridor until we get to the computer room. Once we move Danny, can you back your dragon up past the intersection and hold them off here?"

Karin nodded.

"Great. Jerry, help me move him. We don't have to be too gentle. Stasis is better than a backboard."

"Then what?" asked Gilligan, looking down the corridor in the direction their attackers had fled.

"Then," Wiz said in a hard cold voice, "we're gonna find that goddamn computer and stomp a couple of people flat."

Craig sat glued to his workstation and played as he had never played in his life. Slowly it dawned on him that this wasn't just a couple of early setbacks. He was losing.

It wasn't all one-sided. He was hurting them plenty, but it wasn't enough. His carefully constructed defenses were washing away like sand. His warbots were powerful but the attackers were hitting him in ways they weren't programmed to handle. If he took direct command of a unit he could do pretty well, but he couldn't be everywhere at once and besides, his damn communications kept failing.

A motion at the corner of his screen caught his eye. There, superimposed on the glowing battle display, was a little manlike being perhaps six inches high. Unlike the rest of the screen image it was in full color and high resolution.

The thing turned toward him and pressed its face and palms against the inside of the tube, as if it was looking out. It wasn't an image, Craig realized, there really was something inside his monitor!

The tiny being turned and gestured across the screen. Another manlike little thing stuck its head around the edge of the screen and peered at the world outside. Behind and around it the battle display scrolled on, unnoticed by the gremlins or by Craig.

The first creature tossed a glowing ball into the air and batted it with his free hand. The ball flew across the screen leaving a glowing trail behind it. The second thing leaped up and deflected it before it could touch the far side of the screen. The ball bounced off the bottom and ricocheted toward the upper right corner, smearing a goodly portion of the display. The first creature made a mighty jump and deflected it back toward the bottom left. His opponent dived for it, but the ball bounced over his head and off the side of the screen. The first gremlin chortled and held up a single finger.

Craig watched helplessly as his screen filled up with the lines of the ball tracks.

"Maintenance!" he yelled.

"He's off this way," Glandurg called back to his companions. "Down this side shaft, now."

No more climbing for a bit, Glandurg thought. *That's a piece of good news.* Although he never would have admitted it, he was just about done for. His arms and shoulders ached from clinging to fingerholds in the ventilation shaft and his calves and thighs were cramping from pressing his body flat against the wall. It would be a relief to just walk for a while.

He didn't know how far they had climbed; a league or more, perhaps. But at last the arrow in the talisman had stopped pointing upward and was pointing off to the side.

As he started down the horizontal shaft, Glandurg reached back to touch the hilt of Blind Fury. Soon enough they'd be done with this climbing and sneaking into honest battle.

He wondered if battle was as exciting as the skald's tales made it out to be.

✧   ✧   ✧

It took nearly fifteen precious minutes for the maintenance robots to fix the display on Craig's workstation. By the time he was back in control the situation had deteriorated even more. The last of his air force had been swept from the skies, and with it all of his recon drones. Now he was reduced to viewing the battle through the cameras and sensors mounted on the castle itself. Two critical outposts had fallen and even as he attempted to assert control a third one went.

In the southern quadrant the attackers were almost up to the last line of defenses at the base of the castle walls. Craig turned his attention there. Quickly he switched to one of the cameras on a forward emplacement to try to find a weak spot. He still had a couple of squadrons of warbots he could throw into the battle here, but he would have to command them directly if they were going to be any good.

As he scanned the line of approaching men, a shadow fell over the camera. He swiveled up in time to see a dragon diving straight at him. He flinched and tried to bring a weapon to bear but it was too late. The last view Craig had was of gaping jaws and an enormous golden eye as the dragon crashed head-on into the emplacement.

Cursing, he switched to an alternate view only to get a jerky low-resolution picture that barely resolved itself into blobs of light and dark. Two more switches and he found a camera high up on the walls that was working.

What he saw wasn't good. Lines of dotlike figures, rendered tiny by the distance, were converging on the gates of the castle. Many of them were too close for the artillery, and the machine guns were strangely ineffective.

Some of the figures went down to energy beams or mines, but many more did not. They swarmed over the smoking ruins of his defenses and began to disappear down the tunnels.

Frantically, Craig ordered all his remaining robots to the lower levels to try to stem the attackers.

And then it was all too much. Craig turned and bolted from his war room, leaving the defenses entirely on automatic. He just couldn't face any more fighting and losing.

Mikey! Mikey was working on something. Maybe Panda, the master hacker, could pull this out of the fire for them yet.

Mikey was sitting on a bench cradling something in his lap. As Craig came closer he saw it looked a lot like the figure that had been growing on the computer screen.

"We've got trouble, man."

"No we don't," Mikey said softly. "We've won."

"Goddamn it, they're all over the fucking castle!"

Mikey looked up at him and smiled. For the first time Craig saw the mad, red glint in his eyes. "It doesn't matter," he said almost gently. "It's all working according to plan.

"I was wrong about you, Craig," he went on in the same gentle, hair-raising tone. "You and your robots were important. You were a wonderful diversion. The robots got them to grab the computer. All we had to do was bring them here. Now we'll crush them. We'll just fucking annihilate them."

He caressed the black sphere in his lap. "We own the world. We own both worlds. And we're going to prove it."

Craig drew back in horror.

"You're fucking crazy!"

"No man, I'm sane. Crazy is letting these fucking maggots walk all over you."

He reached out and patted Craig's forearm in a way that made Craig's flesh creep.

"You did good, you know. You kept them so goddamn busy chasing around after your toys they never had a chance to focus on the serious stuff." He caressed the thing in his lap.

"They couldn't get at it. Did you know that? For all

their power they couldn't make what they needed without us. They needed the computer. And they needed us."

Craig stared in horrified fascination.

"You see what that means, don't you?" Mikey was talking to himself now, looking down at the black thing in his lap, crooning to it. "It means they're not all-powerful. We can do things they can't and that means we're more powerful than they are.

"When I get done I'm gonna be master of all I survey." He chuckled and his eyes glinted even redder, like live coals. "I'm gonna rule the whole goddamn world."

Craig backed away from his former friend and then turned and ran.

There were problems, Glandurg admitted, even with an infallible magic direction finder.

It was undoubtedly pointing at the Sparrow, but it didn't show the way to go to get to him. That was a problem when you were in a maze of ductwork that ran only in straight lines and right angles. A half-dozen times now they had followed the arrow directly only to be balked by a dead end. Glandurg suspected the Sparrow was moving around also. But so far they hadn't gotten close enough to be sure.

They didn't want to leave the vents. The roars, screams, explosions and gunfire echoing through the vents—not to mention the smell of burnt flesh—made it clear there was a battle going on out there.

"He is over this way," Glandurg told his weary followers. "Forward."

"We can't go that way," Thorfin protested.

"And why not?"

"Because it's a blind tunnel, that's why."

"He's right you know," Snorri put in. "We've been there twice already."

"I'm the leader and I say we bloody go this way!"

"You may be the leader, but you've got the sense of direction of a blind pig," Thorfin said without heat.

" 'S'truth," young Gimli added. "Remember the sewage tunnel back home."

Glandurg reddened and puffed up like a toad. Then he got control of himself and exhaled slowly.

"Very well," he bit out. "For this job I will appoint a scout. Snorri, you go first to find the way. But I'm still the leader, mind!"

Without a word, Snorri moved past Glandurg and led the party off.

What now? Craig tried desperately to think. The lower levels were already overrun, the control center was out of commission and he didn't even want to think about what Mikey was up to. It couldn't end like this. Not after so much. But now what?

It took him a minute to separate the shrill tone in his ear from the background noise of the battle and a minute longer to realize what it meant. The computer room! Someone had reached the computer room already. He touched a stud on his bracelet and the tiny screen lit up with a view of the computer room. He gaped at what he saw.

Zumwalt and the others were with the computer! Craig slapped his palm against his forehead and swore. A trojan horse! He'd brought them into the castle himself and they'd turned out to be a trojan horse. No wonder half his equipment wasn't working. They must have been sabotaging it for days.

Craig looked at the tiny image and felt his gorge rise. Somehow those sonsofbitches were responsible for everything that had gone wrong since he got here. They were behind his defeat, his every loss.

Well, maybe he'd lose, but they sure as hell weren't going to profit by it!

He turned on his heel and ran down the corridor, away from the War Room and toward his private workshop.

❖　　❖　　❖

Craig met nothing in the halls. The robots and goblins were all fighting elsewhere. Half the lights were out and the elevators didn't work. Now and again the sound of battle or a muffled explosion would reach him by some trick of acoustics, but otherwise the castle was deathly silent. Even the air tasted stale and he realized the air conditioning system had quit.

The automatic door opener wasn't working either, so Craig had to use a spell to burn his way into his own workshop. Once inside, he pulled the door shut behind him and looked around.

There in the middle of the room, surrounded by scaffolding and equipment, was his latest creation: A full suit of Legion battle armor with some special improvements that no game master would ever have allowed.

The bottle-green armor glinted dully in the bright lights of the shop. It was almost twelve feet tall and so broad it looked squat by comparison. There was no neck, only a low rounded dome for a head. The arms were enormous, with oversized forearms to accommodate the blasters and heavy machine guns mounted in them. The hands were six-taloned metal claws, sharp as razors and hard enough to tear through armor steel. The legs were elephantine in proportion with all the actuators hidden behind layers of super-strong flexible armor.

It was hunched forward until its metal claws almost touched the ground and the upper back was opened up like a clam shell. In spite of his anger and haste, Craig stopped to pat the massive knee joint and look up approvingly.

Everything he knew, everything he had learned, was incorporated in this one lethal package. It wasn't as big as his warbots, but thanks to the power of magic it was nearly as heavily armed. It could run at over a hundred miles an hour and slam through walls and buildings as if they were not there. Instead of jump jets it had anti-gravity plates that would let it fly from the surface of the planet out into space if the wearer wished. It could withstand a nuclear explosion and its own firepower was measured in kilotons per second. It was the ultimate warbot, the culmination of his dreams of power.

And now it existed for just one purpose. To destroy the people who had caused his ruin.

Craig mounted the scaffold and chinned himself on the grab bar to ease his legs into the suit. He wiggled the rest of his body in, fitting arms and legs into the sensor harnesses. Finally he touched a switch and the back sections slid noiselessly shut behind him.

He watched the screen displays for a moment as the power gauges rose levels and the view out the front port came alive with a network of glowing lines and cryptic inscriptions. A breath of cool air washed over him as the climate control system activated. This was one design that could stand up to dragon fire and not even feel it.

Once he was sure everything was operational, he stood erect and stepped away from the scaffolding, brushing it aside with a casual gesture that sent pieces ricocheting off the workshop walls. He turned and stepped lithely toward the door. As he passed the workbench he reached down and scooped up the thermonuclear hand grenades lying there. Maybe they would be good for something after all, he thought as he dropped them into a pouch on the armor.

Stigi couldn't use his tail, but that didn't matter much. He very nearly blocked the passage physically. The attackers' only approach was through a mass of fire and straight into the dragon's fangs and claws.

Even if the castle guards had been equipped with dragon-slaying arrows it would have been hard to take Stigi out. As it happened that wasn't part of their equipment and so the problem was very nearly impossible. Warbots might have been able to handle Stigi, but they had all been sent to the lower levels to confront the League forces battling their way up through the castle.

Not that the guards stopped trying. They came on until their charred bodies reached nearly to the ceiling and then they climbed over the smoking corpses to keep coming. By the sheer mass of their onslaught they managed to force Stigi back a pace or two with every attack. But it was a long, straight corridor and Stigi had lots of room to back up.

The door at the end of the corridor was locked, but that didn't stop Wiz. He wasn't fancy about it, he just used a fireball to blow the lock off. Almost without breaking stride he kicked the door open and stepped through. Jerry and Mick were hard on his heels.

The computer was sitting in the middle of the floor, almost exactly where Wiz's double had been standing when Mikey hit him with the fireball. It was up and running quietly away with the image of the key rotating slowly on the screen.

"Is it my imagination," Jerry asked, "or is that thing a lot more detailed than the last time we saw it?"

"Your imagination's not that good. Let's smash the computer and go get Craig and Mikey." Wiz raised his arms to throw another fireball, but Jerry put his hand on his shoulder.

"You're not thinking. Without the key how are we going to close the gate?"

Wiz turned his head and looked at him. "What's your plan?"

"Make a copy of the file first. Binary representation should be as good as any other for the purposes of spell casting."

Wiz dropped his arms and nodded. From down the corridor came roars and yells as Stigi held the entrance. "We've got the time. Let's do it."

Craig heard the fight in the corridor as soon as he stepped off the stairs. The din echoed and re-echoed through the entire level of the castle. His sensors reported combustion byproducts in the air, including some that came from burning flesh. Finally he saw the carpet of bodies in the corridor leading to the computer room. Cautiously he stuck his massively armored head around the corner.

The smoke was so thick he had to resort to his sensors to see what was happening. Up ahead was a packed mass of warriors, some living, some dead and some wounded and down. Every one who could move was pressing ahead. As he watched the scene was backlit by an enormous gout of flame that turned the figures to black silhouettes against a fiery background.

With his battle armor he could undoubtedly charge through the mass and handle whatever was blocking his guards. But that would take time. What he wanted was to get his hands on Zumwalt as fast as possible.

He turned and ran back the way he came. Plenty of time to finish this bunch later.

Several hundred yards and a number of turnings later he was in the corridor leading to the side entrance to the computer room. He had only gone a few yards when he heard a rhythmic banging coming from an alcove ahead of him.

In the alcove two light warbots were beating their heads against the wall, literally. They would step forward, run into the wall, bounce back and then step forward again. From the looks of the wall they had been doing it for some time.

"Halt!" Craig ordered and the robots froze in midstep. Quickly he ran diagnostics and found the robots had a bug screwing up their obstacle-avoidance routines. Fortunately they were light warbots or they would have long since walked through the wall.

A couple of quick commands and the warbots were functional again.

"Follow me," Craig ordered and set off down the corridor with the two killing machines at his heels.

❖   ❖   ❖

"Come on, damn you," Wiz muttered, but the tape cartridge spun on unheeding. He only wanted one file, but the file was enormous. The tape backup was designed for reliability over speed; its designers had never imagined someone would have to transfer information to tape in the middle of a battle.

"They're in there," Snorri reported breathlessly. "I can hear them."

"At last." Glandurg thrust his scout out of the way. He turned to the others. "I will go first. Remember, give me room in battle to wield Blind Fury."

His followers nodded. Glandurg motioned the others to follow him and trotted forward, Blind Fury slapping against his back at every step.

Craig paused outside the door to the computer room. *One more thing.* He took a thermonuclear grenade from his belt pouch and pulled the pin. Now the only thing preventing a multi-megaton explosion was his clawed grip around the grenade. If anything happened and he loosened his hand, everyone in the tower would die in a flash of nuclear fire.

Then he kicked down the door.

The side door to the computer room fell in with a crash and Craig and his robots stormed in. Gilligan was at the main door watching the fight in the corridor and Wiz and Jerry were at the console waiting for the download to finish. All of them jerked up at the sight of the three armored apparitions bearing down on them.

"Kill!" Craig screamed. The robot to his left took one step forward, caught one foot behind the other and tripped headlong with a metallic crash. The second robot raised both its arms to sweep its built-in lasers across the group.

"Drop," Gilligan yelled and all of them pressed themselves to the floor as the beams of ruby incandescence swept toward them.

Wiz felt something gently warm across his back, unsquinched his eyes and looked up. The robot's head swiveled back and forth as it looked from one gently glowing arm to another. It nodded twice, executed an about-face and marched headlong into the wall.

"Oh shit!" Craig screamed. Then he went for Wiz.

He could have used his blasters. He could have used his machine guns. He could have let go of the thermonuclear grenade. Instead he lumbered forward with one taloned hand outstretched. He didn't just want to kill Zumwalt, he wanted to tear him apart, to trample him beneath the battle armor's steel feet until there was nothing left but a thin red smear on the computer room floor.

Wiz dodged the first swipe of the hand by ducking under the massive arm. He got a desk between himself and Craig, but Craig picked the desk up one handed and threw it across the room. There was a terrific *crash* as the flying desk hit the window wall and the sheets of glass collapsed.

Mick Gilligan dropped to one knee and emptied his pistol at Craig. He ejected the empty magazine, slammed another home and kept on firing. Bullets bounced off Craig's armor and ricocheted wildly around the laboratory, knocking up puffs of rock dust when they hit the wall and leaving neat holes in what was left of the big window.

Craig swiveled and pointed the arm holding the grenade at the pilot. A beam of roiling green fire lanced out. Mick dove for cover, but the very edge of the blaster bolt caught his left arm and side. He went down moaning.

Then Craig turned back to Wiz. Inexorably he closed in with one arm outstretched and his claws gaping. Wiz backed away, trying to dodge behind furniture. Craig kicked one piece after another out of his path as he herded Wiz back into a corner.

"Die, Wizard!"

In a single motion Glandurg kicked the grille free and

sprang from the vent, screaming his war cry and brandishing Blind Fury. The enchanted sword hummed through the air in a mighty blow aimed straight at Wiz's neck. At the last minute the blade twisted and struck Craig's battle armor, slicing through the armor plate just above the knee joint.

Craig stopped and looked down in wonder at the oil and fluids gushing out of the cut. Slowly and almost gently the leg collapsed under him and he sank to one knee. Wiz just stared open-mouthed.

Undaunted, Glandurg drew back and struck at Wiz two-handed. Again the sword twisted, this time upward to catch Craig in his massively armored chest. Again the sword bit deep, cleaving through magically enhanced armor and what lay beneath it.

The suit's speakers amplified Craig's scream to a deafening level. Sparks and fluids poured out of the gaping wound in his chest. He rose on his good leg and tried to stagger back. The suit's gyros moaned as they worked to hold him upright, then screeched as the bearings failed for lack of lubricant. Craig rocked backward, caught himself, overcorrected and fell forward just as Glandurg brought Blind Fury down in a mighty overhead chop to cleave Wiz in half.

Instead the enchanted sword connected with the back of the battle armor's domed head. Blind Fury went deep and came out with the tip stained with a wash of crimson. The battle armor jerked convulsively and then lay still.

Glandurg looked down at the fallen metal giant, over at Wiz and up at his bloodstained blade.

"Shit," he said.

Then he looked down at his feet. A gray, egg-shaped object had rolled clear of the armor's lax hand. Now it lay on the floor between the dwarf and his quarry hissing quietly.

The dwarves didn't know what the thing was, but their magic told them it was dangerous. Very dangerous.

"Run away!" Glandurg yelled to his men. It was wasted breath. The dwarves had turned as one and jumped for the air vent. There was a mad scramble as dwarves bounced off each other in mid-air, pushed one another out of the way and tried to squeeze three dwarves through an opening that wasn't big enough for two. Glandurg wasn't the first through the vent, but he wasn't the last either.

Wiz and the others pressed themselves flat behind the console as the grenade hissed evilly. Then the hissing stopped. Wiz jammed his fingers in his ears and squinched his eyes tightly shut waiting for the explosion.

At last he opened his eyes, took his fingers out of his ears and cautiously peered around the corner of the console.

The deadly gray egg still lay in the middle of the room, rocking gently. As Wiz watched, the fuse protruding from one end slowly unscrewed itself and fell to the floor. A tiny head poked out of the fuse hole and peered about, enormous ears flapping.

The gremlin pulled itself out of the grenade and grinned widely at Wiz.

"Wheee," it squeaked.

FORTY-SIX

MIKEY

Wiz leaned against the wall, one hand on his chest, and enjoyed the luxury of breathing deeply.

Jerry came over and knelt by the battle armor.

"Is he . . . ?" Wiz asked.

Jerry stood up. "Yeah," he said flatly. "He is."

He turned to Mick Gilligan. "Are you all right?"

"Just burns," Gilligan panted. "Not too bad, but it hurts." He looked down at his flight suit. "Good old Nomex."

"We'll get a healer to you as fast as we can," Wiz said. "Meanwhile, we've got one other thing to do."

Jerry raised an eyebrow.

"Mikey," Wiz said grimly.

"Someone call me?"

Mikey strolled through the broken door as casually as if it was still his castle. He was cradling a dark, misshapen thing in both hands. Wiz recognized it and sucked in his breath.

Mikey smiled and shook his head. "You poor dumb shits. You never did figure it out, did you?"

He stepped around the fallen robots and moved to the shattered window wall, shards of glass crunching under his feet.

"Now it's too late." He looked down at Craig's corpse. "While that little shit kept you running around in circles, I finished this."

Mikey held his prize high. A trick of reflection from the broken window made it appear that there were two of him, one floating in air and both holding the key.

Gilligan growled and scrabbled for his gun. Mikey looked over at him and he froze. Wiz wanted to scream, he wanted to run, he wanted to go for Mikey's throat. But he couldn't do any of it. Like Mick and Jerry he was rooted where he stood.

Mikey looked up and Wiz saw his eyes were red and glowing like an animal caught in the headlights.

"Always one step ahead. That's the difference between a real master hacker and people like you, Zumwalt. We're always one step ahead.

"Anyway, I just wanted you to know before . . ."

Out of the corner of his eye, Wiz caught a movement in the shattered window wall. Now there were two reflections in the glass. He shifted his eyes back to the room, but Mikey was alone with the key.

Then he looked in the window again. There was someone standing in front of Mikey's reflection.

Duke Aelric.

The elf's silvery armor was marred and stained. There were nicks in the blade of his curved sword and what looked like a burn mark along his helmet. Wiz had no idea where he had been, but he'd obviously been in a hell of a fight.

The elf stepped forward and laid both his hands on the key.

"Mine," he said.

There was still no one in the room but Mikey took the black convoluted thing in a double death grip.

"I made it," he yelled. "I can use it. It's mine!"

The muscles in his arms quivered and the veins in his neck bulged as though he was trying to hold the key against a tremendous pull.

In the window Aelric's teeth were set and splotches of high color stood out on his pale cheeks. His muscles swelled and rippled under his mail as he strove to wrest the key from Mikey's grasp.

Aelric and Mikey both seemed to flicker. Behind them Wiz thought he saw other things, some of them manlike. The sky darkened and began to run like wax—or perhaps it was his vision closing in. Faster and faster the images flickered until it was like watching an old silent movie. Then they flickered faster yet and there were two images superimposed on each other in the glass.

Mikey alternated with something large and vaguely manlike with fur and the pointed ears of an elf. The thing with Aelric was manlike too, but it shone so brightly it hurt Wiz's eyes.

Mikey's breath was coming in harsh gasps and his arms were shaking from the strain. Aelric was straining too, but he wasn't shaking. A fraction of an inch at a time the key moved toward the elf.

With a cry the Mikey in the window broke away. As soon as he released the key it was as if he had been sucked down a tunnel. With a despairing wail he dwindled and vanished in the distance.

The real Mikey whimpered, slumped to the floor and lay still. The black thing he had held was gone.

There was still no sign of Aelric in the room, but in the glass he stood with the key resting in the crook of his arm.

"Well done, Sparrow," the image said.

Wiz found he could move again.

"Are you really there?"

"I am here," the reflection said. "As for reality . . ." He shrugged in the old Aelric manner.

"Now," he said, turning serious, "I think you will find that resistance has collapsed. You will have perhaps another day before this World starts to decay. I would suggest that you and all your people be gone by then."

"And the key?"

"With it we can close the gate forever on these others." He seemed to sway a little and then caught himself.

"Lord are you all right?"

Aelric smiled tightly. "I am as you see me, Sparrow. Now if you will excuse me, it would be best to get this to safekeeping."

And with that he was gone.

FORTY-SEVEN

LOOSE ENDS AND FAREWELLS

Moira was with the first group of wizards and healers to come to Caermort. She and Wiz had time for a brief tearful reunion before the demands of their work pulled them apart. That night they ate a dinner of cold field rations on a terrace at Caermort and stood on the parapet looking up at the strange night sky with only a few odd stars.

"A fell place," Moira said with a shiver. "I will be glad to be gone."

"You and me both," Wiz said, leaning over to kiss her.

"Ah, I hate to disturb you folks," Jerry's voice came out of the darkness. "But there are some people here who want to talk to you."

Wiz and Moira turned. There was Jerry with twelve dwarves clustered around him.

"Oh, wizard," Glandurg called. "We would have speech with you."

Wiz stepped forward. Moira started to come with him but he stopped her.

"Stay back here. It's all right."

"What about you?"

"Whatever happens I'll be perfectly safe," he said with more confidence than he felt. "But I don't want you close to me if he starts swinging that sword."

Surreptitiously Wiz readied a fireball spell, but he stepped up to the group as if he hadn't a fear in the world. "Glandurg, isn't it?"

"Aye," said the dwarf leader. "We have come to bid you farewell."

"Very nice—but not to bring up a sore subject—what about your debt of honor?"

"Oh that," Glandurg said. "We were hired to slay an alien wizard whose magic was wreaking havoc upon the World. The wizard is dead so our contract is fulfilled." He looked slyly at Wiz and Moira. "After all, the trolls did not say *which* alien wizard they wanted killed."

Wiz could only nod.

"We go now," said Glandurg. "The evil wizard is slain, the balance is restored to the World and our debt is paid. Perhaps our paths shall cross again should you need doughty warriors to stand at your back on some great quest."

With that Glandurg and his followers turned and filed through the door. Then they began to sing, jauntily but very off key.

" 'Debts must be paid, ' " Jerry quoted as the dwarf song died out in the distance. "Those guys are the kind who would pay off a debt in subordinated debentures— if they knew what subordinated debentures were."

"Don't tell them," Wiz said. "The last thing this world needs is gnomes of Zurich."

"But those are not gnomes, they are dwarves," Moira said. Wiz and Jerry broke up laughing and she jammed her elbow into Wiz's ribs, making him splutter. "Oh all right! You and your silly name jokes."

"I wonder how they expect to get off this island?" Wiz said, massaging the suddenly sore spot on his short ribs.

"Burrow for all I care," Moira said. "I do not understand how they got here in the first place."

" . . . and you should have seen the wizards' faces when that dragon rider and her dragon, popped up in the chantry next to Major Gilligan," Judith said laughing. The others laughed too and she helped herself to more bread and cheese.

They looked like a halloween party. There was Wiz in his usual tight pants, open-necked shirt and sleeveless tunic. Mick Gilligan was sitting next to him in his Air Force green flight suit. Then came Moira in a long gown of russet velveteen with forest green lining showing in the insides of the flowing dagged sleeves. Jerry was beside her in a medieval-looking tunic with a most un-medieval patch pocket full of felt-tip pens. Finally there was Judith wearing the open-backed hospital gown she had arrived in, now artfully dirtied and torn.

It had been barely twenty-four hours since Caermort had fallen and none of them had gotten much sleep. But everyone agreed that the sooner they got Mick and Judith back to their own World the better.

Pots of blackmoss tea and pitchers of chilled fruit juice shared the table with platters that had held small cakes and other delicacies. There was a sun dial very conspicuously planted in the middle and everyone made small talk while they waited for the shadow to shorten.

"How is Danny?" Judith asked.

"Bronwyn says he will recover well enough," Moira told her. "There is sickness in his blood and the burns were of a dangerous kind. Still, she can pull him through." She bit her lip. "But the energies released did something to him she cannot repair. He will have no more children."

"Damn," Wiz said softly.

"I'm so sorry," Judith said.

Moira shrugged. "Such things happen. Considering the carnage all about them they got off lightly."

"And June?" Judith asked.

Moira smiled. "With him night and day, of course. They have brought the cradle into the sick room so she may tend both of her men at once."

"What about Duke Aelric?"

Wiz shrugged. "He took the key and vanished. I imagine we won't see him for a while."

Judith poured herself another cup of fruit juice, drained it and sighed. "My one chance to meet an elf. Gone."

The all fell silent for a moment.

"Well, anyway, I'm glad I got a chance to see you again," Judith said as she put her cup back on the table.

"And we are glad to see you, my Lady," Moira said. "I only wish it could have been a more pleasant visit."

Judith nodded and looked again at the creeping shadow of the sun dial.

"What are you going to tell them?" Wiz asked.

She looked down at the carefully soiled hospital gown. "That when I woke up I was wandering around downtown San Jose in this."

"That doesn't explain anything."

Judith's eyes twinkled. "I know. That's the best kind of explanation."

"They'll probably think you halfway came out of the coma, wandered out of the hospital and you've just been roaming around ever since," Jerry said.

Judith smiled. "How would I know? I was in a coma."

Wiz turned to Major Gilligan. "I wish I could reward you for your help, but I think anything we gave you would just complicate your life."

"I've been rewarded already," Gilligan told him. "And yeah, it would be a little hard to explain showing up with a bag of gold or something." *As if this isn't going to be hard enough to explain,* he thought.

"Okay, we understand you want to go back to the Air Force as if you'd crashed in the ocean."

"I've pretty much got to."

"You know we would put you down just about anywhere in the world."

Gilligan shook his head. "I've got a duty to go back and it will be easier if it looks like I just crashed."

"We'll put you and your gear down on an uninhabited

island not too far from where you disappeared. From there you can use your radio to get help."

"How far is that island from where I went down?"

"About 200 miles."

Gilligan frowned. "That's thin."

"We could put you and your raft in the water about where you crashed."

Gilligan thought about the freezing, fogbound Bering Sea and how long it would take to get rescued.

"I'll take my chances on the island."

"Okay, one other thing. We could heal your burns completely, but you'd be left with marks you didn't have when you took off." He looked Gilligan over. "Or we can partially heal you, so it will look as if you were burned when your plane went down."

"I've already been over this with your medics. I want to look like I was injured when I bailed out."

"You understand that once you're on the other side the pain spells won't work. Those burns will hurt."

Not half as much as some other things will hurt, Gilligan thought. But he just nodded.

Wiz nodded in return. "Very well, then. Your equipment's in the next room. You might want to check it over and make sure you've got everything you need while you've still got time. Bronwyn will meet you there for the healing."

Just about all his gear was there in a neat pile, even the things he had discarded when he came ashore on the island. It was all restored by magic. Somehow they had even managed to refill the magazines of his pistol.

"Mick."

He turned around and saw Karin in the door. His equipment forgotten, he took her in his arms and kissed her. The burns made him clumsy but neither of them noticed. "Where have you been? Why didn't you come with me?"

"Looking after Stigi and telling my superiors what had

happened," she said in a small voice. "I could not come until my squadron leader released me."

He held her in his good arm close to his unburned side.

"Listen to me. I've got two more years left on this tour." *If they don't courtmartial me over this,* he thought. "I'll serve out my time and resign my commission. Then somehow, *somehow,* I'll find a way to come back."

Karin looked deep into his eyes. "I will be waiting."

There was a discreet cough behind them.

"Time, my Lord," Arianne said. "Trooper, if you wish to accompany him to the chantry you may."

The wizards and others were already assembled when Gilligan and Karin came into the chantry.

As they came in, Wiz handed Gilligan a small wooden tablet. "Before you go, you might want to memorize this."

Gilligan looked down at it. "Is this what I think it is?"

"Yep, it's an 800 number. Direct line to the Wizard's Keep from any phone in the USA. Just don't use it unless you really need to."

Gilligan looked up at Wiz. "I'm not going to ask how you did this."

Wiz shrugged. "It wouldn't do any good. It was one of Danny's projects. We figured we might need to contact people over there again and Danny set this up."

Gilligan stared intently at the scrap of wood and his lips moved as he burned the number into his memory. After a minute he handed the tablet back to Wiz.

"Is this legal?"

Wiz hesitated. "Like I said, it was one of Danny's projects."

This time there were two circles of blue-robed wizards in the chantry. Bal-Simba stood at the head of one of them and Arianne led the other.

Mick and Karin embraced for one final time, then

Arianne waved him to the center of her circle, next to his gear. Judith took her position in the other and the chants began.

I hope to God I can pull this off, Major Michael Francis Xavier Gilligan thought fervently as he faced the three men across the table. He had managed to get his blues on over his bandages and the meeting was in an office rather than his hospital room, but he still felt lousy from the burns and spacey from the pain killers.

This wasn't a formal inquiry. Gilligan had only been back at the base for twelve hours. It was more of preliminary attempt to find out what had happened over the Bering Sea.

"Now Major Gilligan," the debriefing officer began, "you say you can't remember anything from the time you bailed out until you found yourself on the island?"

"Nossir. I think I cracked my head on the way out, but the first thing I really remember is being on that island with the radio." He paused. "Ah, I was delirious most of the time, sir."

The debriefing officer didn't respond, but the black man behind him, the one wearing the flight suit with no insignia, half-nodded. Obviously he had already seen a report of Gilligan's description of his "hallucinations."

It was thin and he knew it. Especially in light of what must be on Smitty's tape. But it was the best story he could come up with and he'd stick to it for as long as he could.

"The cold salt water apparently restricted the damage from those burns. You're extremely lucky, do you know that?"

A flash memory of blue eyes and a little dusting of freckles over a straight nose. "I figure I'm about the luckiest man in the Air Force," Gilligan said sincerely.

The debriefing officer nodded and the man sitting next to him in the flight suit with no insignia remained impassive.

Step by step they went over Gilligan's story—what there
was of it.

"And you say you don't remember anything after you
sent your wingman back?"

"Nossir, not a thing."

"Perhaps this will refresh your memory," the man in
the flight suit said. He leaned forward and handed Gilligan
a folder.

Here it comes, Gilligan thought as he opened the folder.
Then he looked at the photograph.

"Nossir," he said, fighting to keep his composure. "I'm
sorry. This doesn't look familiar to me at all."

The picture was obviously the result of a lot of work
with an image processor. The image had long, thin wings
and a small tail set at the end of a tapering, torpedo-
shaped fuselage. Just forward of the wings was a central
turret with what was obviously intended to be a sensor
array. The wings and body were marked with what were
clearly intended to be phase-array antennas. On top of
the wings were heavily baffled intakes for jet engines
buried in the body. The tail showed additional inlets for
cooling air to dilute the jet exhaust coming from the
shielded tailpipe.

The man with no insignia frowned. "Pity. Some of the
details are conjectural and we were hoping you'd be able
to fill them in for us."

"I'm sorry, sir. I don't remember anything like this."

"Well, it doesn't matter much. *Aviation Week* ran that
picture in last week's issue." His face showed he didn't care
for that at all. "We know now the thing isn't Soviet, so in
the next week or two the Japanese or the South Koreans
or the Israelis or whoever the hell else really did build it
will let the information leak out." He shook his head. "It's
a small world, Major, and you can't keep secrets long."

"Yes sir," said Major Mick Gilligan, thinking of another
World entirely. "It is a very small world."

FORTY-EIGHT

WINNERS AND LOSERS

The now-useless computer sat in a cellar at the Wizard's Keep. The pieces had been unpacked and set together in a pale imitation of a working system. It looked strangely out of place in the low room with the beamed ceiling and the rough masonry walls.

Wiz was sitting at the console with his back to the door, idly tapping on the keyboard with one hand.

"What are you doing, love?" Moira asked as she came up behind him.

Wiz shook himself out of his reverie and stood to kiss her.

"Just thinking," Wiz said after the kiss. "When I was back in Cupertino I dreamed of having one of these things all to myself. Now I've got one and it won't work here."

"I wonder if it is worth keeping?" Moira said with a housewife's practicality.

"I wouldn't feel right throwing it away. Maybe we can find a use for it."

"As a haven for gremlins, no doubt."

"I don't guess the gremlins are interested in machinery that doesn't work."

"Just as well," Moira said. "Else there would not be a moment's peace."

They stood arm in arm looking at the computer for a while.

"Well," Wiz said heavily. "At least that's over."

"Not quite, mortal."

Wiz and Moira whirled. There stood the elf Lisella.

Lisella smiled, cold and beautiful as the full moon at midwinter. "I mean you no harm, mortal. I come with a message. Duke Aelric bids you to him."

Moira moved in front of Wiz like a terrier protecting her master.

"Why does not the duke deliver his invitation himself?"

Ice blue eyes locked onto flashing green. "Because he is dying, Lady."

Duke Aelric lay on snowy linen in a cavern with softly glowing walls. He was so still and composed that at first Wiz thought they were too late. But as they approached he turned his head toward them.

"So Sparrow, we meet again." His voice was as firm as ever but he sounded weary, as if tired out by a great exertion.

"Yes, Lord," Wiz said numbly. Even this close he could not see a mark on the elf duke, but his normally pale skin was now almost chalk white.

"I wanted to see you once more to thank you. You have performed a great service for the whole World, including the ever-living."

"We almost screwed it up, Lord."

"You did very well indeed." His eyes flicked to Lisella. "Much better than some expected."

He stopped speaking and he seemed to drift for a moment. Then his eyes focused and he turned his attention back to Wiz. "You have my personal thanks as well." He sounded even wearier. "Ennui is part of the price the ever-living must pay." He smiled slightly. "Our association has been many things, perhaps, but it has never been boring."

"No, Lord." Wiz smiled through his tears. "It was not boring."

"No," Duke Aelric muttered almost beyond hearing. "Not boring."

Then he was still.

Silently Lisella placed a hand on Wiz's shoulder and guided him away from the bier. Behind him he saw other elves drape the linen over the body.

"It was the key, wasn't it?" Wiz said at last. "That was what those others wanted all along."

"Of course," Lisella said. "You did not realize that it could be used to destroy a World as easily as to close it off?"

"Well, why the Hell didn't he tell me the thing was that dangerous?" Wiz blazed. "We came within an ace of losing it to Craig and Mikey and losing the entire World with it."

She looked at him with amusement. "Would you have dared to use your Mousehole to construct it if you had known?"

"Then why . . . Oh! You can't build one, can you? You can't make a key on your own."

"Not so precisely as to be that powerful, no. Neither could the others. To attempt to make it by magic is to warp the very fabric of the World."

"So you used us," Wiz said dully. "Just like those others were using Craig and Mikey."

"You disapprove, Sparrow?" the elf said coldly. "You find the price high?" She tossed her head in the direction of the still form under the linen draping. "Consider the price *he* knew he would pay."

Wiz gaped. "He knew?"

Lisella cocked a raven eyebrow. "Why do you think he took such an interest in you?"

"But why? I mean if he knew it was going to kill him . . ."

"Because he knew there was a better chance of success with you and your alien magics than working only with the ways of his people. He chose a road of certain destruction because it gave a better chance—not a certainty, only a better chance—that the World would live."

She looked at Wiz oddly. "It must be a strange and wonderful thing to be so attached to a place you would willingly go down to non-existence for it."

Lisella raised her hand and made a gesture in the air. "Go in peace, mortal. Our business is at an end."

And suddenly they were back in the computer room.

For a long time neither of them said anything.

"Well," Wiz said at last, "the prophecy was true. The mightiest among us died and all of us lost."

"Craig lost his life. Danny and June lost the chance for more kids. Mick and Karin lost each other. Glandurg lost his quest. Judith lost months out of her life and we lost . . ." He stopped and swallowed hard, unable to go on.

Moira wiped her eyes. "Not everyone lost, I think. Mikey can be said to have gotten his heart's desire. So the prophecy was truly fulfilled."

Wiz thought about that. "Yeah," he said flatly. "You're right. He did get what he wanted."

Sunlight streamed through the mullioned windows of the Wizard's Keep in golden shafts and painted warm bright patches on the floor. Dust motes danced in the beams.

Mikey looked at the dust, fascinated. He stretched out his hand and tried to catch the dancing specks in his fist. But they would not be caught and he had more important things to do.

Very deliberately he plumped down on the floor and returned to the job of arraying his army. With exaggerated care he added a new tin soldier to the end of the first line of men. Then he took brightly painted wooden blocks from the pile beside him and added a new building to the town behind his men. He rearranged the cutout trees next to the town and leaned back to survey his work.

Looking out at the kingdom of block villages and tiny metal soldiers spread over the floor of his playroom cum prison cell, Mikey the Great beamed and gurgled with joy.

At last he was truly the master of all he surveyed.

THE WIZARDRY CONSULTED

ONE

FLUFF THE MAGIC DRAGON

True, it is nonsense. But it is
important nonsense.
— Philosopher Ludwig Wittgenstein
On His Life's Work
(Quoted on the title page
of *The Consultants' Handbook*)

"You know one of the nice things about peace?" Wiz Zumwalt remarked to his cubicle mate. "It's boring."

Jerry Andrews turned away from the glowing letters of golden fire hanging in the air above his desk.

"Are you being sarcastic?"

William Irving Zumwalt, "Wiz" or "Sparrow" to one and all, twisted his wiry frame in his chair and brushed a lock of dark hair off his forehead. Like Jerry he was dressed in the flowing linen shirt, breeches and high, soft boots that were this world's equivalent of jeans and a T-shirt. In spite of the clothes he still managed to look like a programmer.

"Heck no! I was just thinking how nice it is. No one's trying to kill me, no one's trying to destroy the world. No dwarf assassins, no elvish magic. Just peace and quiet. It's boring, but you know something? I *like* being bored."

Wiz sighed and looked out the traceried window into the rose garden below. Now that there were only three programmers left in the World, the Stablemaster had reclaimed their old quarters for his cows. In place of the Bull Pen, Danny, Jerry and Wiz had a spacious workroom in the main tower, with windows surrounded by climbing roses, and a view of the rose garden and the western wall of the Wizard's Keep. Beyond the towers of the west wall, the green hills ran off into the purple distance.

In Wiz's time in this world peace had been a scarce commodity. His first weeks after being shanghaied here were spent running for his life from the Dark League of the South. What with one thing and another, especially a red-haired hedge witch, he had discovered that the magic in this world could be made to work like a computer program. That led to a hacked-together magic language and a battle of magic that destroyed the Dark League. Then he'd been kidnapped by a remnant of the Dark League and spent weeks dodging wizards in the freezing, deserted City of Night. That was when Jerry, Danny and some other programmers were brought here from San Jose to help him. That in turn led to a couple of computer criminals finding their way to this world and that had ended in another enormous battle. In between there had been the job of teaching this world's wizards how to program and months of delicate, wearing negotiations with the non-humans of the world who were upset by humans' new magical powers. It had only been in the last few months that teaching and negotiating had tapered off and Wiz could get back to serious programming.

"Yep," he repeated, taking his eyes away from the landscape. "It's wonderful."

"You sound as if you're trying to convince yourself." Jerry sounded amused.

"I'm already convinced," Wiz said firmly. "I'm bored and I like it."

Jerry leaned back in his chair, which squeaked in protest, and put his ham-like hands behind his head. He was several inches taller than Wiz and a lot heavier, although he had dropped perhaps forty pounds since coming to this world a couple of years ago. Even powerful wizards here got more physical exercise than their software counterparts in Cupertino. Like Wiz he was tanned, but unlike his friend, who drew his dark hair back in a shoulder-length ponytail, Jerry's lighter brown hair was neatly trimmed above his collar. "I'd rather think of it as having enough time to work on interesting projects. Now that we've got wizards and apprentices trained in the basics of the magic compiler we've got the time for refinements."

"Speaking of which, what is that you've been hacking on so furiously?"

"Kind of an experiment," Jerry said, turning back to the code. "I'm trying to see how well the magic compiler works in a more conventional computer language."

"You're translating the thing into C?"

"Well, no," Jerry said. "I thought I'd try something that was a little less tied to computer architecture. Something more general."

Wiz looked over his shoulder at the lines of luminescent characters suspended in midair. Then he squinted and leaned closer.

The magic compiler was written in a combination of this world's runes, the English alphabet and various made-up symbols. To the uninitiated a spell listing looked like someone's graphics card had barfed on the screen. But even compared to that, this listing was strange. In addition to the "normal" symbols, there were tiny squares, triangles, right angles and things that were even less comprehensible. Wiz scanned the display several times, frowning.

"If I didn't know better, I'd swear that was . . ."

"Yep," Jerry said proudly. "APL."

Wiz groaned.

"Hey, you're a fine one to complain. Who wrote the first spell interpreter in a hacked-up version of Forth?"

"That was different," Wiz said with some dignity. "Forth was exceptionally well suited to what I needed to do."

"So is this," Jerry informed him. "APL is an extremely elegant language. You can express a whole series of complex mathematical operations in a single line of code simply, unambiguously and logically."

Wiz tore his eyes away from the mess above Jerry's desk and poured himself another mug of blackmoss tea. "*If* you've got a computer that can produce hieroglyphics and *if* you never need to remember what you did."

"Nonsense. It's no harder to write understandable code in APL than anything else. You can even write incomprehensible code in C."

"I rest my case."

Before Jerry could reply the door banged open and Danny limped in.

"How's the back?" Wiz asked, grateful for a respite from what promised to be a full-scale language debate.

"Getting better," the young programmer said, plopping himself down in his chair. He leaned forward almost forty-five degrees. "See? No pain."

Considering the extent of his injuries, Danny was lucky to be alive, much less walking around. A blast from a guard's weapon had nearly burned him in half during the great battle for Caermort almost three years before. Magic had saved him and magic had healed him, but not even the world's most skillful healers could restore him fully in safety. So for months he had been going to the healers in the Wizard's Keep for a combination of physical therapy, massage and healing magic. Gradually but steadily he was improving.

The third member of the software development team was several years younger with fresh good looks that made him look younger still. Even before his ordeal he had been slender, but the rigors of his recovery had taken flesh off his bones until he was positively skinny, despite the best efforts of his wife June and the castle cooks to feed him up.

He looked over at the characters above Jerry's desk. "What's that?" he asked, levering himself out of the chair and limping over to join them.

"APL," Wiz told him. "He could have been doing something useful and he's been writing an APL interpreter."

"Well, whatever makes you happy," Danny said with a shrug.

"Like figuring out how to tap into our world's telephone system, I suppose," Jerry retorted.

"Hey, we *needed* an Internet connection. We have to keep up with what's going on back in the real world. Besides," he added, "you're the one who's on that thing four hours a night."

"I have a lot of newsgroups I have to keep up with," Jerry said virtuously. "There's a lot going on there."

"Well, better keep it away from the wizards," Wiz said. "I'm not sure what they'd make of some of those newsgroups."

"You mean like the **alt.sex** groups?" Danny asked.

"I was thinking more of **comp.language.flames**, but yeah, the **alt.sex** groups too. Especially **alt.sex.gerbils. duct-tape**."

"That's bogus," Jerry said. "The real name is **alt.sex. bestiality.hamster.duct-tape**."

It was Danny's turn to look smug. "You mean that's another group. Just because it's not in the official **alt** hierarchy you can't find it."

Wiz wasn't sure whether he was joking or not. The Internet, an international computer network originally built around universities and research institutions, was famous for the depth and breadth of the knowledge contained in its newsgroups. However, even the Internet's staunchest advocates had to admit that not all the newsgroups were research-related—or even serious. Hidden away in various places in the sprawling multi-dimensional message space were some decidedly odd things, including some highly unofficial newsgroups. But you needed to know how to use the net to get to them. Danny's knowledge of the ins and outs of the net was extensive.

Danny was no sooner settled back in his chair than there was a discreet knock at the door. In all the Wizard's Keep there was only one person who knocked so delicately, so discreetly and so exquisitely.

"Come in Wulfram," Wiz called.

"Excuse me, My Lord." The castle seneschal was calm, dignified and more than a little bit stuffy. "But . . ."

Before he could finish the door banged open again and two children and a dragon charged into the room.

"UncaWiz, UncaWiz," shouted Caitlin, the daughter of one of the guardsmen. She was a couple of years older than Danny's son Ian, with dark curly hair, flashing dark eyes and a single black eyebrow stark against her pale, fair skin. She was utterly charming, she knew it and she used it shamelessly.

Right on her heels came Ian. He was barely three and well into the head-down-and-charge stage of childhood locomotion. Without pausing he ran full-tilt across the room and bounced into Danny's lap.

But the real attraction was the third member of the group, who charged into the room just as heedlessly, got his feet tangled up with the rug and his own tail, caromed off a pile of manuscripts and executed a neat bank shot to end up beside Ian and Danny.

Little Red Dragon, or LRD to the programmers, was little only in comparison to the eighty-foot cavalry mounts in the aeries below the castle. He—Wiz thought he was a he—was nearly ten feet long from snout to tail tip. His scales were darkening from scarlet to maroon and the blue edges were going from turquoise toward navy and his combination of exuberance, dragonish temper and size was making him increasingly hard to handle. Dragons do not become intelligent until they are nearly full grown. LRD was a long way from full grown and somewhat further than that from intelligent. But LRD and Ian were inseparable, so the dragon was allowed in the programmers' workroom and their quarters in the Wizard's Keep.

The seneschal knew when he was outclassed. With an exquisite sigh of resignation he stepped away from the door to await the wizards' pleasure.

"The dragon's got a new name!" Caitlin announced. "We had to come tell you because you can't call him LRD any more."

"Not LRD?" asked Danny, looking down at his son squirming in his lap.

"No! Fuf-fee," Ian pronounced distinctly, reaching up and hugging the scaly monster's neck. LRD looked pleased.

"I beg your pardon?" Wiz said.

"He means Fluffy," Caitlin said with five-year-old superiority.

"Fluffy!" Ian repeated with three-year-old emphasis.

"Okaaay," Wiz said, "his name's Fluffy."

"He's taking us on a adventure," Caitlin announced. "We're going across the river to hunt for mushrooms."

"All by yourselves?" Danny asked. "What does Shauna say?"

"Oh, Shauna can come too," Caitlin said. "Fluffy says it's all right."

"Where is Shauna anyway?" Wiz put in.

"Here, My Lord," the nursemaid said, puffing with exertion as she came into the room. She dropped a perfunctory curtsy to Wiz. "Sorry, My Lord, we were down in the orchard and they just took off running. The whole pack of them." She turned toward her charges and planted her hands on her ample hips. "No manners in the lot of them. Just up and whooping off like a tribe of savages. They ought to be ashamed of themselves, bursting in here like that and disturbing wizards at their work. Why it would have served them right if they'd interrupted a powerful spell and been turned into a parcel of frogs!"

The boy, the girl and the dragon recognized their cue and they all managed to look properly abashed.

"Maybe it would be a good idea to take them over to the woods," Danny said. "Let them run off some of this energy."

"Well . . ."

"Please Shauna," Caitlin wheedled.

"Peese," Ian chimed in.

"Whuf," added the dragon.

Shauna considered and then relented. "Well, all right, My Lord. But just to get them out of your hair." She turned and glared fiercely at the children. "And this time that beast—" She jerked her head at the dragon. "That beast has to swim the river. Near to upset the boat last time, he did, and the boatmen won't take him any more."

"Come on," Caitlin whooped and dashed for the door. Ian jumped out of Danny's lap and pounded after her and the dragon followed, nearly knocking Shauna down as he charged past.

"Here now!" she yelled. "Just slow down, the lot of you." With an apologetic glance over her shoulder, she followed her charges out the door, calling to them to come back.

The racket died down as dragon, children and nurse-maid vanished down the corridor.

At that point Wiz's wife Moira came into the room, a wide-brimmed straw hat thrown back over her shoulders, setting off her freckled, slightly flushed skin and cascade of red hair. She was wearing a peasant blouse, a brightly colored skirt and she had a basket of fresh flowers in her hand. To Wiz she looked like a vision out of a Monet painting.

"Was that LRD?" Moira asked as she came over to kiss her husband hello.

"No, that was Fluffy."

Moira arched her coppery eyebrows over great green eyes. "Love, even for you that is incomprehensible."

"Wasn't my idea." Wiz shrugged. "Caitlin and Ian insist LRD's name is Fluffy."

"Where did they get that, I wonder?"

Wiz shrugged again. "Maybe the dragon told them."

Moira just sighed and shook her head.

"Normalcy," Wiz sighed. "It's wonderful."

Jerry snorted with laughter.

"What's so funny?"

"Two kids go tearing out of here chased by a dragon, and you say it's normal."

"The dragon doesn't bother me, I just think of it as an overgrown St. Bernard."

A discreet cough reminded him of the waiting seneschal.

"I'm sorry Wulfram. Now, you were saying?"

"There is a dragon to see you, My Lord."

"A dragon?"

"A *large* dragon," the seneschal amended with gloomy glee. "He is sitting on the East curtain wall and—ah— urgently desires an audience."

For a minute no one said anything.

"Oh boy," Wiz said at last.

"So much for normalcy," Moira said.

"Just think of it as an executive vice-president from the home office," Jerry suggested.

TWO

ENTER THE DRAGON

First, know who you're working for.
—*The Consultants' Handbook*

Their guest was perched precariously on the east curtain wall of the castle. The walkway on top of the wall was wide enough for eight men to pass abreast, but the dragon gripped it with his talons the way a parakeet grips its perch. Its enormous scaled head stretched well above the watchtowers. Wiz couldn't see its tail, but judging by what he could see the dragon was a monster, two hundred feet long if it was an inch.

Although the courtyard and walls were deserted, the dragon had an audience. Wizards and others crowded the windows and doorways looking out into the East Court. There was another group at the double gate that led into the courtyard.

Even in silhouette Wiz recognized the bulk of Bal-Simba, the leader of the Council of the North, in the front. The large black wizard nodded to him over the heads of the others as he came up.

Next to him was the one-armed Master of Dragons who commanded the council's dragon cavalry and Arianne, the tall blond woman who was Bal-Simba's assistant.

The crowd parted as Wiz approached and he saw that the courtyard was not completely deserted. Out in its center sat Fluffy, née LRD. He was gazing up at the visitor and his tail switched back and forth like a fascinated cat's. Caitlin and Ian were back in the shadows at a side door, huddled up against Shauna's skirts like frightened chicks with a mother hen.

Wiz ducked back from the doorway.

"Quick," he said to Bal-Simba, "tell me everything you know about dragons."

The giant black wizard shrugged. "Easily done, since I know little enough. Adult dragons are morose, fierce and solitary creatures. They are greedy for treasure, skilled in magic and grow in size and intelligence seemingly without end."

"How smart do you think that one is?"

Bal-Simba looked appraisingly at the shadow darkening the doorway. "I would say very smart indeed. Like lizards, dragons never stop growing, but their growth tapers off as they age. That one must be very old to be so large."

"Great."

He looked at the Master of Dragons, but the one-armed man just shrugged. "Lord, I can tell you of the care and training of young dragons, but I know nothing of them after they mature. As their brains begin to grow the psychic bond with their riders loosens and they become unmanageable. We release them long before they attain full intelligence."

Wiz looked again. This dragon was not only bigger than the ones he knew, it was different. The scales had darkened to a dull gray-green, there were spines along its back and its teeth were much longer. The body was leaner and the whole effect was more predatory. The cavalry mounts were fearsome, but this thing was positively terrifying.

"Do not worry Wizard," a voice at once warm and soft as honey and hard and cold as iron rang in his head. "I will not eat you. Not yet, anyway."

"Uh, thanks," Wiz said. Bal-Simba frowned and started to speak, but Wiz motioned him to silence. Obviously Wiz was the only one who could "hear" the dragon.

Again the honey-and-iron voice rang in Wiz's skull. "You may call me Wurm."

"Hello Wurm," Wiz said. He took a deep breath and stepped out into the courtyard. The afternoon sun had warmed the flagstones and the air was balmy and sweet with the scent of roses. None of which made Wiz feel any less like a turtle on a freeway.

"Since my presence here seems somewhat disconcerting, may I suggest that we come to the point?"

"Sounds good to me. Ah, what is the point?"

"I have a proposition for you."

"'Proposition' as in 'job'?"

The dragon "shrugged" in Wiz's mind. "If you want to put it so crudely."

Wiz shook his head. "Sorry, I don't hire out. There's enough to do here."

The dragon "sounded" amused. "I think once you have heard the terms you will reconsider."

In spite of the mildness of the afternoon Wiz realized there was a trickle of sweat starting down his back. "Okay, what are the terms?"

"If you do this thing I will reward you richly. Gold, jewels, a heap of treasure higher than your head." A dismissive mental "shrug." "The usual."

"What if I don't take the job?"

The dragon craned his neck high into the sky and peered down at Wiz as if he were something small and soft that had just crawled from beneath a rock. "Then," Wurm said with chilling calm, "I shall burn the town to ashes and ravage the countryside for miles around. And I shall continue until you do agree. Or until I am slain."

Looking up at the monster, Wiz had no doubt Wurm could do it, or that he would.

"Uh, let me think this over, will you?" Wiz ducked back into the doorway where the others were waiting.

"How hard is it to kill a dragon?"

"Difficult," Bal-Simba said in a low voice. "Dragons are inherently magical and their magic is extremely strong. Besides which they are large and powerful beasts." He looked intently at Wiz. "Has it come to that?"

"No, but it might. He wants me to take on a job for him and he's got a real strong negative incentive plan."

"If we must fight him we had best buy time," the giant black wizard said. "I would advise you to ask him his proposition in detail."

Wiz stepped back out into the courtyard. "Okay, look. I can't decide on the spur of the moment, but I am willing to listen. Why don't you tell me the details?"

The dragon paused, as if thinking. "Very well then. Come with me and I will show you what I wish."

"Now I don't know about . . ."

"Do you fear for your safety, Wizard?" Again Wurm sounded amused. "I told you I will not harm you and I will not. Besides," and he lowered his huge head almost to Wiz's level and cocked it like a chicken watching a worm, "what could I do to you elsewhere that I could not do to you here?"

"It's not that," Wiz assured him hastily. "It's just that it's not easy for me to just pack up and go. I mean I've got responsibilities here and . . ." Wurm raised his head above the castle wall. Then he daintily lifted a foreleg and inspected his three black front talons, each longer than Wiz was tall.

"I'm in the middle of these spells, you see . . ." Wiz continued weakly.

Without pausing to inhale, Wurm breathed a roaring jet of lambent blue flame perhaps fifty feet long. Wiz flinched back from the heat and noise. Behind him he heard screams as people stampeded for safety. But the dragon's head was turned away from the Wizard's Keep. Wurm extended his index talon until it was immersed in the fire. He held it there until the tip glowed bright red. Then he reached down and whetted the heat-softened claw on the rough stone of the castle wall. He left three smoking, foot-deep grooves in the stone before he was satisfied. Then he turned his attention back to Wiz.

"Now Wizard," the dragon said mildly, "you were saying?"

"Can you give me ten minutes to pack?"

THREE

HE WHO RIDES A DRAGON...

Initial client contact is often the most
delicate part of the project.
—*The Consultants' Handbook*

"I do not like this," Moira said as she and Wiz walked
back out to the courtyard a few minutes later. Bal-Simba
and the others were trailing by a few yards to give them
some privacy.

Wiz grimaced. "It's not my idea of a summer afternoon's
stroll either, but we don't have a lot of choice."

"We could refuse the dragon now," she said fiercely,
"and fight him if he wills it!"

"And get a lot of people killed unnecessarily." Wiz shook
his head. "You heard Bal-Simba. We can't protect the town
right now, much less the countryside. In a few hours we'll
have the spells ready to hunt him down, but now we've got
to buy time."

"And you are to be the sacrifice," Moira said bitterly.
Then she sighed. "Oh, I know you are right, love. And
so is Bal-Simba. But for once I wish it could be someone
else."

Wiz stopped under the final gate and pulled her close,

almost losing his staff in the process. "Come on, it's not that bad. I've only got to stall him for a few hours and, hey, maybe the dragon wants something easy." He kissed her and felt her relax in his arms. "Don't worry, I'll be fine. Honest."

Moira broke away from him and tried to smile. "I know, love," she said softly.

"Besides, I've got this." Wiz held up his hand to show off his ring of protection. "Anything dangerous happens and this spell kicks in immediately. So quit worrying." He leaned close and kissed her again. Then he let go, turned and stepped out into the courtyard.

Wurm was where Wiz had left him. "Are you ready, Wizard?"

Wiz slipped the leather thong of his staff over his head and shoulder. Then he exhaled and tried to sound chipper. "Ready as I'll ever be."

The dragon bent its enormous neck down and Wiz swung his leg over. Then the beast raised its head and the spines moved together, cradling Wiz gently but firmly between them. Wiz made himself as comfortable as he could and tried not to think what would happen if the dragon arched his neck further.

Instead Wurm raised his head and Wiz was carried aloft with the swooping suddenness of an amusement park ride. Before he could adjust to his new perspective the dragon pushed off the wall and unfurled his gigantic wings with a beat that sent wind swirling through the courtyard, kicking up stray leaves and blowing grit back in Wiz's face. Wiz squinched his eyes shut involuntarily and nearly lost his lunch as his inner ear, deprived of a visual cross check, protested strongly. By the time he got his eyes open, the Wizard's Keep was dwindling toy-like below and the land was spreading out like a patterned quilt beneath them.

Bareback on a dragon was not the most comfortable way to travel, Wiz discovered. At least not when you were riding a monster like Wurm. Unlike the cavalry mounts, Wurm was so large that a human could not straddle his neck comfortably. Trying to sit astride was like doing the splits. By extending his legs forward along the dragon's neck Wiz could bring them comfortably close together, but that left him supporting most of their weight with his stomach muscles. Eventually he settled for a jockey-style seat with his legs drawn up as if his feet were in very short stirrups. If he shifted position frequently his muscles didn't protest too badly.

To keep his mind off his muscles—and his predicament—he studied the scenery passing beneath them. As nearly as he could estimate from the size of the fields below they were about as high as an airliner flies. But airliners are heated and pressurized and there was no sign of either on Wurm's neck. Still, legs and back aside, Wiz was as comfortable—well, as physically comfortable—as he had been back in the courtyard of the Wizard's Keep. Wiz spent a few minutes considering the implications of that for this world's physics and then finally dismissed it as magic.

After an hour or more Wiz began to fidget, and not just from the cramps. They were passing beyond the lands of man and well into the Wild Wood. "How much further is it?" he asked.

"Far enough," his host/mount replied.

"I mean when will we get there?"

"When we arrive." The dragon sounded amused. "You mortals, always so fastened on time and distance."

"I thought dragons were mortal too. I mean you die don't you?"

"Even the ever-living can die, Wizard, as you know. Mortal implies a finite life-span."

"Well, don't dragons grow old and die?"

"Grow old, yes. But I have never heard of a dragon dying naturally."

That had several implications and Wiz wasn't sure he liked any of them. "How old are you?"

"I do not know. Even if I had remembered to count the seasons, we do not become self-aware until we are nearly full grown. Ask the little one in the courtyard how old he is and see what you get for an answer."

"The little one . . . oh, you mean the young dragon."

Again the amusement in Wurm's "voice." "There was no one else in the courtyard as I recall."

"That's the pet, uh, playmate of a friend's kid. He calls him Fluffy for some reason."

"That is because he is," Wurm said in Wiz's head.

"Fluffy?"

"Of course. Can you not sense it?"

Wiz wasn't sure whether the dragon was joking or not and considering the circumstances he didn't want to find out.

"In any event," Wurm went on, "the experience will probably help him. Your kind is spreading everywhere and knowing humans well will serve him even better than it has served me."

"You were a cavalry mount, weren't you?" Wiz asked with a sudden burst of insight.

"I was."

"I thought you said you didn't remember before you became intelligent."

"I said we could not count. Just because we are not intelligent does not mean we do not remember."

Wiz wondered if dragons bore grudges.

"In probability it helped me," Wurm said, so quickly Wiz's next wonder was if dragons could read minds. "Most of my kind die before they attain reason. A few score years fed and cared for undoubtedly bettered my odds."

"But don't your parents take care of you?"

"We are able to care for ourselves from the moment we hatch," the dragon said. "Our mother is long gone before our birth."

"I'm sorry."

"Why? It is the way of dragonkind since time began. We avoid the entanglements of those who are born in groups of their kind and it ensures we will be strong and clever—those who survive."

Wurm didn't say it but the subtext was clear: This was one strong, clever dragon.

They flew a while more in silence.

"Wurm? When you were in the cavalry whose side were you on? I mean who . . ."

"Does it matter, Wizard?" There was a trace of irritation in the dragon's thought. "It was long ago, it happened and it is done. That is enough."

Wiz didn't try to make any more small talk.

Northward they flew, and eastward, for what seemed like hours. The sun rose to noon and sank toward the western horizon as they traveled. Below them the neatly tended fields and villages of the World of humans gave way to the rolling green of the Wild Wood and that in turn to a land of jumbled mountain ranges and steep, narrow valleys. Then gradually the mountains flattened and the valleys widened into gently sloping grasslands. The forest did not come back, save in scattered patches, but the land was green and pleasant. Squinting ahead Wiz could see more mountains rising off in the distance.

"Yonder lie the Dragon Lands," Wurm informed him. "Do you wish to turn back now, Wizard?"

Wiz hesitated. Part of him wanted more than anything to turn around and go home. But there was another part of him that drove him grimly onward. There was a problem here and he had to solve it. *Had* to.

Besides, if they turned around now it meant more agonizing hours riding dragonback.

"No," Wiz told Wurm. "Let's go on."

Wurm's expression didn't change but Wiz felt the dragon "nod" mentally. There was a small, distant part of him that told him he ought to be worried about that.

Wiz glanced at the sinking sun and estimated the distance to the mountains. "Is that where we're heading?"

"Our destination is somewhat closer," the dragon said and, without word or warning, winged over and dropped steeply. Wiz whooped in terrified surprise and wrapped both arms around the spine in front of him. He had a confused, whirling view of a broad grassy valley cut by a meandering river with a substantial village or small city nestled along its banks. Then everything was hidden by Wurm's enormous wings as they locked to brake for a landing.

"Dismount. We are here."

"Fine," said Wiz, trying to throw his leg over the dragon's neck. He found it was numb from hours of sitting and he had to use both hands to hoist the leg over so he could slide off.

He tried to step away from Wurm's side and his knees nearly buckled.

"Where is here?" he asked to cover his embarrassment.

"The Dragon Marches," Wurm told him. "Here the lands of mortals run to the borders of the Dragon Lands."

They were on a grassy knoll beside a dirt road that wound through the valley toward the village in the distance. Dotted here and there he could see clusters of buildings that looked like farmsteads. The fields were laid out in strips, most emerald green with growing grain. The air was cool but not unpleasant and the breeze whispered gently through the grass.

Wiz took a couple of tottering steps. His legs were more or less working again, but his lower back ached terribly and his butt was on fire as the circulation returned.

"I didn't think people could live beyond the Wild Wood because of the magic."

"Humans have spread further than your Council of the North ever knew," Wurm told him. "Here there is magic, but less than in the Wild Wood."

"So I see." Wiz shaded his eyes against the setting sun. Off toward the village he saw movement on the road, as if people were coming this way.

"Okay," Wiz grunted, stretching backwards to try to get the kinks out of his back, "now what's this job of yours?"

The dragon regarded Wiz with an unwinking golden eye.

"It is not my job, precisely," Wurm told him. "Rather it is for them. The ones who live in this valley."

"I thought you . . ."

The dragon breathed a thunderous snort of amusement. "What need would I have of mortal magic? It is the inhabitants of the valley who need you."

Wiz looked down the road. There was definitely a crowd of people headed toward them.

"Okay, why do *they* need me?"

"Why to defend them against dragons," Wurm told him. Then with a sudden motion and a thunderclap of air beneath his enormous wings the dragon launched himself into the sky, leaving Wiz to face the people of the valley.

"Remember, Wizard," Wurm's voice came into Wiz's mind. "Your duty is to them. Fulfill it well."

There were perhaps a hundred people coming up the road in a compact mass. *Welcoming committee?* Wiz thought. *But why didn't we just land closer to the village?* Most of them were carrying things, as if they had left their work to come welcome him. As they drew closer he could hear them, a low rumble that somehow didn't sound like cheering. In fact it sounded downright ugly.

By then the crowd was close enough that he could make out details. They were all men, mostly roughly dressed and all carrying something. Some of them had pitchforks, some of them were carrying flails and pruning hooks and some of them just had big sticks. None of them looked in the least bit friendly.

"Uh, hi," Wiz said, smiling weakly.

Moira fidgeted in the window seat looking north. Outside the bottoms of the clouds were turning pink in the setting sun. To the embroidery in her lap she had managed to add perhaps a dozen stitches.

"Negotiation or not, he should have been back by now," she announced.

Bal-Simba looked over from the oversized arm chair

across the room. "Long before now," the black giant amended. "At the very least he should have contacted us."

By unspoken consent they had gathered in the programmers' workroom. Danny and Jerry worked at their desks, Bal-Simba had settled himself into his special chair and relayed instructions through his assistant, Arianne. June, Danny's wife, was sitting in the corner with Ian asleep in her lap and Moira was in the window seat looking out the way Wiz had gone.

The first several hours after Wiz's departure had been a rush of frantic effort as programmers and wizards alike prepared for battle with the dragon. In several places in the castle wizards of the Mighty were still casting spells and apprentice programmers were still laboring, but in the main preparations had been complete for a couple of hours. Now as the long summer day drew to a close there was nothing left to do but wait and watch for some sign of Wiz or the dragon.

Danny turned from his workbench. "Time for the locator spell?"

Moira stood up. "Past time."

Once before Wiz had been kidnapped. As a result all the programmers carried a spell which would locate them anywhere in the World.

Jerry took down a beaten copper bowl from the top of a corner cabinet. The bowl was nearly hidden by scrolls and papers and he almost caused a small avalanche as he worked it free.

"We need some water," Jerry said looking around.

Moira snatched up the vase she had filled with flowers only hours before, tossed the flowers on the floor and extended it to Jerry.

As Jerry poured water into the bowl, Arianne entered, perhaps summoned by Bal-Simba. She stood beside him while they completed preparations.

Finally Jerry took a splinter from a vial and floated it carefully on the water's surface.

arg wiz locate exe! Jerry commanded.

As the five leaned over the bowl, the needle spun twice around widdershins, quivered and then slowly drifted off until it was pointing firmly south.

"South?" Danny protested. "But they went north."

"The needle points south," Moira said. "They must have circled around when they were out of sight of the castle."

Jerry frowned. "Hold it." He reached into the bowl and nudged the sliver of wood gently with his finger. The needle swung aimlessly and finally stopped, pointing in another direction entirely.

"Northwest?" Moira said, "but . . ."

Jerry tapped the needle again. The sliver bobbed aimlessly.

"Shit! We've lost him."

Almost unnoticed by the others, Bal-Simba whispered something to Arianne. The tall blond woman nodded and hurried from the room.

"But the locator . . ." Moira began.

"Has been masked," Bal-Simba said, rising from his chair to join them.

The hedge witch rounded on Jerry. "You *swore* to me that the spell could follow him anywhere. No matter what."

Jerry spread his hands helplessly "It should. I don't understand it."

"I do, I fear," Bal-Simba rumbled. "The dragon is shielding Wiz's location from us."

Moira clenched her fists and hissed something very unladylike under her breath.

"I suspect he had no intention of attacking us at all," the giant wizard went on slowly. "That was simply a ruse to distract us while he made off with Wiz. And while we prepared for the attack which would never come the dragon wove his spell masking their whereabouts." He scowled fiercely. "As Wiz would say, we have been slurped."

"That's suckered," Danny corrected.

"What it is does not matter," Moira snapped. "We have to find him."

Bal-Simba shrugged. "Easier said than done, I fear."

Danny twisted the ring on his finger. "I thought these things could punch through any counter-magic."

"Any human magic," Bal-Simba said. "Dragon magic is different and of a very high order. This Wurm is extremely powerful even for a dragon, I think."

"What do you think he wants with Wiz?" Danny asked.

Bal-Simba only shrugged. "Who knows the mind of a dragon?" Then he caught Moira's expression. "But I do not think he intends to kill him," he added quickly, "or even harm him, necessarily. Beyond that? I would not venture to guess."

"Wait a minute," Jerry said. "Can't Wiz contact us?"

"He can if he is unconstrained," Bal-Simba said.

They all fell silent. Everyone in the room knew what it took to constrain a wizard from communicating.

"Well, how do we find him?"

"The Watchers are being alerted now," the giant black wizard said. He turned to Jerry. "My Lord, can you release the recon demons?"

"I'll get on it immediately. It will take a while to extend their coverage though."

"As quickly as you can, then. Now if you will excuse me . . ." He turned and hurried from the room.

FOUR

MISDIRECTION FOR THE DIRECTIONLESS

Sometimes the problem you're hired to
solve is not the real problem.
—*The Consultants' Handbook*

Okay, Wiz admitted and he leaned against the bars of
his cell, *maybe it wasn't my best opening line.*

At least they hadn't killed him. On the other hand,
there was no guarantee that they *wouldn't* kill him. And
considering the way they'd acted that was a definite
possibility. In fact that option had strong minority support
in the mob. What had passed for cooler heads had held
out for "The Rock," whatever that was. Wiz had a
suspicion he'd find out soon enough and an even stronger
suspicion he wouldn't like it.

After a brief argument over his fate, they had hustled
him back to town with a pitchfork in his back. Now he
was on the second floor of a fairly substantial building.
More precisely, he was in jail.

Wiz had never seen one of this world's jails before but
he had no doubt that he was in one now. There were bars
running from floor to ceiling on three sides and a windowless stone wall on the fourth. There was a narrow bunk

bolted to the wall and a chamberpot underneath. The layout reminded Wiz vaguely of a Western movie set, but the substantial bars were no stage props. The cells to either side of him were empty. The place was clean enough, but smelled faintly of must and dust, as if it wasn't swept regularly.

From the glimpses he had gotten as the mob frog-marched him through town, the place was larger than it had appeared. In fact it was a good-sized town or even a small city, enclosed in stone walls. Most of the buildings were built of a combination of timber and stone, but a few of the more imposing ones were all stone. That included this very imposing jail off the main square of the town.

There were offices of some sort down on the ground floor and every so often someone would mount the narrow staircase to peek in. Somewhat less frequently the jailer, a thin, sour-looking man with jug ears and a big nose, would come all the way into the room to check on him. He was careful not to get too close, Wiz noticed, and if he had the keys he wasn't carrying them.

Wiz toyed with the idea of creating a spell to unlock the door but he decided the best thing to do was to wait and see. If he was going to solve these people's problem he needed more information and he wasn't likely to get that as a fugitive from justice.

Still, it wasn't a very comfortable situation. Wiz sat on the edge of the bunk and wondered how he had gotten into this mess.

Let's see, he thought. *A dragon wants me to protect these people from dragons. The people who live here want to string me up because I'm working for a dragon—only I'm not working for a dragon, I just agreed to find out what the dragon wanted. Except the people still want to string me up for associating with dragons and I'm still not sure what the dragon really wants and . . .* And he was getting a headache.

For some reason he remembered visiting a psych major

buddy in her lab long ago and far away. Sybil had been running rats through mazes as part of some kind of project and while they talked she kept a stopwatch on the rat and its frantic efforts to escape. It had been a long time ago and Wiz found he couldn't remember what Sybil looked like very well, but he had a crystal-sharp memory of the expression on the rat's face.

There was a stirring in a corner of the room off behind the stairs. Wiz looked again and someone stepped out of the shadows. Someone tall, slender and wearing a jerkin and tight trousers. Then she took another step out into the full light and Wiz saw it was a woman. A young woman, actually, he amended, with dark hair down to her shoulders, dark eyes and fair skin. She strode lightly across the room with the easy grace he associated with gymnasts or dancers. Somehow Wiz didn't think she was either of those things.

She stopped several paces from the bars and put her hands on her hips. "So you're the wizard, eh?"

Wiz nodded. "Who are you?"

"Name's Malkin. I'm here for stealing. What'd you do?"

"Not much of anything, actually. My name's Wiz."

"You came here riding a dragon, didn't you? That's enough."

"Well, if you knew why did you ask?"

Malkin shrugged.

"And," he added, "if you're a prisoner too, how come you're on the outside?"

Malkin grinned and held up a key ring. "Like I said, I steal things."

"And you're still hanging around here?"

His new acquaintance grinned. "Jail's as good a place as any to doss," she said lightly. "Besides, listening is more fun than escaping. They're arguing about you in the sheriff's office."

"What are they saying about me?"

"They want to take you to The Rock."

"What's The Rock?"

"That's where they chain out the condemned for the dragons to eat," Malkin told him. "Supposed to keep the dragons satisfied so they don't eat anyone important."

"Does it work?"

"Nah. But the dummies keep doing it anyway." She shrugged. "You're an outsider, so you're natural."

"Not much tourist business here, is there?" Wiz asked sourly.

Malkin shrugged again. "Anyhow, the folks who brought you want to take you to The Rock right away and the sheriff doesn't want to until the mayor and council have a chance to see you. So far the sheriff's winning. That means you've got a few hours because it will take them that long to get most of the council together."

"Does the sheriff think the mayor won't want to see me killed?" Wiz asked hopefully.

"Nah. But ol' Droopy's a stickler for protocol. If he isn't consulted he'll make the sheriff's life miserable for weeks. So it's better for the sheriff to wait."

Wiz opened his mouth to reply but Malkin faded soundlessly back into the shadows. An instant later the jailer poked his head up the stairwell.

"Who are you talking to?" he demanded.

"Myself," Wiz said brightly. "I often have long conversations with myself. I find I'm excellent company. I play bridge with myself, too. You don't happen to have a deck of cards, do you?"

The jailer looked at him oddly and ducked back down the stairs.

Wiz lay down on his bunk and thought hard. Unless these people had some very powerful magicians, something he had seen no sign of, he could get out of here any time he wanted to. But that wouldn't help solve his problem. Given a little time to prepare spells, his magic would probably let him beat a dragon—provided it wasn't too big or too powerful. But he didn't think that he could take on all the dragons in the Dragon Lands alone and win. That obviously wasn't the answer.

He might be here to help these people but they felt he had a higher and better purpose as dragon bait. They didn't want help, they wanted a sacrificial goat they could hang all their trouble on. Yet he *had* to help them! It was imperative that he solve their problem.

Wiz chased the problem round and round in his mind without finding even the beginnings of a solution. He did, however, find an increasing sympathy for that long-ago rat in the nearly forgotten psych lab. He wondered if the rat had ever found the solution to its problem. Then he wondered what constituted a "solution" to a psych maze from the rat's point of view. The patch of sunlight from the window in the side wall finished its journey up the wall and gradually dimmed out at dusk. Outside the street noises quieted and died as the city settled into sleep. Eventually Wiz did the same.

Gently, soundlessly, the searcher floated north into the graying dawn. Physically it looked like a smear of smoke or a wisp of gray silk about the size of a handkerchief. Magically it was nearly as uncomplicated. All it did was gather sense impressions and pass them on to a slightly larger, somewhat more substantial entity floating along well behind it. It had only limited mobility and moved mostly by floating on the wind.

By itself it wasn't much, but the searching spell cranked them out by the tens of thousands. The searchers fed back into hundreds of the larger concentrators and they fed into dozens of high-level analysis demons. Given time they could find anything in the World that was in the open and unmasked. Slowly, inexorably, the net of magical watchers was spreading over the face of the World.

The rising sun tinted the underside of the clouds orange but the mountains below were still in deep shadow. Soon the sun would break above the horizon and bathe the mountain peaks in fire. It would be a glorious sunrise but the searcher was incapable of knowing or caring. It floated where the wind took it, working generally north on the air currents.

The searcher saw the speck detach itself from a peak and waft into the air, but it attached no more significance to it than to the pinkened clouds or the dark valleys. Analysis was for the higher echelons. So it faithfully recorded the speck's growth and resolution into a dragon, climbing to just below the bottom of the clouds. It watched without apprehension as the dragon approached, its great wings cleaving the air in mighty beats. It felt no fear as the dragon swooped down with its wings slightly folded to increase the speed of the dive, and no terror as a gout of dragon fire blotted out its existence. All of this it simply recorded and transmitted back to the collector, neither knowing nor caring that another dragon had flamed the collector minutes before.

Its killer, a young female only recently sentient, felt a pang of fierce joy at having destroyed the intruder. She gloried in her strength and prowess as she climbed toward the clouds to begin her day's hunting—and to kill any more of the strange creatures who invaded her territory.

Back at the Wizard's Keep, Jerry Andrews studied the results on his display and frowned.

"A problem?" Arianne asked mildly. Bal-Simba had been up late and his assistant had taken the early watch. Jerry had been up all night and probably wouldn't crash for a few more hours.

"Something's happening to the searchers." He took a long pull on the mug of blackmoss tea on his workbench and swiveled to face the tall blond woman. "We've got good coverage on the lands of man and the Wild Wood, but when we move outside that territory we start losing them."

"Losing them?"

"The search demons. Mostly they're being destroyed. Some we're just losing contact with. I think those are local magical effects. But a lot of them are being attacked by dragons."

It was Arianne's turn to frown. "That could be natural. Dragons are common beyond the borders of the lands of man and they do not like other flying objects in their air." She paused.

"Do you think it's natural?"

"I do not know," the wizardess said slowly. "I would not count on it."

"Wurm's doing?"

"It may be. However, dragons are solitary creatures. It takes a great cause to get them to cooperate, even slightly."

"Which means that kidnapping Wiz is a very big deal for the dragons."

"What it means, I think, is a problem for Bal-Simba when he awakens, and possibly the Council of the North. It is far beyond my abilities to decipher. What does this do to your search?"

"Complicates the hell out of it." Jerry swiveled back to the columns of glowing letters above his bench. "We're not getting any searchers more than a couple of hundred leagues beyond the borders of the known world. Unless we can change that we're going to be limited in where we can look." He took another pull on his tea mug. "Somehow I don't think we're going to find Wiz in the known world."

FIVE

A SUDDEN CAREER CHANGE

**Never tell them the truth until you check to
find out what the truth is today.**
— *The Consultants' Handbook*

"You still here?"

Wiz jerked awake and there was Malkin standing just outside his cell.

"Of course I'm still here. I'm in jail!"

Malkin shrugged. "So? You're a wizard, aren't you? Why don't you just magic yourself out of here?"

"I can't do that," Wiz said miserably.

"Well, don't you know other wizards? They could get you out of here."

"I can't do that either," Wiz said.

"Why not?"

"I just can't. I've got to solve these people's problems."

"Look," said Malkin, obviously exasperated, "the folk hereabouts don't want you to solve their problems. They want to stake you out like a pig at a barbecue."

"I can't run away," Wiz said simply. "I've got to stay, don't you see?"

"I see they're right," Malkin said. "Them as says wizards is all cracked."

She was right, he knew. The smart thing would be to magic himself out of the place, walk the Wizard's Way back to the castle and return with enough help to clean up the whole situation. But he couldn't do that. He just *couldn't*. There had to be a better way and he had to find it on his own. Malkin sniffed and Wiz looked miserable as he pondered the trap he was in.

And then, in a blinding flash, he had it!

The misery and indecision were gone and his brain shifted into overdrive as he saw the possibilities. He started to smile. Then he started to grin. Then his expression became positively maniacal with glee.

Like most programmers, Wiz preferred straight talk and plain dealing. But he wasn't a fanatic about it. It was obvious the only thing straight talk and plain dealing would get him in this situation was a quick trip to The Rock.

Malkin edged away from the bars. "Are you all right?"

"Never better," he assured her. "Never better. It's just the solution is so obvious."

"What is it then?"

"Well," he told Malkin slowly. "There's reality, and then there's Creative Reality."

"Creative reality?"

"It's kind of like Creative Accounting—except they don't send you to prison if they catch you at it."

"Meaning what?" the girl said with a frown.

"Meaning that a true master of Creative Reality borrows their watch and tells them what time it is, and then gets paid for it," Wiz told her. "That's the first rule of Creative Reality. You make people pay you to solve their problems—and then you make them like it."

"But these people don't want you to solve their problems," Malkin said in the same exasperated voice. "They want you for a sacrifice."

Wiz's smile got even broader. "That's normally the way

it is for the masters of Creative Reality. Kind of the job's ground state."

"The only thing that's going to get ground is you if you don't get out of here."

"Oh, not at all. Look, the first secret of consulting—that's what we call applied Creative Reality—is that people don't need an outsider to tell them what to do about their problems. They know they've got problems and they usually know what their choices are. What they don't know is how to get from where they are to a place where they have made a choice. So they bring in a consultant and most of the time half the people in the organization don't want advice, they want a scapegoat—a sacrifice. Now they've got an outsider in the game they can blame their troubles on. But the game's rigged against him from the first."

Now Malkin was intrigued rather than exasperated. "Yeah. So?"

"So what the successful consultant does, once he's dealt into the game, is cheat like mad."

"I still don't see . . ." Malkin began, but there was some commotion on the stairs as the warder made his way up. The thief slipped into an adjacent cell the instant before the warder's head poked through the floor, quickly followed by the rest of him. He stood by the stairway, drew himself to unaccustomed attention and announced: "His Honor, Mayor Hendrick Hastlebone, Lord Mayor and head of the wool merchants guild and the honorable members of the city council. Mayfortunesmileonthe-honorablemayorandcouncilors." Then he relaxed and slumped again.

The mayor was a portly individual with basset eyes, a substantial paunch and a considerable appreciation of his own importance. He was dressed in a short robe of green velvet trimmed with gold. Around his neck hung a heavy, gaudy gold chain of office topped off with a jeweled and tasteless medallion.

One of his councilors was tall and lean, one was short

and bald and the others were pretty much nondescript. They wore either the short robe and hose like the mayor or long robes with deep hanging sleeves and they all had heavy gold chains around their necks, only slightly less gaudy than the mayor's. They advanced in a tight knot with the mayor in the lead until they stood before Wiz's cell.

Wiz stood waiting for them, not quite leaning against the wall, but giving the impression that he was completely at ease. He watched the mayor carefully and just as the man drew breath to speak he cut him off.

"Good of you gentlemen to come."

The mayor was caught with his mouth open. He closed it, scowled and tried again.

"Who are you?"

"My name's Wiz Zumwalt."

"A wizard?" one of the councilors interjected. Mayor Hastlebone glared over his shoulder, but Wiz and the others ignored it.

"I'm a wizard by training, but by profession I'm a consultant. I solve other people's problems for a living."

The mayor raised an eyebrow. "Most folks have enough to do solving their own problems."

"That's why we consultants are so rare. And so much in demand."

The mayor snorted.

"Now, I understand that *you* have a problem with dragons," Wiz said. "I can show you how to rid yourselves of your dragon trouble—for a very reasonable fee, of course."

"Of course," said one of the councilors, the lean one, an individual with an oily manner and a puce wool robe that clashed horribly with his complexion.

"What makes you think you know how to handle dragons?" the mayor demanded.

"I come from the Valley of Quartz—Silicon Valley—and we have no problems at all with dragons there."

"We have our own ways of handling dragons," one of the councilors said.

"I'm sure you do," Wiz said, assuming a manner he had seen so many times when consultants made a pitch. "And what you've accomplished here is really remarkable—all things considered. But perhaps you could benefit from a more professional, scientific approach to your problem."

"How did you get here?" a hatchet-faced man in a malachite green robe demanded in a tone that indicated he knew the answer perfectly well.

"By dragon. It's a very expeditious manner of travel." Wiz smiled. "You ought to try it sometime."

That set them buzzing. The mayor turned his back and the whole group huddled together, muttering to one another. Once or twice someone poked his head up out of the pack and craned his neck to get a better view of their visitor. Wiz stayed where he was and tried desperately to look as if he didn't have a care in the world.

"Very well," Mayor Hastlebone said finally. "If—*if* you can completely rid the valley of dragons, what would be your fee?"

"One tenth of the town's produce for a year," Wiz said as blandly as he could manage.

"Preposterous!"

"Hardly. The dragons cost you more than that in a bad year and probably almost that much in most years."

"Absurd," said the mayor, with a little less conviction.

"Quite reasonable, actually."

"It would be worth it if he succeeded," said one of the councilors, a portly man in a forest green short robe and rose pink hose.

"Utter nonsense," said another councilor.

"Are you afraid he might succeed?" asked a silver-haired man in sea blue.

The mayor's face turned red and a vein in his temple started to throb.

"Gentlemen, gentlemen," interposed a pudgy man with a rim of white hair around a sweat-shiny scalp. "Suppose it got about that this wizard had made his offer and we had refused out of hand? Can we afford *not* to let him try?"

The councilors nodded and muttered among themselves and even the mayor seemed momentarily lost in thought.

"Very well," Hendrick said at last. "You shall have your opportunity. But," and he stepped close to the bars and wagged his finger under Wiz's nose, "we expect results. We only pay for results."

The fact that he didn't haggle over the price told Wiz the mayor didn't expect him to complete the assignment successfully.

"Plus room and board, while I work," Wiz said.

The mayor opened his mouth to object, caught the mood of the council and merely nodded.

"Oh yes, I'll need a local assistant."

Hendrick didn't look pleased. "Don't know that I can spare anyone."

"What about the young lady over there?" Wiz pointed to Malkin, sitting demurely in her cell. "I believe she is available."

The mayor turned to look at Malkin and a smile spread slowly over his face. Wiz didn't need to read minds to know he saw a way to get rid of two thorns in his side when Wiz failed.

"Very well. Warder! Release the prisoner into this wizard's keeping."

As soon as the cell door was unlocked Malkin threw herself about the mayor's neck, weeping and thanking him for his generosity. Since she was nearly half a head taller than the mayor, the result was incongruous to say the least.

Mayor Hendrick was still trying to brush her off when someone burst into the office below shouting for the watch.

There was a mutter of conversation downstairs and then two sets of feet came pounding up the staircase.

"Dragon!" panted the lean straw-haired man in the lead. "Dragon's hit the Baggot Place. Got Farmer Baggot and his whole family."

"Ate them all?" demanded the mayor.

"Not yet," the man gasped. "Least not when I left. He's got them penned in the farmyard."

The mayor turned back to the cell and smiled at Wiz in a way that wasn't at all pleasant. "Well, Wizard," he said, "it seems you face your first test."

SIX

MORE THAN ONE WAY TO SKIN A DRAGON

First get them talking.
                    —*The Consultants' Handbook*

The Baggot Place was about a mile out of town. Since the mayor and council didn't offer to provide transportation, Wiz and his new apprentice had to walk.

It was a fine morning for walking. The sky was clear, the air was cool, the sun golden, and the morning light made the dew on the brilliant green grass sparkle and glitter as far as the eye could see.

They weren't the only ones on the road. Ahead and behind them, people were trooping out of town along the road. Occasionally an apprentice or schoolboy would overtake them and run on ahead.

"Are you sure we're going in the right direction?" Wiz asked Malkin.

"This is the way to the Baggot Place and that's a fact," Malkin replied, tossing and catching something shiny as she strode along, her long legs letting her match Wiz stride for stride.

"Then why are all these people coming this way? Don't they know they're headed toward the dragon, not away from it?"

"Course they know," Malkin said. "They want to see the show."

"The show?"

"The dragon burning down the farm. Or maybe even you destroying the dragon." The way she said it made it obvious which way Malkin thought it would go.

"Hmmpf!" Wiz snorted. Then he got a closer look at the shiny thing his companion was juggling. It was a heavy gold chain with a big medallion attached.

"Where did you get that?"

"Pinched it when old baggy eyes wasn't looking," Malkin said gaily. "He never even noticed it."

"Well give it back!" Wiz commanded. "Preferably so he doesn't know you took it."

Malkin turned sullen for a moment and then brightened. "You mean un-steal it? Put it back around his neck so he doesn't notice? Now that could be fun."

Wiz groaned. Obviously his new associate's profession was an avocation as much as a necessity. Kleptomania he hadn't counted on.

"Why'd you spring me anyway?" Malkin asked, tucking the chain away in her jerkin.

"Because I needed someone who knows this place to tell me what's going on. And so far you're the only honest person I've met." Then he eyed the bulge in Malkin's clothing.

"So to speak," he added.

Little knots of citizens had already gathered on the hill overlooking the farm. They stood about in groups of two or three and gossiped and pointed down at the farmstead below. Wiz noticed none of them ventured even a little ways down the grassy slope toward the stricken dwelling.

As Wiz and Malkin toiled up the road the crowd's excitement grew.

"The wizard's coming!" an adolescent male voice shouted. "Here comes the wizard." Heads turned and people shifted to catch a glimpse of Wiz and Malkin as they climbed toward the brow of the hill.

The farmstead at the base of the hill was built of warm yellow sandstone with a dark slate roof. There was a three-story farmhouse, a large stone barn and several stone outbuildings, all clustered tightly around the farmyard. Where the buildings did not touch they were connected by a high stone wall.

Protection against dragons, Wiz realized. Only this time it hadn't worked. Wiz could hear the terrified lowing of cattle in the barn and in the courtyard he saw the flash of sunlight off scales as the dragon moved.

The gawkers edged closer to Wiz and Malkin, some of them shifting their position so they could see both the wizard and the farmhouse at the same time.

Obviously they expected him to produce a white horse and suit of armor out of nowhere and ride down to do battle with the monster. Or at the very least start throwing lightning bolts.

But Wiz didn't have a spell for horse and armor handy and he suspected lightning bolts would only annoy the creature. Besides, he doubted he could kill it before it burned the farmstead to the ground and killed everyone inside.

In fact, Wiz realized, he didn't have the faintest idea just *what* he was going to do next. So far everything had been reaction and reflex. Now he needed something more and he simply didn't have it. He felt the townspeople's eyes boring into him from all sides and he flushed under the weight.

Well, he wasn't going to accomplish anything from up here. He'd have to confront the dragon.

"You wait here," he told Malkin. "I'm going to go down there and try to talk him out of this."

Malkin looked at him. "You're going to go in there?" she asked. "Just like that?"

"Well, yes."

"And you're going to talk to the dragon. Get him to release his prisoners?"

"I hope so."

Malkin eyed her erstwhile employer. "Around here we've got a name for people what talks to dragons."

"Traitor?" Wiz asked apprehensively.

"No. Lunch."

It was a long, long way from the top of the hill to the farmyard gate. Well, Wiz acknowledged, it may have only been a few hundred yards, but it *felt* like a long, long way. By the time he got to the door of age-grayed oak planks in the yellow stone wall he was sweating, even though the dew was still on the grass.

Wiz stood before the gate for a moment, gathering his courage and mentally reviewing his plan. But his courage wasn't cooperating and reviewing his plan only reminded him he didn't have one, so he took a deep breath and knocked on the gate.

The door opened a crack and a three-foot talon hooked through the slit and pulled it wide. Suddenly Wiz was face-to-face with a very large dragon.

It wasn't a monster on the scale of Wurm. Objectively he knew the creature couldn't be much more than a hundred feet long. But objectivity doesn't count for much when you are one easy snap away from a set of jaws that are longer than you are high, all studded with fangs as long as your forearm. It doesn't help any when those jaws start salivating as soon as you come into view.

"Helllooo," the dragon's honey-and-iron voice rang in Wiz's skull. "Do come in." The last part was said pleasantly, but there was no doubt it was a command.

Wiz stepped through the gate as if it was the most normal thing in the world. He found himself standing between two enormous clawed forepaws and staring at an expanse of armored chest.

The dragon stretched his neck out until his head was nearly twenty feet above the ground. Then he cocked his head to one side and regarded Wiz unblinkingly. Wiz resisted an impulse to wave inanely to the beast and a much stronger impulse to turn and run. So he just stood there, hands at his side and with what he knew must be a monumentally silly smile plastered on his face.

"My, you are a bit odd, aren't you?" the dragon said at last.

"I beg your pardon?"

"Normally the only humans who approach us are warriors who come blustering and bashing, or magicians who come hurling all sorts of dreadfully tacky spells. But you're not doing either. I wonder what you could be?"

"I'm a negotiator. I'm here to arrange for the release of the hostages."

"Hostages? Oh, you mean those." The dragon jerked its head toward a corner of the farmyard and Wiz saw several people huddled together. One young man scrambled to his feet as if to dash for safety through the open gate, but without turning his head the dragon lifted his tail and brandished it threateningly. The youth turned white and sank to his knees.

"Actually they're not hostages. More in the nature of provisions."

"That's what I wanted to talk to you about," Wiz said.

"You're not frightened, are you?"

"No," Wiz lied.

"Oh, I do hope you're not," the dragon said. "These—" he twitched his tail at the cowering knot of people "—are frightened positively speechless and I was so hoping for some amusing conversation before dinner."

"Uh, I don't suppose I could convince you to make a meal of beef?"

The dragon licked his chops and his fangs glinted evilly in the morning sun. "Oh, certainly. As a second course."

Then he was all mock civility again. "But I am being churlish. Allow me to introduce myself. I am called Griswold."

"Pleased to meet you," Wiz lied once more. "I'm Wiz Zumwalt."

"Ah, yes," Griswold said, regarding him closely. "And a wizard too, I see. My, my. How opportune of you to come to call."

Wiz was feeling that it was less opportune by the moment, but he didn't say that.

"Yes, ah, now about releasing these people . . ."

"Oh, quite out of the question, I can assure you. But surely you knew that before you arrived?" The dragon heaved a great gusty sigh. "You humans, always thinking that wishing for something can make it happen. You are amusing, but you are so dreadfully illogical."

"And dragons are logical?"

"Of course."

For a mad instant Wiz tried to imagine what the NAND diagram for a logical dragon would look like.

And then he saw his opening.

He hesitated. The last time he had tried this with one of this World's creatures he had nearly lost his soul. But he didn't have much choice. He sure couldn't fight the monster, he didn't think he could out-magic it on the spur of the moment and he didn't have any other ideas.

The people of this world didn't think in the abstract. Abstractions and mathematical thought tended to puzzle and confuse them. Wiz devoutly hoped the same was true of dragons.

He cleared his throat. "Then surely you are skilled in all forms of applied logic. Riddles, say?"

"Dragons are excellent at riddles," Griswold said loftily. "Surely you're not proposing playing the riddle game with me?"

"Yep. And if I win you turn these people loose and agree never to bother them again."

"And if *I* win?" Griswold asked, leaning forward so Wiz had to crane his neck to meet the dragon's eye.

"You get them."

"My dear boy, surely it hasn't escaped your notice that I have them already. No, you'll have to offer something more." The dragon licked his chops in anticipation. "Yourself, for instance."

It occurred to Wiz that the dragon had him too, but he tried to ignore that.

"All right, but if I win I want a larger prize, too."

Griswold looked amused. "Gold? Jewels?"

Wiz almost agreed; then he caught sight of a farm implement leaning against the wall. It was a pruning hook, its two-foot curved blade wickedly sharp along its inner edge.

"Uh, no," Wiz said. "I was thinking of something a little more personal."

"What then?"

Wiz smiled as unpleasantly as he could manage. "Well, dragon skin *does* have a number of magically useful properties."

The dragon hesitated for an instant. "Done and done," he exclaimed.

"Fine. I'll go first,"

Griswold nodded. "Tell me the riddle, then."

"It isn't one I tell you. I have to show it to you."

The dragon brightened. "Charades? I haven't had a good game of charades in ever so long."

"Here are the rules," Wiz told him. **emac.** Instantly a two-foot-tall demon wearing granny glasses and a green eyeshade popped into existence next to him.

Griswold watched him closely, alert for any sign of treachery.

APL dot man list exe, he commanded.

The demon drew a quill pen from behind one bat ear and began to scribble furiously. Line after line of fiery letters grew before them. Each line defined one of the commands of Jerry's version of APL. There were a lot of them and the emac took several minutes to write them all in the air.

"Hmm. Ah, yes," Griswold said.

"Now, have you memorized them?"

"Of course." The dragon didn't sound quite so confident now.

"Fine," Wiz said. **emac.**

? replied the editing demon.

clear end exe. The emac rubbed the air furiously and the characters vanished. The demon bowed and it vanished as well.

"Now." Wiz picked up a stick and scratched furiously in the dirt.

"I'll bet you can't tell me what this does."

Griswold craned his neck forward to stare at the symbols in the dirt.

"Um, ah . . ."

"Come on," Wiz said. "It's perfectly logical and quite unambiguous. What is the result?"

"Well . . ."

The dragon drew his brows together in a mighty frown. He stuck his forked tongue between his ivory fangs and let it loll out one side of his mouth. He cocked his head nearly upside down to get a better view of the characters.

Whistling tunelessly, Wiz strolled over to the wall and picked up the pruning hook. He ran his thumb along the edge nonchalantly and hefted it experimentally.

"You're forfeit, you know," Wiz said, turning back to the dragon.

"Time," Griswold said desperately. "Give me more time!"

Wiz had never seen a dragon sweat before. He decided it was an interesting effect.

"Can't you solve it?"

"Of course I can solve it," Griswold said pettishly. "I just need a little more time." His voice rose to a whine inside Wiz's head. "The rules didn't say anything about a time limit."

"Very well." Wiz laid the pruning hook aside and gestured magnanimously. "I will give you until the Moon is full again to solve the riddle. Now go."

Griswold sagged with relief. "Thank you," he practically blubbered. Then he hesitated and looked back at the humans huddled behind him. "Uh, I don't suppose . . . just one . . . for a snack, you know?"

"GO!" Wiz roared, reaching for the pruning hook. Muttering to himself, the dragon leapt into the sky.

"Whhhoooooo," Wiz breathed and collapsed against the wall, using the pruning hook for a cane. He was immediately engulfed by the hysterically grateful Baggots, all of whom were laughing, crying and hugging him simultaneously. Since the entire family apparently enjoyed garlic as much as they disdained bathing, and since their idea of a thankful hug could snap the spine of an ox, Wiz was less appreciative than he might have been. In fact, by the time he got out the farmyard gate he was limping and holding his ribs.

SEVEN

SETTLING IN

Always live better than your clients.
—*The Consultants' Handbook*

News travels fast. The mayor and council hadn't been at the Baggot Place, but they knew all about it by the time Wiz and Malkin made their way back to town. They were gathered inside the gate in a tight cluster when the pair strode back through.

While the town guard held back the common folk, the mayor and councilors pressed forward, eager to be associated with their new hero.

There seemed to be twice as many councilors as there had been in the jail. A couple seemed to be in open-mouthed awe of him. Most of the others looked gravely pleased. A minority eyed him speculatively, like a group of cats trying to decide what they could do with a new and rather strange baby bird which had just dropped into their midst. With a sinking feeling Wiz realized he wasn't out of the woods yet.

"Well, Wizard, it seems we owe you a debt of gratitude," the mayor said, loudly enough to be sure the crowd heard him.

"All part of a consultant's job," Wiz said airily and equally loudly. "We exist to solve our clients' problems."

"Well, you've made a very good start," said one of the councilors, a handsome silver-haired man with an air of smooth sincerity.

"Almost too good," came a voice from the crowd. "Like it was planned."

"Of course it was planned," Wiz lied glibly. "You don't think even a consultant would face a dragon without a plan, do you?"

"Some folks," Malkin put in, "don't even plan where their next pot of ale is coming from." She turned to face the heckler. "Do they, Commer?"

The crowd laughed and that was the end of it.

"Now as I was saying," Mayor Hendrick went on, "let me be the first to welcome you to our city."

"On behalf of the council," a small, overdressed councilor with a fringe of dark curly hair added sharply.

The mayor looked annoyed. "On behalf of myself as mayor and the council," he amended.

"Thank you," Wiz said. "I'm sure this will be the beginning of a very productive relationship." *Push it when you're hot.* "Oh, and I'll need living quarters for my assistant and myself."

"We have just the place." Mayor Hendrick beamed. "A fine old house in the very center of town. In fact we will give it to you!" One or two of the councilors nodded enthusiastically and a couple of others looked smug.

"Very generous of you," Wiz said smoothly. Actually he was more puzzled than gratified. The mayor didn't seem like the sort to be impressed by the morning's activities, much less the kind who'd be moved to sudden acts of generosity. Still . . .

The mayor beckoned and a large, tough-looking man dressed mostly in black stepped forward.

"This is Sheriff Beorn Beornsdorf," Mayor Hendrick said. "He will show you to your new home."

Wiz smiled and acknowledged his recent captor with

a nod. The sheriff's neck bent a fraction of an inch in reply but he still looked like he was wishing Wiz and Malkin back into jail.

Wiz looked over at Malkin and jerked his head toward the mayor.

Malkin strolled over, still looking back at Wiz, and walked right into Mayor Hastlebone. She bounced off his ample stomach, apologized profusely, brushing off the front and shoulders of his tunic while she did so.

"Dust speck," Malkin said and stepped away to join Wiz. The mayor eyed her oddly then looked down and seemed to realize his chain of office was back around his neck. He frowned, opened his mouth, then shut it firmly.

The house turned out to be a substantial structure of the town's usual stone-and-timber construction just off one of the town's smaller squares. It was narrow but at least four stories high, with a front right on the street and a small, neglected garden in the back.

The garden wasn't the only thing neglected. As they stood on the stoop Wiz could see that the windows were dirty and laced with cobwebs on the inside. There were streaks of rust running down from the door hinges and the brass lock plate was green with corrosion. Even with the door unlocked, Wiz had to put his shoulder to it to force it open. The unoiled hinges creaked and screamed like damned souls as the door swung to.

The hall inside was equally bad, musty smelling and deep in dust and cobwebs. There were doors opening off to either side and a large staircase leading up. Past the stairs was another door that probably led to the kitchen.

Wiz sniffed the stale air. It obviously hadn't been opened in a while but he didn't detect the odor of damp or rot. "This place doesn't look like anyone's been here in years."

"Not in two years," Malkin told him. "Not since Widder Hackett died."

"Still," Wiz said as he looked around, "it seems like

a nice place. I can't imagine why anyone would leave a house like this empty. In the middle of town and all."

Malkin shrugged. "She didn't leave any kin. Besides, it's supposed to be haunted."

"Haunted," Wiz said faintly.

"Probably just rats running around the place."

"Rats," Wiz echoed more faintly.

Malkin considered. "But you never can tell. Old Lady Hackett was a sour sort and that's a fact. If she could come back and haunt the place, like as not she would." She paused. "Maybe she could, too, seeing as how she was a witch and all."

"A witch," Wiz echoed more faintly yet.

"But don't you worry," Malkin finished brightly, "it's probably just rats."

Wiz decided rats were definitely his first choice. "Well anyway, it's home for now so we'll have to get this place cleaned up."

Malkin looked around. "Take a heap of cleaning."

"Oh, I don't know. Sweep it out, scrub down the worst of it and it will be fine. Heck, it'll be a hundred percent better if you just scrub the grime off the windows."

"I don't do windows," Malkin said haughtily.

"I had a 386 system like that once."

She looked at him oddly.

"Okay, I'll do the windows. But we'll need a broom and some rags and stuff."

"I can get those at the market."

"Just be sure you pay for them."

Malkin's face fell. "Where's the fun in that?"

Before Wiz could answer there was a sharp knock at the door. Tugging it open, he found himself face-to-face with an overdressed, balding little man who looked vaguely familiar.

"I need to talk to you, Wizard," the man snapped. He glared at Malkin. "Alone."

Malkin, who apparently knew him, glared back. "I'll get the stuff," she said to Wiz over the top of the visitor's head. "You and Shorty here have a nice chat." With that she swept out the still-open door, leaving the little man purpling in her wake.

"Jailbird bitch should have gone to The Rock long ago," the man said as Wiz thrust the door closed on its still-protesting hinges. "But who you choose to associate with is your business. We've got other matters to discuss."

"What can I do for you Mr . . .?"

"*Councilor*," the man corrected. "I'm Councilor Dieter Hanwassel and I'm someone to be reckoned with around here."

Wiz looked more closely and saw the man was indeed wearing the heavy gold chain of a city councilman over his elaborately brocaded black-and-silver robe. Where he wasn't going bald Dieter had dark curly hair that fluffed out from his head. Since he was bald from his forehead to the back of his cranium, he looked like he had just had a nasty accident with a lawn mower. The whole effect was comic—until you saw the jut of the jaw, the lips pressed into a tight line and the glitter in his dark eyes. He reminded Wiz of an excited terrier in a too-fancy collar. A terrier who was aching to take a bite out of someone.

"Ah yes, Councilor, I believe we met this morning."

Dieter jerked a nod. "We did. And now that the rest of those ninnies aren't around we can talk seriously."

Wiz put on his blandest expression and nodded. One thing consultants never had to search for was the political factions in an organization. Sooner or later they came searching for you. Usually sooner.

"I'm sorry I can't offer you a seat," Wiz said, "but you see—"

Dieter cut him off. "What you can offer me is your support, since just now you seem to have the council's favor." He eyed Wiz. "I'm a plain man, Wizard, and plain-spoken. We can do a lot together, you and I. And I can do a lot for you."

"You mean you can help me with dragons?"

"Dragons," the councilor snorted. "What do I care about dragons? I'm a practical man and we both know there's nothing you can do about them, eh? No, what I'm interested in is revenues. Do you realize this city hasn't had a revenue increase in near a generation? There's all sort of projects, wonderful projects, just stalled because there's no revenue. Why, there's streets, and fountains, and bridges. All just crying out to be built. And they've gone crying for years because of lack of revenues."

"What do you expect me to do about that? I'm an expert on dragons."

Dieter waved that away. "Tell them you need more money to fight the dragons, that's what. They already agreed to pay you a tenth of the city's revenues. Tell them you need more, and now."

"They'll only pay me if—when—I succeed."

"And you know what they'll do to you if you *don't* succeed, eh?" The Councilman leaned close and glared up at Wiz. "Well, let me tell you, you won't succeed without my help. I have weight on the council and me and my followers, we want those revenues increased."

Wiz wondered how much of those revenues would wind up in the pockets of the councilor and his cronies. Considering what the guy was like he decided a better question would be how much of the money would make it past those pockets.

"Now, I'm not a greedy man, Wizard," Dieter continued in what was obviously supposed to be a placating tone. "When the money flows there'll be help for those as helped us. Sort of finder's fees, you might say."

"It certainly sounds like a worthwhile program. What seems to be the obstacle?"

"The mayor's the obstacle, him and that Rolf who's behind him. All they ever do is cry about 'tax burdens' and 'fiscal responsibility.'" The little man snorted. "'Fiscal responsibility.' What about our responsibility to them as support us I'd like to know?"

Wiz nodded. "It sounds as if you have a very strong

case. I can assure you I'll give the matter serious consideration."

"You'll give the matter more than that if you want to
stay off The Rock," Dieter said. "I'll be watching you,
Wizard. And I'm a man who remembers his enemies as
well as his friends."

After his visitor left Wiz spent the next several minutes
working the front door back and forth to free up the
rusted hinges. The hinges squeaked and groaned in protest
and that suited his mood perfectly.

"The runt leave?" Malkin asked when she breezed back
in a bit later, her arms loaded with cleaning supplies.

"He's gone. Did you pay for all this stuff?"

"Charged it to the council," she said, dropping everything in the middle of the hall. "Someone will be around
later with bedding and stuff. What did the little rat want
anyway?"

"My help in raising taxes."

"Figures. Of the whole money-gouging lot Dieter's
about the worst." She paused and considered. "Well,
anyways the most obnoxious."

"That's a problem for another day," Wiz said as he
stooped to pick up a broom. As he stood back up he saw
the flash of gold in Malkin's hand. "What's that?"

"Oh, something I picked up in the market," she said
breezily, holding up an ornate gold ring with a big green
stone. "Do you like it?"

"I thought I told you not to steal anything."

"You told me to pay for the cleaning stuff. And I did—
leastways I charged it all legal-like. But this," she said,
popping the ring down her bodice, "isn't cleaning stuff."

Tomorrow, Wiz told himself. *I'll worry about this
tomorrow.* "Come on, let's try to make this place habitable."

Malkin turned out to be a surprisingly hard worker.
She obviously didn't know much more about house cleaning than Wiz did, but she went at it with a will and before

long dust was flying in all directions. In a little less than two hours they had the front hall and two of the upstairs bedrooms more or less clean.

"Woof! You don't have any spell to clean this place, do you?" Malkin said as she plopped down on the stair beside Wiz to take a break.

"Not really. Well, I do know one, but it takes everything out of the room." *And sends it off in all directions with roughly the velocity of machine gun bullets.* He remembered the time in the ruined City of Night when he and the others had hacked the spell together to move rubble and how they'd ended up cowering in the dirt from the resulting barrage of missiles. That reminded him of Jerry, Danny and most of all Moira, and sent a pang through him.

"You all right?" Malkin asked, catching his mood.

"Yeah, I'm fine." He focused his attention on her. "Tell me about this widow who used to live here."

"Widder Hackett?" Malkin chuckled. "She was a salty one, even for a witch. She had a tongue, that one. If you so much as sat down on her stoop she'd come flying out waving a broom and chase you off. Always complaining about dirt and such, she was." The girl looked around the house and shook her head. "What she'd think if she could see this place now! We could clean and polish until the end of time and we'd never get it back to what it was."

"I'll settle for getting it to where it's habitable," Wiz said. "Let's do some more on the upstairs and then knock off for dinner."

"Let's knock off for dinner and then do some more upstairs," Malkin countered. "It's near evening and I haven't eaten today."

"Now that you mention it . . ."

Malkin looked at him. "Well?" she said finally.

"Well what?"

"Well aren't you going to magic us up food?"

"I'm not very good at that—unless the kitchen's got a microwave?"

Malkin snorted. "Fine wizard you are. I don't suppose you can cook either."

"I do all right," Wiz said defensively.

Malkin snorted again. "I know what *that* means, coming from a man. Look here then, I'll go back to the market and get a few things—charge a few things," she amended hastily before Wiz could say anything, "and I'll cook tonight. I don't want food poisoning on top of everything else today. But tomorrow you do the cooking. Now help me get this miserable door open so I can get back to the miserable market before the last of the miserable stalls closes."

With Malkin's help he tugged the door open again and he watched her as she disappeared down the street. Then he leaned against the door and pushed it to again as the hinges protested like souls in mortal agony.

The door, Wiz thought. *I've got to do something about that damned door.*

Wiz went down the worn stone steps into the kitchen. It had to be the kitchen, he decided, because private houses don't usually come equipped with torture chambers.

It was a high, narrow room in what he would have thought of as the basement of the house. A couple of thin barred windows high up lit the place dimly. The walls and floors were dank stone and the ceiling was rough beams and planks. There was a huge fireplace with a wicked-looking collection of iron hooks and chains hanging under the mantel, plus a contraption of iron spikes and gears and yet more chains off to one side that he vaguely recognized as some kind of spit for roasting meat. There was a stone sink in the opposite wall and in the center of the room a heavy wooden table with a rack full of hooks above it.

Gee, he thought, *clean this place up, light a fire in the fireplace, put some flowers here and there, I'll bet you could brighten it up to, oh, say, dismal.*

Among the pile of supplies Malkin had purchased was a small bottle of oil. Wiz took the oil back upstairs to the door and poured some on the hinges as best he could from the inside. Then he tugged the door open to get them from the outside.

He barely had the door open six inches when a furry gray streak shot through and dashed between his legs.

"Hey!" Wiz yelled, but the streak ignored him. It was halfway up the stairs before it stopped and resolved itself into a cat.

It was a rather bedraggled and quite large cat. A tiger-striped tabby cat, Wiz thought, dredging the terms out of his subconscious. A tiger-striped tabby tomcat, he amended as the cat turned its backside toward him.

The cat sat in the middle of the stairs and looked back over its right shoulder at Wiz.

"What do you think you're doing?" Wiz demanded of the cat. The cat continued to study Wiz with its great yellow eyes as if to say, "I live here. What's your excuse?"

Wiz opened his mouth to say more and then shut it again when he realized there wasn't anything he could say. Not only is arguing with a cat a lost cause, this cat was halfway up the stairs and could easily outrun him if he tried to give chase. Wiz didn't like looking foolish any more than the average cat does, so he decided to leave it for now.

Wiz didn't dislike cats, but from observing his friends who had cats he had arrived at a couple of conclusions. The first was that cats, not being pack animals like dogs or people, do not have consciences. That meant that if you had a cat you were sharing your life with a furry little sociopath.

The second was that every animal had evolved to exploit an ecological niche and in the case of cats that niche was people.

"Well, all right," Wiz told the cat. "But don't get the idea you're staying."

"Who are you shouting at?" asked Malkin as she came in the door with a basket of food.

Wiz nodded toward the stairs. "That."

Malkin studied the cat and the cat studied Malkin. "I

think that's Widder Hackett's cat," the tall girl said finally. "Handsome enough."

"So is a leopard, but that doesn't mean I want to share quarters with one."

Malkin grinned at him. "Looks like he's decided to share quarters with you. And if you're planning on catching him to throw him out you can do it yourself. He's a scrapper, that one, and I've no fancy to get myself clawed up to put out an animal that will come right back in every time you open the door."

"Hmmf," Wiz snorted, weighing his ambivalence toward cats against the obvious trouble it would take to get rid of this one. "Does he have a name?"

"Widder Hackett called him Precious, but I think his name is Bobo."

"Bobo, huh? Looks more like Bubba to me." The cat narrowed his yellow eyes and glared at him as if to say "Watch it, bud."

It turned out there was a stove in the kitchen. It was a ceramic tile box next to the fireplace that Wiz had dismissed as a waist-high work counter. There was also a wooden hand pump that drew water into the sink. Malkin got a fire going with the help of a fire-starting spell from Wiz and she quickly threw together a grain-and-vegetable porridge that turned out surprisingly well. They ate in the kitchen under the glow of a magic light globe Wiz conjured up.

The only excitement came when Bobo cornered and caught a rat in the upstairs hallway. He came trotting down the stairs, head high, with the limp furry corpse dangling from his mouth and settled himself under the sink to eat with the humans. Wiz turned his back to the sink and tried to ignore the occasional crunching noises from Bobo's direction.

"Cat's got his uses," Malkin observed.

"Unfortunately I don't have a violin that needs stringing."

"I don't suppose you've got a spell to clean dishes

either," Malkin said as she scraped the last of the stew from her bowl.

"I can probably whip one up tomorrow."

"Let it be for tonight then. But one way or another, Wizard, you'll clean those dishes tomorrow. And tomorrow it's your turn to cook."

"Who's the boss in this outfit anyway?"

"Depends," Malkin said lazily, "on who needs who the worst, don't it?"

Tomorrow, Wiz thought. *I'll worry about this tomorrow.*

Actually there was a lot to worry about tomorrow, Wiz admitted to himself as he crawled into bed later that evening. He had to get things set up here so he could work, and he had to figure out a way to keep Dieter pacified. And he still didn't have the faintest idea how he was going to solve the village's dragon problem. That last was really beginning to gnaw at him.

Well, Wiz thought as he drifted off to sleep, *it could be worse I suppose.*

"Look at this mess!"

Wiz jerked bolt upright in bed.

"Look at it, I tell you," the voice repeated.

Wiz looked around frantically, but the room was empty.

backslash light exe! he called out into the darkness. The room filled with the warm yellow glow of a magic globe, but there was still no sign of anyone else in the room.

"I don't suppose you're going to do anything about it, are you?" the voice rasped again. It was a particularly unpleasant voice. It reminded Wiz of a rusty door hinge or slowly pulling an old nail out of a piece of very hard wood.

"What are you carrying on about?" came another voice. Wiz whirled and saw Malkin in the doorway, rubbing sleep from her eyes.

"There's someone in the room. I can hear her but I can't see her."

There was a loud snort from the corner.

"There," Wiz said.

Malkin's eyes narrowed. "I didn't hear anything."

"It was a snort. A definite snort."

"Are you sure you've been getting enough rest?"

"I tell you there's someone here. It sounds like an old woman and she's complaining that the house is dirty."

"Well, look at this place!" the voice came again. "It's a pigsty, an absolute pigsty! And what are you doing about it, I'd like to know? You're sitting there in the dirt and not making a move to clean it up."

"Probably Widder Hackett," Malkin said judiciously. "I guess them as said the place was haunted was right."

"You're taking this awfully calmly."

Malkin shrugged. "So far she's not bothering me."

"Why is it I can hear her and you can't?"

"Because you're the owner, dummy," the old lady's voice grated. "No one but the owner sees or hears the ghost. Them's the rules."

Suddenly things clicked. "When you died without heirs," Wiz said into empty air, "who inherited this place?"

"Why, the council, of course," the voice said. "Not that any of that pack of layabouts lifted a finger to keep my house up. Crooked as a dog's hind leg, every last one of them, and don't think I didn't tell them so!"

Malkin was obviously only hearing half the exchange, but she kept swiveling her head from Wiz to the corner he was looking at, like the spectator at a ping-pong match.

"Which explains why they gave the place to me."

"And what are you going to do about it?" the ghost demanded again.

"Well, this is all kind of new to me," Wiz temporized. "We don't have ghosts where I come from. Except on TV—and you can usually fix those by getting cable."

The ghost of Widder Hackett ignored his sally. "A right uncivilized place, it sounds like. Well, we do things better here. And that means taking care of my house."

Wiz thought about pointing out that death usually

severs right of ownership. Then he decided it probably
didn't apply here.

"Look, it's the middle of the night. I can't do anything
about it right now, can I? I promise you I'll get started
on it first thing in the morning."

"I suppose that's the best I can expect from someone
like you. All right then, but first thing in the morning,
mind."

I couldn't get a ghost that rattles chains or moans, Wiz
thought as he tried to get comfortable again in his haunted
house. *I've got to get one that nags at 80 dB. I don't
suppose there are OSHA noise regulations for ghosts either.*

Wiz finally drifted off to sleep while musing on the
most effective kind of hearing protectors to use against
ghost noises.

Wiz was having a wonderful dream, about a place with
Moira and no dragons, when a rocket went off beside his
head. He was bolt upright with the covers off before he
realized that what he had heard was a voice and not a
particularly violent explosion.

"Well?" came the voice again.

"Well what?" Wiz was not at his best early in the
morning and one glance at the rosy hue of sunlight
painted on the wall told him it was *very* early morning.

"Well, it's morning," said the voice in a particularly
unpleasant tone. "What are you going to do about the
house?"

"Ah, the house. Right." He realized he recognized the
voice. He also realized he didn't have any caffeine in the
house. The third realization, less than thirty seconds later,
was that this was not shaping up to be a good day.

True to his word of the night before he fixed breakfast
for himself and Malkin. But Malkin apparently liked to
sleep late as much as Wiz did and since she didn't have
a complaining ghost dogging her footsteps she could stay
in bed. Wiz left a pot of oat porridge on the stove for her,
put down a saucer of milk for Bobo after the cat jumped

in his lap three times trying to get at his porridge and milk, left the dishes in the sink (over Widder Hackett's strenuous objections) and dragged his way upstairs.

Since he still didn't have a handle on the dragon problem, much less the more immediate stuff, he relied on routine. Maybe something would come to him while he worked.

The first order of business, Wiz decided, was to set up a workroom. In the back of his mind he knew that a programmer's work space wasn't really appropriate to someone who was supposed to be a consultant on dragons, but it didn't really matter. It would make the place more homey and help him think about his real problem— once he figured out which of the mountains of problems he faced was the real one.

There were two parlors on the ground floor, one on each side of the entrance hall. Both of them were full of furniture swathed in dusty sheets and it looked like it would be a backbreaking job to move it out. Besides, the front windows were right on the street, which meant working there would be like working in a department store window, unless he kept the drapes drawn all the time, in which case he'd need artificial light. On top of all that he had a strong suspicion the ghost would have something to say if he starting moving the furniture around in the parlor—probably quite a lot to say, in fact.

The second floor, with his and Malkin's bedrooms, had more possibilities. The upstairs front room had obviously been some sort of a sitting room rather than a bedroom. Now it was stark and bare with only a sturdy wooden chair sitting in one corner and a sturdier table against the opposite wall. But light flooded in when Wiz forced open the protesting shutters. It was clearly the best room in the house to serve as his workroom. Without another thought he grabbed one end of the heavy oak table and started to tug it over to the window.

"Don't drag that!" Widder Hackett yelled. "You'll gouge the floor."

The sudden noise made Wiz drop the table. One leg landed on his foot and the other hit the floor with a resounding *thump*. The scream of outrage in his ear almost made him forget the pain in his foot. "You ninny! Look what you've done. That mark will never come out! Oh, my beautiful floor."

It was amazing, Wiz thought, that even when he was hopping around holding one foot the ghost's voice seemed to stay right in his ear.

Finally Widder Hackett ran down and the pain in Wiz's foot subsided to a dull throb. Gingerly, favoring his injured foot, Wiz took the table in the middle and heaved it clear of the floor. He delicately staggered across the room and gently lowered it before the window, bending over in a position that put his lower back in dire peril. He straightened to ease the protesting back muscles and reached out to push the table up against the wall. A sharp sound from Widder Hackett stopped him and he ended up carefully lifting the end to slide it into position.

"And be sure you carry the chair too!" the old lady's ghost added.

With the chair and table in place, Wiz sat down to rest his aching foot and to try to get some work done. Even though setting up his magical workstation went smoothly it still wasn't easy. Every couple of minutes Widder Hackett would be back to complain about another outrage to her beloved house and Wiz's lack of action, not to mention morals, character and general deportment. Since the ghost's voice combined the worst features of a foghorn, a screech owl and a table saw ripping lumber full of nails, Wiz was quickly developing a semi-permanent twitch. He had always pictured ghosts as having high, reedy voices that were just on the edge of audibility. Apparently it took more than dying to modulate Widder Hackett's tones.

"I'm surprised they didn't let me out of jail just to give me the house," he muttered as he leaned back to examine the fruits of several hours of not-very-productive work.

"Don't put your feet on the table!" Widder Hackett

roared. Wiz jerked his feet back to the floor. "And sit up in that chair. You're putting weight on it wrong and you'll break it like as not."

Wiz had gone to public schools, but he had Catholic friends who had gone to parochial schools. From what they had told him Widder Hackett had a lot in common with the nuns.

Bobo sauntered through the door and jumped up on the table to sniff at Wiz's magical spells. He decided that fiery letters probably weren't good to eat. Then he decided he needed petting and Wiz's hand was just lying on the table not doing anything so Bobo butted his head against it until he got a response.

Wiz sighed and scratched the cat under the chin. "I don't know, Bubba. What do you think I ought to do?"

The cat gazed deep into Wiz's eyes. "Feed me." The thought came crystal sharp into Wiz's mind. Wiz sighed again.

"You know, it's probably a good thing cat lovers don't know what their cats are thinking."

"Feed me now," Bobo's thought came clear again. There was no response except some distracted petting. The cat gave Wiz a look that clearly indicated he thought Wiz was mentally retarded for not getting the message. Then he jumped down from the table and stalked out the door, tail high.

"And just when are you going to do something about the disgraceful condition of the front parlor?" demanded a now-familiar voice beside his ear.

Wiz sighed again. He had a feeling it was going to be a long, long day.

EIGHT

CALLING HOME

The problem with being a miracle worker
is that everyone expects you to work
miracles.
                    —*The Consultants' Handbook*

Two hours later Wiz started his latest creation running
and then let out a long, whooshing sigh.

"You all right?" Malkin asked in a voice that showed
more curiosity than compassion.

"Yeah, fine. But if I'm going to get anything done
around here I'm going to have to hire a housekeeper."

Malkin crossed her arms over her chest. "Good luck.
Not many as will want to work for a strange wizard in a
haunted house."

"Well put an ad in the paper will you? Or have the
town crier announce it or whatever you do here."

"I'll take the news to the market." She looked over at
the rapidly scrolling letters of golden fire above his desk
under the window. "Meanwhile, what's that?"

"It's a workstation. I just built it."

Malkin looked at the gray box and keyboard sitting on
the table and the letters of golden fire hanging above it.

"Built it out of what?"

"Well, actually it's a program, a spell you'd call it. See, we've found that in this world a sufficiently complex program, or spell, produces a physical manifestation, what you'd call a demon."

Malkin regarded the things on the desk. "Don't look like no demon I've ever heard tell of," she said. "But you're the wizard. What's it good for?"

"Well, what you see here is really just a user interface. It virtualizes what I was used to in my world and that makes it easier for me to relate to."

"Seems to me any relations you had with a demon would have to be illegitimate," the tall thief said. "But what's it good for?"

"Just about anything I want it to be. Right now I'm setting up an Internet connection so I can talk to my friends."

"More magic, eh?"

"No, it's technology. I need a machine on the other side," Wiz explained to the uncomprehending but fascinated woman. "So I've created a little dialer demon to troll the net for systems I can set up accounts on."

Malkin cocked an eye at him. "I see. So it's demons and trolls but it's not magic."

"No, it's . . . Okay, have it your way. It's magic."

Just then the system emitted a bell-like tone. "Boy there's luck. Less than five minutes and I've found one. Uh, excuse me will you?" With that he turned back to the console.

"Now what are you doing?" Malkin asked. "Magic aside."

"I guess the easiest way to explain it is to say I'm breaking into something that's locked. Something a good ways from here."

For once the tall thief seemed impressed. "Burglary without being there," Malkin said wonderingly. "Wizard, I think I'd like this world of yours."

Wiz thought about Malkin as a computer criminal.

Then he shuddered and turned his attention back to the computer.

Exploiting a hole in the system's security was easy. In a matter of minutes Wiz had two new accounts set up. The final wrinkle was a simple little shell script to take messages from one account and pass them to the other. Anyone who tried to trace him back could only follow him as far as this machine.

"There, that'll give me more protection," he told Malkin as he leaned back from the keyboard. *Not a lot*, he admitted to himself. But until he got Widder Hackett off his back he wasn't going to be able to do much better.

"Protection from who?"

"From anyone at the Wizard's Keep who might want to find me."

His erstwhile assistant regarded him with a look Wiz was coming to know all too well. "These folks are your friends, right?"

"Of course."

"Then I'd think you'd be yelling to them for help instead of hiding from them."

"I can't," Wiz said miserably. "I can't let them find me."

Malkin muttered something about "wizards" and left the room.

The first order of business, Wiz decided, was to tell everyone he was all right. He quickly composed an e-mail message and sent it over the net to **thekeep.org**, the Wizard's Keep's Internet node.

He typed furiously for several minutes, stopping frequently to erase a revealing phrase or to re-read his work to make sure he wasn't giving too much away. Then he spent some time planning the exact path the message would take to reach its destination. At last he hit the final "enter" to send the message on its way and settled back in his chair with a sigh of contentment.

He was promptly jerked erect by Widder Hackett's screech at air-raid-siren intensity.

"Loafing again, are you? The house falling down about

your ears and you lolling at your ease. Wizard or not, you are the laziest, most good-for-nothing layabout I have ever seen in all my days."

There was a lot more in that vein.

Over the course of the day Wiz discovered that the person who said you can get used to anything had never met Widder Hackett. The combination of her awful voice and her complaining nearly drove Wiz to distraction. If she had been there all the time he might have gotten used to her. But she would vanish for five or ten or fifteen minutes only to reappear with more demands just as Wiz was settling in to concentrate on what he was doing.

And there was nothing he could do to satisfy her. Even an attempt to sweep and dust the front parlor ended with the ghost shrieking that he was a useless ninny and all he was doing was moving the dirt from one corner of the room to another. Meanwhile, he not only wasn't getting anything done, he wasn't even able to think seriously about what he wanted to do. Worst of all, Wiz discovered that the exorcism spells that laid demons to rest had no effect at all on ghosts.

Fortunately for Wiz, Widder Hackett shut up at about ten o'clock at night—perhaps because old ghosts need their sleep. Be that as it may, Wiz got several hours of uninterrupted work in late that night.

Unfortunately Widder Hackett was back at sunup the next morning, loud as ever and full of new complaints and demands. Even putting a pillow over his head couldn't shut her out, so Wiz was up and about before the cock stopped crowing.

Meanwhile Wiz's message was on its way to the Wizard's Keep. It traveled a long and convoluted path through two worlds. First it was injected into the telephone lines by magical interference with a digital switch in a telephone company central office. It traveled over the regular phone network to the modem attached to the system he had cracked. There it slipped by security, thanks to Wiz's handiwork, and was received in one mailbox, transferred to another mailbox and sent out on the Internet. It traveled from computer to computer over the net as each node routed it to a succeeding node moving it closer to its destination. After traveling for several hours and touching every continent, including **penguin.edu** at Ross Station, Antarctica, it reached a node in Cupertino where it was stored until the final node made its daily connection to collect its mail. When **thekeep.org** called, the message was forwarded along with the rest of the day's e-mail down a telephone line to the junction box serving an apartment building— specifically the line leading to the apartment occupied by a programmer and fantasy writer named Judith Conally. There it was magically picked off, translated back to the Wizard's World along with most of the rest of the mail and showed up in Jerry's mailbox in his workstation in the Wizard's Keep.

Since Jerry slept mornings he didn't find it until he came into the workroom about mid-afternoon. He was still yawning over his second mug of blackmoss tea when he sat down at his terminal. He looked over the job he had left running, found it was progressing satisfactorily and punched up a list of his mail.

Jerry called the message up and started reading. By the time he had finished the first screen he was biting his lip.

"Danny! Moira! You'd better come look at this."

Hi Jerry and everyone (especially Moira!):

I can't tell you where I am or what I'm doing, but I'm safe—at least for now.

I don't know how long this job is going to take, but I'll have to stick with it until I'm done.

As to what I'm doing, let's just say I'm taking a lesson from Charlie Bowen.

> Say hi to everyone for me and don't worry
> about me.
> Give my love to Moira.
>
> PS: Please don't try to find me. It's very
> important.
>
> -W

"Who's Charlie Bowen?" Danny asked.

"Someone Wiz used to work with at Seer Software," Jerry told him, abstractedly. "Another programmer."

"A real hotshot, huh?"

"No, that's the funny thing. He was a lousy programmer. He wrote their accounts payable routine and he made a royal mess of it. The module kept fouling up assigning purchase order numbers, choking on invoices and if there was the least little problem in the paperwork, it kicked the thing out and it had to be processed manually. It was taking Seer Software six or eight months to pay even a simple bill and they kept having to explain to everyone it was the software's fault."

Danny took a swig of tea. "So did they fire him?"

"That's the other funny thing," Jerry said. "They promoted him."

Just then Moira came dashing into the room, face flushed and flour up to her elbows. "You've heard from Wiz!" she panted.

Jerry gestured to the message on the screen. She craned forward to read it over Jerry's shoulder. As she read her face fell and then she started to frown, deeper and deeper as she read along. By the time she reached the bottom she was scowling.

"There is something very wrong here. Why didn't he tell us where he is?"

Jerry shrugged. "He said he didn't want us to know."

"He also said he did not want us to worry," Moira said grimly. "Those are mutually exclusive and he knows that."

"Then maybe," Danny said slowly, "he *can't* tell us."

Jerry frowned. "You mean he doesn't know where he is? That's crazy. Wiz's magic could tell him in an instant."

"So maybe he knows and can't tell us," Danny said, groping.

"A geas!" Moira exclaimed. "Of course! He cannot tell us because he is magically forbidden to do so."

"He doesn't sound like anything is stopping him," Jerry objected. "It sounds more like he's being secretive of his own free will."

"That is the problem with a geas," Moira told him. "You do not necessarily know you are under it. Everything seems normal to you and you think you have the best reasons in the world for doing what you do, no matter how badly you want to do the opposite."

Jerry rubbed his chin. "Well, it sure fits with Wiz's behavior. He wants to tell us, so he contacts us. But he can't so he comes in through the net and then won't say where he is."

"Is there any way to trace him?" the hedge witch asked. She gestured at the message header. "Wiz told me once that gives the location of the sender."

"Normally it does," Jerry said. "But take a look at it."

Danny frowned as he ran his finger along the line. The further he went, the deeper his frown became. "That can't be natural," he said at last.

"It isn't! That isn't a routing path, it's a shaggy dog story."

"Meaning what?" Moira demanded.

"Meaning he deliberately set up this routing to be as difficult and obscure as he could make it," Danny said before Jerry could answer. "See, normally a message is routed automatically by the most efficient path—given the location of the source, location of the destination, topology of the net and the amount of traffic. But you can force the route by using bang paths."

Moira didn't understand much of that, but she was game. "Bang paths?"

"Yeah. Site names separated by bangs." He pointed to an exclamation point between two names. "That's a bang." He studied the list for an instant and pointed at one sequence. "Here he's going from a U.S. site belonging to a Danish industrial concern to the Los Lobos League for Love and Understanding, the sex researchers. So that part of the path is **bang!llulu**."

Jerry groaned. "I wonder how long he searched to come up with that one?" Moira glared at him for the distraction.

"Anyway," Danny went on hastily, "I don't recognize all these site names but from the looks of it this message traveled a couple of times around the planet. Here's a site in Ukraine. That one's in the science city just outside of Tokyo. This one is the Coke machine at Rochester Institute of Technology—they put the Coke machine on the Internet so the computer science majors could find out if there were any sodas in the machine without having to walk all the way to it."

"Personally I always preferred the one at Carnegie-Mellon," Jerry said. "It's the original and it's got a graphical user interface."

Moira wasn't about to let the conversation wander off into a comparison of computerized vending machines. "Well, can you trace him or not?"

Jerry rubbed his chin. "That's hard. See, the path shown on a message isn't completely reliable. You can fake some of it. It's going to be hard to figure out where he's connecting to the net, much less where he is in our world."

"Maybe not," Danny said. "If we can rig up a little perl script and plant it on all these sites we may be able to trace him back to where he's really connecting."

Moira's face lit up. "Can you do that?"

"Well, we're going to have to get into a pile of computers, including that Coke machine, but . . ." His eyes focused on something far away. "Let me think about this and see what I can come up with. But we should be able to do it."

"And then?" Jerry asked.

"Then," said Moira grimly, "we go to his rescue whether he wants it or not."

NINE

A BRACELET, SOME CHICKENS, AND A PRETTY MAID ALL IN A ROW

Don't think of it as a distraction.
Look at it as an income opportunity.
—*The Consultants' Handbook*

Wiz was hard at it again the next morning when Malkin stuck her head into his workroom.

"Someone at the door wants to see you."

The interruption made Wiz lose his place, but by now he was so used to it he just sighed and followed Malkin downstairs. There was a dumpy, middle-aged townswoman snivelling on the doorstep. From her posture and sniffling Wiz figured she was either very upset about something or she was suffering from a really bad allergy. As soon as Wiz appeared she grabbed one of his hands in both of hers.

"O Great Wizard, you see before you a poor woman in great affliction." Whatever it was, it wasn't a problem with her lungs, Wiz thought. Her voice rattled the windowpanes. "Oh, the tragedy," she wailed. "Oh me! Oh me! O Wizard, I beg of you, save me."

"Save yourself and put a stopper in it," Widder Hackett

snarled in Wiz's ear. "That woman's voice can peel paint and she's got the brains of a titmouse besides."

Wiz had noticed the first and was willing to take the ghost's word for the second. But by this time they were over the threshold and into the hall. Clearly the only way to get rid of their guest now was to hear her out.

"Uh yes, Mrs. ummm . . . ?"

"Grimmen," the woman proclaimed, without lowering her voice. "Mrs. Grimmen. I stand before you a vessel of woe, a pitiful shell, a—"

"Yes, but what happened?"

Mrs. Grimmen, her concentration broken, glared at him. "That's what I'm telling you, Wizard. My gold bracelet has been stolen."

"Your bracelet?"

"You heard me. You ain't deaf are you? Oh woe! Oh sorrow! Oh . . ."

"Fertilizer!" snapped Widder Hackett—or something very close to that, at any event.

Stolen? Wiz looked back at the stairs where Malkin was standing and raised his eyebrows in unspoken question. The tall woman pinched up her face as if she was insulted by the very thought and shook her head.

"Uh, look Mrs. Grimmen, I'm not really a finder of lost objects. I'm a consultant on dragon problems."

"Well, how do you know a dragon didn't steal it?" the woman demanded. "It was gold after all."

"It was gilded pot metal," Widder Hackett amended.

"Yes, but . . ."

"Oh woe!" Mrs. Grimmen declaimed. "Oh sorrow! Oh alack!"

"Oh tell the ninny to look in the flour barrel," Widder Hackett said. "That's usually where she's hidden it when she can't find it."

"Uh, have you looked in the flour barrel?"

Mrs. Grimmen stopped in mid-wail. "Why would I do a silly thing like that?"

"Well, maybe that's where you left the bracelet."

The woman looked at him like he was crazy. "I didn't leave it anywhere. It was stolen from me. Oh woe! Oh woe!"

"Look, just go home and look in the flour barrel, okay?"

"But it's stolen away, my treasure. Oh woe! Oh woe!"

"Right," said Wiz, taking her by the elbow and gently guiding her toward the door.

"Sheesh! What next?" Wiz muttered as he turned away from the door.

"Chickens, most likely," said Widder Hackett in his ear. Wiz looked out the door and saw a man coming down the street with a live chicken in each hand.

He was scrawny and balding, with a big sharp nose and a receding chin. The way he strutted along with his head thrust forward put Wiz in mind of a chicken as well. Needless to say he stopped at Wiz's front door.

"I'm here to see the wizard," the man announced.

"I'm the wizard," Wiz admitted.

"Kinda young ain't you?"

"I was fast tracked in wizard school. Look, I'm kind of busy right now, so if you don't mind . . ."

"Not so fast, Wizard. I've got a job for you."

"I've already got a job."

Ignoring that the man thrust the chickens in Wiz's face. "Just look at them."

Since the birds were about level with Wiz's nose there wasn't any way to avoid it. From the way they struggled and cackled the chickens weren't any happier about the situation than he was. Aside from that they looked just fine. Of course, Wiz admitted, the only thing he knew about chickens was they came in three kinds: Regular, extra-crispy and spicy Cajun style—plus kung pao if you ordered Chinese.

"What's wrong with them?"

"Well, look at them! They don't lay hardly any eggs and no matter how much I feed them they stay scrawny."

Wiz looked over his shoulder into empty air.

"Don't ask me," Widder Hackett grated. "The old fool's been to every witch and magician for miles around. No one knows what's wrong with those stupid chickens."

"To be honest," Wiz said, "I don't know that this is my kind of problem. I'm really here as a dragon specialist."

"You're the municipal wizard ain't you?" he demanded.

"Actually," Wiz began, "I'm a consultant."

"Wizard, consultant, what's the difference? Point is you're paid out of my taxes to solve our problems. Well, this here," he said, thrusting the protesting chickens forward, "is my problem. So earn your money and solve it!"

"Those aren't dragons," Wiz pointed out.

"Any fool can see that, Mr. Wizard."

"Well, since they're not dragons they are not my problem. I only deal with dragons. Goodbye." Before his visitor could say another word, Wiz put all his weight against the door and forced it closed. Outside, the man made a couple of loud remarks about "uppity employees" and then the sound of his footsteps and the cackling of his chickens receded in the distance.

"Good grief," Wiz muttered weakly.

"Better get used to it," Widder Hackett told him. "There's going to be lots more of them. Word gets around you're a wizard working for the council and you'll have every lamebrain who thinks he's got a problem camped out on your doorstep demanding you solve it." She snorted. "And there's lots of lamebrains in this town, I can tell you that."

"But how am I supposed to get any work done if I'm constantly being interrupted by people with lost bracelets and sick chickens?"

"That's nothing. Wait until the love-sick ones start coming to you. Rattle on for hours, they will, and not a word of sense to be found in any of it."

The way she said it left Wiz with a sinking feeling she was speaking from experience.

There was a knock at the door. Wiz whirled and jerked it open.

"I told you I can't do anything about your damned . . . chickens," he finished weakly.

There was an angel on the doorstep. An angel in a drab brown dress.

"I beg your pardon, My Lord," the angel said in an angelic but timid voice. "I, I heard you are looking for a housekeeper."

Wiz realized his angel was actually a girl, perhaps eighteen years old. The plain brown homespun dress concealed a trim figure. Her skin was creamy white with just the right touches of pink. A fringe of wheat-gold curls peeked out from her bonnet. Her eyes were wide and blue as Wedgewood saucers.

Wiz finally managed to get the circuit from his brain to his mouth working again and closed his jaw. "Uh, well, yes," he said. "What's your name?"

"Anna, My Lord."

"Well, I'm Wiz. Wiz Zumwalt. Come in, won't you?" He stepped aside and managed to keep from bowing as the girl ventured over the threshold.

Wiz suddenly realized he had never interviewed anyone for a job other than a programming position and he wasn't quite sure what the etiquette of hiring servants was.

"Ah, nice day isn't it?"

Anna gave him a wide-eyed stare. "Of course, My Lord." The way she said it made him look a little closer. Not only were those eyes as blue as a Wedgewood china plate, Wiz realized, the owner possessed about as much intelligence as a china plate.

"My Lord . . ." Anna ventured tremulously. Then she stopped and gathered her courage. "My Lord, I know I am not very clever, but I will work hard."

"Oh, let her stay," Widder Hackett's voice grated in his ear. "She can't make more of a mess than the pair of you."

Wiz looked at the forlorn beauty and sighed. The first rule of successful housekeeping is you've got to be smarter than the dirt. Looking at her, Wiz figured Anna was probably brighter than the average dust bunny. They'd just have to live with the intellectually superior dust bunnies.

Besides, there weren't any other applicants, and Wiz wasn't going to get anything done with Widder Hackett complaining in his ear.

"All right," he sighed. "You've got the job."

"Oh thank you, My Lord!" Anna's smile made her even more angelically beautiful. "You will not be sorry, I promise you."

"Uh, you're not afraid working for a wizard?"

"Oh no, My Lord," Anna said innocently. "My granny was a witch. I've grown up around the craft, you see."

"That was Old Lady Fressen," Widder Hackett informed Wiz. "Child's her only grandchild and she tried to teach her the Craft." Widder Hackett snorted. "And her with not the sense to come in out of the rain. Not that Old Lady Fressen was any great shakes when it came to brains, mind you." With that the ghost was off on a long, rambling, and none-too-favorable reminiscence about a dead former colleague.

In their own ways and in their own times all of the occupants of the house settled in. Even Widder Hackett complained less once Anna set to work.

As if by magic the dirt and dust disappeared from the house. The sheets came off the furniture in the front rooms and light streamed through the newly washed windows. The wooden floors developed a mellow glow and the odors of dust and age were replaced by the scents of furniture oil and sweet herbs that hung in bunches in all the rooms. The beds were less lumpy and the bedding fresher.

Wiz knew it wasn't magic, of course. The girl worked from morning until night with a fierce concentration and a single-mindedness that he found a little awe-inspiring. If Anna was no mental giant, she knew how to keep house and she had the energy of a dynamo to boot.

Anna even made a difference in the kitchen. Not only

was it considerably cleaner after she arrived, it seemed brighter as well. Part of that was that the girl spent an afternoon whitewashing the walls—which earned Wiz an earful of Widder Hackett's complaints about the younger generation and their new-fangled notions—but part of it was simply her personality. New-fangled notions or not, Anna fitted this house far better than Wiz or Malkin did.

Malkin was usually available when Wiz needed her, but the rest of the time she kept to herself. Anna was in awe of the tall thief, but clearly didn't approve of her. Malkin clearly didn't feel any kinship for Anna either. In fact both the women seemed to get along better with Wiz than they did with each other.

The one member of the household who really welcomed Anna was Bobo. For some reason the cat developed an instant bond with the girl and spent hours each day around her or sitting in her lap on the infrequent occasions when she sat down to rest. Considering that Anna also did the cooking and spent much of her time in the kitchen, Wiz reflected, that probably wasn't so odd.

For his part Bobo had made himself at home as only a cat can. Which is to say with total disregard for the rights or feelings of the human inhabitants.

For one thing, Bobo had the typical cat criteria for a place to sleep. To wit, it should be warm, soft and inconvenient. The most inconvenient place of all was Malkin's pillow because she was allergic to cats. After she threw him out several times, learned to keep her door closed always and to search the room before going to bed, Bobo transferred his attentions to Wiz. Since even in his current emaciated state the cat weighed nearly twenty pounds and since his favorite way of getting into bed was to take a running jump and try to land right in the middle of Wiz's stomach, this was a less than ideal arrangement from Wiz's point of view. However it suited Bobo fine and like most cats he had a strong sense of the proper order of the universe.

When Bobo wasn't happy he complained and he had obviously taken voice lessons from his mistress. When he was happy he purred. Since Bobo's purring had the volume and timbre of a Mack truck at idle, happy Bobo wasn't much of an improvement over unhappy Bobo.

For all that, it worked somehow and life settled into a routine.

From the top of the mountain you could see for miles. Myron Pashley couldn't see any further than his computer screen in front of the window.

Special Agent Myron "Clueless" Pashley, FBI, utterly ignored the vista of pine forests stretching down to the tan desert and the blue and purple mountains on the far horizon. Instead he hunched further forward in his swivel chair and ran his finger down the screen. His lips moved silently as he worked the elementary subtraction until he arrived at the final, fatal, number on the last line.

"Whipple, come take a look at this."

Ray Whipple, Pashley's office mate, pulled his head out of the latest copy of *Astrofisicka*. He made a show of reading the journal in the original Russian because he knew it annoyed Pashley.

"Look here," Pashley's finger stabbed down onto the computer screen. Whipple sighed, put the journal down and looked over Pashley's shoulder.

"What happened, get lost in the directory tree again?"

"No, I got something. There's an error in the user accounting."

"So what?"

"What it means," Pashley growled, "is that a hacker's gotten into the system."

"What it means," Ray shot back, "is that the accounting program screwed up again and the roundoff errors are accumulating."

Pashley smiled a superior smile. "Look at the amount of the error. Eighty-seven cents! You read *Cuckoo's Egg* didn't you? You know what that means."

Whipple, who had not only read the book but had helped the author in a small way during his hunt through the Internet for an international spy, couldn't get his jaw back up in time to protest.

"We got us a hacker and we're going to nail him." With that he bent to the computer with a will, punching keys frantically.

Ray retreated to his chair and his journal. He had a sinking feeling he wasn't going to make the deadline for this year's computer Go competition.

Myron Pashley had been born to be an FBI agent, but he was born too late. He belonged in the Bureau in the days of narrow ties, short haircuts and J. Edgar Hoover; the days when a straight-arrow personality, a gung-ho attitude and a suspicious mind could substitute for intelligence and judgment.

After graduating next-to-last in his class at the FBI academy, Pashley had pictured himself on the streets of urban America, fighting crime that was poisoning the nation's body politic. Instead he was assigned to computer fraud and copyright violations. Not the best use for a technological idiot, his superiors admitted privately, but at least he wasn't likely to get shot or blow an important organized crime investigation. Keep him there for a couple of years, they figured, and eventually he'd get fed up with the Bureau and quit.

His superiors had reckoned without Pashley's zeal. Assigned to combat computer crime, Pashley convinced himself this was the new plague sweeping through America and he threw himself into the battle with the boundless enthusiasm—and the brains—of an Irish setter. He began hanging out on computer bulletin boards, running up huge phone bills as he trawled for the evil "hackers" who were insidiously spreading through the nation's computer networks, committing all sorts of nefarious deeds.

He quickly discovered that hackers were as subtle and devious as they were dangerous. The fact that he could find absolutely no trace of any illegal activities on the bulletin boards he frequented was tangible proof how devilishly clever these "hackers" were.

He would have been more effective if he hadn't needed someone to untangle his electronic screwups on the average of once every fifteen minutes, but he persisted.

Finally his patience was rewarded. On an obscure computer bulletin board in the Southeastern United States he found his master criminal. The messages Pashley had collected were enough to convince his boss that he really had something and a full-scale investigation was launched.

Three months later a daring and well-coordinated dawn raid on the North Carolina hideaway seized nearly a million dollars' worth of computer equipment plus over fifty firearms. At the press conference that morning Pashley had cheerfully posed in front of tables loaded with seized items while brandishing what he called "a blueprint for techno-terrorism."

That brief shining moment was the high point of Pashley's career.

Unfortunately it was immediately followed by the low point. It turned out his "master hacker" was actually a science fiction novelist who wrote for computer magazines on the side and collected guns as a hobby. Not only were all the weapons the FBI had seized perfectly legal, but the "blueprint for techno-terrorism" turned out to be the notes for the author's latest novel.

Needless to say the author was not happy. He also had a considerable talent for invective and a pen dipped in vitriol which he used to lambaste the Bureau and Special Agent Pashley in several national magazines. For one awful week even Jay Leno had been making jokes about him. Somewhere in that terrible period he had been dubbed "Clueless" Pashley and the name had stuck ever since.

It wasn't as bad as the DEA agent in the gorilla suit, but at least the DEA agent got a solid arrest out of it. All Pashley got was a multi-million-dollar lawsuit,

naming him, "John and Jane Does 1 through 999," and
the Bureau as defendants.

It hadn't helped matters when Pashley's superiors found
he had been rather selective in the bulletin board messages he had shown them. The full message base proved
"to anyone but an utter idiot" (in his boss's memorable
phrase) that the computer bulletin board was merely a
way for fans to communicate with their favorite author.

His boss was demoted, his section chief took early
retirement and his chief's supervisor was transferred to
a job in the Aleutian Islands. But Pashley, whose head
should have gone up on a pike over the main entrance
to FBI headquarters, wasn't even reprimanded, thanks to
the multi-million-dollar lawsuit pending against the
Bureau. Instead he was given an "independent assignment" and sent to this observatory in the desert south-
west to continue his fight against computer crime.

Thus, on this brilliantly sunny afternoon, Pashley was
sharing a cubbyhole office with the rather bewildered
astrophysicist who had been assigned to "coordinate" with
him. After three months in the same office Ray knew all
about what Pashley had done, but he still wasn't sure what
he had done to be punished like this.

For preference Ray Whipple didn't deal with anything
closer than about five light years. People were especially
difficult for him and riding herd on Pashley was straining his skills at interpersonal relations.

Putting the magazine in his lap Ray decided to try one
more time. "Look," he protested, "it doesn't work that
way."

"You mean you don't know how to make it work that
way," Pashley said. "These kids are geniuses."

"But," Ray repeated feebly. "But . . . but . . . but . . ."

"Don't worry. You hold up your end and we'll nail these
hackers yet." He hit a few keys and looked at the results
on the screen. "Uh, could you get this untangled for me?
Computer's screwed up again."

TEN

PROGRESS REPORT I

Never Let Them See You Sweat.
—Consultants' Slogan

Normally a consultant presented a proposal in writing.
These people preferred a face-to-face approach. *Like
making a presentation to the prospective client*, Wiz
thought, *only I've already got the job.*

Something over a dozen councilors had assembled in
the Mayor's office for the meeting. In addition to Mayor
Hastlebone and Dieter there was a distinguished-looking
man in a tasteful blue tunic whom Wiz remembered
vaguely, one or two other sharp-looking characters and
a few old codgers who looked like they had come because
they didn't have any place better to be.

Dieter was off to one side with a couple of other
council members hanging at his elbows, talking to a
slightly taller, younger man who managed to be handsome
in a beefy blond sort of way and still look like Dieter.
The councilor was punctuating his words with short, sharp
hand motions and the other was focusing on him
intently and occasionally nodding to show he more or
less understood.

As soon as Wiz entered the room Dieter jerked his

head around to stare at him and, followed by his
entourage, pushed his way through the group over to
him.

"Ah, Wizard," the little councilor said just a shade too
loudly, "I'd like you to meet my nephew Pieter Halder.
My sister's son. Fine boy and my heir." He clapped the
young man firmly on the shoulder. Pieter smiled vacantly
and nodded.

Dieter fixed Wiz with an eagle's glare. "Have you
considered what I told you?"

"Ah, I have the matter under advisement."

"And?" the little man asked sharply.

Out of the corner of his eye Wiz saw that the mayor
was watching them. He didn't look any too pleased.

"Well, as you know, this is a serious matter. . . ."

"Serious for you if you go against me, you mean."

"While I'm sure we share many basic objectives . . ."
The mayor cut him off by rapping his gavel to call the
meeting to order and Dieter and the others retreated to
the councilors' benches. Wiz suddenly found himself
standing alone in the middle of the room.

"I asked the wizard here to tell us what he's going to
do," the mayor announced. "You all know what happened
at the Baggot place." There was general muttering and
nodding. "Now he's going to explain to us how he's going
to fight these dragons."

"Well, actually I wasn't planning on fighting them," Wiz
corrected. The temperature in the room seemed to drop
ten degrees and the councilors started to mutter among
themselves again, this time a low ominous mutter.

Wiz recognized his cue for fancy footwork. He steepled
his hands, dropped his voice half an octave and nodded
to the council.

"Obviously, to solve a problem of this magnitude it is
necessary to grasp the entire solution space by completely
reinventing the initial propositions. As you can see this
is a major undertaking and to be effective the work flow
must be carefully managed."

The councilors were listening intently now, all of them nodding to show their neighbors that they understood perfectly, even if no one else did.

"Now," Wiz went on, "currently we are in the initial definition phase of the project."

"What definition?" Dieter objected. "The problem's dragons and how much money we're going to spend to protect ourselves."

"Money?" another councilor put in. "Who said anything about spending money?"

"Well, there is the wizard's fee . . ." Mayor Hastlebone started, but he was drowned out by three other councilors trying to talk at once. He pounded the table with the gavel trying to restore order. Wiz noticed the oak table was dented and battered in front of the mayor's seat.

"As you can see," Wiz said when the mayor finally restored order, "there are some fundamental issues which must be addressed before we can precisely define the problem." Dieter opened his mouth to protest, then snapped it shut and settled for glaring at Wiz.

"We consultants know that before we can address solutions we must quantify the problem."

"Quantify?" asked one of the councilors.

"Reduce it to numbers. We must have something we can measure and count so we will know how much progress we are making."

"Seems like an odd way to go about solving a problem," one of the councilors near Dieter grumbled, "counting things."

" 'Specially for them as can't count and ends up with eleven in a dozen," one oldster piped up. That got a chuckle from most of the councilors, a red-faced mumble from the objector and a glare from Dieter.

"There are a number of proven statistical or numerical techniques we could use," Wiz went on. "First we must choose the appropriate one."

"We could count the number of people that get eaten," a councilor suggested.

"No, that's much too insensitive. We need something far more accurate."

"The number of dragons sighted each week?" suggested another.

"Subject to misinterpretation. I propose using a composite index extracted from baseline data which we will collect. By applying appropriate analysis techniques we can reduce the multi-dimensional dataspace to a single, easy-to-understand figure of merit by which to judge our dragon-reduction strategies." *Not to mention being so complicated nobody will be able to figure out what it means,* Wiz thought.

"And what do you propose to do about the dragons while you're gathering all this information?" Dieter's stooge demanded.

"Why nothing at all," Wiz said blandly. "That would invalidate the baseline sample and disturb the entire database."

"Ayup," an old councilor nodded wisely. "Them databases get right testy when they gets disturbed." He continued to nod and stroke his beard. Everyone ignored him.

"And how long is this baseline period going to be?"

"Normally you want at least one year's data. You have to allow for seasonal disturbances you understand." The councilors muttered and shifted in a way that told Wiz he had overplayed his hand.

"But since this is a rush job we will telescope that," he continued smoothly. "Let us say three moons after the program is fully functional."

"And meanwhile we do nothing," Dieter put in.

"No, while we are gathering data we can start an educational campaign to explain to people the dangers of dragons."

"But they all know dragons are dangerous," another councilor protested.

"Yes, but do they know how to avoid dragons? Oh, I'm sure they have some strategies they learned by hook or crook. But we have a responsibility to teach them optimum dragon-avoidance strategies."

"How are we going to do that?"

"Why, with an education campaign, of course. We will prepare pamphlets describing the dangers of dragons and how to avoid them."

"Most of the folks around here are illiterate."

"Quite all right. We will use iconographic representations for the literacy-impaired."

"What did he say?" muttered one of the councilors.

"He means they'll be full of pictures for them as can't read," explained his neighbor, who was quicker on the uptake.

It was a very long meeting.

Well, there's another hurdle crossed, Wiz thought as he stepped out of the town hall into the main square. *Or maybe another bullet dodged.* He wasn't sure he liked the second analogy even though a nasty little voice inside told him it was probably more accurate.

"Ah, Wizard Zumwalt!" came a smooth voice behind him. Wiz came out of his fog and saw the distinguished silver-haired councilor in the blue tunic standing at his elbow.

"Just Wiz, please."

The other smiled and nodded. "Very well, Wiz. And I am Rolf Rannison, head of the cloth merchants' guild and president of the Guild Association." He favored Wiz with an especially sunny smile. "I was hoping you could be my guest for lunch at the Guild Hall."

"Well . . ."

"Please accept," his would-be host urged. "Finest food in town, I can assure you."

Wiz knew he was being hustled, but he also knew that was part of a consultant's job. So he nodded and smiled as best he could. "I'd be honored."

The Guild Hall was a massive stone-and-timber building across the main square from the Town Hall. The private dining room on the second floor was paneled below and decorated with murals above. The paintings showed muscular folk going about the business of commerce in a style that reminded Wiz of WPA post office art.

The table was just a little bit too small so the two were forced close together. Not close enough to be uncomfortable but enough to encourage intimacy. The linen was starched and perfectly pressed, the liveried waiters were expert and unobtrusive and the food was very good, if rich.

It was all so well handled that it took Wiz a while to figure out what it was about the place. It wasn't just that it was old: The room and the Guild Hall felt, well, faded, like some once-great old downtown hotel. The murals were dulled with time and lack of cleaning and the paneling below them showed wormholes here and there. Like a lot of other things in this town, the Guild Hall obviously wasn't what it once was.

By the end of the first course Rolf was on a first-name basis with Wiz. Once or twice in his career in Silicon Valley Wiz had been wooed by some very high-powered headhunters. That was what this meeting with Rolf was like. The man was working on him, trying to bring him around to—what?—and in spite of his cynicism, Wiz found himself responding to the man's charm. If Dieter was born to sell used cars in San Jose, he thought, Rolf could sell bonds on Wall Street. Wiz smiled, pleasantly, tried to enjoy the meal and waited for the shoe to drop.

"I noticed you've already met Dieter," Rolf said casually as they worked their way through a dessert that was mostly berries, whipped cream and some kind of strong liqueur.

"After a fashion. He came to see me the first day."

Rolf smiled knowingly. "He is *dynamic*, isn't he?"

Wiz put down his spoon. "He is also about as subtle as a hand grenade in a barrel of oatmeal."

Rolf chuckled. "I think I understand the reference, but what is a 'hand grenade'?"

Wiz thought about how to explain high explosives to

a culture that didn't even have gunpowder. Then he
thought about what Moira said about his explanations.
"Let's just say it's something that doesn't belong in an
oatmeal barrel."

Again that engaging toothpaste smile. "You know one
of the things I enjoy so much about you, Wiz? Your
outlook is refreshing." He gestured from the wrist. "Like
a breath of clean air into a musty closet that has been
closed up too long."

Considering his performance this morning a breath of
hot air was more like it, Wiz thought. But he made an
appropriately modest reply.

"Refreshing nonetheless, Wiz. We have been a back-
water for too long. It has narrowed us, cramped our
vision." He leaned forward over the table. "Wiz, we need
to change and I think you are going to help us make the
changes we need so badly."

He used my name twice in two sentences, Wiz thought.
Here it comes.

"Wiz, that is one of the reasons I hoped we could meet.
I wanted to offer you my support in your program. You're
going to do great things for us, I know. In fact I'd go
so far as to say your coming marks a new beginning for
this town and its people."

Great, Wiz thought. *I am not only supposed to slay
dragons, I'm supposed to work bloody miracles.*

"You understand I have a very limited brief. I am a
consultant on dragon problems, not a general management
consultant."

"Your formal brief, true. But I think you underrate your
importance just now. As a wizard of great power, a defeater
of dragons and an outsider with new ideas, the whole
Council is compelled to listen to you." He paused and
cocked an eyebrow. "And very frankly I doubt the present
regime will allow you to do much about dragons."

That was so true that Wiz could only nod.

"Where do you fit in all this?"

"Fundamentally I think we want the same things."

Just then what Wiz *really* wanted was to go home to
the Wizard's Keep and Moira. But that wasn't one of his
options until he got this mess straightened out and he
couldn't do that unless he stayed alive. He jerked his
attention back to what Rolf was saying.

"You bring us change. But the change has to start at the
top. We need new blood on the Council and especially we
need a new mayor." He waved a hand in a self-deprecating
gesture. "Oh, not necessarily me. But someone with the
vision to see the way we must go and the determination
to see that we can get there."

"What's wrong with Mayor Hastlebone?"

Rolf sighed. "I am afraid he is too much under Dieter's
influence. He can see nothing but old solutions to our
problems."

"Dieter does have some ideas for doing things differ-
ently," Wiz pointed out.

"Dieter's solutions are more of the same old medicine.
More taxes to strangle the life out of what little trade
we have left." He shook his head. "No, money will not
solve our problems. Not without a complete restructur-
ing and a reawakening of civic discipline."

He leaned across the table and touched Wiz's hand.
"Wiz, we must—what was your phrase?—reinvent ourselves. Yes, 'reinvent.' A new city, a new culture rising out
of the ashes of the old. Why, the possibilities are . . ." Rolf
trailed off, seemingly transfixed by something infinitely far
off over Wiz's right shoulder. Then his attention snapped
back to Wiz and he was all business again. " . . . rather
remarkable," he finished smoothly.

A chill ran down Wiz's spine. "Look, I'm flattered that
you think so highly of me, but . . ."

Rolf held up a hand. "When someone says they are
flattered it means they are preparing to turn you down.
Don't, I beg of you. You don't have to say yes, but leave
the matter undecided, please."

"I will certainly try to keep an open mind."

✧   ✧   ✧

Let's see, Wiz thought as he made his way back across the square. *I've been in town less than ten days and I've already made two powerful enemies.* At least Rolf would be his enemy as soon as he figured out that Wiz had no intention of supporting his schemes. Dieter wanted to loot the town. Wiz suspected Rolf's desires ran deeper and more dangerously. The man didn't want money, he wanted power. Probably a lot more power than a mayor had ever had before.

Of the two Rolf was probably the more dangerous. Dieter's hostility was open. With Rolf you'd never see the knife coming until it was buried in your back. You could see Dieter coming, but that didn't mean you could dodge. He touched the ring of protection on his finger. It would place him in stasis if he was under immediate physical threat. *If the damn spell had any sense I'd have been frozen solid a couple of days ago,* he thought sourly.

Not a living soul was waiting to greet Wiz when he got home. Widder Hackett, however, was.

"Well Mr. Wizard, I hope you enjoyed your stroll around town because there's been the netherworld to pay while you've been gone."

"What's wrong?"

"That demon of yours is holding the girl prisoner up in the upstairs parlor," Widder Hackett said. "What the fiend has planned for her," the ghost continued virtuously, "I wouldn't want to guess.

"It's what comes from consorting with them low-class demons," Widder Hackett added as Wiz pounded up the stairs to rescue Anna.

He came into the room and found a hysterical maid facing off with a very determined scaly green demon.

"What's going on here?"

"I, I was just trying to . . . and it, it . . ." Anna was hyperventilating and for a minute Wiz thought she was going to faint on him.

Wiz recognized the demon. It was the one he had set

to guard his desk and it manifested if anyone tried to touch his papers or equipment. Apparently Anna, not knowing better, had tried to clean off the desk.

He put his arm around her shoulders to comfort her, and to catch her if she did faint. Anna was trembling like a leaf and she pressed her face into his shoulder so she wouldn't have to look at the demon.

"Hey, it's all right. He won't hurt you if you don't try to touch anything on the desk."

"But he won't let me leave!"

Wiz looked around and realized that to get to the door they would have to pass the desk. The demon wouldn't attack unless someone tried to touch the things on the desk but it would certainly come alert if anyone but Wiz got close. *I'll have to turn the sensitivity down on the spell,* he thought.

Malkin stuck her head in the door to see what the commotion was, saw Wiz and Anna, and disappeared before Wiz could say anything.

"He won't hurt you if you don't touch what's on the desk," he told her. "Look, I'll dismiss him, okay?" A quick gesture and the demon vanished, looking smug. "There, it's fine." He gently pried her face out of his shoulder and turned her toward the desk. "See? No more demon." With his arm still around her shoulder he walked her past the desk to the door.

"Now, you don't have to clean around the desk, all right? That's not part of your job anyway and I'm sorry I didn't tell you that before. Are you okay now?" Anna sniffled and nodded.

Wiz drew a line on the floor in softly glowing blue light. "Look, anything inside this line I will take care of, okay? Just don't touch any of it and I'll make sure the demon doesn't bother you."

Bobo sauntered into the room, looked at the line and sniffed.

"Now just go on down to the kitchen and rest for a while. You'll be okay?"

Anna sniffled and nodded.

"I'm sorry to be so much trouble My Lord, it's just that . . ."

"I know," Wiz said encouragingly, "it wasn't your fault. Now go on."

Still sniffling, Anna made her way downstairs toward the kitchen.

"Malkin," Wiz called, "can you come in here a minute?"

"What's up?" the slender thief asked as she strode into the room. Malkin showed no fear but Wiz noticed she kept just far enough away from the desk to keep from triggering the demon. For an instant he wondered how she knew the distance so exactly.

"Uh, about what you just saw. It wasn't really what it looked like."

Malkin waved a lazy hand. "Forget about it."

"But I wanted to explain . . ."

"No need," Malkin said. "The child's safe with you."

The way she said it, Wiz wasn't sure whether to be relieved or insulted.

"You'd better be careful though. The little ninny doesn't have the sense to be afraid of magic. She's likely to blunder into something you'd rather she didn't."

"I'll take extra precautions," Wiz assured her. "What about you? Aren't you afraid of being around all this magic?"

Malkin laughed. "Afraid? Not hardly. I respect it is all." The way she said it, and the way she smiled, left Wiz with a slightly uneasy feeling in the bottom of his stomach. He decided at the same time he turned down the demon's sensitivity he was going to increase the protection.

ELEVEN

MEANWHILE, BACK AT THE OBSERVATORY

Just because someone is hard-working and
ambitious doesn't mean that person has
the least idea what is going on.
—*The Consultants' Handbook*

It was another sunny day in the desert. Of course, it's
almost always sunny in the desert, which is why this
particular desert mountaintop sprouted telescopes like
lawns sprout toadstools. With telescopes come astronomers, naturally, and just now this particular astronomer's
mood was anything but sunny.

"You," Ray Whipple said, "have got to do something
about that FBI agent."

There was a pause while the observatory director took
his artfully scuffed ostrich-skin cowboy boots off the corner of his desk. "What's the problem?" he asked mildly.
Actually he had a pretty good idea what the problem was
and he was only surprised it had taken this long to
happen.

"He found an eighty-seven-cent error in someone's

account and now he's convinced he's on the trail of the mother of all conspiracies."

The director made a show of lighting his pipe. "That's his job after all."

"But the man's an idiot!" Ray protested.

"I know. So does his supervisor. She asked us to keep him here as a 'special favor' to the Bureau."

"He's chasing all over the net looking for some imaginary 'hacker' he thinks he's found and he's dragging me with him!"

"He's not breaking down any doors or shooting people, is he? It's safer for everyone if he stays here where he's out of the way and mostly harmless."

"But I've got to deal with him," Ray groaned.

"Look," the director said sympathetically, "I know this is hard on you. I'll tell you what. When this is over I'll make it up to you. How would you like some extra observing time? How would you like to get your project up on Hubble next year?"

Ray's eyes widened. Time on the Hubble Space Telescope was somewhat more precious than gold in the astronomical community. "You could do that?"

"Just keep our agent happy and keep him out of everyone's hair."

In the event, Clueless Pashley kept himself out of everyone's hair for the next three days. He was so busy tramping through the Internet in pursuit of his master hacker and screwing up his account that he was only an electronic pest for everyone but Whipple.

Pashley's performance on the Internet was reminiscent of the old saw about a thousand monkeys at a thousand typewriters, which is to say it was nearly random and mostly produced garbage. However, as in the case of the monkeys, there is always the element of blind chance and sheer, dumb luck. Pashley's original error was, as his office-mate surmised, an accounting glitch. But in the course of his thrashing around, Special Agent Myron Pashley stumbled and fell face-first into a heap of gold.

Not surprisingly it started with a total disaster.

Like most astronomers, Ray Whipple was used to working at night and sleeping during the day. Even though his current job was "temporary system administrator for administrative support services" (or, as he put it, "computer janitor") he saw no reason to change his habits.

Pashley, on the other hand was an early-to-bed, early-to-rise type who was in the office religiously at 7 A.M. This particular day he managed to be in the office all of thirty minutes before he did something especially stupid and crashed the entire system. Which of course resulted in Ray having to drag himself out of bed and drive back up the mountain at an ungodly-o-clock in the morning to fix what Pashley had done.

To add insult to injury, Whipple had to listen to Pashley the entire time he was trying to bring the system back up.

"I almost had him," Pashley kept insisting. "I was onto something and the hacker crashed the system to cover his tracks."

Ray knew damn well what had caused the crash almost as soon as he sat down at his terminal, but yelling at Pashley wouldn't get him any closer to time on the Hubble. To try to shut out his office-mate, he kept his attention glued to the screen as the system booted back up.

Because he was concentrating so intently on his workstation he actually read the list of demon processes as it scrolled up. The last one was one he didn't recognize.

Whipple frowned. He should have known all the demons on the system and here was one he'd never seen. He called it up and found it was a perl script that scanned for incoming traffic with a particular name in the "from" field and forwarded information about it to a site he'd never heard of, **thekeep.org**.

This was getting stranger and stranger. A quick check of the mail queue showed a couple of messages with the right name in the "from" field that hadn't yet been forwarded when the system went down. He called one of those up and scanned through it. Then he came to the routing.

"What the hell?" he exclaimed.

"What?" demanded Pashley, hurrying over to peer over his shoulder. "What did you find?"

The routing was absurd. It looked as if the message touched every continent, including Antarctica, and was routed through the weirdest collection of sites he had ever seen.

This was completely lost on Pashley, but he did pick up on something else.

"Look at the name," Pashley said, jabbing his finger at the screen so it blocked most of Ray Whipple's view. "**Thekeep**. One of those fantasy names is a sure tipoff that it's a hacker site. I'll bet we'll find this is a major hacker nexus."

Whipple, who had played D&D until he got into graduate school, kept quiet. He had learned that arguing with Pashley on one of these subjects was useless.

"Whatever it is, someone got into our system," Whipple said.

"YES!" Pashley shouted in his ear. "I told you we had a hacker on the loose."

Ray Whipple gritted his teeth. "It looks like you're right."

Meanwhile the programmers at **thekeep.org** pursued their own search for Pashley's "hacker." It was slow, tedious work. There were a lot of systems on Wiz's routing list and not all of them were easy to plant a search demon in. A few were flat impossible so the programmers had to resort to other shifts. Fortunately Wiz was so homesick he e-mailed a message almost every day. Unfortunately it still took inordinate amounts of time and work.

"You know what I really resent?" Danny said one evening as the pair was hard at work. "All that work we put into dragon-slaying spells that we'll probably never have the chance to use."

"That is a consequence to be sought rather than mourned," Bal-Simba rumbled from his extra-large chair where he sat reviewing a scroll with Moira and Arianne.

"Well, yeah," Danny agreed. Then he added disconsolately, "But I've got such a *good* one."

"I was even hoping to learn something," Jerry said. "I have this theory about the black-body temperature of dragons."

"Most dragons are not black," Moira told him. "Why you should be interested in just the black ones, I do not know. Much less their temperature."

"No, you don't understand. See, a black body temperature is a physical property of all things, even dragons, no matter what their color. And . . ."

"My Lord, if this is another one of your explanations I am in no mood to hear it."

"But," Jerry said plaintively, "it's such an *interesting* question."

"The only question I am interested in regarding dragons is how to get Wiz back," Moira told him firmly.

Ray Whipple had an easier time of it. Being a legitimate system administrator at a legitimate site, not to mention being actually in this world and being able to invoke the name of the FBI, Whipple had resources Danny and Jerry didn't. By using them and calling in a few favors, Ray was able to trace Wiz back to the system he had broken into very much faster than the people at the Wizard's Keep.

In a matter of days he had a result to show the FBI agent.

"Cute," Ray said as he displayed his find. "It's a cutout using two mailboxes. Incoming mail goes into one, the script automatically transfers it to the other one and then it gets forwarded out of there. But if you trace it back the trail ends at this mailbox."

"Cutouts huh? That's an intelligence trick. And you thought it wasn't spies."

"A lot of people know how to do that," Ray muttered into the screen.

"Now, how do we track him from here?"

"That's going to take a little more work," Ray said, ignoring the "we." "But what I can do is modify his script so that we can see his traffic." The keys rattled under his fingers. "There. Now the script makes an extra copy of all messages that go through that mailbox and sends one to you."

"Hot dog!" Pashley breathed, visions of reinstatement dancing before him, "I told you we'd get this hacker." He stopped. "But wouldn't it be simpler just to ask the people at that site to track where the other side mailbox leads to?"

"I tried that," Whipple told him. "But I didn't get anywhere. I think there's something funny about that site."

TWELVE

BUREAU-CRATIC COMPLICATIONS

If you can delay solving a problem long
enough, one of three things will happen:
The problem will become so large that it
destroys the organization, everyone gets
so used to living with the problem that it
ceases to be a problem, or the problem
solves itself. In cases two and three you
win. Meanwhile you don't make enemies
by rocking the boat.
                    —*The Consultants' Handbook*

It was a bright muggy morning in Washington, D.C.
The kind of morning that finds legions of bureaucrats hard
at work in their air-conditioned offices and trying not to
think about what the drive home will be like.

The director of the Federal Bureau of Investigation
was hard at work in her air-conditioned office, but she
wasn't worried about the drive home. For one thing she
probably wouldn't go home until well after sundown. For
another she was deep in a review of industrial espionage

activities in the United States, trying to decide how much of the report represented a legitimate danger and how much was eager beavers pumping for a bigger share of the department budget.

The Phone rang.

Not just any phone, The Phone. Popular legend to the contrary it was not red. It was a very ordinary looking tan telephone with a funny mouthpiece and an unusually thick cord connecting the handset to the base. It was the director's main link to the White House and the higher echelons of the Justice Department and the national security apparatus.

The director eyed The Phone. Not even the President normally used that telephone to contact her. It rang again and she picked it up.

"Director, do you recognize my voice?"

The director pulled what looked like a cheap pocket calculator out of the top drawer of her desk, checked the date and time and punched in a highly improbable mathematical calculation. "Give me confirmation."

"Alpha," The Voice said, "gamma rho woodchuck three-four."

"Confirmed. I recognize you."

Actually the director had no idea who the person on the other end of the phone was. She only knew he represented No Such Agency, the officially non-existent organization charged with communications and cipher security. The outfit was a couple of rungs up the intelligence food chain from the FBI.

"We have a domestic security problem," The Voice said. "Someone has been using one of our accounts on the computer network. A rather sensitive account. I am afraid we need your cooperation on this one." There was real regret in The Voice.

"We'll be happy to assist you," the director said, trying to keep the excitement out of her own voice. A favor like this to No Such Agency could be worth a lot in the barter market that made official Washington tick.

"We can have a team ready to meet with you inside of an hour."

"I understand one of your people is already working on this from the other end, Special Agent Pashley."

"Pashley?" she asked in a voice that didn't betray anything.

The director was trying to quit smoking, but she groped in her desk for the crumpled remnants of her last pack and lit a slightly bent Camel.

"Yes. He apparently found evidence of the penetration at another site and has been tracing it back."

"I'm sure he doesn't realize the significance. I'll put a team of specialists on it instead."

"We think that would be inadvisable just now," The Voice said. "Perhaps it would be better if we worked with this Agent Pashley alone."

"Of course we'll need a small group to liase," the director said hastily.

"Of course," The Voice agreed. "Have your people contact ours at a suitable level and keep us informed of anything Pashley turns up."

After The Voice hung up the director ground out her cigarette and glared at the phone. *Damn that man. And damn Pashley!* Somehow that moron had stumbled into something.

The Bureau had teams of computer experts who could handle this. Real experts, not street agents who had been through a two-week course at the academy. No matter what No Such Agency wanted, she'd get them on the case and pull Pashley and . . .

Her hand stopped halfway to the phone. She *couldn't* pull Pashley. The Bureau's whole defense in the lawsuit depended on the fiction that Pashley was a competent, trusted agent. The Justice Department attorneys had explained to her that, on paper at least, she didn't dare do anything to suggest the Bureau had less than full faith in the turkey.

All right, she'd compromise—on paper. Pashley would

stay on the case, conducting an independent investigation from his damn mountaintop. Meanwhile she'd put together a tiger team to work with No Such Agency.

Wiz was staring at the screen when he heard a peremptory knock at the front door. Since he was staring at the screen because he was fresh out of ideas, he pushed his chair back from the desk and went out on the landing to see who it was. *I really ought to write a screen saver for that thing, just to give me something to look at,* he thought.

He got to the stairs just in time to see Anna opening the door for Dieter Hanwassel. The councilor was flanked by his nephew Pieter and a gawky young man Wiz didn't recognize who was clutching a rather grimy roll of parchment.

Anna had been scrubbing the front hall. She was wearing an apron over her brown dress and a kerchief over her golden curls. A pail of soapy water stood halfway down the hall and she still had the scrub brush in her other hand. As the three entered she realized she was still holding the brush and blushed crimson.

"Good afternoon, gentlemen," Wiz said in his best snow-the-suits manner as he descended. "What can I do for you?"

Even in tights and velvet bathrobes, these guys were suits.

Suit or not, Dieter wasn't snowed. "I want to talk to you, Wizard. On business."

"Of course."

"You know my nephew Pieter. This is Alfred Alfesbern. He's a brilliant young man and he's got the solution to your problem."

"Well . . ." Wiz began.

"We'll talk in your office. Come along Pieter."

"Do I have to?" Pieter whined, looking over Dieter's shoulder to where Anna had gone back to scrubbing the floor.

"All right," Dieter snapped. "Wait here then. But be ready when we're ready to go." The other nodded, his eyes never leaving the maid.

Somewhat uneasily Wiz led his guests up the stairs and into his workroom. There weren't any chairs for visitors and Wiz didn't want to encourage these visitors to stay anyway.

"Now what can I do for you gentlemen?"

"It's what we can do for you," Dieter said. "We can solve your problem for you. Show him Alfred."

"I call it the Dragon-Stopper," the lanky man said, unrolling the scroll.

Wiz peered over his arm. "It looks like a town with a wall around it."

"It is a town with a wall around it," Dieter put in. "This town."

"You see," Alfred continued, "I have determined that dragons cannot pass through solid material. So if we interpose solid material between the town and the dragons, they cannot reach us." He stood up and beamed triumphantly. "And our problem is solved!"

"But dragons can fly right over a wall."

"Not if we build it high enough," Alfred said. "We just extend the wall up until it is beyond the dragons' ability to fly over it."

Wiz wondered what the altitude ceiling on a dragon was. Even if they couldn't do any better than a Piper Cub that still meant a 10,000-foot wall.

"That's going to be an awfully high wall."

"Details," snapped Dieter. "Quibbling. This will solve the problem and we'll be done with it."

"How are you going to build a wall that high?"

"The same way you build a low one," Dieter said. "What's the matter? Have you gone stupid?"

"No, I mean how are you going to get the work done?"

"We'll hire a good contractor. I know one or two."

I'll bet you do, Wiz thought.

"Gentlemen, I'm not sure this is practical."

"It's perfectly practical," Dieter said. "You're the one being impractical here."

"We've built lots of walls," Alfred put in. "It's a well-known technology." Dieter glared at him and the young man shut up.

"Look here, Wizard," the councilman said, "you can't say absolutely, positively this won't work, can you? So what's the harm in trying? It will put people to work, get money flowing and revive the economy. Besides," he added slyly, "there'll be something in it for you."

"Gentlemen, I really don't think . . ." Before he could finish there was a feminine shriek from downstairs followed by a male bellow of pain.

Down in the hall Pieter Halder was doubled over clutching his groin. Anna was standing with her back against the wall, her face scarlet and her skirt rumpled up against her petticoat. She looked up, saw Wiz and Dieter standing at the top of the stairs, turned and fled sobbing to the kitchen.

Wiz glared at Dieter and the little man backed partway down the stairs under the force of his gaze.

"Get out. All of you. Now."

"She's lying," Pieter gasped, still clutching himself. "I didn't do anything."

"Tried to put his hand up her dress is all," came Widder Hackett's voice out of thin air. "Oh, if only I was alive and still had me magic!"

Wiz faced Dieter again. "You are here as my guests." He bit each word off hard and sharp, advancing as he spoke so Dieter and Alfred kept backing down the stairs. "That will protect you for precisely ten heartbeats more. If you are still here you will be trespassers and I will deal with you accordingly."

Dieter paled. "You can't treat me this way," he yelled.

"Five heartbeats," Wiz said. "Four, three . . ."

By then all three of them were out the door, Dieter in the lead and Pieter limping doubled over behind.

"You haven't heard the last of this," Dieter shouted as

Wiz slammed the door on them. "You'll pay for this! I'll make you pay for it!"

With a final glare at the door, Wiz turned and went down to the kitchen.

Anna was slumped over the kitchen table weeping. She raised her head as Wiz came down the stairs and wiped her reddened eyes.

"I'm sorry, My Lord, but he . . . And I didn't do anything to provoke him. I swear I didn't."

Seeing her shame and misery, Wiz was very glad Pieter and the others were out of his reach.

"I know you didn't," he said gently. "No, you did exactly the right thing. I'm only sorry you didn't hit him harder."

Anna looked up and sniffled. "My granmama told me to do that whenever a man got, got too . . . forward."

Wiz stepped toward her to comfort her and then stopped. The last thing she needed just now was to be touched by a man.

"You're a very brave girl," he said. "And your grandmother was a wise woman. Go on and pull yourself together. Take your time, and if you want to go up to your room and lie down, go ahead."

Anna sniffled again and tried to smile up at him. "Thank you, My Lord, but I need to get dinner started."

"You don't have to."

"Please, My Lord. I'll be all right. Really I will."

Wiz left her in the kitchen and came back up to his workroom. All the while Widder Hackett carried on a monologue about young Halder's moral shortcomings. Clearly it wasn't the first time something like this had happened and apparently Widder Hackett had made a hobby of collecting gossip about his misdeeds.

He had barely gotten settled when Malkin came striding in. "I met the shrimp and a couple of his flunkies on the street," she said. "He was in a worse mood than usual and that miserable nephew of his was walking like he'd run into a banister."

"It wasn't a banister. It was Anna's knee."

"Like that, eh?" the tall woman shrugged. "Serves the copulating little swine right. She's not the first skirt he's tried to lift unwilling."

"So Widder Hackett has been telling me."

Malkin nodded. "Aye, she'd know. The old cow was the biggest gossip in the town. She must have kept records of everything everyone did."

"You thieving little strumpet!" Widder Hackett rasped.

"Careful," Wiz said to Malkin.

"She was an old busybody and I'd tell her so to her face."

Wiz looked around the room. "I think you just did."

Malkin snorted. "So what? She's dead and she can't touch me."

"Why you little guttersnipe!" Widder Hackett roared. "You're a fine one to talk, what with . . ."

The ghost went on for some time and in some detail. In the middle of it Wiz discovered that putting his hands over his ears did absolutely nothing to block out her voice. Malkin watched his antics with some amusement.

"Anyways," she went on when Widder Hackett finally ran down into a mumble, "you've got bigger things to worry about. That half-firkin councilman is going to hold it against you no matter how much provocation his pig nephew gave the girl."

"He's unhappy with me already. Just before Anna kneed Pieter I told him I wouldn't support his latest graft opportunity disguised as a public works project disguised as a dragon defense."

"In that case you've probably made yourself a mortal enemy. Dieter may dote on that little swine but he truly loves the chance to get money out of someone else's pocket."

"Well, it was inevitable anyway," Wiz sighed, "once he figured out I wouldn't go along with his scheme to get his hand into the public treasury up to the arm-pit."

Malkin nodded and turned to go out. She paused in

the doorway. "There's another thing you'd better think about, Wizard. Young Halder's not the only one who's going to come sniffing about after Anna."

"She seems to handle them pretty well."

"Oh, aye. She'll protect herself. If she understands what's about in time. Problem is she's as cow-witted as she is pretty and she might not see the danger. Not all men are as easily discouraged as Pieter Halder. That's why she needs protection."

Wiz sighed. *Another responsibility I don't need.* "Look, go down there and comfort her, will you?"

"Me? What do I know about comforting hysterical females? You do it. You've got the knack and she looks up to you."

"I'm not what she needs just now. Besides, I think she'd take it better if a woman told her she did the right thing."

"All right then. I'll look in on her."

"Malkin?"

"Yes?"

"Do you suppose people will get the wrong idea about you and Anna living here with me?"

"Oh, there'll be talk. Always is. But you're a powerful wizard and you're expected to be strange and mysterious in your ways. Besides, no one except chronic gossips are going to believe that you'd take advantage of the girl." She eyed him. "I don't know if you're too married, under a spell or—Fortuna aid me!—a gentleman. But it's obvious you're not going to do her any harm."

"What about you?"

Malkin threw back her head and laughed. "Me? Fortuna, I've got no reputation to lose, being a thief and all. And you could do better than a long stick like me in any establishment in town." She sobered slightly. "Besides, men want women they can look down on and that's a fact."

Wiz started to protest that he found Malkin attractive and then decided this wasn't the time. It was true about her height, Wiz realized. Malkin was easily the tallest woman he'd ever seen in this world. She was over six feet and her slenderness made her appear taller.

By the time he got all this together in his head, Malkin was gone.

THIRTEEN

CHAT MODE

> While ignorance and stupidity may debar a
> person from solving a problem, it is no
> handicap at all when it comes to screwing
> up someone else's solution.
> — *The Consultants' Handbook*

Wiz was bored, restless and, most of all, homesick for
Moira and the Wizard's Keep. E-mail was wonderful
but it was no substitute for being there. It wasn't even
a substitute for talking on the phone.

He toyed with the idea of trying to set up a telephone
call to the Wizard's Keep, but hooking into the other world's
phone system was really Danny's area of expertise. Wiz
wasn't sure he could establish a voice connection and still
keep his location hidden

On the other hand, he thought, *I can do something
almost as good.*

Computer chatting would give a much more immediate
connection and he knew a way to make that secure.
What's more, he knew where he could find what he
needed to do it.

506

He spun back to his workstation and started connecting to the Internet.

Danny was bored. As often happened when he got bored he was surfing the Internet, hanging out on his favorite talk channel. As usual it was barely controlled chaos, with perhaps a half dozen conversations going on at once, like a printout of a cocktail party.

> FREEKER: Anyone got any good codez?
> DRAINO: So he says 'first assume a spheri-
>   cal chicken'
> PILGRIM: The P-153 is a piece of shit. Use a
>   canopener.
> RINGO: Does anyone have the DTMF codes
>   to do that?
> DEATHMASTER: Hahaha
> A.NONY.MOUS: Look in the last issue of
>   2600.
> WIZ: Hey Danny how are things at the Keep?

The message scrolled by so quickly he almost missed it. Then he called up the buffer, read it again and goggled.

"DRAINO: Wiz," Danny typed, "is that you? Where are you? Are you all right?"

"Fine," the answer traced out on Danny's screen. "Maybe we'd better go to a private channel."

"Jerry, Moira come here!" Danny yelled over his shoulder. "It's Wiz."

"Well, they've had a problem all right," Special Agent Marty Conklin told the FBI director. In the corner Conklin's boss nodded approvingly. "They've got their butts in a sling so they want us to pull a rabbit out of the hat to save their bacon."

The director winced at the mixed metaphors. She wasn't sure she approved of Conklin either. He was obviously pushing the Bureau's weight restrictions hard and the director had a strong suspicion he couldn't pass the annual physical training test either.

But in Conklin's case the title "special agent" was especially appropriate. He was the FBI's brightest, if arguably weirdest, specialist on computer and telecommunications crime. His boss had managed to make him look halfway presentable in a rumpled gray suit, but he had still come along just in case his prize charge got too far out of hand.

The director lit another cigarette and blew smoke out her nose. *I've got to quit these—as soon as this business is settled,* she thought. "What exactly happened?"

"They left a back door ajar at a black site and now they've got newts in the firewall."

"Can you put that in English?"

Conklin paused to do a mental translation. "Okay, they have a site that's physically highly secure. Everything's guarded and under lock and key. For some reason they need Internet access from the site, but obviously they don't want the next net newt who comes along to take the system home with him."

"Don't want a what?"

"A net newt—slimy little uglies that you find under rocks."

The director nodded. "Oh, you mean hackers."

"No, I mean system breakers, computer criminals." Conklin was about to launch into his canned lecture on how most hackers are not criminals, but his boss cleared his throat meaningfully.

"Well, anyway, what you do in a case like that is set up a firewall. That's a computer that connects to the net on one side and to your secure system on the other. All it does is pass messages back and forth. It acts as a barrier to keep out the net . . . uh, the bad guys.

"Now normally a firewall doesn't have any user accounts on it. It is strictly there as a gateway to the main system. But in this case someone did something real dumb."

Conklin smiled broadly at having caught the nation's top communications security agency in an error. "When a computer comes from the factory there's a standard password installed, something like 'password' or 'administrator,' something the field engineers can use to set the system up. Anyone using that password has superuser privileges on the system—they can do anything, because you need that kind of access to get the system up and running. Of course, since the password is the same on all machines of that kind it's a major security hole and you're supposed to erase it as soon as the system's set up."

Now the director was smiling too. "And they didn't?"

"No ma'am they did not. So some slimy little newt comes along, uses the password to set up his own accounts and starts helping himself to all the free computer time he can carry. Now they've found it, they're embarrassed and they're scared it's a major security breach so they want us to nail the little sucker."

The director was still smiling. Bureaucratically this was better and better. Not only did No Such Agency need a favor—it didn't have law enforcement powers and couldn't arrest the system breaker even if it could find him—but the problem was the result of a bone-headed blunder by their people. When the FBI cleaned up this mess No Such Agency would owe them big time.

"In fairness to them," Conklin's boss broke in, "it was an easy thing to overlook. The system has only been operational a few weeks and since the firewall doesn't have any users there was no reason to check the password file."

The director shook her head. She wasn't interested in being fair to No Such Agency, she was interested in milking this for all it was worth. Unless . . .

"Is this really a national security problem? I mean is there a possibility the main system was penetrated by an outside agency?"

Conklin shook his head. "That's what No Such Agency is afraid of, but that's a bunch of professional paranoids playing Cover Your Ass. Fundamentally this was a dumb stunt, the sort of thing a fourteen-year-old kid would do from his Macintosh. There's no sign of any other tampering with the system or of any attempt to get from the firewall back to the main system. I'm ninety-nine percent sure it's a run-of-the-mill newt."

"But not one hundred percent sure? Then of course we need to pursue it." *And put those arrogant SOBs even further in our debt,* she thought. "What are the chances we can catch this, uh, 'newt'?"

"If he keeps using those accounts, about a hundred percent. That's why No Such Agency hasn't canceled them. We're watching, waiting and tracing him back."

"I don't understand," Moira said. "If Wiz is talking to us 'real-time,' as you say, why is it harder to track him in chat than when he sends us messages?"

Moira was sitting with the programmers in their workroom. She tried to spend as little time there as possible to let them work in peace. So she only popped in a dozen or so times a day. Jerry had rigged a panic button to summon her and any of them who weren't in the room if they got a message from Wiz, but Moira still checked constantly.

Danny shook his head and compressed his lips into a tight line. "It shouldn't be, but Wiz got real clever. He's using a program called IRC to chat and he's connecting through the freenet in Cleveland. Dialing in on the phone system to one of the freenet's numbers and using their IRC facility."

"But you said if you could get back to the telephones in your world you could easily find where he is tapping in from our world," Moira said plaintively.

"And normally we could. We can use the software built into a digital phone switch to let us trace someone's connection point in about three seconds." He made a face. "Problem is, Wiz knows it too."

Jerry nodded. "It's as if he's deliberately making this as hard as he can."

Moira's mouth quirked up in something that wasn't quite a smile. "Most likely he is. If the geas commands that he keep his location secret then he will bend all his efforts to that end. He cannot deliberately go against the geas."

"Anyway," Danny said, "Wiz always said he didn't know much about how we tapped into the phone system."

"That's because he didn't want to know," Jerry said. "The whole thing's blatantly illegal."

"So what are they going to do? Send the FBI to arrest us?"

"His conscience bothered him."

Danny shrugged. "Anyway, he must have understood more than I thought. See, we can use the automatic trace facility in the switch to find him, provided he's coming in through a digital switch. Digital phone switches are just about universal in the United States so I took that as a given."

"And it is not?"

Danny made a face. "His first link is to the local phone company. The next one is into the private phone system of a major oil company, where normal trace facilities don't go. Okay, we got that one. But the next link is via the oil company's leased lines to its satellite link to one of its exploration offices in Ulan Bator, Outer Mongolia. Needless to say, that is not a digital switch."

"Oh," Moira said in a small voice.

"It gets better. The next link is from the Ulan Bator switch to a switchboard someplace else in Outer Mongolia. We think it's in a yurt. Anyway, that one is not only not digital, it's still run by a human operator." Danny made an even worse face. "Currently we are trying to figure out how to get through that one. Then we'll see what other surprises he has in store for us."

"It does not sound hopeful then," Moira said.

"There's one more complication you should know about. Even once we slog through all that we will have to run a trace from the switch he is using to his connection point back in this world. That will take a couple or three hours from the time we locate the right switch.

"Needless to say," Jerry added, "we are still pursuing the e-mail link as well." He reached out and patted Moira's hand. "Don't worry, we'll find him whether he wants to be found or not."

"Is this place secure?" the FBI director asked, looking around the conference room deep in the bowels of the FBI building.

"As secure as we can make it," the staffer at the foot of the table told her. His name was Wilkins and he was in charge of such things.

The director grunted and pulled a package of cigarettes out of her purse. The room was supposed to be a no-smoking area but no one objected.

She lit up, inhaled and blew smoke out through her nostrils. "Before we get to the regular business we have a non-agenda item."

Everyone leaned forward expectantly. If it was too sensitive to go on the agenda it was very sensitive indeed.

"Moron Pashley," the director said, taking obvious relish in mangling the name. "He's still making trouble."

Everyone leaned back. Several staffers stared down at the papers before them. One or two looked up at the ceiling, as if hoping to find the answer written there. No one in the room had to be told who Pashley was. He wasn't at all important in the grand scheme of things, but since the call from the head of No Such Agency he had become a major burr under the director's saddle. As a result, the top echelon of the FBI spent an inordinate amount of time trying to keep him discreetly under control.

"How?" asked Paul J. Rutherford, her special assistant and troubleshooter. "He's stuck out in the middle of the desert."

"He's less than two hours from a major airport and he wants to go investigate this new hacker case personally."

"That could be tricky," said James Hampton, her legal adviser. "We'd need a very good reason to forbid him."

"If we can't forbid him we can sure as hell transfer him," the director said. "Send him to some place *really* remote."

"Well, there is a site in Antarctica," Rutherford said. The director brightened visibly.

"Won't work," Hampton put in. "It's outside the U.S. and we're legally forbidden to operate anywhere else."

"Well, what can we find *inside* the U.S.?" The director asked. "There's gotta be a deep, dark hole somewhere we can stick this clown."

"Just any hole won't do," Hampton reminded her. "It's got to have a major computer link to the outside world so we can maintain Pashley is working on computer crime."

"The Aleutians!" someone further down the table said. "There are a couple of places out on those islands with major computer links and nothing else but fog, seagulls and Kodiak bears."

The director thought of Pashley meeting a giant bear in the fog. She brightened again.

"Won't work," Rutherford said glumly. "Those computers are too important. If he screws them up we've got major problems, national-security-wise."

"But the Cold War is over," the director protested. "We're not worried about the Russians any more."

"We use them to eavesdrop on the Japanese and Koreans," Hampton said apologetically.

The director ground out her cigarette and muttered a highly politically incorrect phrase from her childhood. One that used "mother" as an adjective three times.

"All right, this clown wants to go to San Francisco 'to pursue a hot lead.' Any suggestions?"

For a long moment no one at the table said anything. Then Hampton voiced the inevitable. "Since it's a legitimate national security case I don't think we dare stop him," he said apologetically.

The director used the phrase again.

❖   ❖   ❖

Well, Ray Whipple thought, *at least I'm getting some time in San Francisco out of this.* Ray liked San Francisco, especially when it was summer in the desert, but he wasn't looking forward to this trip at all.

He looked around the office to make sure he hadn't forgotten anything—and to keep his mind off what the rest of today was going to be like.

For one thing it involved a ninety-minute automobile ride with Myron Pashley, followed by a wait in an airport and a two-hour flight with the man. That was a lot more than the Recommended Daily Allowance of Pashley and damn close to the LD-50.

Which was the other thing. The man would *not* shut up about this system breaker he was tracking. Since most of what he had to say was palpable nonsense and he seemed utterly immune to anything he didn't want to hear, his chatter was like fingernails on a blackboard to the astronomer. Ray was taking his Walkman and a selection of his favorite Bach tapes in the hope he could drown Pashley out. He suspected strongly the FBI agent wouldn't take the hint.

Look on the bright side, Whipple thought. *When we get to Silicon Valley he's someone else's problem.*

Finally, Ray turned on his vacation demon and logged his terminal off the system. The vacation program would automatically respond to any e-mail messages with an electronic form letter telling the sender he would be gone for a while. He looked around the office for the last time and realized Pashley's terminal was still active and connected. *Idiot!* Ray Whipple thought. As a final gesture he turned on the vacation demon on Pashley's system as well.

Unfortunately Ray was distracted and didn't think it through. The vacation demon didn't think at all. It just did what it was programmed to do.

It was mid-morning when Wiz came into his workroom. Since Anna had started working here he was actually able to sleep in most mornings and he enjoyed the sensation immensely.

Just because he slept late didn't mean others did. Anna was usually up at first light of dawn and even Malkin didn't often sleep later than he did.

This morning both of them were in his workroom staring at the screen saver he had finished the night before. Anna was standing carefully behind the blue line on the floor, broom in hand, obviously interrupted at her work. She was staring at the display like a child seeing her first Christmas tree. Malkin was just behind her, also watching the ever-changing patterns.

Anna saw him and blushed. "Oh, I'm sorry, My Lord, I didn't mean to . . . It's just that it's so beautiful."

"It's a screen saver," Wiz told her. "Although there's really no screen there to save."

Malkin examined the glowing pattern and grunted. "What does it do?"

"Well, it doesn't really do anything." Wiz looked back at the swirl of color. "You know, if they had invented those things back in the sixties when everyone was dropping LSD the intellectual history of the Western World would have been considerably different."

Malkin grunted again and turned away.

"If you'll excuse me, My Lord," Anna said tentatively. "I'll leave this room until later." With that she turned and hurried out.

Wiz watched her go and shook his head. He was no more immune to physical beauty than most men, but like a lot of men he rated other things higher than looks when it came to female attractiveness. Intelligence, for instance—which definitely put Anna out of the running. Besides, the girl's vulnerability triggered his protective instincts.

And always and above all there was Moira. He sighed at the thought and set to work.

As usual, the first thing Wiz did was to check his mail. The very first message was from a net id he didn't

recognize. *Spam or junk mail?* he thought as he
called it up.

> **Special Agent Myron Pashley will be out
> of the office and unavailable for the next two
> weeks. Please forward any urgent mes-
> sages to fbi@fbi.gov**
>
> **Myron Pashley,
> Special Agent, FBI**

Wiz went cold. They were on to him! Someone must
have found his mailboxes on the broken system and called
in the Feds. He recognized the form of the message as
a vacation demon. It was just sheer blind luck that the
FBI agent who had been getting copies of his messages
had gone on vacation and hadn't bothered to exclude his
drop from the demon's reply list.

Wiz slammed his hand to his forehead and damned
himself as an utter idiot. He had been stupid to use that
mailbox setup for so long! It was only a matter of time
before someone traced him back, found the cutout and
caught him.

But in spite of the danger he needed that e-mail link
to the Wizard's Keep. He'd have to come up with something to make it secure from snoopers in both worlds.

System breaking had never been Wiz's idea of hacking.
Danny could probably have come up with a much more
sophisticated way of hiding while using the net. But you
can't become intimately familiar with systems without
learning things that are useful in less-than-legal ways.

Wiz thought hard for a couple of minutes and then
he smiled. Yeah, there was a way. Something that would
be just about untraceable unless they figured out the
trick—and drive them nuts if they tried to trace it.

A few minutes work at the keyboard and a net of
purple and green lines flashed into being above his
work table. Several more key clicks and a few of the

intersections burned fiery red. Wiz looked at the glowing orange letters next to the red points of light. Each red dot indicated a computer on the Internet that doubled as a router. *Not bad. The only question is which one to use?*

"Yes!" he whispered. Even Jerry would never think that the system might be lying to him. If he was careful, they'd never have any reason to suspect at the Wizard's Keep.

That first line of defense would be tough, but it was simple enough that he could put it into effect almost immediately. That would buy him some more time while he added extra layers of security behind it.

Wiz bent to the magical workstation with a will, his fingers flying over the keys. *Just a few more hours,* he thought. *Give me just a few hours and I'll be damn near invulnerable.*

Joshua Weinberg felt like hell. His throat was raw, his cough was worse and he felt like someone was sitting on his chest even when he was standing up. If he hadn't had a damn good reason to come in this morning he would have stayed home in bed, maybe even called the doctor the way Dorothy had been nagging him to do.

But as head of the Silicon Valley office of the FBI, he had responsibilities. Just now he was standing next to one of them.

"It's an honor to have you, Agent Pashley," he said as he led his guest into the main office. He said it loudly enough to set off another coughing fit, but he was sure at least some of the agents in the bull pen heard him.

Privately he was much less impressed. The guy was certainly living up to his advance billing. But as he introduced him to his other agents Weinberg was careful not to betray by so much as the twitch of a muscle that Myron Pashley was anything other than an out-of-town expert on computer crime.

Weinberg knew all about Pashley. He had gotten a

personal telephone call from the director of the FBI
explaining about Pashley at some length. In fact she had
called him at home at 4 A.M. to make sure the call didn't
appear on the office phone logs.

*Cooperate. Treat him like he knows what he's doing.
And watch him every minute.*

As soon as Bill Janovsky, his second-in-command, got
back he'd take him aside and explain about their guest
and how he was to be handled. Just now Janovsky was
up in San Francisco conferring with the U.S. Attorney
about a technology transfer case. Their talk would have
to wait until this afternoon.

Weinberg wished devoutly he was still chasing Soviet
agents around the semiconductor plants. He felt like hell.

In the event, Weinberg didn't get to talk to Janovsky
that day. Janovsky was delayed in San Francisco until after
5 P.M. and Weinberg felt so awful he went home sick
before Janovsky got back. He felt worse the next morning and stayed home all that day and the next day. By
Thursday his wife took him to the doctor and the doctor called an ambulance to take him to the hospital.

One consequence of Weinberg's illness was that it took
somewhat longer than usual to get things squared away
on Pashley's hacker investigation.

There were a couple of less obvious consequences. For
one thing Weinberg hadn't had a chance to tell Janovsky
or anyone else about his conversation with the director.
His people had seen their boss acting as if Pashley was
a big gun expert so naturally they assumed he was.

For another, no one bothered to tell the director that
Weinberg was out of commission. There was no reason
why they should, after all, since no one in the office knew
about her interest in Pashley.

Ray Whipple could have told them a lot about Pashley,
but Whipple had gone off to visit some colleagues at Cal
Berkeley's Leuschner Observatory to get a first-hand look
at some anomalous data collected by the Kuiper Airborne
Observatory. Pashley had assured him he would call him

when needed and Whipple figured the FBI could do a better job of restraining Pashley than he could.

The net result was that Clueless Pashley was loose in Silicon Valley with the full force of the Federal Bureau of Investigation behind him.

FOURTEEN

RAIDING ON THE PARADE

Expert: Anyone more than 100 miles from
home carrying a briefcase.
—*The Consultants' Handbook*

It is a truism well-known to lawyers that while the law
may be uniform, all judges are not alike. It is a corollary equally well known to prosecutors that some judges
are easier than others when it comes to search warrants
and such. In San Francisco District Court, Judge David
Faraday was what the local federal prosecutors privately—
very privately—called a patsy. A law-and-order Nixon
appointee, he could be counted on to grant search
warrants on nearly any grounds.

So it was hardly surprising that FBI Special Agent
George Arnold showed up in Judge Faraday's office with
Special Agent Clueless Pashley in tow to seek warrants
to raid Judith's apartment.

"And this person has been breaking into government
computers?" Judge Faraday asked after looking over the
papers Pashley and Arnold presented to him.

"Highly sensitive government computers," Pashley
amended. "Your honor this is a major national security
case."

Arnold nodded. "Your honor, if need be, we have a civilian expert on computer networks and security waiting outside who can testify to the importance of this warrant." Actually it was Ray Whipple cooling his heels in the outer office, but he was an expert in Pashley's eyes and Arnold was following the lead of the bureau's out-of-town "expert."

"I know about computer crime, Mr. Arnold," Judge Faraday said mildly. "I saw that movie, *War Games*." The judge scanned down through the pile of affidavits.

"Search warrant for subject's apartment, wiretap on subject's telephone, electronic surveillance of premises. Well, this seems in order," he said as he reached for his pen. "Very well, gentlemen, the warrants are granted."

Pashley managed not to cheer.

"Did you get it?" Ray Whipple asked as Pashley and Arnold emerged from the judge's chambers. Pashley tapped his breast pocket significantly, even though the warrant was really in Arnold's briefcase.

"When are you going to serve it?" Ray asked as soon as they were out in the corridor.

"I'd like to hold off on the search warrant for a week or so," Arnold said. "We'll put the wiretap in place immediately and get a snooping van in the parking lot tonight to start executing the surveillance. That van can pick up the electromagnetic emissions from ordinary computers and decode them from five hundred feet away."

The astronomer gave a low whistle. "That's scary."

"Oh, we've got our methods," Pashley assured him jauntily, missing the expression on Whipple's face.

"We can lift information right out of a computer without the user knowing it," Arnold added. "If we listen for a few days we may get to watch this hacker in action before the bust goes down."

"When's she going to do something?" Myron Pashley wondered aloud for roughly the eighth time that evening.

George Arnold squirmed around to get a better view of the readout. "So far she's still watching television."

Pashley and Arnold were crammed into the surveillance van along with the regular operator and several racks of equipment. "Cramped" was too generous a word for conditions in the van. "Badly ventilated" didn't really cover the subject either, especially since Pashley had found a Yemeni restaurant near the hotel and dined on a vegetarian dish that was mostly chickpeas and garlic. So far they had been sitting almost in each other's laps for almost three hours and even Pashley was getting tired of it.

The directional antenna hidden in the van's roof rack was pointed at Judith Conally's apartment less than three hundred feet away. At that distance it could easily pick up electronic emanations from Judith's apartment.

"Wait a minute," the technician said. "The television's just gone off. Hold it, okay, she's starting to work on the computer."

"Here we go!" Pashley crowed. For an awful instant Arnold thought Pashley was going to hug him.

"What's she doing?"

"Looks like loading a program," the tech said, keeping his eyes fixed on the displays. "Okay, she's just put a file up on the screen. I got it now."

Pashley, Arnold and the technician wriggled around until they could all see the display screen.

```
# include <iostream.h>

template <int T>
struct A{A(){A<T>>1>B;cout<<T%2;}};
struct A<0>{};
void main(){A<99>();}
```

"It's screwed up," Arnold complained.

The tech checked the instruments. "No, that's what's on her screen all right."

"What do you make of this stuff?" Arnold asked.

"Code," Pashley assured him. "This is all in code. When we raid the place we'll probably find a code book that translates all these code words."

Neither Pashley nor Arnold knew it, but it was indeed code they were looking at, although not in the sense they meant. Inside her apartment Judith was settling down to work on one of her private programming projects. Since for preference Judith used C and since her C style was both idiosyncratic and highly personal, it was hardly surprising that the FBI agents couldn't make sense of it. Since the particular program Judith was laboring over was her entry in this year's Obfuscated C++ Contest it was to be expected. Since one of the utilities Judith had developed to help her was an uglyprinter, which turned even the best-structured C code into an utter muddle, it was inevitable.

Judith Conally was playing relativistic Tetris when the knock came at the door.

"Damn!" she muttered as the distraction made her miss an especially intricate maneuver in the time direction. The rest of her carefully constructed edifice came tumbling down even before she was out of the chair to answer the door.

Judith had never met Myron Pashley, but as soon as she opened the door she knew what he was. For one thing he was wearing that dark-suit-narrow-tie-white-shirt outfit no one wore anymore but government agents and EDS employees. And EDS employees weren't allowed to wear wrap-around sunglasses.

"Special Agent Pashley, FBI," the man announced, holding out his identification. "We have a warrant to search these premises." He thrust a paper into Judith's hands and pushed her aside. "Stand out of the way, please."

He was followed into the apartment by six other men and a woman, all dressed in the same style if not the same clothing. Since Judith's apartment was not large, it was suddenly very crowded. Judith found herself crammed back against a book case.

One of the agents sat down at her computer and started calling up directories. Others fanned out through the apartment.

After a quick run-through of her more recent sins, Judith relaxed. There was nothing in the apartment which was the least bit incriminating. Then she looked at the search warrant and nearly burst out laughing. A national security case? Get real!

Then she stopped laughing and started worrying. She hadn't done anything, but what had the people in the other world been up to? Wiz was apparently in some kind of trouble and you never knew what Danny was going to do. There wasn't anything illegal here, but the laws didn't anticipate contact with alternate worlds where magic worked. If someone halfway competent had even a hint of a suspicion something like that was going on, the stuff in this apartment would be enough to blow it sky high. Whether that would mean jail or years in protective custody as a "vital resource" she didn't know, but she wasn't eager to find out.

Pashley moved to her desk and Judith's heart caught in her throat. There, lying on top of the stack of unpaid bills and unanswered mail, was her documentation for the magic compiler for Wiz's world. With its mixture of programming and magic that book alone would be enough to give the whole show away.

"What's this?" Pashley demanded, hefting the book.

"That's the design document for magic in my novels," Judith told him as blandly as she could. "Do you want it?"

Pashley knew all about seizing writer's notes after his experiences in North Carolina. "That won't be necessary." He turned to put the document back on the desk and missed seeing Judith slump in relief.

The agents went through the apartment like a polite hurricane. They always said "please" and called Judith "ma'am," but they were relentless and unstoppable. After turning the place upside down, taking her computer, boxing up all her disks and tapes, photographing everything (including the dishes in the kitchen sink and the bra hanging on the bedroom doorknob), giving her a carefully itemized receipt with serial numbers, and making an appointment with Judith to come in for questioning "with your attorney present if you desire," the agents finally left.

"Hit me," Wiz said glumly to the demon crouched on his work table.

The demon in the green eyeshade, gaiters and violently checked vest gave Wiz a toothy grin before flipping down a ten. That made twenty-three and Wiz was busted out. The demon gathered the cards in and shuffled them. Then he cocked an eyebrow at Wiz, waiting for the signal to deal again.

Wiz slumped back in his chair and sighed. It was still early afternoon, but it was not a good day. Not that that was unusual. The townfolk had learned by now that "their" wizard wasn't available before noon, but as soon as noon arrived there was a small line of them on his doorstep, demanding to see him.

He had tried refusing to see anyone, but that meant either being a prisoner in his house or being stopped on every street corner by someone with a long, incomprehensible tale of woe. So he had gone back to seeing a few people every morning, even though there was nothing he could do for most of them.

This morning's crowd had included a farmer who wanted him to find the pot of gold his grandfather was supposed to have buried on the farm, a lovesick young man who wanted his beloved to notice him and a nervous middle-aged woman who apparently expected him to guess what she wanted since she never did get around to telling him.

Meanwhile, in spite of the building urgency he was at

a complete and utter standstill on the dragon problem. He tried to tell himself he was too overcome with distractions to focus on it, but the fact he was playing blackjack rather than working told him how accurate that was. The truth was he didn't have even a notion of how to begin.

Wiz knew from experience there was a hierarchy to working on a software problem. There was hacking, there was programming, there was playing, there was doodling and there was what a British friend of his rather inelegantly described as "code wanking." He had been reduced to code wanking days ago and now he had lost his enthusiasm even for that.

He sighed and looked over at the demon. The demon leered back and riffled the cards suggestively.

"Busy, I see." Wiz turned to see Malkin standing in the doorway.

"Not really. What's up?"

"Message from Ol' Droopy. He wants to know how you're coming."

It took Wiz an instant to identify "Ol' Droopy" as the mayor and somewhat longer to formulate an answer.

"Tell him things are progressing at a satisfactory pace."

"So I see. Anyway, you can tell him yourself. I'm not your messenger. He just stopped me on the way back here."

As she moved Wiz noticed a slight bulge in her tunic.

"Wait a minute! Did you steal his chain of office again?"

"Naw. Did that once, didn't I?" She reached into her tunic and produced a wide leather belt with an ornate gemmed buckle. "I do wonder how far he'll get before his breeches fall down, though."

Wiz groaned. "One of these days you're going to get us all thrown right back in jail."

"That's all right," Malkin said cheerfully. "I've still got the keys hidden away."

Wiz groaned again.

"Besides, you're a fine one to talk. With your messing about with dragons and the Council you're likely to get us staked out on The Rock."

"Well, why do you stay, then?"

Malkin smiled in a peculiarly sunny fashion. "I want to see what's going to happen next. Hanging around here is more fun than a mummer's show. Besides, it gives me a base of operations, so to speak."

Wiz thought about what that last meant. Then he decided he didn't want to know. He also remembered why he had never had roommates. Then he thought of the rats in the psych lab. The more he thought about them the more sympathy he felt.

"Of course, if you want me to leave . . ."

"No, no. I need you for background resource. But try to be a little more discreet, will you?"

Malkin draped the belt over her shoulder, buckle resting on her breast. Wiz noticed it hung nearly down to her knees behind. "Oh, I'm always careful," Malkin said cheerfully. "You have to be in my business."

With that she was gone. Wiz sighed again and turned back to the demon, who raised a pair of scaly eyebrows and riffled the cards. Wiz dismissed him with a gesture. Somehow he'd lost all his taste for taking chances—any more chances.

Judith wasn't the only one upset by the FBI raid. If she was annoyed, the mood in the Wizard's Keep verged on panic.

Bal-Simba frowned when a breathless Jerry and Danny told him, in alternating choruses, what had happened.

"How serious is this?" the big wizard asked when his visitors finally reached a stopping place.

"Pretty serious," Jerry told him. "If **thekeep.org** goes off line we lose our communication link to Wiz." *And probably all chance of finding him,* he thought. But he saw the look on Moira's face and he didn't say that.

"Is Judith in any danger?" Moira asked.

"Danger? No. She's probably not even in trouble, well not much. She's not doing anything illegal. Wiz might be in trouble if they could catch him, but there's not much chance of that."

"The Sparrow told me once that you keep records on these devices," Bal-Simba said. "Is there anything there which would arouse their ire?"

Danny grinned. "There aren't any records on that machine. We keep all that at this end, just in case. As far as the domain is concerned, Judith's system isn't much more than a dumb terminal, even though it's officially listed as the main server."

"That was Judith's idea," Jerry reminded his younger colleague. "After she saw some of the stuff you'd been up to she didn't want any record of it on her system."

"Anyway it was a pretty smart move," Danny said. "There's no way they can pin anything on her. There's even a complete set of domain software on her system."

"We've also got a backup way to reach Judith. We're setting up a modem link over a regular telephone line. She just calls a phone number we give her and logs in."

"Can we give that number to Wiz?"

Danny frowned. "That's going to be trickier. You can bet the FBI has a wiretap on the connection to **thekeep.org**. If we use the current Internet connection to tell Wiz about the new number we'll be telling the FBI too. Since we, ah, weren't completely aboveboard in getting that number it wouldn't do to have them tapping that line too. We may be able to rig up a code or something, but it will take more time."

"Then how do we tell Judith about the number?"

"Easy. We call her, preferably at a friend's house."

"Is this like the number we gave Major Gilligan when we sent him back to your World?"

"Not exactly. That was an 800 number." Danny made a face. "Big mistake. I found out the hard way they monitor those real close. They found us and shut us down in just a couple of weeks. According to some of the people

I've been talking to on the net they're not as careful about local numbers, especially the ones that don't show long-distance charges."

"Meaning you've been hanging around with the phone phreakers again," Jerry said.

"Be glad I was," Danny shot back. "Otherwise we'd have worse problems."

Jerry didn't have a good answer for that one, so he let it slide.

"But can they sever the link?" Moira persisted.

"They may think they have already since they don't know we're tapped into her line."

"Can they cut it entirely?"

"Yeah, by disconnecting the line. But they probably won't do that. There's no reason for them to do it." He sighed. "You know there was a time when government agents were pretty dumb about these things. I understand they've gotten smarter."

"But they still might cut us off from Wiz?"

"Theoretically," Jerry said. "But don't worry. It would take an absolute idiot to do something like that."

It was not a good day for Special Agent Pashley. He had spent the morning interviewing Judith Conally with her lawyer present and he felt he was further behind than ever. After two hours of questioning and several very pointed inquiries by Judith's lawyer as to the exact charge, he had turned her loose. The results from the examination of Judith's computer and related material hadn't helped any.

"Technicalities," he grumbled into his coffee cup. "Tied in knots by damn technicalities."

"I told you it was a mailbox," Ray Whipple told him.

"It's a top secret government mailbox and these hackers are breaking into it!"

"Look," Ray said slowly and carefully, as if explaining something to a child. "We only know that some messages from that mailbox passed through her system. The messages we have were addressed to other accounts on that domain, she says she never got any messages from that account, there's no sign of any such messages on her system and she doesn't know where to find the people the messages were sent to."

"Yeah, but someone had to send the message in the first place and that person had to break into the mailbox."

"But she didn't send mail to herself," the astronomer said patiently. "The messages weren't for her and she didn't know that address was some sort of government secret. Hell, she claims she didn't even know those accounts were on her machine. That makes her as much a victim as the government. You can't arrest her for that. Especially since the thing's so secret you can't admit it's a secret in the first place."

"Hah!" Pashley said.

Whipple shrugged. "You can't prove otherwise."

"Technicalities," Pashley repeated. "Picky little technicalities. They're what's ruining this country."

"Myron, she's innocent."

Pashley snorted. "With a record like hers? She disappears, right out of a locked hospital ward, and no one knows where she's gone, and she's innocent?"

"She had a head injury. The hospital screwed up when she came out of the coma, she wandered around for a while before they found her. The hospital admitted they were wrong by settling with her, didn't they?"

"For all we know she was kidnapped by aliens for experiments or something," Pashley retorted.

Actually Pashley was closer to the mark than Whipple, although neither of them would have believed the real story. Judith had been taken to Wiz's World as part of the battle against computer criminal magicians at Caermort. She had been healed there and returned to our world when the situation was stabilized.

Suddenly Pashley brightened. "A brain probe! Maybe she's jacked into the net directly through her brain. We can find out with an X-ray or MRI or something." He stood up and strode out into the main office. "Hey John," he called, "have we got an X-ray machine around here?"

Ray Whipple put his head in his hands and groaned.

By mutual consent, the programmers and Judith Conally kept word of the FBI raid from Wiz. So naturally Wiz kept sending e-mail and chatting with **thekeep.org** as if it was still there.

Which it was, of course. In spite of what it said in the paperwork, the real server for the domain had always been in the Wizard's Keep in another world. True, there was now no computer in Judith's apartment, but that didn't matter to the signal. It was tapped off magically between the junction box and the apartment. First, however, it traveled through the local telephone office, where the FBI was monitoring the line.

Clueless Pashley looked at the surveillance report and slammed it down on the table. "We didn't get it," he said disgustedly. "Someone's still using that computer link."

"But that's impossible," Arnold protested. "We got her computer."

"Well, she's still on-line. Look at this. She must have another computer in there."

The other FBI agent went over the transcript and shook his head.

"But we got all the computer equipment in the apartment."

"Then it's got to be disguised as something else." He riffled through the sheaf of pictures of Judith's apartment. "What about that wall of electronic stuff?"

"That was a stereo system."

"Are you sure? You can disguise a computer to look like anything. These hackers are diabolical. Come on, let's go back to the judge."

This time the agents carried off a complete stereo system, a big-screen television complete with video game console, and anything else in the apartment that looked electronic, including a clock radio. Again they gave Judith an itemized receipt with serial numbers. Then they departed as quickly and officiously as they came.

"This," Judith said to the bare wall where her stereo had been, "is bloody ridiculous."

FIFTEEN

COMPETITION

Utter incompetence never kept
anyone from underbidding and
over-promising to get the job.
—*The Consultants' Handbook*

Wiz was having another lousy morning. He had left the house to escape the usual flow of people who wanted him to solve their problems only to run into the mayor at the town hall, who wanted to know how the dragon program was coming, and by the way did he have anything for a head cold? Wiz barely got out of that when he encountered Dieter Hanwassel and a couple of his council flunkies in the square.

"There you are, Wizard." Dieter made it sound like an accusation.

"Here I am," Wiz agreed glumly. Then he waited.

"I'm giving you one last chance, Wizard," Dieter said at last. "You can see things our way or suffer the consequences."

"Gentlemen, I have already told you I will give your position all the consideration it deserves."

"You mean you'll try to stall us," Dieter said. "Well, we won't be stalled. You'll either cooperate or else."

"I wonder how the rest of the council would take it if they knew what you were proposing?" Wiz asked with a slight smile. "I understand they are not all in favor of increasing taxes."

The little man turned purple. "Defy me, will you!" Then with a visible effort he controlled himself. "Well, we'll see." He turned and stalked up the steps into the town hall. His hangers-on followed. "I've a trick that's worth two of you," he said to his cronies as they drifted out of earshot. Wiz wasn't sure whether he was supposed to hear that or not.

Wiz spent another hour or so wandering around town, looking at things and fending off a couple of requests for magical help. Malkin was waiting for him when he got home.

"Messenger came from the council for you just a few minutes ago," she told him as soon as he walked in the door. "Ol' Droopy and some of the others want to see you in the mayor's office right away."

"Great. I just came from there. Now what?"

The tall woman shrugged. "Nothing good, I'll warrant."

There was a group gathered in the mayor's office by the time Wiz arrived. Dieter, the mayor, Rolf and several others were talking to a blond young man Wiz didn't recognize. The stranger's back was to the door but Dieter's wasn't. As soon as Wiz walked into the room he peered around the young man's shoulder and smiled at Wiz, not at all pleasantly.

"We have found another magician," Dieter said, gesturing to the young man. "Llewllyn here is skilled in the new magic."

On that cue the young man turned and swept a deep bow in Wiz's direction. The newcomer was undeniably handsome. Blond hair fell in ringlets to broad shoulders. Pearly teeth peeked between ruby lips as he smiled and his blue eyes sparkled. He was only a little shorter than Wiz, not as heavily built, which made him decidedly slender—but elegant rather than skinny. Handsome,

personable and utterly devoid of sincerity. He reminded
Wiz of every used car salesman and mortician he had
ever met. Instinctively Wiz looked for the white belt and
shoes. Then the significance of what Dieter had just said
sunk in.

"The, ah, new magic?"

The young man inclined his head in assent. "Yes, the
powerful new magic of the south. I am a direct disciple
of the Sparrow, the mightiest of all the southern wizards.
It was he who taught me personally."

"That's very interesting," Wiz said noncommittally.

"We are like brothers, the Sparrow and I. Why he even
calls me the Eagle—just a joke between us, of course."

With an effort Wiz managed to keep his mouth closed.
To almost everyone in the lands of the North, Wiz
Zumwalt was known as the Sparrow, a name Bal-Simba
had given him when he first arrived. Apparently this joker
not only hadn't met Wiz, he had never talked to anyone
who knew him.

Part of Wiz's mission had been to teach magic to
more than just wizards. Wizards and apprentices were
now teaching the system to hedge witches and others.
Obviously this guy had learned the new magic at third
or fourth remove—assuming he knew it at all, which Wiz
wasn't willing to grant without proof.

Over Llewllyn's shoulder Wiz saw Dieter nodding
approvingly. The mayor looked worried. Rolf simply
smiled benignly. The implication was clear. This guy was
competition and some of the council would love to dump
Wiz and sign on Llewllyn. Dieter because he hated Wiz,
and Rolf because he saw the young man as easier to
manipulate.

Wiz gritted his teeth. His first instinct was to expose
the phony. But he remembered the consultants he had
seen in his world and how they dealt with these situa-
tions. He could always expose Llewllyn, but Dieter could
always find another stooge. Maybe there was a more
effective way.

Llewllyn, recognizing an opportunity, made a small gesture with his right hand. A sparkle of rainbow light flashed from his finger tips. Several of the councilors gasped and he smiled like a toothpaste commercial.

"There," said Dieter triumphantly. "You see?"

"Oh it's all very well, I suppose," Wiz said carelessly. "Quite remarkable, really, considering."

"You can, of course, do better?" Dieter shot back.

Wiz smiled at the venomous little man. "Well, since you ask . . ." He thought quickly. Most of the magic he knew either wasn't spectacular or was much too powerful. But there was a spell he had come up with to amuse Danny's son, Ian. He tilted his head back and took a deep breath. Then he blew multi-colored bubbles that rose gently to the ceiling and burst into points of rainbow light.

"A conjurer's trick," Dieter snorted. He looked expectantly at Llewllyn. The young man glared at Wiz with what was obviously intended to be an intimidating stare. However Llewllyn was too young and too pretty to intimidate much of anyone. Wiz smiled back.

"May I suggest a compromise?" Rolf put in smoothly.

"What?" the mayor asked suspiciously.

"Why not a competition?"

"Here?" Wiz asked. "Now?"

Dieter smiled. "Here and now. Why not?"

Wiz, who knew a good deal more about wizards' duels, could have given him a couple of good reasons. First, a wizards' duel usually started with lightning bolts and moved quickly to earthquakes. After that they tended to get *really* destructive. That's why wizards generally had it out on mountain tops or blasted heaths or other pieces of low-value real estate. Setting up an indoor wizards' duel was like trying to get ringside seats for a hand grenade fight in a broom closet.

The other reason was that wizards' duels were almost always to the death. That might not have bothered Dieter or Rolf, but Wiz didn't want to kill Llewllyn just because he was a charlatan.

Llewllyn, sensing he had an advantage, decided to push it. "Behold," he cried, "the power of the new magic!"

He moved his lips as he mumbled a word and letters of glowing rainbow fire appeared in the air between them. Dieter and the others gasped at the display and Mayor Hendrick looked worried. The new magician paused, obviously enjoying the sensation he had created.

Wiz was considerably less impressed but intently interested. All Llewllyn had done was list out the spell. A nice effect, but anyone who understood Wiz's magic language could read the listing and see how the spell worked.

As Wiz ran through it he was even less impressed. It was really one very simple spell, dressed up by some subroutines. Further, Llewllyn didn't have the thing written to respond to one command. He had to issue a series of commands and that meant there were opportunities for another magician to interfere. Wiz smiled politely and worked out a couple of lines of code in his head.

Llewllyn smiled at his appreciative audience and made the listing vanish with a flashy swipe of his hand.

"Beozar!" Llewllyn declaimed. "Cautich!" he added. Wiz watched intently, his lips barely moving. "Deodarin." Llewllyn's voice rose to a crescendo and he threw wide his arms. "Behold!"

There was a weak *pop* and then a fizzling sound like a lightbulb burning out.

Llewllyn went pale. "Beozar! Cautich!" He thundered out again. "Deodarin!" and flung his arms out. "Behold!"

This time the fizzle was accompanied by a dim reddish spark that died with the sound.

Dieter shifted uncomfortably and the Mayor frowned.

"Maybe if we drew the curtains to darken the room," Wiz said helpfully.

Llewllyn had gone pale and he was mumbling, but he didn't try the spell a third time.

"I'm sure it's just a temporary problem," Wiz said. "Why don't you take off and work on it a little. I'm sure it will be better in the morning."

"Ah, yes, of course," Llewllyn said to his now visibly unimpressed audience. "This far north one must allow for the effects of the different stars. Tomorrow would be more propitious." The mayor and Dieter both scowled at him. "Or maybe even a little later today," the young man added hastily. "Yes. Now if you'll excuse me." As he bowed quickly and turned toward the door the mayor nodded to the guardsman lounging there.

"See that our guest doesn't wander off," the mayor commanded. "Meanwhile we will decide what to do with him."

The guard followed Llewllyn out and there was a strained silence in the room.

"I'm sure he's quite good, actually." Wiz sighed for effect. "But magic is tricky, after all, and it is so hard to really master beyond the merely superficial."

"He ought to be sent to The Rock for impersonating a magician," Dieter said venomously.

The last thing Wiz wanted was to be responsible for the man's death. "Oh, surely that's somewhat extreme," he said hastily. "After all he was only, ah, 'overly enthusiastic' about his skill at magic."

"He's a liar and he ought to go to The Rock for trying to fool the council," Dieter replied.

"Wiz is right," Rolf put in. "No harm was done. Surely the council can show mercy in this instance."

"Then what?" Dieter snapped. "Is he going to hang around here and steal chickens?"

Mentioning chickens seemed to have an unusual impact on the councilors, as if they knew something Wiz didn't.

"Well, I could take him on as a junior assistant," Wiz said. "He could probably handle some of the minor details, under careful supervision, of course. Naturally I'd need an office on the square here."

"I don't know that we need two wizards now," Mayor Hendrick said.

"Consultants, please," Wiz corrected. "And it would have certain advantages." *Like keeping this guy where I can watch him.* If Llewllyn stayed around he was likely to be trouble and he obviously intended to stick around.

The mayor rubbed his chin. "Still . . ."

"I say let's put it to a vote," Dieter snapped.

Obviously the hassle of another council vote didn't appeal to the mayor. "Oh, all right, but only under the wizard's supervision."

Wiz nodded. "Naturally."

Dieter looked at him suspiciously, but he only nodded.

"Now there is the matter of the fee."

The mayor frowned. "I thought we settled that."

"For the basic dragon situation, yes. However, on closer inspection it has become obvious that job will require services not covered in the original contract."

"I don't remember us signing any contract," Dieter said sourly.

Wiz smiled a superior smile. "Oh, you don't *sign* a contract with a wizard. It is implicitly made manifest. Here, let me show you." He made a sweeping gesture at the wall and under his breath muttered **list apl.man exe**. The wall was covered with fiery letters as the command list for Jerry's version of APL appeared. The reflected light cast a sickly pallor on the mayor, Dieter and the others. Surreptitiously one or two of the council members made signs to ward off evil.

"Now here in section three, paragraph five, sub-paragraph C, item three, you can clearly see . . ."

"All right, Wizard, I see," the mayor said hastily. Dieter and the others didn't seem disposed to argue the point, so Wiz gestured again and the "contract" disappeared.

"I think under the circumstances an additional four gold pieces a week would be reasonable, don't you?" he said blandly.

The mayor obviously didn't think it was all that reasonable, but he nodded nonetheless.

"Very good. Now if you gentlemen will excuse me I need to go find my new assistant."

❖   ❖   ❖

Wiz found Llewllyn in the hall looking like he couldn't decide whether to bolt or brazen it out.

"How did you do that?" Llewllyn asked. "Interfere with my spell, I mean."

Wiz just smiled.

"Come now. Fellow professionals and all that."

Wiz thought that Llewllyn's racket had more in common with a bunco game than magic. Then he remembered what line of work he was in just now. "Oh it's quite simple really. I guess the Sparrow forgot to tell you that."

The young man's eyes widened. "You know the Sparrow?"

"Well enough," Wiz told him.

"Oh," he said in a small voice, eyes shifting left and right. Then he straightened and his voice firmed. "I wonder that I never met you when I was with him," Llewllyn said. "But you must tell me about him sometime—ah, about your experiences with him, I mean."

"Oh, it wasn't very interesting," Wiz said. "You know the Sparrow. Dull as dishwater, really."

"Well, yes, of course, but . . ."

"That wasn't what I wanted to talk to you about. I'm afraid your performance just now offended several rather powerful members of the council."

Llewllyn looked even more apprehensive. "Oh, but surely . . ."

"I know you didn't intend to, of course. But, you know how clients, ah, councilors are. So very, very petty about things like results.

"Now," Wiz went on, "in spite of that I managed to convince them that you have potential. That given supervision and a little guidance you could be an asset to the operation here. So as an alternative I got them to agree to let me take you on as a junior assistant."

Llewllyn was more apprehensive than ever. "Alternative?" he asked faintly.

Wiz smiled. "Why dwell on unpleasantness? Especially when it need never happen?"

"Of course. Assistant you say?"

"*Junior* assistant, but still a consultant with all the rights, privileges and duties thereof." He smiled even more broadly. "I'm sure the Sparrow would advise you to take it, were he here."

The young man's eyes widened. "You don't mean he is likely to come here, do you?"

"Llewllyn," Wiz said sincerely, "I can guarantee the Sparrow will never get any closer to this place than he is right now."

"Oh." The young man sighed. "I mean, what a pity."

"I know what you meant," Wiz said. "Now let's get on with it, shall we?"

"Uh, a moment, My Lord. What about my remuneration?"

Wiz did a quick calculation in his head, based on what junior consultants in his world made versus what the consulting companies charged. "Okay," he said, "I'll pay you one gold piece a week. You'll work in the office here under my supervision. Your primary job will be client contact and low-level problem solving. Be in the office for at least four day-tenths a day, five days a week. You can set your own office hours, but keep them."

Llewllyn's nose wrinkled. "That sounds like a clerk, not a magician."

"It's a consultant. And the less magic you use the better."

"I don't know . . ."

Wiz shrugged. "Consider the alternative."

Llewllyn's face fell. "The alternative?"

"Dieter thinks you sold him a bill of goods. As my assistant you are under my protection. Otherwise . . ." Again the shrug.

Llewllyn swept a graceful bow to Wiz. "My Lord," he said grandly, "you have a new assistant."

Wiz tried to look happy.

✧   ✧   ✧

Anna was upstairs cleaning when Wiz got back, but Malkin was in the kitchen, brewing a pot of herb tea.

"What do you know about a magician named Llewllyn?"

"Never heard of him," the tall woman said cheerfully, cocking one leg over the corner of the table and sitting on the freshly scrubbed surface.

"Slender, long blond hair, really white teeth. Handsome and a born con man."

"Oh, *him*." Malkin said. "He's from around here. Used to hold himself out as a bard but I never heard of anyone who paid him for his singing. I'm kind of surprised he showed his face in these parts. Here, you want some of this? It's a mixture Anna made up."

"Thanks," Wiz said and poured himself a mug of the tea. It was mostly peppermint with a lemony-orangey overtone. A little weak but not bad, he decided. "I take it he had a good reason for leaving."

The thief gave a snort of laughter. "Only a due regard for his own skin. Seems he'd been stealing old man Colbach's chickens and bouncing his daughter at the same time." She grinned and shook her head. "I don't know which made him the madder."

Wiz took another sip of tea. "I'm surprised he came back at all."

"Well, thinking on it, he's safe enough. The girl's married respectable now and the first child looked like her husband, so no one much cares on that score. Farmer Colbach probably still harbors a grudge about the chickens but he don't come to town much. Besides, he's not likely to push it because it would just remind folks about his daughter." She took another sip from her cup. "I guess you ran into him."

"Actually I hired him as my assistant."

Malkin looked down at him hard. "Then you've got mighty strange tastes in your assistants."

Wiz looked back very deliberately. "I know," he said.

SIXTEEN

BLACK BAG JOB

> Forget what you read in the papers. These
> are not very bright guys.
> —Deep Throat to Woodward,
> *All The President's Men*

Another morning, another surveillance report. By now Pashley was beside himself.

"Look at this!" he shouted. "She's still on the net."

"Take it easy," Arnold said. "Just simmer down and let's think." Pashley paused and took a deep breath. His face turned a lighter shade of red.

"Now, how is she doing it? We got every piece of electronic equipment in the place."

"You're sure she hasn't brought a computer back in?" Ray Whipple asked. He was spending a lot more time than he liked at the FBI office and was even discovering he had common interests with some of the agents.

"No way," Arnold said. "We've been watching."

"What has the van turned up?"

"Absolutely nothing. If there's a computer in there it's

got Tempest-class emissions security. We know there's no computer in there."

Pashley was frantically thumbing through the eight-by-ten glossy color photographs of Judith's apartment the agents had taken on the first raid. Suddenly his head snapped up.

"Wait a minute! There is another computer in here." He stood up so fast he nearly knocked the chair over. "Come on, let's go back to the judge."

"You want a warrant to seize *what*?" Judge David Faraday said in an utterly bewildered voice.

"A toaster," Special Agent Pashley repeated confidently. "We believe it is a vital piece of evidence in this hacker case."

"But it's a toaster!" Judge Faraday almost wailed.

"Yes, Your Honor, but there's a computer hidden inside." He stepped up to the desk and held out a repair manual. "As you can see here there is a microcontroller—that's a computer—in the toaster. Further," he pulled out a couple of clippings, "this is the exact make and model which hackers at a hackers' convention actually connected to a communications network, like a telephone system."

"This happened in 1990," Judge Faraday said as he glanced at the clipping.

"Yes, sir, at a secret hackers' convention called InterOp, which was held not far from here."

"This clipping is from the *San Jose Mercury*."

"Yes, sir."

"So this secret convention of," he ran his finger down the clipping, "ten thousand or so computer criminals was covered by the local newspapers."

Pashley was oblivious to the change in Judge Faraday's voice. "Yes, sir. There were some television stories, but we couldn't get the tape as evidence. But you can see it talks about the toaster oven right here."

"Mr. Pashley," Judge Faraday said mildly.

"Yes, sir?"

"Get out of my sight." The judge's voice rose. "Get out of this courthouse!" His face got red and a vein began to throb in his temple. *Don't ever let me see you again. On anything.* Judge Faraday was screaming now. *"IS THAT CLEAR?"*

"But do we get the warrant?" Pashley asked over his shoulder as Arnold hustled him out of the judge's office.

Ray Whipple shifted nervously on the chill vinyl seat. There was something going on here but he wasn't sure what.

Uncharacteristically, Pashley had sought him out to offer him a lift back to the hotel. Instead of driving him nuts with innane chatter while he drove, Pashley wasn't saying anything. Whipple didn't find that to be much of an improvement.

Ray's knowledge of the city was minimal and his sense of direction useless for finding anything smaller than a star, but eventually even he realized they were heading in the wrong direction.

"Where are we going?"

Pashley didn't take his eyes off the road. "I've got a little errand to run."

Two more turns in quick succession brought them into a neighborhood the astrophysicist recognized vaguely. Then another turn and Whipple went cold as he realized where they were. By that time Pashley had turned off the headlights and pulled over to the curb less than a block away from Judith's apartment.

"What are we doing here?"

"We're here to get that toaster," Pashley said.

Whipple went even colder. "I thought the judge denied the warrant."

Pashley thrust out his jaw and gave the astronomer a steely stare. "There are issues of national security at stake. I'm not going to let a technicality stop me."

"That's burglary!"

"No sweat. It's what we call a 'black bag job' in the FBI."

It occurred to Ray that that was also what the Watergate Plumbers called it at the Nixon White House.

"What if she's home?"

"She isn't. She's off playing games with some friends. You just wait here and if you see her coming honk the horn, okay?"

"I dunno about this."

"Look," Pashley said in the voice exasperated mothers use on small children, "just sit here and blow the horn if she comes. Nice and simple. What can go wrong?"

Ray's suddenly overheated imagination came up with dozens of possibilities. "Leave the keys in the ignition, okay?"

Pashley shook his head. "Sorry. You're not a government employee. You can't legally drive this car."

Whipple decided to pass on that. "I don't want to drive it, I just want to be able to honk the horn."

Pashley tossed the keys on the seat. "All right then, but don't go anywhere." He got out of the car and started up the sidewalk, his trench coat flapping against his knees.

"I wonder how big the astrophysical library is at Folsom Prison," Whipple muttered and settled in to wait.

Clueless Pashley was muttering too as he turned into the apartment complex. "Damn pissants and their technicalities! Ruin the damn country."

There was another problem Pashley hadn't mentioned to Whipple. Since Judge Faraday had turned him down for the warrant the mood at the local FBI office had turned decidedly chilly. The surveillance team had been withdrawn and the electronic listening van was back in the government garage. Pashley suspected it had something to do with the fact that AIC Weinberg was almost ready to come back to work. For some reason Weinberg didn't seem to like this investigation.

Actually the incident with Judge Faraday had pushed Janovsky to visit Weinberg in the hospital and tell him what Pashley had been up to. Weinberg hadn't been able to fully brief his second-in-command on Pashley because he was still hooked up to a cardiac monitor when Janovsky told his story, and the monitor thought Weinberg was having a heart attack. The emergency team hustled Janovsky out of the room before Weinberg could get out anything coherent, but Janovsky got the drift.

Pashley skulked by the gate for a couple of minutes, oblivious to the way the street lights highlighted him. It wasn't quite 10 P.M. but the court was deserted and most of the porch lights were off. The apartments had their drapes drawn tightly against the chill evening and he could faintly hear the sound of a television yammering out some game show at the top of its electronic lungs.

Judith's apartment was on the ground floor about halfway back. Her porch light was on but the tall bushes to either side of the door gave him some cover. With a final look around Pashley dropped to one knee and produced a black vinyl case containing a dozen lock picks. He selected one, put the tension wrench in the keyhole and went to work.

If Pashley wasn't smart, he was clever with his hands. He also knew how to pick locks. Unfortunately lock picking is not like riding a bicycle. You need to keep doing it to keep in practice and Pashley hadn't practiced for a couple of years. It took him longer than he expected to tickle the tumblers and get the lock to turn.

Meanwhile Ray Whipple was getting more nervous by the minute. "Think about the Hubble," he breathed, like an acolyte reciting a mantra. "Think about time on the Hubble." He thought about it. He thought hard about that observing time. Then he thought about doing time—three-to-five as an accessory to burglary. Somehow he thought about that time more than he thought about the time on the Hubble Space Telescope.

❖   ❖   ❖

Judith's drapes were drawn and her apartment was dark. Pashley had forgotten a flashlight, so he groped blindly toward the kitchen. The first thing he found was a coffee table loaded with magazines. He found it by tripping on it and knocking the coffee table completely over, making an unholy racket in the process. His further progress was somewhat impeded because he kept stepping on magazines and nearly slipping on their slick pages.

After a few more bumps and stumbles Pashley found the doorway to the kitchen. He made his way through, kicking over the trash can and strewing garbage all over the floor. He felt his way along the counter and after knocking off a box of corn flakes, a stack of dirty dishes and two glass canisters, he finally found the toaster. He yanked the cord out of the wall, sending an array of cans, jars and bottles crashing to the floor and made for the door with his prize.

The police car at the end of the block made Ray Whipple's heart pound. Then a helicopter came over, low and without lights. Ray knew a losing cause when he saw one. With a twinge of regret he silently bid farewell to time on the Hubble. Then he started the car and slowly, carefully drove away.

Pashley saw the policemen as soon as they saw him, which was as soon as he stepped out of Judith's apartment. They were just coming in the front gate so he whirled and ran for the back gate, toaster tucked in the crook of his elbow like a quarterback running for daylight and the policemen pounding after him.

Without breaking stride Pashley straight-armed the gate, knocking it open, and sprinted into the apartment parking lot. He was nearly blinded by the sudden glare of the police helicopter's spotlight, but he ran on, dodging between parked cars. There was a six-foot concrete block wall at the back of the parking lot and Pashley scrambled over, almost into the arms of two more policemen.

"Drop that toaster!" Pashley whirled and found himself with his back to the wall facing two cops with drawn guns. Reluctantly he set the toaster down and raised his hands.

"You don't understand," Pashley shouted over the noise of the helicopter. "I'm an FBI agent on a secret mission."

One of the cops was short, chunky and Asian. The other cop was tall, lean and black. Neither of them looked the least bit friendly. "Turn around, spread your legs and put your hands against the wall." As Pashley complied the black cop moved toward him cautiously, well to one side and out of his partner's line of fire. Keeping his eye on Pashley he nudged the toaster away with his foot.

"Be careful with that. It's vital evidence in a national security matter."

The cops just looked at each other.

"Man," the Asian muttered to his partner, "these designer drugs are bad stuff."

Things got a little complicated once they got Pashley back to the station. While the police definitely had him on burglary, the dwelling was unoccupied. That bumped the offense down to something one step above a misdemeanor. The value of the toaster was less than a hundred dollars so it didn't even qualify as grand theft. For a while the police thought they had Pashley on a charge of impersonating an FBI agent. Then they found out he *was* an FBI agent. Pashley's urgent insistence that the toaster was vital evidence in a national security case didn't help.

True to his word, the mayor found an office for Wiz and Llewllyn in the town hall. Granted, the room was so small the rough trestle table practically formed a barricade across it, but it was conveniently located just inside the main entrance. Both the location and the row of pegs for hanging cloaks and hats hinted at its former use. With Llewllyn sitting in the rickety chair and Wiz standing beside him the place was decidedly claustrophobic. Still, it would do.

Word had obviously spread about the new consulting service. A man was waiting for them when they arrived that morning. Wiz had wanted to spend a few minutes briefing Llewllyn, but obviously he wasn't going to get the chance.

Llewllyn, however, seemed to have no doubts at all. "Come in," he called to the man waiting in the hall. "Never mind my associate here," he said, with a dismissive wave of his hand at Wiz. "What is the nature of your problem?"

"I've been hexed is my problem," the man declared. "Werner the Butcher, he put a curse on me."

It took Wiz a minute to realize that "butcher" was the hexer's occupation, not a nickname.

"How do you know?" he asked.

The man looked at Llewllyn and he nodded for him to answer Wiz's question.

"Me business is gone to blazes, that's how I know. Hardly a customer since that black-hearted miscreant cursed me. Worse, I can't get to sleep no more. I toss and turn through the night. I want that curse lifted."

"When did you notice you were having trouble sleeping?" Wiz asked.

"After I was cursed, of course!" The man looked at Llewllyn. "He simple or something?"

"No," Llewllyn assured him, "merely an assistant."

Wiz cleared his throat.

"Ah, associate actually," the sometime bard amended hastily. "A specialist in another area, but quite competent I assure you."

The man snorted and turned his attention completely to Llewllyn.

"Ah, yes," the young man said, "it so happens I have a special amulet, hewn from the heart of the black oak that grows by the Southern Swamp, prepared by the great wizard Actantos himself. A sure cure. And I can let you have it for just . . ."

Wiz cleared his throat more forcefully.

"But I'm sure you don't need anything so powerful," he finished hurriedly. "Now suppose you tell me what led up to the cursing."

"Will this really help?" The man sounded skeptical.

"Magic is a matter of information," Llewllyn assured him. "The more information the more effective the magic."

"Well, Werner's a surly one. Got his skill in magic from his gran on his momma's side. She was a first cousin once removed of Old Lady Fressen, and . . ."

Llewllyn cut short his reminiscences. "On the other hand, there is such a thing as too much information. Perhaps you can skip ahead to the day the curse was laid."

"That was nigh on two week ago, when I caught Werner picking my whiffleberries."

"He was in your orchard?"

"No, no. The whiffleberry bush is right by the garden wall and some of it hangs over into his garden. Well, since time immemorial there's been an agreement that what's on his side of the wall belongs to him. But I look out this afternoon and here's Werner poaching. He had a whole limb pulled over to his side, he did and he was clearly taking berries that were on my side of the wall."

"And you confronted the, ah, miscreant?"

"Of course I confronted him! I'll not stand for anyone taking what's mine. Well, he denied it, he did, claimed the berries were on his side of the wall and never mind my pointing out the branch near broken off where he'd pulled on it so hard. He protested he wasn't poaching and I pointed out to him that a man'd put his thumb on the scales when folks was buying, as everyone knows he does, mind you, why a man like that couldn't be trusted nohow."

To Wiz it sounded like both parties needed a good talking to and he couldn't for the life of him see what whiffleberries had to do with magic or curses. Of course, he admitted, he'd never heard of whiffleberries before and maybe they had some magic property and . . . Then something Llewllyn said, or rather the way he said it, jerked his attention back to the conversation.

"So you expected him to steal the berries when you weren't looking?" Llewllyn asked in a carefully neutral voice.

"Stayed in the back of the house the whole day to watch the bush," their client confirmed. "Only came into the shop in front when a customer called. Even watched most of that first night, expecting him to come sneaking over the wall."

"And you still think he will plunder your whiffleberry bush?" Llewllyn prompted in the same tone.

"The berries are still there, ain't they? As soon as his miserable curse has me worn down I expect he'll come creeping over the wall some night and make off with the whole lot of them."

"Hmm," Llewllyn said, and rubbed his chin. "Hmm," he said again.

Their client leaned forward anxiously. "Can you help me?"

"Oh, of course," Llewllyn said with an airy wave of his hand. "Not that it is not a difficult problem, mind you, but you have come to the right place. I have the perfect answer for you." He leaned over the table toward the man.

"First, I shall place a curse on the whiffleberries. By magic or by stealth the thief may make off with them, but they will do him no good. For if he should partake of the stolen fruit, his bowels shall loosen, his intestines shall bloat and he shall pass the night in the most intense suffering. Fear not, for your berries shall be guarded by the most puissant magic."

Llewllyn held up a finger. "But understand, such curses are most powerful. To protect yourself you must not go into your garden, nay, even look into your garden for the next fortnight."

The man shifted uneasily. "That might be hard. The privy's back there."

"Oh, for that, of course. But do not linger and do not so much as look out your back window at the whiffleberry bush for fourteen days, you understand? I'd suggest you spend your time in your shop as much as you can. Fear not, business will pick up as soon as I lift the curse."

The man nodded.

"Now as for the curse on you, I must lift it gradually lest the powers invoked rend you limb from limb." The man went slightly pale and nodded again.

"You must stuff your pillow with catnip and place a sprig of tansy under it. This evening I will perform certain mystical operations to banish the invisible demons which are plaguing you. You must drink a cup of wine each night and go to bed at your accustomed time. Over the next two or three nights the curse will dissipate."

"That's all?"

"For you, yes. My part will be much more difficult, but never fear, it will be accomplished."

The man stood and reached for the purse on his belt. "Wonderful! What do I owe you?"

Wiz cleared his throat again.

"Oh, nothing," Llewllyn told him. "Our fees are paid by the town council."

"Then may Fortuna smile upon the honorable council!" the man exclaimed and hurried out.

"Okay," Wiz said after the man was out of earshot. "I understand about the pillow. Catnip's good for helping you sleep. I understand why you told him to spend time in his shop, to get his business back, and I understand why you told him not to keep watching that bush, to relieve his anxiety . . ."

Llewllyn arched an eyebrow. "Do you not believe in the Sparrow's magic?"

"What I just saw was another branch of magic, what I call applied psychology—which by the way you have a talent for—" Llewllyn acknowledged the compliment with a gracious nod, "—but what was that business about a curse on anyone who steals those whiffleberries? The bloating, suffering and stuff?"

"Those are the usual effects of eating green whiffleberries," Llewllyn said dryly. "And if you were from these parts, and if you were not distracted by some stupid neighborhood feud, you would know that whiffleberries will not ripen for another moon or so."

Wiz looked at his assistant. "You may have more talent for this than I thought."

Next, not at all to Wiz's surprise, was the chicken man. He strutted through the door, neck out like a bantam rooster, and two chickens clutched in his skinny hand. He nodded to the two consultants and plunked the two birds down on the table. The birds squawked and shifted and tried to stand up, something they couldn't quite manage with their feet tied together. So they settled for sitting on the table and complaining in an undertone.

"I'm here about my chickens," he announced. "They still won't lay eggs." He jabbed a bony finger at Wiz, "And don't give me none of your lip about dragons, boy, the mayor hisself says you're to help me."

I'll bet the mayor loved having someone to palm you off on, Wiz thought, but he only nodded pleasantly. "I wouldn't dream of it now that the council has renegotiated the contract. My associate here will take care of your problem."

The man scowled at Llewllyn. "He's younger than you are," he grumbled. "Prettier too."

Llewllyn simply nodded and picked up one of the chickens. "Hmm," he said stroking the bird's feathers. He prodded the fowl gently. "Ah, yess." Then he studied the bird's eyes. "Quite so," he said, lifting the chicken higher to study its feet. "Uh huh."

By this point the chicken was thoroughly confused by these goings-on, and Wiz and the bird's owner weren't much better.

"Yes," Llewllyn said at last, "I see the problem clearly."

"If you can do that you're better than the rest of them so-called magicians," the chicken man said. "But what are you going to do about it? That's what I want to know."

The bard put the chicken down on the table. "Why my good man, I'm going to solve your problem. That's what we wizards, ah, consultants, are here for. Now this is a difficult case. The causes are obviously complex and subtle. I will not go into the boring details, but suffice it to say that the cure is straightforward. Simply pluck a sprig of tansy and place it above the door to your henhouse."

"That's it? That's all?"

Llewllyn smiled a superior smile. "The secret is in knowing the cure, not in performing it." Then he leaned over the clucking chickens and waggled his finger under the man's nose. "But this is most important. Do not go into the hen house until the moon has waned and waxed again. Feed and water your chickens outside the coop but otherwise do not go near them."

"Why?"

"Because during this delicate period it would not be safe. You might contract the dread—" his voice lowered to a near whisper "—chicken pox."

"Oh, right. Of course. I'll do just as you say. Thank you sir. Thank you." With that the man gathered his chickens and strutted out.

"Chicken pox, huh?" Wiz said when the man had left, birds dangling.

Llewllyn shrugged. "Not my most inspired invention, I will admit, but it should suffice."

"And tansy?"

"The stuff's a roadside weed around here and it stinks. The smell makes them think it's powerful. Like putting alum in medicine so it will taste bad."

"What do you think he's going to do if his chickens don't improve?"

"Oh, they will improve." Llewllyn's face screwed up as if he was thinking of something unpleasant. "My Lord, I have a certain experience with chickens. The only thing wrong with those birds is that he is pestering them to death. If he leaves them alone they will settle down and all will be well. And if not—" Again the shrug. "I will simply tell him he must obtain a coal black cock without a speck of white upon him. That should occupy him for a few moons."

Their next client was a heavyset young woman with a bad complexion and a red nose. She ventured through the door as if she was afraid that the two men would bite her. In one plump hand she held a handkerchief which looked as if it had seen recent use. Wiz decided that was a bad sign.

Llewllyn didn't seem to notice. He rose and made a sweeping bow to their client. "Come in young lady. Please sit and tell us what has brought you to us."

The young woman twisted her hanky and bit her lip. "I don't know," she said in an undertone. "It's such a small thing, really."

Llewllyn's smile grew even brighter. "There is no problem too small for us, dear lady. We are here to serve your every wish. Please be seated and tell us about it."

Thus encouraged the girl eased herself down into the chair.

"Well, I, I hardly know where to begin."

"Begin wherever you feel like, dear lady," Llewllyn said gently. "The magic will tell me the rest."

"There is the young man," the girl said in a low voice.

"Ah," Llewllyn nodded. "A special young man? Perhaps one who does not notice you?"

"How did you know?" the girl asked.

"Magic tells me many things. But do go on."

"Well," the girl relaxed in her chair, "he's our neighbor you see . . ."

By the time Wiz left fifteen minutes later Llewllyn and the girl were head-to-head across the table. He hadn't given her any advice that Wiz could see, just a lot of encouragement, but she seemed to think he had the answer to everything from her love life to the riddle of Dark Matter—or she would have if she'd known what Dark Matter was, Wiz thought.

Obviously his new assistant had a future in this end

of the business. Now if Wiz could just keep him from bilking the customers or trying to practice unauthorized magic, he'd have one less thing to worry about.

That morning the director of the FBI had a *lot* of things to worry about. As her assistants filled her in on Clueless Pashley's latest exploit, she stubbed out her cigarette and lit a new one. She was back up to a pack-and-a-half a day and headed rapidly for two packs. Her fingers were stained, her breath stank, she had burn holes in her clothes and twice she had nearly set her desk on fire when she missed an ash tray.

"Where is this clown now?" she asked Paul Rutherford when he finished his report.

"The local office bailed him out," her assistant said. "They've got him stashed in a safe house to keep him away from the newspapers."

This was a public relations disaster.

"Senator Halliburton's office called this morning. His committee wants to hold hearings on violating civil rights in national security cases. This Judith Conally and the science fiction writer are going to be his star witnesses."

A public relations disaster and a political nightmare, the director amended. "Could this get any worse?"

"Only if Pashley gets back out on the street," Rutherford ventured. The director glared at him and he wilted. "Uh, no ma'am, I don't think it's likely to get much worse."

Unbidden a snatch of a country song came into the director's head. *You gotta know when to hold 'em, and know when to fold 'em.* She hated country music.

"All right." She mashed out the half-smoked cigarette. "Settle!"

"Settle?"

"That writer's case against us. Tell the Justice Department to settle with him. And settle with this Conally woman. Make apologies, blame it on a rogue agent. But settle."

"Ma'am," Rutherford said carefully, "that sets a very bad precedent."

"It will set a worse precedent if the director of the FBI murders an agent," she growled. "Just pay whatever it takes."

SEVENTEEN

INVITATION TO AN AUTO-DE-FE

At ——— Bullshit Is Our Most
Important Product
—*graffiti on the lavatory wall*
at a major consultantcy

Wiz got home just after noon to find the mayor sniffling on his doorstep. At first Wiz thought someone had died. Then His Honor produced a well-used handkerchief from his sleeve and blew his nose again.

Wiz invited the man in. As they crossed the threshold Malkin was just coming up from the kitchen. They eyed each other with mutual distaste for a moment and the mayor put a protective hand on his chain of office.

"You wanted to see me, Your Honor?" Wiz asked, as much to break the tension as anything else.

"I came to warn you, Wizard." He stopped, his face screwed up and he sneezed thunderously.

"What? That it's pollen season?"

The mayor sniffled and wiped his watering eyes. "No, it's Dieter. He's moving against you in the council. At our next meeting, two days from today, he plans to call for your resignation."

There was nothing Wiz would have liked better than to resign. But since his resignation would doubtless be followed immediately by his condemnation to The Rock, it didn't seem like a good idea to follow his desires.

The mayor looked even more like a basset hound than usual. "He's gathering votes on the council. I'll support you, of course, but it will be close, I'll tell you that."

"What do you want me to do?"

"Could you perhaps be at the meeting? You know, talk to them the way you did before."

"Of course. Can you get me some time on the agenda before the vote?"

After the mayor departed, sniffling and mumbling, Malkin looked at her boss. "Well, O great Wizard, what are you going to do now?"

"I am going to do what any consultant does when he gets into trouble," Wiz said. "I am going to give a presentation."

Malkin snorted. "If I was you I'd give a thought to a quick escape. You heard the mayor. Dieter's got enough votes on the council to have your guts for garters."

"Maybe now he does. But the council will have to take a formal vote and they won't do that until they hear me out because there's always the chance I'll come up with a miracle. A successful presentation doesn't just impart information. It changes attitudes."

"Look," Malkin said slowly and carefully, as if explaining something to a small and none-too-bright child, "Dieter wants to be cock of this dungheap and get more money from taxes. Ol' Droopy wants to stay cock of the dungheap and he doesn't want more taxes. Cross either one of them and you're a dragon's breakfast. Now how in blazes is this presentation of yours going to change any of that?"

"Presentations don't change things," Wiz said airily, "they just change perceptions."

"And just how do they do that?" she demanded.

"Generally by confusing the issue."

The tall girl chewed on that for a while. "Well," she

said at last, "if you're set on this, I want to be there when you make this presentation of yours."

Wiz quirked a smile. "An expression of loyalty?"

"No, I want to see which way it goes so I can get out of here while they're still busy tearing you to pieces."

"Oh, it won't come to that," Wiz assured her. *I hope!* "Before this is over I'll have them eating out of my hand."

Malkin eyed him under raised brows. "Maybe, but my question is how many fingers you're going to have left on that hand."

Bright colors and pretty pictures, Wiz thought. *That's the essence of a successful presentation.* He looked at the code taking shape in glowing characters above his desk and sighed. *Especially when you don't have any content.*

The conventional wisdom was that the more images, graphically displayed numbers and visual tricks you packed into a presentation, the more effective the presentation. Of course the logical implication of that is that the average executive has the attention span of a three-year-old and the analytical skills of a magpie. Normally Wiz would have found that a very depressing reflection. Just now it was comforting. The only thing standing between him and doom in an utterly impossible situation was his ability to sling creative bullshit.

It would certainly be well-illustrated bullshit. Using the spell Danny had developed so long ago and far away, he had set up an Internet connection back to what he still thought of as the "real world" and set an ftp demon to downloading graphics files from sites all around the world. He already had a library of hundreds of images and they were still coming in.

Even so, it was slow going. Wiz was the sort of programmer who had always preferred substance to form. Here the substance was that he had to use form to cover the fact that he had no substance. That meant writing a bunch of new tools. With the council meeting the day after tomorrow Wiz was going to have to bust his butt to save his neck.

Well, that worked too. As a programmer he was no stranger to all-nighters to meet tight deadlines. This was just one more all-nighter. He tried not to think about the stakes.

The day turned to evening and evening shaded into night and still Wiz toiled away, developing the routines to give a presentation that would knock the Council's eyes out.

Anna brought him sandwiches and tea along about dinner time, but otherwise he worked undisturbed until well into the evening.

"Get your head out of your spells, Wizard," the ghost of Widder Hackett rasped in his ear. "You've got a problem."

"It's a tight schedule, but that's not a problem," Wiz said without turning to look at his invisible kibitzer.

"Oh, no?" Widder Hackett grated. "Just you look at that window." Wiz moved to open the shutter.

"No, you dummy!" the voice rasped in his ear. "Don't want him to see you. Look through the crack."

Putting his eye to the crack between the shutters and peering out into the moonlit street Wiz saw they had a visitor. Or more precisely, he realized, they had a watcher. One of the Watch, the tall skinny one, was leaning against the house on the other side of the street.

"What's he doing there?"

"Watching is what," Widder Hackett snapped. "There's another behind and two more at each end of the street. My own house watched by the police like some common den of thieves. I never thought in all my living days . . . I never!"

Wiz forbore to mention that Widder Hackett's living days had ended some time before. "I'm going down there to find out what this is all about."

Widder Hackett snorted. "What makes you think he'll tell you anything?"

"If he won't the council will."

Subtlety wasn't Wiz's strong point and he was both too curious and too angry to be circumspect. As soon as he opened the front door the guardsman stepped back into the shadows.

light exe Wiz commanded and a sphere of brilliant white light appeared over his shoulder. The light was behind Wiz, but it shone right into the eyes of the now-revealed watcher, who squinted and turned his head away. Without a word Wiz strode across the street. The globe of light floated right with him.

"Good evening," Wiz said crisply.

"Evening, My Lord," the guard said, trying to shield his eyes with his hands "Uh, would you mind . . ."

"Sorry I can't turn it off," Wiz lied. "Now, what are you doing here?"

"Well, I'm ah, watching, My Lord. So to speak."

"Watching for what?"

"Criminals, begging My Lord's pardon. We've had criminals around here in this neighborhood and we thought . . ."

"'We' being the council? Is that it?" *Meaning Dieter*, Wiz thought. *But why?*

"Well, ah, as to that, My Lord, I really couldn't say. All I know is I'm supposed to keep watch here until the thieves are apprehended."

Thieves, eh? Suddenly it fell into place. "I appreciate your concern, but it isn't necessary. Tell the sheriff I can guard my own property."

"That's as may be," the guardsman said stolidly, "but I have my orders, My Lord."

"Oh well, if you want to watch, I'm sure you may. But I will tell you now you won't find anything."

"That's as may be, My Lord."

Wiz nodded and returned to his house. He left the light globe on until he was back inside.

"Where's Malkin?" he demanded into thin air as soon as the door closed behind him.

"How would I know?" Widder Hackett rasped. "Out tarting it up I have no doubt."

"She didn't go out the door. I would have known."

"She usually doesn't," Widder Hackett said with obvious satisfaction.

With that there was nothing to do but wait until Malkin got back. Wiz went back to his programming, pausing every so often to peer through the crack in the shutters at his watchers.

It wasn't a terribly productive evening. Between fuming over the watch, worrying about Malkin and starting at every squeak of a floorboard or rattle of a windowpane, Wiz didn't do nearly the amount of work he had planned. Since it was well after midnight when he heard Malkin on the stairs he lost most of the night's work.

When Wiz confronted her in the hallway she was dressed in dark trousers, dark soft boots and a dark pullover. Her dark hair was stuffed up under a dark knit cap and there was a dark burlap sack over her shoulder.

"Where have you been?"

"Oh, out and about," Malkin said nonchalantly. She set the sack on the floor with an audible clank. "Sightseeing, you might say."

"And the stuff in the bag is souvenirs, right? In case you don't know it, lady, there is a cop across the street watching this place and two more at each end of the block."

"And two more on the street behind," Malkin added. "But they never watch the roofs. Half of them's too fat to climb and the rest is scared of heights."

"So you've been coming and going over the roofs."

"Sometimes. The sewer's good too, if you don't mind a few rats."

"Are you trying to get us all killed? The cops are on to you, the place is being watched, half the council is looking for an excuse to put me away—and you with me. Lady, we are just one small slip from disaster here."

Malkin's eyes glowed. "I know," she said breathlessly. "Isn't it exciting?"

"An adrenaline junkie," Wiz groaned. "I had to get hooked up with a kleptomaniac adrenaline junkie."

"Serves you right for hiring folks out of jail."

Wiz growled in frustration.

"Besides, I don't see what you're so worried about. I got in safe with the stuff didn't I? They never saw me."

"Did it ever occur to you that their next logical move is going to be to search the house?"

"Law says they can't search no private home held freehold without a warrant signed by the mayor upon presentation of probable cause. Said probable cause to be solely within the discretion of the mayor. They gave you this place so you have it freehold." She grinned. "And you think the mayor's going to issue a warrant to search this place? You being his ally and all? Old Iron Pants will have to wait a month of blue moons before that happens."

As it happened the month of blue moons ended at about seven o'clock the next morning. Wiz was pulled groggily awake by the sound of a thunderous pounding on the door. Stumbling downstairs he found Anna confronting a gang of armed ruffians. When he looked a little closer he realized that the lead ruffian was the sheriff and that he was brandishing a piece of paper as if it were a shield before him.

"Stand aside, Wizard," he announced before Wiz was even off the stairs. "We're here to search the place for stolen goods. Got a warrant."

Wiz's brain was at best severely challenged at this time of the morning, especially when his blood caffeine level was low, but that woke him up and sent his mind into high gear.

"The mayor signed a search warrant?"

The sheriff grinned nastily. "Mayor's home with a cold. A real bad cold that's got him incapacitated. So this was signed by three council members like the law provides. All legal and proper."

Meaning Dieter, Wiz thought, a sinking feeling in the pit of his stomach.

"Well, I can't stop you from searching," he said standing aside from the door. "But I can't protect you either," he added as the sheriff and his men pushed into the hall. "This is a wizard's house, you know," he shouted to their backs as they thundered up the stairs.

For the next two hours the sheriff's men went over the house eaves to cellars. They found a notebook Wiz had lost, an old copper pan that had belonged to Widder Hackett, a number of rats and an indignant pigeon who was trying to nest in the attic, but not one bit of stolen property.

The only excitement came when Bobo decided that for some inexplicable reason the sheriff's highly polished boots belonged to him, and proceeded to mark his property in the time-honored tomcat fashion. Luckily for Bobo he was a good deal faster than the sheriff or any of his men.

Meanwhile Malkin stood around looking smug, Anna was wide-eyed with terror and Widder Hackett hurled abuse at the searchers at the top of her nonexistent lungs. Unfortunately the searchers couldn't hear her. Even more unfortunately Wiz could. By the time the sheriff's men finished, Wiz was a nervous wreck.

"Well?" the sheriff demanded as he strode into Wiz's workroom. "Are you done in here?"

The two guards who had been tapping the floor for loose boards nodded in unison and stood up. "Every place but this table," the guard in front said. "You want us to dig up the garden next?"

"What's wrong with this table?" demanded the sheriff.

"Looks as if it's magic like."

"That's my desk," Wiz added. "You'd better not touch it."

"Bah!" barked the sheriff.

"Hey, I won't be responsible . . ." Wiz began, but the sheriff was already reaching for the pile of parchments.

No one but the very brave, the very skilled or the very

foolish messes with a wizard's working equipment. The sheriff might have been brave but he was certainly not at all skilled.

As soon as his hand moved over the top of the table there was a twisting in the air and a small green demon materialized below the glowing letters. A small green demon with a very large mouth. Lined with large, pointed and very sharp teeth. Before the sheriff could react the creature chomped down hard on the proferred hand.

The sheriff yelped and jerked his arm away. On the back of his hand in a neat semicircle were eight round puncture marks. "It bit me!" he screamed.

"Actually there are eight of them, so that's a byte," Wiz said, examining the wounds.

The sheriff pulled his hand back. "That's what I said!" He pointed toward the table with his good hand. "Arrest that thing!" he commanded.

The demon crouched on the edge of the table and grinned at them. It had an unusually large grin that showed off its pearly white and pointy teeth to excellent advantage. All three rows of them.

The guards shifted back and forth but made no move toward the grinning entity crouched on the table.

"I dunno," the first one demurred.

"Law says we're only supposed to arrest people," the second one said. "Don't say nothing about things like that."

"You can arrest strayed livestock," the sheriff retorted. "Well, impound them anyway." He gestured at the demon again. "*Impound* that thing."

"Don't know that it's rightly livestock," the first guard said.

"Don't think it's strayed either," his companion added.

"It's right where it's supposed to be," Wiz added helpfully.

"Well, then," said the second guard.

The sheriff was nearly beside himself with fury. "This is an outrage! A complete outrage against the majesty of the law." He was bouncing up and down and his face was so red Wiz was afraid he was going to have a stroke. He decided it was time to pour some oil on the water.

"Look sheriff, you can see there's nothing on that desk but papers. No stolen property, right? Now I'm sorry the demon hurt you, but I'm sure he won't do it again. Why don't you and your men go down into the kitchen and Anna will see to your wound."

"But, but, but . . ."

"It looks nasty, sheriff. The only cure for a demon byte is to have it flushed by a beautiful woman. I'm sure she can find some ale for you and your men while she tends to it."

The sheriff glared at the demon, who glared back. He glared at Wiz, who smiled. Then he glared at his two subordinates. Without a word he turned and stalked out of the room with the guards close on his heels.

Wiz collapsed against the wall and let his breath out in a great *whoosh*.

"Don't know what you're so worried about," Widder Hackett's voice rasped in his ear. "Malkin had the stuff out of the house before they got in the door."

"What'd she do with it?"

"Buried it in the garden."

"The garden?" Wiz yelped. "Didn't you hear them say they were going to dig up the garden?"

"I didn't say *our* garden," the Widder Hackett said gleefully. "Old Trescott's garden next door." She cackled so hard she went into a coughing fit. "Oh, I'd love to see the look on Mrs. High-and-Mighty's face if they was to dig up the loot under her cherry tree. Say, why don't you . . ."

"Uh, let's save that for an emergency, shall we?" Wiz said hastily.

EIGHTEEN

PRESENTATION

Any sufficiently advanced technology is
indistinguishable from magic.
— *Clarke's Law*

Any sufficiently advanced magic is
indistinguishable from technology.
— *Anderson's Reformulation of Clarke's Law*

Any sufficiently advanced anything is
indistinguishable from utter nonsense.
— *Digby's Generalization of Clarke's Law*

Especially if it is sufficiently advanced
nonsense to begin with.
— *Zumwalt's Corollary to Digby's
Generalization of Clarke's Law*

The council kept Wiz and Malkin waiting for over an hour. While Wiz fidgeted in a too-hard chair in the hall and Malkin ostentatiously checked the place for escape routes, the councilors met behind closed doors. Every so often the sound of shouting or an especially ringing bit of oratory would penetrate through the thick carved doors. Wiz fiddled with his notes and tried not to think about the corners he had to cut.

Some of the pieces, such as the buzzword generator, were beautiful. But other details he had been forced to leave to demons because of the time he lost to the sheriff and his searchers.

True to his word, the sheriff had spent most of the rest of the day digging up the garden. Or, more correctly, the sheriff lounged under a tree while his men dug holes more or less at random in the garden. They didn't find anything but they didn't quit until nearly sundown. Wiz was on pins and needles all day, afraid there was something Malkin had overlooked. But in her own way Malkin was as thoroughly professional as Wiz. There was nothing and the sheriff left empty-handed.

At last the doors swung open and the usher beckoned them within. The expression on the man's face did nothing for Wiz's confidence.

The council was seated around a long U-shaped table. Their mood was a cross between a lynch mob and the crowd at a formal execution. Which is to say some of them were looking forward to what they were going to do, some of them would reluctantly do their duty and some of them were there for the show.

Wiz started talking before he even reached the center of the U. "Gentlemen, I cannot tell you what a pleasure it is to come before you today," he said as he strode into the room. His confidence was of a piece with his sincerity, but so far they seemed to be buying it.

He gestured grandly and the daylight streaming in through the windows dimmed to twilight. Another gesture and a demon appeared at the back of the room with a slide projector. The projector was already on and a slide flashed on the wall bearing the words "Success And Prosperity" in vivid red and yellow on a bright blue background—a combination carefully chosen to be arresting without quite giving the viewers a headache.

There was a brief murmur from the council and Wiz charged on before they could recover.

"My research has shown that you face a unique set of opportunities. To meet them I propose a dynamic, pro-active reinvention of the organization to empower the teams using 60-second skills to address for success the strategic planning requirements in light of the Theory Z competitive strategy in time to produce a win-win-win situation."

Maybe I shouldn't have spent so much time on the buzzword generator, Wiz thought. But damn! The out-put was lovely. If the slide-picking demon had done its job nearly as well, they just might, *might* get out of this with a whole skin.

All the while the demon was flashing slides on the wall, medieval streets crammed with modern tourists, waving fields of grain, several interior shots of the Cloisters medieval museum in New York City. Happy children. Wiz thought he glimpsed a shot of Mickey Mouse at Disneyland but he wasn't sure.

The torrent of words and pictures had the desired effect. Everyone was so stunned no one thought to ask about dragons.

"Clearly," Wiz continued, "what is called for is to install a reorganization that promotes a new strategic vision, a tightly focused vision that energizes the new tomorrow.

"While continuing the traditions of the past—" the mayor smiled and nodded "—we must meet the challenges of the future—" it was Dieter's turn to smile "—and provide bold new approaches to the organization's needs." That brought a nod from Rolf.

"We must empower ourselves to consistently use our organizational resources to install this vision. This means using team management-focused techniques to create the need to change and to produce organizational systems which reinforce the vision."

The picture on the screen showed a USDA map of the

United States with the dates of the average last frosts marked.

"That doesn't look like anything around here," one of the more alert councilmen put in.

"Those are magical isoclines," Wiz said hastily.

"Still don't look like the country around here."

"It's a transmorphic projection. Maybe we'd better come back to this later. Next."

The next slide was a pie chart, showing sales of Sara Lee pies for 1993.

The trouble with trusting a demon's judgment, Wiz realized belatedly, is that it doesn't have any. He was damn glad none of his audience could read English.

Wiz smiled brightly. "By now you are doubtless interested in the specifics of my recommended action plan. As soon as I have finished, my assistant," a nod to Malkin, "will distribute copies of the white paper emphasizing the highlights. Meanwhile, let us examine the critical challenges we must meet to empower our vision of empowerment."

The demon flashed up a slide showing someone going over Niagara Falls in a barrel.

"The first challenge is organizational. The traditional organization emphasizes musty, sterile parliamentarianism at the expense of action which would clearly reflect the true makeup of the council." That brought nods from the mayor, Dieter and Rolf, all of whom were absolutely convinced the council was really behind them.

"This means your present decision-making process is diffuse and suboptimal. We must proactively react to counteract this tendency with a broader vision which is only available at the top." The mayor beamed and Dieter frowned.

"However, given the present organization this is clearly impossible because of the workload such a top-down environment imposes on the mayor. Therefore the key to repositioning the products and services to build a corporate advantage is install an action-direction vision by creatively teaming together. To that end, we create an Office of the Mayor to actualize the latency by creative teaming. Working directly with the mayor on this critical team will be innovation powerhouses representing the major resources within the present council. While the mayor will clearly be the team leader he will benefit from the synergy and creative flow of ideas from the team structure."

Again smiles from the critical three. The mayor saw it as a way to subordinate his main rivals to him and the other two saw it as giving them a power base close to the top. That alone should guarantee absolute gridlock, Wiz thought as he paused for breath.

That was a mistake. "What about the rest of the council?" demanded one of the councilmen off to the side. "What about money?" demanded another.

"Yes, money. What about money? What about taxes?" several other voices chimed in.

"I'm glad you raised that critical point," Wiz said brightly. "That is the second platform of my recommendations, but perhaps we can deal with it out of turn.

"The important fiscal consideration is to provide revenue enhancement without increasing taxes. In fact, as you can see clearly from this revenue elasticity chart—" up went a phase diagram of the melting point of lead-tin-antimony solder alloys "—the projected revenue needs can be met with a decrease in current taxes.

"Clearly what is needed is a proactive, projective infrastructure investment of the revenue stream."

"There ain't no revenue," one of the councilors objected.

"That is precisely why you apply the revenues projectively," Wiz assured him. "As you can see from this next chart—" up flashed a bar chart showing the amount of track laid by the Indian railways from 1850 to 1900 "—the revenues can be applied to development in a fashion which will encourage and develop the trade."

That produced an approving mutter from Dieter's

faction. The mayor's people sat in puzzled silence and Rolf's followers looked to their leader for their cue.

"Let us go back to the organization for a moment," Rolf said smoothly. "I believe there is more."

"There is indeed," Wiz said, relieved that he didn't have to do his New Age Bugaloo around the difference between "revenue enhancement" and "tax increase."

Up on the screen flashed an organizational chart of the Supreme Soviet.

"Now this," Wiz said, gesturing with his pointer, "is your present structure. I'm sure all of you can see the inefficiencies and conflict potential implied here so I won't dwell on them. Next slide," he commanded before anyone could object.

Up on the screen flashed the current Miss July, blond, pneumatic and airbrushed to perfection.

Wiz closed his jaw with an audible snap. "Uh, that was just to make sure you were awake. Next slide."

Up came an even more baroque organizational chart. Glancing at the legend Wiz saw it was for General Motors circa 1965.

"Here is my recommendation. A more modern, teaming approach to today's challenges. Rather than concentrating the burdens, it spreads them throughout the organization to make management more effective.

"As you can see, this emphasizes creative teaming to empower all the members of the council to make the crucial decisions needed to create tomorrow. By establishing internal task forces, the Office of the Mayor can be freed from the day-to-day detail of running operations to concentrate on developing an action-directed migration plan to create tomorrow. These teams will prioritize opportunities for infrastructure enhancements using the new revenue stream as it comes on-line." That got a stir of approval as the council members considered the opportunities for graft. "Naturally, every council member will have several team assignments to fully tap into the organization's creative resources. I won't bore you with the details of these teams," *mainly because I didn't have time to work them out*, "but I would like to point out the compensation committee, which will determine remuneration for the council members."

"You mean we'll get paid for sitting on the council?" someone asked.

"It seems only fair," Wiz said blandly.

"And just who's going to be on this compensation committee?" demanded a voice from the side of the room.

Wiz tapped the image at random with his pointer. "That is up to the personnel committee, here."

"And who's on the personnel committee?"

"That is the responsibility of the organizational committee. As a consultant it would be unethical of me to advise you on the makeup of these committees. I'm sure you will be able to work out these details among yourselves."

A quick glance from the mayor to Dieter to Rolf showed them all deep in thought. Rolf was smiling benignly, Dieter was looking sideways at the other two and the mayor was rubbing his chin and nodding.

"Gentlemen, the tide has turned." Up came a tidal chart for New Bedford, MA. "Opportunity awaits us. Fortune favors the brave."

Up came the GM organizational chart once more.

"More importantly we must team together to form an empowerment matrix which will reinvent the corporation, uh, organization, in an entrepreneurial model to reach beyond the present to grasp the opportunities of the future!"

They didn't quite give him a standing ovation, but there were one or two tentative claps from the back of the room.

Wiz let out his breath with what he hoped was a not-too-audible sigh. "Very well. Are there any questions?"

"Can we go back to that last-but-two slide?" came a tremulous voice from the back of the room.

✧   ✧   ✧

Malkin didn't have much to say on the way home. That was fine with Wiz. He was weak with relief and completely exhausted from everything that had happened in the last three days. What he wanted now was sleep, not conversation.

However, Malkin did have one observation. "I don't know if you're the greatest wizard I've ever met," she told him as soon as they came through the front door, "but you are sure the luckiest." With that she turned and went up the stairs.

Wiz started to reply, but then he realized that she was right and that left him with nothing to say.

After a minute he also realized he was hungry. He vaguely remembered eating something after the sheriff's men got through searching the house, but he wasn't sure if he'd had anything since then. Rather than going upstairs to bed, he went downstairs to the kitchen.

Down in the kitchen his assistant wizard was enchanting his maid.

" . . . so we escaped before the bandits even realized what had happened."

"That's so exciting," Anna breathed.

Llewllyn waved a hand dismissively. "Oh tut. All in a day's work for a journeying wizard."

He had a wonderful rich voice and talked enchantingly with hand gestures, smiles and just the right amount of eye contact. If you treated the content as some kind of fairy tale, it was great.

Anna obviously thought it was great. She sat at the table with her chin in both hands, her pale blue eyes fastened rapturously on his face. He didn't have his arm around her waist yet but things were definitely moving in that direction.

Wiz cleared his throat. Both of them started and turned toward the door. Anna blushed and for an instant Llewllyn looked flustered. "Ah, My Lord, how was the meeting with the Council?" he asked before Wiz could say anything.

"Productive. Very productive." *Produced more confusion*

than anything I've seen since the last Total Quality Management seminar. "Can I see you upstairs Llewllyn?"

The young man turned and bowed to the still-blushing Anna. "Forgive me My Lady, but duty calls."

"Okay," Wiz said as soon as they were in the front room, "the council's going to be reorganizing following a proposal I presented to them. Since you're the one in the office most of the time they'll probably be coming to you with questions. Refer any and all questions to me. Don't try to answer them yourself. The situation's kind of, ah, delicate."

Llewllyn smiled knowingly. "Am I to be permitted to know the nature of this plan?"

"Malkin's got copies of the materials I gave the council. You can get one from her."

"Very good, My Lord. Is there aught else?"

"Yes. One other thing." Wiz thrust his face very close to Llewllyn's. "If you mistreat Anna in any way I will personally break you in two."

The younger man's eyes widened. "By magic?"

Wiz flexed his muscles. "That wouldn't be nearly as much fun."

"And you think that I . . . ? For shame."

"Spare me the speeches. Just don't, okay?"

With that he turned on his heel and went upstairs to his workroom.

Wiz ran into Malkin in the upstairs hall. "Our favorite house pest was in the kitchen," Wiz told her. "I filled him in and he's probably going to ask you for a copy of that presentation. Give it to him, but don't let him get any ideas about doing anything on his own, especially answering questions."

The tall woman nodded.

"Oh yeah, one other thing. Llewllyn seems to be making a play for Anna."

Malkin snorted. "You finally noticed that did you? You may," she said, stressing the word *may*, "be a mighty wizard, but you're still blind as any other man. Well, you have nothing to worry about on that score."

"I know," Wiz said. "I told him I'd break him in two if I caught him messing with Anna."

Malkin grinned nastily. "I told him I'd have his balls for earrings and do it with a dull butter knife." The grin got broader and nastier. "Slowly. With a red-hot butter knife."

Looking at her expression, Wiz felt a certain tightness in a very sensitive spot. "Oh," he said in a very small voice.

NINETEEN

CONTACT

Networking is a vitally important
part of the consultant's craft. Never lose
touch with former clients or colleagues.
—*The Consultants' Handbook*

Danny swore a particularly sulfurous oath just as Moira
walked into the programmers' workroom.

"I'm sorry, My Lords," she said and turned to go.

Jerry looked up. "Oh, hi Moira. No, that's all right. We
weren't swearing at you. We were swearing at the system."

"More problems?" she asked in the resigned voice Jerry
and Danny had come to know all too well since the search
for Wiz started.

"I'm afraid so. We've been checking the sites on that
wacko routing path of Wiz's and checking them regularly. But now we keep pinging and we keep getting nonsense."

Danny went over the routing list item by item. Then
he stopped dead. "Wait a minute! According to this he's
going through **shark.vax**."

"That's the North Australia Oceanographic Institute.
So?"

"So **shark.vax** is down. They had a typhoon or something. There was a message about it on the net."

"Let me see that!" Jerry grabbed the tablet from Danny's hand. He traced down it and frowned. The frown grew deeper as he compared the tablet to the screen.

"Ping **shark.vax**." Danny nodded and typed frantically.

"What is it?" Moira demanded, pressing close.

"I think . . ." Jerry began, but Danny cut him off. "See. **shark.vax** isn't there. But how is he using it if it's not there?"

"Magic?" Moira suggested.

Jerry slammed his hand down on the table so hard a pile of manuscripts slid onto the floor. "No, a gimmicked router table! He got into one of those routers and redid the table."

"Slick. No wonder we couldn't find him."

"Does this help?"

"Yes, it helps a lot. All we've got to do now is find the router he tricked and see where the entries in the table really lead. With that we can find the switch he's using and from there we can trace him back to this world."

"But not quickly?"

Jerry forced a smile. "Oh, it's not automatic, but we'll find him. He can't keep hiding like this for much longer."

TWENTY

THE PRANCING PIG

Good advice is where you find it.
—*The Consultants' Handbook*

I can't keep going on like this, Wiz Zumwalt thought wearily. It wasn't just that he had lost another solitaire game. He was stuck on the project and stuck fast. Even if he could keep a lid on things with the town council, which was doubtful, he still hadn't made any real progress on protecting humans from dragons.

In fact, he realized, a lot of what he had done since he came here was in the nature of avoiding work on the problem hoping something would bubble up from his subconscious. But his subconscious was as flat as an open can of Coke left on a programmer's desk over the weekend.

Maybe his subconscious didn't have enough to work on. The truth of the matter was that he didn't know much about dragons and he hadn't really learned much about them since he came here.

"Hey, Malkin," he called over his shoulder, at the same time he clicked his mouse to deal another game.

"What?" came a voice in his ear.

Wiz jumped. There was Malkin at his shoulder.

"I wish you wouldn't sneak up on me like that when I'm working."

The tall thief shrugged. "I'm not sneaking. It's my normal way of walking. Kind of a professional asset, you might say."

"You might say sneaking, too," Wiz retorted. "Anyway, I wanted to ask you about dragons."

"Why ask me? You're supposed to be the expert."

"Yeah, but I've noticed the people around here don't talk much about dragons, or even seem to know very much about them."

"They don't know because they don't want to know. As far as most folks hereabouts are concerned the time you learn anything about dragons is usually when someone gets eaten."

"Still, there must be someone."

"Well now, since you mention it, there is one fellow who probably knows more than most."

"I wonder if I can talk to him."

Malkin shrugged. "Easy enough. If you're up for a little walk."

When they left the house they turned away from the main square and the town hall and headed downhill, toward the river. Wiz, who hadn't been this way much, looked around with interest.

"There's a lot I don't understand about the way humans and dragons relate to each other here," he told her.

"It's simple enough. Dragons eat humans when they feel like it."

"Yeah, but beyond that. For instance why haven't the dragons attacked the town?"

In answer Malkin pointed to a stretch of the street before them. The paving bricks were rougher, darker and shinier. Vitrified, Wiz saw, as if fired at too high a heat. Looking further he realized there was more than one such patch on the street or on the sides of buildings.

"Folks salvage what they can when they rebuild,"

Malkin told him. "Usually there's only bricks and not too many of them."

The tall woman led him further down into the city. Soon he could smell the river and the mud flats that lined it. They must be almost to the end of the town, Wiz thought.

The river flowed under the bridge between mud banks that took up most of the bed. In spring it must be a torrent, but now, in late summer, there was only enough water to fill a narrow channel.

In the failing light Wiz could see that the earth the town sat on wasn't ordinary dirt at all. It was heavily mixed with bits of brick, old paving stones and rubble. Here and there vitrified pieces glinted dully in the light of the setting sun.

Wiz realized the entire hill the town sat on was composed of the remains of earlier towns, like ancient Troy. Except here it wasn't earthquakes and human enemies who had laid down layer after layer of debris to serve as the base for the builders, it was dragons.

"Malkin, look at that."

"What?"

"The river banks. That's not dirt. That's rubble from older towns."

"So?"

"So this place has been destroyed and rebuilt a number of times."

Malkin shrugged and kept walking, unconcerned by her hometown's history.

How many times had the town been destroyed by dragon fire? Wiz wondered as they proceeded across the bridge. How many times had the survivors returned to try to rebuild?

Yet Malkin didn't seem to care. To her it was just a fact of life, even though it could happen again at any time.

That, Wiz decided, was the scariest thing of all.

The stone bridge was wide enough for two wagons abreast, and well-maintained. The town on the other side

of it wasn't. Almost as soon as they stepped off the
bridge the streets narrowed into muddy lanes and
began to twist like the tracks of a herd of drunken cows.
The aroma told Wiz they weren't cleaned regularly either.
The smell of sun-warmed garbage and ripe raw sewage
held a compost-like overtone that suggested they hadn't
ever been cleaned.

"Bog Side," Malkin explained as Wiz tried to shut off
direct communication between his nose and his gorge. "It's
the place to come for entertainment."

The tall tumbledown houses and maze of narrow
garbage-strewn byways didn't look like Wiz's definition
of Disneyland. The characters who swaggered or skulked
or slunk along the streets didn't remind him much of
Mickey and Snow White either. In fact, they made the
inhabitants of North Beach and Sunset Strip seem inno-
cuous. Wiz found himself pressing close to Malkin for
protection.

Malkin swaggered along, ignoring the others or should-
ering them out of her way like so many gawking tourists in a shopping mall. A couple of the more flashily
dressed women eyed Wiz and a few of the larger men
looked him up and down speculatively, but either Wiz's
reputation as a powerful wizard had preceded him or they
knew Malkin too well to try anything. Except for an
occasional hand lightly brushing his belt for the pouch
that wasn't there, no one interfered with them.

Malkin led him deeper into the twisty maze of lanes
and alleys, between houses that sagged out over the street
to support each other like staggering drunks, down
alleys over piles of garbage and through open spaces
where buildings had collapsed into heaps of broken
brick and rotted timbers. Once they passed a long row
of substantial brick buildings, sturdy and windowless but
stained with time and marred by graffiti and abuse.

"Almost there," Malkin said as she turned into an alley
even narrower and more noisome than the last. Wiz was
utterly lost, but from the overtone of mud and long-dead

fish permeating the general stench, he thought they had doubled back toward the river.

The alley suddenly opened out into a square facing the river and Wiz blinked as he stepped from the gloom into the mellow light of the setting sun. Not that the view was much of an improvement. The open space was small and piled more than head-high with rubble and garbage. The buildings on either side leaned alarmingly and one of them had already slumped down into a pile of brick spilling out into the square. The opposite side was formed by the burned-out shell of another of the windowless brick buildings. Looking at the blackened brick and fire-damaged mortar Wiz wondered how much longer it would stay standing.

Halfway down the square, Malkin turned suddenly and ducked into a low doorway. Hanging out over the door was a carved wooden sign depicting a rampant and wildly concupiscent pig, its head turned sideways and its tongue thrust out. The hooves, tongue and other parts were picked out in gold leaf, now faded to a mellow brown. Whether through lack of skill or excess of it, the sign carver had turned the conventional heraldic pose into a gesture of pornographic defiance.

Wiz ducked through the doorway and nearly fell headfirst down the short flight of uneven stone stairs that led into the room.

The place was long, narrow and mostly dark. The reek of old beer and stale urine told Wiz it was a tavern even before his eyes adjusted well enough to see the barrels stacked along one wall. A few mutton-tallow lamps added more stench than light to the scene, and here and there the fading rays of the sun peeked through cracks in the bricks. The three or four patrons scattered around at the rough tables and benches all possessed a mien that did not encourage casual acquaintance and a manner that made Wiz want to stay as far away from them as possible. The only one who paid any attention to the newcomers was the barkeep, a big man in a dirty white smock who looked them up and down and then went back to picking his teeth with a double-edged dagger.

It was definitely not the kind of drinking establishment Wiz was used to. There wasn't a fern in sight, although Wiz thought he detected a smear of moss growing out of a seep of moisture on one wall.

Malkin put her hands on her hips, looked around and breathed a deep, contented sigh. She plopped herself down on the nearest bench and bellowed for the barkeep.

"Hi, Cully! Jacks of your best for me and the wizard here." The big man grunted acknowledgement and turned to his barrels. It seemed Malkin was known, if not welcomed, in this place.

"Come here often?" Wiz asked casually.

"Often enough. The Prancing Pig's the place to be if you want to meet folks in the Bog Side."

Glancing around, Wiz couldn't imagine going up to anyone in this place and asking him his sign.

Cully slapped down two leather mugs before them. From the stuff that slopped on the table Wiz could see the contents were beer. He picked his up and took a sip. It was thick, potent and flavored with some kind of bitter herb besides hops. The pine pitch used to seal the leather gave it a resiny aftertaste. Wiz was no judge of beer, but the stuff wasn't bad.

"This is the real city," Malkin said. "The folks down here don't put on airs and there's none of that social scramble and bicker, bicker, bicker you get on the other side of the bridge. Folks in the Bog Side stick together."

"When they're not slitting each others' throats you mean."

Malkin shrugged. "That's in the way of business." She took a long pull on her mug and slapped it down with a lusty sigh.

Wiz followed with a smaller pull on his tankard. "That reminds me. Those big buildings on this side of the river. Are those warehouses?"

Malkin shrugged. "Some were. A long time ago. Farmers'd

bring in wool. Some of it would be spun and woven here and more would be traded downriver as it was."

"What happened?"

Malkin looked at him as if he was a touch slow. "Dragons is what happened. You can't grow much wool when there's dragons using your flocks as a lunch counter, not to mention snapping up the crew of a riverboat or two. The farmers still graze sheep, but there's not so much wool as there used to be. Not so many come to buy, either."

It made sense, Wiz thought as he took another pull on the oddly flavored beer. Dragons matured slowly and few survived to adulthood. But in a place with little natural magic there was nothing to threaten an adult dragon and they lived a very long time. Over the centuries there would be a slow, steady increase in population and that would mean more dragons to bedevil their human neighbors.

"It couldn't have all been one-sided, though. Otherwise people would never have gotten established in the valley. You had to have ways of fighting back."

Malkin snorted into her mug. "Buying peace, more like. Used to be the council would make a deal with dragons. So many sheep, or cattle, or maidens a year and the dragons would leave the rest alone—mostly."

"But that doesn't work any more?"

"Seems like there's a different dragon every year."

Population pressure again, Wiz thought. Somehow Malthusian economics looked different when you were part of the consumable resource instead of the expanding population. Pretty clearly buying off the dragons wasn't the answer. All that got you was more dragons exploiting the resource.

"You must have had other ways of fighting back."

Malkin thumped down her now-empty mug and considered. "There's children's tales of heroes who could kill dragons. I suppose they're true because there used to be statues to them in half the squares in town."

"Used to be?"

"Dragons didn't like it. They'd swoop down and melt the statues where they stood. Burn down a lot of the town in the process." Again the shrug. "That was a long time ago, too."

It didn't feel like a solution to Wiz, but he persisted. "Still, you could kill dragons."

"A hero could. Had to be a hero who would face a dragon in single combat. Sometimes the dragon'd win and burn the town. Sometimes the human would win and we'd be free of dragons for a bit. But heroing ain't what it used to be. Not so many of them any more and there's more dragons, seems like."

"I understand why you have more dragons, but why aren't there more heroes?"

" 'Cause win or lose most of them are only good for one fight." She jerked her head back toward the bar. "Cully here. He's the only one around now."

"Cully fought a dragon?"

Malkin nodded. "He's the one I want you to meet. Hey, Cully," she called over her shoulder. "The wizard here wants to meet you. And bring us a couple more while you're at it."

As the bartender made his way over with a pitcher of beer Wiz looked at him closely. He was a big man, run to fat now in late middle age and his skin blotchy from sampling too much of his wares. He moved with a pronounced limp with his withered left arm pressed close to his side. For all that he must have been formidable in his youth.

"So you're the wizard, eh?" Cully said as he plopped the pitcher of beer down on the table. Wiz saw he had brought a jack for himself.

"More a consultant just now," Wiz said. "I'm working with the council on their dragon problem."

"Scared a dragon right out of the Baggot Place," Malkin put in. "Frightened him so bad he flew away without harming anyone."

Cully looked Wiz up and down. "So I heard," he said in a tone that wasn't quite a challenge.

"It's a skill," Wiz shrugged. "But you actually fought a dragon and won."

Cully filled his own jack and passed the pitcher to Malkin. "Aye. It's a dragon's treasure that got me this place. And as for winning—" He shrugged his good arm. "Well, I'm here and the dragon ain't."

Wiz leaned forward. "Did you have some kind of special weapon?"

"What's the matter, Wizard? Your own methods not good enough?"

"Oh, my methodology for dragon abatement is perfectly adequate. But like any practitioner I seek to add to my knowledge base."

The big man digested that while he drained most of his tankard.

"Oh, aye, there's all kinds of lore on killing dragons." Cully grinned. Since half his face was a mass of burn scars the result was not only lopsided, it was something to terrify small children. "Thing is, most of it don't work." He twitched his bad arm and Wiz saw the skin was mostly scar tissue. "That's how I got like this, following some of that advice."

Wiz wondered if the dragons exchanged tips on fighting humans.

"Still, you beat a dragon in a single combat."

Cully's grin grew even more lopsided. "I never said it was a straight-up fight. That's not in the rules, you see."

"There are rules?"

"Of a sort. If you don't follow them the dragon won't fight you. It's his choice, you know, seeing as how he can fly and you can't."

"What are the rules?"

"Only show up at the appointed place at the appointed time, all by yourself. After that anything goes."

"How'd you do it?"

"How do *you* do it, Wizard?" Cully shot back.

"I do what any good consultant does. Mostly I talk them to death."

Cully considered. "That's a new one anyway. I wish you the luck of it." He paused. "As for me, I started by hiding in some rocks and braining him with a boulder. Then?" The big man shrugged. "Then it was just one hell of a fight." He looked over Wiz's shoulder as if seeing something miles away. "One hell of a fight."

The mood held for a long minute as Wiz considered the implications.

"And no one's done it since you?"

Cully's eyes focused back on Wiz. "Not for more than forty years. There's some as have tried. But none with any luck, you see."

"Are the dragons getting smarter?"

"There's them as says that," Cully admitted. "Or maybe those would-be dragon slayers is getting dumber. Or softer." He let out a gusty sigh and drained the last of his beer. "I'll tell you one thing, Wizard. Dragon slaying ain't what it used to be." Then he grinned again. "But then neither's much else."

Again silence as both men sat lost in thought, Cully in his memories and Wiz in the implications of what he had learned. He needed to absorb all this and the heavy beer was going to his head.

"Well," he said, pushing his end of the bench back from the table, "thanks a lot Cully. You've given me a lot to think about."

The big man grinned his terrifying grin. "Any time you need advice on killing dragons, come and see me."

"Thanks, Cully." Wiz turned to go but the tavern keeper cleared his throat.

"You forgot to pay for the beer."

In a sinking instant Wiz realized he didn't have any money with him. But Malkin reached into her belt pouch and flipped a silver coin down on the table.

Cully scooped up the coin, bit it, and nodded. "He's got you paying for him, eh?"

"Wizards don't use money," Malkin said carelessly.

"Yeah?" the big man said skeptically. "What do they use then?"

"Plastic," Wiz blurted. "Ah, little cards, like so," he opened his fingers. "When you want something you just show them your plastic."

Cully looked at him with eyes narrowed and Wiz felt foolish.

"And they take this plastic stuff? Just like that?"

"Well," said Wiz, remembering the times he had gone over his limit, "mostly."

For the first time the big man's face showed respect. "You must be a mighty wizard indeed."

"Where'd you get that silver?" Wiz asked as he and Malkin emerged into the cool evening air.

"One of those pickpockets back at the bridge wasn't as good as he thought he was," Malkin said with a radiant smile. "He had money in his pouch too."

"You picked a pickpocket's pocket while he was trying to pick your pocket?"

"It was a challenge."

Wiz just sighed and followed his guide back down the alley, his head full of beer fumes and his mind full of dragons.

So the dragons were getting harder to kill, eh? That made sense too, in a way. The older, more powerful dragons staked out their territories in the center of the Dragon Lands and forced the younger ones to the periphery. That meant that the dragons the humans faced were less powerful and less experienced—less intelligent too, if Griswold was any example. But as population pressure increased bigger, smarter and more dangerous dragons were trying to grab territory on the edge. They'd be harder for human warriors to beat.

He nearly stumbled into a sewage pit and he had to rush to keep up with Malkin.

"Cully is the last of the dragon slayers, huh?"

Malkin nodded. "Far as anyone knows." Her tone changed slightly. "He may be my father too. Big enough anyway."

"You didn't know your father?"

"Nah," Malkin said. "Left or died or something before I was born."

"Didn't your mother tell you anything about him?"

A snort of laughter in the dark. "Barely knew my mother. I was too young to ask questions like that."

"I'm sorry."

"For what? She 'prenticed me to Mother Massiter when I was bare old enough to walk. I was a slavey there for a few years. Then I came into some growth, discovered my talent and I've been on my own ever since."

"But don't you ever wonder . . ."

Malkin's voice roughened. "The world's full of wondering, Wizard. Now let it be and we'll be home soon enough."

They walked along in silence, each wrapped in thought, until they emerged at the foot of the bridge that led out of the Bog Side. There was but a sliver of moon and the bridge was dark. Wiz listened to the water rushing along beneath them and considered what he'd learned. *No wonder these people need help,* he thought. *They're losing to the dragons and they don't even know it yet.*

He never even saw the shadow that detached itself from the gloom and brought the raised club down on his head with skull-smashing force.

Wiz never saw the blow coming, nor the four cloaked figures that came charging out of the dark. He didn't have to. The protective spell in his ring sensed the danger and wrapped him in a stasis field, leaving him frozen in the center of the band of attackers.

The first man's club bounced out of his numbed fingers. Before he could bend to retrieve it, a second, smaller figure twisted in and struck with the speed of a cobra. His dagger flashed down, struck the magic field, skittered off and buried itself in the wielder's thigh. The man screamed and fell back. The other two stopped their headlong charge and stared at the motionless figure of the wizard, considering their next move.

"I'm struck down," wailed the little one with the knife. "Laid low by a cowardly wizard's blow."

"Ah, it's nothing but a scratch," growled the man with the club.

"A scratch?" the wounded man yelped. "A scratch?" His voice went higher and quavered. "It's a Fortuna great wound in me leg, it is. Nigh mortal, I tell you."

"Well, stand away and we'll finish him," said a third man. "All of us striking together." He hefted his cudgel and fitted his actions to his words.

The fourth and last assassin had a sword. The three remaining men struck Wiz simultaneously and in turns. They hit him high. They hit him low. They pounded and hammered and thrust and sliced and hacked and hewed. Wiz just stood there, frozen in time and oblivious to their efforts.

"Doesn't seem to matter what we do," the shortest one gasped at last. "It hurts us worse than it does him." He rubbed his shoulder. "Got me bursitis going again, it has."

"We could set him on fire," the tall one with the sword said speculatively.

"Not likely he'd burn," said the third. "He's an expert on dragons after all."

"Let's throw him in the river then."

"Don't look at me," the aggrieved voice came out of the shadows. "I'm wounded out of commission."

"Three of us can handle him all right. Come on boys."

The men clustered around Wiz and tried to jerk him aloft. But the stasis spell worked in proportion to the applied acceleration and Wiz would not move.

"He's heavy as lead," one of them grunted.

"Let's tip him, then," said the man with the sword. "Maybe we can move him that way."

By slowly tilting the frozen Wiz back on his heels and

working him forward inch by painful inch the thugs got Wiz to the stone rail.

"Now," the tall one panted, "how we going to get him over the railing?"

"Maybe we could hoist him up and tip him like?" the one with the sword said dubiously.

"Won't do any good if he lands in the mud bank," the third said, having regained his breath.

The two looked at each other and then leaned over the rail to peer down to the river.

A strong hand grasped each man by the belt and boosted both assassins up and over the rail before they knew what had happened. The third man rushed to the aid of his friends only to be seized and propelled over the stone railing after them. Three splashes from below confirmed that they had indeed been over the river and not the mud bank.

"Now," said Malkin, turning to face the fourth thug.

"No need." The man hobbled to his feet and held out a hand to ward her off. "No need. I'm going." With that he hoisted himself over the stone rail and disappeared into the darkness below.

With the threat vanished, the spell relaxed its grip and time speeded up to normal for Wiz. He blinked as his eyes refocused, realized he was facing in a different direction and then saw Malkin looking over the bridge railing.

"Something happened didn't it?"

Malkin looked at him oddly. "Four Bog Side bullies just tried to kill you is all. I guess that qualifies as 'something'—at least for normal folk."

She strode ahead briskly. "Come on," she said over her shoulder. "Let's get off this bridge before something else happens."

"Who?" said Wiz as he caught up beside her.

"Hired help," Malkin told him. "And not of the best, either. Seems as if someone wants you dead, but they don't want to spend a lot of money on the project."

"Dieter?"

Malkin considered. "Mayhap. But as like Mayor Hastlebone. Or one of the others."

"Wait a minute. The mayor's my strongest supporter."

"He's tied his wagon to your star and that's a fact. But mayhap he's afraid your star will fall and wants to hedge his bet. After all, if you die accidental-like, you can't rightly be said to have failed, now can you?"

"Hendrick?"

"Or maybe one of the common folk, who's afraid of dragons."

"Well, if they're afraid of dragons," Wiz said despairingly, "don't they want me to succeed?"

"They're likely afraid you'll stir the dragons up to burn the town again."

"Great. Try to do them a favor and they try to kill you."

Malkin grinned. "You expected gratitude?"

TWENTY-ONE

FANFARE FOR KAZOOS AND DRAGON

Just because it doesn't work the
way you expected doesn't mean it's
useless.
                    —*The Consultants' Handbook*

Wiz stewed about the incident on the bridge for the next three days without coming to any kind of conclusion—except that someone here *really* didn't like him. Since he had known that almost from the moment he set foot in town, the information didn't help him any.

He was still stewing when the mayor showed up on his doorstep. He was hoarse and made liberal use of the handkerchief in his sleeve, but he looked better than he had the last time Wiz had seen him.

"What can I do for you, Your Honor?" he asked once they were settled in his workroom.

"It's this new organization," Mayor Hendrick said. "Oh, I'm sure it's wonderful and all that. But it's so, well, complicated, we meet and we meet and we meet and nothing ever seems to get done."

"Reinventing and re-empowering an organization does take some time to get up to speed," Wiz said. "But I'm sure once the initial formalities are out of the way you will find it a vast improvement."

"Maybe, but that's not exactly what I wanted to talk to you about. I need something to help me maintain my position."

Thoughts of a palace coup flashed through Wiz's mind. "Maintain your position?"

"With this new executive committee. I need something to increase my dignity," the mayor said. Wiz thought about suggesting a face-lift and a personality transplant, but he decided against it.

Wiz shrugged. "Well, I'm not much on public speaking."

"Oh, but you handled that presentation wonderfully," the mayor said. "Anyway, I speak well enough as it is. What I need is something more, well, *imposing*, if you know what I mean? Something magical. I was thinking, perhaps, a halo?"

Wiz thought that a halo would make the mayor look more ridiculous than dignified. "Fine for a darkened room, but what about broad daylight?"

Mayor Hastlebone sniffled. "Yes, that is a problem. What do you suggest then?"

"Well, how about some background music?"

"You mean like a fanfare of trumpets?" The mayor brightened. "Yes, that would be just the thing." He waved his hand. "Make it so, Wizard."

"It's not quite that simple. Let me think for a minute. What do you want it to sound like?"

"Oh, something like Ta-daa tum tum tum TAA." The mayor waved his hand in time to the imaginary music. "You know, important."

"I guess so," Wiz said, punching keys on his workstation and watching the fiery letters scroll past. "Can you do that sound again?"

"TA-DAA TUM TUM TUM TAAA." The mayor was louder this time.

"Okay got it. Now . . ."

"You mean you're not going to make a hundred trumpets materialize in the room?" The mayor sounded disappointed.

"No, I've captured the sound and I'll use that. After I juice it up, of course."

Calling up his synthesizer module, Wiz set to work. Eventually he came up with something that combined the theme from *Masterpiece Theater* with the post call from a horse race. Even to Wiz's musically untrained ear it sounded more like a chorus of kazoos than a trumpet call.

The mayor's face fell.

"Needs something more," Wiz said quickly. "How about a three-part echo effect?"

Wiz noticed that the sound of the trumpets had brought Llewllyn to the doorway. He didn't seem awed, but he was very interested.

A few more minutes of fiddling and Wiz tried again. Now it sounded like some of the kazoos had bass voices and they weren't quite playing together. The mayor brightened at the noise.

"Now I just say *fanfare exe*?"

"That's right. Try it."

Mayor Hendrick puffed out his chest and struck a pose as if delivering an oration. **fanfare exe!** Flinging one arm outward he began to address a non-existent crowd.

As soon as he opened his mouth the invisible trumpets brayed. His Honor stood with his mouth open for a minute and then closed it just as the fanfare finished. "My friends," the mayor began and was immediately drowned out by the trumpets.

"Ah, I think this needs a little more work," Wiz said. "Let me play with it some more and perhaps we can do better."

The mayor's reply was drowned out by a volley of trumpets.

"Say 'fanfare cancel exe,'" Wiz shouted through the noise.

"What?" Immediately another round of racket burst on top of the existing one.

"FANFARE CANCEL EXE," Wiz shouted.

"*FANFARE CANCEL EXE?*" the mayor asked. The trumpets cut off in mid-bray.

"This needs a little work," Wiz said into the ringing silence.

"I thought a wizard simply waved his wand, or staff, to make things happen."

"I'm afraid there's a little more to it than that, at least on such complex spells. This may take a couple of days, but I'm sure I can cook something up you'll like."

He had just seen the mayor out the front door, still sniffling, when a noise in the kitchen caught his attention. He went downstairs and found Llewllyn and Anna sitting at the table with a large basket between them. There was a blanket neatly folded on top of the basket.

"You wanted to see me?" he asked Llewllyn.

"Ah, a trifle really. Nothing of any importance I assure you."

Wiz gestured at the blanket and basket. "And this?"

"We're going on a picnic," Anna said brightly. Her face fell. "That's if you don't mind, My Lord. I'll be back in plenty of time to fix dinner and all my work's done, except for washing the walls and I can't do that until the soapmaker finishes her next batch of cleaning soap and that won't be for another two days, so . . ."

"No, it's fine with me." Then he eyed Llewllyn. "Just remember our discussion."

The young man gave his boss a toothpaste smile. "Of course, My Lord."

"Oh, by the way," Wiz said casually to Anna. "Have you seen the butter knife anywhere?" Then he smiled insincerely at Llewllyn, who had suddenly gone a little pale and developed a distinct hunch.

A pleasant way out of town a jumble of rocky spires reared from the countryside. It was a common destination for picnics and other more private affairs, as Llewllyn knew from his previous residence nearby.

Anna had packed a lunch in a wicker basket and neatly covered the provisions with a spare blanket to serve as a tablecloth. She had fixed the lunch herself, but Llewllyn was the one who suggested the blanket.

"My gran would never let me come here," she told Llewllyn as they turned off the road onto the path into the rocks.

"Oh, it's perfectly safe, I can assure you," the putative wizard said carelessly. "I've been here many times."

"Many times?"

"Picnics," Llewllyn added hastily, catching her tone. "I've been here on picnics."

"Oh, this is a lovely spot," the girl said, as they came to a glade in the rocks.

"There's a better one a little ways up. More private— ah—better view." He took her hand and helped her up the steep trail among the pink granite boulders. The path twisted and climbed until it reached a spot just below the top of the main spire. Rocks jutted up around them, forming a natural bowl enclosing a flat spot just large enough for a cozy picnic.

"Here, you see? You can see for miles and no one can see us at all."

"No one?"

"Completely private." He moved closer to her. "And look at the view." He stood behind her and extended one arm over her shoulder to point out the sights. "There's the river, and there's the town over there, you see?" Somehow it was completely natural that Llewllyn's other arm fell around Anna's waist.

"Are you sure we'll be all right?" she asked wide-eyed.

"Never fear," Llewllyn said. "I am here to protect you."

"Oh, Llewllyn," she whispered softly.

He drew her to him and held her in his arms. "You know I would give my last drop of heart's blood for you. I love you more than life itself."

"Oh, Llewllyn."

Anna's eyes were dewy and her lips soft and partly open. Llewllyn bent forward to kiss her.

A shadow passed before the sun.

Anna's eyes grew round and she went rigid in Llewllyn's arms. The wizard wasn't used to getting that kind of response so it took him a second to realize she was looking over his shoulder and not at him. He turned around in time to see a dragon settle down among the crags below them.

Peering around a rock Llewllyn could see the dragon, or part of it, nestled among the rocks below them. It had curled up, blocking the trail.

Anna shrank back against him, cowering in his arms. Llewllyn clasped her tightly to stop his own trembling.

"Be brave, my beloved," he said to her. "I will protect you." She made no sound but clung to him more tightly.

Llewllyn's first instinct was to sneak away. But he knew this place well enough to know there wasn't anyplace to sneak to from here. The only way out was the trail they had come up. They could stay where they were, but sooner or later the dragon was sure to see or smell them. There really wasn't anything else to do, he decided. Especially not with the girl here.

"I will face the monster."

Anna turned even paler. "Oh, but you can't. You'll be killed."

The wizard took her in his arms. "If I am it will be in a good cause. I will gladly offer up my last drop of heart's blood to save you."

"Oh, be careful," Anna breathed. "Come back to me."

He patted her cheek. "Never fear my darling. All will be well."

A quick peek around the rocks showed the dragon was lying down and couldn't see the trail. Llewllyn took a deep breath and moved toward the dragon, dodging from boulder to boulder and sometimes crawling on his belly.

His first thought was that he might be able to find

another way down the rocks. Or perhaps, if the dragon was truly asleep, they could sneak by it. By the time he reached the place where the dragon rested he knew both hopes were in vain. The rocks were much too steep and while he could hear the dragon breathing regularly, it was obviously not asleep.

Llewllyn stopped and thought hard. He had scant experience with dragons. But he knew Wiz had handled one by talking to it and if there was one thing Llewllyn was confident of, it was his ability to talk.

No help for it, really, he told himself. Then he stood up, straightened his tunic, brushed the grass out of his blond hair and squared his shoulders. It never hurt to make an impressive entrance.

In fact, he realized, he had a spell of his master's to make the entrance even more impressive. All the trumpets might even make the dragon think he had an army behind him.

fanfare exe! he whispered. Then he took a deep breath and opened his mouth to go forth and do battle with the dragon.

The dragon, meanwhile, was mostly interested in getting a nice nap. He had fed that morning on a dozen or so sheep at an outlying farmstead and taken light exercise by flying a few dozen leagues. Now he was ready to settle down and digest his meal. The rocks were nicely warm from the sun and the scenery suited his dragonish nature.

He was just relaxing into gentle slumber when the blare of trumpets yanked him awake.

The dragon's head jerked up and he roared in surprise and anger. A lance of flame shot from his jaws directed at nothing in particular but passing over the rock behind which Llewllyn waited. The bard was unharmed but the blast of superheated air cost him what little courage he had remaining.

Unfortunately, when Llewllyn became frightened he stuttered uncontrollably. Every time he tried to get a syllable out it touched off another peal of trumpets. The rocks rang and resounded with the noise of a trumpet fanfare played as a twenty-part round and the dragon's head darted this way and that seeking the source of his torment.

Finally it was too much. With a roar of frustration the dragon leapt into the sky to try to find a quieter place for his nap.

Llewllyn was still watching the dragon go when Anna came running down the trail and into his arms.

"You're all right! I saw the fire and the dragon, and I was afraid." She stopped with her eyes even wider as the significance sank in. "You did it," Anna breathed. "You defeated a dragon."

Llewllyn opened his mouth to say something modest but the trumpet fanfare cut him off.

Anna's eyes grew even wider. "Oh, you are a mighty wizard! And my hero." Llewllyn just smiled and held Anna tighter. Occasionally, given enough hints, he did know when to shut up.

Winging away from the rocks the dragon came to a somewhat different conclusion. *A pretty pass indeed when you can't even take a nap without being disturbed by these pesky humans and their stupid magical jokes,* he thought. *I'm going to have to do something about them. And this new wizard of theirs.*

TWENTY-TWO

DRAGON TROUBLE

> The Consultant's Three Rules of Crisis
> Management:
> 1) When Life Hands You A Lemon, Make
>   Lemonade.
> 2) When Life Hands You A Hemlock,
>   Don't Make Hemlock-ade.
> 2a) Always Know The Difference Between A
>   Lemon and A Hemlock.
> —*The Consultants' Handbook*

" . . . and then the dragon flew away," Anna told Wiz and Malkin, her blue eyes round as saucers. "And we were saved!"

"Oh, it was nothing really," Llewllyn said modestly from where he stood at her side, his hand resting on her shoulder. Anna reached up and placed her hand over his. Then she beamed up at her savior.

Wiz and Malkin exchanged glances and then stared down at their plates and the remains of dinner. Obviously both of them thought that for once Llewllyn's description of events was more accurate than Anna's.

The pair had been through the incident three times

and Wiz still wasn't completely sure what had happened. For one thing, the story had grown with each retelling. For another he trusted neither Llewllyn's veracity nor Anna's powers of observation. He was reasonably certain there had been a dragon involved and that the dragon had flown away, perhaps in response to something Llewllyn had done. He suspected from Anna's description of the sound of trumpets that his fanfare spell had been involved as well. Beyond that, he wasn't willing to speculate—except about the reason for the grass stains on the blanket and the dried grass in Anna's hair and the flush on the girl's cheeks.

Obviously something more was called for, so Wiz tried. "Well, I'm glad you're safe."

Anna sighed. "I owe it all to Llewllyn. Isn't he wonderful?"

Malkin kept her eyes on her plate.

"Quite remarkable," Wiz said dryly, rising from the table. "But if you'll excuse me, I have work to do." *Like trying to keep my dinner down*, he thought as he headed up the stairs.

Since Llewllyn had developed the habit of cadging meals with them the scene was repeated at lunch the next day.

Since the mayor had summoned Wiz to discuss the fanfare spell, the scene was prolonged because Llewllyn insisted on accompanying him to the town hall. The young man paused several times to ostentatiously greet important people, keeping Wiz close so he could bask in his reflected glory. Somehow he managed to work the fact that he had defeated a dragon into each conversation, so Wiz had to listen to more or less the same story three or four more times. By the time they reached the street that led to the main square Wiz was thoroughly fed up with his assistant.

"You know that what you did was stupid," Wiz told him finally. "I mean terminally stupid. Why didn't you just wait for the dragon to leave?"

"Were I by myself I might have," Llewllyn admitted with a disarming smile. "But Anna was there."

"So you risked her life as well as your own to impress her."

"No, to protect her. Better for me to face near-certain death at the fangs and claws of a dragon than for anything to happen to her. Were I slain perhaps the monster would be satisfied and not look further among the rocks."

"Still it was stupid."

Llewllyn nodded, as if to show he was too well bred to argue with his employer. "Perhaps, My Lord. I can only say that love makes a man do strange and wonderful things."

Wiz snorted.

"But I do love her," Llewllyn proclaimed. "Why, I would shed my last drop of heart's blood for her."

"Yeah, but will you marry her?"

"Of course, My Lord, in due time. Do you doubt me?"

"Your record in that department isn't exactly sterling," Wiz said as they turned the corner into the main square.

"Ah, but I was young and callow then, a mere stripling. You see before you not a boy, but a man full-grown, a man redeemed by love."

Wiz thought that what he saw before him was a pompous windbag and he was about to say something to that effect. But just then the world stuttered.

One instant Llewllyn was beside him and the next he was in front and staring open-mouthed. Everyone was running and screaming and there was dust in the air that hadn't been there before.

Wiz started to ask what had happened. Then he saw the brick. No, not a brick, a piece of worked stone. Like part of a cornice. It was lying in the street behind Llewllyn, surrounded by the dust it had raised when it fell. There were several other pieces of freshly broken stone nearby. Looking up he could see that a big chunk of the stonework on the building was missing.

Wiz looked back and saw Llewllyn had progressed to

working his jaws, but not far enough to actually make noise. He also saw they had drawn a crowd.

"It, it, it . . . bounced," Llewllyn finally managed. "It just hit you and it split to pieces and it bounced right off the top of your head."

Looking around, Wiz saw that several councilors and the sheriff had joined the excited group.

"Think nothing of it," he said over the rising buzz of conversation. "As a great wizard I am protected by a spell that renders me invulnerable to mortal danger." The conversation grew even louder.

"But you froze. Like a statue," his assistant said.

Wiz had been hoping no one would notice that. "A side effect," he said with a wave of his hand. "So long as the danger lasts I am immobile and invulnerable. Now come. Let us be on our way."

Maybe that will stop people from trying to terminate my contract with extreme prejudice, he thought as the crowd parted before them. *At least it might if I can find someplace to sit down before I get the shakes.*

Wiz didn't see the bald little man with the leather sack of mason's tools lounging at the edge of the crowd and wouldn't have recognized him if he had. Nor would he have attached any special importance to the thoughtful way he rubbed his chin as Wiz and Llewllyn proceeded on their way.

Having a piece of rock dumped on his head may not have hurt Wiz physically, but it sure didn't do anything for his mood. Between Llewllyn's bragging, the mayor's insistence on having the new spell before the next executive committee meeting and being sneered at by Pieter Halder on the town hall steps, he was in a foul mood when he got home that evening.

Anna, however, was still starry-eyed and bubbling. For once Llewllyn wasn't hanging around, so Wiz was spared that, but the maid's innocent prattling about the wonders of her true love was just as hard to take.

" . . . and someday we'll be married," the maid finished up her latest, albeit short, line of thought.

"You hope," Wiz said in an undertone, unable to contain himself further.

Not enough of an undertone, unfortunately. "Why of course we will," Anna said innocently.

"Look Anna, I don't mean to burst your bubble or anything, but are you sure Llewllyn is the marrying kind?"

"My bubble?" Anna said blankly.

"A figure of speech. I mean your illusions about Llewllyn." As soon as he said it, he knew it was the wrong thing to say, but by then it was too late.

"But they're not illusions. They're real. As real as Llewllyn's magic that saved me from the dragon!"

"Uh, yeah, his magic is another thing. I mean . . ."

"Oh, I know what you mean," Anna burst out. "You're jealous of Llewllyn's powers and I think you're awful!" Then she remembered she was talking to her employer and dashed from the room in a flood of tears.

Wiz watched her go and turned back to his tea. "Women!" he snorted.

"Men!" Malkin retorted. "Well, that was nicely done. What do you intend for an encore? Pull the wings off flies?"

"Now wait a minute. You're the one who brought up the dull butter knife."

"Aye, and I would too. But that doesn't excuse being cruel to the child. That was cruel and all it's likely to accomplish is driving them closer together."

"Little trollop's right," Widder Hackett chimed in. "All you did was hurt her feelings."

"But I was trying to let her down easy. To help her."

"By making her miserable?" Malkin replied.

"Help her my left foot," Widder Hackett grated. "Of all the shoddy, ill-done . . ." There was a lot more.

Wiz looked to either side at the women, one visible and now silent, one invisible and just working up a good head of steam.

"All right have it your way," he snapped. "I'm a miserable failure as a human being. Now if you'll excuse me, I'm going to get some air." With that he stormed out of the kitchen with Widder Hackett still railing in his ear.

Wiz stood on the stoop for an instant, looking out along the dark street. There were no street lights and the moon was only half-full. There wasn't so much as a candle showing in a window, which made the street gloomy and forbidding. It was as if the houses were bombed out and abandoned, he thought. Somewhere several streets over a dog howled, adding to the effect.

He turned and started away from the square, head down and lost in thought.

The truth was, he did feel bad about making Anna cry. But dammit! The girl was his responsibility and he couldn't let her get too mixed up with someone like Llewllyn.

The other truth was he didn't want the responsibility, he admitted as he picked his way along the dark, deserted way. In fact he didn't want any of the responsibilities he had acquired since he got here. Yet he was stuck with them and he was juggling like a madman trying to meet them. That was one of the reasons he'd been so hard on Anna.

Ever since he got here he had been writing checks furiously. Sooner or later some of them were going to come due and he was way overdrawn at the luck bank.

It wasn't just that, this wasn't *fun* any more. In the beginning this had all been a big game, but now the joke was old and not particularly funny.

He couldn't even take pride in his job, like he could writing a good tight module of code in something like COBOL. At heart he just wasn't a con man and playing the role was taking its toll on him. He sucked a breath of the cold night air and sighed gustily. This wasn't working out at all the way he had anticipated.

He was cold and tired and frustrated and a little

scared and more than anything else he just wanted to go home.

Wiz never even saw the shadow that separated itself from the wall as he passed. And he never heard the hiss of the blade through the air. The edge landed squarely across his shoulders and as he froze into immobility a sharp whistle rang out from the darkness from whence the shadow had come.

"Ow!" said the shadow. "My wrist."

"I told you not to hit him, didn't I?" retorted a second cloaked man as he emerged from the darkness. He was shorter and for an instant a moonbeam gleamed off his dark pate. "Just tickle him in the ribs, I said. But no, you have to take a mucking great whack at him."

There was a rattling on the cobblestones just around the corner.

"Here comes the cart," said the first one. "Let's get this business over with."

Heaving and straining the three men loaded Wiz's immobile form into the cart. The spell didn't increase Wiz's weight, but it did do funny things to his inertia. The footpads found they could only move him slowly and that made him seem even heavier. It didn't help that one of them had to keep his sword pressed against Wiz at all times lest the spell break. That left two of them to do most of the work, including burying the frozen wizard under the turnips that made up two-thirds of the cart's load.

It was not a quiet business, especially since all three men had a tendency to curse and mutter at every little bit of work. But not a shutter banged open nor even a light showed at a window, as if these kinds of goings-on were commonplace here.

Finally, with Wiz stowed and covered, the pair mounted the cart and rattled off in the night, leaving the occasional turnip behind to mark their passage.

A few minutes jolting over cobblestones brought them to the city's west gate. It was lit by flaming torches on either side and before it stood a representative of the city's guard. He was tall, gangly, wearing a steel cap and leather-covered jack. In the crook of his bony arm he carried a halberd that had definitely seen better days.

"And where do you think you're going?"

"Out to my granny's," said the tall one. The medium-sized one next to him nodded vigorously and the short one sat twisted on the seat to keep his knife on Wiz's throat under the pile of turnips.

"At this time of night?"

"We had to finish work," the tall one said. "Then we had to eat dinner and harness the cart and load it, and . . ."

The guard peered past the driver. "What have you got in there?"

"Uh, turnips."

"Why are you taking turnips out of the city?" he demanded.

"Granny lost her entire turnip crop," the tall man said smoothly. "Weevils got them, they did."

"Turnip weevils," added the driver helpfully. "Terrible things, turnip weevils." His companion, who recognized lily-gilding when he heard it, poked him in the ribs to shut up.

The guard had never heard of turnip weevils, but then he was a city boy. More importantly perhaps, in this city the best and brightest did not become city guardsmen and out of that lot, the best and brightest of the not-so-good and not-so-smart weren't assigned to gate duty after curfew. Still, this was irregular and he had the reputation of the city guard to uphold.

"What's the rest of that stuff?"

"Building supplies. We're going to make some repairs on her cottage while we're about it."

"Fixing the fireplace," the man in the back added helpfully.

"It's after curfew. You won't be able to get back in until morning."

"That's all right. We'll stay at my granny's."

The guard still thought the whole thing was extremely fishy, but his orders were more about people and things coming into the city than people and things going out.

"All right. Pass on then. But I'm going to remember the lot of you."

"Well?" said the tall one at last.

"Well what?" the guard replied.

"Aren't you going to open the gate?"

"If you want the gate opened do it yourself. There's three of you."

The driver started to protest, thought better of it and nudged his companion to get down off the seat.

"Takes two to manage. Can you at least help him?"

The guard jerked his chin at the man in the back of the cart. "What's wrong with him? And why's he sitting funny like that?"

"Hurt meself loading the cart," the little one said. "Set off me lumbago, it did, and sitting any other way hurts." The guard snorted and turned to help the third man open the gate. The cart creaked through and off into the night with Wiz still magically frozen under a load of turnips.

"Hurry up with that cement, will you? My arm's getting tired."

A fire provided light and kept off the chill. A couple of hundred feet away the horse, still hitched to the cart, munched grass placidly. Wiz was standing in a tub half-full of cement, gesturing to empty air. One of the thugs was holding a sword to his throat and the other two were bent over another tub stirring the contents with wooden hoes.

"You want another turn at it?"

"All this work. I think we're underpaid, charging for this like a simple kidnapping. Between the hauling, the mixing and the rest I swear stone cutting's an easier living."

"Where is he anyways?" the third one put in. "I want to count me money and see the back of this job."

"We're supposed to meet him at Bottomless Gorge, and we're still a good half mile from Bottomless Gorge."

"And who was it who decided we'd stop and do it here, eh?"

"I didn't decide. Here's where the cart broke down."

"I knew it would," the third one said gloomily. "Overloaded it was, and as soon as we got off the main road . . ."

"It will ride lighter with nothing but him in it," the tall one told them. "Just get that stuff mixed up good and we'll have plenty of time to fix the cart while it sets hard. Meanwhile our client will just have to wait."

"I dunno. Not good business practices to keep a client waiting. How's that cement coming?"

"Still more like soup than cement."

"You put too much water in," the tall one said from where he held the sword on Wiz.

"I did not!" the shorter man retorted.

The third one stuck his hoe blade in the trough and watched the milky concoction run off the end. "This lot's got chalk mixed in with it. Adulterated, that's what it is."

"Came right out the city warehouse, it did," the short man said morosely. "Councilman Hanwassel's best. You can't trust no one nowadays. The decline in honesty in our society is shocking. Positively shocking. Me, I lay it all to the parents."

"Me, I lay it all to you," the tall one said acidly. "Last time I let you get the supplies for a job!"

"And who was it who was too busy nattering over his ale in the Blind Goat to go out and get the necessaries?"

"That was planning," he answered loftily. "Something like this takes planning—and delegation. It's up to the subordinates to fulfill the tasks delegated to them."

"You can delegate all you want," the short man answered sullenly. "But next time *you* steal the flipping cement."

The other one started to reply, but the third man gestured them to silence.

"Hsst. Here he comes."

Pieter strode into the firelight.

"Where have you been?" he demanded. "And what are you doing here?"

"Cart broke down," the tall one told him. "We figured we'd set him up here and then take him the rest of the way." But Pieter had quit listening as soon as he caught sight of Wiz.

He stood in front of Wiz, arms akimbo. "So Wizard, not so high and mighty now, are you?" He followed it up with a stinging slap to the face.

At least Pieter's hand stung. It was like slapping a rock and the young man winced in pain.

"He can't hear you," one of the footpads said.

"Can't feel what you do to him either," another one added.

"Well, wake him up then. I want him to know the author of his fate."

"Wake him up?" the shortest one quavered. "He's a wizard."

"And he's tied so tight he can't wiggle a finger and gagged so tight he can't utter a word. Release him, I say!"

Hesitantly the one with the sword removed it from Wiz's ribs.

Suddenly Wiz was there again, tied up, gagged, surrounded by three armed thugs and a grinning Pieter, and up to his knees in cement. Not for the first time it occurred to him that the protection spell's definition of "mortal danger" left a lot to be desired.

The short, balding one, whom Wiz mentally tagged "Curly," was edging away from the reanimated wizard. The one beside him was holding his sword warily, ready to thrust it between Wiz's ribs at the first sign of movement. The tall one was looking back and forth between Wiz and Pieter.

"Throw me out of the house, will you?" Pieter snarled and drew back his hand to slap Wiz again.

The blow never landed. Wiz was gagged, but that didn't matter. He could form the words in his throat and that was all it took.

The spell for "loose knots" worked in part by making things self-repulsive and in part by reducing the coefficient of friction of everything in the neighborhood to something less than teflon on plate glass lubricated by greased owl shit. Which is to say that any friction fastening in the vicinity stopped working instantly.

Which is to say that everyone's pants fell down as their belts came untied. Actually it is to say more than that. Sewing can be loosely defined as a form of knotting, so the clothes not only fell off, they fell to pieces.

That left Wiz, Pieter and his three henchmen standing there stark naked. In this crisis the thugs reverted to their natural behavior: They turned to run like frightened rats. Pieter just stood with his hand stopped in mid-air and his mouth open. Wiz spoke another word and all four of them were frozen in place.

Wiz took a step forward and nearly tripped over the edge of the tub he was standing in.

light exe he commanded and a witchfire globe cast an even blue light over everything.

It made an interesting tableau. The tall man had lost his footing and fallen to his hands and knees. The balding one was trying to scramble over the tall one's back, which left them poised as if playing a slightly obscene game of nude leapfrog. The middle-sized one was straightening up with arms pumping, like a sprinter coming out of the blocks.

Wiz shook the wet cement from his legs and considered his next move. A chill evening breeze reminded him that his first priority was finding something to wear if he didn't want to catch cold. He looked at the piles of fabric littering the ground around them but none of them were large enough to cover much.

The cart had been outside the range of the spell, so the horse was still placidly cropping grass. Wiz pulled off the horse's blanket and, ignoring its condition and its odor, draped it over his shoulders toga style.

Leaving Pieter frozen, he gestured to unfreeze his

stooges. The three returned to awareness facing a wizard surrounded by glowing blue light and wearing a tattered horse blanket. Just then Wiz's sartorial shortcomings meant less to them than his obvious power.

Their first act was to collapse in a heap as their momentum caught up with them. Curly covered his head with his hands and moaned.

"Stand where you are!" Wiz commanded in a stern and majestic manner—or as stern and majestic as you can be when the cold night air is nipping at your bare backside. "Go on, stand up, all of you."

The three thugs pulled themselves erect and sorted themselves out facing Wiz. They were all about the color of the cement in the tub and Wiz didn't think they were shivering because they were cold.

"I ought to turn you all into frogs," he said sternly. The tall one blanched and the short one whimpered more loudly.

One of these days I've got to write a spell to do that, he thought. However, just now the threat was enough.

He pointed at the trough. "What's this stuff?"

"Cement, My Lord. It's a little thin because . . ."

Wiz cut him off with a wave of his hand. "Okay, you're going to take this cement and you're going to paint a coat of it onto Pieter here. All over, so he's thoroughly covered. Then, when it's dry, you're going to load him into the wagon, take him back to town and set him up in the square in front of the town hall. Got that?"

"The wagon's broke," Larry said sullenly.

"Then carry him," Wiz said and turned away into the night. He took two steps and then turned back to them. "But if he's not standing in the square by noon, you're all going to be pigeon roosts by evening."

He took two more steps and turned back again.

"Oh, and one more thing."

The three quailed before him.

"Which way is it to town?"

❖   ❖   ❖

God what an evening, Wiz thought as he trudged down the dusty road toward town. The moon gave enough light to keep him on the road and out of potholes, but not enough to see every rock and tree root. As a result he had stubbed his toes and bruised his heels a half dozen times before he had gone as much as a mile.

The only good thing is, it's too late for anything else to happen to me tonight.

Just then a shadow passed over the moon. Wiz looked up to see a dragon settling down on a hillock beside the road. The moon was behind the creature so it loomed nightmarishly large and black before him.

"Starting a new fashion, Wizard?" Wurm's "voice" rang in his head.

"Right now I'm trying to get back to town."

"Still, this is opportune. I have been meaning to speak to you at a time and place which would not upset your, ah, clients."

Wiz had a sudden premonition the night's events so far had just been a warm-up. "What do you want?" he asked wearily.

"An opportunity to discuss your progress, and perhaps your future actions. I understand for example that you personally convinced one dragon to give up his prey. That in itself is a notable accomplishment."

"Ah, to tell you the truth it wasn't that difficult. Not with that particular dragon."

Wurm nodded his enormous head. "Griswold is a moron. Even for a hatchling."

"Well, at least my run-in with him helped get me in solid with the council."

"Oh, you have accomplished more than that," Wurm said, amused. "In two days there will be a dragonmote to decide what to do about you."

"Dragonmote?"

"A meeting of dragons, or of all who choose to attend." He cocked his enormous scaly head. "Quite an honor actually. The first dragonmote in several hundred years.

Dragons dislike gatherings and prefer single combat to the constant clumping and bickering of humans. Besides, dragons seldom feel the need to take concerted action."

Suddenly it got even colder under the horse blanket. "Concerted action?"

Wurm nodded again. "I believe the currently favored solution is incinerating the town and you with it."

"Is this where I came in?" Then he thought furiously. "Look, can you get me in to that meeting? To speak to them I mean."

Wurm cocked his enormous head. "I think it can be arranged." The way he said it left Wiz no doubt that had been his plan all along.

TWENTY-THREE

DRAGONMOTE

The number of screw-ups in a
presentation is directly proportional to the
importance of the audience and inversely
proportional to their belief in what you're
selling.
> —*The Consultants' Handbook*

Never meddle in the affairs of
dragons, for they are subtle and see right
through bullshit.
> —Marginalia in a copy of
> *The Consultants' Handbook*

The place was a narrow chasm between two towering
sandstone cliffs. When it rained the sandy bottom was
probably under several feet of water. About twenty feet of
water, Wiz judged from the bits of driftwood and debris
caught in cracks and ledges up the wall. He devoutly hoped
it didn't rain while the dragonmote was in progress.

Not that it would matter to the dragons. They dropped
in through the narrow crack of sky above and settled themselves along the cliff faces, hanging head-down like bats.

The smell of snake and sulfur was well-nigh overpowering and garbled bits of dragon speech rang in his head.

With a minimum of hissing and squabbling the dragons settled into their places. There didn't seem to be any strict hierarchy, but the larger, older dragons clearly got the best seats in the house.

A smallish dragon slipped in through the crack of sky, but instead of choosing a spot on the sandstone walls, it dropped down onto the sand next to Wiz. All dragons looked pretty much alike to Wiz but as soon as the creature "spoke" Wiz recognized Griswold.

"You cheated me!" the young dragon said. "Cheated me out of my rightful prey. That spell you showed me was a phony."

"No it wasn't."

"But it doesn't do anything!" Griswold protested.

"I never said that it did," Wiz said blandly.

"But, but, but . . ." Griswold did a fair imitation of a turkey gobbling. Wiz just smiled sweetly.

The young dragon drew back his head as if to say something else, but Wiz shushed him as the meeting came to order.

"This mortal is here under my protection," Wurm declared as the dragons settled in. "Are there any objections?" There was a certain amount of shifting and hissing, but apparently no one objected strongly enough to try to tackle Wurm.

There was no introduction. The dragons fell silent and stared at Wiz, waiting for him to begin.

Wiz gestured and his equipment appeared. It included an overhead projector, complete with a green demon to operate it, a screen, and a large easel holding flip charts. *Beats heck out of lugging this stuff down the hall,* he thought. He picked up the pointer lying on the easel and launched into his prepared spiel.

"Uh, good afternoon ladies and, uh, well dragons. My name is . . ."

"We know who you are," a steely voice rang in his head. "Get on with it."

"Certainly, Mr. ah . . ."

"Ralfnir," came the cold voice. Looking up and to his right Wiz identified the "speaker" as a dragon nearly as large as Wurm and just as ferocious looking.

"First slide, please. Now, as you can see here . . ."

The demon flipped on the projector and a gorgeous rainbow-tinted slide appeared on the screen. It was not, however, the title slide. Wiz didn't recognize it at all. Then he looked harder and realized it was in upside down. At least it seemed to be upside down. Since it was titled in Japanese it was hard for Wiz to tell.

"Uh, next slide please. Now, as you can see here . . ." He stopped. This one was the Miss July picture from the presentation to the council. Trying to look at the slide from the dragons' perspective, Wiz realized her pose and lack of clothing made her resemble something on a buffet. The dragons seemed mightily unimpressed.

"Uh, next chart please."

Finally, mercifully, the demon got the right slide.

"Now as you can see . . ." But that was as far as he got. Ralfnir drew back his head and aimed an incandescent blast of dragon fire down at him.

The world blinked as Wiz's protection spell cut in. When it cut out Wiz found himself standing beside a heap of smoking ashes holding the charred stub of a pointer. Behind him the reflected heat from the canyon wall warmed his back unpleasantly.

Damn. There have been times I've wanted to do that to a presenter.

"Ah, perhaps it would be better if I dispensed with the visual aids," he said weakly.

"Now," said another frigid, metallic "voice," "tell us something we wish to hear or begone."

Always stress the advantages to the client. But he couldn't think of any.

"All right," he said desperately. "I'm here today to talk

to you about a matter of mutual concern between humans and dragons."

"Not all dragons think there is a problem with humans," Ralfnir put in, looking at Wurm. "Humans multiply and dragons eat them."

Wiz got the strong impression that Ralfnir and Wurm were rivals in some way. The very fact that Wurm was sponsoring him seemed to make Ralfnir oppose him.

"You have until now," Wiz said. "But things are changing among the humans."

"Oh yes," Ralfnir said, "the 'new magic' we have heard of. Why should we fear anything you humans do?"

"It's already defeated two of you," Wiz said levelly.

"That's a lie!" Griswold "shouted" so loud Wiz flinched. "I was hornswoggled, not defeated."

There was a ripple of laughter from the other dragons. Griswold bridled with rage, but Wurm checked him with an easy gesture of his wingtip. The young dragon subsided, glaring murderously at Wiz.

"The point is," Wiz went on, "that humans are much more potent magically than they have been. It would be in all our interests for dragons to recognize that and to renegotiate your contract with humans."

That produced a babble of dragon speech that made Wiz's head ring. Finally Ralfnir cut through the din.

"Nonsense!" he roared. "I have no 'contract' with humans." There was another head-splitting chorus of assent from the dragons up and down the canyon walls.

Gradually the noise, both acoustic and mental, died away. "Not all of us are afraid of humans," Ralfnir continued, turning his head to look at Wurm. "Dragons dealt with your kind for ages and dragons will deal with them for ages more. Magic or no, dragons will continue to handle humans as it pleases us to do so."

"That won't be as easy with the new magic," Wiz said.

"So far, your 'new magic' has only disturbed Shulfnim at his nap." He paused and nodded toward Griswold. "Oh yes, and bested that one."

Griswold's renewed protest was cut off by a roar of dragonish mirth. The other dragons flapped their wings and slapped their tails against the rock to show approval.

Ralfnir waited for the noise to die again before he went on. "I do not think we have to fear such powers as these."

"This was just a taste," Wiz warned. "The new human magic is very powerful. You will have to reckon with it or I cannot be responsible for the consequences."

"If humans interfere with us," came another steely voice, "it will be we who are responsible for the consequences— to the humans."

Another cacophony of approval with more wing flapping and tail slapping burst out from the assembled dragons.

"But if you look at the long-term trend . . ." Wiz began, but Ralfnir cut him short.

"A human talks to dragons about the long term? We who live for age upon age?"

Wiz gathered his remaining courage and tried again. "Even dragons can die," he pointed out. "They can be killed by magic and humans now have magic that can, ah, severely limit your scope of action."

"Then prove it," Ralfnir said. "Show me the power of this new magic you think of so highly."

"I'll be glad to demonstrate," Wiz said. As soon as the words were out of his mouth he realized he had made a mistake. "Uh, what did you have in mind?"

"Why," Ralfnir purred, "if this new magic is so dangerous to us, surely you cannot object to a simple duel."

Having no lips, dragons cannot smile. But Ralfnir did an excellent imitation, drooping his lids over his golden eyes and opening his mouth slightly to run a blood-red forked tongue over his gleaming ivory fangs.

Wiz looked at Wurm but the great dragon remained impassive. The chasm had gone very, very quiet.

"Okay," Wiz lied. "How about tomorrow?"

❖   ❖   ❖

Their business concluded, the dragons left the canyon like a cloud of startled bats. At last only Wurm and Wiz remained.

"It was perhaps unwise to challenge Ralfnir to a duel," the dragon said in a tone of mild reproof.

"Did anyone ever mention your genius for understatement?" Wiz said sourly.

"This was not your object, then?"

"No. I was suckered. What now?"

Wurm seemed surprised by the question. "Why, that is up to you. You can fight him or not."

"Any advice?"

"Advice? That would be presumptuous indeed of me. You must do as you think best."

Wiz thought Wurm had been presumptuous as hell already by getting him into this mess. However he didn't see any point in saying so.

"But if I fight him and he kills me, I haven't solved the problem."

Wurm considered. "Your death would be a solution of sorts."

For an instant Wiz wondered if this entire episode might have been Wurm's elaborate plot to get him to commit suicide. He dismissed that as unnecessarily baroque, even for a dragon.

"I don't suppose I could talk him out of this?"

Wurm cocked his enormous head. "Unlikely. The challenge was formally issued and accepted. Now it is a matter of honor." He paused, as if considering. "True, there is not much honor to be gained by killing a single human, but Ralfnir enjoys sport for its own sake."

"But if I win do I have a deal?"

"Why should you? If you win you will only eliminate Ralfnir."

"Then what's the point?"

"No point, really," Wurm said, "unless you like slaying dragons as much as Ralfnir likes slaying humans. I told you before, Wizard, dragons do not form groups as humans do. There is none who can speak for all of us."

"So why should I even show up for this duel?"

Wurm gave a mental "shrug." "Perhaps no reason at all. Save that if you do not Ralfnir will undoubtedly hunt you down and quite likely burn down that town you humans are so fond of in the process."

"And if I do face him?"

"If you win you have nothing to fear from him. If you lose—" again the "shrug" "—he will probably not bother with the town."

"Great. And if I do beat him, I'll still have to best every single other dragon in order to get them to leave the people alone?"

Wurm paused, as if considering. "Probably not. I imagine that after you have slain forty or fifty dragons most of the rest will decide humans are not worth bothering with." He cocked his head. "It would be an effective strategy, were you able to carry it out."

"There's gotta be a better way," Wiz muttered.

"If there is I would suggest you endeavor to find it," Wurm said. "It would be best if you found it ere dawn tomorrow."

"I'm working on it," Wiz told the dragon and turned to start down the canyon.

"Oh, and Wizard . . ." Wurm's "voice" rang in his head.

Wiz turned back to the dragon.

"Do not count on your ring of protection. Even a hatchling could defeat that spell."

"Thanks," Wiz mumbled, and turned his face again toward town.

TWENTY-FOUR

NET GAINS

The essence of successful consulting is
knowing when to bail out.
—*The Consultants' Handbook*

Wiz spent most of the night staring at the screen and
doodling meaningless bits of code. He knew he should
be coming up with some dynamite dragon-killing spell,
but instead he kept reviewing the spells he did have.

*Let's see. I've got lightning bolts . . . probably not much
good against a dragon . . . suck energy . . . maybe that
would do something . . . frictionless surface . . . nope, not
against a flying creature . . . attract fleas . . . I wonder if
dragons get fleas?* Occasionally he would compound something out of the spells at his command, combining the
old spells to be called in sequence or simultaneously by
a single code word. He spent rather more time working
on a fire-protection spell that looked pretty good. But
mostly he just sat at the terminal and stared into space.

Time and again his fingers would stretch to the keyboard and he would start the sequence to reach the
Wizard's Keep over the Internet. Time and again he
hesitated and his hands dropped away. He knew he wasn't

626

thinking clearly but trying to think more clearly only made things less clear. *Like trying to squeeze a handful of jelly,* he thought morosely.

Anna spent the night sleeping the sleep of the completely unworried—or the really stupid, which may have been the same thing in her case. Bobo spent the night doing tomcat things. No one knew how Widder Hackett spent the night except that she wasn't talking to Wiz.

The only really active one in the house was Malkin. She spent most of the hours before first light gathering up the booty she had secreted about the place. Even though she'd turned most of it to gold coins through One-Eyed Nicolai it still made a substantial load.

Live for some time on that, she thought as she swept the last of the gold into a leather sack. *Time to move on anyway. I was tired of this town.* The prospect wasn't very satisfying somehow and Malkin realized it wasn't just because this was where she had been born. With a sigh of frustration she dropped the bag on the table. It toppled and spilled a cascade of coins onto the tabletop. Malkin didn't bother to sweep them back into the bag.

Restless, she wandered down to the kitchen to get something to eat. Once she descended the narrow steps she found she wasn't hungry. Maybe a cup of hot mulled wine would help her sleep.

She busied herself blowing up the fire and drawing wine from the small cask on the sideboard. She took down a lovingly polished saucepan and put in the wine with cinnamon, cloves and other spices to steep over the still barely glowing coals.

"Smells good," came a voice behind her. "Can I have some?"

Malkin whirled and there was Wiz, dressed for traveling with cloak and staff.

"Startled me," the tall girl said. "But yeah, there's plenty."

"On second thought I'd better not. I'll need a clear head this morning." He didn't sound at all confident.

Malkin ladled out a cup of the hot, spiced wine. "Getting an early start eh?"

"No sense in postponing things." Malkin just nodded and sat down at the table.

For several minutes neither of them said anything or moved, Malkin drinking her wine at the table and Wiz standing on the stairs.

"Look," he said at last. "I'm not much good at these things, but I just wanted you to know that you've really helped me here. And I wanted to thank you for that."

Malkin only nodded, not trusting her voice.

Wiz sighed heavily. "Well, I'd better get going if I'm going to make the spot by sunup. Thanks again."

"Good luck Wizard. And thank you." Then she stared down into her wine cup so Wiz couldn't see her tears.

Wiz went back up the stairs. A moment later she heard the front door open and close.

Well, she thought to herself, *that's that.* It was possible Wiz would beat the dragon, of course. But in Malkin's world winning a fight with a dragon was a near-impossibility. Besides, the wizard hadn't sounded nearly as confident as he had when he'd been tackling human foes.

She sighed and drained the last of the wine. She still wasn't sleepy so she poured the rest of it into her cup and headed back upstairs with it. She still had packing to do.

Wiz had left the workroom door ajar and his workstation on. The colored light from the screen saver pattern streamed onto the floor in rainbow patterns of cold fire. Malkin paused at the door, intrigued. A combination of thief's caution and a certain sense of honor had kept her away from Wiz's work table so far, but now Wiz was gone and she was going as well. She no longer felt bound and the thing had always intrigued her.

A glance out the window showed the sky just turning pink, so she had a while. She spoke the word that turned off the guardian demon. Then she slipped into the chair, set the wine cup on the desk and started to experiment.

Unlike most of the non-magicians in her world, Malkin could read. Literacy is a handy skill for a thief who wants to know what she is stealing. Thus the keyboard on Wiz's workstation wasn't completely alien to her. Further, burglary is as much a matter of attitude as technical skills. Malkin knew nothing about computers and security, but she had seen Wiz type his log-on sequence repeatedly and she had memorized it.

Unfortunately her memory wasn't that good. The keys were small and fairly close together. What's more, Wiz's program didn't echo the password on the screen and to top it off, Malkin's typing technique was primitive. Twice she blew the password and she was hesitating with her index finger hovering over the keyboard when Widder Hackett took a hand.

"Not that one dummy!" the Widow Hackett screamed in her ear. Malkin didn't hear of course, but Bobo jumped up on the desk and walked across the keyboard, placing his paws very deliberately.

Malkin sneezed as the cat's tail brushed under her nose and when she opened her eyes she was in.

The fiery letters above the desk formed a list of items, each with a number after them. At the top of the list, blinking in and out of existence, was a tiny black demon with a spindly tail and long nose wearing red shorts with two big white buttons in front. When she moved the steel mouse on the table the demon moved. Obviously it was what Wiz called a "mouse," although it looked like no mouse she had ever encountered.

She moved the mouse and the on-screen mouse skittered over the first item on the list. As she had seen Wiz do so often, she pressed the steel mouse twice. The screen changed and she saw a series of messages. Another push on the mouse and the mouse demon on the screen flipped the first message down to reveal the next one. Malkin

started going through them and puzzled out the messages
as they came up.

What she got was extremely confusing. The first group
of messages seemed to be jokes, except they were about
pieces of knotted string—frayed knotted string—and
mouse testicles. Malkin couldn't understand why that was
supposed to be funny and most of the stories didn't make
any sense anyway. There was another series which consisted mostly of a four-way argument with the participants
hurling vituperative abuse at each other. The subject was
obscure and she didn't recognize all the words but she
guessed that a complete translation would have made a
fishwife blush.

The next batch of messages consisted of a host of
extremely creative ways to kill off a being who was
apparently some kind of demon—at least it was
described as large and purple and the only things Malkin
could think of that matched that description were
demons. Judging from the hatred in the messages it must
be an exceptionally evil demon. It also seemed to have
a fondness for children. Perhaps it ate them, she couldn't
be sure.

Several of the messages mentioned a being called
"Kibo" who seemed to be an extremely powerful demon.
At least these people seemed to believe that mentioning
the name brought them luck.

There were even some messages that seemed to bear
upon magic. But they were obscure and often couched
in strange combinations of runes which made her eyes
water just to look at them.

Finally, unknowingly, she clicked out of the stored
messages and into the next item on the menu, which
happened to be chat mode.

Jerry was working late. Which meant it was dawn and
he was still at his desk. He was deep in a piece of code
when a slate-blue demon wearing a dress and sporting
a telephone headset in her 1940s hairdo popped up at

his elbow. "Wun-ringy-dingy," the creature pronounced in a nasal voice, "teew-ringy-dingy."

"Gotta get a new chat demon," he muttered. Then he saw who was asking to chat and hit the call button for Danny and Moira.

Danny had been in the kitchen getting a snack before he went to bed. He showed up with a slab of gingerbread liberally smeared with butter in his hand, a mouth so full he could barely breathe and a generous trail of crumbs leading down the hall.

Moira was right on his heels. Her face was puffy, her red hair a tangled mess and a green silk robe had been wrapped hurriedly around her.

"He's on IRC," Jerry said over his shoulder. "But so far he hasn't said anything."

"Here," Danny said around the gingerbread, "let me take it."

"But . . ."

"Get the search demon started," Danny hissed. "Use my workstation." Somewhat reluctantly Jerry gave up his seat and Danny set down his snack and began to type.

A message formed itself in fire at the level of Malkin's eyes.

"How you doing?" it said.

Malkin had seen this happen with Wiz before but it was still a little surprising.

"All right," she picked out on the keyboard.

In chat mode a person's method of typing is almost as distinct as a telegrapher's "fist," especially when you're expecting a very fast typist and you get someone whose method is obviously more hunt than peck.

"You're not Wiz," Danny typed.

"Shut up," Jerry hissed. "Keep him on the line until we've got the location." Beside him the tracing demon was scribbling furiously as it unraveled link after link.

"Right about that," came the laborious reply. "I'm Malkin."

"Where's Wiz?"

"In over his head is where," Malkin typed. "He's out fighting a dragon."

Moira gasped, Danny paled and Jerry craned his neck to read the message from Danny's workstation.

"Is he all right?" Danny typed.

Moira snorted when she read the question. "I told you he's fighting a dragon," she picked out. "In these parts that ain't healthy. Who are you?"

"I'm Jerry," Danny lied, "Wiz's best friend. It sounds like he can use all the help he can get."

"You got that right," came the reply.

"Look, he's under a spell cast by a dragon to keep him from telling us where he is. Can you tell us where he is?"

Malkin hesitated, then her thief's caution won out.

"Look, I don't know why but for some reason Wiz didn't want you to know where he is. I don't think I should tell you either."

"Shit," Danny muttered as he read the message. Behind him Moira said something considerably stronger.

"But he's under a spell," he typed.

"So you say," was the answer. "Maybe you're telling the truth and maybe you're not. But it's not for me to give away his secrets."

Danny looked over his shoulder and tried to gauge the progress of the tracking demon. "All right," he typed. "I guess we have to respect that."

Back in Wiz's workroom Malkin had a sudden flash of insight. "You can find me through this, can't you?"

"How could we do that?" came the hasty response. "We just want to talk is all."

"No," Malkin typed, "I've talked too long as it is. Goodbye." With that she moved to sign off.

"NO YOU IDIOT!!!" shrieked Widder Hackett but no one could hear her.

It was Bobo who rose to the occasion—literally.

Before Malkin could complete the logoff sequence, he uncoiled from his spot on the windowsill, levitated across the room in a single bound and skidded to a four-point landing on the table next to the "computer." A quick lash of his powerful tail sent the cup of hot mulled wine splashing into Malkin's lap.

With a curse Malkin jumped to her feet. Bobo hopped off the table, clawed her solidly on the ankle and ran out yowling. Malkin grabbed the fireplace poker and chased the cat down the hall. She didn't realize she had forgotten to log off.

Back at the castle the programmers realized it immediately.

"Line's still live!" Danny shouted. "Quick, get the trace going."

"That will take hours!" Jerry didn't exactly shove Danny out of the chair but he squeezed in so quickly the smaller programmer almost landed butt-first on the floor.

His fingers blurred as he rattled through a sequence and the fiery letters flew from the demon's pen.

"What do you think you're doing?" Danny demanded as the message began to take shape.

Jerry stopped typing and backspaced over a mistake. "I've turned off the routine that splits spells into pieces on the screen so you don't activate them just by entering them."

"I can see that."

"As soon as this spell appears on Wiz's terminal it will activate. Just printing it out is the equivalent to reciting it." Another pause and more frantic backspacing. "It'll produce a big flare of magic to show us where Wiz is."

"It is also gonna produce a big flare of magic here," the younger programmer pointed out. "That's likely to raise all kinds of hell with the spells around here."

Jerry didn't take his eyes off the screen. "I know."

"Bal-Simba is not gonna like this."

Jerry hit the last key and completed the spell at the Wizard's Keep, and sent it on its way.

The magical lights in the workroom dimmed and then came back with an unhealthy greenish pallor. There were various poppings and cracklings, unearthly wails and one or two outright explosions from other parts of the Wizard's Keep, accompanied here and there by yells from wizards who had been working late or were at work early.

At the abandoned terminal in Wiz's office Jerry's typing poured out of the screen. There was no one there to read it, but since it was a spell and not a message that didn't matter. Unknown to the inhabitants of the house, magical forces gathered and twisted around them as an invisible tornado of magical energy rose toward the heavens. The emac reached the last line of the spell and sent the requested acknowledgment.

"It worked!" Jerry yelled triumphantly. He spun to face Moira. "Quick, tell the searchers to scan the World for a flare of magic. Big magic." Moira nodded and dashed from the room.

"And tell Bal-Simba too," Jerry called after her. He raised his voice to follow her down the hall. "And apologize to him for the mess, will you?" Then he turned to Danny. "Get your staff. I think we're going to fight a dragon."

When a dragon says dawn, does he mean daybreak or sunrise? Wiz wondered.

It was past first light and already the sun was peeking over the eastern hills. There was still no sign of the dragon. Wiz didn't know if that was because the duel wasn't supposed to start until sunrise or if it was a psychological move on Ralfnir's part. If it was psychology, Wiz thought, it was sure effective.

The dawn air was heavy with dew and still as death. Not so much as a zephyr ruffled the tall green grass or the yellow meadow flowers. A few puffy clouds hung high in the summer sky and here and there a butterfly or bumblebee went about its business among the patches of buttercups and field mallow.

Wiz licked his lips, took a tighter grip on his staff and nearly died in an eyeblink.

With a pop of displaced air Jerry, Danny, Moira and Bal-Simba flashed into existence in Wiz's workroom. A quick glance showed them the room was empty but the sound of cursing downstairs told them there were people about. As one they dashed for the door.

Malkin was standing at the sink, sponging the wine out of her dress and describing in lurid detail all the things she was going to do to Bobo, when Bal-Simba and the others came pounding down the stairs with Jerry in the lead.

"You're Malkin, aren't you? Where's Wiz?" he got out in a single breath.

Malkin's mouth fell open.

"My Lady, please," Moira said as she pushed around Jerry. "Where is Wiz?"

"Where, Lady?" Bal-Simba demanded over Jerry's shoulder.

No one argued with Bal-Simba. Not only did he have the presence and voice of a mighty wizard, he was nearly seven feet tall with bulk to match his height. For the first time in her adult life Malkin found herself dwarfed and intimidated by another person.

"Tell them, girl!" shrieked Widder Hackett.

Over in the corner Anna gaped at what had invaded the kitchen.

"At the dueling field," Malkin stammered. "You take the west road . . ."

"No," Bal-Simba commanded. "No time for words, just think of the place. Think clearly."

"Got it!" Danny shouted. "Let's go." The four gestured as one and vanished.

There was a *pop* of inrushing air and the kitchen was empty again save for its normal inhabitants.

"Fortuna!" muttered Malkin. The stains on her dress forgotten, she reached for an empty wine cup, eyed it, tossed it back on the drainboard and took a beer tankard down from its peg. She filled it to the brim from the wine keg and downed nearly half of it without taking the tankard from her lips.

"Excuse me, My Lady," Anna quavered when Malkin came up for air, "but who were they?"

"Friends of the master's."

"How did they get here?"

Malkin shrugged.

Bobo sauntered into the kitchen looking pleased with himself. But since Bobo always looked pleased with himself neither woman noticed.

Malkin took another long pull on the wine. "Best prepare the spare bedrooms, girl. We're going to have company this night." *Either that or dragon fire ere sundown,* she thought as she turned away. But no sense in saying that. Nothing they could do about it and the poor child was already frightened near out of what little wit she had.

TWENTY-FIVE

WE WHO ARE ABOUT TO . . .

The essential difference between a consultant and an owner is that it's not the
consultant's butt on the line.
                    —*The Consultants' Handbook*

And if it is your butt on the line you've
screwed up big time.
                    —Marginalia in a copy of
                    The Consultants' Handbook

Wiz sensed rather than heard the movement behind
him and flung his staff out in an instinctive warding
gesture. A wall of flame washed over him, charring the
grass and scorching the earth beneath. The sky darkened
for an instant and then the shock wave nearly knocked
Wiz off his feet.

Shaking his head to clear it, Wiz realized Ralfnir had
come in behind him right at ground level and very fast.
His instinctive guard was the only thing that had saved
him. Looking the way the shadow had gone he sought
Ralfnir. At last he saw the dragon, so far away it was only
a speck in the blue. The dragon hauled around in a tight

turn, mighty wings beating the air. Then he seemed to drop down on Wiz like a stooping hawk. Again Wiz raised his staff and this time he didn't let the dragon close.

Bolt after bolt of lightning struck Ralfnir square on and splattered harmlessly off his armored chest. The dragon replied in kind and Wiz's anti-fire spell glowed dull red around the edges. Wiz turned his head away from the blast of heat radiating off the shield and countered with a rainmaking spell. The dragon steamed and sizzled in the sudden downpour, but shook off the water like a dog and kept coming.

Wiz raised his staff and gestured again. Four things like old-fashioned beehives made out of steel appeared at the cardinal points around Ralfnir. As soon as they winked in they exploded, releasing a horde of steel bees aimed straight for the dragon. Ralfnir shot a great gout of flame, slewing it back and forth to play over the oncoming metal insects. Most of them glowed red, then yellow, then fell from the sky like a rain of molten steel. The few that penetrated Ralfnir's defenses bounced harmlessly off the beast's armored hide.

Now he swooped close and reached out with gaping jaws. Wiz dropped flat on the ground and heard the dragon's jaws close above him like a rifle shot. The pressure from the wingbeats made Wiz's eardrums ring and then the dragon was gone again with a lashing of lightning bolts to speed him on his way.

Ralfnir winged over and dived behind the hill. For an instant Wiz thought he had gotten him, but the dragon popped up seconds later, spraying Wiz with fire from close range and jinking down again before the human could get a spell off.

backslash spindizzy exe! Wiz muttered. A blue haze enveloped him and he rose, a hundred, two hundred, three hundred feet straight into the air. The ground fell away from him and the hilltop where he had stood became a black smear on the rolling green meadow.

It was a calculated insult. Dragons hate other flying

things near them, especially flying humans. Ralfnir swelled his neck and hissed like a runaway steam whistle. Then he dove for Wiz with all his strength.

Jaws agape and talons spread, Ralfnir dived for Wiz Zumwalt. With a mighty roar he struck the flying wizard square on with the full force of his two-hundred-foot-long armored body.

Wiz bounced. Bounced and skittered away from the dragon, light as a windblown leaf. Ralfnir clutched at him with his talons but Wiz popped out of his grasp like a watermelon seed.

The dragon roared in frustration and fury and unleashed a column of fire straight at his would-be prey. The incandescent blast curled around the blue haze and Wiz was simply borne away like a feather on a puff of breath. Again and again Ralfnir spewed mighty gouts of flame at his victim. Each time Wiz was borne lightly away by the force and unharmed by the flame.

Hot damn! It's working. When he had developed the spell it had seemed just too tricky, but it was not only protecting him, it was obviously puzzling the hell out of the dragon. The bubble-of-force component kept the searing heat of the dragon's fire away from him and the repulsion spell kept the dragon from grabbing him, but the real secret was the inertia-canceling spell. Without inertia the dragon couldn't hurt him no matter how hard he hit. Even the force of Ralfnir's fiery breath simply blew him gently away.

Now maybe he'll get tired and give up.

Ralfnir hung motionless, wings beating and armored chest heaving. He cocked his head and considered the human in the blue bubble floating a few hundred feet away. Then he straightened his neck as if he had reached a decision.

On the other hand, Wiz thought, *maybe he won't.*

Slowly, methodically, the dragon began to stalk the human across the sky.

✧   ✦   ✧

If Ralfnir couldn't harm Wiz, he quickly discovered he could knock him around a lot. The dragon batted Wiz in his blue bubble from paw to paw and then lashed him with his tail. The force of the blow drove Wiz down to the earth. The spell bounced him back up again like a rubber ball and rattled Wiz's teeth, spell or no.

Again and again blows from Ralfnir's tail hammered Wiz to the ground, and again and again he bounced back up. In effect Ralfnir dribbled Wiz the length of the meadow and back.

His spell might have rendered Wiz immune from physical force, but it did nothing at all for his inner ear. Somewhere between the second and third dribble Wiz discovered a hitherto unknown predilection to airsickness.

While he fought to keep his stomach in place Wiz realized he hadn't been as smart as he had thought. He couldn't even think straight in the middle of all the bouncing, much less cast spells. Perhaps worse, the protection field severely limited the kinds of spells he could cast at all. The best he had was a standoff and he had a suspicion that wouldn't last forever.

It didn't. After bouncing Wiz off the terrain one last time the dragon lay back and regarded him briefly. A garbled bit of dragon speech formed in Wiz's mind and suddenly his bubble burst, leaving Wiz hanging unsupported and unprotected several hundred feet in the air.

There was a brief, sickening drop as the world rushed toward him.

backslash paracommander exe! Wiz cried and his fall slowed to an easy descent. Ralfnir, however, didn't. The dragon dived again on the now-helpless wizard, intent on finishing him before he reached the ground.

Wiz sucked in his breath when he saw the dragon coming. *Doesn't shooting a man in a parachute violate the Geneva Convention or something?* He realized Ralfnir had probably never heard of the Geneva Convention and wouldn't abide by it if he had.

Wiz watched the dragon bore in on him, looming ever larger in his vision. **backslash uncommander.exe!** he whispered and the spell released him, letting him fall free again. The sudden burst of speed confused Ralfnir and instead of nailing Wiz squarely, he passed several feet over Wiz's head. As the dragon spread his wings to brake and come around again he twisted his head over his shoulder and shot a quick burst of fire at Wiz. The shot was badly aimed and missed, but it came close enough to fill Wiz's nostrils with the reek of singed hair.

Wiz was so intent on watching Ralfnir he almost forgot to reactivate the spell. He was only a few feet off the ground when he switched it back on and hit hard enough to drive him to his knees. He barely had time to grab his staff before the dragon was on him again.

This time Ralfnir settled to the ground with two mighty wing beats that threw up so much dirt Wiz flinched away. Then slowly, ponderously, he waddled across the meadow to confront his adversary.

A quick spell reduced the friction beneath the dragon to almost nothing, but the dragon simply glided on like a skater on ice. He nearly fell into the gaping pit that opened before him, but he hopped over with a quick half-flap of his wings. Tendrils of meadow grass tugged at his feet, but the dragon broke their grip without seeming to notice. Wiz used an illusion spell to fill the meadow with duplicates of himself. Ralfnir ignored them and came straight for the real Wiz.

A basketball-sized meteor blazed out of the sky and struck the dragon squarely between the eyes. Ralfnir shook his head as if to dislodge a fly. An iceberg congealed around him and shattered instantly. Ralfnir plowed through the pile of ice shards and kept coming. Barely a dozen feet from Wiz he stopped, raised his head high over Wiz and looked down at him.

Wiz felt as if he was suffocating. The dragon's glare seemed to press down on him like a rock on his chest. He felt his will, his magic and even his life draining away from him under the impact of those great yellow eyes.

Gasping, Wiz managed to form one more word and the world went black and freezing cold.

Ralfnir roared in rage and frustration as his prey disappeared in the rapidly expanding black cloud. He drew his head even higher and breathed a gout of flame at the spot where Wiz had been.

The resulting fireball blew Ralfnir clear across the meadow. Technically it was a misfire since the carbon black and liquid oxygen Wiz's spell had dumped around him hadn't had time to mix fully. However, the result was impressive enough. The carbon was very finely divided, almost monomolecular, and the liquid oxygen not only propelled the carbon black outward in all directions, shutting out light, it also made a dandy oxidizer for the carbon fuel.

Another part of the spell protected Wiz from the explosion. Ralfnir wasn't so lucky. He lay stunned for an instant where the blast had flung him. As he rolled to his feet Wiz saw he was moving slowly, as if in pain. But he sprang into the air as agilely as ever.

This time the attack was purely magical. Again the dragon closed in on Wiz, beating and battering at him with magical blow after magical blow. Wiz was able to deflect some of them with his staff, but there were so many and they came so quickly he could not ward them all off. Under the inexorable pressure Wiz was beaten to his knees, waving his staff in one hand in an increasingly futile effort to protect himself. His chest constricted, his vision blurred and he gasped for breath, leaning on his staff to keep from falling. Ralfnir came ever closer, moving in for the final kill.

There was a sound like machine-gun fire from the edge of the meadow, four quick sharp explosions.

And Jerry was there.

And Danny.

And Moira was there.

And Bal-Simba was there.

As one the quartet raised their staffs and hurled death and destruction at the dragon bearing down on Wiz.

If he'd had time to prepare Ralfnir might have had a chance. He was an old dragon and greatly skilled in magic. But he was in the midst of battle and he was focused on Wiz with a predator's intentness. He barely noticed the other humans before their spells hit him.

Bal-Simba was quickest off the mark. A bolt of black lightning flew from his fingertips and wrapped itself around Ralfnir. The dragon was brought up short in midswoop as if he had been lassoed, and he jerked violently against the sooty black bonds drawing tighter and tighter around him. The more he struggled the more closely he was held. Before the others' spells could reach him he was already weakening and sinking toward the earth.

Jerry's spell was an outgrowth of his speculations about the physical nature of dragons. It enclosed Ralfnir in a perfectly reflecting sphere that rapidly brought its contents to the black body temperature of a dragon. Of course, since there was no energy sink available in the sphere, the dragon died a heat death, which is sort of the thermodynamic equivalent of heat stroke.

Moira wasn't fancy. She just threw the three worst death spells Wiz and his friends had taught her. She topped it off with the worst spell in the old magic she remembered from her days as a hedge witch—a spell guaranteed to give the victim a case of hives.

Danny's spell was probably the most ingenious. It took all the random molecular motion in the dragon's body and pointed it in one way—toward the highest gravity potential. What was left of Ralfnir didn't just drop out of the sky, he hurtled with ever-increasing speed. In the space of a few hundred feet the dragon went from zero to Mach eight. Straight down.

Where he hit, Ralfnir literally left a smoking hole in the ground.

❖   ❖   ❖

Wiz sagged against his staff and stared dumbly at the hole where the dragon had been. Then he stared at his friends coming across the meadow to him. Neither event registered very strongly.

"You shouldn't have come," Wiz mumbled as Bal-Simba reached him slightly ahead of the others. "You weren't supposed to come. I didn't want you here. You've ruined everything."

He was still mumbling when Bal-Simba laid a huge hand on his shoulder. "Sparrow look at me," he commanded. Wiz met his eyes and his mouth dropped open. He shuddered, staggered and would have fallen if Bal-Simba had not taken his arm.

"Wha . . . what . . . ?"

"A geas," Bal-Simba said. "A magical compulsion. Laid on you, I have no doubt, by a certain dragon."

Wiz's jaw dropped again. "Oh," he said. "So that's . . ." He didn't get a chance to finish. Moira was in his arms, kissing him and crying and all he wanted to do was hold her close forever and ever.

"Hey, Wiz," Danny said after an appropriate interval.

Wiz raised his face from Moira's mane of copper hair. "Thanks guys. I think you just saved my life."

The giant wizard made a throw-away gesture. "It was a piece of pastry."

"That's 'piece of cake,' " Danny corrected.

"Whatever."

"Come on love," Moira murmured in his ear, "let us leave this place."

Wiz shook his head without taking his nose out of his wife's hair. "I can't just yet. There are a couple of loose ends I need to tie up here."

Moira looked over Wiz's shoulder at Bal-Simba.

"No geas," he told her. "Only a sense of responsibility."

"Responsibility to whom?" Moira asked.

"The town council," Wiz told her.

"The town council?"

"Yeah, I'm a consultant to them on dragon problems."

"Sparrow," the giant black wizard rumbled, "I am almost afraid to ask what you have been doing."

"Well," Wiz admitted, "it's kind of complicated."

Bal-Simba eyed his friend. "Now I *am* afraid to ask."

"I'll explain it to you when we get back to town," he said. "It's really not that bad." Then he stopped. "At least it seemed like a good idea at the time. But it's not dangerous." He stopped again. "Well, okay, there are these three thugs who were trying to kill me and a couple of people on the council who want my hide. And I guess Pieter, the guy in the cement overcoat who's standing in the town square, is going to come looking for me once he gets unfrozen. But it's really not that bad." He realized all four of his companions were staring at him, hard. "Honest," he finished lamely.

"You had best tell us about it when we get back to town," Bal-Simba said.

"Uh, I've got to make a kind of a detour first." Wiz looked over his shoulder at the trickle of smoke coming from the fresh crater in the sod. He took a deep breath.

"Okay, now for the hard part."

TWENTY-SIX

DRAGON DECISIONS

History does not always repeat
itself. Sometimes it just yells "Can't you
remember anything I told you?" and lets fly
with a club.
                                        —John W. Campbell

Again Wiz Zumwalt faced the assembled dragons. This
time he had arrived under his own power along the
Wizard's Way. He had come alone, but Bal-Simba and the
others were watching him closely.

This meeting being called on short notice, there weren't
as many dragons along the walls of the canyon as there
had been the day before. But there were still a satisfying number.

"Well," he said to the mass of monsters, "you've had
your taste of the new magic. Satisfied?"

"It was not a fair duel," one of the dragons complained.
"You had help from others of your kind."

"Not fair at all," Wiz agreed cheerfully. "But then
you're not going to get a fair fight with a human. Don't
you see? Humans cooperate. They work together

naturally." He thought of the town council. "Maybe not always easily and not always well, but they manage to do it."

He threw his head back to look up at the assembled dragons and raised his voice so his words echoed off the cliffs. "It won't be one dragon against one human. It will be one or a few dragons against every human in sight. And most of the time the humans will win with the new magic."

There was a great shifting and slithering as the dragons absorbed the idea.

"Then we should kill you all now," a voice rang harshly in his head.

"You could try," he said levelly. "But there are many more humans than there are in this valley and a lot of them already have the new magic. Even if you got every human in the valley, others would replace them."

More shifting and slithering.

"What do you propose then?" a new voice asked.

"Simple. You're going to make a treaty with the people in the valley. And this time you're going to abide by it." He turned round to face the mass of assembled dragons. "All of you."

"And how shall we bind all dragonkind by our agreement?" a "voice" like an iron kettledrum asked.

"That's your problem. Maybe the seniors could take turns patrolling the border. But you're going to solve it or in a few generations there won't be any dragons left in the Dragon Lands."

He looked up at the assembled monsters. "Think it over," he said. Then he turned on his heel and left.

It wasn't yet noon but the group was worn out by the time they returned to the house. They were too tired to walk so they took the Wizard's Way back and popped into the front hall just as Anna came up the stairs from the kitchen.

She wasn't the least fazed by the apparition in her front

hall. These were wizards, wizards did strange things, therefore anything wizards did was normal. She merely curtseyed.

"Will there be anything you need, My Lord?" she said to Wiz. As usual Anna looked utterly charming in a brown work dress and dirty apron. There was a smear of soot on her cheek just below one china blue eye and blond curls peeked out from the kerchief that protected her hair.

"No, nothing now, thank you," Wiz said. "There's ale in the keg in the kitchen isn't there? We'll probably be down there for a while."

Anna curtseyed again. "I'll finish preparing the guest rooms, then, My Lord." With that she turned and hurried up the stairs, oblivious to Moira's eyes boring into her back.

"Who," Moira demanded, "is she?"

"That's Anna. She's my housekeeper."

The red-haired witch fixed him with a fishy eye. "Your house had better be all she has been keeping, My Lord."

In the event the explanation in the kitchen took somewhat longer than Wiz had anticipated. About three hours, in fact, by the time he answered all the questions, straightened out everyone's chronology, found out about Judith's troubles with the FBI, and gave Jerry and Danny a very detailed and highly technical explanation about exactly how to gimmick an Internet router.

"What do you intend to do about this Pieter, the one you left in town square?" Bal-Simba asked when he finally ran down.

"Well," Wiz said, "I don't suppose it would be really right to leave the little oinker frozen for all eternity." He sighed with genuine regret. "So I guess I'll have to take the spell off him."

"I would suggest doing it the last thing ere we leave the town," Bal-Simba said. "Otherwise he will like as not try to attack you again."

"Oh, I wasn't thinking of being around at all," Wiz said. "I figured I'd create a timer demon to unfreeze him after we've left."

"Wise," Bal-Simba nodded.

"I was thinking of having the demon unfreeze him— oh, I dunno, say at high noon on the next market day. The square should be nice and crowded about then."

"That's nasty," Danny said. "I really like it."

"You get that way when you play consultant," Wiz grinned back. "That and hanging around politicians." He snapped his fingers. "Speaking of which, I'd better get down there and set up the spell. Don't want to leave it to the last minute. Also I've got an errand to run at the town hall."

Bal-Simba cocked an eyebrow. "More consulting?"

"No," Wiz told him as he stood up from the table, "I've got to see a man about a house."

Wiz's errand at the town hall took somewhat longer than he had expected. *But not nearly as long as it would take in Cupertino*, he thought as he pushed his front door open. The council may have had politics down to a blood sport but at least they hadn't invented lawyers yet. As part of his efforts to gum up the works Wiz had considered introducing them to the concept, but he had saved it as an emergency tactic if things really got dire. *Common decency if nothing else*, he thought. Llewllyn hadn't been in his office at the town hall and Wiz was just as glad.

As he tugged the front door closed Malkin came up from the kitchen.

"Where is everyone?" he asked as she reached his floor.

"Oh they're around," she said breezily. "Your wife's down in the kitchen, 'helping' Anna."

"'Helping'?"

"Allaying her suspicions about what you've been up to with her. The big black wizard is in the front parlor, along with one of your friends." She grinned. "They're supposed to be meditating, but every so often they get so deep in thought they start to snore. Your other friend is upstairs working at your desk. Says he's surfing, but there's not a wave to be seen."

"That's just a figure of speech," Wiz told her. "What about you?"

"Oh, I've got some errands to run." She paused. "Leaving, eh?"

"Probably tomorrow. I'm done here."

She nodded. "That's the way of it."

There was a longer pause.

"What about you? What are you going to do once I've left?"

Malkin laughed. "Oh, I'll go back to the Bog Side, away from all these high-toned folk like the town council and their fancy ways. I'll be taking the air, as you might say. You've stirred up a right hornet's nest here and I'm minded to see how it goes on for a bit."

"I mean, you'll be all right and everything?"

Malkin laughed again and Wiz thought it sounded a bit brittle.

"Me? Fortuna, I've looked out for meself all these years. I'll do just fine on my own. Now if you'll excuse me, I've got an errand to run." She loped up the stairs toward her room.

"Malkin."

The tall thief paused at the top of the stairs and looked back. "Yes?"

"I meant what I said about appreciating your help. Thanks again."

"Any time, Wizard. Any time." With that she disappeared down the hall.

As Wiz turned back toward the kitchen there was a hammering on the front door.

"What in the . . . ?" Anna was halfway up from the kitchen, but he waved her back and tugged the door open himself.

As soon as the door cleared the latch it flew open, sending Wiz reeling backward. Llewllyn burst through, waving his arms. He was flushed, sweaty and almost completely out of breath.

"Flee!" he gasped. "There's a dragon . . . Anna. Run. We must . . . run or be . . . burned where we stand."

He tried to push past to the kitchen but Wiz put his arm around him.

"Relax. The dragon's dead. It's all over."

Llewllyn turned back to Wiz and blinked. "Dead?"

"Very dead. There's no danger."

"But . . . but, but . . ."

"Look, we've got houseful of company, so if you can just put off seeing Anna until tonight I'm sure she can explain the whole thing." He gently turned the sometime bard and would-be magician around and guided him back toward the front door.

Wiz almost had him out the door when Bal-Simba came out of the parlor, rubbing the "meditation" from his eyes.

"Sparrow, I . . ."

Llewllyn gaped. He might never have been near the Wizard's Keep, but even people who had barely heard of the Council of the North recognized its leader on sight. Even in our world how many six-foot-eight, 380-pound guys do you see—outside of the NFL? And even NFL linemen don't file their teeth to points.

"I am sorry, Sparrow," the huge wizard said, "I did not know you had a visitor."

Llewllyn's head was swiveling back and forth between them convulsively. His mouth hung open and he had suddenly gone pasty white.

"Uh, leave us for a minute will you, My Lord?"

"Of course," Bal-Simba rumbled. "I will be in the parlor."

"You knew," Llewllyn said dully as soon as Bal-Simba closed the parlor door. "You knew what I was all along."

"It was a little hard for me not to," Wiz said dryly.

Llewllyn struck a noble pose, chin-high. "Well, go ahead. Denounce me to the council. Have them stake me out for the dragons to rend and tear. Or will you simply turn me into a toad?"

It was awfully tempting, but Wiz shook his head.

"I've got a better idea. I'm leaving tomorrow and I'm going to make you my successor."

Llewllyn stopped posing and gawked. "But, My Lord, I am a liar! A charlatan! A back-stabbing schemer!"

Wiz smiled and clapped him on the shoulder. "I can't think of a better set of qualifications for this job."

It is also, he thought, *called making the punishment fit the crime.*

"Besides," Wiz continued, "Anna needs you."

Llewllyn looked blank. "Anna, My Lord?"

"My housekeeper. You know, the woman at whose merest whim you'd lay down your life. The very light of your existence. You are in love with her, aren't you?"

"You know I am, My Lord," Llewllyn said quietly. "But why is she your concern now that you are leaving?" His eyes narrowed. "Or was there something between you?"

"Would it make a difference to you if there was?"

Llewllyn looked at him levelly. "Only that I'd have your heart for trifling with her, be you wizard or no."

Wiz suddenly discovered Llewllyn could be amazingly convincing under the right circumstances.

"No, there was nothing between us. But she's a good kid and she deserves to be happy. You are apparently what makes her happy, so . . ." He shrugged.

The blond man bowed. "I will endeavor to see that she is happy, My Lord."

"Do that. Meanwhile, come back later." With that he pushed him out the door.

TWENTY-SEVEN

DRAGON TALE HOME

**Always end projects on a positive note, no
matter what they were like.**
—*The Consultants' Handbook*

"Excuse me, My Lord," Anna said from the top of the
kitchen stairs. "But Llewllyn, what did he want?"

"Mostly to tell you about the dragon. I asked him to
come back this evening."

Anna frowned, prettily. "The one you killed? But I
already knew that."

"Yes, but he didn't."

"My Lord?" It was a good thing Anna looked so pretty
when she was confused, Wiz thought, because she spent
so much time being confused.

"He'll explain it to you this evening. But I wanted to
talk to you anyway."

A shadow darkened the maid's beautiful, empty brow.
"Have I done something wrong, My Lord?"

"No, no. Not at all. It's just that . . . Look, you know
I'm leaving here tomorrow with my friends?"

The maid nodded. "I know and I'm so happy." Then
she went crimson. "Oh, that's not what I mean at all. I
mean . . ."

"I know what you mean," Wiz said reassuringly.

"I mean it has been a pleasure serving you, My Lord, but I, I mean," then the words came in a rush. "I mean Llewllyn has asked me to marry him and I said yes and oh, I'm the happiest girl in the world!"

Wiz ignored the disembodied snort from over his shoulder. "Congratulations. When is the happy event?"

"As soon as can be." Her eyes sparkled. "He is wonderful and I love him so. Besides," her voice dropped. "I have been so alone since Grandma died. Oh you have been kind, My Lord, but there's been no one for me to turn to for advice and Llewllyn," she sighed, "why he knows *everything*!"

Wiz held up his hand, checking the explosion of spectral wrath behind him.

"Well, since I'm not going to be here for the wedding, I'd better give you your present early."

The girl flushed again. "Oh My Lord, that is not necessary."

"Still, I am going to give you this house. As a wedding present, you might say." Anna's jaw dropped and her face lit up like a child's at Christmas. He waved a finger. "Now mind, I am giving this to you personally. Not to the two of you. I've arranged it with the council that it shall be yours alone."

Anna hugged him and started to cry into his shirt pocket. "Hey, it's okay," Wiz protested and tried to move her away. "It's all right."

"Well, My Lord," Anna said with a smile and a sniffle. "I'd best go and finish in the kitchen."

"Yes, do that." *Before Moira catches you hanging all over me and turns us both into toads.*

"Smart," Widder Hackett said at last. "If she owns the house I'll be able to advise the poor child. And she'll need it, married to that empty-headed popinjay."

"That's kind of what I was thinking," Wiz said. *That and I don't want to find out if the ghost stays with the owner if he leaves the house.*

✧   ✧   ✧

Malkin was gone for a long time doing Malkin-ish things. The principal one of those things was a visit to her fence to turn the last of her swag into gold. Since One-Eyed Nicolai didn't open for business until after dark, she took her dinner at a dingy little food stall in the Bog Side. On the way home she was diverted by a couple of opportunities to ply her trade and ended up returning with more loot than she left with, plus the gold from the fence, and coming in quite late to boot.

Thus it was that Malkin was sneaking up the back stairs with her latest acquisitions when a looming shadow blocked her way.

Jerry, who was wide-awake after the day's nap, had been net surfing on Wiz's workstation. He had taken a break to stretch his legs—and see if there was anything to eat in the kitchen. He wasn't expecting to meet anyone on the stairs and he nearly stepped on Malkin before he could stop. As it was he half-stumbled, half-fell into her and they ended up clinging to each other to keep from falling completely downstairs.

"Oh, hello," Jerry said mildly, releasing his hold on the girl.

"Hello yourself," said Malkin, looking up at him. Not only was she one stair lower on the stairway, but even on the level Jerry overtopped her by perhaps half a head. "Let's see, you're the one called Jerry, right?"

"That's me."

"And you're a wizard too?"

"Well, a programmer but around here it pretty much comes to the same thing." Between the darkness in the stairwell and Malkin's dark clothing Jerry couldn't see much of his new acquaintance, but the combination of dark hair working its way out from under the knit cap, the pale, fair skin and lithe figure he had wrapped his arms around to keep from falling all made a very favorable impression.

"I was just taking a break," he explained. "From work

on the computer, ah, workstation, I mean." It occurred to Jerry he was babbling, but if he shut up she might just pass him by on the stairs. "I do that a lot. Work, you know. Besides I'm kind of a night person," he explained. "I do most of my best work then."

Malkin smiled up at him. "I know just what you mean. I'm that way myself."

Somehow the big programmer and the tall thief ended up sitting side by side on the stairs, talking. Somehow it was getting light outside before they reached a stopping place in their conversation and went their separate ways.

It is possible they were overheard. But Danny was sleeping in the front parlor and Wiz and Moira were far too occupied to hear anything. If Bal-Simba heard he gave no sign. Widder Hackett didn't talk about it and Bobo just looked smug.

It was barely dawn, but Wiz was already up and packing to go. He was taking clothes out of the wardrobe, folding them more or less neatly and putting them in a thing he persisted in thinking of as a duffel bag, even if it was made out of sueded leather rather than canvas. There wasn't much besides a few clothes. He hadn't accumulated many possessions in his time here, just as he hadn't grown particularly attached to the place.

There was a shadow at the window, as if a cloud had passed before the rising sun. But a cloud doesn't usually send the early risers in the street running and screaming. Nor does a cloud rattle the windowpanes.

Shirt still in hand, Wiz went to the window. There was a dragon settling daintily into the square, oblivious to the townsfolk scattering like a herd of terrified sheep. He didn't have to be told it was Wurm.

"Leaving, Wizard?" the dragon's voice came in his head.

"Yes, now that I'm free of your damned geas."

Wurm waddled across the square until his head was just outside Wiz's room. It was a small square and Wurm was a large dragon, so it was only a few steps.

Wiz watched him come. He discovered he wasn't intimidated by dragons any more, but he was awfully tired of them.

"You had solved the problem so I would have removed that anyway."

"Big of you," Wiz said and turned back to his packing.

The dragon cocked an enormous golden eye at Wiz through the window.

"You have not claimed your fee."

Wiz put a stack of shirts into his pack and hissed in irritation as one of them slid onto the floor. "I'm not interested in a fee," he said stooping down to pick up the shirt.

Wurm raised an enormous eyebrow. "If you are not paid how do you expect to remain in business?"

"I'm out of business as of right now," Wiz told him. "The next time I feel the urge to do this I'll take up a more honest branch of the profession, like television evangelism."

"Nevertheless, you are entitled to payment."

"The only payment I want is a little peace and quiet, like about fifty years worth. I don't want ghosts screeching in my ear, I don't want to have to worry about the cops busting down my door because of my housemate's hobbies, I don't want to have to put up with a bunch of quarrelsome children masquerading as politicians." He threw the shirt into the bag and it promptly slid out again. "And most of all, I don't want to have to deal with dragons."

"That is a rather large reward indeed," Wurm said. "Even for a task such as you have performed."

Wiz stuffed the shirt into the bag again, more carefully this time, and turned to face the dragon. "You knew this, didn't you? You knew the new magic was spreading to the north and you knew that with it humans could beat the dragons."

"Let us just say I found the probabilities inopportune," Wurm said lazily.

"So you went right to the source of the new magic and kidnapped me to fix things before they got out of hand."

"And you fixed them. That is vindication enough, I think."

Wiz opened his mouth to protest and then closed it again. Dragons being cold-blooded in more ways than one, nothing else was likely to matter to Wurm, least of all the danger Wiz had been in.

"So you dragged me in here against my will to help the humans with their dragon problem."

"I prefer to think of it as dragons having a human problem," Wurm said.

"Well, why didn't you just tell me that?"

Wurm's "voice" was coldly amused. "Would you have bent all your skill to protecting dragons from humans? Even under geas?"

There was enough truth in that that Wiz didn't have a reply, so he changed the subject. "By the way, what are you going to do?"

"I? Oh, you mean dragonkind. We will solve our own problem—now that we agree it is a problem." The dragon sounded amused. "That is the essence of consulting, is it not? To, ah, 'borrow someone's watch and tell him what time it is'?"

Wiz wondered where the dragon had heard that. He had an uneasy feeling Wurm had heard, and knew, a lot more than he was telling.

"Goodbye Wizard. I do not think we will meet again, but I predict you will have an extremely interesting future." With that Wurm turned sinuously, took three running steps and launched himself into the air with a beat of wings that rattled the windows and made the shutters bang against the walls.

"If I have anything to say about it," Wiz said to the dragon's rapidly dwindling back, "my future will be about as exciting as watching grass grow."

❖   ❖   ❖

"I see you had a visitor," Bal-Simba said as Wiz came down to breakfast in the kitchen.

Wiz leaned over and kissed Moira soundly before replying. "Yeah, Wurm. He wanted to say goodbye."

Moira arched a coppery eyebrow and the big wizard accepted this without comment. Wiz helped himself to the porridge on the tile stove. He added some sliced apples and peaches from a bowl on the table and drizzled honey over the mixture.

It was a remarkably full kitchen, considering the programmers' normal working hours. Anna was still bustling about finishing up the last of breakfast. Moira was sitting next to Bal-Simba and Jerry and Malkin were off to one side, talking intently. Only Danny hadn't come down yet and that wasn't surprising. Yesterday was probably the earliest he had gotten up in months.

Wiz took a mouthful of porridge and fruit and sighed. "A few more hours and we'll be back at the Wizard's Keep and peace and quiet."

Moira raised her eyebrows and gave Wiz one of her patented smoldering looks with her enormous green eyes. "So it's peace and quiet you want, My Lord?" Bal-Simba guffawed.

Wiz reddened. "Relatively speaking, I mean. And speaking of relations . . ."

Anna set another bowl on the table and Moira looked at the girl significantly. "We shall have plenty of time to discuss that when we get home."

"Home," Wiz repeated. "I can't wait to get back. I've missed you so much. I've missed all of you." He quirked a smile. "Heck, I even got to missing Little Red Dragon, I mean Fluffy."

Moira raised an eyebrow and smiled. "I take it you have not enjoyed your adventure? Seeing strange lands? Battling dragons? Doing great deeds of heroism?"

Wiz smiled back. "I only battled dragons when it was absolutely necessary, I rigorously avoided deeds of heroism, great or otherwise, and this place may be strange enough, but I wish I'd never seen it and I bet you all do too."

Moira turned to where Jerry and Malkin were deep in conversation.

"Well, not all of us perhaps."

Watching the pair Wiz felt a sudden chill.

"Well, we'll be out of here soon enough. Let me finish eating, grab my staff and we'll be leaving inside a half-hour." He smiled at the prospect and leaned back to take another pull from his mug of tea.

"Oh, that reminds me," Jerry said. "I've got some news too. Malkin's agreed to come back to the Capital with us."

Wiz spewed tea all over the table.

"*WHAT?*" he demanded indignantly and lapsed into a coughing fit that somewhat diminished the effect.

"I have decided to come with you," Malkin said gaily. "This Capital of yours sounds like an interesting place. Full of opportunities."

Wiz thought of Malkin's definition of "opportunity" and blanched. "I don't think you'll find any opportunities in the Capital. Nope, no opportunities at all. It's a dull place really. Full of all kinds of boring guards and burglar alarms and . . ." He trailed off when he saw he obviously wasn't making an impression. Then he looked at her more closely, over at Jerry and back at Malkin. "There's more to it than just opportunity, isn't there?"

Malkin looked shy. "He's the first man I've ever met I didn't have to look down on."

Wiz was tall by this world's standards and Malkin could look him square in the eye. Jerry was a head taller than Wiz, which made him about the biggest man around, save Bal-Simba. He was still heavy, but after several years of more exercise and the diet full of vegetables, grains and fiber eaten in this world he was no longer exactly fat.

Wiz looked at his friend.

"I've never met anybody like her before," Jerry said simply.

Considering that Jerry had never been in jail that was probably true, Wiz reflected.

Wiz turned to Moira. "I don't suppose this is some kind of infatuation spell?" he asked with a tinge of desperation in his voice.

Moira looked amused. "Infatuation, yes. A spell, no. Only the age-old magic between man and woman."

Wiz put his head in his hands and moaned.

"Is there aught I can do?"

"Yes, warn the people at the Wizard's Keep to nail down anything they want to keep." He considered. "And tell them to use *big* nails."

Jerry and Malkin had moved to the corner, intent on some private matter and oblivious to the other people in the room. She had her hands on the rough stone walls and was apparently explaining to him how to scale a wall at a corner. Jerry was just looking at her, ignoring what she was saying.

"I think Jerry has finally met his match," Moira said approvingly. "She seems quite taken with him as well."

"She probably just wants a place out of jail," Wiz said sourly.

Moira looked speculatively at the couple in the corner. "No, she is really in love, I think."

"Worse," Wiz groaned.

"Well," rumbled Bal-Simba. "At least it shall not be boring."

"That," said Wiz Zumwalt, "is exactly what I am afraid of."